# A GENTLE TYRANNY

**wander**™
An imprint of
Tyndale House
Publishers

# A
# GENTLE
# TYRANNY

NEDÉ RISING SERIES

# JESS CORBAN

Visit Tyndale online at tyndale.com.

Visit the author online at jesscorban.com.

*TYNDALE* and Tyndale's quill logo are registered trademarks of Tyndale House Ministries. *Wander* and the Wander logo are trademarks of Tyndale House Ministries. Wander is an imprint of Tyndale House Publishers, Carol Stream, Illinois.

*A Gentle Tyranny*

Designed by Eva M. Winters

Edited by Sarah Rubio

Published in association with the literary agency of Wolgemuth & Associates, Inc.

*A Gentle Tyranny* is a work of fiction. Where real people, events, establishments, organizations, or locales appear, they are used fictitiously. All other elements of the novel are drawn from the author's imagination.

For information about special discounts for bulk purchases, please contact Tyndale House Publishers at csresponse@tyndale.com, or call 1-855-277-9400.

Printed in the United States of America

| 27 | 26 | 25 | 24 | 23 | 22 | 21 |
|----|----|----|----|----|----|----|
| 7  | 6  | 5  | 4  | 3  | 2  | 1  |

*In memory of my mother, MaryAnn. Could I turn back time, I'd kiss you more and sass you less. Thank you for loving me unconditionally. See you on the other side.*

*For a glossary of terms and pronunciations,*

*turn to page 370.*

# Prologue

FEBRUARY 16, 2067

MIAMI

IT'S FINISHED, she thinks. *It's really finished.*

Tristan Pierce's fingers move quickly along the patchwork of headlines, photos, and quotes covering the wall-sized bulletin board in her office. The tall brunette yanks the mementos from staples and tarnished pins and stuffs them into a small metal case within an army surplus duffel. According to Melisenda, they could have company sooner than planned. Her best friend is rarely wrong.

*But they're too late,* she muses with satisfaction, smiling for the first time in months. *No one will find us once we board the boat, and even if they do, what's done is done.*

The clippings are crisp between her fingers, and spotted brown, like her own creasing skin—aged beyond her forty-one years by the horrors she's witnessed. She considers reattaching them, leaving the wall as a memorial—a reminder to the monsters of what they've done. But, compulsive or not, she can't bring herself to part with her *why*—the impetus which propelled her to form the

ix

Safety Coalition almost seventeen years before. This montage has pushed her, sustained her, through each nightmarish discovery and daunting obstacle she has faced as leader of the Coalition.

The headlines still ignite as much fury as the first time she read them: "9 out of 10 Girls Molested before Age 15," "'Daughter Sex' Most Searched Internet Term," "Police Find a Dozen Four-Year-Old Girls in Brothel." Her gaze moves to a photo of thirty-six women in a heap of blood and black cloth, beheaded for "crimes against Allah," then to a faded picture of a younger Tristan, arm draped around a smiling young woman, pinned beside the headline, "Mutilated Teen Identified as Sasha Pierce."

Once again, she allows rage to check the tears threatening to spill, neither her pain nor her fury dimmed decades after losing her sister to a man who showed no remorse for his crimes.

As she slips the picture of Sasha into the case, a final headline stares back from the now-blank wall: "Will Women Ever Be Safe Again?"

Even now, when she knows the answer to that last headline is *yes*, women will finally—*finally*—be safe again, more horrific memories bleed into the corners of her mind. She remembers her father—the first man who should have offered protection but betrayed her instead. The others who made a living degrading her. Waking up in an alley, aching for death. If she were the only one violated, perhaps she could live with that. But she can't stand by while two-thirds of all women are stripped of their dignity—abused in countless ways—because of genetics. Simply because they're female, born to be prey for men. Innocent prey like Sasha.

*Those brutes,* she curses silently, heat flushing up her throat and into her cheeks.

She rubs the back of her neck and inhales deeply, forcing herself to push down the dangerous spiral of fury.

*Breathe, Tristan. Breathe.*

She has practiced the coping technique a million times, and taught it nearly as many, to women around the world who found solace in the underground efforts of the Coalition. All those women—battered, abused, frightened to lose their basic human rights—were an easy sell. In only a decade she had gained the commitment of key women from each nation on every continent. Desperation fueled them to end the perversion, their passion coercing the moderates. When it was time to execute the Liberation sixteen months ago, worldwide implementation was seamless, completed two months earlier than scheduled.

And now, a new world is dawning.

Tonight Tristan, along with twenty other Coalition members from the United States, will sail for their new home in Central America aboard a covert vessel. Fifty-four international members will make their own journeys to the site, embarking from twenty-five countries around the world—from Australia to China, India to Haiti. They will transport their daughters, as well as any infant sons they gentled during the Liberation, to begin again at a safe haven disguised as a top-secret military base.

The rest of the world will live out its final generational cycle. Every detail has been accounted for. Thanks to the efforts of the Safety Coalition, no remaining male will be able to reproduce, and hundreds of Coalition leaders, representing millions of members, will stay behind to handle media manipulation and unforeseen issues. Most have agreed to live out their days among the savages, knowing their sacrifice will enable the future they've worked so hard to secure for future generations. But as for Tristan, and the brave few who accepted her invitation to create a world free from fear, they will begin again. And this time, they will do it right.

She rolls up the constitution drafted at their last international council meeting in Rio de Janeiro, and squeezes it into the duffel, along with a well-worn leather journal. Then she straps the bag atop a large, reflective metal case—the key to their present success and future survival—and wheels it toward the door. Outside, the screeching of tires announces Mel's arrival.

Tristan steals a final glance at the lone headline on the wall, pondering the enormous responsibility she carries to usher in a renewed era—an era safe from the depravity of men. As founding councilwoman of the Coalition, she has been given the task of naming the new society.

According to the religion she once believed in, it was in an ancient garden, the Garden of Eden, that men first poisoned the world with patriarchy.

*They've tried to rule over us ever since*, she thinks, grimacing. *But we'll reverse all that. We'll do it all differently—create a system opposite of everything that screwed up this backwards world. We'll even reverse the name of its origin. Eden stood for repression, but . . .*

"Nedé," she whispers, her decision made. "Nedé will stand for women."

# The Constitution of Nedé

*We, the seventy-five founding women of Nedé, do hereby establish the laws and code of conduct for our great society, to abolish the evils of patriarchy and to rid the world of the Brutes who have harmed women for millennia due to their biologically driven lust for pleasure and power. The following five Articles shall serve these purposes:*

I. **MATRIARCHAL SYSTEM.** The peace and prosperity of Nedé shall be maintained by three cords of government: the Matriarch, the Council, and the Alexia.

  A. **MATRIARCH.** We hereby appoint Tristan Pierce, founding Council member, to serve as the first Matriarch of Nedé. The Matriarch shall hold executive power to act in the best interest of Nedé, in partnership with the Council.

    1. **SUCCESSION.** At such time as the Matriarch should choose to retire from service (but before she reaches eighty years of age), she shall possess the right and responsibility to choose a successor. Each of the four Provinces—Fik'iri, Lapé, Amal, and Kekuatan—shall supply one Candidate, selected by senatorial vote, for the Matriarch's consideration. Upon evaluating the merit of each Candidate, the Matriarch shall

choose one woman to become her Apprentice for a duration of one year, after which time executive powers will be transferred in full to her successor. Should the Matriarch perish or be rendered incapacitated before such a Succession can take place, the Council shall elect a successor by vote.

B. **COUNCIL.** The Council shall consist of four senatorial houses, each representing one of the four Provinces. Each provincial Senate shall comprise twelve members, elected by popular vote. A Senator's term shall last eight years, with one re-election possible. Senators shall advise the Matriarch in matters of state, serve as judges in civil matters within their Provinces, and serve as examples to all Nedéans of the Virtues we strive for.

C. **ALEXIA.** To guard Nedé against any threat—within its borders or without—we hereby appoint Siyah Assad to establish and organize a peacekeeping force, hereafter termed the *Alexia*, to uphold the Articles of this constitution, to maintain order within Nedé, and to protect our borders from any threat, present or future. The leader of the Alexia will report directly to the Matriarch, who will select and appoint future Alexia leaders.

II. **GENTLES.** Males born to the women of Nedé, hereafter termed *Gentles*, having been liberated from their aggression and lust, shall contribute to the good of Nedé—and maintain their enlightened state—through the important tasks of public and private service, as deemed beneficial by the Matriarch and Council. These duties shall not deny nor diminish the dignity of life but aim to make provision for the inherent frailty of Gentles and supply them with meaningful labor. For the good and safety of all, in perpetuity, the women of Nedé do make these sacrifices:

A. Between the ages of three months and one year, Gentles will be relinquished by their birth mothers to a Materno finca, where they will live until the age of seven.

B. Between the ages of seven and fourteen, Gentles will reside in special facilities called Hives, where they will be educated and trained to serve Nedé.

C. To prevent undue or inappropriate attachment, interaction with grown Gentles shall be limited to necessary instruction.

III. **DESTINIES.** To spread the abundant capabilities of Nedé's women across all necessary sectors, at eighteen years of age each woman shall choose, based on her own interests and abilities, a particular field of expertise, where she shall serve Nedé until she is physically unable to do so. These destinies shall include: Ad Artium, Agricolátio, Alexia, Fabricatio, Gentles Regimen, Innovatus, Materno, Politikós, and Scientia & Medicinae. A detailed description of these fields of employment can be found in the forthcoming document *Nedéan Customs and Practices*.

IV. **MATERNO COMPENSATION.** Without denying a woman's right to refrain from childbirth, to ensure the longevity of our population, special honor shall be bestowed on women who choose as their destiny the bearing and nurturing of children during the span of eighteen to thirty-eight years. These honors shall include: substantially comfortable lodging, a stipend for each delivery, and a stipend for each baby she breastfeeds for one complete year. Any woman who births ten or more children shall receive a pension for the remainder of her years. All others shall choose another destiny in which to serve the remainder of her years.

V. **VIRTUES.** Contrary to the rampant immorality of our respective origin societies, Nedé shall cultivate a haven of incorruptible ethics. All Nedéans, led by the Matriarch, shall endeavor to embody the core Virtues of diversity, harmony, ingenuity, simplicity, and self-restraint. The development of these Virtues shall remain the free responsibility of the people, whether through their religion of choice or without it.

  A. **DIVERSITY.** Because Nedé combines the cultures and languages of dozens of countries of origin, to create a new, diverse yet unified society we shall:

    1. Establish English as our common tongue, precious-metal coin as our common currency, and the metric system for measurement.

    2. Preserve distinctive relics of our respective heritages, including food, dress, art, and religion.

    3. Treat all women equally.

    4. Rely heavily on the ancient roots from which many of our cultures of origin arose (i.e., the Greeks and Romans, with special attention given to Latin, mathematics, and music) while not ignoring the contribution and influence of ancient Eastern cultures.

  B. **HARMONY.** Nedéans shall strive to live by this guiding principle: treat other women as you would treat yourself. Furthermore, because harmony shall prevail as long as our citizens adhere to these Articles of the constitution, the Matriarchy shall guard them at all costs. Failure to adhere to these Articles shall result in fines, loss of privileges, or imprisonment. While capital punishment shall have no place in Nedéan justice, either for woman or Gentle, the Matriarch reserves the right to ensure—by any other means necessary—that all Nedéans benefit from our collective peace and prosperity.

C. **SIMPLICITY.** Nedéans shall endeavor to live in harmony with Mother Earth, respecting and cultivating nature in ways the old world—dictated by Brutes—failed to do. The location of Nedé, with its limited access to man-made resources and technology, shall foster the virtue of simplicity, as well as contribute to the previous Virtues. Gentles shall provide the manual labor necessary to work the land, care for animals, and enable a simple life for all Nedéans.

D. **INGENUITY.** In order to thrive in Nedé's locale, Nedeans will apply their minds to creative problem-solving, make do with what is available, and refuse to give up when setbacks arise. Without compromising simplicity, our limited technological resources shall be focused first and foremost on creating and maintaining life, public sanitation, and fostering harmony. Should additional resources be discovered in Nedé, they shall be repurposed at the discretion of Innovatus to increase convenience without compromising our core virtue of simplicity.

E. **SELF-RESTRAINT.** Recognizing the dangers and evil of primal lusts in every form, and to demonstrate our superiority over the Brutes who abused, suppressed, and mistreated us, the women of Nedé will adhere to the highest standards of self-restraint by denying any and all base urges; instead redirecting our passions into productive contributions for the good of Nedé. Unlike our brutish predecessors, women are capable of enjoying all the merits of platonic friendship and sisterly affection without digressing into crude gratification. Those not exercising self-control will be punished as deemed appropriate by the Matriarch and, if necessary, the Alexia.

*Protect the weak. Safety for all. Power without virtue is tyranny.*

*Signed,*
*Representatives of the Safety Coalition,*
*founding members of Nedé*

*Tristan Pierce, Florida, USA*
*Melisenda Juárez, Florida, USA*
*Li Na Kuang, China*
*Stephanie Becker, New York, USA*
*Meera Lopez, Belize*
*Alicia Lavoie, Canada*
*Farah Museau, Haiti*
*Amelia Chavez, California, USA*
*Charlotte Taylor, Australia*
*Camila Roberts, Texas, USA*
*Prisha Ananda, India*
*Fernanda Varela, Brazil*
*Margherita Santoro, Italy*

*Consuelo Medina, New York, USA*
*Liz Carolina Rivera, Colombia*
*Siyah Assad, Iran*
*Chisimdi Okonkwo, Nigeria*
*Stella Williams, Australia*
*Annika Novak, Russia*
*Amadi Makeda, Ethiopia*
*Adaku Musa, Nigeria*
*Cora Cunningham, California, USA*
*Ana Silva, Brazil*
*Maria del Carmen Cruz, Mexico*
*Fatima Mohamed, Morocco*
*Elena Chan, Canada*

Jaqueline Harris, United Kingdom

Dimitra Alexopoulos, Greece

Mila Ivanov, Russia

Islande Pierre, Haiti

Candela Moreno, Spain

Emily Carroll, Georgia, USA

Tamaya Khalil, North Sudan

Yael Dayan, Israel

Bjani Ngalula, Democratic Republic
of Congo

Margot Du Plessis, South Africa

Zana Jafari, Iran

Mingmei Tan, China

Min Cho, South Korea

Ishaani Bakshi, India

Rebecca Allen, Texas, USA

Lee Nguyen, California, USA

Maria Alvez, Brazil

Grace Lynn Macdonald, Georgia,
USA

Amira Suleiman, Syria

Lex Sterling, Kentucky, USA

Zala Tesfaye, Ethiopia

Anwen Hughs, United Kingdom

Susan Jones, Virginia, USA

Mae Lee, United Kingdom

Shandice Castillo, Belize

Andrea Tourmaline, Washington,
USA

Blair Williams, United Kingdom

Adèle Leblanc, France

Sofia Dominguez, Spain

Genevieve Fox, Illinois, USA

Ji-woo Kwan, South Korea

Naomie Nadeau, Canada

Tahara Ahmed, United Kingdom

Caron Leblanc, France

Aliyah Morrison, California, USA

Soo-jung Pak, South Korea

Guilia Russo, Italy

Lauren Diaz, Louisiana, USA

Novah Ramos, Nevada, USA

Laurence Tremblay, Canada

Adriana Torres, Mexico

Claire Evans, Utah, USA

Ceylon de Silva, Sri Lanka

Alana Herrera, New York, USA

Zhi Ruo Xue, China

Olivia Fraser, United Kingdom

Thea Spanos, Greece

Tanner Bryant, Nevada, USA

Alipha Oliveira, Brazil

Part One

# CHAPTER ONE

JANUARY 2267
NEDÉ

THE STICKY-SWEET SCENT of orange blossoms quickens my pulse, triggering a nervous twist in my gut. We're almost there. Callisto, my pinto horse, weaves a little faster through the rows of citrus and mango trees, as eager as I am to reach our destination.

Howler monkeys announce our arrival, crouching in the tall, broad-leafed teak trees that stand sentinel around a large clearing. It's a poor replica of the real Arena in Phoenix City, but it's mine. Bright sunlight illuminates a maze of makeshift jumps, barrels, hoops, and other obstacles. When Mother had this section of the teak forest harvested five years ago, I begged her not to replant it.

"What do you want it for, Reina?" she had asked, concern wrinkling the corners of her hazel eyes.

3

I didn't answer, but I knew she'd already guessed. She let me claim the field anyway—let me have the very thing she knew could take me away from her.

Callisto stamps a hoof as I adjust my legs over her bare back. A click of my tongue sends her happily running around the barrels, high-stepping over lattices of branches and logs, and ducking through a curtain of dried vines. She hesitates at the jumps, but I don't have to urge much to get her to acquiesce. She is the best of horses.

After half a dozen laps, I retrieve homemade weapons from a sun-bleached wooden shed: a rough-hewn short sword, a bow, and a hip quiver of arrows. I arrange targets around the clearing for my session, pinning a leaf to a trunk here, balancing a rock on a stump there. My weapons would garner smirks from anyone who knows anything about the real things, but I've never had the heart to ask Mother for authentic ones. So I'm left with this roughly-carved bow made from an ipê branch and a linen string, arrows fashioned out of thin branches and fletched with chicken feathers, and a short sword that couldn't pierce a pillow. But I'm partial to my weapons because of the Gentle who crafted them for me—in secret, like everything about our friendship. Anyway, at least they've helped me learn the basic mechanics of archery and swordplay, in case I muster the nerve to . . .

A rustle pulls my attention to a pile of leaves. A lizard skitters up a stump, and I quickly take aim. I'm about as good at hitting moving targets as I am at keeping the Articles, but I try anyway. No surprise, the lizard lives to see another day.

Behind me, Callisto makes a noise that sounds suspiciously like a laugh.

"What are you snickering at?"

She stares back, feigning innocence. Sometimes I wish she could talk. But not now.

I mount her again, this time with sword tucked into my belt and bow at the ready, and begin to trot the course, shooting poorly as I go. *Focus, Reina.* I squeeze the bow's grip harder, but sheer determination won't make the arrows hit true. The next shot misses its target by a handbreadth. *Ugh.* I wish I had someone to teach me.

What I lack in skill, Callisto more than makes up for. She does her part brilliantly, breezing through the choreography of each obstacle. Ever since my first visit to the real Arena—almost ten years ago now—I've been obsessed with Nedé's peacekeepers and their sleek horses, tempted by a dream that would crush Mother.

I fine-tuned Callisto's footwork for almost a year before I even tried to shoot a bow from her back. Now I can trust her to weave and jump through weathered posts and vine-wrapped hoops with little guidance from my lower body, even without a saddle. My torso and arms can focus on my weapons. Well, except on the last obstacle, the breach, named for the challenging gap between two inclined ramps, and it's coming next. I'm not yet steady enough to make this jump and shoot at the same time. Maybe I never will be. But if I maintain my focus, I can keep my seat across the breach without holding onto the circle of rope around Callisto's neck. I position my legs, sway with her movements, and prepare to soar across two meters of nothing.

Just as Callisto's hooves hit the bottom of the ramp, another rustle snatches my attention, this one bigger and farther away, toward the edge of the teak rows, where thick brush and leafy vines mark the edge of our property. My eyes follow a flash of brown that darts from behind a wood target toward the thicket. Two legs. Not an animal. The figure is brown all over and covered in dirt and—Callisto lunges forward in a mighty jump—I feel my legs come loose, and I'm thrown through the air. It all happens so fast. One second I'm twisting and falling, the next my head collides with a support beam on the far ramp.

Sparks shoot through the darkness like the pain ricocheting around my skull. I vaguely feel my face rub into the dirt . . .

———————

I register pain first. Then something—cloth?—being wrapped around my head. I should try to open my eyes, but before I muster the strength, a sound freezes me solid. A voice. I've never heard one like it.

"We should take her to the house in the valley. That's where she lives."

The tone rumbles like rock against rock, deep as the River. It's quickly followed by another, even thicker voice.

"Are you crazy? Torvus would kill you. *Kill you.* We're not even supposed to be here."

"What do you suggest—we just leave her here, unconscious?"

"Yes? She's fine. Girl or not, that hit wouldn't kill her."

"It doesn't feel right leaving her like this, Rohan."

"Fine. I'll put her in some shade. You watch from that thicket till she wakes up if you want. But you better not let her see you, or I swear, Jase, I'll skin you myself."

"Alright."

One set of footsteps trails away, and I'm lifted like a sheaf of dry grass. I vaguely realize this should terrify me. Even in my pain-induced fog, there's a nagging awareness that my limp body hovers unnaturally over the ground, held in midair by two impossibly strong arms. No Gentle could do that. Those weren't women's voices either. My pulse quickens to a distant, double-time beat, which only makes the pounding in my head worse. I claw toward coherence, gathering just enough clarity and courage to open my eyes the tiniest sliver.

The face is as foreign as its voice: shaped more like a Gentle's than mine, but squarer, with bristles on its cheek, and wild, dark hair, pulled back but not tamed. It's a he, I think, though his strength far surpasses a Gentle's. Eclipses even mine. Am I dead? Dreaming? His bare chest sticks to my cheek, and feels rough with . . . hair? On his chest? *What the bats?*

In the blurry corners of my narrow vision, I can just make out his neck and one shoulder, muscles tensed from their load. They're pronounced, like a stallion's flank after a run. Whoever, whatever, this is, I think I should be afraid. I tell myself to do something—to swing or kick or yell—but my body won't listen.

He lays me down as softly as a kiss on a pile of teak leaves. I sigh into it, relief washing over me. *Don't try to move now. He's going to leave.*

But he doesn't seem in a great hurry. First he adjusts the cloth wrapped around my head and then, for some reason, his fingers linger near my face.

"There's resemblance," he mumbles in a husky whisper, to himself or the other one, I'm not sure. "But she's . . . *beautiful.*"

He gingerly wipes a trickle of blood from my forehead, and I flinch involuntarily, sending him running for the thicket. His footsteps fade, but I still don't—can't—move.

My head aches like it got kicked by a mare. I lie still in the cool leaves for who knows how long—immobilized half from throbbing pain, half from lingering panic—letting my heart slow and giving whoever-that-was the chance to disappear. He told the other one to wait and watch in the brush. Are they both there now?

*There is nothing to be afraid of, Rei.* I grit my teeth and will myself to believe it. I'm not accustomed to fear; the sensation irritates me. *Relax.* Whoever they were, they didn't want to hurt me. *You're fine.* Still, when I finally get to my feet, I head straight for Callisto. I am braver with her. I heave myself clumsily onto her sweaty back. Only then do I find the courage to scan the thicket at the edge of the clearing. No movement.

"Of all the stupid . . . ," I mumble, touching a finger to the tender lump on my head, gashed down the center and still throbbing. I lean against Callisto's neck for support. "I suppose that's enough training for today."

Perched on my horse, still frozen in indecision despite the lack of immediate threat, I replay the bizarre events. It all happened so fast. I slog through the sequence again and again, searching for any clue that might shed light on the strangers' identity, their purpose for being there, the reason they emerged from the shadows to help me, the odd words spoken by the one who carried me. No answers come.

Eventually the dizziness ebbs, and I unwrap the cloth tied around my head. The bleeding has stopped. The fabric is a shirt of sorts—made of a stiff material, dirty, and now stained with my blood. That explains the bare chest. But it doesn't explain who they were, or why they were at Bella Terra. I drop the cloth on a half-hidden stump, not wanting to worry anyone or raise questions about my whereabouts this morning by bringing it to the villa.

"Come on, girl. Let's go home."

---

The next morning, my first conscious thought as my mind sheds sleep explodes as a muffled yell into my pillow:

"Ciela! I'm going to *kill* your rooster!"

Light barely filters through the sheer curtains of my bedroom window, if you can call it light at this hour—more of a dusky gray than true morning. Another crow from Diablo, and I start thinking about chicken and rice, barbecued chicken, chicken stir-fry, and a feather pillow made from the rest of him.

I know better than to think I'll fall back asleep, so I decide on the next best thing: an early ride.

I'm in the large pasture behind our villa by the time the sun properly wakes. Despite my fussing at that cursed chicken, there's a small satisfaction in beating the sun at her own game. I haven't beaten Tre, though. I never do. As a Gentle, he's always up before the sun to begin work around the finca: tending the animals, trimming overgrowth, hauling water. Well, unless he's sick, which happens as regular as the rains. Gentles might be amiable, obedient, and helpful, but they're also fragile, weak-bodied, and often ill. I hate to say it—Mother insists I shouldn't—but some are frustratingly dim-witted too. It's like their minds are riddled with holes, losing streams of thought, forgetting the simplest instructions. Tre, though, he's not as bad as the others. He can't grow muscle, any more than I can change the Article that forbids our friendship, but when fate threw us together almost five years ago, his relative boldness caught me off guard. He was sharp for a Gentle—or, perhaps, what he risked helped me see beyond what I expected him to be.

He had stumbled upon me near the riverbank that day, next to a giant fig tree, where I had found one of our baby goats lying dead. The soft fur on its tiny body was mottled with blood, and flies were already gathering. I'm not usually overly emotional, but I had just fought with Mother, the sight really was awful for a thirteen-year-old, and for whatever other reasons I found myself sobbing over it. Like, *really* sobbing. The blubbering-mess kind of cry.

Tre was walking a short distance from the bank with an armful of wood when he noticed me. He dropped his load and approached, timidly, without a word. Then he knelt down beside the tiny kid goat, took a broad stick, and started scraping the moist soil, stroke after stroke, until sweat trickled down his sun-leathered, freckled cheeks. When I realized what he was doing—giving a burial to an animal we would have burned or fed to the dogs—I knelt down too, helped him dig the deep grave and pile it with rocks to protect the corpse from scavengers. By the end, Tre's thin body was shaking with exertion, and that caught my attention too. Most Gentles would have given up far sooner.

I knew what I was risking by interacting with him. Despite my great respect for the Articles, I guess I was too impertinent to keep them perfectly, even then. Or perhaps Mother's influence really had made me soft, as other women whispered when they thought we couldn't hear.

After a while, I even got the nerve to ask him his name. I knew he had one; Mother always names her Gentles.

"Treowe," he had said.

"That's a funny name," I said, wiping the remnants of my cry on my shirt sleeve.

"Dom Pierce gave it to me. She said she hoped I'd live up to it."

"What does it mean?"

"Faithful."

He chanced upon me at the riverbank again after that, more and more often, until our meetings were orchestrated less by chance and more by intention. Unlikely though it is, our secret friendship works somehow. We enjoy each other's company, when we can manage it. I speak to him as an equal, and he treats me as more than one, which, admittedly, feeds my ego. He's always looking for ways to make me laugh behind my tutor's back, calms me down when my temper flares, leaves little treasures where I'm sure to find them. I don't know why Mother chose "faithful" for this Gentle, but he's lived up to it.

I see him now across the field, his shaggy, straw-colored hair flopping over his face as he leads a row of semi-obedient sheep. When he sees me, he crosses his eyes and blows out his cheeks, trying to coax a laugh. He doesn't dare wave, and I don't dare call to him, but his gesture lets me know I'm seen, and my smile tells him the same.

I resume my search for the object of my predawn expedition and find her cropping grass between four other mares. When Callisto hears me coming, she walks over with a pleased whinny.

"You're not sleeping either, huh?" I rub her forelock, then down her neck, fingers pushing through one of the white patches on her tobiano-patterned coat.

"Maybe you'll accidentally step on that nasty rooster while we ride." I slip the braided neck rope over her head and swing onto her bare back. "Let's go, beautiful."

Callisto walks west through the pasture as her muscles warm. Howler monkey calls cut through the hum of insects and bird chatter. The air is heavy this morning. It may be the dry season, but we'll probably still get drenched with rain by noon. The endless wet is what makes Nedé so beautiful, so lush, Mother says, but I prefer the dry days. Just another way we're complete opposites.

Outside the south gate, Callisto moves faster, anticipating a return to my teak forest arena. Me, on the other hand? Paranoia might be cousins with weakness, but I don't have the urge to return to my training grounds today—not yet. I decide to follow a trail past the teak forest instead, opting for my favorite place on Mother's three hundred hectares: a ridge overlooking Bella Terra. When I pass my obstacle course, my eyes thoroughly scan the thick wall of foliage for movement. Seeing nothing, I wonder again whether being lifted off the ground could have been a hallucination, brought on by the smash to my still-tender skull. I seriously consider this possibility for about four seconds. Then I notice the shirt I left on the stump yesterday is gone.

That strange bare-chested . . . person . . . and the other one—whether or not they were as strong and strange as I imagined, they did exist outside my mind. And they'd come back. Or maybe never left. *Quit panicking, Reina. Of course they would come back for the shirt*, I tell myself, irritated by the way my breaths have shallowed. I didn't get the impression they had much to spare. *That doesn't mean they're still here.* Still, I give Callisto a click and a squeeze with my calves, urging her to pick up her pace until we pass the teak forest entirely. I spend the next ten minutes trying to puzzle out a logical explanation for what I saw yesterday: my sister Ciela, home from the city and playing a trick on me? A Gentle wearing goat skin? Each possibility sounds even more ridiculous.

Once we reach the treeless ledge perched high on the edge of a foothill, boasting sweeping views of Bella Terra and beyond, my questions still. This place never fails to overpower whatever weighs on my mind.

From the overlook, the white buildings of Bella Terra resemble the dollhouse set my oldest sister, Jonalyn, used to play with when she was young. The smooth, white walls of the casitas and out-buildings seem to glow from within, topped with perfectly symmetrical rows of red-brown clay tiles. Papery bougainvillea shades arched doorways, and a tiered fountain shines like a new coin in the pebbled courtyard. Sheep, llamas, and horses graze in their respective fields, and a small column of smoke curls up in wispy fingers from the outdoor kitchen.

The villa, schoolroom, stables, and other outbuildings lie tucked in the center of the surrounding fields, which are sectioned like a rolling, tightly stitched green quilt. The property is hemmed on the north and east by the coiling, twisting Jabiru River. I can just make out a large crown of leaves along its banks belonging to the fig tree where Tre and I often meet during his afternoon break. The pastoral scene is familiar, though not particularly inspiring. For a muse, I turn my attention east.

Squinting toward the sun, I search for the only tall buildings in all of Nedé, which mark our capital, Phoenix City. I find their out-line, flanked by the shimmering Halcyon Sea. The city has always felt thrilling, a melody that sings to me, tempting me to dream of more than I have and more than I am. Today is different, though. Today I know that change is finally coming, and I welcome it.

This simple life on the finca is quaint, serene even, but it isn't for me. The view is tolerable this morning, I'll give it that. But morning and evening light show off everyone's good side, and I don't trust them. Love a thing at noon, and your amor is real.

Next week, I will have to decide on a destiny: my vocation and, ultimately, lifestyle. I know what Mother wants. She hopes I'll become a Materno, like her and like my sister Jonalyn. Ciela chose Scientia and Medicinae, working at the Center for Health Services, which isn't far removed, especially since she still comes home some weekends. She can't stand to be far from Mother for long. I don't resent them for their choices. Their destinies comple-ment them, like lime to avocado. Not only are there perks to being a Materno—like our own rural finca—but nurture and care come naturally to the women in my family. Three of them, anyway.

I was eight years old when I realized I was different from my sisters and Mother, as unnatural as a filly born to a herd of sheep. We had attended a demonstration at the Arena, where the Alexia, all beauty and fierceness, rode their dark Lexander horses through intricate obstacles, pelting moving targets with arrows like their bows were extensions of themselves. I've been enamored with the Alexia ever since, hence my makeshift arena and weapons. If I'm honest, the Alexia scare as much as inspire me, but that life rings vastly more exciting than raising babies and managing a finca. And none of the other destinies—Scientia and Medicinae, Politikós, Ad Artium, Gentles Regimen, and the like—intrigue me much. Dom Bakshi, my tutor, urges me to reconsider—I suspect because of her loyalties to Mother. Some days, her certain disapproval is enough to steer me clear of the Alexia; others, it draws me toward them. Today? Today I'm not sure I'm ready to face the disappointment my choice would spark, and that makes me wonder if I understand the Virtues at all.

It's true that most of the other women in my family seem made to nurture. The clearest exception? Grandmother. It's a wonder she had a child at all, let alone two. I asked Mother about it once. She said Matriarchs are required to give birth twice, to improve the appeal to potential Materno recruits. It's difficult enough to maintain thirty percent of Nedéans in that destiny, she had said grimly. I wondered if she resented being a child birthed by law rather than choice. Regardless, the thought of Grandmother choosing to mother anything goes against all sensibilities. "Mother of Nedé" or not, she's about as tender as a teak tree.

Mother once told me I remind her of Grandmother. I wonder if that's what she meant.

I must be taking too long admiring the view, because Callisto gives a soft tug on the rope in my hands. She's often the more responsible of our duo. I reluctantly let her lead us down the trail, past my arena—quickly now—and back through the groves of fruit trees, towards home. Chores are waiting, then studies, followed by the murder of a certain bronze-tailed rooster.

---

"You smell like you've been in the sheep field, Reina." Dom Bakshi's voice drifts flatly over the top of a large book, opened in front of her face so that a bouffant of shiny, grey-streaked black hair is the only visible part of her.

"Then your olfactory senses serve you well, Domina Bakshi," I tease, using her full title with a nasally, academic delivery. I only use *Domina*—rather than *Dom*, the shortened version of a distinguished woman's prefix—when I'm being falsely dramatic. I drop the accent to add, "I marked the lambs, fed the dogs, and swept the villa too. I swear, if Mother had her way, we'd do all the Gentles' work for them."

Dom Bakshi snaps shut the book, which appears drab and ancient next to her purple sari, draped over a peach-pink cropped bodice. She often resembles a passionflower next to Mother's simple Materno clothing, and I only wear what I can ride in, if I can help it. But Dom Bakshi's great, great, great, great-grandmother—or was it five greats?—was a foremother from a land which wore such clothing. Not that all Nedéans wear the dress of their foremothers. Our climate isn't suited for most. Others carry on food traditions, still others dialects and songs. And some, like the Pierce line I descend from—a family marked by Matriarchs and Senators— prefer a blend of the best diversities Nedé offers.

My tutor raises her chin, and I know what's coming even before she says, "We'd be better off if *more* daughters of Nedé knew how to take care of themselves, as in the earliest days of our Matriarchy. Back then, the Gentles were too young to work, and our survival depended on our own ingenuity, ability, and grit. You're lucky your mother knows the value of such things."

Her words are so predictable I have to force down a laugh. We've had this conversation dozens of times over the years. Mother makes us learn some of the Gentles' tasks—farming, cleaning, washing clothes, and the like—me and my sisters complain, and Dom Bakshi reminds us of the virtue of hard work and the rarity of our mother: a woman who came from privilege yet values character and all life. And then we roll our eyes while knowing full well she's probably right.

"Besides," she adds, "you clearly haven't been worked *too* hard, or that attitude of yours would have been curbed by now." It's her turn to smile.

Dom Bakshi is at least twice my age, speaks five languages, and is usually a model of professionalism, but every once in a while I catch the faintest bit of sass, hinting that her sharp wit doesn't always squeeze into the perfect tutor mold. After nearly eighteen years spent under her teaching, I've learned more from her than Latin, mathematics, history, and music. I've also inherited her intensity and questioning spirit, and I'm proud of it.

On my way to the far side of the room, I pass half a dozen small desks arranged in rows. Those are for the Gentles, though we're never taught at the same time. My own, larger desk is littered with charts, books, papers, and a wooden monkey I carved with my first knife when I was ten years old. Got my first stitches whittling it too, and as Mother tied off the last knot, I vowed I'd never get rid of that monkey—being bonded by blood as we are—so there it sits. He grins up at me with a crooked smile.

The two other desks positioned adjacent to mine have been collecting dust since my older sisters finished their tutelage and began their destinies. If I were a more sentimental person, I might get choked up at the thought of my own desk's fate, which—following today's final lesson—will follow suit. But I'm not, so I don't.

No, I'm not sentimental, or so I'm told. I take in the familiar smell of oiled wood and the flower garden behind the schoolhouse. I notice the large map of Nedé on the wall; the shelves of books, so rare; my inkwell and favorite curassow-tail-feather pen; the plaques of Nedé's Virtues, taken from Article V of our constitution. I notice them all without sadness. I celebrate what I've accomplished here, but the future is coming too fast to waste tears on what's behind me.

"Dom Bakshi," I say, thankful she will have already moved past my initial ingratitude, "how did you know you wanted to be an Ad Artium? And why be a tutor instead of—I don't know—a painter?"

She sighs, sympathy replacing her irritation with me. "You still haven't decided yet, have you?"

I shake my head.

Perhaps she realizes that one more day of lessons won't define my educational career, because she pushes aside the chart intended for today's teaching and sits down beside me.

"Well," she says, "the important thing, you'll remember, is that you can't make a wrong choice, Reina. Every destiny is vital to the success of Nedé, and every woman has a dignified role to play. The jobs we do are as unique as the women we are: all colors, all sizes, all peculiarities, all languages, all heritages, brought together as one people, of equal worth, for the safety and good of all. So whether you choose Scientia and Medicinae, like your sister Ciela, or Ad Artium like me, or even Alexia," she gives me a knowing smile, "your only task is to follow your heart. How lucky we are to live in the days of Nedé!"

I've heard the speech before, but I'm grateful to her nonetheless. Yes, lucky. I can't imagine what it would have been like to live in the world before Nedé, in those faraway places where Brutes ruled over women, hurting them by . . . well, I don't know how, but it must have been terrible, because the foremothers declined to record the atrocities in our history parchments. I can't imagine what those women went through before most of them and all the Brutes were wiped out in the Great Sickness. If the foremothers hadn't already been fighting the Brutes and working on important medical advances, they would have died too, and never have found the key to curing their sons from the inferior genetics that caused Brutishness. Because of the foremothers' courage and insight, the sons of Nedé were freed once and for all to be their true, Gentle selves, able to use their best gifts for us.

Unlike the women of long ago, I've never been anything *but* safe. I mean, Nedé isn't perfect, but I've never been in any real danger. Most women are happy to abide by the Articles of our constitution, and the Alexia would make a short history of any dissenter. The Alexia . . . just the thought of the slick-clad, bow-wielding, imposing but impressive peacekeeping force of Nedé fills me with both excitement and fear. Not fear of what I would face—squabbles between finca owners, the rare Materno who won't part with a Gentle, or an occasional wild animal venturing from the Jungle are hardly terrifying—but with whom I'd face them. The Alexia are known to be stern, strong, and steely. The whole group of them is tough as a coconut: rough and hard, unless you're on the inside. I'd like to think I'm strong enough to make it in, but . . . what if I'm not?

Dom Bakshi continues, "Imagine if no one chose Fabricatio. Who would teach the Gentles to make and sew cloth, fashion carts, or press the very paper on your desk? We need women in Innovatus as well, to use the few natural resources and repurposed materials we have at our disposal to create new technologies and maintain those the foremothers inherited when they arrived—like the phone in the villa, or the Center's important medical machines. And of course, where would any of us be without the Maternos, the faithful women who sacrifice their bodies and decades of their lives to bring new life into this world?"

I try not to let my mind camp on the word "Materno," but despite Dom Bakshi's rousing speech, the name itself is so boring compared to the other destinies that I can't help but feel it doesn't belong. *Materno.* Might as well be called "predictable." "Soft." Or maybe just "Leda," after Mother herself. As soon as I think that, guilt pricks my insides. That wasn't fair. See? I'm not patient or kind enough to be any good at nurturing, not even for the incentives.

"I'm sure I'll figure it out. I have a whole week anyway—that's practically a lifetime." I waggle an eyebrow at Dom Bakshi. She shakes her head.

I feel better for her words of encouragement, though, just like I do after every time I fret with indecision and she gives me the "all of Nedé is at your fingertips" speech. Because she's right—Nedé is a remarkable place: diverse, safe, and full of possibilities. Whatever destiny I choose, I'll be okay.

So why do I fight this inner worry that none of them suit me *exactly* right?

We spend the rest of my foiled lesson talking about life, and destinies, and Nedé. Dom Bakshi has taught me well, and I see her look of satisfaction as she dismisses me. I'm another job completed, I suppose. I gather the few books and papers I wish to keep, plus one wooden monkey, and leave the Bella Terra schoolroom for the last time.

# CHAPTER TWO

THE SIZZLE OF THE FRYING PAN and the smoky-sweet smell of plantains greet me before anyone in the kitchen notices I've slipped in.

Mother says Marsa's the best chef in Nedé. Granted, they've been friends longer than I've been alive, but the compliment can't be solely biased. Mother grew up at Finca del Mar—the Matriarch's seaside estate—where she had access to the finest luxuries of Nedé. Chefs—unlike kitchen hands, who are Gentles—earn high regard in Nedé. A subset of Ad Artium, chefs give their foodcraft the same devotion singers give their songs, or dancers imbue their dance. Given the enticing aroma filling the kitchen now, I'm convinced the benefits of culinary art surpass them all. Usually only wealthier women can afford chefs, never Maternos, but some perks still reside with the Matriarch's daughter. Mother convinced Marsa to take the position at Bella Terra before I was born. Over the years, her role has expanded from preparing enticing meals to second mother. She doesn't let us girls call her Dom Museau—only Marsa. And since she and Mother have known each other since childhood—Marsa's own mother was a chef at Finca del Mar—she's basically family anyway.

Her full, colorful voice—matching her thick body, wrapped in a multi-colored apron—rises above the sizzle. "Don't even think about sitting down to lunch until you've washed that filth off your hands, petit!"

I'll always be "petit" to Marsa, never mind my nearly eighteen years. She still calls both my sisters "petit" too, as if we were no different from the actual children of the house, the nine little Gentles currently assigned here by Gentles Regimen. Marsa sometimes calls them "petit" too, but only the ones she especially fancies, like Gentle 85272, who we've taken to calling Little Boo. Mother is the only woman I know who names all her Gentles— both the little ones in her care and the finca workers who care for us. Sometimes she gives deep thought to their monikers, but usually she just picks something that seems to fit. When Little Boo was smaller, maybe three years old, he loved to play peekaboo with anyone who would join in the game. He's six now, just a year away from leaving us for a Hive, but the name has stuck. Apart from Tre, I don't usually spend much time with the Gentles—no one is supposed to, per Article II—but as far as the little ones go, Boo's my favorite.

I brush past one of the Gentle kitchen hands to get to the sink. "It's just a little sheep dung," I tease.

"None of that talk in this kitchen, petit. Wap kon Jorge!"

I've never actually *gotten* the "thing that's coming to me," even though she's threatened it nearly every time I've exasperated her my whole life long. If her two hands weren't occupied on the frying pan and whisk respectively, I'd get a thick finger wagged at me for good measure too.

"Alright, I'll wash them," I say, with a bit of false reluctance.

I like Marsa. She nags me like a nanny goat, but the food she crafts for our little finca, and her genuine care for our family, make up for it. From the sink, I can see she's got a pot of coconut rice and beans warming on the back of the iron stove; a pan of finished plantains, ready to top the rice; and chicken with vegetables and herbs simmering in the frying pan. The meal will be simple—fit to serve our little mob—but elegantly garnished.

"I hope that's Diablo in the pan," I say, not at all joking.

"Real mature, Reina," Ciela shoots back from her seat at the table. Ciela is three years older than me. Accusing me of being immature is the only comeback she knows.

"He woke me up again today. He's louder than the monkeys! I'm serious, Ciela. If he goes missing, you'll know what happened to him."

She narrows her eyes. "Not everything that annoys you has to be disposed of, little queenie."

On second thought, Ciela has two comebacks: accusing me of immaturity and making derogatory plays on my name. Reina means "queen" in one of the old languages. The first time I remember her using this comeback, she was mad because I stomped my four-year-old feet at her when she wouldn't let me have the red scarf for our Alexia play. Okay, sure, I like to have things my way. But she can be a beast too.

I roll my eyes, proving my immaturity, I suppose, but I don't care. I tolerate Ciela's existence little more than Diablo's.

"Arrêté! That's enough!" Marsa barks.

Marsa has little patience for our family squabbles, and her large, quasi-stern presence has squelched countless quarrels over the years. A woman with a metal skillet can be quite persuasive.

"Yes, Marsa," we say in unison. Though we don't sound it, we both mean it.

Though Mother is a Materno, she also travels frequently because of her role as one of two Center directors, specifically overseeing the Materno operations of Nedé. Usually her job just takes her to Phoenix City for a few days, but sometimes she's gone for a week or more visiting other towns or fincas scattered throughout the Provinces. When she's away, Marsa fills the void by tightening up the ship. "None of your nonsense when Leda's away," she'll say. But she doesn't have to say it often. We don't seem to argue as much when Mother's away; her absence has a way of making us act like the adults we are. Well, like the adults Ciela and Jonalyn are, and I will become once I choose my destiny.

My destiny . . .

The thought produces a familiar knot of anxiety—not exactly because I don't know what I'll choose—though there's *that*—but because, as much as I push against Mother's opinions, I don't want to disappoint her. Speaking of . . .

"Good afternoon, Marsa, girls." Mother slides a leather satchel from her shoulder onto the tile floor. Despite the many miles she must have ridden this morning, she still enters the room like sunshine incarnate. Which, conversely, instantly darkens my mood. She crosses the room and takes a seat at the head of the rough-hewn wood table. Ciela and I rise to take turns kissing her cheek.

"Hi, Mother," I say, more flatly than I mean to. I don't know why, but I generally turn sour as buttermilk when she's around. She smiles at me despite my lackluster greeting.

"Hello, Reina." Her voice sounds even warmer on the heels of my coldness. Her patience with me is admirable; I don't know why it makes me even grumpier. She lifts her chin and turns slightly, giving me easier access to her cheek. I brush aside a chocolate wave of her hair and kiss her quickly.

All women are honored in Nedé, no matter their destiny, but Maternos hold particular esteem. At least, we are *taught* to show honor. We've been told that Maternos have the hardest job of all: enduring pregnancy, birthing children, raising daughters, and, for those who manage fincas, caring for Nedé's youngest Gentles until they're transferred to Hives. Every Materno—whether she manages a rural finca or prefers a flat in Phoenix City—gives much of herself: her body and her time. Children are taught to show reverence by kissing their mother when she enters a room, bringing her flowers "just because," or by serenading her on special occasions.

I don't deny that Mother works hard and has given much of herself to us. I suppose I just figure all women labor for the good of Nedé, no matter their destinies. Each contributes to society. Why should Maternos get more recognition?

Mother's peaceful expression furrows when she notices the gashed lump near my hairline, still swollen after the blow to the wood ramp yesterday.

"Reina, what have you done to your head?"

I take my seat as I consider how to respond. I could tell her about my accident—about the strange, frightening people in the teak forest who—despite the missing shirt—I still suspect I may have hallucinated into existence, or at least somehow exaggerated. I could ask if she knows anything that might explain who they were or whether we should be concerned. But it's as if all rational thought and civility dries up when I'm around her, and I can't bring myself to say any of that. Instead I shrug my shoulders.

"Nothing. It's fine," I claim, curt and dismissive. I'm stupid not to tell her, and I know it. If those people *are* dangerous, Mother should know they were on Bella Terra land. But my stubborn pride keeps me from changing course now.

Sparing me from further inquiry, Dom Bakshi walks through

the doorway with nine trailing Gentles ordered by height. The boys take turns kissing Mother before taking their seats. She acknowledges them each by name, not number, with a smile and a nod.

Once everyone is seated, one of Marsa's kitchen hands, a stout Gentle with a limp, brings overflowing bowls and platters to the table. We eat family style at Bella Terra, as Mother prefers: our family, plus the little Gentles, Marsa, Dom Bakshi, and a few other staff. The rest of the Gentles—those who have been assigned to work at Bella Terra—will eat later. As we pass the bowls of beans and rice and the platters of plantains and chicken pieces, cheerful anticipation grows from the young ones. Mother's Gentles are happy nearly all the time, but never more so than when they are about to eat.

While Mother says a prayer for our food, I hear a noise coming from the Gentles' side of the table. I open my right eye a pinch and catch Little Boo shoving a piece of plantain into his mouth. I raise an amused eyebrow at him, and he grins, then shuts his eyes tight and reverent-like.

Mother's "amen" is followed by a raucous clinking of silverware and nine sets of cheeks stuffed full. Little Boo watches me. I wink back.

Once Mother has asked the boys about their morning with Dom Bakshi, and they seem occupied with each other, she turns to me.

"I got a call from your grandmother today."

My fork halts midway to my mouth. "Is something wrong?"

Phones are rare, in holding with one of Nedé's most important core Virtues—simplicity—and those who have them reserve them for urgent matters. The last time we had a call from Grandmother was two years ago. She was concerned about a report regarding the Center and wanted Mother to take care of it before the day was up. Mother had quickly packed a few things in a rucksack and ridden to Phoenix City before lunch. If Grandmother has called, it must be important.

Mother pauses before answering, as if weighing whether or not she can avoid telling me. "She wants to see you, Reina."

"Me?" She has my full attention now. "Why?"

Mother's shoulders sink just a little. I only notice because it's so unlike her. "She wouldn't say. She wants to talk with you about something, and when I pressed, she said it was not my concern. You know my mother."

*No, I don't,* I want to say, but instead I give a small nod.

I've only had maybe a dozen interactions with my grandmother since I've been old enough to capture memories. One particularly clear recollection was the day of the big Alexia demonstration; I was eight years old. When she noticed me watching the horses before the event, she invited me to sit in the Matriarch's box with her. I remember Mother looking skeptically at Grandmother, as if trying to weigh her motives. "She'll be fine, Leda. I'm just giving her a better view," Grandmother had said, and Mother relented. I felt important, watching the show next to my grandmother, the Matriarch, in her flowing, colorful robe and beaded jewelry. I think she found amusement in my delight too, because every so often she would incline toward my ear, pointing out the pedigree of a horse, or the agility of its rider.

"These women are trained to protect us, Reina. It is the highest honor of all," she had said.

I had been taught, by Dom Bakshi I suppose, that being a *Materno* was the highest destiny, but I knew better than to question the Mother of Nedé. Besides, I think I rather agreed. Something about the Alexia, or their dark, shiny horses, or both, felt courageous and bold. I was already bold. And I thought I might be courageous someday. Watching the demonstration next to Grandmother, I wondered for the first time whether I might have the *brio*—the spirit, determination, vivacity—to run with the Alexia when I was grown.

That was almost ten years ago. Since that encounter, I've only had reason to speak to Grandmother at our annual dinners at Finca del Mar. Every September she invites my family, including my aunt and great-aunts, to a feast after the Initus Ceremony, where all of Nedé celebrates the fourteen-year-old Gentles' departure from their respective Hives to begin vocations. She doesn't usually talk to me or my sisters much at those dinners, but last year was different.

At the feast Grandmother asked me, "Reina, Leda tells me you'll turn eighteen this year. Have you chosen your destiny? Will you be a Materno like your mother and eldest sister? Or . . . " Here she paused and narrowed her eyes, as if evaluating me. ". . . Or perhaps the Alexia for you?"

Heat crept up my neck, and I'm sure I flushed as crimson as boiled lobster. As much as I clashed with Mother and my sisters sometimes, I hadn't yet told them that I could never be a Materno. It never felt like the right time to break the news, but something in Grandmother's look gave me a rush of adrenaline, and I found myself saying more than I meant to.

"I'm not sure which destiny I'll choose yet, Grandmother, but . . . it won't be Materno." I wanted to look at Mother, curious what my admission caused her to feel, but kept my eyes locked with Grandmother's instead. The corner of her mouth had raised slightly, and she sounded amused.

"Ah! A rebel in the family. You know, Reina, that every woman in Nedé is free to choose her destiny. If you want to be a Politikós, or run with the Alexia, Leda will not stop you." She shot a pointed look at Mother, as if to quell any thought she might have had of swaying my decision.

"Yes, Grandmother," was all I managed. Strong personalities

vied at that table, least of all mine. But I had felt vindicated by Grandmother's enthusiasm. At least one relative wouldn't be disappointed by my probable defection.

That was five months ago. Could that be why she wants to see me now? To find out if I've mustered the courage to "rebel?"

I eat the rest of my lunch rather distracted with the thought, hardly noticing the usual lunch noises—the Gentles' quiet chatter, Marsa's humming, Mother and Ciela talking about Center business.

Whatever Grandmother wants, I'll soon find out.

---

Treowe is already leaning against the fig tree when I arrive at the riverbank carrying two bananas and a leftover breakfast pastry.

"I brought us something," I say, sliding down the trunk to sit next to him. I hand him a banana, then tear the soft, bubbly empanada in half to share too.

"Well, thank you, Rei." He takes the fruit by the stem and smacks mine with it, initiating a banana sword fight.

"You're so immature," I tease. Still, I don't surrender until both our bananas slump in mushy defeat.

"If I'm immature, that means you have bad taste in friends!" He makes himself laugh with his joke, producing one dimple on his right cheek.

He reminds me of a taller, slightly wider version of Little Boo when he laughs. Even the oldest Gentles don't look much different from the little ones. Just more wrinkly and with less hair, but ever thin-framed and baby-faced, with a frail quality that makes me uncomfortable if I dwell on it. So I don't—at least, not when it comes to Tre. If I ignore the way he gets winded after brushing down the horses or harvesting the orchards, I can avoid facing

what'll happen when he gets older. I can pretend we can always be friends.

I huff playfully at his insult. "That's it—give me my food back," I demand, extending my palm.

He slaps my hand instead. "You can't have it. That's our deal. I risk the whip to be your friend, and you reward my daring with culinary delights."

"Whatever. No one's going to whip you—not at Bella—and you know you don't come for the food."

He grins at me, accepting his defeat. I grin back. "I win."

"You always do," he says, kicking my foot.

We sit quietly for a time, eating our squishy bananas, relishing the shade of our tree. Across the river, an iguana climbs a thin branch dangling precariously over the green water. His feet move slowly, his body waddling across the limb. I hope he falls in so I can watch him swim up the slow-moving current.

I wonder how many afternoons we've spent along the riverbank over the past four years. We never stay more than twenty minutes or Old Solomon, the lead Gentle here at Bella, would notice Tre was gone. A Gentle taking more than the allotted morning or afternoon rest is not tolerated, not even by one of their own. Tre would probably be given extra chores, of the less desirable variety. Mother would never let Solomon whip him, though. She's too kind for that. I know because she caught us here once, when she was out looking for me at just the wrong time. She stared at us, said hello to Treowe, asked me her question, and, though it seemed she wanted to say something else, turned and went back to the house. She's never mentioned it since.

Even though I don't adore Mother as Jonalyn and Ciela do, I can see she is a good woman. Leda Pierce is more magnanimous with Gentles than anyone else I know. I've seen a Gentle in the stocks for not picking up trash fast enough, not bowing his head

when a Dom walked past, or being away from his Hive past curfew. The stocks are in Phoenix City.

So is my Grandmother.

"The Matriarch wants to see me," I say, hesitant to interrupt our quiet reverie.

"What for?" he asks absently.

"I have no idea."

This gets him to sit up and face me. "No idea at all?"

I shake my head.

"Are you going to go?"

"Of course I'm going to go. She's my grandmother. She also happens to be the Matriarch. No one says no to the Matriarch, Tre."

His back finds the tree again. "Are you nervous?"

I yank a stem of grass and wind it around my finger. "Maybe. Yeah, a little."

Treowe doesn't respond right away, but I know he's thinking because of the way his brow creases. When he speaks, I know he's chosen his words carefully.

"I don't think you need to worry. I bet it has something to do with the Succession."

My eyes stretch wide. I had never once considered that possibility. Not ever, in my whole life, considered that possibility.

"Think about it," he continues, "the Matriarch's got to be what, in her seventies? And she hasn't chosen a successor yet. I'm no historian, Rei, but I'm pretty sure that's a record. She's got to be thinking about starting the competition."

"Even if she is thinking about it, what does that have to do with me? I'm too young. Anyway, Mother would be a better Candidate from our Province. Everyone loves her, and she's the Matriarch's daughter."

"Dom Pierce would be . . . an amazing leader. But if Matriarch

Teera had wanted her, she could have started the Succession years ago."

He's right—Grandmother is seventy-six, well past the usual age when Matriarchs begin the process of selecting an Apprentice. If she had wanted Mother to be one of the four Candidates, why wait this long? I still think Tre is crazy, though. Me? Represent Amal Province? It's laughable.

"Even if Grandmother did want me to join the Candidates, she wouldn't undermine the Provinces' sovereignty," I counter.

I know I have a point, even without his nod of assent. Nedé's eighth Matriarch might be stern and brazen, but she respects the system our foremothers set in place. At the time of a Succession, each of the four Provinces is required to select a Candidate of their choice. Any woman in a Province may be nominated—though there are schools dedicated to training suitable contenders—but the final vote lies with each Province's twelve-woman senate, just as the senate members were voted in by the women of their respective Provinces. The Matriarch wouldn't disrupt our flawless system, especially not for a granddaughter she has barely spoken to.

Tre considers my argument. "Yeah, she's pretty by the book. Maybe I'm wrong."

"Obviously wrong," I say, bumping his shoulder with mine. His dimple reappears.

"When do you leave?"

"In the morning."

"Taking Callisto?"

"Of course." I add, "She likes Phoenix City."

Tre huffs. "Right." He knows my horse can't stand the city.

Six years ago, Mother's finest mare, Estrella, was studded by an overeager Paint stallion who didn't care about Old Solomon's breeding plan. The result was Callisto: the smartest pinto Solomon had ever seen, but whom he couldn't sell or breed because of her equine mutt-ness. Sure, half of her is Lexander, a thoroughbred-Criollo mix—the most desirable bloodline in Nedé. But the other half is Paint. In Phoenix City, because of the Alexia's preference for dark, sleek coats, that would get her a job hauling loads. None of that matters to me, of course, because she's one hundred percent mine. Old Solomon started her, then gave her to me to complete her training, saying I was the only one of Mother's daughters who could handle her spirit without crushing it. We've been inseparable since. Anyway, Callisto dislikes the city about as much as I relish it, but I will never take another horse if I can help it.

Tre brushes some crumbs from my leg. "Then I'll make sure she's rubbed down and ready for you in the morning."

I nod my thanks.

"I better get back," he says with a sigh. "A llama busted a fence, and Old Solomon wants me to fix it this afternoon." With that, he stands, stretches, and turns toward the house.

I'm suddenly overcome by a strange reluctance to let him go. "Tre?"

I don't know what I want to say, exactly. That I appreciate him? That I'll miss his company while I'm away? That I wish we could spend more time together than the occasional chance meeting or these short picnics on the riverbank allow? That he's the only friend I have, and I'm afraid once I choose my destiny I'll lose even that?

He turns back toward me. "Yes, Rei of Sunshine?"

I roll my eyes. Whatever nice thing I was trying to put my finger on vanished the moment he used Mother's pet name for me. He knows I barely tolerate it when *she* says it.

The moment passes, taking my nerve with it. "I'll see you later."

He doesn't say anything, just stands there, looking at me through the clump of flaxen hair that is prone to flop over his face. Then he smiles again, walks up the bank, and disappears.

—————

After dinner, I head to my room to pack a few things. I figure I won't need much. Mother is using the trip to Phoenix City as an opportunity to check in at the Center, but we'll still only be gone a couple of days.

I've put my nicest two shirts and a long linen dress into a leather rucksack when Mother knocks softly on the solid mahogany door.

"May I come in?" she asks.

"Sure," I say, dropping in a pair of seamless riding pants for the journey home.

Mother takes in the room, her gaze lingering on a portrait of me and my sisters, painted when we were small enough to hate sitting still that long.

"Reina, are you sure you want to go?"

I try to weigh why Mother would ask this. I'm nervous to talk to Grandmother, sure, but not afraid. I'm not a child. I bet she's just reluctant to let me go because she's being overprotective, as usual. A familiar resentment quickly heats my blood.

"Let me guess—you're afraid I'm going to fall madly in love with the city and never come back. Or are you worried that Grandmother might start giving me grand ideas about noble destinies besides Materno?" I don't give her time to answer. "That's it, isn't it? You're afraid that I'll be different from you—that I'll make a life of my own that doesn't include you or this . . . this . . . *finca*." I say it like a curse word. My voice is loud now, my face flushed.

She looks hurt, but not confused. She is a saint, and I am a devil. For the love of Nedé, why does Mother always bring out the worst in me?

"No, Rei. I'm not worried about you choosing a different path. I just want to make sure you know which path you are choosing."

I try to meet her calmer volume, with little success. "I'm not choosing any path right now. I'm just going to see what Grandmother wants."

She sits down on the end of my wooden four-poster bed, the very spot she used to sit when she'd tuck me in and lead prayers when I was a child. After our "amens" she'd lean over and kiss my forehead, and I would wrap my arms around her neck and beg her to stay "just one more minute." She always would. I loved her then. I still do. I know I do. I'm just terrible at showing it.

"My mother can be very persuasive, Reina. That's all. And while I want you to show her the respect she deserves as Matriarch, I also want you to be . . . wise. Discerning. Keep your eyes open and remember who you really are."

What a funny thing for her to say.

"How do you know who I 'really' am? I don't even know myself."

"I know you are strong. That you can do anything you put your mind to. And deep down you are kind. I see it in the way you treat Callisto. And . . . Treowe." She doesn't pause at my startled expression. "Yes, I know you still meet with him, Reina. You might think I'm aloof because I'm often away, but don't for a minute think I don't know everything that goes on at Bella Terra."

I do think she's aloof, but not just because she's gone a lot. I simply think she's naive about how life works, and especially about how I work. I suspect she doesn't understand my adventurous spirit because she doesn't have one. She could have done anything—*been* anything—but she chose the easy way out. She chose babies and this boring, rural life.

When I don't answer, she continues, "I also know you think

I'm weak because of the destiny I chose. I just hope your view of me doesn't cause you to do something rash."

Is it possible she has heard my thoughts?

"I just don't understand why you'd pass up the life you could have had as the Matriarch's daughter. You could have done anything you wanted to—had a nice house in Phoenix City or been a senate member like Aunt Julissa. Or yeah, even an Alexia. I can't fathom what would make you give all that up for a finca and some Gentles and mundane work at the Center."

I watch her face carefully. Even now, strained with concern, it's lovely. Despite the small wrinkles and sun spots, no one could argue otherwise. Her features curve softly, so different from my thin nose and wide cheekbones. But we have the same eyes. I'm the only one of my sisters who inherited Mother's hazel eyes, which stand out sharply against our cattail-colored skin. People tell me they are beautiful, but they remind me of weakness because they remind me of her.

Those eyes are trained on me now, but they don't give away her thoughts. She seems to be sifting through them, deciding which to share and which to keep locked away. Still protecting me.

"I chose my life on purpose, Reina," she finally says. "I felt it was the right thing to do at the time. And I don't regret it. I certainly don't regret you or your sisters, or the many Gentles I've raised here at Bella Terra. Your grandmother doesn't understand that because . . . she and I have different ideas about true strength, and what ultimately makes us free and happy. Soon you'll be making your own decision about which path to choose, and you'll have to live with the consequences that accompany it." She says that last part with sympathy, which infuriates me. Is she so sure I'll choose a path that will make me miserable?

I turn away and busy myself stuffing items I don't intend to take into my sack.

Finally she sighs and stands to leave. "I love you, Rei of Sunshine," she says softly, then closes the door behind her.

Yes, I am definitely a devil.

# CHAPTER THREE

WHEN I REACH THE STABLES the next morning, Callisto whinnies and stamps a hoof in greeting. True to his word, Tre has already brushed her coat and mane and outfitted her with my best leather headstall and reins, which will serve more for show than function. A red hibiscus crowns her brown and white head, the stem tucked under her browband. It's just like Tre to adorn my favorite horse with my favorite flower on a day when I need extra pluck. But Callisto looks ridiculous. I remove the delicate bloom and tuck it behind my ear instead, then run my fingers down my horse's neck.

"I know it was for you," I tell her, "but you don't want Grandmother's horses to tease, do you?"

Tre's thoughtfulness inspires me to be a better person. Not quite enough, though, to apologize to Mother for my attitude last night. When she walks into the stable a moment later, I give a short, "Good morning," as I kiss her cheek. It's too small a gesture, but it's the best I can do.

"Good morning to you too, Reina." Mother offers a warm smile, though I hardly deserve it.

In a rush, nine little figures come running through the open barn, reprimands from an uncharacteristically disheveled Dom Bakshi trailing behind them. Her vibrant sari instantly brightens the earthen floor and weatherworn stalls of the stables, like a jolt of yellow on a black-and-white sketch.

"Back in line! Slow down! Watch out for the horse muck!" she instructs. The eager Gentles swarm Mother, all trying to hug her at once. Their voices tumble over one another.

"How long will you be gone?"

"Do you have to leave?"

"Can we come too?"

"Can Dom Museau make us pastries for dinner?"

Mother chuckles as she tries to answer all their questions.

I slide both arms into the rucksack I packed last night, leading Callisto out of the barn while Mother kisses and hugs each little one. Between Dom Bakshi and Marsa, the Gentles will be well taken care of, if a little less pampered. Why does she carry on so? Maybe she likes being needed.

Once the Gentles are satisfied with their hugs and farewells, Dom Bakshi regains control and shoos them out of the stable. They wave at me as they walk past, in a line like little chicks. Then Little Boo breaks ranks, and before I can prepare myself, he has wrapped his small arms around my waist.

"Goodbye," he says, squeezing once with all the strength he can muster.

I barely have time to drop my free hand to pat his back before he sprints back to the others, walking single file toward the whitewashed schoolroom for their morning lessons.

"He has taken a liking to you," Mother says, riding Estrella toward me.

"I don't know why." I grab a handful of Callisto's two-tone mane, then swing onto her bare back. I'm not being self-deprecating. I truly can't fathom why Little Boo likes me so much. I hardly encourage it. He must sense I care for him, despite my efforts not to.

"He shouldn't," I say. "He's in for a rude awakening when he leaves this place, Mother. You're setting them all up for it."

Mother gives Estrella a nudge. My attempt to unsettle her with reality backfires. She only straightens and lifts her chin as she says, "I've explained they may not always be treated kindly once they leave. But while they live at Bella Terra, under my care, they will know what it means to have value."

---

The road to Phoenix City takes five hours by horse. In the dry season, as it is now, the hard-packed dirt of Highway Volcán is easy enough to travel. It's also wide enough for two carts to pass one another, which means precious little shade relieves us from the muggy, mid-day heat. I pour a little water over my wide-brimmed hat, letting the runoff trickle through the woven jipijapa down my sweaty neck and back.

Nedé is roughly rectangular, dissected into four Provinces by two major geological features. The Jabiru River divides north from south, cutting a twisted path from the uncharted Jungle lands in the west and emptying into the Halcyon Sea at Nedé's easternmost edge. A range of low hills divide west from east, Amal and Kekuatan Provinces from Lapé and Fik'iri. Uncleared Jungle wraps Nedé's northern, western, and southern perimeters, left wild because we don't need it. When the foremothers arrived, they were gifted with more than enough cleared land. Few Nedéans populate those outlying edges, for obvious reasons. The closer one gets to the Jungle, the greater the probability one—or one's livestock—could become dinner for a jaguar or puma. Fer-de-lance vipers and other venomous spiders and snakes make their homes in the dense Jungle too, posing a threat to anyone living too close to Nedé's fringes. But there's little chance of seeing anything more dangerous than a scorpion or occasional coyote here in the center.

Mother and I ride silently, passing banana farms, orange groves, and wide swaths of grassy fields flecked with lazily chewing, long-eared cows. There are a few horses too, but none fit for more than cart-pulling or riding into town.

Most women in Nedé have no use for superior equines, with the exception of Mother and a handful of others. The Alexia, though—they breed and train the most magnificent horses in Nedé. Old Solomon told me they have over two thousand head of Lexanders, dispersed among facilities in all four Provinces.

Before Old Solomon got old—before he got a name at all—he was one of the lead Gentles tasked with caring for the Alexia's horses, at their Arena training grounds in Phoenix City. When Mother heard they had dismissed him—to live out his remaining years at a phase-out facility or take the stinger, a "humane" way to end a Gentle's suffering—she offered him a vocation at Bella Terra. I don't think she figured he'd live more than another year or two. Gentles don't often make it past forty-five. Most of them succumb to heart attacks or get brittle bones and die before then—no one seems to know why. Seven years at Bella Terra, and he hasn't gone belly up yet. He probably won't live much longer, but he's the oldest Gentle I've ever seen—maybe a record setter.

Mother couldn't have known he'd live so long or prove so useful. Grandmother essentially cut her daughter loose when she gave up her high status to become a Materno. But other Nedéans still see Mother as tied to the Matriarchy. That's how she was able to secure fifteen Alexia horses when I was very young. And with Old Solomon's help, she bred a fine herd. The horses at Bella Terra may not have the extensive training or fancy tack of the Alexia's, but my Callisto could contend with the best of them. She's smarter, too. I'd bet my riding boots on it.

Another benefit of being the Matriarch's daughter: Mother was given one of the nicest Materno fincas in all of Nedé. I don't remember the particulars, but it belonged to a Senator—a relative of Grandmother's, I think—before being converted for Mother's use. Bella Terra is no Finca del Mar, but it has ample amenities, land, and Gentle staff for a comfortable life.

Mother's singing voice rises through my thoughts, though she has likely been singing all the while. Her voice is like the birds' songs to me—so often present that I only notice the melody when I focus on it.

*Come, you weary, restless women,*
*You're much stronger than you know;*
*I will lend my strength to guide you,*
*Lead you to your haven home.*

*Harmony will bind together*
*Every culture, every race;*
*Simple living, bold creating,*
*Self-restraint our saving grace.*

I recognize the words. It's one of the many songs from the old world, songs the foremothers of Nedé brought with them nearly two hundred years ago. This one's called "Tristan's Song." Dom Bakshi says they sang to forget the horrors of their previous life, when most of the world died from the Great Sickness. We don't worry about diseases like that today, because of Nedéan advances in medicine, but the songs have stuck. Dom Bakshi also says music is "an immovable pillar of Nedéan culture." I just know we sing a lot. Festivals, exhibitions, funerals, around the house—we don't need an excuse to make melody. Mother continues,

> *Leave behind us every danger,*
> *The world's hope we now restore;*
> *Forge ahead, a new day dawning,*
> *Better than the years before.*
> *Better than the years before.*

Her voice is lovely and soft, like so much of her, but clear. That softness would lull me to sleep when she'd sing over me, little Reina, all nestled in my four-poster bed. Mother begins another tune, one I easily recognize, though I couldn't name it.

> *You take one, and I'll take three,*
> *And I'll meet you there, at the mahogany tree,*
> *Where the fire don't burn, and the dark water's deep,*
> *We'll save them there, at the mahogany tree.*

I've heard the words dozens of times. I suppose it's another of the foremothers' songs, though I can't remember hearing it anywhere else. The cadence matches Callisto's hoofbeats, and I unintentionally hum the tune while Mother sings.

> *You follow the mare, and I'll follow a stream,*
> *And we'll leave them there, at the mahogany tree;*
> *If there comes a day when you can't find me,*
> *Lay my flowers there, by the mahogany tree,*

*I'll be buried there, by the mahogany tree.*
*I lost my love at the mahogany tree.*

Hearing Mother sing takes me to another time: a time when I was too young to resent her.

———————

With each passing mile, the buildings I spied from the lookout yesterday stretch higher. Wide swaths of grassland replace the tall trees of Amal, and we leave behind the hum of insects and noisy bird chatter. The air still weighs warm and humid here in Lapé Province, but a sea breeze blows it across the coastal plane. Eventually houses multiply—simple, whitewashed buildings roofed with clay tiles, spaced comfortably under swaying palms. Colorful clothes dance along wash lines in the fresh breeze, and an occasional dog sniffs curiously at the road as we pass.

Callisto's shoulders tense slightly when the dirt road changes to cobbled stone and the buildings grow taller and finer, peppered with shops and vendors. Unlike my horse, I've always loved the transition, signaling a welcomed break from boring Bella Terra, but today the thrill runs alongside apprehension.

Eventually we turn right onto Calle del Sol, which will lead directly to Finca del Mar's gates. The road also serves as the epicenter of Phoenix City's culture and business. Our capital buzzes with all the energy I remember. Here, enormous urns overflow with vibrant foliage, sprinkled with purple, orange, and pink flowers. Women walk tall up and down the wide street, their rainbow-colored tunics, rompers, and serapes presenting a lively contrast to the glowing white buildings. Some women wear their hair in long braids; others don weightless scarves or wide-brimmed hats to keep the sun at bay. The assortment of colors pop against the women's rich skin tones—some lighter, like weathered thatch; others deep as oiled mahogany—all collectively known as "Nedéan brown," with no small measure of pride. I've been taught that two hundred years of diversity have erased the physical and societal racial lines that once divided the world. In Nedé, we're free to enjoy the best of everything the foremothers brought us—from our clothing to our food, from the religions we practice or don't, to the dialects still passed down throughout the Provinces, like Marsa's patchy Creole.

The crowded streets, bustling with the pace and excitement of the capital city, remind me of Dom Bakshi's words: Nedé is a diverse place indeed, a common sisterhood, unified by our joint heritage.

All Nedéans belong . . . *though I suppose not equally*, I muse, noticing the other citizens peppering Calle del Sol.

Outside a dress shop, a stooped Gentle follows a large Dom, his arms stuffed with packages. She flares with irritation at him, no telling about what. Across the street, a uniformed Gentle pulls a cart of produce toward a restaurant, where smells of fresh-baked flatbread and fried plantains waft through the open front of the building. Next to a row of apartments, I notice a Gentle about Treowe's size emptying a trash bin into the back of a donkey cart. He snatches at the air, trying to catch a rogue paper escaping on a fresh gust of wind.

The sight makes me wonder anew how life would be different for my friend if he wasn't assigned to Mother's finca. I shouldn't care. I mean, every Gentle contributes to the good of Nedé in one way or another. All the same, I do. If his life must be one of service, I'm glad it's with us, where at least someone appreciates his kindness, his humor, his efforts to make our lives better.

"I'll stop at Finca del Mar first, make sure you're settled, before I head to the Center," Mother offers.

"That's okay. I know the way from here." Does she sense my apprehension? I don't want her pity, don't need her protection.

All the same, when she smiles softly and says, "I know you do," I don't protest. Matriarch Teera, grandmother or no, would intimidate a puma. Even though I don't relish the inevitable drama that results from the two of them in the same room, at least it will deflect some of the attention from me.

"Thanks," I manage.

By the time we reach the end of the cobbled street, our shadows stretching long to touch the bottom of Finca del Mar's gates, my stomach reacts to what I have refused to let my mind dwell on: I still have no idea why Grandmother wants to see me. And the sheer grandeur of the Matriarch's villa intensifies my insecurities. I feel small, out of place.

A Gentle in the thatched gatehouse recognizes Mother and presses a button. The serpentine metalwork swings inward without a sound, like magic. A long, smooth driveway, lined with perfectly straight palm trees, leads to the main villa, though "villa" seems a grotesque understatement. Three sprawling, stark-white stories rise before us, supported by immense columns, adorned with wood-trimmed glass windows, and featuring several curved balconies. The dark roof tiles, matching the mahogany wood trim, perfectly contrast with the spring green and vivid pink bougainvillea crawling up and over the pergolas on either side. A few hectares of cropped grass surround the villa like a smooth, green lake, a frivolity afforded only here. Geometric hedges line mosaic-tiled paths, and sprays of colorful flowers burst from windowsills, hang over ledges, and engulf the many trellises.

Despite walking this path a dozen times over the years, the sight of Finca del Mar still causes a lungful of air to stall mid-breath.

I've heard some whisper that Grandmother's taste for luxury smacks of hypocrisy for a Matriarch touting the Virtues of

Nedé—that no Matriarch before her has fussed with the finca or thrown parties the way she does. Even if that's true, I have trouble faulting her for it. What can it hurt to create living, fresh elegance like this?

At the end of the driveway, we dismount next to a large, raised pond. I've always liked this fountain, and the bulbous orange and silvery fish that call it home. Water courses through a wood trough suspended over the radius, spilling a steady stream of water into the basin. When we were young—and sure no one was watching—my sisters and I would toss small sticks into the trough and then bounce anxiously until they reappeared, riding the waterfall like twiggy catfish.

Two Gentles—one dressed in an indigo linen suit, the other in drab stable attire—cross the vast south lawn toward us. While we wait for their assistance, I can't resist the urge to poke at a lily pad floating in the gently swaying water. Mother clears her throat as they approach, and I reluctantly straighten.

"Good afternoon, Dom Pierce, Reina Pierce. The Matriarch is expecting you. My associate will take your horses to the stables. Please follow me."

I want to argue that I'd rather take Callisto myself than trust her to a Gentle I've never met, but I know better. Grandmother would never approve of me doing a Gentle's task. Besides, if this stablehand works at Finca del Mar, he can't be completely inept. I hand him the reins.

"Her name's Callisto. Water first. Then brush her down before she grazes." He probably doesn't need my instructions, even though most Gentles *are* a little slow of intellect, but I won't take the chance.

"Yes, Dom."

I almost remind him I'm not yet a Dom—won't be until I choose my destiny—but decide I like the sound of it. I rest my head on Callisto's neck and pat the other side with my hand.

"You're a good girl, Callisto." Then, lowering my voice, "I'll visit you later." She may not understand my promise, but I'd never go back on my word.

As the stablehand leads the horses away, I turn to face the next obstacle.

Riding into Finca del Mar on Callisto was one thing. Now, walking up the marble steps to the oversize mahogany doors, I feel vulnerable, like a piece of me—the bravest piece—has been stripped away.

Mother guides me through the front doors, which also seem to open of their own accord. A large panel hangs over the threshold, emblazoned with Nedé's motto in scrolling bronze letters: "Praesidete debiles. Salus omnibus. Vis sine virtute tyrannis est." *Protect the weak. Safety for all. Power without virtue is tyranny.*

"Just remember who you are," Mother encourages.

Right. Remember who I am. Now, if I could just figure out who that is.

# CHAPTER FOUR

GRANDMOTHER'S SCARLET MACAW greets us with a squawking, "Hello."

"Hello, Winifred," Mother replies. After we hear her own mother's muffled voice in another room, Mother takes a seat on a large leather chair facing the floor-to-ceiling windows which frame the Halcyon Sea.

I feed Winifred a handful of seeds from a pink seashell near her cage and notice her long, red tail feathers have grown. I've always loved giving the cantankerous bird treats, even when I was so short Jonalyn had to lift me up to reach the cage. The few fond memories of this place dispel some, albeit little, of my unease. Finca del Mar has always conjured in me equal parts awe and terror. Whether more due to its own splendor or to Grandmother's formidable presence, I can't say.

When minutes pass without Grandmother's appearance, I meander the perimeter of the room, pausing to glance at each sculpture and painting displayed. Tristan Pierce, our first Matriarch, so wise and determined. Her daughter Acacia, second Matriarch, with wild curls and thick eyebrows. A large depiction of Phoenix City, before our foremothers rebuilt the concrete, mismatched buildings into the jewel of Nedé. In it, I recognize the tallest, cube-shaped building as the predecessor of our current Center for Health Services. The canvas portrays an unappealing, uninviting city, a shadow of its present splendor. I'm pondering the next portrait, a masterful painting of the modern Alexia Arena, when I overhear Grandmother's voice, rising with anger.

"I don't care if we lose a hundred head, Adoni. Fear brings questions. Finish this, or I will find someone who will. Do I make myself clear?"

Despite her volume, I'm confident we weren't meant to hear this conversation.

"Yes, Matriarch Teera," replies a strong voice. "We'll return to the site immediately and continue our search."

A door opens, and heavy boots click against tile toward the front entrance. I resist the urge to turn around, partly to remain inconspicuous, and partly because I've already guessed whom Grandmother was addressing. There is only one group of people in Nedé who wear heavy boots. Only one destiny who prefer not to be addressed as Dom, regardless of their distinguished status. And there is only one Adoni: leader of the Alexia. She doesn't bother to close the door softly.

A moment later, Grandmother emerges from her office.

"Welcome, Leda, Reina." Her voice is calm and stately. She allows us to kiss her cheek but doesn't offer an embrace. Grandmother has never been one for unnecessary affection, at least not since I outgrew her lap.

"How are you?" Mother asks.

"Well enough. I trust your journey was uneventful."

By phrasing it as a statement rather than a question, I notice, Grandmother avoids continuing the conversation.

Their expressions divulge the effort it takes to keep even this trivial small talk civil. Mother's face is guarded but without malice. Grandmother's wrinkled face shows precious little emotion. But the sharp arc of her eyebrows conveys an air of superiority. I wonder if she has them groomed that way.

"Well," Mother says, "I have business at the Center I must attend to. I'll be back late, Reina. No need to wait up for me."

I kiss her cheek, just shy of reluctantly. I may not covet Mother's company, but all that is familiar and predictable in this room is about to walk out the door.

When she leaves, Grandmother turns her attention to me.

"I have a few unexpected matters I must attend to. Domus will show you to your room so you can . . . *freshen up*. Meet me for dinner in the garden promptly at five." She doesn't wait for an answer before turning back toward her office.

Domus, the well-dressed Gentle who showed us into the house, reappears.

"If you would follow me," he says, starting toward the large marble staircase leading to the guest wing on the second floor. I know Major Domus—Domus for short—from my yearly visits. I believe he's the only Gentle at Finca del Mar given a name, and even his counts only if being called by your occupation—"chief household Gentle"—qualifies as a name. It likely serves more as a convenience for Grandmother, who would view rattling off his number a waste of breath.

As we ascend the stairs, I notice a scar over Domus's left ear, a bare squiggle through his gray hair. The old wound is as familiar to me as he is. I remember the night Grandmother gave it to him. She had bumped into Domus after consuming one too many glasses of chicha at dinner. She flew into a rage, culminating in smashing her glass against his head. Domus has yet served Grandmother faithfully, and he is getting old, maybe close to forty. I wonder how much longer Grandmother will keep him.

On the second floor we pass a dozen wood doors before approaching the room I have always shared with Ciela during our visits. Surprisingly, Domus carries on, stopping instead before high, double doors at the end of the hall.

"Matriarch Teera welcomes you to Finca del Mar, Reina Pierce."

As he swings the large doors inward, a word I'm not proud of slips out. It's the room's fault.

The space is almost as big as the Bella Terra stables, but that's where the comparison ends. Floor-to-ceiling windows encompass most of the east wall, trimmed with delicately embroidered curtains and boasting magnificent views of the rippling turquoise sea beyond the expansive, lush gardens. The bed—which could fit me five times over, despite its mountain of overstuffed, gem-colored pillows—beckons me like a silken cloud. Jasmine flowers creep up trellises on the attached balcony, their thick, sweet scent pouring in through the open windows. Everywhere is gleam and richness, and I just stand there awestruck, taking it all in.

Domus seems amused by my speechlessness.

"The Senator's Suite is reserved for the Matriarch's most honored guests," he explains, interrupting my stupor.

"Then why . . . ?" I cut the question short, reprimanding myself for forgetting where I am. At Finca del Mar—anywhere other than Bella Terra, really—Gentles are only addressed when one is giving commands or needs information. I'd best not forget that, especially within Grandmother's earshot.

Once, when I was very young, she saw my eldest sister conversing with a Finca del Mar stablehand while he prepared our horses for a ride. Jonalyn engaged him in her kind way, laughing innocently at an unintentional joke he made. Grandmother stormed across the lawn like a hurricane, her jaw bulged from clenching her teeth.

"You'll do well to remember the Articles, Jonalyn," she said, her pointy eyebrows raised to the sky. "This is not your mother's feeble excuse for order."

I was embarrassed for Jonalyn, and more, for all of us. I didn't run and hide in my room like Jo did, but I suddenly lost the urge to ride. And even my six-year-old self rarely missed that opportunity.

The next day, we heard the stablehand was in the stocks for his impudence.

Appropriate or not, I wish I could ask Domus why I've been given the high honor of staying in the Senator's Suite, because I bet he'd know. He must hear things, secret things, as he passes through the villa's rooms, noticed little more than the lavish finery by the Matriarch or her distinguished guests. Why I would now be numbered among the latter baffles me.

He doesn't acknowledge my unasked question. "The Matriarch will expect you for dinner at five o'clock in the garden." And with that, Domus exits, leaving me to, as Grandmother put it, *freshen up*. I'm as grimy as a pig after a mud bath.

I pull open a drawer in the high wooden dresser opposite the windowed wall. It smells of lemon and beeswax. I feel guilty emptying the contents of my dusty bag into it, contaminating its grandeur with my things.

As I change out of my riding clothes and slip into the claw-foot tub, already filled with cool water, I turn possibilities over in my mind. Why would Grandmother treat me differently than any other time I've visited her finca? Maybe she wants to give me a send-off before I choose my destiny. Did she do that for Jonalyn or Ciela? I don't remember. Though, if she did, why would Mother be nervous about my coming? And what of the heated exchange I overheard between Grandmother and Adoni?

I sort through unanswered questions best on the back of a horse. But as I can't very well come riding to dinner on Callisto, I slip into the simple linen dress I brought, twist my hair into a side knot, and then pass the few remaining moments until five o'clock on my balcony, chewing on a thumbnail and watching the sun play catch with the waves.

A mosaic path leads me from the villa to the gardens. It meanders through plumeria, heliconia, cohune palms, bird-of-paradise, and two topiaries pruned to resemble pineapples. A tunnel of papery-pink bougainvillea finally deposits me at the outdoor dining room. I assume I am alone until I hear Grandmother's voice, her body obscured by a high-back chair.

"You're late," she says, her voice as steely as the utensils glinting on the table.

"I . . ." I'm about to tell her that I am right on time, but wisely abort the challenge. " . . . am sorry, Grandmother." And then add, for good measure, "'Freshening up' was more daunting than I anticipated." I kiss her cheek—hollow compared to Mother's—then sit across from her, in the only other chair at the long table. She sits tall and stern in an airy, deep purple dress. I didn't realize we would be alone. I've never been completely alone with Grandmother.

She eyes me silently for a moment, as if trying to decide something.

"Good," she finally concludes, whether to my apology or another inner consideration, I can't tell.

I bow for prayer out of habit, remembering too late that

Grandmother has no use for religion. I casually lift my head, hoping she didn't notice.

No such luck. She raises a disapproving eyebrow at me. "When you get to be my age, Reina, you realize you could die at any moment. I no longer have the luxury of frivolity." I can't help but notice the contrast between her philosophy and Mother's, the latter believing that the older you get, the less you have the luxury of ignoring religion.

*Get it together, Rei. Don't make a fool of yourself.*

As Grandmother unfolds a starched napkin onto her lap, a Gentle sets a plate of exquisitely garnished lobster tail in front of her. The scents of butter, cilantro, and garlic mix with the balmy evening air.

"I am interested to know if you have decided on your destiny."

So that's it. She wants to know what I've chosen to do with my life. I sigh a little inside, relieved my worry has been needless, then remember that I am not entirely sure how I *do* plan to spend my life. I hope she won't be too disappointed that she has wasted her efforts—the summons, my gorgeous room, this mouthwatering dinner—on an indecisive seventeen-year-old. Still, I must answer. Why not the truth?

"I believe you know me well enough to guess I'm not meant to be a Materno," I begin, surprised by my own candor. "I've always been drawn to the Alexia, and I know Mother wouldn't stop me, but even so, they're . . . "

"Slightly intimidating?" Grandmother offers, dabbing the corner of her mouth with a napkin. I see the first hint of a genuine smile I can remember—maybe ever—on her face.

"Yes. Exactly." My shoulders relax a little, and I lean on my chair's armrest. Maybe Grandmother understands me better than I realized. Perhaps she and I really are alike, as Mother says. Is that so awful?

"I can ride, and I'm not afraid. I find their fierceness beautiful. But sometimes I wonder if . . . I don't mean to sound prideful, but I . . . " My mind works furiously to put words to the inklings I'm still sorting through myself. "Part of me feels I was made for something . . . *else*. I want to serve Nedé, and do something good, but I'm also hesitant to be confined to any one destiny. Am I wrong to feel that way, Grandmother?" I'm eager now, almost hopeful. Perhaps this woman understands my uncertainties in a way no one else can.

My question hangs in the air. The glimmer of normality in Grandmother has already dimmed, the crack sealed. She seems in no hurry to answer. I sense I'm being measured, considered, weighed, much like the bite of lobster she turns over in her mouth. Finally she swallows, then looks directly into my eyes.

"I once felt as you do now, Reina. I learned, however, and you must always remember, that the success of Nedé depends on its leaders valuing the good of all above the desires of one."

"Of course," I say, lowering my eyes. *Don't be stupid, Reina! Why were you so frank? You know better.*

"However," Grandmother continues, "if you can learn that one, all-important lesson, your unconventional attitude will serve you well. I see promise in you, Reina. And I have an opportunity that might be of interest."

I place my fork next to my untouched plate and sit up straighter, determined to compensate for my recent lapse in judgment.

"As you know, it is every Matriarch's duty to select and train a successor to carry on the traditions of Nedé, maintain order, and ensure our prosperity. Despite my protests, my age continues to advance. As such, I've decided to begin the Succession. I will announce my selection of Apprentice at our country's two hundredth anniversary celebration in two months' time."

She pauses to take a long drink of bubbly amber chicha before continuing. My nerves prick in the interim. Tre was right: she's ready to begin the Succession—call on each of the Provinces to select a Candidate who will compete for the honor of replacing the Matriarch after a one-year Apprenticeship. Though "compete" is a loose term. I believe the Matriarch simply trains all four Candidates for a few weeks, then selects whomever she deems most qualified. But what does that have to do with me? My palms stick to the thin fabric of my dress. Why would she tell me . . .

"You are aware that each of the four Provinces has the honor and obligation to vote on one Candidate to represent them. You may not be aware that a . . . *recent* amendment to the constitution allows me to select one additional Candidate, a wild card if you will, to compete in the Succession."

My fingers tremble with adrenaline. I twist the cloth napkin in my lap to steady them.

"I have decided to exercise my right to a Candidate, and I have chosen you, Reina."

She has got to be kidding.

"I have seen and heard enough about you to believe you could one day make an excellent Matriarch."

The garden spins around me, flowers and lights swirling in glowing arcs of color. This is a dream. It has to be a dream.

"The station of Matriarch requires four essential qualities: intelligence, courage, strength, and . . . the fourth is the principle I just mentioned. A Matriarch *must* put the good of all before her own desires—whatever the cost."

She accentuates the words, as if willing them to penetrate my skull.

"I'm taking a chance on you, Reina. You will contend with four qualified Candidates, and I make no promises. I will select the best choice for Nedé. Only time and training will tell whether you can overcome Leda's influence and meet my expectations."

She pauses. Is she waiting for me to say something? Yes, I should definitely say something. But what? I scramble for a response, hoping to exude humble gratitude instead of the complete shock that threatens to spill out.

"I'm . . . honored you'd choose me. I'll try to make you proud, Grandmother." I attempt to sound as fully confident as I am certainly not.

"*Try*? You will do more than try. Whatever the final outcome, I will not be embarrassed by you, Reina. Do I make myself clear?"

"Yes, Grandmother."

"Then it's settled. The Provinces' senates have been instructed to provide their Candidates for training, beginning in five days' time. Have your mother send anything you require from home. Only essential personal items. Suitable clothing will be made for you. If you are to represent me, you must shine." Her last words carry the tiniest hint of sarcasm.

"Yes, Grandmother."

When she speaks again, I don't detect even a hint of sympathy for the turmoil she has just unleashed in my world. "One last matter: from now on you will address me as Matriarch, not Grandmother."

At that, she drains the last of her chicha, stands, bids me goodnight, and leaves me to stew with my uneaten dinner.

---

Evening light washes the wood frame of the open stable in a subtle glow. Callisto stretches over the crossbeams of her stall as I approach. Her white patches shine with ethereal light. Fitting. She's the salvation I need tonight.

I didn't know where else to come.

Anything was better than sitting alone at that table, left to sort through the overwhelming implications of Grandmother's offer under the watchful eyes of the servants. I need something familiar to ground me—ideally the smell of an open barn and well-worn leather. I want to touch the rough hair of my mare's neck, be carried by her strength beneath me.

I don't bother with tack, just swing onto Callisto and go. She doesn't mind the familiarity, and I feed on it. Thankfully, my breezy skirt bunches easily around my waist.

I find a groomed path behind the stables. If I remember correctly, it leads through a palm grove and down to the sea. That suits me just fine.

My stomach churns as if I ate shock for dinner. Grandmother asked me to be a Candidate. No, she didn't ask—she told. Did I have a choice? Do I *want* a choice?

I might be the Matriarch's granddaughter, but I have never once considered what it would be like to fill her role. She was always . . . *other*. We had our life at Bella Terra, and the emotional distance between her and Mother underscored that otherness. No, entering into Grandmother's world was never the remotest possibility. Now it is. And the question is, *Do I want it to be?* Could I, a seventeen-year-old from rural Amal, take on the duties and pressures of Nedé's Matriarchy?

Maybe I'll never have reason to find out. Grandmother made very clear she offers no promise of actually choosing me as her Apprentice. Each Province has at least one elite school to educate, train, and prepare women for the remote possibility of being elected to represent their home. I won't stand a chance. So all I really have to do is hold my own and not embarrass Grandmother. Then I can join the Alexia, push down the foolish inkling I'm somehow above the system, as Grandmother rebuked, and meet my destiny as if none of this ever happened.

The evening wind sweeps cool against my bare arms and legs. I unpin my hair and let the salty gusts have their way.

Still, Grandmother chose me. She wasn't required to select an additional Candidate. She must see something in me that warranted the risk. She *must*. I might struggle to believe there's anything exceptional about me, but if the Matriarch of Nedé is willing to take a chance on this headstrong girl, I aim to prove I'm even more than she suspects.

We reach sand, and I sense Callisto's urge to run. I let her give in to the impulse, for both of us. Flying across the beach, my heartbeat races in time with her four-beat gallop. We glide above the sand, above the water, above my insecurities. Here, in this moment, the wind whipping past me, my fingers wrapped in Callisto's tangled mane, I am brave. I'm strong. I will prove to Grandmother, and to myself, that I have what it takes to succeed.

───────

Dusk gives way to darkness as we reluctantly leave the beach. I lingered as long as possible, knowing we could count on electric-powered lights to illuminate the path back to the stables—another luxury unheard of at Bella. Yet even Finca del Mar's stables smell of horse and manure, just like home. As we enter the breezeway, I almost expect to find Tre there, greeting me with a one-dimpled smile and, if we were alone, a question about my ride.

Instead of my confidant, the Gentle who took our horses earlier sits atop a three-legged stool, oiling a saddle. He startles at my approach, then scrambles to take Callisto off my hands, his gaze never meeting mine. He is as short as I remember, but he seems younger—maybe twenty. His dusty, earth-colored clothes fit this setting better than the villa entrance. He belongs here.

Then again, I suppose I do too. I certainly feel more relaxed standing between horse stalls than sitting on cushioned furniture in the villa. Maybe I'm a little too comfortable here, because when he reaches for Callisto, I don't ignore him like I should. Instead I insist, "No, I'll groom her."

The Gentle's eyes grow round. "Yes, Dom."

"My name's Reina." My voice dwarfs his.

He gives a slight nod. "Yes, Dom Reina."

"No—" I start, about to correct his confusion, but I kind of like the familiar-formality of mixing the proper title with my given name. It inspires me to ask, "What's your name?"

"Gentle 549—"

"No, I mean, what do they call you? The other Gentles?" This is a question no woman has likely ever asked this stablehand, and I understand his hesitation. But growing up at Bella, where Mother always gave her Gentles names—it gave them dignity, she would say—I can't bring myself to address him by a number. I suppose you don't realize which curiosities of home wear off on you until you leave.

He turns a cloth over in his hands twice as he considers, but I know he'll answer me eventually. He has to. I'm Dom Reina—his superior—even if, presently, we're both tending to horses.

Finally he says, "They call me Neechi."

"Neechi? I've never heard it before. Does it mean something?"

"Friend."

"Then I'm in luck," I say. "Where do you keep the brushes, Neechi?"

He retrieves a boar-hair brush from a rack on the far wall. As he places it in my hand, his gaze lifts slightly above the ground. Progress.

As he returns to the saddle and oil, I cross-tie Callisto and busy myself brushing the sweat and loose hairs from her coat. Only now, noticing a few dozen horse hairs stuck to my linen dress, do I realize how absurd I must seem to Neechi. Not only am I taking over a Gentle's job, I'm doing it in my dinner clothes.

The exhilaration of the beach gallop quickly fades as I consider the possibility of Grandmother discovering her recently appointed Candidate lingering in the barn with the stablehand.

"You can't tell anyone about this, okay? Grandmother would have a fit."

Neechi doesn't look up from his work. "Yes, Dom Reina," he says, but even his caramel-smooth, quiet voice can't hide the amusement he finds in all of this. He seems kind. It shouldn't surprise me—nearly every Gentle I've met is kind. And why shouldn't they be? They live for the good of Nedé. Still, that they remain cordial when it's rarely reciprocated—does that show weakness? Or strength?

We work silently for some time, he on a series of saddles and me on my beloved mare. Neechi breaks the quiet with a question.

"You always ride bareback?"

"Mostly." I've already answered before I realize how much courage it took him to ask me anything. Perhaps my boldness, my irreverence for formality, gave him the nerve. Well, if he's not afraid, then neither will I be.

"Old Solomon . . . I mean, Solomon, taught me. He's—"

Neechi cuts me off, "I know who he is, Dom Reina. Every groom in Nedé knows 'bout Solomon, and what Dom Pierce did for him."

I didn't realize. "Oh. Well, he believes a horse is waiting to be understood. And if a rider will take the time to get to know her, earn her trust, speak her language, she'll do anything for you." I nuzzle my face to Callisto's. "And I would do anything for her."

It's quiet again for a time.

"Will you use the saddle when you ride with the Alexia?" Neechi's second question stops my hand midstroke.

I don't know much about the Succession process—I've never had need nor curiosity. But this much I do know from my Nedéan History class with Dom Bakshi: to aid the Matriarch in the selection of her Apprentice, each of the four—or in this case five— Candidates takes an abbreviated training in Nedé's core industries. The rationale goes that any Matriarch of Nedé must be competent in various fields if she is to rule the people wisely and represent them fairly. One of those trainings will be with the Alexia, the peacekeepers of Nedé.

"I guess I'll have to," I say, the bigger reality of what lies before me sinking in. I'll have to train like an Alexia after all. And, pure irony, like a Materno too. "But riding on a saddle is the least of my worries. Wait, how did you know . . . "

Neechi looks bashful, though no blush shows through his earth-toned skin. "Among the Gentles, news travels like a river in the wet season."

The servants at dinner. They would have overheard our conversation. That their scavenged news would reach Neechi in the time it took for me to ride the beach is rather impressive, in its own way.

"Then you probably know more about it than I do," I say.

I wonder how much the Gentles gather about the inner workings at Finca del Mar. If Domus hears everything in the villa, and they have some underground gossip network, what else might Neechi know? I decide to test it out. Trying to look absorbed with selecting a pick for Callisto's hooves, I toss my next question lightly into the air.

"Adoni was speaking with Gran . . . Matriarch Teera when I arrived this morning. Does she come to the Finca often?"

His silence validates my theory. He has information but

thinks better of sharing, or he wouldn't ignore the question. I don't press. I'm risking Grandmother's rebuke for my candor with this Gentle, but Neechi could be put in the stocks or whipped.

Directing the precarious conversation to a somewhat safer topic, I ask, "I've ridden in saddle some. What should I know about the Alexia way?"

Before Old Solomon came to Bella Terra, I wouldn't have dreamed of taking advice from a Gentle. But his wisdom with horses proved I'd be foolish to refuse learning from an expert, Gentle or not. And if Neechi works at the second most prestigious stable in Nedé, surpassed only by the Alexia's equine facilities, there's a good chance he knows more about it than I do.

Neechi rubs a set of reins with the oiled cloth. "Like you said, you have to speak their language. Alexia saddles and stirrups free their hands for weapons, but distance them from the horses. You have to close the separation."

"A different way to communicate," I muse. "Callisto can handle that. It will just take some getting used to."

"You have a fine horse, Dom Reina, but . . . "

"What?"

"I don't see them letting you ride your pinto in the Arena. Their Lexanders are as much a part of their . . . *presentation* as the rest of their uniform."

That hadn't occurred to me. Not surprising, given I hadn't considered any of this before dinner. But riding into the greatest challenge of my life on a horse other than Callisto? That might put me over the edge. I slide my hand down her freshly-combed mane, trying to smooth the agitation welling up inside.

"Don't let it worry you, Dom Reina." He really looks at me, for the first time, and adds, reassuringly, "You're strong and you know horses. That will serve you."

"Thanks."

He gives a small nod, then returns to rubbing the saddle. I stall Callisto but can't leave her just yet. She nudges my shoulder with her velvety chin, and I rub her nose in turn. I've ridden other horses, but they didn't understand me like this one. None have her spirit, or anticipate my commands like she does. If I must enter the Arena, how can I do it without her?

I suppose I should take Neechi's advice and not waste worry on what can't be changed. Four other Candidates will arrive in less than a week—a more imminent obstacle.

*I can handle obstacles. I can overcome them.*

Yet my newfound confidence rings false, flimsy, probably just remnants of the salt wind and free riding on the beach. Deeper down I'm scared. But acknowledging fear won't do an ounce of good now. I have to make Grandmother proud. I don't want to find out what happens if I don't.

---

A soft knock startles me where I sit at the vanity in my nightclothes, combing out the repercussions of riding with my hair down. I know that knock. It's the same I heard last night, a million miles away, before my world was turned upside down.

"Come in."

Mother enters the suite, looking a bit wilted, as she always does after a shift at the Center. She lowers herself onto the bed.

"How was your evening?" she asks, watching my reflection in the vanity mirror as I wrestle with another wicked snarl.

"You first." I'm taken aback by the pleasantness in my own tone. But that makes sense—it's often easier to be agreeable away from home. Or perhaps my tightly-wound attitude has loosened a bit, knowing I won't be returning to Bella Terra with her.

"Fairly routine," she says, rubbing the back of her neck. "I had a directors' meeting with Dr. Novak, checked several birthers' progress, and catalogued the vaccines for this week's infants. The new Materno Finca in Fik'iri Province opens next month, so we had preparations for that as well." She sighs. "Enough about all that. How was dinner?"

I place the comb on the polished stone counter and turn to face her. I'm at a loss for where to start, or how to phrase it, so I just blurt it out.

"Grandmother wants me to be a Candidate in the Succession."

She closes her eyes, lets out a slow breath. I've seen her do that only once before, and the memory pricks me.

Three years ago one of Mother's Gentles—we called him Tiny because he was—went missing. Three days later, Dom Bakshi had rushed into the living room, sobbing that a village down river found his drowned body caught on a log. Mother had this face then, had let out the same slow breath, as if reminding herself to inhale and release oxygen.

At least this time it doesn't appear tears will follow. In fact, her next words are respectably even keeled.

"And what do you think about that?"

Now I'm the one who must fight to keep my emotions in check. Her seemingly simple question is, in fact, the most complicated she could have asked. I have very little idea what I think about it. Will I do it? Yes. Am I scared? Absolutely. But try to dig below the obvious and my mind sinks into a thick muddle, unable to tell up from down.

"I don't know," I try. "I'm honored she'd select me. I doubt I'm Matriarch material, but she must see some strength, or skill, or *something* in me to risk it. But she'll have four perfectly good options from the Provinces to choose from, and I'm only turning eighteen this week. Why would she want me to join the Candidates?"

"Reina, she'd be crazy not to want you. You are sharp and capable, strong and kind. Nedé would be lucky to have you as Matriarch." She says this forcefully, with conviction. "But my mother . . . " She pauses, looks to a corner of the room, then lowers her voice. "My mother likes to be in control, Rei. She has always surrounded herself with people she knows will do what she wants without questions."

I try to process this, but the connections come slowly. When they do align, I'm hurt by the assumption, and it shows in my volume.

"So you think she wants me only because I'd be easy to manipulate?"

Mother puts a finger to her lips and responds even quieter, probably so I'll get the hint. Is she worried about somebody hearing us, all the way up here?

"No, Rei. Not *only*. I know you're strong. I also know my mother. You look up to her, but . . . " She stares at the ceiling, once again carefully deciding how much to share. She still doesn't trust me with whatever she knows. She sighs, then says, "Everything isn't always as it seems."

The words hang in the air because I have no rebuttal—no experience to confirm or deny—no way to pull them down.

She moves toward me, kissing the top of my head.

"You can do anything you put your mind to, Rei of Sunshine. That has never been a question in my mind, and it shouldn't be one in yours. Anyway, you'll need that brain space to find answers to other questions—questions maybe you don't even know to ask just yet." She crouches down so she can look me in the eyes. The urgency in her expression surprises me. "Remember who you are, Reina. Please remember. And may God go with you." With that, she kisses my head again and leaves the room.

I think about her last hope—that God go with me. I've never

given much thought to Mother's religion—to her mealtime prayers, or to the crusty book of scriptures she keeps on her nightstand, a relic from the old world. Not many Nedéans believe in God. Most of the foremothers, I understand, thought that if he existed, he wouldn't have let the Brutes of old wreak havoc on the world. Safer to trust in themselves. So *we* trust in ourselves. But I've seen how Mother believes in something bigger than us, and now, in the face of an unknown future, I figure it can't hurt to try. I bow my head and mumble a silent plea for help.

# CHAPTER FIVE

THE NEXT MORNING Mother and I take breakfast at a small table tucked in yet another corner of the vast gardens I've previously never explored.

Grandmother is away on business, which suits me fine. Maybe my unease will dissipate in the weeks ahead, but for now she still intimidates the bats out of me.

Mother looks fresh and cheery after a good night's sleep, her skin dewy and bright, her dark hair wrapped up in a papaya-colored scarf. A small pendant rests in the hollow between her collarbones, a circular wooden carving of a tree, strung on a braided jute cord, thinning with age. I don't know if I've ever seen her without the necklace. We don't talk much—Mother's gift to me. She only comments about the exceptional sweetness of the dragon fruit, and I about Grandmother's horses—safe topics that won't spark another quarrel.

Despite our uneasy congeniality, her presence soothes my nerves. She is a single relic of home in this strange world of fine clothes and too much leisure time. With her quiet company, I let myself enjoy the sweet scent of plumeria and the relative cool provided by enormous manicaria palm fronds hovering over the space like umbrellas. Several pendulums of bright red and yellow lobster claw flowers dangle from heliconia shrubs, as gaudy as jeweled necklaces. In the Finca del Mar gardens, peculiar, fragrant plants are as common as cow pies at Bella Terra.

Mother used to belong here. It's not *so* difficult to remember when she cuts her egg frittata like *that*—butchering the innocent dish into minuscule pieces, chewing each bite as if she has all the time in the world. Still, it's strange to imagine her growing up here, being coddled and groomed, wearing silk serapes and taking her breakfasts alfresco.

She must have been very different then. Or did she leave this life because she was *already* different?

*Like me?*

She notices me staring at her and tilts her head.

"What is it?"

"Nothing," I mumble. "Just thinking."

She smiles gently, with the familiar kindness that heaps endless shame on my head, and returns to mutilating her breakfast.

If I enter this world—if I somehow become Grandmother's Apprentice—will I wake up one day eating my frittata in itty-bitty bites? Will this strange opulence and bounty someday feel like home, the way Bella fits Mother like good riding boots?

———

When we finish our meal, Mother prepares to leave, promising to deliver the items I'll need from home. I want to ask her to tell

Treowe something too, but I don't know what, and—even though she's aware we spend time together—I'm nervous about bringing him up. Mother has proven compassionate, but admitting my best friend is a Gentle might cross a line, even for her.

I hug Mother, really hug her, before she mounts Estrella. The slightest glimmer of a feeling I haven't experienced around her in years surfaces: *love*. Why must she ride away for me to feel it?

Perhaps we don't realize what we have until change comes to steal it away.

As Mother disappears down the palm-lined driveway, Domus finds me.

"Dom Tourmaline is prepared to see you, per the Matriarch's request, to undertake your . . . *attire*."

I have heard the name before. If I'm not mistaken, Dom Tourmaline, a prestigious Ad Artium, oversees Grandmother's own wardrobe. She styles the Matriarch's hair and makeup for special occasions too—another frivolous "luxury" of which I've heard whispers. But the dissenters on this point have all been Amal women; we value simplicity and comfort perhaps even more than the other Provinces. Here in Lapé—particularly Phoenix City— women pink their cheeks and wear silks and embroidered scarves if they want to. Ad Artiums appreciate ample pizzazz most of all. I've never been one to fuss with such things, but apparently that's about to change.

I smooth invisible wrinkles from my plain brown pants as Domus leads me back into the villa, through the three-story vaulted foyer, past the marble staircase, then, turning right, toward the north wing. This part of the villa is appointed primarily for entertaining: the botanical dining room on the right, followed by a large kitchen bustling with smartly dressed female chefs and Gentles in aprons; on the left, an enormous hall, used for dancing, parties, and plays. Past the hall, at the far north of the wing,

Domus motions toward an ornate door with a bronze plaque labeled "Dressing Room." I thank him and let myself in.

Dom Tourmaline reclines on a velvet couch, in statue-like repose, her back curved, chin tilted slightly up and to the right to counterbalance a large, blue-and-yellow-feathered fascinator. Her skin, generously dusted with pearlescent powder, is smooth as a statue's too. Only the odd orange-gold of her hair, coifed in a bob beneath the plumage, reveals she isn't made of stone. One gets the impression she may have been holding that pose for hours, waiting to be admired, because she waits a full three seconds after being discovered to come to life. I've never seen anyone like her.

"Dom Pierce, it's my pleasure," she says. Her words slide as smooth as her skin.

"I'm not a Dom yet."

She holds out a gloved hand. I assume she wants to clasp my forearm—a Nedéan greeting—but instead she raises my fingers to her lips, which match the strange hue of her hair, and kisses them.

"Being chosen as a Candidate is a distinction in itself, wouldn't you agree?"

She takes two steps back and assesses her new project. Her gaze flits quickly from one part of me to another, and as she makes internal calculations, her head sways slowly from side to side. In fact, her every movement resembles an iguana's: slow, fluid, deliberate. She examines my arms and gathers my loose hair into her fist, inspects my eyes, squeezes a cheek, measures *every* circumference.

What has Grandmother sentenced me to?

We spend the next hour in relative silence, except for the swish of silk fabrics, the scratch of a feather pen against parchment, and Dom Tourmaline's occasional "Hmmm," or "That will do nicely." Once satisfied with her notes, she ushers me to a station along the far wall where she applies a thick yellow liquid across parts of my face and each of my arms and legs. The substance begins to harden on contact, tightening and pulling against my bewildered skin.

"This may sting just a little, dear," she says and jerks one end of the hardened coating, ripping off every existing hair in the process. I grit my teeth to keep from yelping.

Alexia training is starting to look less intimidating. This stuff—this might kill me.

I am genuinely curious to know the reason behind all this primping. "Why—?" My question is cut short by another yank on the tender skin of my upper thigh. I don't stop the yelp in time. "Ow!"

"Matriarch Teera has given very clear instructions," Dom Tourmaline says, without glancing up from her work. "You must outshine the other Candidates in every way, which includes abandoning your rural look for something more . . . *regal.*"

"Regal? Is that code for torture?"

She answers with another tug.

I decide right here and now that if I ever become Matriarch, I will banish this nonsense—whatever it is—from Nedé. The thought placates me . . . until the next yank.

When Dom Tourmaline is satisfied that my skin has been sufficiently stripped of hair, she examines the ones on my head. Her fingers slip through the long, smooth strands, letting them fall over my shoulders, then lifts a pair of metal shears. I've always loved my hair long, like a horse's tail: thick and straight and blown by the wind when I ride. But I hold my tongue, along with my breath, and close my eyes.

*Snip. Snip.*

I shudder with each cut. Eventually I work up the nerve to peek at her progress. To my everlasting relief, she hasn't cut more than a fingerlength.

When she opens a makeup case, my nerves return. Judging by Dom Tourmaline's face, she enjoys a good slathering of paint. I find it silly. I don't particularly want to look silly, even if it *is* "regal." Having no way to tell what she's doing, I close my eyes once again and focus on the soft brushes smoothing over my cheekbones, eyelids, and lips, while my hands soak in a bowl of warm liquid. This pleasure almost makes up for the earlier trauma. Maybe a little pampering isn't so bad after all.

The minutes tick by. My stomach tells me we are nearing lunch by the time I change into a sleeveless dress the color and richness of chocolate and stand obediently in front of a mirror.

"Well." Dom Tourmaline is clearly pleased with herself. "What do you think?"

What *do* I think?

Personal beauty rarely crosses my mind, regard for it even less frequently. In Nedé—at least where I come from—women value strength, smarts, and wit. Amal women don't have time, and certainly no need, to fuss over our appearance. But now, the girl in the mirror enthralls me, like a sunset or a newly opened hibiscus. She's . . . *beautiful.*

Apparently interpreting my silence by my expression, Dom Tourmaline beams. "Lovely," she says. "I'll have Domus take up a few items that will fit you for now. The rest of your clothes will be tailored and delivered in three days." With that, I am dismissed.

I steal one more look in the mirror and stand a little taller. A new look for a new destiny.

---

Late-morning three days later, the selection of new clothes from Dom Tourmaline arrives. I rifle through the dresses, rompers, shirts, and trousers that line the armoire in nearly every shade

imaginable. The different textures of silk, linen, and bamboo slide delightfully between my fingers. I've never seen so many clothes in my life.

After too many minutes deliberating, I reach decision fatigue and so settle on an outfit embarrassingly similar to my usual riding clothes. No matter: it's my birthday, and even if the Articles keep us from fussing over such occasions, I will wear what I want. And I will spend it on a horse.

As I reach the second-floor landing, the stomp of boots stops me even before I catch the dark figure storm through the front door toward the south wing. The woman bangs a bare forearm against the first door, the Matriarch's office. A network of tattoos covers most of her right arm and shoulder. Her hair is shaved on the same side, the rest trailing in a thick braid beginning above her left ear and ending at her waist.

"Come in," Grandmother replies.

I assume the tall woman in black leather, a sheathed short sword hanging from her belt, a quiver of arrows strapped to her thigh, is Adoni, leader of the Alexia. When she speaks, I am sure of it. I recognize the deep tone as the voice I overheard the first day.

"There has been another incident," I hear, just as the door closes.

I know I shouldn't listen in, but as I descend the last few stairs, curiosity wrestles restraint and wins. I tiptoe across the great room and pretend to admire a large portrait of Matriarch Teera next to Winifred's cage in case I'm spotted.

"Hello!" the blasted bird squawks.

"Shh!" I hiss, shoving a palmful of seeds into her cage. I squeeze my eyes shut, painfully aware of the quiet pause in the office, as if Grandmother is straining to hear something too.

Seconds pass with only the sounds of Winifred's beak prying open shells.

Finally Grandmother asks, "Where?" with a coolness only she could effect.

I let out a breath and slip a few more seeds to the macaw to ensure her cooperation.

"Kekuatan. They are getting bolder, Teera. They took a number of metal items, some tools and animals, then burned the place down."

Another pause.

"The women?"

"Three were . . . attacked. Another was injured fighting them off. And they killed two Gentles."

Footsteps echo down the hall of the south wing towards me. *Don't panic, don't panic, don't panic.* I move quickly toward the closest exit, which happens to be the front door, trying to appear intentional rather than guilty. I pull it closed, ever-so-quietly, behind me.

*Kekuatan? That's where . . .*

Two figures and a horse stop me midthought. The first I recognize immediately as Domus. The second is a light-haired Gentle that belongs at Bella Terra, not standing by the pond. *Treowe.*

Our eyes meet, but we don't say a word. Not in front of Domus.

"Dom Pierce had your things sent," Domus explains.

Tre produces a leather satchel, which Domus slings over his own shoulder.

"Thank you," I say, trying to sound uninterested.

When Domus turns toward me to ask whether he should take the bag to my room, Tre takes the opportunity to mouth one word: *stable.*

"Yes, thank you, Domus. I am on my way to the stables. I will show this Gentle where to take his horse." I make my words tight, terse, trying to mimic the tone most women take with Gentles.

Domus gives a little bow before returning to the house.

Tre and I walk silently, acting the parts of submissive Gentle and aloof Nedéan. Not until we reach a long hedge of bushes does Tre chance stopping.

"Rei, listen to me," he says, all muted and rushed. "There's been an attack."

I'm confused. Why would Tre know about—

"It was Jonalyn's place."

I hear a guttural sound; maybe it came from me. The conversation I just overheard comes rushing back: *three attacked, one injured, two dead.*

"Is she . . ."

"She's hurt bad. And La Fortuna burned to the ground—the whole finca. The staff and Gentles are being relocated, but she was brought to Bella this morning with her daughter. Your mother had me bring your things so she could stay with her."

"Of course. Thank you."

Ciela and I have always been too close in age and temperament to get along well, but Jonalyn, five years my senior, was distant enough for me to adore. Even when I outpaced her height, she looked after me, chiding me for my gloom toward Mother and Ciela, but in a way that made me know she cared. Once, she found me at the teak forest, soon after I set up my crude training elements. I thought for sure my secret shire had met a premature end, but Jo didn't tell Mother. I always figured she understood better than Mother or Ciela that I was different—that I had my own path to follow.

I don't realize my eyes have filled with tears until they spill over with warm grief. Tre puts his arms around me, pulls me into a hug. I suck in a breath, taken aback by the foreign feeling. He's never hugged me before. And I have *certainly* never hugged him.

"It's okay," he whispers. "Everything will be okay."

His embrace feels akin to a mother's hug when a child has

scraped her knee. No—more urgent, like if he holds me tight enough he can unravel all my pain. Tre has never done anything this bold. He risks much to give me the gift of solidarity.

Voices interrupt our strange collision of warmth and grief. I pull away, quickly wiping my face with my hands.

Two gardeners duck through an arbor a stone's throw away. They're preoccupied with a bundle of withered palm fronds they carry between them, but their presence reminds us both that we don't have the luxury of privacy. Finca del Mar doesn't offer safe nooks for chance meetings, not like Bella. I don't need to say it; I can tell Tre is thinking it too.

His words rush together. "Rei, I probably won't see you for a long time. Maybe never, depending on how things go for you. So I need you to know something. It . . . has been an honor to be your friend. And I think you'd be the best Matriarch Nedé's ever had. You've got what it takes, Rei. You have to believe that."

I don't know if I agree, but I can tell he's sincere, so I try to accept the words for his sake.

Before I think about it, I kiss his cheek, lightly, quickly. "Thank you, Treowe," I say. And I mean it.

Tre smiles bashfully, the way he always does when he finds a way to brighten my life with his thoughtfulness.

We walk on toward the stables, playing our parts once again. I try to follow the pattern in the mosaic tiles underfoot—hexagon, hexagon, diamond, repeat—so my worry for Jonalyn doesn't spiral into panic. For the briefest moment I consider asking Grandmother for more information, to make sure my sister is okay, but that would incriminate my eavesdropping. Hardly the impression I want to make. No, Mother will ensure she has the best care. But the words "hurt bad" keep bobbing to the surface of my mind, dragging with them a host of questions. I've never heard of anything like this, not even in my history studies. Nedé has always been peaceful. Always. Could Gentles be involved? What kind of monster would . . .

I nearly pitch forward, tripping over my own foot. Siyah almighty—what if the people in the teak forest had something to do with it? The one who carried me was unlike anyone I've ever seen—yet, I'm still not entirely sure what was real and what was injury-induced delirium. Describing what I *think* I saw might land me in the insanus wing at the Center. I'd better not mention it to Tre—not to anyone—until I can tease out what actually happened. Besides, it's too late to talk to him privately, out in the open as we are.

When we reach the stables, we must part ways without so much as a goodbye. While I ready Callisto, Neechi talks quietly with Tre and helps him care for his horse.

How strange to see my longtime friend here, with a new one.

" . . . Too far to travel tonight," Neechi is telling him. "We have a spare bed in the Gentles' quarters. You can stay here tonight and ride back in the morning."

So this will be the last I'll see Tre. I can't resist glancing back at him, just once, as I ride away. He is already looking at me, and as our eyes meet, I try to say what I hope can be understood without words—that he matters to me. That I wouldn't ride away from him if we weren't here.

Yes, change does have an annoying way of revealing what we've had all along, just as we lose it.

# Part Two

# CHAPTER SIX

WORRY CHASED SLEEP AWAY most of the night, like a blasted bleating nanny goat. And when I did finally fall asleep, I dreamed of fire and panic, a face with prickly hairs, and a shirtless chest bulging with disproportionately large muscles—big as boulders. I woke up terrified and wondering again if they could be related—the attack on my sister's finca and the mysterious visitors to my teak forest. Now, though, in daylight, the ridiculousness of someone lifting me off the ground makes me wonder anew whether I imagined the whole thing.

But I don't have the energy to deliberate now—I'm too bleary-eyed and weary.

As I finish my bowl of fresh fruit on my balcony, the first Candidate and her Province's send-off party arrive. You'd think they were joining me for breakfast for the volume of their excitable racket. Or maybe that's just tiredness amplifying my irritation. I only catch bits and pieces of the merry bunch between the railing and columns of jasmine, but all their cooing and embracing is enough to make me glad for my secluded space.

The clamor ceases when Grandmother approaches, her Matriarchal robe marking her as the Mother of Nedé. The featherweight silk panels drape nearly to her feet, awash with complex swirls of orange butterflies, craboo yellow flowers, lime green leaves, and turquoise waves. The back panel is emblazoned with a thin, nine-pointed star, representing the destinies of Nedé, and the collar and slanted cuffs are trimmed with dragon fruit–red embroidery and shimmery beadwork. She clasps forearms with a striking woman with a long face, upturned eyes, and shiny black hair that falls over her shoulders in loose waves.

Lapé Province's offering, I gather. No one else could have traveled the distance to Finca del Mar this early in the day.

She's the first Candidate to arrive, and already I'm questioning why I agreed to do this. By the look of her—polished appearance, proper posture, being fawned over by the accompanying Senators—she was clearly born for this. I spear the last pieces of papaya and pineapple slowly, quietly, for fear of alerting them to my inferiority with loud, un-Dom-like chewing.

Only once Grandmother excuses herself and the twittering crew disappears around a corner, do I dare move from my lookout. I head straight for the stables, and Callisto and I play hooky until the first mandatory lecture.

———

Seven hours later, the Candidates sit around a horseshoe-shaped wooden table, capable of seating three times as many, in a room down the hall from Grandmother's office. I guess the generous distances between the five of us discourage small talk, because only the scratch of a pen against parchment disrupts the silence. The pen is held by the Candidate I saw through the balcony at breakfast. She's already taking notes, which only confirms my earlier assessment.

In my periphery, I can just make out a broad-shouldered woman a few seats left of the first, staring steadily toward the front of the room. Her arms—the rich brown of dried allspice—complement her orange, boxy tunic. She reminds me of a younger Marsa, and I'm tempted to like her because of it. But her arrogant expression bridles my trust. Between her and me, the curve of the table prevents a clear view of the two remaining Candidates. I could glance sideways to look them over, but that might be *slightly* obvious.

Finally Matriarch Teera enters the room, accompanied by a woman in a rosette-patterned dress, like silken jaguar's fur. I'm so busy feeling conspicuous, I realize a second too late that the four other Candidates have already stood out of respect. As Grandmother pauses, waiting for me to do the same, her left nostril flares ever so slightly. Only I would notice this, her granddaughter, trained in the art of the Matriarch's irritations. To her credit, she is too discreet to reprimand me in front of everyone. I try to look penitent as we retake our seats.

"Congratulations, women of distinction," Grandmother begins, "and welcome to Finca del Mar. You have been selected to represent your Province in one of the oldest tenets of Nedé: the Succession. I needn't tell you the honor that has been bestowed on you. I will select from among you the most competent, brave, hardworking, and resourceful Candidate as my Apprentice, heir to the Matriarchy of Nedé."

The woman in the tunic sits a little straighter. I want to disappear into my chair.

"In order to guide my decision, over the next seven weeks you will be given a vastly abbreviated training in all nine of Nedé's core destinies: Scientia and Medicinae, Gentles Regimen, Politikós, Innovatus, Ad Artium, Materno, Fabricatio, Agricolátio, and— new to this Succession—an expanded course in Alexia. As you progress, I will judge your intelligence, leadership, empathy, and determination—all essential qualities in governing our land. The Candidate with the readiest wit, courage, and skill will succeed. The rest will be returned to your Provinces. Of course, I don't expect my Apprentice to master everything in seven weeks. We'll have a full year following the announcement for that."

Grandmother meets each of our gazes, one by one, as she speaks.

"Ideally, in keeping with the traditions of Nedé, I would facilitate this training. However, because of—" Here she pauses and taps the table with a gnarled knuckle— "because of an unexpected, particularly urgent matter, I will not be conducting your training myself."

Surely that "urgent matter" involves the attacks. All remain composed, but I can feel the other Candidates' disappointment. Me? I can't say I'm too broken up about avoiding Grandmother's constant tutelage, or her critical eye.

"I have selected my advisor Dom Russo to oversee your studies and travel schedule." She motions to the bony-faced woman beside her, who looks to be almost Grandmother's age, and about as dour. "Much of your education will be facilitated through lectures here. You'll complete other elements of training at various sites across Nedé. I will announce my final decision at our two hundredth anniversary celebration in two months' time."

I admire the way Grandmother talks: clearly, succinctly, with authority. The others hang on her words, as if spoken by a goddess. I wouldn't mind being honored that way. Definitely not a sufficient reason to want to be Matriarch, I muse, but an undeniable perk. I wonder which of the women sitting at this table will earn the title.

When Grandmother takes her leave, Dom Russo begins.

"First, introductions are in order," she says.

And with those five words, I discover it's possible to distrust someone in the span of a sentence. Perhaps I should blame Dom Russo's outfit for making the suggestion, but she seems to have the cunning of a jaguar. She peers at each of us with coal-lined, calculating eyes, as if deciding which one of us to devour first. Thankfully, she begins with the woman on the far end of the table, who tucks her feather pen behind her ear and turns toward us. To her credit, she's as calm and steady as morning rain.

"My name is Nari Kwan, and I represent Lapé, working in Innovatus. I'm honored to Candidate alongside such capable women." There's a warmth to her words, which makes me feel a little less threatened by her. Which makes me distrust my own judgment a little more.

The woman in the orange tunic follows. Close-cropped tight curls frame her broad forehead, wide nose, and unsmiling, full lips.

"Jamara Makeda. I represent the strong women of Kekuatan, where I contribute to the good of Nedé through Gentles Regimen," she says, her eyes still trained on the front of the room.

After Jamara, I finally get a proper look at the third Candidate, who says, "I am Yasmine Torres, from Fik'iri." Her voice is more timid than I expected, and she must be the eldest of the Candidates; a bit of grey peppers the hair peeking from a silken maroon scarf. "I'm a Politikós," she adds. I make a mental note not to allow Yasmine's unassuming countenance to fool me. As a Politikós, she has probably been trained at one of the elite schools.

The last Candidate must hail from my home Province, then. She clears her throat with dramatic flair.

"My name is Brishalynn Victoriana Pierce." She says it like she's talking to a Gentle—disinterested and slightly condescending. "But you can call me Bri."

Pierce is also my surname, and the surname of the current Matriarch, and the surname of several Matriarchs before her, including the first Matriarch of Nedé, Tristan Pierce. So I guess we're distantly related, though I've never met Bri before today. When the seventy-five foremothers founded Nedé, they brought with them seventy-four surnames. We still use only seventy-four surnames; every Nedéan can trace her heritage to one of those women, even though our population currently nears one hundred sixty thousand, including Gentles, who aren't given surnames.

Brishalynn looks to be in her early twenties, with unusually blonde bangs that curve over her forehead, kissing the tips of her dark eyebrows. Her shoulders, revealed by the drop-sleeve blouse she wears, are light compared to most Nedéans', and peppered with amber freckles.

"I'm a Politikós, and I represent Amal," she continues, with the same patronizing superiority. "Well, I *did*, before she came along." Bri glares at me, not bothering to hide her disdain. "Now I'm just here for the ride."

Dom Russo appears taken aback, unsure how to respond. She takes an uncomfortably long time to muster, "That ride will be over if I hear another disrespectful accusation against *any* of the other Candidates, Dom Pierce."

Funny thing about threatening words: they only *threaten* when accompanied by the right tone. Contrastingly, Dom Russo's words puff from her lips like soft, rainless clouds. So much for the intimidating office of Matriarch's advisor.

Brishalynn offers an obligatory apology. "I'm sorry if you're offended."

Cleverly phrased, I notice, to avoid any acknowledgment of

wrongdoing. She casually wraps her hair into a knot at the nape of her neck.

I'm so rattled by Brishalynn's barb and Dom Russo's apathy that an uncomfortable moment passes before I remember I'm supposed to introduce myself now. I stutter through the first few words.

"Hi . . . I'm Reina . . . Pierce. I'm from Amal too. And . . . I haven't chosen a destiny yet." I sound like a delicate orchid, too meek and flustered to be taken seriously. The strength in me slaps my pride for such a hideously timid beginning. I'm going to have to pull it together—and soon—if I'm going to have any chance at this.

The rest of the lecture is a blur of details, itineraries, instructions, and to-dos. I try to focus, but my head spins with self-doubt by the time we are excused for dinner.

———

The five of us are to take our evening meals together in the large dining hall. If tonight's dynamics are any indication of how that will go, I'm tempted to fake an illness so I can eat alone in my room. Or maybe share Callisto's feed in the barn.

Thankfully the surroundings make up for the company. The dining hall ingeniously doubles as an arboretum, in case the Matriarch and her guests crave an open-air dining experience during the wet season, when outdoor meals might otherwise drown in a sudden, irreverent downpour. Orchids and bromeliads, dwarf orange trees and giant elephant ears encircle the thirty-seat table like a living crown. One wall shivers with water as it trickles down a vertical, mosaic waterfall. Despite the earthy vibe, the space is well appointed, with shiny wood, plush textiles, and an enormous capiz-shell chandelier, laden with flickering candles.

Jamara, who continues to display impeccable posture, stares straight ahead. Yasmine looks pensively at her plate, chewing slowly. Bri slumps in her chair, with an air of complete annoyance. Only Nari attempts small talk, which to this point has been rebuffed. She turns to me in one last effort.

"Reina, when did you find out you would be a Candidate?"

I find it hard to read Nari. Her tone is even and polite; she's either making a genuine effort at civility or sizing up her competition. I finish swallowing a bite of stuffed fish—delicious, though not quite as good as Marsa's—before answering.

"Five days ago."

The sudden elevation of Nari's eyebrows implies she might say something else, but Bri interrupts.

"Well, it looks like you were the last to know then, Rei." She says my name with a familiarity we do not share. "The Senators in Amal already knew when they held the vote. I guess I should thank you, though. I got three more votes because they figured if the Matriarch was going to throw *you* into the mix, she must not care about a Candidate's age, or might even want a younger Apprentice. But they're a bunch of overstuffed parrots. The only reason Matriarch Teera would choose someone under thirty is to keep the rule in the family. Why else would she give you the best room in the house? Hmmm? Being here is a waste of my time." With that, she pushes off from the table and storms out of the room.

That's it then. Brishalynn hates me because, while my being chosen got her the candidacy, she thinks I've eliminated her chance of Apprenticeship. The tips of my ears burn. I want to yell at her but bite at what's left of my thumbnail instead. I won't give her the satisfaction of a response.

Nari mutters, "She's a howler, isn't she?" The word sounds so foreign coming from one so polished that I laugh out loud, despite the stifling atmosphere.

"She's *something*," I say, thinking of a few other choice words that fit better.

Nari smiles. "Don't let her get to you. If Matriarch Teera chose you as a Candidate, she has her reasons. In the end, we all want what's best for Nedé."

I appreciate her words. Jamara, apparently, does not. She stays silent, but I see her look at Nari with . . . what is it in her face? An air of superiority, maybe? Whatever it is, I don't like it. Maybe her arrogance comes from her destiny. Or vice versa. Either way, I've never met a Gentle's Regimen worker who wasn't sour as star fruit.

"So, you're from Lapé," I say to Nari, changing the subject.

"I work in Innovatus. Mostly new developments. We haven't had many raw materials to work with for the past few years, but we recently discovered another ancient city site in Kekuatan that had a load of metal, wiring, screens, that sort of thing. So we're working on repurposing that."

I find it interesting that an Innovatus would get Lapé's vote over a Politikós. Then again, Nari seems the type of woman others must flock to. I've only known her a few hours, and I'm already keen to be around her. Likability is a good quality in a leader. I wonder if Grandmother had it once.

Nari tells me more about the device she's working on, some kind of machine you can control with your voice, as we finish our last bites of fish and spicy slaw. It sounds like magic, but then, much of Innovatus does.

Perhaps I was paranoid to be intimidated by Nari. I doubt I'll make any friends in a competition like this; still, it's nice to have someone to converse with.

———

After dinner I make a beeline to the shore to enjoy the last splendor of sunlight. My lack of friends at dinner turns my thoughts to Tre. I'm almost glad he left this morning; I couldn't have handled seeing him tonight without being able to talk to him. I might have forgotten myself again and wound up too close for polite company.

The clear water of the Halcyon Sea cools my feet, releasing the tension I didn't realize I was still carrying. If I stand very still, flat silver fish come and peck at my toes. The gently-lapping surge of water brings them in—nibble-nibble—then sucks them back with its retreat. In it comes, out it goes. In they come, out they go. Breathe. Breathe. I could stand here all night, inhaling the scent of seaweed and wild, feeling the air move around my bare shoulders.

Brishalynn said the Senators knew about me when they took their vote. That would have preceded my arrival at Finca del Mar. Was Grandmother so sure I would accept? Well, she was right, anyway. I didn't even think about refusing her. I didn't ask any questions either. My only real consideration was to not disappoint her—to make her proud.

I suppose that's still my motivation—the reason I'll do my best tomorrow, and the day after that, and again the following day, for seven weeks of tomorrows. *I have to make her proud.*

# CHAPTER SEVEN

OUR DAYS SLIP INTO A RHYTHM. I take breakfast alone in my silken, sunlit suite, followed by history and civics classes all morning; lunch with the Candidates in the outdoor dining room, then destiny-specific classes and a short break before dinner in the botanical dining hall, where I make small talk with Nari and some-times try with the others.

Classes aren't terrible. Dom Bakshi was an excellent tutor, yet every day I absorb bits of information she never had need to teach me. Yesterday I learned that before Matriarch Teera's rule, the Alexia were one-fifth their present number. Teera also built the Arena and initiated the first demonstrations, for Nedéan enjoy-ment and morale, only a few years before I was born. The Alexia have always been mounted peacekeepers, traveling through the vil-lages to maintain harmony, deal with problem animals, and settle disputes among landowners, but during her rule they have become reputed for their discipline, skill, and affinity for fine body art and even finer horses. Not to mention their shedding of the Domina title. I wonder if I would have been drawn to join them back then, before the daring Arena displays of their force and ability—before they were so . . . Alexia.

Even though our heritage interests me, four days of Nedéan history, Politikós studies, and Innovatus information has jumbled my mind with dates, facts, processes, and technology systems. So when Dom Russo announces we'll be leaving Finca del Mar to tour one of the Hives today, I feel what Brishalynn vocalizes.

"*Finally*," she moans, like an irritated twelve-year-old.

I can't say I like Bri, but I envy her boldness. She usually says what we're all feeling, and for whatever reason, Dom Russo ignores her sarcasm and general disrespect. Seeing derisiveness on someone else, though, makes me question my own attitudes. Does my disrespect to Mother and Ciela smell as foul as Bri's? *Ugh.*

We travel to the site, just southwest of Phoenix City, in a horse-drawn surrey with the Matriarch's seal carved on the flank. Most Nedéans walk, though the Alexia and some finca-holders ride horses, but the sight of a gleaming bamboo carriage, trimmed with crimson velvet seats and thin ivory curtains, attracts stares from those we pass.

Jamara takes the front seat, next to Dom Russo, her back as stiff as her personality. I'm in the third row, paired somewhat uncomfortably with Yasmine. She hasn't said a word since we left the finca. She hasn't even looked at me, for that matter. She's either really shy or hates me. Hard to tell with Yasmine.

Brishalynn sits ahead of me, babbling sourly about the irritation-of-the-day to her seatmate, Nari. Each of her tirades makes me further question how she was chosen, and even more so, why her impertinence is overlooked. I guess Tre was right about

Grandmother's devotion to our system. If Amal chose Bri, then Bri will stay. Or has Dom Russo even *told* Grandmother how immature she has acted?

As if sensing my silent evaluation, Bri swivels around, crossing her arms over the back of her seat, and tilts her head to one side.

"So, *Rei*." This time she says my name like it's funny to her. "Have you ever seen a Hive? Or would your sweet mother not let you?"

If she meant to strike my insecurities, she's a good shot. I *haven't* seen a Hive, and I'm a tad nervous about the prospect, though I don't know what that has to do with Mother. And I certainly don't know how it's any of Brishalynn's business. For better or worse, the surrey comes to a stop before I have time to smack her.

I'm not sure what I expected of a Hive, but the long rectangular cement building makes a poor first impression. Patches of formerly yellow paint cling stubbornly to crumbling masonry. Only a few tenacious native plants even bother growing in the gravel lot surrounding the building. As if from the weight of its own misery, a chunk of brittle mortar topples from the third story, exploding with a puff of dust on the stony ground below.

A pit forms at the base of my stomach and creeps upward. *This is a Hive?*

Dom Russo, sporting another feline-inspired outfit—how many does she have?—leads us through the front entryway into the enormous stone bowels of the building. The inside reeks of musty dampness, body odor, and, by my guess, a dead rodent. Cement walls, staircases, and hallways section the building like a beehive. Dim light struggles through square window openings, devoid of standard netting. How do they keep the mosquitos and beetles out?

Gentles file past us in a straight line, led by a tight-suited Gentles Regimen Worker, who nods at our party as she marches past. I see where Jamara gets her posture.

"For the benefit of those not familiar with our Hive system, I'll start with an introduction," Dom Russo begins, her heels echoing down the long corridor. "Gentles spend the first seven years of their lives at one of our many Materno fincas, after which time they are transferred to one of nine Hives. This is Hive I, the oldest of the compounds, dating to our foremothers. As the Gentle population grew, additional Hives were constructed in each of the four Provinces." She pauses to remove a stone from her heel. "Once transferred to a Hive, a Gentle's training begins, first in general education, manners, and character development, and then, based on a placement evaluation, training for a specific vocation: sanitation, public works, agriculture, building, house cleaning, etcetera." She chuckles suddenly, as if struck by something funny. "Anything we don't wish to do!"

Though Dom Russo seems to be the only one who got any real pleasure out of the joke, I might be the only Candidate downright repulsed by it. Her humor feels as foreign as we are in this crumbling excuse for lodging.

As Dom Russo continues, we pass classrooms where rows and rows of Gentles sit attentively in matching brown trousers and white short-sleeved tunics. At least they were probably white at one time. Now the filth of this place sticks to them, drenching them in drab.

We pass another doorway, and I catch a glimpse of a tutor striking a mop of dark hair. I've never seen a young Gentle hit; it pains something in me. The Jaguar, as Bri has taken to calling Dom Russo, doesn't skip a syllable.

"Only the Gentles who require reading and writing for their vocation are taught those skills. Gentles work best when their minds are filled with only the tasks at hand. Some vocations entail more extensive training than others, but all Gentles remain in the Hive until the Initus following their fourteenth birthday. I am confident each of you has attended at least one Initus ceremony, where every Gentle pledges their allegiance to the good of Nedé, and we celebrate their 'important contribution to society.'"

The last is a wry statement, and we all know it. I have attended the Initus every year I can remember. Most of Nedé comes to the events. Though attendance isn't mandatory, most women make the journey for the plays, concerts, and parties that lend an air of festivity to the week. Free chicha compels the rest. I doubt anyone really comes to celebrate the Gentles—Mother excepted. Grandmother always makes a big show of gratitude anyway, reminding them of their "important contribution," their vital role in Nedé's success. Then we go back to Finca del Mar for dinner, and she treats the Gentles as she always does: a necessary nuisance at best, an object of wrath if she's had too much chicha. The scar over Domus's ear serves as a permanent reminder that a Gentle's "important contribution" only gets him so far.

The next room we enter, uncomfortably crowded for its immense size, is striped end to end with dozens of long, splintering tables and matching benches. A whistle blows and the already-cramped space absorbs even more Gentles as they stream in for a meal.

Dom Russo shouts over the din, but I don't hear her words. I'm too mesmerized by the cold efficiency of the noon meal. Older Gentles scoop rice and beans into bowls and slide them across metal counters to eager hands. Regimen workers pace behind the servers, instructing and occasionally scolding their charges.

The air is stifling in this room. A sparse row of windows along one wall provides dim light but no cross-ventilation. A drop of sweat trickles down my back. What I wouldn't give for comfortable clothes instead of this prissy romper. And yet Dom Russo drones on and on about the inner workings of Gentles Regimen: assignments, transportation, uniforms, and the like.

A slight, freckled Gentle two tables away catches my attention. His small hand grips the spoon tightly, shoveling his meager meal into his mouth, as if it's his first in days. Is it the flaxen shade of his hair? Or the freckles dotting his cheeks and the bridge of his dark nose? Some familiar quality fools me into imagining it's Tre sitting there, a little Gentle, greedily consuming his lunch. The thought rips at my heart like a reamer tearing the flesh from an orange. Why have I never wondered about his life before it crossed mine?

This would have been Tre's world before he came to Bella Terra. One Gentle among hundreds, thousands. Herded, snapped at, rushed, and hit. None of this feels right. I notice each timid face now—hollow, dirty, resigned. The tired gazes barely moving from their meals. I want to do something for them. I don't know what. Just *something*. Something for all the Treowes in this whole cursed place.

The walls press in and I'm suffocating from heat, stench, and injustice. I need air.

I scan the perimeter for an exit, only to find our group already nearing a door in the far wall. I double my pace to catch up, hoping no one has noticed my distraction. No such luck.

Bri smiles coyly and whispers, "What's wrong, Rei? Not what you expected? Better not let the Matriarch see you go soft." But her tone lacks its usual edge; the slightest twitch of her lip makes me wonder if this bothers her, too.

When we clear the doorway, bright sun strains my eyes, so that I can't immediately see what she means. When I do, my breath catches.

Matriarch Teera stands in the center of a square courtyard, looking even more severe than usual. Her billowy Matriarchal robe couldn't be more conspicuous, standing out like a bird-of-paradise in a dust bowl. And there's another form too. I blink, and blink again, trying to understand the shape.

As focus returns, I make out what it is: a Gentle, kneeling in the dirt at the Matriarch's feet. Two Alexia stand guard, arrows trained on his chest, though his defeated slump hardly looks threatening. Dom Russo motions for us to file around in a semicircle, facing the Mother of Nedé. I steal a glance at the other Candidates. Jamara is the only one who doesn't look uneasy; but then, she never does. Yasmine's hand flies to her mouth.

"Good morning, women of distinction," Grandmother begins. Her voice is cool and calm, as if toasting guests at a party. "Despite being shown great care and treated with, I daresay, more kindness than perhaps deserved, occasionally a son of Nedé repays us with treachery."

The huddled lump struggles to lift his head, and I glimpse his face—bruised and swollen, a line of blood trickling from his brow to his chin. He can't be older than fifteen. Dust mixes with the tears on his cheeks. I look away before I start producing my own.

"This Gentle injured a girl who caught him stealing food from his patron. Our foremothers gave their very lives to create a society where all women may live in peace and safety. Every Matriarch must possess the ability to sustain those ideals, elevating the good of Nedé above all. Inner weakness in a Matriarch would lead to our flourishing society's ruin."

She scans the semicircle of Candidates as she speaks, her hands clasped solemnly behind her back. Now she motions to the Alexia on her left, who shoulders her bow and produces a black metal object, twice the size of her hand, from a leather cloth. Grandmother takes it to Nari, whispering something near her ear.

For a moment, I wonder if the Matriarch told her not to move, because she doesn't so much as blink. She just stands there, staring uncertainly at the foreign object in her hand. Then she walks slowly behind the Gentle and points it at the back of his head.

When I recognize what she holds, my whole body pulses with heartbeat.

I have only seen one gun in my life, the summer of my twelfth year, while we were visiting a Materno's finca near the western border of Nedé—near the Jungle. I heard the Materno tell Mother that the Alexia had given her the weapon in case a problem jaguar returned to steal more of her sheep or Gentles. Dom Bakshi told me that when the foremothers arrived, they found many guns in Nedé. But since they had no use for them, Innovatus repurposed the metal into more useful products: horseshoes, coins, and farming tools for the Gentles' use. Why would Grandmother have one?

Sun glints off Nari's dark hair and the metal in her hand. She's not shaking, which is more than I can say for Yasmine at the moment, who stifles little sobs. Only the thoughtful knot between Nari's brows discloses her uneasiness about this scenario.

She wraps four thin fingers around the handle, looping the fifth through a metal ring as she aims. How does Nari even know how to use a gun? I hold my breath and force my building emotions from my face. Grandmother can't see me squirm. And why should justice bother me, anyway? He's a guilty Gentle. This is for the good of Nedé. Our safety. He must be eliminated so others don't follow suit, but . . . *this way*?

Maybe behind her calm demeanor Nari wrestles with the same question. She stares at the gun another moment, then, as if the answer comes to her, offers it back to Matriarch Teera.

"According to Nedéan law," Nari says, with remarkable steadiness, "an offending Gentle will be punished with thirty-five lashes or placement in the public stocks. A Matriarch may well have to make difficult decisions, but I also believe it is the duty of every Matriarch to uphold the statutes our foremothers put into place."

It's a test. It must be. Grandmother wants to know what Nari is made of, that's all. And she did beautifully. Better than the rest of us likely would have. I'm proud of her, and I'm proud of my people—the foremothers who wrote laws protecting against brutality. I anxiously glance at Grandmother, expecting to see pleasure in—maybe even admiration toward—Nari's courage. Instead, her left nostril flares, and the sharp peak of one eyebrow slightly elevates.

I know that look. And I fear whatever will follow.

Grandmother relieves Nari of the gun. "Your knowledge of Nedéan law is admirable, Dom Kwan. However, circumstances may arise in every Matriarch's rule which fall outside the bounds of black and white. In those situations, she must decipher what action will uphold the key values of our society—" She raises the gun to the Gentle's head— "and *act.*"

The peal of the shot reverberates against the cement walls around us. I swallow a scream. The young Gentle crumples into a heap of dust and cloth and blood. Grandmother hands the gun to one of the Alexia, and they follow her out of the courtyard, dragging the dead body behind them.

---

I watch Nari as we ride back to Finca del Mar. Her expression isn't steely, like Jamara's, but it's equally removed—a stark contrast to Yasmine's puffy, red-rimmed eyes and cheeks still streaked with tears. Even Bri rides silently, her fingers twisting and pulling the same piece of blonde hair.

But how should we respond to what we just witnessed? *This doesn't happen in Nedé.* There must be something I don't know, some piece of information that explains why Grandmother would take a Gentle's life for stealing. No, not just for stealing; she claimed he had hurt a girl. Is that even *possible?* Gentles are by nature nonviolent, passive, living to help and serve us. And yet . . .

the attack on Jonalyn's finca. If Gentles were responsible, then maybe it *is* possible for them to become violent.

The Gentle resurfaces in my mind again and again, his young, pitiful face contorted with tears and fear. I watch him slump to the ground, bleeding red into the thirsty dust. No, he couldn't have hurt anyone. And that leaves only one conclusion: Grandmother killed him without just cause, to make a point.

*A Matriarch must put the good of all before her own desires—whatever the cost.* Her words take on a new, unnerving meaning. Does "the good of all" now include shedding innocent blood?

Nari shifts uncomfortably, still staring through the sheer curtains of the surrey. I don't know whether she wishes she had done something differently, but I admire her for standing her ground, for doing what she believed was right.

Mother warned me that Grandmother surrounds herself with people who will cave to her bidding. I have a feeling Nari just disqualified herself from the Apprenticeship. And—a new premonition sends prickles down my spine—*who will be next?*

When the surrey makes its way down the cobbled driveway of Finca del Mar, the whole picture feels wrong somehow. The bright white villa, studded with gleaming glass and oiled mahogany, is monstrous, offensively clean. Carefully manicured lawns, bursting with a dozen shades of exotic flowers—all too perfect. I run a finger along my dusty arm, remnants of the squalid Hive, and rub the brown grit between my fingers. I come from dirt too, from the dirt of a finca. From a finca where Gentles are treated with kindness and cared for by a woman who—though I occasionally resent her for it—seems made to nurture.

Mother told me to remember who I am. I don't think I know the answer to that yet, but I do know where I am from. And it's not here.

It's too early for dinner, but too late, I lament, for a ride, so I wander through the villa to pass time. Since we spend most of our days on the first floor, in the windowless room Dom Russo uses for our lessons, or in the great dining hall, where the plants seem to have more to talk about than we do, I climb a marble staircase to the second floor. There's nothing new here either. The level is divided evenly between the Matriarch's suite, which comprises the entire north half of the second floor, and a dozen other bedrooms in the south half, including the extravagance where I sleep, the Senator's Suite.

I slip into my room for a change of clothes, then return to the staircase and climb to the third and final floor. I'm not even sure why the third floor exists. There are enough offices, nooks, meeting rooms, bedrooms, sunrooms, and the like on the first two stories to house half of Nedé. Jonalyn, Ciela, and I were glad for the excessive, empty top level as kids, though. We used to play hide-and-seek here when we were very young. It was our safe haven—a place we could steal away from Grandmother's critical watch and act like the children we were. The memory reminds me that I still haven't received word about Jonalyn. She must be doing better or Mother would have sent a letter, or given a message to Grandmother for me. That has to be the case. I don't have the capacity tonight to entertain any other scenario.

The third floor reminds me of a room Jo might have arranged in her dollhouse—meticulously designed for nothing but show. The plastered walls boast fanlike strokes and bouquets of cinnamon-scented peace lilies wait to be inhaled. Embroidered pillows top tooled leather chairs, arranged for invisible guests. Despite the lack of use, not a single end table harbors dust, the work of equally invisible Gentles. Only the faint clatter of dishes from the dining room far below interrupts the eerie quiet, the sound rising through a three-story vaulted atrium in the center third of the villa. I had better mind the time, or I'll be late for dinner. Though Dom Russo doesn't dine with the Candidates, she mysteriously knows when we're late and never misses an opportunity to chastise—unless, of course, you're Bri.

I meander down a hallway absently. Large windows overlook the fountain in front of the villa. To my left, old paintings pique my curiosity: a collage of miniature portraits of the seventy-five foremothers; the very Hive we visited today, though bright yellow and less dilapidated; a group of Alexia, I assume, mounted on gorgeous horses, but wearing plain clothes and holding strangely shaped bows.

The last picture brings me to a small sitting room. I recognize the distinctive furniture, posed at right angles. How could I forget those red velvet sofas? Awfully ugly things. And I bet no one has sat on those feather-stuffed cushions since my sisters and I did somersaults across them ages ago. We were so happy then, flipping and bouncing until our staticky hair stood on end. Jonalyn would smooth our braids and clothes before we went downstairs, a Materno even then. The memory of my sister reignites worry, but I try to force it down. *She's going to be fine, Reina. You would have heard otherwise if she wasn't. You have to focus on what's in front of you now.*

I run my hand along the gaudy, velveteen fabric. One minute you're a kid and having the time of your life, the next you're leaving home for an uncertain future. I bet the ancient, crisping books lining the far wall would agree: Where does time go? Once devoured by eager eyes, now forgotten in an abandoned room, on an abandoned floor, reduced to status symbols and touched only by the cleaning staff who can't read them anyway.

Ridiculous pity for the neglected volumes tugs at me, urging me to pull a book from the shelf—to enter someone else's memories. I consider the spines of half a dozen titles, daring each one to convince me of its merit. But these appear to be mostly

dull instructional volumes: *Sustainable Living on a Large Scale,*
*Models of Government, Agricultural Methods of the Ancient World,*
*The Mariner's Guide to Sailing.* Such puzzling titles. *Field Guide*
*to Central America* especially intrigues me. What is "Central
America"? I flip through the musty pages of fading plants and animals I know well—banana palm, iguana, toucan, howler monkey,
monstera, and a hundred other familiar sights. *Interesting.* I replace
the book and continue reading spines: *Chemistry 101, The History*
*of Vaccination, The Illustrated History of Weaponry, Encyclopedia of*
*Horse Breeds and Horse Care.*

I almost wonder . . . I retrieve the field guide again, flipping to
the first page: "Copyright 2042." Book printing is sparse in Nedé,
and the first presses didn't begin production until the 2150s. These
must have come with the foremothers. Could Tristan Pierce herself
have handled these very tomes? I'm taken aback by the weight of
what I've discovered: a preserved piece of our history, growing ever
more brittle in a forgotten corner of the third floor.

"Dom Reina." A meek voice startles me out of my awe. I wheel
around to find a familiar Gentle dressed in a pressed suit waiting
behind the atrocious red leather sofa, his hands clasped behind
his back.

"Domus," I splutter.

"Dom Russo sent me to find you. Dinner has begun," he says
matter-of-factly, then adds, "and you know how she dislikes tardiness." He finishes with a wink. A wink! Well isn't this day full of
surprises?

I can't restrain a smile. "I'm sorry. I got distracted. I'll come
down directly."

With the book safely returned to its contemporaries, I follow
Domus downstairs.

———

I expect to hear only the usual bubble of the wall fountain when I enter the dining hall a few minutes later. Instead, I'm met with actual voices, engaging in a real conversation. I slide into my seat, trying not to draw attention to myself or my tardiness. Jamara notices me but doesn't say anything. The others seem too engrossed in their discussion to care whether I'm present or not.

Yasmine speaks in her small voice. "It's nothing like I thought it would be. For fifteen years I have been the top student in Fik'iri's School for Politikós, but none of my training prepared me for . . . for *that*."

I assume by "that" she means the atrocity we witnessed in the courtyard.

She squeezes her hands tightly in her lap, brown eyes still ringed with tear-swollen lids. I doubt she has stopped crying since we left the Hive this afternoon.

I've wondered how unassuming, fragile Yasmine was chosen by Fik'iri to represent them. I mean, Nari is personable and sharp, Jamara practically seethes strength, and Brishalynn is bold and young. But until now I've wondered what hidden quality warranted Yasmine's Candidacy. To be the top student at her Province's feeder school for *fifteen years*, though, is nothing shy of impressive. She must be ridiculously smart.

"No, I suppose none of us were prepared," Nari agrees, tipping her glass to finish the last gulp of chicha. I didn't take Nari for a drinker, but I suppose today could have turned anyone into one.

"How did you know how to use a gun, Nari?" I can't help the question. Her ease with the weapon—if not the task—has been dogging me since the initial shock wore off some.

Nari nods slowly, drawing her thin fingers along her jawline.

"In my Innovatus detail, we were given one of the last known cases of guns to disassemble for possible repurpose. We were hoping to find new uses other than common tools. I never actually used one, but I've read enough operation manuals to know how they work."

She pauses, a new realization hitting her at the same time I whisper, "She knew."

"Of course she *knew*," Bri snorts. "She knows everything about us. Oh, don't look so surprised, Rei. You can't tell me you haven't suspected she's keeping tabs on you, her own granddaughter! Teera knew exactly what she was doing, handing Nari the gun out of all of us."

Yasmine catches my eye from across the table, her lower lip quivering. "You know the Matriarch better than any of us, Reina. Why would she do such a thing? Why would she violate Nedéan law?"

A forkful of roast curassow stalls midway to my mouth. *How am I supposed to know what goes on in the Matriarch's mind?* Seriously—if I'm the expert on her inner thoughts, we're really in trouble.

As I sift through possible answers and whether I should give one at all, Jamara breaks the silence, clearly irritated with this whole conversation.

"He was a threat to Nedé," she says, with cool finality.

The table goes silent. The broad woman from Kekuatan rarely speaks unbidden. I rather prefer it that way. Now, her dismissive tone bears too much resemblance to the Matriarch's. Has Jamara been practicing? The thought of the withdrawn, stiff Candidate rehearsing speeches in front of a mirror strikes me as funny.

"There you have it," I say, unable to hide a smirk.

But Yasmine isn't satisfied. "I'm not sure he *was* a threat. Do you really believe he was a threat?"

Bri slams her fork onto the table. "For the love of Nedé, Yasmine! If you keep going on about it, you'll be next."

Jamara actually smiles—the first I've ever seen on her stoic face. It's not a nice smile, of course. Her cruelty reminds me of Bri's defiance in one way: they both make me uneasy.

After a long silence, Nari attempts to defuse the mounting tension by changing the subject. "I'd be curious to know your thoughts, ladies, on ways the Matriarchy could improve inter-provincial relations."

I join the conversation for Nari's sake, though I have little input about interprovincial anythings, because I admire her steadiness and because I probably should start considering matters of state if I'm going to have any chance of staying on Grandmother's good side. And after today, that should *probably* top my priorities.

# CHAPTER EIGHT

THE PAST WEEK HAS PROGRESSED as if we never visited the Hive. Lectures have continued without incident, as has the quasi-peace among the Candidates. One could almost forget that Nari held a gun in her hands seven days ago. If she questions her standing as a Candidate, it doesn't show.

Coinciding with the completion of our Ad Artium unit, tonight Grandmother will host an Exhibition of the Arts for the Council and Province influentials. Finca del Mar has been a hurricane of activity all week in preparation. The gala will be quite an affair, serving the dual purposes of highlighting what we've learned about the most poetic destiny of Nedé and allowing Grandmother to endear herself to her prominent subjects with chicha and finery.

The grounds crew have been buzzing frantically around the finca today, snipping stray leaves, scrubbing tile paths, hanging lanterns from trees, and eradicating even the tiniest of weeds from garden beds. Inside the mansion, cooks labor over exotic dishes, the savory smells daring us to keep focused on our studies this morning. The almost continuous clamor of musicians tuning instruments and rehearsing songs in the great hall made it nearly impossible.

This afternoon their never-ending practice persists through the wall of the dressing room, where Dom Tourmaline revisits the daunting task of making me look like I didn't spend the past three hours riding Callisto, which I did. Truthfully, I'd trade most of my possessions to be with her now, rather than suffer through this déjà vu with the yellow goop.

The Dom with the statuesque skin—which today is draped with a sleek, gold dress—slathers oil on every millimeter of my bare body. I marvel as she works, simultaneously aghast that anyone would care to spend this much time primping, while also having to acknowledge the pure art she infuses into this madness.

One of the first things Old Solomon taught me about horses was how to gauge their intelligence by their eyes. Some horses, you can tell they're taking everything in. Their eyes are sharp and eager. Others, especially poorly bred or overworked horses, have dull eyes—disinterested, unaware.

Dom Tourmaline's eyes hint at the intelligence hiding under her statue-perfect facade. Despite the seeming pettiness of creams, powders, and hair removal, her talent must be fueled by that acuity. What a strange person she is. Not what I would call *approachable*, but neither is she steely, like Dom Russo or Grandmother.

She takes a solid hour to sweep my hair into a waterfall braid, which cascades into a cluster of waves over one shoulder. Next comes the darkening of eyelids, powdering of skin, slight reddening of lips, and a dozen other seemingly superfluous procedures. Finally, with a nod of satisfaction, she helps me change into a dress she removes from a satin sheath.

The bodice is strapless, made from a stiff, silken material that shimmers like sun on water. The skirt flows from it like petals—five panels of multi-layered, slightly pleated, coral-colored chiffons. It's as if Dom Tourmaline knew my favorite flower and chose to make a fabric representation of it. If I could wear a hibiscus, it wouldn't be any lovelier.

She leads me to a full-length mirror and spins me to face my reflection. I barely recognize the girl who meets my stare.

"It's gorgeous," I breathe.

Dom Tourmaline doesn't respond, but a smile plays across her lips. She is pleased with herself, as she should be. The dress is perfect.

The resemblance to my favorite flower reminds me of the hedges of hibiscus at Bella Terra. And Treowe. And other familiar comforts that seem ages away—routines that once drained me but now prick nostalgia. And people who in that other place irritated the snot out of me but now squeeze my heart with . . . *longing*.

With all the simplicity and goodness of Bella Terra contrasted with the uncertainty and unease I've felt since watching the Gentle die in the courtyard, I continue to chew on Mother's insistence that I remember who I am. I'm still not entirely sure what she meant, though I think I catch a glimpse as it flutters by. Bella is irrevocably part of me—the beauty and light, the love and the strength of home.

But tonight—tonight I must play a chameleon, blending in while standing out. And if I want to catch Grandmother's attention at the Exhibition, Dom Tourmaline's skill with brushes and fabric has become my best asset.

---

The great hall explodes with opulence. Brightly dressed guests mill around the space while Gentles serve hors d'oeuvres of grilled breadfruit, spiced octopus, and tender lobster cakes. They sway through the crowd, this way and that, in time with the lilting folk music. The musical ensemble—Ad Artiums in matching embroidered caftans and feathered hairpieces—play a lilting tune with flutes and stringed instruments. Several crystal-clear barrels, balancing atop waist-high, stone bases, shimmer with gold-amber chicha, made bubbly by the best of Nedé's fruits and months of fermentation. The sight of that much chicha at a party would normally incite my nerves—you never know who is going to lose their better sense under the influence of the drink—but this is high society. They should know when to stop. *Theoretically.*

Grandmother reclines in a high-backed chair draped with silk on a platform facing the stage. Several Senators sip from delicate glasses while conversing with her, including one familiar face: Aunt Julissa, Mother's only sibling. Though her expression is slightly less dour than her mother's, she has the same high eyebrows, which have the look of always appraising. Even amidst this glut of grandeur, she, like the other Senators, has abstained from flashy jewelry or fancy clothes and so appears particularly drab next to the Matriarch's sparkling sheath dress topped with her colorful robe.

I recall my lessons with Dom Bakshi about the five core Virtues of Nedé: diversity, harmony, simplicity, ingenuity, and self-restraint. Those tenets made Nedé great, Dom Bakshi would say, and they remain essential to our well-being. Most share these sensibilities, and I imagine there will be discontented whispers tomorrow—*Did you see the Matriarch, shining like her electric-powered bulbs? The opulence! Tristan Pierce would roll in her grave.* Perhaps they're right to question Grandmother's legacy of pushing against the confines of simplicity. I wonder what Aunt Julissa thinks. Perhaps she pardons her mother's taste for finery because she has double the passion of most.

Suddenly insecure about my perfectly tailored dress and the makeup darkening my features, I scan the room for the other Candidates, hoping they've shined up for the evening too. Brishalynn chats with another woman I recognize as a Politikós from Amal. Even from this distance, I notice a difference in Bri. She must respect whoever that is, because I don't detect an ounce of bravado or sharp sarcasm. She carries herself like a proper Dom, making her selection as a Candidate somewhat easier to understand. And, to my relief, she *has* taken pains to dress up. In fact, she looks stunning in a floor-length, black sheath dress.

Jamara and Nari speak with leaders from their respective Provinces too. It must be nice to see people they know. Something familiar to steady them. Not that Jamara needs steadying, but I'm glad for Nari.

I'm trying to spot Yasmine when I catch a dark figure storm through the arched doorway instead. Her black leather boots and tangled tattoos strike an unsettling chord amidst all the silk and updos of the hall. She holds the hilt of her dagger with one palm as she strides toward the Matriarch, leaning close to address her privately.

I'm near enough to hear Grandmother answer, "Very well. Keep to the back."

Adoni leaves the room and returns with half a dozen Alexia, who file in along the furthest wall from the stage. Snug, sleeveless black shirts show off their muscular arms, a few of which display intricate ink like Adoni's. Their unconventional hairstyles—some bald, others with shaved patterns or Fulani braids, rows of two-strand twists or Mohawk fades—couldn't be more out of place.

A hushed murmur ripples through the guests like a rock displacing water in a pond, starting at one end of the room and finishing abruptly against the other. Each successive wave of guests undoubtedly asks themselves the question dogging my own mind: *Why are they here?*

A chorus of instruments promptly strikes a festive tune, returning our attention to the gaiety of the evening. Dom Russo directs me and the other four Candidates to a row of chairs arranged on either side of the Matriarch. As I take my seat, I notice Grandmother appraising me. She offers a slight nod, though the affirmation could be directed at me or at Dom Tourmaline's superior skills. Either way, I sit a little lighter as my body finds the chair, and I focus my attention on the stage.

The music builds in a rush, then drops to a melancholy dirge. A woman with rich skin and unnaturally blonde hair in a flowing red dress commands our attention. I recognize the tune as one of the old songs. Her voice rides the haunting, fluid melody as surely as I ride Callisto. Behind her, an eight-woman ensemble echoes each line with a repeating refrain:

> *Sorrow follows me where'er I go,*
> *Take me away, I must get away;*
> *Can't trust a Brute far as I can throw'm,*
> *Take me away, I must get away;*
>
> *Don't make me do it, already did,*
> *Take me away, I must get away;*
> *No way to hide what cannot be hid,*
> *Take me away, I must get away;*
>
> *If I live through this I'll see the day,*
> *Take me away, I must get away;*
> *I'll do what I must to make you all pay,*
> *Take me away, I must get away,*
> *I'm going away, I just can't stay.*

The soloist bows demurely to a round of applause, and another woman takes her place under the dazzling, sparkling glass lamps overhead.

When the first note passes over her pale-pink lips, a flood of surreal delight courses through me. Music—it's magic. How else could it bring every sense alive, pull emotions from thin air and make them mine?

She sings "Tristan's Song" like I've never heard it before:

*Come, you weary, restless women,*
*You're much stronger than you know;*
*I will lend my strength to guide you,*
*Lead you to your haven home.*

I close my eyes and drink in the bewitching melody. Like water searching over rocks, the music dances and bubbles, gracefully smooth. As the stream builds, a chorus of voices joins her. They tell the story of a woman who finds strength she didn't know she had to help others who were in need—to create a home where diversity, harmony, simplicity, ingenuity, and self-restraint could rule rather than fear and danger. It was written in honor of Tristan Pierce, our first Matriarch, the brave woman who overcame so many obstacles to found Nedé.

The next act incorporates three core performing arts: music, dance, and theatre. Dom Russo ensured we were properly educated in the historical and modern expressions of art before today's Exhibition. I'm grateful for the instruction. Knowing the rigorous training and long-standing tradition of Ad Artium heightens my present enjoyment.

The lyrical drama tells a story about our first Matriarch—played by a graceful dancer in a flowing dark costume—outsmarting the brutish males who found pleasure in their unspeakable crimes against women. The Brutes are portrayed by pairs of dancers, one on the other's shoulders and covered by a cloak, creating large, fierce foes. Tristan leaps and ducks around the stage, narrowly escaping capture by one Brute, then hitting another over the head with a pole. Her dancing continues what the soloists began: I am swept away by every rise and fall of her skilled body, captivated by her strength and fluidity.

The music crescendos as she reaches a prison door where a group of women huddle together in a slow, mournful dance. As their heroine opens the bars, the women flood out, their dingy costumes magically transformed into radiant robes of lime green and brightest orange. They circle around Tristan, then collectively raise her above their heads in a new, jubilant dance.

The liberated women follow their new leader around the stage. As the Brutes continue the chase, they suddenly grip their chests, convulsing as they melt to the floor, overcome by the Great Sickness. Tristan blows a glittery powder over each crumpled form, and in their places "Gentles" arise, bowing to Tristan and joining the trailing company of dancers.

The lights, costumes, music, and choreography leave me breathless, but it's the story—one woman whose bravery changed everything—that lifts my heart like a feather in a sea breeze. I might not fully understand who I am yet, but now I know who I want to become.

---

When the final curtain drops, my head still swims with wonder. I understand now why Nedé places such a high value on Ad Artium, giving it a place among what might be considered more essential destinies. The arts have a way of acknowledging life's horrific events while simultaneously glossing them with hope.

I head to one of the tables piled high with the delicacies I spent most of the day dreaming about; to my delight, they appear as mouthwatering as they smelled. I select a two-toned chocolate pastry drizzled with frosting and am just about to enjoy the object of my desire, when Bri's testy voice foils my pending nirvana.

"Nice dress, Rei."

I pretend not to hear her, but she's hard to ignore when she snatches my pastry, sinking her own teeth into it. If there weren't a whole platter of them nearby, I'd smack her. Her cheek stuffed with chocolaty phyllo, she mumbles, "Don't look now, but I think it's Yasmine's turn in the Matriarch's hot seat."

Of course I do look, as discreetly as I can, toward Grandmother. She converses alone with the timid Candidate, her mouth very close to Yasmine's ear, in the same fashion she spoke to Nari last week. Then the Matriarch pulls away, returning to a cluster of women nearby, ever stately and collected.

Tucked within a swirling mass of guests, Yasmine stands completely still, trying to decide what to do, or in shock, or both. Her face gradually drains of color, and she presses her hands against her stomach. Then, in a flush, she rushes from the hall, nearly bumping into an Alexia standing guard at the door.

"A hundred gold coins says she just got tested," Bri wagers. "Double that says she failed."

"Poor Yasmine," I whisper, watching the empty doorway, wishing she'd reappear, knowing she won't.

"I told her she should have kept her mouth shut."

"Don't you ever quit?"

"Why should I?"

*Ugh.* She drives me crazy. But I'm too preoccupied with a new question to walk away just yet.

"Do you think she'll test all of us?"

"Probably," Bri replies, with the indifference of predicting the dinner course. I don't know how she can stay so calm about it. I envy her detachedness sometimes. This is the nature of our relationship: one moment I hate Bri, the next I can't help but admire her pluck. The scale swings from disgust to wonder and back again, often by the hour.

"Doesn't matter to me," she continues, taking a glass of chicha from a passing servant's tray. "I know with you around I don't have a chance of winning, but that won't stop me from taking you down with me." She smiles menacingly over the rim of her glass, then toasts the air before tossing it back.

This is also the nature of our relationship: more often than not loathing tips the scales.

I don't excuse myself or offer any niceties. I just walk away, biting my lip so I don't say something I'll regret.

———

Darkness covers the gardens like an inky blanket, illuminated only by glowing paper lanterns that hang from trees and line the paths like tethered stars. I find Yasmine at the end of the bougainvillea tunnel, where I had dinner with Grandmother my first night at Finca del Mar. I felt like I should look for her. She strikes me as a kind, fragile soul, like one of the baby lambs birthed at Bella Terra each spring. Naive and gentle, they'd be eaten before nightfall if our farmhands didn't watch over them so diligently. Now, as I watch Yasmine with her arms folded around her middle, her body trembling from rage or fright, the similarity saddens me.

"Are you okay?"

She doesn't answer right away. The seconds tick past, and I'm starting to think she's not going to. Just as I turn to leave, her trembling voice, roughened by the croak of many tears, disrupts the still, balmy night air.

"No. I'm not okay." A fresh sob shakes her shoulders.

I wait, but she doesn't offer more. *Brilliant idea, Reina. What did you think you were going to accomplish when you found her? Ease her pain with your presence?*

"I'm sorry," I fumble, "I'll let you—"

In a rush Yasmine blurts, "Matriarch Teera asked me to offer . . . *special favors* to a Senator of Lapé Province. She said it is the duty of every Matriarch to ensure her most loyal allies remain loyal." She adds, practically spitting the words out of her mouth, "*Whatever* the cost."

I don't entirely know what Grandmother meant by "special favors," but apparently Yasmine does, and the implications I *can* figure out turn my stomach: whatever Grandmother meant, she must have wanted Yasmine to engage in some act of "crude gratification"—to violate Article V. For the Matriarch to abuse one of Nedé's highest Virtues—an act worthy of imprisonment—she'd have to be crazy.

Perhaps it shouldn't shock me so violently. Grandmother's reverence for our laws—particularly when they get in her way—has already proved questionable. But to sink to this level . . . What happened to the Mother of Nedé who supposedly embodies our ideals? Without self-restraint, we're no better than the Brutes of old.

Another bout of tears draws the attention of several Exhibition guests meandering the fragrant garden by lantern and moonlight. I shift uncomfortably under their stares, wishing Yasmine would pull it together, feeling bad for thinking so.

"What are you going to do?"

The incredulous shock on her face shames me. "What do you mean, 'What are you going to do?' I will not disgrace my Province or myself, even if it costs me the Matriarchy."

A paradoxical fire burns in her eyes. Meek, gentle Yasmine has a limit to her compliance, and good for her. But the repercussions she'll face for her refusal . . . well, I can see she's already guessed what they might entail.

"You're braver than I realized," I say, and before I think better of it, I give her a light hug. Maybe it will comfort her the way Tre's hug reassured me in my moment of shock and grief not far from this very spot.

"I'm sorry," I say again.

"Don't be foolish," Yasmine whispers, the blaze extinguished as quickly as it was lit. "It is I who should be sorry for you, Reina Pierce. I will return to my people when this cursed Succession is over. But you—how do you escape danger when the viper lives in your own nest?"

She's concerned for *me*, pities *me*, and that unnerves me most of all. It implies I should be afraid. And maybe she's right. I've always been a little wary of Grandmother, intimidated by her stern presence even as a child, but this Succession has revealed in her a disregard for the Virtues—a wickedness, even—I didn't know existed.

As Yasmine flees to deeper, invisible corners of the garden, my chest tightens with worry of my own: Will our common blood save me from becoming Grandmother's next prey?

# CHAPTER NINE

WHEN I RETURN TO THE STABLES after my customary evening ride a week later, Neechi's cheerful whistle echoes from inside. I nearly always find him here when I come for Callisto—oiling a saddle, brushing a horse, or, as he is now, mucking a stall. In fact, the short, caramel-skinned Gentle has become as familiar as the lecture room, where we spent the majority of our day taking notes about our country's infrastructure. Today's new information: the Gentles contribute to the good of Nedé partly by dealing with Phoenix City's dung—literally—through a system of sanitation that has been maintained since the foremothers. And now here is Neechi, cleaning up horse dung too.

We don't have plumbing at Bella Terra—none of the rural towns do—but still, how did I make it eighteen years without pondering the fate of the city's waste after it disappears down the toilets I use when visiting? And that's just one sacrifice of many I've never considered. I almost wish I could go back to not knowing. Becoming aware has awakened an uncomfortable conscientiousness I sense could undo me. Compassion, if left unchecked, might sabotage another emotion I'm counting on for my victory: determination.

Yes, victory. As I rode along the beach tonight it all became clear. I want to win—I *have* to win—I know that now. Not to make Grandmother proud. My desire for her approval bled out and died in the dust with that Gentle. Now I want to win so she can never do that again. To protect the next innocent targeted by "the greater good" of Nedé.

But in an unfortunate irony, now that I want to win, the fear of failure winds around my heart and squeezes tighter than a boa constrictor.

I didn't want to talk with Neechi this evening, worrying his softness could sink my resolve. Still, when he stops whistling to speak, I welcome it. I'm not great at ignoring him.

"You will train with the Alexia soon, yes?"

I take it back. Ignoring him would be better than talking about training.

Even though I've been drawn toward the Alexia for as long as I can remember, their training would intimidate anyone. Running a self-made course with toy weapons is one thing. Standing in the real Arena, surrounded by stone and superior skill, will be quite another. And the more I've encountered the broad-shouldered, stern-faced Alexia the past few weeks, the less I relish the thought of entering their territory.

"In two days' time. We visit the Center tomorrow, then report to the Arena the following day."

As I lead Callisto from her stall, I imagine for the thousandth time wearing the Alexia uniform—black leather riding boots, seamless breeches, close-fitting vest, wide belt, sheathed dagger, carrying a bow as casually as a handbag. One uniform, symbolizing all I've both longed for and dreaded half my life.

"Callisto will be there when you arrive," Neechi says, the usual lilting timbre of his voice as smooth as if he hadn't just spoken the impossible.

"How . . . ?"

"Domus convinced Matriarch Teera it would be in her best interest to allow you to ride your own animal, allowing the others to see what you can do."

Confused hope muddles my mind, and I'm sure it shows.

I will ride Callisto? If Grandmother has sanctioned it, no one can protest. But . . . a *Gentle* convinced her? For Domus to initiate an audience would be risky—even for the major domus—which is largely out of character for a Gentle. And the only way he would know is if Neechi . . .

"Thank you," I say, understanding dawning on me. Perhaps Tre isn't the only Gentle with notable wit.

He gives a slight tilt of his head, wrinkles forming at the corners of his eyes.

"Why?" I ask.

"Because she's your best chance to prove yourself, Dom Reina. Adoni won't like it. You should be careful not to cross her in any way other than this. But she won't refuse to let you ride your mount—pinto though she is—when the order came from the Matriarch."

I lean into Callisto, relief flooding me like a dry-season rain. I draw so much of my spirit from hers. With her, I am brave. I have courage. I can prove to Grandmother, and the Alexia, that I have what it takes.

"Thank you, Neechi," I offer again, though the sentiment rings fiercely inadequate. If I can, someday I'll repay him for his kindness to me.

---

The next morning, we board the bamboo surrey once again, taking our usual seats as the creatures of habit we are. Though a small comfort, I am relieved four other Candidates still fill the seats. I fully expected Grandmother to send Nari and Yasmine home after their respective refusals. But so far, nothing. If they're lucky, she'll let the Succession play out before deciding whom to dismiss. If they're not, who knows what Grandmother might conjure up.

Within ten minutes we've approached our destination, and I'm happy to give my concerns a rest.

The Center for Health Services, aptly named for both location and function, rises above the city houses and shops like a square volcano, stretching towards the sky. Nine stories of intermittent glass windows reflect the morning light, thick clouds drifting along their mirrored surfaces. Compared to the Hive, the freshly painted beige building resembles a palace. You'd be hard-pressed to find a crack in the eggshell-smooth walls, and abundant palms, trees, and flowering shrubs encircle the perimeter. A dozen story-high arches, nearly engulfed with flowering flame vine, usher us through a fiery-orange tunnel to the entrance. Apart from Finca del Mar and the Arena, the Center is the most impressive building in the most impressive city in Nedé.

We've barely disembarked from the surrey when Dom Russo begins her lesson. She has a special "lecture voice," I've noticed. Bri has noticed too, and I smirk at how annoyed she gets when the Jaguar uses it.

"The Center is the most vital operation in Nedé," she begins. "As you will no doubt remember from your lessons—" she fixes us with a pointed look— "a great epidemic, resulting from the Brutes' inferior genetics, decimated the world of old in a single generation. The foremothers were only able to save themselves and cure their own would-be Brute children of their inferior makeup through a lucky advance in medicine. To prevent a recurrence of the blight on human history—both of sickness and of Brutes—we place the utmost importance on maintaining the physical hardiness of our population. At the Center, we create life, then maintain vibrant lives. Today you will see this at work."

As she concludes, we pass under the final arch and step into the lobby. A woman in a creamy white lab coat greets Dom Russo by the front desk. Though the wiry curls escaping the twist of her bun shine silver, she carries herself with the confidence of youth. Thick lips offer neither smile nor frown, and narrow-rimmed glasses perch on a hearty nose, revealing disproportionately large eyes. *I'm almost certain* we've met before.

"Welcome, Candidates," she greets us, with surprising warmth. "I am Dr. Karina Novak, codirector of the Center."

*I knew she seemed familiar.* I've only visited here two or three times, when we were in town and Mother had to check in on things, but now I remember being introduced to Mother's codirector. However, as Dom Russo makes introductions, the doctor gives no indication of making the connection.

"I'm honored to lead your tour of our Center facilities today. We have much to see, so we had better get started."

The doctor turns west, leading us down a hallway lit as bright as noonday with electric bulbs. We pass waiting rooms and offices, and as we do, she explains our surroundings.

"Floors one through three comprise our General Health Clinic. We encourage women to practice basic care and homeopathic medicine at home, using the abundance of plant material we have at our disposal in Nedé. We have facilities in each Province to train them in medicinal herb use and basic hygiene. However, if a woman comes with a more serious complaint, we evaluate other treatment options and will occasionally prescribe stronger medicine, which we develop in our research labs on the ninth floor."

Their strategy must work. I rarely hear of disease or serious illness in Amal. Even here, most of the women walking the halls or sitting patiently in comfortable waiting rooms seem fairly healthy; in fact, old age seems to be a prerequisite for frailty. I am proud of Nedé for taking such good care of its women. And, though I have to rein my pride to admit it, I'm proud of Mother for contributing to this. Ciela too.

*Ciela.* She should be working today. I'm *almost* glad at the thought of my sister nearby. I guess absence has softened my feelings toward her a bit too.

We wind our way around the first floor in a circular sweep. Before we reach the lobby again, I notice a sign painted over double-wide closed doors: Gentle Care. Dr. Novak prepares to walk past the room, but my curiosity stops my feet from continuing.

"What's in there?" My voice echoes across the floor-to-ceiling tiles of the hallway.

The doctor pauses, then turns, looking slightly pleased. Without taking her eyes from mine she says, "Dom Russo, I know we are on a time schedule, but Dom Pierce would like to see our Gentle Care facility. Will you permit me to show this important work to your Candidates?"

The Jaguar looks highly annoyed, which in turn makes Bri suddenly thrilled with the possibility of going inside. She never misses an opportunity to irritate our tutor.

"I want to see it too," she demands.

"Very well," relents Dom Russo, crossing her arms. "But be expedient, please."

As Dr. Novak swings open one of the large doors, I immediately understand why they keep them shut. The smells of unwashed bodies and rubbing alcohol nearly flatten me. Forcing down a gag, I step into the large waiting room, packed with too many chairs. Ailing, frail Gentles fill the seats and lean against walls. One coughs into his arm. Another lies across three chairs. Everywhere is sickness and fatigue and . . . *sadness.*

"This is our Gentles clinic, where we treat curable illnesses, with the aim of returning workers to their vocations. However, we've found that once a Gentle falls ill, usually by his late thirties to early forties, he rarely fully recovers. For this reason, we allow chronically ill Gentles the option of receiving quietus early."

Yasmine speaks up, if you can call it that. Her voice barely rises above a whisper these days. "What's *quietus?*"

Dr. Novak tilts her head to one side, considering. "Ah, yes, you probably know the injection as 'the stinger.' It's the euthanasia option we provide Gentles when their health begins to fail, as a more comfortable alternative to spending their remaining months at a phase-out facility."

I openly stare at a leathery, thin-boned Gentle slumped in the chair closest to me, his eyes half-closed. He can't be older than Jonalyn.

"They come here to die," I say, half question, half realization.

The doctor's large eyes peer at me through her glasses. Are they tinged with lament? Resignation? More likely she's just trying to read me.

"Many of them, yes," she finally says, in a matter-of-fact tone befitting a doctor.

My throat tightens, and the corners of my eyes sting with heat and salt. I blink back the tears. *Not here, not in front of the others.*

I keep from crying but can't stop the question: "Why can't you make them better, the way you help the women?"

I've never considered the question before, and my naivete

shames me into a pea-sized lump. Why *do* women live so much longer than Gentles? And why are we healthier?

"Unfortunately, I can't give you a definitive answer, Dom Pierce. Some suspect the same *deficiencies* in male genetics which made them susceptible to the brutishness of old may be the culprit now. Others of us are undecided. But we all agree that we must do what we can to help them, even when the most compassionate course is to let them end their misery."

I silently scan the room full of Gentles, servants of Nedé—made pathetic by inferior genetics? My mind flies to Treowe. How many years does he have before some phantom illness brings him here? He would choose the stinger over wasting away at a phase-out, I know he would. I set my jaw and bite my thumbnail hard to push back the rising dread. There must be something we can do for them, for *him*.

Dom Russo starts toward the doors, signaling the end of our detour. I follow willingly, grateful for a respite from these unsettling new realities.

For the next hour we travel up staircases and through countless hallways, canvassing three floors of general health, followed by two floors of hospital facilities, where we witness all manner of routine procedures. I'm sick to death of sterile rooms and endless tile hallways by the time we reach the sixth floor.

But when we step onto the landing, this level—instead of resembling a medical clinic—looks like we took a wrong turn and ended up in someone's great room.

Dr. Novak lowers her voice. "We won't tour this floor or the next, for the sake of our residents' privacy. Floors six and seven contain our Materno flats—more than one hundred, actually. In the past thirty years, as our population has rapidly expanded, we have constructed dozens of other complexes through Phoenix City—6,500 flats as of last year, with another thousand already under construction. We offer these residences to Maternos who prefer city life to the rural existence of finca owners, which can be somewhat isolating. Here, women can come and go as they please, enjoy the company of other Maternos, and benefit from all Phoenix City has to offer. In addition to offering community spaces, our flat complexes provide the added luxuries of cafeterias and daycares to minimize domestic duties. These women have chosen to give Nedé the priceless gift of new life, and in our abundant gratitude, we cover every expense and endeavor to make their twenty years of service to Nedé as comfortable as possible."

"Why wouldn't every Materno choose to live here, rather than on a finca in the boondocks?" Bri asks.

"Both options have merit. Rural life—particularly the autonomy which accompanies managing a finca—appeals to many Maternos, my codirector included." She glances briefly at me. "Fincas are also better suited to large numbers, for those who wish to take advantage of the ten-birth pension. But to your point, most Maternos do prefer our flats, which can accommodate up to four daughters at a time. Gentles are transferred to fincas after a nursing period."

"How old are they when they are transferred?" asks Nari.

"A few months to a year, depending on the Materno's interest in the nursing stipend. Most flat-dwelling Maternos appreciate the arrangement, recognizing the benefits of sending Gentle infants away sooner than later, both for the Gentles and for themselves. It allows them to focus on their daughters' upbringing and minimizes the risk of any . . . *attachment* issues down the line."

I'm about to ask what "attachment issues" they've encountered when a flat door swings inward and a young woman, scarcely older than me, steps out, her hands cradling her bulging abdomen. She only makes it a few steps before grasping at a wall to steady herself. She grimaces, breathing out slowly. Dr. Novak quickly assists her to the stairs, instructing us to follow.

"Where are you?" she asks the woman, unalarmed but urgent.

"Four minutes."

"Good enough. Let's get you to delivery."

We climb the next two flights of stairs in fits and starts, pausing twice for contractions. During each interim, Dr. Novak schools us in the finer points of baby delivery at the Center, while occasionally checking her watch. Apparently, knowing when to go to the eighth floor—not too soon, but certainly not too late—is an art form which older Maternos master. When we halt a third time, forced to watch the young woman breathe slowly through another painful contraction, I worry she may not yet be adept at the particulars. I'm none too keen on the idea of witnessing a birth, especially one in a stairwell.

With a half-dozen sighs of relief, we clear the stairs with baby still tucked inside. A receptionist casually directs the shaky mother to a birthing room. Dr. Novak whistles at a nurse.

"Get ready to catch that one," she instructs. The dark-haired nurse nods and picks up her pace, without the slightest hint of concern. They must deal with this all the time.

"The eighth floor. My favorite," she says wistfully. "Here we initiate life, deliver life, nurture life, and preserve life. I believe it is the most important mission of the Center."

Her enthusiasm about babies reminds me of Mother's. I've never understood it. Even when I was young, while Jonalyn and Ciela took turns holding the littlest Gentles, soothing their cries and changing cloth diapers, I preferred to be out romping with the horses, scaling a tree, or shooting at stump targets with my toy bow and arrows. I'm just not made to nurture. Never have been.

"While the some five thousand Maternos who live in rural fincas largely give birth at home," she continues, "those who choose to reside in the flats, as well as any women who experience complications in pregnancy, deliver here. We see mostly the young ones.

After three or four deliveries under her belt, a Materno generally feels confident enough to tackle the later ones at home with a midwife."

For those aiming for the ten-birth pension she mentioned earlier, I suppose that saves them a lot of trips to the eighth floor. That's also a lot of babies. Bats! Ten apiece?

I've never given it much thought, but now I'm curious: How many children has Mother birthed? Surely not even close to ten. I can't imagine her aiming for a pension if it meant giving up her work either as a Materno or as Center codirector. But how many exactly? I'm confident, at least, that I was the last baby born to Leda Pierce. I would remember a pregnant Mother. And before me were my two sisters, but were there any Gentles in between? Or have all the Gentles who lived at Bella over the years been birthed by other Maternos?

Fragments of forgotten conversations resurface, merge, and yes . . . yes, there was at least one—a Gentle who died as an infant, not uncommonly, before Jonalyn was born. Did she have others before Ciela and me? I'll have to ask her.

We pass a dozen or more rooms resembling the hospital floor with their curious technology, each containing a bed surrounded by instruments and monitors. The woman we escorted to delivery lies on one such bed, the dark-haired nurse poised at the foot, watching a screen punctuated by squiggles. Another woman, wearing normal clothing and a serene expression, holds the birther's hand and whispers soothing encouragement. The squiggles intensify along with the birther's moans. My stomach lurches.

I've never witnessed a birth—by choice—and, though the unfolding drama gives me a greater appreciation for Maternos, I'm relieved when Dr. Novak moves us on.

After touring a thankfully *empty* delivery room, we continue down the hall, past the records room, until the corridor splits in front of a glass wall. Dr. Novak pauses here, tenderly placing a palm against the three-meter-high panes. Beyond the barrier, dozens of bassinets form tidy rows, each cocooning a tiny human. Several of the babies lie swaddled in colorful blankets—swirling floral prints of banana yellow, breadfruit green, and fuchsia pink. The remaining babies, presumably Gentles, sleep cozily in drab taupe wraps.

"The nursery," beams Dr. Novak. "Most babies begin their lives here, receiving the best of care. Except in cases of medical abnormalities, daughters are reunited with their mothers to bond and begin nursing as soon as possible, either in their Materno apartment, or, for our finca managers, at their homes. Roughly a half-dozen girls are born here each day."

"And the Gentles?" I ask. "Why are there so many in here?"

"Except for their scheduled nursing times in designated rooms, Gentle infants remain in the nursery until transferred to a Materno finca—up to a year for those whose mothers are capitalizing on the nursing stipend, and three months for the rest. Again, we've found everyone benefits from this arrangement."

A nurse enters the nursery, arms cradling a bundle of taupe fabric. Peeking out from an open fold, a tiny wrinkled face yells in distress, though we can't hear his protests through the thick glass. After setting the baby in an empty bassinet, the nurse leaves the room, and a pair of nurses amble toward him. One produces a vial no bigger than my thumbnail and gives it a good shake. When the baby's mouth opens wide with another trembling scream, she takes the opportunity to administer the vial's contents, squeezing the liquid into his mouth. Her partner makes notes on a parchment.

"What are they doing?" Yasmine asks.

"Administering the health vaccine to today's newborns. All children are inoculated at birth—with a different formula for Gentles and daughters. The vaccinations form the cornerstone of Nedé's health and subsequent prosperity. We have completely eliminated the primary diseases of pre-Nedéan history, all without the use of barbaric needles. As a result, we have reduced the mortality rate among Nedé's daughters to an impressive 2.5 percent, and of the Gentles' to an equally admirable 14.2 percent. Of course, it would be impossible to completely eliminate the disparity between those numbers, because of the Gentles' weaker dispositions. But a team of highly qualified technicians are even now making adjustments to our vaccines to provide Gentles the greatest chance of healthy lives."

As she motions us to continue, I glance back at the newest nursery arrival, wondering if he came from the woman we accompanied up the stairs. The bundle of taupe lies still now in his bassinet, calm as a sleepy kitten.

At the end of the glass nursery wall, we pass under another sign—"Life Serum Clinic"—and into another waiting room. Here, several women recline in upholstered chairs, two conversing, a third reading a book. Dr. Novak speaks with a nurse behind a counter, then motions us to follow her. While we pass a number of small exam rooms, she explains, "This is where Maternos become mothers. The life serum is inserted into a Materno's uterus in a painless procedure resulting, nine times out of ten, in a successful pregnancy."

Dr. Novak beams over the statistic. I've never heard of *life serum*, but I'm putting the pieces together. I knew Maternos came to the clinic to get pregnant; now I know how.

We don't stop in any of the exam rooms, and that's just fine with me. I've learned enough about birthing today without a visual tutorial of initiating pregnancy. The last room we pass, a corner office, is different from the others. The two external walls are floor-to-ceiling windows like the nursery. Inside, shiny microscopes glint atop steel workbenches. A square-meter box perches on a wide table in the corner, condensation dripping down the glass door, obscuring its contents. I want to ask Dr. Novak about the room, but she has already rounded the next corner. No matter—I'm not curious enough to bother tracking her down.

We circle back to the stairwell and up a final flight to the ninth floor. As we turn a corner into a large laboratory, I'm surprised to run into a pair of black-clad Alexia, armed and at attention. Their presence seems to catch Dr. Novak off guard as well; she stumbles over words, explaining the purpose of our visit.

*If the Alexia are here* . . . I search uneasily for Grandmother, certain another test is waiting for us. When I don't spot her colorful robe amidst the monotony of cream-colored lab coats, I exhale my needless panic. *She's not here.*

But someone else is.

Even with her back to me, I recognize Ciela's dark chestnut hair, twisted into a high bun, her petite shoulders hunched over a microscope. A wave of homesickness I don't quite understand washes over me. For all our quarreling, she's a welcome sight. I need to talk with her, find out if she smells like home, ask her about Jonalyn. I want answers to the questions this place has raised, and more than anything, I want her to tell me there's something we can do for Tre, and for Little Boo, to keep them from ending up here, wishing to die.

Having appeased the Alexia, Dr. Novak leads our group down a corridor on the west end of the lab. I fall back little by little, attempting nonchalance as I weave through tables and partitions to my sister.

"Ciela," I whisper behind her.

She whirls around. "Reina? What are you—"

I shush her with a finger to my lips. "I only have a minute. Is there somewhere we can talk?"

Judging by her pinched eyebrows, our atypical surroundings haven't fostered a sudden sisterly fondness in her as they have in me. She's as annoyed as ever. To her credit, she caps a beaker, stands, then escorts me down a hallway and into an empty office, closing the door behind us.

"Alright. What do you want, little queen?" she snips.

I almost wanted a hug three seconds ago, but a familiar resentment begins swelling instead, threatening to spill unheeded from my mouth. *No.* No, I won't give into it. A Candidate is above petty sibling squabbles. Sort of. *Ugh!* This stuff runs deep.

The internal dialogue between my pride and better sense takes a moment, and Ciela, no doubt expecting a quick comeback, seems rattled by the quiet interim.

"What?" she repeats.

"Jonalyn?" I will my voice not to crack. "Is she okay?"

It's strange how mutual suffering can patch leaky relationships, at least temporarily. When Mother's lost Gentle was found drowned in the Jabiru, I didn't understand the depth of her sadness. But her tears doused the coals of my rebellion, putting the fire out for a time. Marsa didn't have to break up any fights between me and Ciela for at least three weeks. We pulled together for the sake of Mother's grief, filling the vacuum created by her weakness with our own strength.

Maybe Ciela sees my own fragility now, because her next words come softly.

"Mother says she's going to make it. It was awful, Rei, seeing her unconscious and covered in blood, and little Cassia was terrified, but they're doing better now. Mother dotes on them, of course. And I'm . . . dealing with it in my own way."

"What do you mean?" I'm used to Ciela's brow scrunching ten different ways in frustration at me, but the hard line across it now isn't like her.

"The . . . *people*—whatever attacked her finca—she said they looked like Gentles, but they were bigger and obviously stronger, and they hurt some of the women." Her voice drops so low I can barely hear her. "I think they were Brutes, Rei, and I'm determined to figure out what's going on."

"*Brutes?* Like in the old days?" Disbelief drips from my words as I remember the cloak-draped actors at the Exhibition, bulky and angry, chasing and imprisoning the nymph-like dancers. That was a story—*history*, but still a story. The notion they could be real, alive, here in Nedé, is preposterous.

"What else could they be?" Ciela insists. "True Gentles would never hurt a woman. That's not their nature."

She's right about that: what happened to Jonalyn isn't in a Gentle's nature. It's why I suspected Nari's assignment from Grandmother was a test. Gentles rarely speak out of line, let alone show anger. Let alone *hurt* people. They are the essence of *safe*.

So the attackers weren't women. They weren't Gentles. But Brutes? That's not only illogical—it's *terrifying*.

I've been dogged by a handful of fears in my eighteen years: drowning, losing my Callisto, failure, to name a few. But I have never feared harm from another human being. Never had reason to. Women aren't perfect, to be sure, but they generally follow the Articles, and I've always been cocooned by safe people. Even the intimidating Dominas—like the Alexia or, more so, Grandmother—have never threatened my physical safety. No woman would hurt me—certainly no Gentle. But if Ciela is right—if there are Brutes out there, they are decidedly *not* safe. Their existence would change everything.

*But it's impossible.* Brutes died in the sickness that wiped out the world of old. They've certainly never been spotted in Nedé.

*Unless* . . .

A frightening possibility slams into me like a blow to the head.

*The teak forest.* For the first time in weeks I remember the encounter with a sticky bare chest, and a brand-new fear spreads through my veins like spider webs, pulsing in my ears, making me dizzy. What if I *wasn't* hallucinating? What if they . . . Could *I* have seen—been helpless in the arms of—a *Brute*?

*No.* Those couldn't have been Brutes. They seemed too . . . too *human.* Besides, they didn't hurt me. Don't Brutes hurt women?

*That doesn't mean they haven't hurt someone else.*

I'm about to spill a bucket of confusion on Ciela when familiar voices outside the office door remind me I'm on borrowed time.

"Listen, Ciela, I have to get back. Will you tell Jo, and . . . Mother, that I love them?"

Her eyes linger on me a long moment before answering. "Of course."

I don't think it's lost on either of us that we just had a real, adult conversation. No bickering, no pettiness.

"Be careful out there, Reina. If I'm right, you need to be careful."

I slip out the door just as Yasmine's short frame turns the corner at the end of the hall. I try to rejoin the group casually, as if I haven't been sneaking around a high-level laboratory. Dom Russo isn't fooled.

She growls, "Where have you been, Dom Pierce?"

"I got distracted, taking everything in, and I lost the group. I'm sorry," I say, feigning sincerity. I worry she won't buy it, until she unexpectedly lets it go.

"Don't let it happen again," she directs, then saunters ahead, her mid-calf, feline-print skirt swaying in time with her steps.

The conversation with Ciela steals my attention from the rest of the ninth floor. I vaguely note the many offices, various-sized labs, and a supply room that feels deliciously cold, almost too cold. Dr. Novak calls the effect "refrigeration." The technology here at the Center far eclipses any other in Nedé, simplicity bowing to ingenuity. At home, we're lucky to have a telephone. Here, machines hum, electricity powers lights and temperature, and technicians tinker with microscopes and vials. I guess Dom Russo wasn't kidding: Nedéans are serious about our health.

I'm still not really listening as we descend all eight flights of stairs back to the lobby. More pressing concerns blur everything else.

I try to push the terrifying question of the Brutes from my mind and focus instead on the good news. Jonalyn is recovering. I'm sure I'd have been informed if she wasn't, but still, I needed to hear it. Concern for her has weighed heavily on me, pestering every peaceful moment, ever since Tre told me about the attack. She will make it; she has to. But as much as I try to focus on her, one unnerving reality taints each positive thought: danger lurks in Nedé. Grandmother knows it. Adoni knows it. But *what* exactly do they know? And how can I find out?

As we exit the Center, passing under the last high arch of fiery-orange flowers toward our waiting surrey, I force myself to shake free of the what-ifs and focus on the immediate. Dr. Novak clasps each of our forearms in turn, thanking us for coming and wishing us luck in the Succession. When she grasps mine, I prepare for a standard farewell. Instead, she leans closer as she says, "If there's ever anything I can do for you, Dom Pierce, don't hesitate to ask."

I'm taken aback by her intense sincerity.

"Thank you, Dr. Novak."

I can't imagine needing to take her up on the offer, but there's something sharp about this doctor. I get the sense she is being more than polite.

As the surrey pulls onto the street, the Alexia Arena looms scarcely a quarter mile north, snapping my senses to attention.

One of those other fears of mine—the fear of failure—displaces the alleged Brutes for now. Training begins tomorrow, and I can't give Grandmother any reason not to choose me. I have to make life better for the Gentles—for Tre and the others. I have to do better than she has done.

# CHAPTER TEN

THIS MORNING, under an unusually cloudless sky, the world of childhood make-believe collides with the smell of leather, the tight cinch of a wide belt looped across my hips, the thud of leather boots against the stone tiles as I enter the Arena. I try not to wear my nerves as plainly as my temporary uniform.

Like a line of matching ants we pass under the enormous archway of the south entrance: Jamara, Brishalynn, Nari, Yasmine, and I. No one speaks, for nerves or out of reverential awe—maybe both.

Except for Jamara, whose close-cropped curls need no securing, we each have our hair pulled up, twisted into braids or knots for ease of movement and relief from the coming heat of training. Our styles don't come close to the intricately braided or etched designs of the Alexia's hair, and our arms are noticeably devoid of inked artwork, a clear reminder that we're not *actually* Alexia. We're Candidates in Nedé's seventh Succession. Outside of this Arena, that might make us superior. Here, it means we have much to prove.

As I step from the last stone tile of the breezeway and onto the hard-packed sand of the Arena floor, a goose-bumpy shiver shakes my shoulders. Layer upon layer of gray stone benches encircle the training field, rising like a circular staircase to the heavens. The columns of the Matriarch's personal viewing balcony jut out from the stadium on the far end, and I remember viewing the demonstration from that very spot.

But today the Arena yawns strangely hollow, deprived of raucous cheers reverberating throughout the stadium in adoration of Nedé's warrior women, or drunkenly celebrating the Gentles' Initus Ceremony. This morning only the thwap of boards and terse commands puncture the quiet, the noises made by a dozen or so Alexia busily hoisting targets and arranging obstacles, preparing for our arrival.

A tall woman strides toward us with a dominating confidence rivaled only by Matriarch Teera's. I recognize that gait, the muscular arms, the tattoos that cover most of her right arm and shoulder. The long, single braid falling from the left side of her head brushes a silver hilt at her hip. She is fierce. She is beautiful. Adoni, leader of the Alexia.

As she nears, the tattoos on her arm converge, revealing a singular shape: one elaborate dragon, an arrow piercing its scaly flesh. The image on her arm suddenly pulses with significance. They say her name means "she who fights with dragons."

Adoni draws the dagger—a metal blade as long as her forearm—from the sheath on her belt. She spins it nonchalantly while addressing us.

"Welcome to the Arena, Candidates. Because of the high profile of the Succession, the Matriarch has tasked me personally with teaching you the ways of the Alexia. In this company, I would expect one of you to know the meaning of our order's Greek name?"

I want to impress Adoni, but I'm not fast enough. Nari has already taken the opportunity.

"Alexia means defender," she says matter-of-factly.

"Correct. Alexia are the defenders of Nedé. Any Matriarch, then—or future Matriarch, in this case—would be wise to become acquainted with our ways. She, too, must be a defender of her people. No one expects you to become fully Alexia, but for the next three weeks you have the opportunity to prove to Matriarch Teera that you are stronger than your opponents—that you are the best Candidate to lead and defend Nedé, from *any* threat."

Maybe I know more than I should, but I can't help but wonder if a particular threat fills Adoni's mind. I also wonder whether the disproportionate amount of time we'll be training with Alexia—three whole weeks—is due to that threat, or simply because of the intimacy the Matriarch and Alexia must share. In order to appoint an Alexia leader, after all, a Matriarch should have a detailed understanding of the role.

"Meet Trinidad, my second-in-command." Adoni motions toward a younger Alexia who joined us a moment before. "She will outfit you with weapons."

Though half a head shorter than Adoni, Trinidad has the same muscular build and commanding presence. Metal bands circle her biceps, matching her short, copper-tipped curls.

"Follow me," she orders us.

She leads us to a rack of bows and quivers, and we line up dutifully, waiting for our new toys. When Trinidad turns to face us, I glimpse her eyes for the first time. What an unusual color they are—like liquid gold, pooling around her pupils. The whole of her arrests me. She appears to have stepped off a page of Dom Bakshi's mythology book—a dark-skinned Greek goddess, accented with splashes of gold.

Those intriguing eyes measure us quickly and skillfully, matching each Candidate with the appropriate weapons. She hands me a quiver of arrows and a light, midsize mahogany bow. I test the string. The low-pitched twang awakens memories of childhood target practice and sprinting through green fields in colorful scarves, like those the Alexia wear for the demonstrations. It all seemed so magical then—the Alexia's strength and accuracy, the wicked agility of their fine horses. Even my worry of disappointing Mother gave the destiny a fantastical quality only a forbidden dream can lend. Now, dust sticks to my bare arms, already sweaty in the rising morning heat, and irritating gnats circle our heads, grounding this full-circle moment in reality.

I haven't shot a bow in weeks—and even then my poor specimen could only afford me the crude mechanics. I have no illusions about the challenge ahead of me. Judging by the way Nari gingerly grasps her weapon, though, I don't think she's ever shot one. Ironic, that a bow—the most common weapon in Nedé—would be foreign to her, when she knew how to hold a gun. Jamara doesn't seem familiar with her bow either, but her strength and coordination make her someone to watch. Yasmine and Brishalynn test their strings and examine their arrows, suggesting they've taken basic weaponry courses at their Politikós schools for Candidate hopefuls. I can't let them intimidate me. I won't. I have to excel at whatever challenges Adoni presents.

Trinidad directs us to form a line facing a block of targets, concentric circles painted on sacks of dry grass. After a brief lesson in mechanics, she instructs us to fire at will. I've barely drawn an arrow before I hear the thud of a tip plunging into a target. Bri smirks with satisfaction. Yasmine hits dead center a second later. I try to block out the competition, focusing instead on steadying my left hand, nocking an arrow and letting it fly. *Zzwing.* A complete miss. *Bats.*

I can practically feel Bri gloating three stations away. I shoot another, this time grazing the bottom right corner of the sack. Another. No better. A fourth arrow produces a puff of dust three meters short of the target. Am I getting *worse*? I angrily yank another arrow from my quiver.

Trinidad, who has been pacing behind us, appears at my left shoulder before I can embarrass myself again. "You're overthinking it, Candidate."

"Reina," I say, trying to gather a shred of dignity from the pile of splintered ego on the Arena floor.

"Like I said, *Candidate* . . . "

Bri interrupts, her eye not wavering from the target, "You should remember your manners, Trinidad. One of us might be your next Matriarch." Her arrow hits its mark, and she adds, "How will you want to be remembered?"

My eyes bug out of my head at her audaciousness, but I manage to stuff down a baffled laugh before it incriminates me.

The muscles of Trinidad's jaw tighten, but she doesn't validate Bri with a response. That has to be the first disrespect she's received from a trainee—like *ever*. On one hand, I admire Bri's gutsy brash bravado, but I wish she wouldn't have interrupted. Whatever advice Trinidad was willing to offer has been nipped by pride, and she turns to resume overseeing our progress.

"Wait," I plead. "What do you mean?"

Though obviously irritated, she considers for a moment, then makes her way back to me.

"I can tell you've had some experience with a bow. You know the technique. Get out of your head and just do it."

Not exactly the instruction I was hoping for, but I nock another arrow, not bothering to analyze my posture before sending it. This time the tip buries into the outer ring of the target. I resist the urge to whoop and dance in celebration, though I can't hide a *little* swagger as I head to a barrel to restock my quiver.

"Better," she says. "Now do it again another, oh, hundred times. A Candidate will practice until she gets it right. An Alexia will practice until she can't get it wrong."

I take her seriously, gathering my arrows, shooting, and repeating for the better part of three hours. I hit the center mark only four times, but at least the dirt has escaped repeated pummeling. As ease with the bow returns, wild frustration gives way to determination. *Work harder. Get better. You can do this, Reina.*

Bri and Yasmine moved on ages ago and have already completed a more complicated set of targets—a system of painted boards and pulleys that hurtles targets across the Arena at surprising speed. They're now drinking water under the enviable shade of the awning.

Jamara tries her hand at the moving targets now. I'm suddenly not so embarrassed at my subpar beginning. The bow is not her strong suit. If our future holds hand-to-hand combat, though . . .

I take a spot adjacent to Jamara and swallow my nerves as a target rushes past. *Now would be a really good time for a lucky shot.* My muscles threaten mutiny as I take aim, energy sapped from the ridiculous number of repetitions they've already completed. I will them to hold steady, following the next target as it flies past. *Zzwing.* The arrow nicks the end of the board and drops like a stick to the Arena floor. The next two completely miss. I'm nocking another, biting back frustration, when Adoni's authoritative bark sends us to another section of the Arena. I'm glad for the excuse to rest my arms, but as I turn from the moving targets, I promise my new nemesis, *I'll be back for you.*

En route to the assembling crew, a slight breeze carries a familiar, earthy smell that heightens every sense. Horse sweat. Stables.

The familiar aroma bolsters the confidence shoved down by the last challenge. I scan the Arena for equines, disappointed to find none. The teasing scent must be traveling from the stables outside the Arena walls.

I shake off my longing for Callisto, giving Adoni my full attention.

"Alexia's greatest weapons are our horses and our bows. They offer speed and accuracy. Next comes the short sword, or dagger, which we will cover in the days ahead." She begins to pace among us. "However, situations may arise when your only weapon will be your own strength. In that situation, you had better know how to use your assets."

You could use Jamara's back as a plumb line, so stiff is her spine. Her bulk isn't honed with muscles like Adoni's or Trinidad's, but her sturdiness makes her formidable nonetheless. When we're told we'll be paired with an Alexia as a sparring partner, I'm relieved I won't have to fight her—not yet, anyway.

As bodies shuffle to form duos for the exercise, I catch Adoni whisper something in Jamara's ear. What could she . . . ? A glint of sun on metal piques my curiosity just as Trinidad steps in front of me.

"You ready to learn, Candidate?"

You've got to be kidding me. With all the ordinary, averagely skilled Alexia in this ring, did I have to get Trinidad?

I nod, adrenaline coursing at the probability of having every weakness exposed by her superior skill. But I am ready to learn.

From a raised platform, Adoni demonstrates strikes, blocks, and counterattacks. I try them out on Trinidad, imitating Adoni's mercifully patient pace as we grow accustomed to the unfamiliar movements. After several dozen practice runs we have the basic blocking down, and Adoni instructs us to increase the force and intensity.

Trinidad raises an eyebrow. "Alright, Candidate. Let's see it."

She waits for me to take the offensive, which I begin with a right jab. She knocks my hand out of the air with her right hand then slaps the side of my head with her left, almost playfully. My ineptitude stings more than the blow. Embarrassment fuels my next swing, which I aim at her ribs. She easily steps aside, rolling around to my flank, and smacks the other side of my head, then grabs my wrist and twists my arm behind my back, just hard enough to make me wince.

"You're not going to make this easy on me, are you?" I wheeze through gritted teeth.

"Would you want me to?"

In answer I swing my leg back and hook hers, trying to knock her off balance. The attempt fails, but she offers, "Good," then releases my arm and resets our positions. We go at it again and again, and time after time she bests me with strength, speed, and stamina. My muscles scream with exhaustion, my tongue swells with thirst, but I repeatedly take my stance and give her my all.

Finally Trinidad says, "Enough for now. Get some water." I'm too weary to thank her; all I can manage is a small nod.

As I drag myself to the awning, I notice the other Candidates have stopped too—all except one. Jamara and her partner wrangle as if in a real fight, nearly matched in ability. This Alexia doesn't possess Trinidad's or Adoni's skill, but the trickle of blood running down her cheek is not from weakness. Veins bulge across Jamara's neck, her body moving surprisingly fast for her size. Her expression placid, the only indication of fatigue is the sheen of sweat on her dark skin.

We're all watching now, absorbed in the matchup. When Jamara pins the Alexia to the ground, fist poised above her face, Adoni calls them off.

"Enough," she says, though as casually as if finishing a meal.

"Alexia train with each other to prepare. We save excessive force for the real enemy."

The Alexia stands and gives a slight nod to her opponent, conceding her skill. Jamara doesn't return the respect. She simply wipes her expressionless face with a palm while walking away.

Yes, if it comes to hand-to-hand combat with Jamara, I'm in serious trouble. And what was that Adoni said? *The real enemy.* I don't know who or what that is, but I get the sense she does.

---

That evening, a cool shower in the bathhouse outside our Arena barracks melts the dust from my skin. Our new accommodations pale in comparison to Finca del Mar luxury, but I don't mind. The familiar collision of my body against uncomfortable elements— heat, dirt, physical exhaustion—soothes me. Familiar creatures strike me as relics from home. While housed in the Senator's Suite at the finca, I didn't encounter a single beetle or gecko in my room. Now a camouflage tree frog keeps my feet company, taking his own shower in the splashes of water ricocheting off the cement floor against his striped legs. His kin join the twilight songs, serenading me through the hollow block walls. Above the spigot, which protrudes from one wall, palm leaves rustle and sway across the deepening indigo sky. I inhale the night song along with balmy-sweet jasmine, breathe out the fatigue of archery and sparring with Trinidad.

What an anomaly she is. Stunning, tough, and sharp-witted. She could have mopped the floor with me but attentively pushed my limits instead. Not that she went easy—the blooming purple bruises on my arms and shins attest to that—but neither did she exhibit Adoni's off-putting arrogance.

I tilt my face toward the spigot, letting the thick, soft stream overrun my forehead, cheeks, lips, and body. Well, I made it through the first day, anyway. Only twenty left: thirteen here at the Arena, then one week on patrol.

Even with a final week at Finca del Mar, that still gives me less than four weeks to prove to Grandmother that I am the one she wants—the Apprentice Nedé needs. To show her I can outshine Nari, overpower Jamara, and outwit Brishalynn. And that I can best Yasmine, too, though at this point, I honestly just hope she survives the next two weeks. And then, if I convince Grandmother, before the year is up I will lead Nedé, and figure out who torched my sister's finca, and find a way to give Treowe an option besides self-inflicted death or long-term misery.

I let myself wonder what he's doing at this moment. Probably playing a game with the other Gentles in their quarters at Bella Terra, or walking along the banks of the Jabiru. No, he wouldn't be wandering the shore at this time of night, but the thought makes me smile anyway. I bet he'll see the big fig tree and think of me. Of course he would. He is a loyal friend.

Am I?

If I fail to become Apprentice to the Matriarch, how true could I remain to Treowe? I would have to choose another destiny. Alexia is plausible as ever, since I didn't fold under the pressure today. But as an Alexia, I'd never see Tre. Oh, there'd be the occasional holiday to return home for, but no other reason for our lives to intersect. No more picnics by the Jabiru. No more quiet conversations in the stable. The only path to remain close to him—the only way for me to repay all the kindness he has shown me—is to possess the power to sidestep our Nedéan conventions. And for that, I must become the ninth Mother of Nedé.

# CHAPTER ELEVEN

W<small>ITHOUT THE</small> S<small>ENATOR</small> S<small>UITE'S THICK SILK CURTAINS</small> to block the morning light, I awake as early as if feathered Diablo were my bunkmate instead of Nari. Dawn still deliberates over what color to wear for the day when I make my way quietly from my bunk to the Arena, being careful not to wake the others.

Outside, seven other large bunkhouses line a gravel path that leads through the residential quarters and toward the largest equine center in Nedé. The sight of dozens of horses grazing in the field next to the stable tempts me to abandon my mission in favor of wrangling one for a ride. I wonder when Callisto will arrive—*if* she'll actually arrive. It takes some effort to tear my eyes from the dark, sleek-coated Lexanders, forcing my feet to follow the path past the paddocks and stable to my predetermined destination.

The slate gray outline of the massive Arena looks cold and

even less inviting in the low light of predawn. But my resolve beats out apprehension. *I have to get better,* I remind myself as I enter through the archway and into the quiet emptiness.

As I pull yesterday's bow from a rack of similar weapons, the thought occurs that perhaps I should have secured permission to be here. I'll take my chances. I'll use whatever excuse, whatever leverage I need to, for Tre's sake.

With no one to man the moving targets, I warm up on the infernal sacks that soundly humiliated me yesterday. After a dozen shots triumphantly meet straw, not dirt, the seclusion of the empty Arena ups my nerve. With the spunk of a younger Reina, I experiment with maneuvers I've observed at Alexia demonstrations. First I run past the target, keeping the center mark in my sights, then turn on my heel and shoot. Sprint, shoot, repeat. Roll, shoot, repeat. My effort quickens with my heartbeat. The arrows, however, laugh at my confidence, every one of them refusing to hit true. I grip the riser more tightly. When yet another arrow narrowly misses the target, I grunt in exasperation.

I hear Trinidad's words echo in my mind: "Quit overthinking it, Candidate."

No, not in my mind. I whip around to find her leaning against the Arena wall, hidden by shadow under the awning. Upon being discovered, she uncrosses her arms and closes the distance between us. As she enters into the soft radiance of early light, her arm bands glow golden.

My cheeks warm. How long has she been watching me? Fantastic. If she wasn't convinced before, now she *knows* I'm incompetent. I consider racking my weapon and pretending I didn't see her, but that's about as stupid as what I'm doing now.

Trinidad grabs a bow and quiver on her way to me. "You have the determination of an Alexia," she says, no flattery in her tone. "But you're getting ahead of yourself. Quit dancing around like you know what you're doing and remember the basics. Until you can hit the target consistently, forget that fancy stuff."

Beside me, she models again the proper posture, the correct drawing motion. She wields the bow as skillfully as a third arm; her movements powerful but laced with the nuance of a master archer. She hits dead center once, twice, thrice. Then she sets her bow aside and instructs me to shoot, occasionally smacking the flat of my stomach or the underside of my arm to remind me to flex, lift, or relax.

My arms ache with fatigue, the tips of my three shooting fingers swell hot and sore by the time voices build in the distance. *Bats.* I lost track of time. I silently question Trinidad. I have no idea if this is okay—me early, her here.

Her eyes flit in the direction of the sound. "Take the north exit. Circle around behind them, quietly. I'll get these put away." I guess that answers my question. She grabs our gear and starts toward the weapons rack.

"Trinidad?" She doesn't look at me, but I know I have her attention. "Will you help me again tomorrow?"

Her eyes brush the now blue patch of sky over the Arena, considering.

"Be here at zero-six-hundred."

---

When I reenter the Arena to join the other Candidates, Bri saunters toward me.

"Where'd you prance off to this morning, Sunshine?"

I don't think I broke any rules, but I don't want her to know about the morning training. I'd rather none of them know.

"I woke up early. I . . . needed some air."

Her eyebrow arches as she scans the dust on my vest. "Of

course you did," she says, with mock understanding. "Just like you were oblivious that you were going to be a Candidate."

That's it. I don't care if she hates me for being here; this is ridiculous. I push into her, tempted to indulge the fist that itches to rearrange her snide face.

I yell, "What's your problem? It's not like I asked to—"

"Looks like some of you are ready for today's training," Adoni interrupts, her strong hand grasping my shoulder, pulling me away from Bri.

I try to compose myself, the flush of anger melting into the heat of embarrassment. Adoni releases me and mounts a meter-high, circular raised platform on the south side of the Arena before continuing.

"Today you will test your hand-to-hand combat skills on each other."

Even though I'm keen on the prospect of having permission to hit Bri, I question the wisdom of giving us Candidates an opportunity to get our hands on one another. I try to discreetly read the others' opinion of this development, but Adoni's already continuing, "In the real world, your opponent won't give you the courtesy of a fair matchup. In fact, a smart adversary will ensure inequality. You must prepare your mind and body to fight anyone—regardless of size or ability."

Am I the only one wondering what kind of opponent the Alexia would face, other than a senile, enraged woman or rogue wild beast?

"Using the combat techniques you've been taught, you will attempt to pin your opponent or render her immobile for ten seconds. You'll be the judge of how much you can take. The match ends when one of you admits defeat, falls off the platform, or goes unconscious."

*Goes unconscious?* Is she serious? I take mental stock of the other

Candidates, calculating how far each would go to win. I don't trust Bri or Jamara to hold back from hurting someone. And Yasmine will be as helpless as a two-legged iguana. Yes, this is definitely a bad idea.

Adoni continues. "Our first matchup is between . . . ," my heart quickens, afraid of what I will hear. "Dom Reina Pierce and Dom Torres."

I close my eyes and sigh in relief. *Thank goodness.* At least Yasmine only has to face me.

I easily spring onto the platform. Yasmine struggles to do likewise, her arms shaking from exertion or fear—likely both. I want to assure her it's okay, to promise I won't hurt her more than what's necessary to win, to remind her she can concede at any time. But I can't let the others think I'm soft. I'm already disadvantaged against two of them in bow, and against Jamara and maybe Nari in combat. I can't let my tenacity slip. It's the best weapon I have.

With the snarl of a feisty barn cat, Yasmine takes a defensive stance, bracing herself for a fight. Fik'iri Province should be proud of their Candidate. I am. And I respect her valor enough not to go *too* easy on her. She might be timid and fragile, but she deserves to lose with dignity. With a slight nod of reassurance, I come at her with a three-quarter-strength punch. She counters with a slap to my right cheek, then tries to claw at me with her other hand. I guess that's the end of form or technique. Yasmine seems eager just to survive, wildly swinging, grasping, grunting.

I skirt around her, slipping behind her squat body. Being considerably taller, my arm slides easily around her neck. I squeeze, being careful not to hurt her, then kick the back of her knees so she buckles. She crumples beneath me, still squirming, trying to find a way to break free. I stare at the gray streak in her hair, aware of every one of my muscles. A little tighter and I could cut off her air supply. How fragile is life? A single strand of spider silk, snapped with the flick of a forearm.

Nedé's motto has never felt more essential: *Protect the weak. Safety for all. Power without virtue is tyranny.*

Within seconds Yasmine's resolve disintegrates, and she rasps, "Enough." I immediately release the pressure, and she collapses on the splintered wood platform.

"You did good," I whisper for her alone. I mean it. She did as well as could be expected of her. How was she—or anyone in Fik'iri—to know Grandmother would introduce such a rigorous Alexia component to the Candidacy?

I jump from the platform, breathing quickly, more from adrenaline than fatigue. Adoni reviews our technique, analyzing Yasmine's lack of control and abandonment of form. I don't really hear much. I'm distracted with trying to pinpoint a slippery emotion. I believe it belongs in the same genus as shame and regret. Should I have refused to fight her? As my adrenaline slows, scratches begin swelling and stinging across my face and down my arm. I did try to protect her, to act with virtue. Still, it didn't feel right to dominate a frantic, helpless Yasmine.

Adoni's voice pulls me back to the moment. "Next up: Dom Makeda and Dom Brishalynn Pierce."

A grin spreads across my face. Maybe I should, but I *don't* feel shame about looking forward to this one.

No doubt Jamara will give Bri a good sobering, and she deserves it. Bri's usual brash facade doesn't crack, but she must be nervous. Adoni whispers something in Jamara's ear as she walks toward the platform. The Kekuatan woman mounts it with ease. I watch Adoni a moment longer. Is it just me, or does she seem angry or frustrated about something?

Jamara's frame dwarfs her opponent's, and she sneers as they take their stances. Bri smiles demurely in turn. Then, in a flash,

Jamara rushes at Bri, unexpectedly taking the offensive. Smart move. She just eliminated the one thing Bri had going for her: speed. They collide with a smack, thud to the wood platform, then roll and maneuver, each Candidate trying to gain the advantage.

A minute into the match, Jamara has Bri pinned like a butterfly. She punches her square in the face once, twice. My stomach turns. Bright red blood streams from Bri's nose, her lip. It's one thing to hear about violence—or even to wish it on another person. It's quite another to witness brutality firsthand.

Jamara lifts Bri by her vest and slams her head onto the wood, splattering blood. When Bri still doesn't concede, I search for Adoni again. She watches with arms crossed, a strange, determined hardness blanketing her face. Another thud of Bri's head against boards, and she all but stops squirming. Could she still concede, even if she wanted to? Consciousness slips from her body like the blood draining from her nose.

The anger I've harbored toward Bri for the past three weeks drains in an instant. No one should be beaten like this, not for a training game. Adoni said so herself.

Trinidad turns toward her leader, speaking quietly but with fierce urgency. Adoni only shakes her head, her concentration never wavering from the platform. But even she doesn't look happy about this. Why doesn't she *do* something?

Jamara slides her hands from Bri's vest to her neck, cutting off her air supply. Bri gives several weak attempts to dislodge Jamara, then goes completely limp.

That's it. At least it's over. *Bats*, I have to admire Bri's courage. There's no way I would have made it that long.

But instead of rising in victory, Jamara reaches for her belt. The metal blade of a dagger glints as she unsheathes it.

*No.* No, something isn't right.

Without a thought, without a plan, I rush toward the platform, feel myself stumble toward Jamara, instinct propelling me to stop her before she does something unthinkable. Just before her raised arm can strike its target, I barrel into her side. My momentum is barely enough to knock her off Bri's body, but the dagger rattles to the deck. For the briefest moment I have the advantage, her mass under me. Then, faster than a coconut falls, I'm forced onto my back. Panic seizes every sense, and I'm overwhelmed by heat and light, the hardness of the boards under me and the stench of sweat above. *Think, Reina. Think.* But no revelations come in the oppression of Jamara's strength. I swing a knee up but don't have enough force to dislodge her. When she shifts slightly, I manage to retrieve my arm and connect my knuckles with the side of her head. The blow proves too little too late. A solid fist is the last thing I see.

---

I welcome the cool stream of water especially this evening. It massages my head and trickles down my face, stinging where it irrigates the cut over my left eyebrow. My muscles scream anarchy after the early morning hours spent training with Trinidad, followed by the combat session gone wrong, and then several hours of blade training following my return to consciousness.

As I left the bunkhouse on my way to the shower this evening, Nari had followed me outside.

"Reina," she said. "What you did for Brishalynn—that took guts." Nari has a steady sincerity I appreciate. I'd say I've even grown to trust the Innovatus from Lapé.

"Thanks," I replied, a little embarrassed. It was the first I'd heard someone speak of the incident since it happened. When I came to under the awning, the others had already started blade training—business as usual, the Alexia way.

"Did you see what happened after I . . . uh, got my face rearranged?"

As luminosity drained from the last clouds overhead, Nari recounted what transpired after Jamara knocked me unconscious. Apparently, as soon as Jamara clocked me, Trinidad sprinted toward the platform and was mid-mount when Adoni called them both off.

"Jamara was going to *kill* Bri," Nari said. "And probably you too. If you didn't go after her, and if Trinidad didn't go after you . . . by Siyah! What was she *thinking*?"

I shook my head, equally puzzled. "Did anything else happen?"

"Any more unsanctioned fights? No. They carried you and Bri to the awning so a medic could examine you. She bandaged up the cuts—Bri's were worse."

The medic—a middle-aged woman with elaborate plaits of silver-black hair framing her lined face—had welcomed me back to consciousness. Her rough hands dabbed at the cut over my eye, patched it up, and then sent me back to training as if I had simply taken a water break. Bri, whose face resembled a slab of raw lamb, was excused for the rest of the afternoon. How kind of Adoni.

"Oh," Nari continued, "and I convinced Adoni to give us separate lodging for the rest of Alexia training. I didn't think Bri should spend the night under Jamara's bunk after what happened. Who knows what she might do next?" She chewed at her lip. "Adoni seemed strangely unconcerned. Do you . . . " She paused, then rushed on. "Do you think Jamara was put up to it?"

"Maybe."

I wasn't trying to keep information from her. She's probably the closest thing to an ally I have in the competition. The truth was, I really didn't know.

But now, as my muscles uncoil in the shower spray, my thoughts become more lucid. I remember Adoni's private aside with Jamara yesterday, the glint of metal just before I was paired with Trinidad. . . . Did Adoni *give* her the dagger? I struggle to picture the knife Jamara held poised above Bri—it all happened so fast. But the small blade wasn't like the short swords we used in training this afternoon. And Adoni had said something to Jamara again, just before she mounted the platform to fight Bri.

But that doesn't make sense. Why would Adoni put her up to it? What would she gain? Nothing. The only plausible answer is that Adoni was under orders.

The connection slams into me like the Candidate from Kekuatan: *Grandmother.* Could she have been testing whether Jamara would do "whatever it takes" for the good of Nedé? My stomach lurches. If I'm right, it would seem Jamara is the only Candidate who has passed her test.

My amphibian shower mate croaks, perhaps to let me know he's finished bathing. I crank the valve closed, listlessly pushing the slimy frog aside with my toe, then dry off enough to dress.

When I step out of the shower house into the darkening twilight, I'm suddenly aware of every stirring in the leaves, every distant monkey call, every individual croak and grate of invisible insects. If I'm right, if killing a Candidate was sanctioned—no matter who gave the directive—none of us is safe, least of all me. I've gone nearly eighteen years without experiencing fear on any substantial scale, but between the encounter at my teak forest arena, the information Ciela gave me, and Jamara's recent ruthlessness, jumpy nerves are becoming familiar companions.

# CHAPTER TWELVE

THE WELCOME, THICK SCENTS of horses and leather assail my senses when I step into the Arena six days later. Unlike the traces of stable smells that have taunted me the past week of training, today I am certain horses wait nearby.

During the dry season of my twelfth year, Old Solomon beckoned me into the round pen at Bella Terra, where he waited with a feisty pinto filly. He always maintained that a horse, being a flight animal, must learn to trust, rather than fear, its handler. Fear may produce results, but trust inspires a horse to want to please, to give her very best effort. Under Solomon's instructions, I learned to speak the young horse's language, using my body positioning, eye contact, and hand signals to assure her she could trust me; I was in charge but wouldn't hurt her. Within thirty minutes she was following me around the pen like a puppy, nuzzling my shoulder and letting me lie across her back.

I spot that little filly now, all grown up, as I pass under the stone archway of the east entrance. She stamps a hoof in the center of the Arena, her white and chestnut coat a blaze of light against the chicory and black of the dozen Lexanders around her, a seagull among frigate birds. Her ear flicks toward me—she senses me, is ready for my instruction. *Good girl.* The fatigue of Candidate training—the conflicts, hours of bow and blade training, my secret early-morning sessions with Trinidad—fade instantly at the sight of her. This is about to get fun.

But I see no mirth on Adoni's face as she eyes the equines. From what I've learned of the Alexia leader, I'd bet my best leather halter she's not so much annoyed that my pinto looks different but that her authority was undermined by executive order. Twice now, I suspect, after Jamara's test. Neechi was right—I had better not cross her in any way other than this.

Except I already did, didn't I, when I plowed into Jamara last week.

Never mind. Callisto's here now. Just seeing her reenergizes my brio. And I'm going to need it, because here comes Brishalynn.

The sinewy master of sarcasm saunters nearer, her face blotchy with still-healing bruises. I try to ignore her, hoping she's en route to anywhere other than here. I don't need any of her barbs ruining my excitement. She stops next to me, though, facing outward so we stand shoulder to shoulder. I brace myself for a typical snide remark. Instead a beat passes in silence.

"Thanks," she finally says. I marvel at her ability to make even gratitude sound insincere. "You know what for."

"Sure." I try to sound nonchalant, like I didn't save her life last week. I don't want to be played for a fool if this is just a charade. And if she is sincere, it won't do any good to mention she should have thanked me sooner.

Adoni raps the flat of a sword against a barrel to get our collective attention, graciously concluding our awkward moment.

"Meet your new best friends," she says, taking a set of reins from a Gentle. She mounts the horse's fifteen-hand height as if it were a pony in a petting pen. Adoni's black leather and tattoos present an even more striking image against the steed's shiny, all-black coat, tail, and mane. As if she weren't intimidating enough before, now I really don't want to make her mad.

"Dom Kwan," she says, looking at Nari. "What are the Alexia's greatest assets?"

"The bow and the horse," she answers, without hesitation.

How does she do that—talk to Adoni with the confidence of an equal? I make a mental note to try to do the same.

"Correct. Most of you have gained some proficiency with your weapons." Is that a nod in my direction? "Now we turn to an equally important asset. You will each be paired with a horse for the remainder of your Alexia training." She motions toward the cluster of muscular, dark Lexanders—plus Callisto—saddled and bridled in the signature Alexia style: clean lines of leather, accented with intricate beadwork in jewel-toned colors. Magnificent.

"You won't form a full union with your horse in the brief time remaining, so your goal is teamwork. Nyx and I have been training together since she was old enough to saddle. I have earned her obedience. You, however, will have to assert your dominance." Nyx shifts under her, and Adoni adds, "Without cruelty. All creatures deserve your respect."

Her final words sound paradoxically soft for one so hard. Then again, the dichotomy of the Alexia is precisely what has drawn me to them since I was a girl. They've mastered the fusion of strength and beauty, fierceness and equity. Most Nedéans possess some form of this, and I am proud of my heritage. Even the less "nurturing" of us, like Adoni and Grandmother—like me, perhaps—display a certain kindness toward fellow creatures. We respect life.

*We respect life* . . . A flash of a crumpled, bloodied Gentle interrupts the thought, and the disconnect—that Nedéans treat our horses with more humanity than our Gentles—instantly heats my blood. Naturally, my mind drifts to a certain unwieldy clump of golden-flax hair, and I have to force myself to focus on Adoni before concern for Tre steals my concentration. But the sour taste of hypocrisy lingers. I can't be like them—like Grandmother, cold and void of care for any but her own; like the thousands of Nedéans who use Gentles for their service without seeing them as people. *I can't.*

I physically shake my head to get it back in the Arena where it belongs.

"Over the next week, you will complete your exercises exclusively on your horses: bow, short sword, maneuvers, and combat," Adoni continues. "When you can shoot with deadly accuracy from horseback, we'll talk." With that, she urges Nyx to a full gallop around the perimeter of the Arena. She slides her bow from her shoulder, draws an arrow from the flat leather quiver against her thigh, and hits the first target dead center. She repeats the feat in rapid succession, riding a wide arc around the Arena. Nyx's muscles pulse under her sleek hide, like ripples on the Jabiru at midnight. Horse and rider work as two halves of a whole, gliding in perfect synchronization, galloping and shooting as one dark, mythic being, piercing target after target.

When she reaches the last, marking its center with the tip of a lightning-fast arrow, Adoni turns in her saddle and hits it a second time, just to make sure we know who's in charge. As if there were any doubt. She brings Nyx to a sliding stop in front of us, dislodging a cloud of dust.

"Any questions?" she asks, motioning to another Alexia to retrieve her arrows.

I have about a dozen—starting with, *how do you* do *that?*—but I'm too awed to speak. No one so much as twitches.

"Very well. Have at it, then."

Trinidad summons us one by one, pairing each Candidate with a horse the way she matched us with weapons the first day of training. I notice she places Yasmine on the quietest of the mares, hinting at compassion to match her remarkable intuition. I wonder if all Nedé's defenders have benevolence buried under their brazen exteriors.

When Adoni barks orders at another Alexia, I'm cured of the theory.

As Trinidad pairs Bri with a smoky-brown stallion, Bri mock complains, "But I wanted that pretty brown and white horse over there." She sticks out her still-swollen bottom lip at me. "I wonder who will get *that* one?"

I guess gratitude hasn't changed her disdain for me after all. I wonder why she even apologized. Trinidad slaps the stallion's flank, obviously as irritated with Bri's never-ending snark as I am, sending her horse galloping. I stuff down a laugh as she bounces and flails, trying to regain control.

With the others on horseback, I'm left with Trinidad and our two animals. She motions toward Callisto with a sweeping pass of her hand, and I resist the urge to bury my face in my horse's mane. Instead I pat her neck and whisper, "I've missed you, my love."

Mounting her feels like home, familiar in every way except the leather saddle between us. Trinidad adjusts my stirrups.

"She's beautiful," I say, tipping my head toward her dark-chestnut horse with a peculiar golden ombré mane and tail.

"That's Midas. And yes, she is." She finishes notching the other stirrup and takes a step back to evaluate my posture.

Our morning sessions have afforded me a bit more familiarity with Trinidad. Today she told me to call her Trin when not with the others. Still, I feel bold when I tease, "You match."

She grins, wrinkles forming at the corners of her golden eyes. "When you spend as much time with your horse as we Alexia do, you start to lose yourself to the bond. Sometimes it's hard to tell who molds to whom."

Whether Trin turned golden for Midas, or they chose the mare for the golden-tinged Alexia, either way, the pair of them create one of the most arresting sights in Nedé: dark skin, deep coat, both gilded and gleaming in the morning sun. They define *stunning*.

Trin adds, "I can't say the same for you. She must be some horse for you to insist on bringing her into the Arena. She sticks out like two bare cheeks in the moonlight."

"I didn't . . . "

But there's no point arguing the details, no explaining the brashness of two Gentles who convinced the Matriarch to give Callisto access.

"Do you have any advice for me?" I ask instead, taking advantage of the brief moment of privacy with the Alexia's second-in-command, my unlikely mentor. Her answer comes quickly, as if she was waiting for me to ask.

"A horse tops your best weapon. They're intelligent. They know their limitations and sense opportunities, sometimes better than we can. No bow or blade can do that. If she's a bold horse, not full of fear, then trust her instincts." Satisfied with my seat, she mounts Midas and directs me toward the obstacle course filling the inner two-thirds of the Arena.

The apparatuses are simplified versions of the obstacles used to show off the Alexia's skills at the demonstrations. Callisto will recognize most of the hurdles from my practice course at Bella Terra: the barrels, logs, hoops, and jumps. Except these are bigger. Higher.

Wider. More intricate. Better built. So, basically nothing like my course. Especially that ten-meter-long suspension bridge, and the half-moon raised platform with a three-meter gap in its middle. It makes *my* gap look like jumping a puddle.

The other Candidates dot the length of the course. Bri regained control of her horse and isn't far ahead, walking a zigzag pattern through a dozen barrels. Yasmine and her horse are further along, just finishing a series of low hoops, and Nari is midway across the suspension bridge on the north end of the course, having completely stopped to attempt the corresponding target.

Jamara leads the pack, bouncing around on the back of her dark chocolate stallion between four increasingly high jumps. She's nearly thrown on the last one and is so rattled she forgets the target altogether. She's just trying to keep her seat as she reaches the final obstacle: the gap. The horse knows what to do, increasing his speed along the inclined ramp. As the horse takes the enormous leap, Jamara's body whips back, wrenching free from the saddle and landing with a thud on grass-stuffed safety sacks. She hustles to her feet in a rage. As she exits the course that just served her lunch, Adoni yells from the shaded awning.

"Where's your target? It just killed you, Dom Makeda."

Jamara's expression remains blank as she draws an arrow, but her fingers shake so violently she can barely hold it against the bow string. She misses by at least three meters.

I don't feel a shred of sympathy for her. There's something satisfying in watching a cruel person fail, and I don't doubt her ruthlessness anymore. After what she tried to do to Bri, I can no longer attribute her quietness to anything but arrogance and malice.

I talk to Callisto and run my fingers through her mane while I watch the others fumble through the remaining obstacles. I wasn't holding out for a clear course, but when Bri clumsily clears the gap and I'm still watching, I realize I have one.

"Is your mutt taking a leak? What are you waiting for, Dom Pierce?" Adoni mocks from across the Arena.

I grimace at the insult, but I'll let it fuel, rather than intimidate, me. I push down the trapped sensation of stirrups hugging my feet and assure myself Callisto will still be able to feel the nuances of my requests through the saddle.

"You can trust me," I soothe us both. "Show them why they should be jealous of you."

Callisto doesn't need any more than a squeeze from my calves and a shift in body weight to know what to do. Within three steps she's up to a lope, gliding from barrel to barrel with the agility of a monkey in a rain tree. Her cadence, our collective focus, transport me to the teak forest clearing: wind sucking heat from my body, running over the shadows of big green leaves, senses acute in the abandon of the moment. As Callisto skirts the tenth barrel, I slide an arrow from my thigh quiver and position my body toward the left-hand target. Trinidad's voice echoes in my mind, *Don't overthink it, Candidate*. And for once, I don't. I simply nock the arrow, trust my senses, and let it fly. I don't have time to see if it hit; Callisto is already halfway to the next obstacle, slowing only when forced to pick through the logs spilled at all angles. With high steps here and a hop there, we maneuver through them quickly. At this slower speed, I easily pierce the moving target with another arrow. My valiant pinto charges through the four wooden hoops at a slow gallop, then mounts the incline to the suspension bridge.

"You've got this, Callisto," I urge.

She hesitates a moment before placing her forefoot on the first unstable board. I lean back and nudge her again with my calves and a click. *Please don't embarrass me now*. She seems to know what's at stake, walking timidly but without a stumble across the length of the jittery bridge. Her trust is a gift I hope to repay someday.

After shooting a vertically moving target, we move into the jumps, each wooden bar higher than the last, culminating in a fence well over a meter high. Callisto is not a natural jumper, but she can do this. I know she can.

She sees the coming jumps and tosses her head just enough to let me know she doesn't like it, but she'll do it. She lopes to the first, and I feel her body lift off the ground, rounding in bascule. She clears that one easily, then the second. As she nears the third jump, I note this obstacle's target placed about ten meters left of the fourth. I draw an arrow and quickly get back in position to make it easier for Callisto to clear the highest fence. She flies over it brilliantly, but as I swing my bow toward the target, I fumble with the arrow and drop it. A curse explodes from my lips as I frantically draw another, but I'm forced to slow Callisto to get a shot in before we move out of range. The arrow hits the bottom left of the target. I grit my teeth in frustration.

The final and most difficult obstacle comes next. The one I could never quite best at my own arena, though it was a fraction of this gap. I push Callisto to increase her speed as we race up the long, semi-circular wood ramp. I sway in time with her rhythm, heart beating wildly. My fingers tighten around the bow grip when I spot the last target dangling above the fourth row of empty seats. My frustration hardens into determination. I draw an arrow and nock it seconds before Callisto's forelegs leave the ground, her body stretching beyond what I thought possible. *Don't think about it, Rei.* I trust my body to secure me to my horse; I trust my arm to steady my bow. For a moment in time we fly—rider and horse suspended above the Arena—and I release my arrow.

As we land, I quickly swing around to look over the course. An arrow protrudes from every target, a feat no other Candidate accomplished.

Adrenaline and muggy heat draw sweat from every pore of

my body. Callisto's breathing hard too, but I can tell she's as proud of herself as I am. I collapse into her neck, grinning and praising her efforts.

As my heart slows, a sound gradually comes into focus: Bri, clapping slowly in mock praise. Only she taunts, but everyone else is watching. Every Candidate, every Alexia. They've seen what Callisto can do. What I can do.

———

Prior to leaving the Arena, I steal a few extra moments with Callisto before the Gentles can claim her. My shoulders ache so intensely from the final lesson of today's training—an hour spent throwing daggers from horseback—that when I slide off her back, I collapse into her neck instead of stroking it.

"Where'd you learn to ride?" I recognize Adoni's rough voice before her shadow darkens Callisto's hide. If my heart weren't so sick of racing today, it might have the energy to quicken now. Instead, it's surprisingly steady as I consider her question.

"From you," I finally answer.

I don't offer more, to protect the innocent. I doubt she'd favor Old Solomon—a Gentle, her former head stablehand at that— giving me formal instruction. It's mostly true, besides. Watching Adoni and the other Alexia birthed my hunger for riding, even if Solomon gave me tips. Their demonstrations spawned my obsession. I watched them intently—memorizing each gait, every combination—then mimicked what I saw when I returned home to Amal. My subpar weapons prevented me from much success there, but with Callisto as a partner, who couldn't learn to ride?

"You're good," she says. "If things don't work out with the Succession, you have a place with me." Adoni's scrutiny shifts to Callisto. "I don't extend the offer to *her*," she adds with a smirk, "though I admit, she's not as pathetic as she looks." She doesn't wait for a response—just walks away.

Seconds later, Trinidad appears next to me with Midas. After standing in front of—rather, beneath—the Alexia leader, Trin feels as comforting as a fire in the kitchen oven. Which is saying something.

"Am I dreaming, or did Adoni just give me a compliment?"

"If she didn't, she should have. You did well out there today, Candidate."

"Thanks to you."

"Thanks to yourself. Your determination served you well." She holds my gaze for a moment, and I'm struck again by the arresting color of her eyes. Her irises are like pools of gold, speckled with light. She nods toward Callisto. "And that horse might be ugly, but she's smart."

I suck in a breath. "Cover your ears, Callisto! The rude Alexia doesn't mean it."

Trinidad smiles and shakes her head. "You're a piece of work," she says, walking away.

"Trin?" I call after her. When she turns, I mouth a silent plea, "Tomorrow?"

A slight nod is all the yes I need.

I press my hands together and touch them to my lips in thanks. With only five days left of training, I need every minute of guidance she'll give me.

---

The air is thick with dawn's yawning balminess as I make my way to the Arena five days later, but a hot vein in the breeze hints at the changing seasons—the drier months to come. As I follow the now-familiar gravel path through the residential quarters and past the stable and field of horses, I pass a row of hibiscus bushes, dotted with bright red blooms. A half-smile tugs at my lips as I remember the flower Tre tucked under Callisto's browband the morning I left home. Bella Terra is ages away now, the quiet life I lived there replaced by the unknown future I'm chasing.

I pluck one of the delicate, ridged flowers and twirl it in my fingers, spinning the broad petals left, then right, and back again. As I walk, I chide myself for taking all I had for granted. Maybe I can have it again, though, if I—*when* I am chosen as Apprentice.

*Matriarch Reina.* The pairing of words sounds so ridiculous, even in the privacy of my own thoughts, that I snicker out loud. The title fits my name no better than my dusty possessions belonged in the lemon-scented wood dresser of the Senator's Suite. But whether I deserve the opportunity or not, I'll do everything in my power to succeed my grandmother—to become the ninth Matriarch of Nedé—for the Gentle who knows my favorite flower, and all the sons of Nedé like him.

My success or failure will be revealed soon enough. This is my last secret session with Trinidad. Tomorrow we ride out for a week of patrolling Nedé with the Alexia, and then . . . and then all this will be over, and Grandmother will make her choice, and I will know if I'm it.

I flex muscle groups as I walk, surprised by their strength after only two weeks under Adoni's training. I suppose between early mornings with Trin and long days with the others, I've earned these muscles. Still, I can't help but wonder how strong I could become if I were a true Alexia, spending my life as a defender of Nedé.

I enter through the east gate to find Trinidad, already laden with training weapons, adjusting Callisto's stirrup.

"What are you doing? We'll get caught for sure," I stammer. As much as I love my horse, I'm not stupid enough to think we can keep this quiet.

She raises an eyebrow, smirking at me. "You think I'd risk training you without Adoni's permission? I don't like you *that* much, Candidate. I asked her after the first morning I found you here."

"She knows?" I ask, mouth agape. "And she agreed?"

"She's not stupid, Reina." My name sounds foreign on her tongue. "Matriarch Teera wouldn't have chosen you to Candidate if she wasn't hoping you'd succeed. With recent developments, Adoni understands the advantage of having a skilled, savvy, Alexia-friendly Matriarch follow Teera." She shrugs, grinning wide. "At least, that's what I told her."

I run my hand down Callisto's neck, letting Trin's words sink in, sorting through their implications. Adoni let Trinidad train me, so that I'd get better, so that I can win. So that she'll have an ally and can keep her position. The thought of working closely with the woman who can shoot an arrow through a coconut while galloping shadowy Nyx full speed—shouting orders besides—is more than I'm ready to deal with at the moment. Instead, I focus on the golden-tinged Alexia in front of me, who is *slightly* less frightening.

"Thanks, Trin. I owe you."

"Yes, you do. But maybe I'll go easy on you when it's time to cash your debt."

"And maybe *I'll* save your reputation by not leaking that you're actually nice."

Her smile catches me off guard. Perhaps she enjoys talking with someone normal, someone devoid of the stern steel that marks most Alexia.

Trin's use of the phrase "recent developments" echo Grandmother's words the first day of the Candidacy, when she revealed she wouldn't conduct our tutelage. It also calls to mind Adoni's heavy boots against the tile floor of Finca del Mar's great room, when I arrived with Mother, and again at the Exhibition. And then there were the Alexia stationed at the top floor of the Center.

Curiosity compels me, though I'm smart enough, at least, to phrase the question carefully, attempting casual indifference.

"I heard there were some sort of raids. Is it safe for us to go on patrol?"

She doesn't seem shaken by my question but still takes a moment before answering. "I'm surprised Adoni decided to continue with the plan for border patrol, but I don't think you have anything to worry about." She motions for me to mount Callisto, signaling our conversation is over. I don't press further. I'm anxious to get my fingers on some arrows anyway.

She puts me to a half-dozen drills, purposefully chosen, it seems, to test the sum of two weeks of training: mounted sprints, jumps, and the obstacle course, replete with moving targets for both arrows and short swords. When I complete them without missing more than a few targets, I surprise even myself. Trin simply nods her approval, adding a matter-of-fact "Good," every so often.

We walk Callisto to the hitching post just as the stablehands deliver the rest of the horses. I pat her forehead while Trin wraps the reins around the pole. Callisto and I are both going to have our work cut out for us today. I'm already exhausted.

Before I duck out the south gate, Trin says, "I've requested you for my patrol group. I don't want you and that mutt of yours getting into any trouble."

"Right." I grin at her. "I bet you just want to steal her when I'm not looking."

She shakes her head, and I duck into a hall to brush the dirt from my clothes and smooth my hair into a fresh braid before circling around to reenter the Arena with the others. She's surprising, that Trinidad. But bats, I'm glad to have her on my side.

Part Three

# CHAPTER THIRTEEN

I AM RELUCTANT TO LEAVE THE BUNKHOUSE the following morning, despite the promise of Callisto's constant company for the next week of patrol. The truth is, I've taken to the long days in the Arena even more than I suspected I would. Before training under Adoni's watchful eye and sharp tongue, I knew the Alexia honed their skills with sweat and tenacity, but I didn't understand the half of it. They do more than ride horses and shoot arrows—these women embody the Virtues in a way I didn't realize I craved. The barracks are full of diversity, uniting women from all over Nedé in a common cause. Simplicity undergirds their schedule. Ingenuity improves weapons and horsemanship. And self-restraint—for Siyah's sake—the discipline they possess in training their bodies and minds puts most of us to shame. If it weren't for the prospect of becoming Nedé's ninth Matriarch, I'd beg to stay—to submerge myself in the challenge of mastering my mind and body, of living in community, and keeping peace in Nedé. To become fully Alexia.

But, ready or not, our group hits the road by dawn, leaving the stone Arena to resume testing its usual students without us. We head west from Phoenix City on Highway Volcán, the same road that brought Mother and me to Finca del Mar so many weeks ago. As often as I have eagerly anticipated arriving in Phoenix City, today I am equally pleased to leave behind the shops and houses, the ever-present bustle of Nedéans, and especially the Finca and its residents.

Our patrol comprises Trinidad, me, Brishalynn—*fantastic*—and four other Alexia whom Trin introduces as Fallon, Merced, Angelica, and Valya. I recognize Fallon and Valya from our training sessions. They worked as combat partners and operated the moving targets. The other two I don't recognize, but they are Alexia through and through, the usual hard exterior contrasted with the beauty of the female form, accented by close-cut uniforms. Valya's long braid falls from the back of her head like an intricate rope. Fallon's is cropped short as grass the goats have sheared. I've always been fascinated by Alexia hairstyles. They prove that whether a woman enjoys fussing with style or not, she can be equally fierce and beautiful.

The six Alexia horses, sleek and dark—except for Midas's ombré mane and tail—keep a quick pace, much faster than I'm used to on lengthy rides. Lexanders are bred for strength and stamina, meaning today's seventy kilometers to the outpost? They'll ride it and ask for seconds. Callisto has no breeding advantage, but I'm confident her brio—or plain old pride—will motivate her to keep up.

I settle into the sway of my mare's back, my lower body mirroring her movements. I still dislike the saddle, but I can't complain about the extra padding today. Though, even with that luxury, I suspect Bri's bony rear end will be feeling the kilos tonight. She already shifts uncomfortably. Is it wrong to enjoy her flustered discomfort? Surprisingly, she doesn't carp, though. In fact, she seems to have abandoned her obnoxious alter ego this morning. I'd even say she seems *thoughtful*, if I thought her capable of introspection. Maybe she suspects Trinidad will mysteriously "lose" her between Phoenix City and the outpost if she gets out of line. Trin just might. She has often rewarded Bri's disrespect with double conditioning or a superior combat partner.

The wide, dirt Highway Volcán more or less parallels the Jabiru. It keeps at least four hundred meters south of it, but never more than two kilometers, allowing the road to run a straight course, unlike the coiled river that, I've heard, would be twice as long if pulled taut. We'll follow the highway all the way to our patrol assignment which, in a stroke of good luck, happens to be the western edge of my home Province. When Trinidad conveyed our assignment in the predawn light this morning, I didn't even try to hide a smile. I've always been curious about that area of Nedé. Today I'll finally get to see it.

According to Trin, we'll spend the next seven days patrolling the western swath of Amal, along Camino del Oeste, checking in on the sparse little towns and fincas brazenly occupying the outer edges of the Province. Jamara, Nari, and Yasmine were assigned with another handful of Alexia to patrol the northern border of Fik'iri Province.

The day stretches on, heat and pungent horse sweat our constant companions. By noon we near the center of Nedé, where the four Provinces touch. This is familiar country. Bella Terra lies scarcely a kilometer north, tucked between us and the Jabiru. When we pass the twin rain trees that mark either side of the road home, I strain for a glimpse of Mother's finca, though I know it will remain obscured by the gentle rise of a hill.

Strangely, the place I was so anxious to leave now beckons me.

I long to stroll through the neatly cropped rows of cacao plants, breathe in the tall canopies of orange tree blossoms, run recklessly down the hill to the stark-white villa, nestled in the center like a milky quartz stone on a bed of moss.

Bella may not be "home" anymore, but it must be part of who I am, because being near it soothes me, like one of Mother's songs. I can almost hear the little Gentles' happy mealtime chatter, see Mother's soft face smiling at their antics. And Tre. Something deep in my heart aches when I imagine his one-dimpled smile, laughing at something I've said, under our fig tree on the riverbank. I miss him. I miss them all. Having tasted the coldness of Finca del Mar, having witnessed the twisted agenda of an aging Matriarch, the warmth of Bella—the light and the love I once experienced there, *once despised there*—feels as much a part of me as the horse that carries me past it.

*Stupid Rei.* I had a place I belonged but didn't see it. Certainly never appreciated it. Now I'm on my own, and I must shoulder whatever comes next with the independence I fought so hard for.

By midafternoon we pass the last recognizable landmark: a Materno finca I visited once with Mother. With each step, I venture farther west than I've gone before.

Highway Volcán is maintained by Gentles, but ripples and crevices from recent rains force us to slow our pace. The area's hardwood trees were cleared long ago—during the foremothers' time—and the fallow interim has allowed bushes, grasses, and vines to overtake the remaining clusters of palms, abandoned structures, and younger hardwoods. In every direction, nature devours nature. Only the occasional village, or a finca's tidy fields, hold back the overeager foliage.

The monotony of tangled green and oppressive heat dull the novelty of our adventure. I sing quietly to myself to keep from nodding off.

*You take one, and I'll take three,*
*And I'll meet you there, at the mahogany tree,*
*Where the fire don't burn, and the dark water's deep,*
*We'll save them there, at the mahogany tree.*
*You follow the mare, and I'll follow a stream,*
*And we'll leave them there, at the mahogany tree . . .*

"What's that song?"

Trinidad's voice snaps me back to attention. She brings Midas alongside, her gold-tipped curls bouncing in time to the horse's steps.

"I don't know the name. Mother used to sing it to me."

"I like it. One of the old songs?" she asks, seeming genuine. Everything about Trinidad is genuine, though. She can come across hard as teak, but never false. She says what she means, does what she says. I like that about her. I *trust* that about her.

"It must be. You haven't heard it?"

She shakes her head.

Strange. It's a tune I've heard since infancy; the words as familiar as Mother's dark hair and hazel eyes. If it's not one of the old songs, where did she learn it?

I ponder the words as I hum it again, but their meaning remains ambiguous. I'm not surprised. Most of Nedé's songs border on cryptic, like so many poems written for beauty before sense; otherwise, I'm told, the Brutes would have punished the women for the songs' bold indictments against their cruelty.

Trin keeps riding, silently, beside me. The others are far enough before and behind that I chance a more personal question. "Did you always want to be Alexia?"

After a moment, she stretches a hand to her boot, retrieving a short dagger. Its metal handle sparkles with inlaid turquoise and bone-white quartz.

"This was my Nana's," she says, rubbing her thumb over the stones. "She was Alexia, many years ago. It was her only weapon . . . and she never had to use it." She slides the dagger back into her boot as she continues, "When I was small, she told me stories of her travels, how being Alexia gave her the opportunity to explore Nedé, helping women settle disputes—she was good at that, the old softie—bringing news to the outlying towns and such. When it was time for me to choose a destiny, I knew I wanted to serve Nedé like Nana did, help others and see everything it has to offer."

I smile at the thought of Trin knee-high to her Nana, dreaming of one day becoming who she is now. And I smile because I can relate.

Trin shifts her weight and tips her head toward the bow slung over one shoulder. When she speaks again, her voice is quieter, for privacy or out of sadness, I'm not sure. "But the Alexia are no longer what they once were."

She seems lost in memory, or caught up in the realization. I wonder if she's ever shared that with anyone. Whom else could she talk with so candidly? I doubt Adoni. Not her Alexia recruits either. That leaves me—a headstrong Candidate who has somehow come to consider her a mentor . . . maybe even a friend.

"What are they now?" I ask, not sure I want to hear the answer.

"We are both more and less."

I recognize the clipped tone as her way of finishing the conversation. Though I'm dying to press further, I restrain my curiosity. Instead, I attempt to decipher her meaning.

*More.* Because of my own Grandmother's patronage, the Alexia are stronger, better trained and armed, than at any other time in Nedé's history. That part of Trin's answer is easy to guess. But *less*? How are the Alexia inferior to what they once were?

I mull on the question for the better part of an hour before a tentative answer surfaces in the form of a memory. The day Jamara almost killed Bri, Trinidad had approached Adoni. I remember her concern, the frustration twisting her face. She wanted Adoni to call it off, but the leader wouldn't budge. She would have let Jamara murder a Candidate in the Succession, on what I assume were the Matriarch's orders.

Trinidad joined the Alexia for adventure and peacekeeping, like her Nana, but it seems their role has morphed into Matriarch Teera's personal militia. Grandmother has turned them into a weapon. And that brings another puzzle, one I may be unable to solve no matter how many kilometers we ride: *Why?*

———————

By evening we near the junction where Highway Volcán tees into Camino del Oeste: a north-south road that parallels the Jungle. Though I've never seen it personally, Dom Bakshi insisted we study the maps in the schoolroom until we knew Nedé's geography as well as our own home's. Unlike the two-dimensional maps, this vantage point vividly illustrates how Highway Volcán got its name: the enormous cone-shaped remnant of an ancient mountain rises menacingly out of the Jungle Wilds straight ahead of us. It's known as El Fuego, and I've heard it occasionally smokes, though it hasn't erupted in the history of Nedé.

The Divisadero Mountains—this morning just small lumps on the horizon—rise east of the border like green giants, rock faces peering out from tangles of hair, guardians of the Jungle. Thick clouds pass over their heads like swirling crowns, backlit with golden light. A waterfall pours uninhibited from a lush, rocky outcropping halfway up El Fuego to the Jungle below, rebounding in a swirl of white mist. Birds soar and swoop, searching for their next meal. The mountains roll into the distance, and I've never seen such gradients of green: fresh as new grass here, almost black in the unknown beyond.

I never expected the Jungle to look so . . . *beautiful.*

The sheer wildness of it produces a strange, hollow feeling inside. *Beautiful,* yes, but disquieting and fearsome too. I'm in unknown country now, having to trust the Alexia around me to know what they're doing and where they're going. I trust Trin, at least.

As heaven's lights fade, the glass windows of a small finca about half a kilometer ahead burn with warm lamplight.

"We're almost 'home,'" Trinidad assures us.

"Are we staying *there*?" Bri asks, motioning toward the villa. They are the first words we've heard from her in hours.

Trin smirks. "If by 'there' you mean the camp along the river, yes we are."

I strain to distinguish shapes in the dying light, and can just make out a clearing between the road and a closer section of the Jabiru. The camp, as Trin called it, comprises a twenty-by-thirty patch of ground, cleared of brush and mostly hidden by the surrounding foliage.

We set up for the night just as the last graying light gives way to blackness. Fallon retrieves a bundle of dry kindling from her pack, then works with a few logs to grow a flame, though it's still so hot I want to jump in the river.

"What's that for?" Bri grumbles. "You trying to roast us?"

Fallon is roughly Trinidad's size, though at least ten years older. She points to three fat scars that nearly encircle her otherwise impeccable bicep.

"So this doesn't happen to you."

A shudder runs through me, and Bri's eyes widen, but neither of us respond. They must be claw marks—puma, jaguar, who knows. The Jungle mountains loom above us, dark and mysterious now, keepers of unseen predators likely just waking up, hungry after a long day's nap. I unroll my blanket as close to the flickering flames as I can get. I'll sleep by the fire, even if it roasts me like a plucked curassow.

As the world goes dark, the steady buzz of insects comes to life, louder and more layered than I've ever heard before. I try not to think about the Wilds or what might prowl there, focusing instead on the red-orange flames curling over the wood. Other than the outdoor kitchen, we rarely had reason for fires at Bella Terra; I can't remember ever sitting and simply staring at one. Now I'm mesmerized by the collision of flame, fuel, and oxygen, entranced by the tongues of orange licking the sticks clean, burping up clouds of smoke in satisfied billows, leaving behind bony embers pulsating red and white as they cool.

When my face burns too hot and my eyes sting from dryness, I roll onto my back and watch the spirals of smoke and sparks float up to the stars. Ten thousand shining pinpricks dust the black canvas, but I find familiar friends in the heavens.

When we were children, Dom Bakshi would make up stories to help us remember our lessons. They illustrated history, language, geography, and the like. I've long forgotten most of them, but one story refused to be lost to childhood. I can still picture Dom Bakshi's shiny bouffant of hair, the slight bob of her head as she recounted the tale, eyes full of wonder and intrigue:

"Long ago, the gods issued Nedé a challenge," my tutor began, with her usual flair for frequent dramatic pauses. "If an Alexia ever successfully shot the sun, they would grant her to become an immortal goddess. However, were she to miss, she would be swept up instead to the heavens and transformed into a starry warning to others. The gods were very arrogant, you see. Siyah, the first Alexia defender, was said to have been so strong and so accurate that she determined to do it. So she pulled that string back with all her might and shot her arrow high with a prayer. It flew fast, straight, and true. But when the gods realized that a human was about to claim immortality, they changed their minds and sealed up the heavens. Her arrow struck the layer of atmosphere between the sky and the expanse beyond and stuck fast between the worlds, like a needle in a pincushion. The Nedéans were outraged, naturally, but the gods ignored their accusations of injustice and set Siyah in the sky regardless, where she blinks overhead tonight, bow at the ready, blade at her hip."

It's a silly story, I know, but the true bits—Siyah being our first Alexia, the starry dot-to-dot that resembles her—served their purpose: I've always been able to find the Siyah constellation in the night sky.

I find other star patterns, and each one makes me feel small, even the comparatively tiny cluster of stars at Siyah's heels called the Rooster. I hate roosters. But from his tail . . . My eyes trace the glowing pinpoints of light to find the pronounced hind-quarters and outstretched tail of The Great Mare as she gallops across the sky. I've always loved the Mare best, for obvious reasons. I begged Dom Bakshi to tell me a story about that one too, featuring my Callisto, made immortal in the skies by a God who knew she'd be mine before time began. Mother always said he made Callisto and me for each other. I didn't wonder then whether she was right about his existence, or if the Virtues were our highest calling, as I later learned most Nedéans believe. No, back then I was content to pretend I was Siyah, riding my divinely appointed, shimmering mare through the heavens, galloping trails of stardust till dawn.

But now—sleeping on the ground far from my childhood home, training in a Succession I'm desperate to win—*now* I wonder. The answer feels important somehow, and not just because I could really use some help. As I'm drawn down the hazy tunnel ushering my mind into sleep, I find myself hoping she's right.

———————

A violent slicing sound startles me awake. It's almost as dark with my eyes open as closed, but I just make out Bri's snarling face over me, her eyes glistening in the dying firelight, before she hurries away. A silver short sword pierces the dirt next to me, glinting centimeters from my chest. I scramble to my feet in shock, staring at the sword, trying to orient myself: it's night; everyone else is asleep; I think Bri just tried to kill me.

No, she would have sliced through my skin if she wanted to kill me. Her aim's not *that* poor. I squint in the darkness, expecting to see her gangly limbs sprinting away in the distance, but instead she's leaning against a tree overlooking the river.

I yank the sword from the ground and sneak, trembling and breathing hard, toward her, with every intention of doing something rash. As I close the distance, raising the blade to shoulder height in anticipation, she lifts her eyes to me. But instead of fighting, running, or even speaking, her mouth turns down, and she stares out at the river again. Moonlight reflects off the water, giving her face an eerie glow. The illuminated tear track down her cheek does nothing to quell my fury. My arm accelerates toward her, and I bury the tip of the blade into the tree trunk just beside her own chest.

"You're welcome," she says, trying to sound snarky, but her voice quivers.

It had to have been her test, and she willingly failed. This girl— I'll never figure her out.

"Why didn't you do it? You *hate* me. You could have gotten rid of me and been rewarded for your obedience."

She draws herself up, forcing a half-hearted smile.

"You don't give my jealousy enough credit, Rei. The Matriarch didn't put me up to it. I wanted to kill you all by myself. . . . At least, I thought I did." She tugs her sword from the tree and sheathes it. "Turns out, I'm not as wicked as I thought I could be. You know, killing the saint who saved you—there's probably a special place in hell for people like that. I couldn't do it. Ironic, right? I was going to take you out so I could have a shot at Apprentice— had the story all figured out too, how you were conspiring with the Amal senators to do Teera in, how she would reward me for my loyalty—but my cowardice only proved I'm not worthy of the position. I don't have it in me to do 'whatever it takes.'"

"That's not weakness, and you know it." I exhale the dying embers of adrenaline and lean against the tree trunk in her place. "Removing your enemies is easy. Learning to live with them takes strength." I'm surprised at my sudden wisdom.

The quiet rushing of the river fills the silence as the minutes pass, until there's little room for more talk.

"Do me a favor," I quip, standing to leave. "Don't wake me up again?"

She rolls her eyes, but relief seeps through the show.

I leave her alone with her regrets, wondering which failure pains her more: that she wanted to kill me, or that she couldn't.

Returning to my place by the fire, a sleepy Trinidad questions me with her eyes.

"Everything's fine," I say. And I think everything is. Somehow I don't believe Bri will plan another attempt on my life.

*At least not tonight.*

Sleep proves too slippery to catch, though, so I watch the pulsing embers for a while. If Grandmother still hasn't given Bri a test, maybe my obnoxious co-Candidate is right. Perhaps Grandmother isn't giving her due consideration. But what of me? Still no challenge. Could I be so favored that Grandmother doesn't see the need to test me? The possibility both relieves and unsettles. I'd rather not be forced to prove my allegiance in some contrived trial. But if she doesn't see the need, what does that say of her assessment of my malleability? Is she so convinced I'd do anything—*anything*—she told me to, for the good of Nedé?

As I wait out the darkness, I go round and round with a slippery quandary: *Will I?* What am I prepared to compromise in order to rule Nedé, to remain friends with Tre, to help other Gentles like Neechi and Little Boo? Do *I* have what it takes to win, if victory forces me to betray the very conscience I'm trying to follow?

# CHAPTER FOURTEEN

BY DAY TWO OF PATROL, the shiny gloss of novelty had dulled to a lackluster matte. Today marks our fifth day monitoring countless hectares on horseback, checking in on the fincas and small villages positioned near the edge of the Wilds. The most remarkable surprise I've encountered in our travels—besides the otherworldly size of the bug bites—is the courage of the women who face isolation and the threat of predators in exchange for lush, fertile farmland in the shadow of the foreboding Divisaderos. The rest has proved painfully anticlimactic.

This evening we travel north, returning to Highway Volcán and the camp we utilized the night we arrived—the spot where Bri almost did me in. How removed that seems now. The endless hills and valleys, barely touched by Nedéans, the days stretching as long as the wild grasses, have all but erased life before this week.

The Arena, Finca del Mar, the Succession itself—they could be a dream, with my real life an eternal Alexia patrol.

As we ride, the light warms and then fades, draining the fields of color and shrouding the Wilds beyond in shadow. We'll be lucky to reach our site by dark, but the prospect doesn't worry me as it would have five days ago. I'm growing accustomed to pitch black nights and uncertain sleeping arrangements. I am also getting used to the mist thickening around the mountaintops each evening, as if the peaks sleep best wrapped in a cool, gauzy blanket. As we ride, I watch the thin clouds encircle the largest mountain, then fill the hollow crater that was once its peak. Mist also rises from a distant point on the horizon. That haze is thicker, grayish, and rises like a plume from the earth.

"Fire!" Trinidad yells. She digs her heels into Midas, galloping away like a shot.

We take off after her. Fallon, Angelica, Valya, and Merced trail fifty meters behind but keep pace. Bri might not be a great rider, but her horse knows how to run, and she barely lags behind. The superior stamina of the Lexanders shines through. For the first—and hopefully last—time, I wish I was riding one. I keep my own Callisto at a full gallop, but within five minutes the others have shrunk to pebbles on the horizon. She's simply not fast enough. I urge her on; I may not be able to keep up, but I can't lose them completely.

The column of smoke grows taller with each passing minute. The others are out of my sight now. When I reach the top of a rise in the road, the small finca next to our camp comes into view, maybe half a kilometer ahead, angry flames engulfing the villa walls.

Adoni's voice echoes in my mind, the information I overheard her give Grandmother: "... *then burned the place down.*" I rein in Callisto as I consider: *Could this be an attack?*

A few dark figures dart across the road thirty meters ahead. One startles at the sight of me and shouts something at the others. The pack picks up speed. They've seen me, and yet they run. That narrows the possibility of their identity. If I waste time getting Trinidad, they'll disappear into the thick Jungle, and we'll never know for sure. If there's even a small chance these raiders are the same savages that attacked and burned Jonalyn's finca, I can't let them get away.

As soon as I lead Callisto off the packed dirt road, thick grass and growing darkness slow her pace. I urge her on, carefully, quietly, and ready my bow. Trinidad told me once that my horse was my greatest weapon—that if she wasn't prone to fear, I should trust her instincts.

"Be brave, Callisto," I whisper. "Take me to them."

I coax her into the unknown, hoping to overtake the figures before they reach the wall of Jungle that marks Nedé's boundary. But when we collide with the seemingly impassible tangle of Wilds, I still haven't spotted them. I scan the area, looking for signs of movement. Instead I discover a barely cleared path heading due west, straight into the belly of the Jungle. Freshly trampled grass at the trail's opening hints that Callisto has proven Trinidad right.

I weigh my options. Abandon this mission—go back to the burning villa and lose the chance to learn their identity—or press on? *Quickly, Reina—think.* If I find out who is doing the raids, we have a chance of stopping them, don't we? And if apprehending a raider wouldn't prove to Grandmother that I have what it takes—that I'm Matriarch material—I don't know what would. She wouldn't need to test me. I could prove my competence *and* avenge my sister.

I press into Callisto, moving us forward into the unknown.

The trail scarcely cuts a path through thick, encroaching brush. We pick our way through the walls of darkening green, ducking under vine-covered branches and skirting around an occasional boulder. Minutes pass, my every sense painfully alert. I can practically taste the hum of life around me—plants, animals, and insects, all aware of my intrusion, but refusing to hint at my targets' whereabouts.

Entering a surprisingly open glade, we move faster. Then I see it: a flash of movement, darting behind one of many trees on the far side of the clearing. I push Callisto into a run, readying my bow. *Faster, faster.*

I am a centaur, my human body running on equine legs. I lift an arrow to my bow, ready to release as soon as I get the shot.

Then, without warning, Callisto buckles under me. I'm thrown from her and hit the ground hard, fire shooting through my left shoulder. Scrambling back to her, pain blurring my vision, I find her front legs tangled in lengths of rope attached on each end to leathery spheres the size of my fists. I have to free her, and fast. I unsheathe my sword, but before I can touch the blade to the rope, a massive force barrels into me, knocking me flat on my back. Before I realize what's happening, my attacker grabs my wrists and pins my legs under him—too easily. I squirm and twist frantically, trying to pull a limb free, but he's stronger than me. *He's stronger than me.* What in Siyah's name? Adrenaline pumps through my shaky limbs as I struggle in vain. If I was helpless against Jamara, now I'm prey. I've never been more scared in my life.

"Well, well . . . what do we . . . have here?" he says, the staccato of his mock-playful words the only sign that keeping me down requires effort. His upper lip curls curiously as he looks me over.

My face blazes with heat; blood pounds through my ears. *Think, Reina! Think like an Alexia.*

I force myself to slow my lungs and suppress the seizing panic so I can assess the situation, like Adoni taught us. *Observe, decide, act,* I hear her say. I register the fiery red of his hair first, illuminated in the moonlight that settles on the open clearing. It curls and twists at odd angles, like the flames engulfing the villa just a few kilometers away. Then the dark freckles mottling his strangely pale skin. But it's the attack itself that points to his identity. Ciela was right. There is no other possibility.

He *must* be a Brute.

He's too strong, too dangerous to be anything else. And that means I need a weapon.

My sword glints atop a clump of stringy grass close enough to reach if I can manage to free an arm. I channel every iota of strength into a quick twist of my right hand. My wrist slips from his grip, and I strain for the hilt, but before I can curl my fingers around it, he wrenches my arm back. Lightning-sharp pain shoots through my injured shoulder, down my arm and across my back. I can't hold back a scream.

"No, no, no," he chides, breathlessly. "You don't want to do that."

Laughter erupts from unseen accomplices, gathering closer. One cackles, "A little sooner with the bolas next time, Dáin? She almost skewered me."

Another voice, "What are you going to do with her?"

The red-haired Brute pushes his tongue into his cheek, pretending to give this question deep consideration. Is this a game to him? While he toys with his catch, a trickle of blood torments me, itching fiercely as it rolls across my forehead and into my hair. My limbs grow tired from straining against him, but I won't give up trying.

Finally, he issues his verdict: "She's seen us. She can't live. Bring me my club."

A scraggly, smaller Brute thrusts a stout club toward my captor. The head of the intricately carved weapon resembles a harpy eagle, its beak tapering steeply into a menacing hook. Sharp, bony teeth protrude down the entire ridge of its back, mimicking neat rows of deadly feathers. The carved wooden chest bears symbols and swirls. I try not to dwell on how the weapon will feel colliding with my head, instead readying myself to surge with one last escape attempt should he release his hold on me for even a second.

But instead of reaching for the club, he tilts his head to one side, seeming to reconsider.

"But she's a pretty one, she is. Maybe I should keep her a little longer."

He bends low, his face so near mine his hair forms a canopy over my head, and I can smell the stench of his breath, can see thin scars beneath peeling scabs.

"Would you like that, girl?" he whispers. "Would you like to stay with me?"

He licks my cheek, as if tasting me. Bile stings my throat, revulsion instantaneously morphing into a fresh wave of panic.

*What . . . what is he going to do?*

My body shakes with wild fear, but I won't die without a fight. I resort to the only act of defiance I can: I spit in his terrifying face.

His dark eyes narrow, and his grip tightens with renewed hatred. He wipes his cheek with his shoulder, then shifts his body so he can choke me with one hand while still immobilizing both my arms and legs. His fingernails dig into my flesh, constricting my windpipe and pressing the breath out of me.

*He's going to kill me. By Siyah, he is going to kill me.* I writhe frantically, to no avail. *I have to get away.*

A sudden rustling at the edge of the clearing, followed by a loud voice—somehow familiar—interrupt my attacker. "Rohan, over here!"

The monster jerks toward the sound, revealing the slightest flicker of worry. His grip slackens—just enough for me to arch my back and slam my head into his with all the force I can muster, transferring the energy of my hysteria to the strength of the blow. Stars explode in a galaxy of pain through my head. My captor yells—a deep guttural sound. In a flash of anger, he releases a hand, raising it in a clenched fist, intending to strike. But before the blow reaches my face, someone knocks the savage off me, colliding with him like an arrow piercing a target. They roll over and over, limbs intertwining and swinging, but the red-haired Brute isn't as big or as strong as his assailant.

I fight against dizziness and pain, fumbling for my sword in the grass with the arm that still functions. I have to free Callisto. We have to get out of here.

"You did it again, didn't you? Stupid peccary!" With Dáin pinned under him, a large, dark-haired Brute shouts into his face. I recognize that thick hair, the angular face, the broad shoulders . . . the teak forest. He was the one who carried me. *He was the one who carried me.* If I wasn't beside myself with fear, frantic to escape, curiosity might get the better of me. But as it is, I have only one aim: *get far away.*

"So what?" Dáin barks back. "It's better than waiting around for Torvus to do something!"

The larger Brute punches him in the face, and I hope he never stops. But to my terror, after the first blow he gets up, releasing his hold on Dáin. I instinctively scramble toward Callisto, away from the Brute that . . . that . . . that was going to kill me or I don't know what if these others didn't show up. I won't let him get me again—I won't.

But he seems to have lost interest in me. Now he focuses his fury on the dark-haired Brute, who stands a full head taller. Dáin wipes his bloodied nose with the back of his hand and grabs his club, but he doesn't take the offensive. In fact, I notice he doesn't even meet the larger Brute's eyes.

"What were you thinking?" the big one shouts. "Torvus warned you what would happen. You don't think he'll find out?" He shoves a hand into Dáin's chest again and again, pushing him toward the clearing's perimeter as he speaks. "Don't come back to Tree Camp. You have no place with us anymore." He scans the darkness for the accomplices I trailed here, who now cower beneath the watchful eye and outstretched spear of his companion. "None of you do."

Dáin spits red into a bush. "You know it's time," he hisses. "You can't wait for Torvus forever." But he gathers the rest of his weapons and hurries into the tangled Wilds with the other attackers.

The biggest Brute yells something else after them, but I'm not listening anymore. Instead, I'm working furiously at the ropes around Callisto's forelegs. When the last strand breaks, I help my frightened horse to her feet.

"Quick, girl. We've got to get out of here."

I want to stroke her neck. I want to bury my face in her mane and disappear from this nightmare. But I grab the saddle instead, getting ready to swing myself onto it—as best I can with one busted shoulder.

"Easy there," the same deep voice reverberates behind me, only a breath away, as strong hands grab my hips, preventing me from mounting the only safety I have. "You're in no shape to ride. You're hurt."

He may have saved me from one terror—maybe even helped me before—but now I know he's a Brute too; I can't trust him. I understand now, firsthand, why they could never be trusted—why the foremothers feared them and the world was better without them. They're all dangerous. Stronger than us, and dangerous.

The other one—whose voice first stopped Dáin—joins us now. "We're not going to hurt you," he says. "I'm Jase. And this is Rohan. We won't let Dáin get to you again."

Something about Jase's face seems familiar, though I'm sure I only got a proper look at his dark-haired partner, Rohan, in the teak forest. The shape of this Brute's eyes—no, the sound of his voice? I can't place it, but it calms me somehow.

No—*I have to get out of here, one way or another.* I reach for my sheathed sword, preparing to fight for my life.

"We're going to help you," Jase continues, hands held up in surrender. "But you have to trust us." His eyes plead with me, and I waste precious time wondering where I've seen them before. I'm so preoccupied with the battle between familiarity and terror that I fail to see the hand come from behind and prick my neck with a needle-like object.

I whirl around to find Rohan—yes, I recognize that striking face—a dart poised between his fingers. I strain to reach for Callisto, but my limbs turn to water, and I melt into his waiting arms.

So much for trust . . .

# CHAPTER FIFTEEN

*CROOOAK. Croooak. Croooak.* The familiar, grating rhythm of a toucan acts as a cord, and I use it to pull myself hand over hand out of unconsciousness.

When my eyelids finally respond, fluttering open, they're met with a network of palm thatching zigzagging down from a steep apex. I find I'm lying on a stiff cot in a small, rustic space. A room, I think, because two more beds line opposing walls, and hanging baskets overflow with bedding, clothing, and weapons. But this is not like any room I am used to.

The top half of the stick walls and door are covered with sheer netting, revealing dense leaves and branches just beyond. Dappled sunlight filters through the foliage and into the tiny dwelling, settling in blotches on cluttered shelves and a form that jerks me wide awake.

*Brute.* The dark-haired one who carried me to shade weeks ago, that knocked the red-haired beast off of me—when? Last night? Last week? Rohan, I think. Grogginess lingers, but the pain across my forehead has dissipated to a dull throb. My shoulder tingles strangely. I probe the area with shaky fingers, startled by a wet, squishy . . . poultice?

If he wanted to hurt me, why bother helping me? Perhaps he's not an immediate threat; maybe I should restrain my urge to run, at least until I figure out what's going on. With the way this Brute beat up Dáin, I wouldn't stand a chance of escaping anyway.

My voice sounds thick, foreign, when I ask, "What did you do to me?"

The hulking form sits in a corner, bent over his hands, not three feet from me. At my question, he simply glances up, as if expecting me to wake at this very moment.

"Sordy root. A tranquilizer. We tip our darts with it for hunting. We couldn't chance it—you knowing where we were taking you."

"And where *have* you taken me?" I ask, dully.

"Tree Camp," he says, as if that's supposed to clear things up.

"Where's the other one—Jase?"

"Trying to convince Torvus not to skin him for bringing you here." He chuckles. It's a deep sound, not like Treowe's light laughter, but carries the same sincerity. His brevity disarms me, *a little*.

I try a different approach. "Why *did* you bring me here?"

Rohan slides a blade around the tip of a stick he's holding. Wood peels away, in a wide curl, like the strand falling from his forehead into his eyes.

"You were hurt. And you would have gotten lost trying to get out of the Jungle in the dark. Besides, it woulda hurt like crazy to get that shoulder into place if you were awake." He puts the stick down and looks at me, a sly smile on his lips. "Though, the way you bashed Dáin, maybe I underestimated your pain tolerance."

Trying to prove him right, I clench my teeth and sit up. The room spins, and my body sways like a wind-blown palm. Rohan reaches a hand to steady me, but I jerk back. Even his hand is larger than it should be, never mind his bulging forearm. I don't think he's more than a few years older than me, yet he makes Adoni look like a filly. But where she is strength and beauty, this Brute is strength and . . . *strength*. His shape intrigues me—so bulky, foreign. It's frightening and . . . appealing, all at once. His body *is* beautiful, I suppose, in its own frightening way.

"Not all of us would hurt you," he says, more quietly. But he doesn't reach toward me again. Instead he takes a mango from the cot next to him, pares it with his knife, and hands me a slice. "Here. Food will help the dizziness."

I take the fruit hesitantly. "You're not going to drug me again, are you?" I ask, only half joking.

He grins wide, rubbing the short, prickly hairs on his cheek. "I guess you'll find out." Under thick eyebrows, his dark eyes dance with mischief. I smile, in spite of myself.

The soft, stringy mango flesh tastes sweet as honey. Juice fills my mouth and runs down my palm. The familiar flavor takes me home—to a hundred family meals at Bella Terra and picnics on the riverbank with Tre. Then home reminds me of Callisto.

"My horse?" I feel guilty for not remembering her before now.

"Fine. It's tied up and eating banana leaves like it's never seen food before."

Thank Siyah. I steady my mind, attempting to formulate a plan. I just have to get to her, and then she can get me back to the others. *The others . . .* Where will they be? Trinidad—she will come looking for me. Yes, she will search, but she has no way to guess where I am. By the time she realized I didn't make it to the burning villa, how would she follow me? *I* don't even know where I am.

My stomach turns sour, and I have to force down the last bit of mango. If I can't find my way back on my own, I'm at the mercy of these Brutes.

Can I trust them? This one, and Jase, they don't seem to want to hurt me. Granted, I know little of Brutes. Perhaps they use kindness as a ruse, earning their victim's trust before striking. Or maybe they turn evil against their will, suddenly snap because of their inferior genetics.

Despite the paralyzing possibilities, he was right about the food. Fresh life rehydrates every fiber of my body.

"Are you going to let me leave?"

"You ask a lot—" Before he can finish, the door swings open and another Brute squeezes in. He's a bit shorter and narrower than Rohan, with curly, medium brown hair and a wide smile: Jase. I'm struck again by some familiar quality. His grin reminds me of . . . Treowe's? Is that it? No, it's something else . . . something about his light eyes.

"You're awake!" he says, with surprising enthusiasm. "Good."

"What did he say?" Rohan asks.

Jase's smile fades a little but he nods. "He wants to see her, later. I told him she was hurt, that she should rest today, and we'll take her back tomorrow."

*Take her back* . . . that's good. They don't plan to keep me here forever. My shoulders relax a little, sending a pain down my left arm.

One of Rohan's eyebrows arches high as the thatched roof. "Tomorrow?" He looks Jase over suspiciously, then pulls him aside. Though he lowers his voice to a raspy whisper, I can hear every word. What—does he think I'm deaf?

"What are we going to do with her until tomorrow? She's not *that* hurt."

"I dunno. Keep her here. Or . . . maybe show her around a little."

Rohan gawks at him like he's lost his mind, and I pretend not to notice, though they're arguing right in front of me.

"*Show her around?* So she can go back and tell the rest of them all about us? It's stupid, Jase, I don't care if she is . . . " He glances at me and trails off.

I'm too baffled by everything going on to do anything but stare back.

Jase winces apologetically. "Sorry about his manners, Reina, it's just that, we're not used to bringing outsiders to camp." He flashes another warm smile, and I can't help but distrust this Brute less than the others I've encountered so far. Which, granted, isn't saying much, since that count has only reached three.

Rohan shoots him another what-are-you-thinking glare. Wait . . .

"How do you know my name?" The words come out slowly, laced with growing suspicion.

"Uh . . . I heard it . . . ah . . . " Jase stammers, clearly caught off guard.

"It doesn't matter," Rohan interjects, ending the matter with one final, pointed look at Jase.

They want to change the subject? Fine.

"I want to see my horse," I say, trying on the Matriarchal tone I've heard often the past few weeks. Only, it comes out more spoiled child than commanding leader.

"No way," the larger Brute retorts. But Jase seems to be considering my request.

"Why not? She's smart—she knows she'd never make it out of here on her own. We'll just show her the horse and then bring her back. Everybody's busy with the new huts anyway. It'll be easy to keep her out of sight." In Rohan's silence he adds, "Torvus doesn't have to know. Besides, she's not our *prisoner*. It's Dáin's fault she's here in the first place."

Rohan shakes his head. "Fine. Just—help me get her down."

Rohan reaches for my arm, but I brush him off. I can walk on my own. How hard can it be to go "down"?

As I stand, I notice my bow, quiver, and short sword leaning in one corner of the room. "I don't suppose I get to have those back?"

Jase shrugs at the same moment Rohan hastily answers, "No," then adds, more patiently, "not yet."

I suppose I can't blame him. I wouldn't give my prisoner her weapons either, even if she was nearly half my size. I guess I could take it as a compliment.

When Jase swings the door inward, I'm instantly aware why the netted walls reveal only exceptionally long leaves and thick branches. If a small platform didn't greet us beyond the threshold, I'd plummet two hundred feet to the ground. Their room is perched at the top of a colossal broad-leaf mahogany tree, laden with similar huts and platforms, all connected by ladders, ropes, and thin bridges. At least twenty dwellings cling to the tree below us, and we are at the very top of them all.

At the edge of the small landing, the Brutes usher me onto an even smaller platform. When Jase tugs a thick rope, it drops two feet. I lose my balance and, although a railing encircles us, I'm forced to grab Rohan's arm to keep steady. Gratefully he doesn't throw an "I told you so" in my face. In fact, he seems to stand a little straighter, his muscle flexing under my touch. I try not to think about the feel of his arm, like a rock wrapped in skin, or what it could do to me. Or how silly I must have looked on the way *up* the tree—presumably thrown over his shoulder—and instead take in the rest of my surroundings.

If I was unsure before, now I am certain: they have absconded me deep into the Jungle Wilds. From our high vista, smaller trees and hills roll like endless waves in every direction, interrupted only by the crests of knobby mountains. A good distance to the east, the waves end abruptly in a flatter expanse of cultivated land, crisscrossed with rivers and roads. That must be Nedé.

When we dip below the other treetops, I hold my breath, as if I'm being submerged in a green sea—a thick, jungle ocean. I want to swim away, to paddle toward that shore—toward the familiar patchwork of farms and villas and people who are safe. If it weren't for Rohan's strong grip, now firmly holding my good arm, I might dive over the side and make a swim for it.

Our platform descends through the massive limbs in halting drops as Jase draws the rope. The other tree huts, some built around the trunk, some seemingly entwined with sturdy branches, appear empty.

"Do other Brutes live in those?"

"Bru—? Oh, right—that's what you call us," Jase says, his brow furrowed. "Yeah, mostly three or four to a hut. Oldest at the top of the tree, youngest near the bottom. Except the cubs. We take turns caring for the little ones when they come. We're building new huts for them now."

Rohan scowls at Jase, trying to shut him up with a glare. Though I see it, Jase apparently does not, because he continues, "I'm the oldest, at twenty-four dry seasons, then Rohan—twenty-two for him—and we share—*shared*—a hut with Dáin before he got his stupid butt in trouble again. Well, I'm the oldest besides Torvus, I mean. He's—I dunno—*old*. You'll meet him later."

Lucky for me, it seems Jase talks when he's excited. Why *is* he excited? His blabbing clearly irritates Rohan—the smarter of the two?—but I'm glad for the information. I want to keep Jase talking, get him to leak more information I might need later, but questions overwhelm my mind, making it hard to narrow them down. I skip over the most obvious question, *How in bats do you exist?*, and settle instead on something more likely to get past Rohan's increasingly wary guard. It's still an answer I want desperately to know anyway.

"Is Dáin behind all the attacks, or are there others of . . . *you* who burn innocent fincas?" I don't do a very good job of keeping anger from my voice, and I wince at my hastiness.

*Probably not a good idea to make your Brute captors mad, Rei.*

The question hangs with us, suspended halfway up this massive tree. Jase silently consults Rohan, seeming unsure whether to continue.

To my surprise, Rohan's the first to offer an answer, his brow furrowed with conviction.

"Dáin never had Torvus's blessing for what he did—what he's done. He thinks with his anger, not sense. Like I said, not everyone would hurt you."

I hold his gaze, unflinching, trying to read him. He scares me because he *could* hurt me. Even now I am keenly aware how close his towering body is to mine—near enough to feel his heat, which means he is close enough to hoist me over the railing like a sack of plantains. Still, there is something compelling in the way he looks at me. I could almost believe him.

He continues, "But he's not the only one who figures we've waited long enough. Others have joined him, and now that he's forbidden from camp, more will probably take his side out of curiosity, or pity."

I have more questions, but before I can choose one, the platform halts, a full three feet above the ground. After scanning the area, Rohan unlatches one corner of the railing so we can exit our floating transportation. He releases his grip on my arm, but offers me his hand for the jump, willing to help, unsure whether I want his assistance. I set my jaw and hop down without it, immediately regretting my stubbornness when a fresh wave of dizziness and pain almost topples me.

Dozens of similar platforms hover above the ground, grouped in clumps, like lily pads floating on a shady pond. From this vantage point, the mahogany tree on which they all hang looms above like a massive being—strong and otherworldly, not unlike the Brutes who hide my body with theirs as we zigzag a route through uncrowded parts of camp.

A type of rustic village spreads outward from the tree. Several thatched buildings dot the clearing, some enclosed, others open-air. Everywhere is green, and wood, and *Brutes*. Dozens of Brutes. They are all smaller than Jase and Rohan, some barely so, others much younger. There are even small children who look identical to Mother's Gentles, except that they wear virtually no clothing. All work busily, some digging in raised garden beds, others building another thatched hut. One pours water into a large watertight basket, and two others play a game with a handful of the tiniest ones. What strange universe have I been dropped into? A world where boys work without Gentles Regimen to drive them.

Though difficult to judge by the sun, shrouded as it is by the leafy canopy overhead, I'd guess it's early afternoon. We skirt a clearing centered around a large stone pit. Wisps of smoke curl upward from gray ashes, enveloping a blackened animal which hangs suspended over the dying fire by poles. The smell of roasting meat mingles with the smoke, counterbalancing the ever-present sweet aroma of wet earth. And then I see her.

"Callisto!" I breathe, running toward her.

Tethered to a tree ten meters from the pit, she has already stripped half the plants within reach of her rope. Her ears twitch wildly, taking in all the new, unnerving sounds. She seems simultaneously foreign and familiar, so small against the largeness of her surroundings. Her brown- and white-patched hair appears out of place in this setting—so different than any backdrop from which I've viewed her.

She nickers as I run one hand down her forehead, then rake my fingers across her neck. The Alexia saddle still cradles her back, and for one brief moment I consider swinging onto her and making a break for it. But Jase is right—I am smart. I know the odds of getting past Rohan and Jase, finding my way out of the Wilds, and avoiding attack from a nocturnal predator along the way are thinner than a whisker. So I unbuckle the black leather cinch strap and slip the saddle from her instead. She seems unharmed, and I am satisfied. For now.

"We'd better go," Rohan says, glancing warily around.

"Let's get her some proper food first."

Rohan sighs, shaking his head, but doesn't protest.

I eye the roasting whatever-that-was over the firepit, not keen to find out what constitutes "proper food" around here. Thankfully we walk past the charred hunk toward an open-front hut resembling a kitchen. Under the thatched canopy, rows of wood slabs rest on rock legs. Those must serve as tables. The rear of the hut is equipped with a large stone oven, a wood rack of mismatched pots and crude utensils, and a deep basin. A young Brute fills the reservoir with a jug of water. Rohan keeps me out of sight while Jase sneaks up from behind, distracting him by mussing his hair playfully. The small Brute grins, balances his jug in one arm, and takes a big swing at Jase's stomach with the other.

On impact, Jase mock groans, "Uggh, you got me!"

The boy scampers off for more water, proud of his might, and, the coast clear, Jase lifts a fiber mat from the ground, revealing a rock-lined pit filled with fruit. Rohan opens a similar cache, this one covered with a board and weighted down with several large rocks. A half-carved carcass hides inside, which he splays with a knife, removing several large chunks. I take the one he offers hesitantly.

"What is it?"

I'm no stranger to meat, but we eat mostly lamb and chicken, and Marsa's kitchen hands always deal with the messy job of preparation. I'm not sure what to think about this blackened body of flesh in the leaf-lined hollow, with its prickly snout and holes where eyes used to be.

Rohan tears into his piece. "Peccary," he replies, through chews.

"Ah," I say, like I know what that is. I take a bite of the leathery meat anyway. The flesh feels dry on my tongue and smells of smoke, but it either tastes good, or I'm too famished to tell otherwise.

Jase grabs two mangoes and a rough, brown ball of a fruit called mamey. They lead me to a table mostly screened by shrubbery, and we eat our meat pieces and the refreshing, ripe fruit, which Jase slices into wedges with his knife. Both Brutes carry no shortage of weapons. My recent Alexia training makes me curious about the various knives strapped to their bodies; I try not to stare.

"How's your shoulder?" Rohan asks, finishing the last bite of orange-pink mamey.

"It hurts when I move my arm, but it's not unbearable."

Without responding, he stands and walks away.

"He'll be back." Jase smiles reassuringly. It seems he is always smiling, as if fueled by some internal joy. Few people have that disposition. It reminds me of Mother's cheeriness, though less infuriating for some reason.

"I'm sorry about Dáin and everything last night, but I'm glad you're here, Reina."

I nod, unsure how to answer. I'm grateful for his kindness. This one-sided familiarity still unsettles me, though.

"Jase, how *do* you know my name?"

He chews his lip, like he wants to tell me everything he's ever known in his life, just put it all out there, but something holds him back. When he speaks, his words are tinged with genuine apology.

"That's not for me to tell you."

We stare at each other for an awkward moment. I don't know

what he's thinking, but I—I am trying to put my finger on why it seems I know this Brute, and why that familiarity nudges me toward trust.

Rohan returns, breaking the silent inquisition, and sits facing me.

"Here," he says. "Hold your arm like this."

He lifts my forearm to a right angle, with surprising tenderness, then uses a large, rough piece of fabric to make a sling. He leans close to tie the ends behind my neck, then stops short. Reconsidering, he moves behind me, gingerly reaching down for the fabric ends. His proximity unnerves me a bit, but watching him fumble because of my standoffishness is worse. The adjustment was a thoughtful gesture, giving me the space I made clear I wanted. Maybe I should loosen up a bit.

"Thank you," I say, for both his gifts.

As we finish the last of our meal, a group of Brutes passes by, not five meters from the kitchen hut. They're too preoccupied to notice us veiled behind the bushes. But I see them, and I'm fascinated by what I observe.

Two Brutes, slightly younger than Rohan and Jase, lead a gaggle of little ones—cubs. The leaders each carry a baby strapped to their backs, swaddled in a leather pouch of sorts. All but the leaders weave and wiggle, the group shifting like a swift cloud as they move through the clearing. I'd guess they're about Mother's Gentles' ages—none of them older than seven. The idea of these children holding a straight line—the way Dom Bakshi marches the Gentles around Bella, or the way they filed in for lunch at the Hive—is laughable. Even these pint-sized Brutes exhibit a wild unruliness. A dirt-covered cub grabs a stick and slashes at the bushes around him. Another breaks ranks completely to chase a lizard that eventually skitters up a tree.

The older Brutes, broad and brown-skinned, stomp through

the brush, slowing every so often to allow the others to catch up. I marvel at their loads: one of the babies is quite small, the other perhaps a year or so old. What a strange sight: such small humans attached to such large ones.

The irony is not lost on me. I've always equated nurturing with weakness, and yet here are Brutes—perhaps the most formidable beings in all of history—using their strength to care for little children. There's nothing soft about Brutes, and therefore nothing weak about their care of the cubs. Perhaps I've been too harsh on Maternos.

"You know what we should do?" Jase says eagerly, that endearing smile of his returning. "We should take her to the chute."

When Rohan's skepticism melts into a mischievous grin of his own, I wonder what I am in for.

---

Thirty minutes later, the swish of our legs against encroaching plants and the constant chatter of birds is finally interrupted by a new sound: water. The longer we thread along this barely cleared path toward the chute—whatever *that* is—the louder the bubbling rush.

The trees seem to grow atop each other, some heavy with stray vines, others laden with massive brown termite mounds, wrinkled and bumpy, like an old Dom's knee. Palm fronds spread wide overhead, and orange and blue bird-of-paradise flowers flock playfully amid the green undergrowth.

The Jungle is wild, yes. A little frightening? Absolutely. But an unexpected magnetism ignites my blood too.

I watch Rohan's figure four paces ahead of mine. *Wild. Frightening. Magnetic.* The Jungle's allure isn't the only surprise in the Wilds.

I brush my fingers along the fringe of a fern-like shrub. The tiny leaves shrivel at my touch, startling me.

"Sensitive plant," Jase says behind me.

He slides his rough palm across another frond, and I wrinkle my nose at the transformation, mesmerized by the slow movement of leaves, folding in on themselves of their own accord. He seems pleased by my delight in this small thing. We play with the leaves so long that we have to walk double time to catch up to Rohan.

We reach the source of the watery music soon after. Bordered by a gravelly swath of exposed bank, a green-blue river rolls past, not rushing like a wet-season tributary, but swift enough to sweep a careless person downstream. Speaking of downstream, a hundred meters to my right the river disappears into a rocky outcropping at the base of the hillside—a black hole nearly concealed by loose vines and shadow. I'm suddenly sorry I didn't get more clarity about the nature of "the chute" before I followed two Brutes deeper into the Wilds.

They don't bother to explain what comes next—whether they'll be abandoning me here or drowning me in the river and stashing my body in the rocks. Instead they rummage around in the brush above the bank and return with three good-sized boards. On closer inspection, each "board" consists of multiple bamboo poles lashed together with thin vines.

"What exactly do you plan to do with those?" I frown, guessing and dreading the answer at once.

"Float!" grins Jase, throwing his shirt over a boulder.

I freeze, peering between him and the dubious instrument of my certain death, then hurl the first excuse I can think of.

"I'm hurt, remember?"

"You can ride with me," Rohan instructs more than offers. He has also removed his shirt, and I try not to stare at the prominent bulges on his chest and abdomen. "Jase, take the torch?"

"Sure."

He grabs the long stick tipped with a bundle of dried plant material, shrugging off my incredulousness.

"See? No excuse," Rohan says, his eyes playful. "You'll be fine. Surely we've earned enough trust to take you through a little cave?"

"A *cave*?" I gasp. I know what caves are: rare formations that carve small sections out of rock, making room for animals to burrow in, or—at the most—a person to walk into. We have a few of them in Nedé. *This* is not a cave. This is a gigantic abyss filled with churning water, ready to swallow us and our rafts whole. My better sense warns me to refuse, but Rohan has already situated "our" raft at the edge of the water. Jase pushes off the shore, lighting the torch with something from his pocket.

"Come on," Rohan insists. "We don't want to get too far behind our only source of light." He grins at me, waggling an eyebrow, and I let myself be convinced by his playful urgency.

They wouldn't take me if it wasn't safe . . . *would they*?

Once I take a wobbly seat on the small raft, Rohan gives it a push. For a second I wonder if he's sending me down by myself, the devil, but at the last second he jumps on deftly, taking a seat behind me. The raft is so small—or Rohan is so big—that he's forced to place one leg on each side of my body to fit.

We glide swiftly now as the river narrows. The raft shifts over a white crest in the rapid water, and I instinctively hold onto one of Rohan's knees with my good arm for balance. The coarse hair covering his skin feels strange, but I don't have time to dwell on it. Already the cave yawns open, ready to swallow us and our rafts whole, dooming us to what I am sure is a certain and ghastly death.

As we enter its dark mouth, vines brush over my face and snag in my hair. I yank the last free just as a sudden dip in the river catapults me forward, nearly dumping me overboard. I yelp, the cry echoing against the enclosing rock walls. He probably thinks me a child, but I don't care—I've lost the will to maintain my dignity. Now I just want to survive.

Rohan laughs behind me, but grabs my shoulder when I pitch forward, preventing me from tumbling off the raft, then slips an arm around my waist. I don't resist. Frankly, I welcome the security of his strength at the moment. Doesn't mean I trust him, but . . . maybe I do, a little, because here I am.

"Relax," he says.

And with him anchoring me to the bamboo beneath us, I do. Enough, at least, to take in the midnight world around me. Jase drifts a few lengths ahead of us, bobbing with the shifting current, his moon-like torch casting flickering light on the pale stone walls and ceiling, except the towering sections which escape its reach.

What a strange place. Even the sounds are otherworldly: dim, magnified by echoes. The crackle of the torch fire. Water dripping from gnarled rock fingers that dangle overhead. The occasional whoop or holler from one of the Brutes as we careen through the darkness. And the smells—if dark were an odor it would be just as wet and musty, and cool, blessedly cool.

On and on we glide, past a small waterfall, under a low over-hang, and through another enormous room, and as we do my ter-ror morphs to adrenaline-infused exhilaration. Now I don't want the ride to end. I've never imagined anything remotely like this place. A beautiful blackness, hiding strange and wonderful sights, invisible to the world outside.

Forward we sail, along an invisible, watery road, the once blue-green river only appearing in shimmering, metallic ripples around Jase's raft.

We pass a bulging stone knob on our right, and a sudden, vio-lent flurry of a hundred wings rushes past me. Panicked, I turn my body into Rohan's, using his bulk as a shield. He laughs again, but leans down over the top of me, making us as small as possible while the living mass flows over and around us, chirping and flapping.

I feel his breath in my hair when he speaks. "Bats. Hold still; they won't hurt you." His hand runs gently up and down my arm, just once. He's trying to comfort me, I think, trying to assure me that everything will be okay, and it works, I guess, because I'm not afraid of the bats—I'm not thinking of them at all. Instead I'm consumed with the smell of woodsmoke and sweat, and the feel of his chest against my cheek. Again.

But this time Rohan's touch doesn't make me shrink away. A strange warmth courses through me. His hand smooths my hair—to untangle it from the scruff on his chin—and a feeling I've never experienced reaches into my consciousness, coaxing something to life in me. I don't know what it is, what to call it. Fondness? Friendship? Trust? No—I'm familiar with those—I experience them for Treowe. This is something else entirely, a feeling bigger and stronger than affinity. An emotion that wars against the virtue of self-restraint, and I know instinctively I'm in danger of falling into it completely.

It seems the twitching, flying animals will never stop, though probably less than a minute passes before the shrill chirps cease echoing around us. In the new quiet I'm afraid he'll hear the throbbing *thump, thump* of my heart.

Rohan doesn't seem in a hurry to sit up again, and I wonder if he felt it too: the jolt of whatever-that-was that blindsided me. But then he does sit up, and shifts a little to give me more space. So . . . no, then? It was just me? All the better. Something in me suspects that the . . . *feeling* I just experienced falls under the realm of the Brutes' inherent danger.

*And they are dangerous, Rei. The one thing you know for certain is how dangerous they are.*

But even as I think it, I know that's only half true. Everything

I *used* to know about Brutes is their danger. But "everything" changed when I met Rohan and Jase at the edge of a teak forest.

We glide on, my nerves replaced by a comfortable silence. Eventually weak light spills into the cave like dawn, growing stronger and brighter with each passing moment. Soon I can distinguish the grainy texture of the walls, and the ceiling dances with marbled light reflected off the water. The river itself returns to its proper color as we are spit into the vivid green of a wild paradise.

As the river widens, the current slows enough for Jase to dismount his raft and lead it through the waist-deep water to shore. Rohan moves to disembark ours, but the shift in balance nearly topples me.

"You better be careful!" I tease.

The command no sooner leaves my lips than a wicked scheme flashes in Rohan's eyes.

"I'd better *what*?" he asks, simultaneously lifting an eyebrow and the edge of the raft.

"Don't you da—" but the rest is cut short by a tumble, splash, and mouthful of tangy water. I scramble to my feet, soaked and spluttering, "You . . . you . . . "

"Brute?" he suggests, erupting in a deep-belly laugh.

I splash him in protest, chasing him and our raft with sloshy strides to the bank, where Jase howls with mirth.

"Glad *you* think it's funny," I scold, but I'm smiling too.

"What did you think?" Jase asks expectantly.

"It was . . . *fun*," I admit.

"I knew she was a brave one. Didn't I tell you, Rohan?" Jase beams, seeming genuinely proud.

Rohan nods approvingly. "Ah, but is she brave enough to jump?"

Jase's good-natured, cheerful laugh rings out. "I bet she would, if she wasn't hurt."

But I am hurt, as my makeshift sling still attests, so they insist I sit on a raft on the shore to watch them demonstrate "jumping."

I roll cool, smooth river stones under my toes while they swim to the far bank and begin a long scramble up a series of rock faces and boulders, half covered in foliage, to a small ledge maybe ten meters above the river. Rohan goes first, shuffling carefully to the edge, then crouching and springing into the air. I hold my breath as he falls, falls, falls headlong into the water, his body slicing through the surface like one of his many knives. He surfaces a moment later, grinning wide, water matting his hair and streaming down his face.

Jase goes next, cutting through the air with a mighty holler before splashing down into the water. I yell for him too. These two, they are crazy, and dauntless, and . . . *full of life*.

They climb and jump, yell and splash a half-dozen times before swimming back to my side of the river.

"I've never seen anyone do something that dumb," I grin. "I want to try."

"Next time we'll show you how to do it," Jase promises.

The words hang in the air: *Next time*. Jase looks so hopeful that I expect Rohan to elbow him or rebuke him or something, but he looks away instead. And I chew on the words, wondering, *Will there be a 'next time?' Do I want there to be a next time?* It seems Jase does. Why?

Rohan hoists one of the rafts over his head and starts down a brushy trail that winds parallel to the cave we just conquered. I assume they'll deposit the boats at the bank where we began. Jase takes the other, and I follow. I notice they didn't position me between them this time. Are they so sure I won't run for it? Of course I won't. They might not know I could never leave my horse, but they're well aware I'd get lost or eaten by dinnertime without them.

*Dinner* . . . do Brutes eat an evening meal? I suddenly find the thought funny. Two days ago, I knew nothing of Brutes other than what Dom Bakshi taught me in history class and what I picked up from Candidate training—admittedly not much. I knew they were dangerous, that the foremothers founded Nedé precisely because something inferior in their genetics caused them to hurt women. Yesterday a Brute attacked a finca, and then pinned me to the ground, underscoring everything I understood about them. But today—today these Brutes have also become people. I have seen their kindness, humor, humanity. So much so that I am wondering whether I will have dinner with them, and the prospect doesn't terrify me.

I watch Jase's back as we walk. His arms are tensed under the weight of the raft, but he manages it well. Jase doesn't bulge with muscles like Rohan, but his body is well-built and strong. Wet hair sticks to his neck, a little stream of water trickling down between his bare shoulder blades. His skin resembles mine: warm and smooth, like a sun-drenched cattail cob. It also matches the cloth wrap around his waist, which drips onto the hard-packed trail underfoot.

Jase seems all kindness. I can't imagine anyone *not* liking him, and not solely because of that endearing, familiar quality. He favors me too, though I can't imagine why. Just like I can't understand how he knows my name, or, if that's not for him to tell me, who will.

———

Late-afternoon sun casts steep shadows across the undergrowth by the time we reach the outskirts of Tree Camp. The plays of light and silhouette all but hide the network of camouflaged platforms and ropes overhead—like an aerial version of ants' subterranean

tunnels—while lower mahogany boughs splay like foliage fingers unsuccessfully hiding a secret.

What other marvels do these Brutes hide?

We're not yet to the kitchen hut when a group of three Brutes, slightly younger than my escorts, enter the clearing from the thick Jungle, limp animals slung over their shoulders. When they see me, they freeze and stare openly, mouths agape.

"What's *that* doing here?" one of them snarls. Mud conceals most of his face. His catch's fur resembles a jaguar's, though a much smaller cat.

Rohan steps casually in front of me. "She's none of your concern, Fin," he says, low and even. The muddy Brute grunts but relents, fixing me with a sideways glare as the three move on.

When they're out of earshot, I ask, "What would they do to me if I was alone?"

"Probably nothing," Jase smirks. "Except Fin. He doesn't see what's wrong with what Dáin's getting ready for—" He stops short, wincing, and I catch Rohan lifting his foot from Jase's.

"What is Dáin getting ready for?" I insist.

Jase addresses Rohan. "She's going to have to know sometime."

Rohan looks away, which Jase seems to take as half-hearted consent. "Dáin thinks we've waited long enough—that it's time to do something about . . . our situation. He's stupid to think he can take down the Matriarchy by himself, but that's what he's planning."

"Take down the Matriarchy?" Fear rises in my chest, reminiscent of the panic I felt when I learned about the attack on Jonalyn's finca. "Is that what those raids are supposed to do?"

"No," Jase shakes his head. "That's just to get what he needs, though he probably wants to scare some women too."

"*Scare* them? You mean *kill* them?" I set my chin, resisting the sting of salt threatening to spill from my eyes. "He torched my sister's finca. He killed Gentles. He would have murdered her too if she wasn't such a fighter."

"Your sister?" Jase asks quietly. A pained expression clouds his face as Rohan takes over.

"What the Matriarchy has done to men—it isn't right. It has to stop. Dáin's right about that." Though his volume remains constant, the force behind it intensifies, and I stiffen at his aggression.

"What are you talking about?"

"Come on, Reina," Rohan says, equally urgent and condescending. "You're smart. Put the pieces together. Whatever you've been told isn't the whole truth." He flaps a hand against Jase's chest. "We're here, aren't we? I don't know what they do to them, but I'll tell you one thing: Gentles aren't born gentle."

"But . . . " I search for the hole in his reasoning, aching to refute him, but I can't deny their existence. And these Brutes—these "men," as Rohan called them—muddle everything I've known to be true. They are so very different from Treowe, with his soft . . . *gentility*. Tre is safe, and thoughtful, and compliant, and *safe*. Rohan and Jase, they have shown me kindness, but they are also rough, and unpredictable, and while I feel a certain safety with them, I also fear what they are capable of. They *could* hurt me, but I don't think Tre ever could.

Why *are* they so different?

And then there's Dáin, who *did* hurt me. And though I fear him most of all, at least he acts like a Brute. His behavior makes sense to me, even if his existence doesn't. He uses his strength to hurt others—to hurt women. If the Brutes in the play at the Exhibition danced their way into real life, they would have wild red hair and furious eyes.

Yet Rohan's last words echo in my mind, reverberating like drops of water in the cave: *Gentles aren't born gentle.*

My head spins with the faces of every Gentle I've ever

encountered, meek souls dedicated to serving the good of Nedé. Then one particular Gentle replaces them all—the one with a dimple and sun-spotted cheeks, who has never so much as raised his voice, let alone posed any threat to my safety.

What if Treowe *wasn't* born that way?

Rohan doesn't press the issue further. Maybe he sees the storm he created surging and spinning inside me—a hurricane of doubt and uncertainty, set in motion by four little words. In my stupor I barely notice Jase slip an arm around my shoulder, leading me onward.

"Come on," he says. "Torvus will be waiting."

As we walk, the curious sights and sounds of camp tear my thoughts away from the puzzle of the Gentles' nature. Instead I consider these Brutes, how they seem born to *do*. Not one is unoccupied. Mud-covered Fin and the other two we encountered earlier skin their game in the large fire ring. Three others pound boards into the new hut, while two cubs braid long roots into rope. Brutes tend to the garden, and Brutes sharpen the tips of long sticks. There's even what appears to be a reading lesson underway beneath the shade of a cohune palm, a long-haired Brute writing charcoal letters on a slab of wood for a semicircle of squirrelly young ones. Even here, in the middle of nowhere, for no one's admiration or use but their own, they have created a world of rustic form and impressive function. No one could accuse them of idleness.

I'm baffled by the ingenuity required to construct this secret place. Apart from the odd metal pan, the netting in the huts, or a few other stray curiosities, it seems to be built entirely from Jungle materials. Water runs through hollow bamboo to irrigate a park-like garden where wood poles trellis climbing edibles and trees bulge with fruits, some foreign, some familiar. Raised boardwalks connect the various huts and cabanas, presumably to avoid mud and high water in the rainy season. The kitchen and other buildings are simple, but serve their purposes.

And then, of course, there's the giant tree, laden with a network of shelters hanging in the limbs like the fruit in the orchard. I can't imagine how they managed *that*, but there it is, looming over camp as its pièce de résistance.

We pass a shed where several Brutes rummage through weapons, and I wish there was more than Rohan and palm fronds to hide me from sight. Apparently the Brutes' affinity for such tools is surpassed only by their ability to make them. The cache nearly overflows with neatly categorized spears, bows, clubs, darts, bolas, and nets. The weapons don't compare with the Alexia's, but must do nicely for hunting and skinning, given the number of pelts I've spotted around camp, and that carcass still smoking over the fire.

In Nedé, women joke about the Gentles' apathy—their lack of initiative. Even Mother will occasionally bemoan to her female staff, "If you don't make them do it, nothing will get done!" That's why we have Gentles Regimen—to keep Gentles on task. I thought only women were self-motivated, but no one drives these Brutes, and they clearly don't need any push. Even more surprising, it seems as if they collectively manifest the spectrum of Nedéan destinies, though adapted to suit their environment: Innovatus, Agricolátio, Alexia, Fabricatio, and the others—even, shockingly, Materno.

Jase stops before a small wooden house a short distance from the mahogany tree.

"This is it."

My stomach drops again, a sensation I've grown increasingly accustomed to since smoke rose from the horizon last evening: *fear*. What sort of Brute is this "Torvus"?

Strangely, the structure resembles a Nedéan house. Solid wood walls form a perfect rectangle, and netting covers proper windows. The front door, made of solid wood, is etched with a single plumeria blossom. Someone put a lot of care into this building's construction, though—judging by the brittle thatching, weather-worn walls, and encroaching plant-life—that was some time ago. It's the first dilapidation I've seen in camp.

Jase raps on the door but doesn't wait for an invitation to enter. He offers a reassuring smile as he leads the way. When Rohan doesn't follow, nodding me toward the door instead, I ask, "You're not coming?"

"I'll wait here." He pushes a hand through his hair, which has dried in clumps over his forehead and against his neck. He leans against the railing, but when it creaks under his weight he relocates to a sturdy wood crate with wide slats and a latch. Is Rohan trying to look nonchalant? I'd find that extremely funny if I weren't so nervous.

I assumed he would come with us, and now that he isn't, I *want* him to. I want him to be there, ready to step between me and whatever waits inside, like he did with Fin earlier. But I force myself to push down the desire, gather my courage, and cross the threshold into the house.

Jase takes my arm and gently leads me forward a few steps. My eyes work to adjust to the dim light. When they do, the form that materializes makes me want to run back outside.

# CHAPTER SIXTEEN

LIKE ALL LITTLE SISTERS, I suppose, I craved association with my older siblings, though more so with Jonalyn than Ciela. My eldest sister walked into beauty's bloom just as I entered the age of noticing my own shape. I vividly remember the first time I dared to hope I would resemble her as I grew up.

We were sitting around the rough-hewn kitchen table at Bella Terra, I was about eleven years old, and Aunt Julissa was visiting. Council business usually kept her from seeing us outside Grandmother's annual Initus dinners, though Mother said the sisters used to enjoy summers at the finca as children, when it belonged to their "Aunt" Salita, a cousin of Matriarch Teera's. Despite Julissa's infrequent stays—years passing between visits—her return to Bella seemed to stoke a forgotten sentimentality in the typically stern woman. As we sat around the table that evening, eating Marsa's exquisite herbed lamb chops and creamy risotto, she had peered at Jonalyn and me intently and then twittered in her sing-song fashion,

"Well, no one will take them for strangers, Leda. I've never seen sisters resemble each other the way Reina and Jonalyn do. Like two kittens from a litter, they are."

I took it as a great compliment. Though I'd much rather be known for superior riding than beauty—the latter of little benefit in Amal—I was proud to be tied to Jonalyn. After hearing Aunt Julissa's observation, I noticed Jonalyn's and my similarities more acutely: the way our dark hair streaks honey gold from the sun; our thin noses and high cheekbones; the roundness of our eyes, though Jo's irises are brown, while mine are hazel like Mother's. Sibling sets usually highlight Nedé's diversity; Aunt Julissa found our striking similarity peculiar because it's uncommon.

Now, as I look from Jase to the hulking Brute beside him, I think of Aunt Julissa's words. They are two kittens from a litter. Though Torvus is an old cat, no longer prone to chase his own tail, who could miss the resemblance? Both Brutes have broad faces, with wide noses and thick lips, and their hair has the same curl and color, though Torvus's grays at the temples. They even stand similarly: legs shoulder width apart, weight perfectly centered over their feet, shoulders drawn slightly back.

They are different, to be sure. One scowls while the other seems pleased even without a smile. Torvus also looks to be nearly twice Jase's age, and he is thicker and harder and more muscular than a human should be. He's so unlike an aging Gentle that I gawk at his otherworldliness—a demigod with slightly-graying facial hair.

When Torvus speaks, his voice rumbles low as distant thunder; my heart pounds like the ensuing rain.

"Who are you?" he booms.

"I told—" Jase begins, but the older Brute silences him with a raised hand.

"I want to hear it from her." He stares at me with penetrating, watery-grey eyes. I need to answer. I don't have time to think about whether I should.

"I'm Reina Pierce," I manage, with more strength than I feel.

He considers my clothing. "You're Alexia?"

"No. Yes. I . . . " His intensity makes me nervous, and I don't think through my words as carefully as I should. "I'm a Candidate for the Matriarchy. We're currently training with the Alexia."

Jase's mouth drops open a little, his eyes growing wide. Torvus's, on the other hand, narrow into thin slits.

"Who knows you're here?" he asks.

*Way to go, Rei. Why don't you tell him about all your childhood fears while you're at it?*

Now they know I'm a Candidate—that I'm close with the Matriarch, that I could know things. What if Torvus plans to take down the Matriarchy too? If he knows I'm isolated, what might he do for information? I should tell him they will all be out looking for me, that they'll be here any minute. But for some maddening reason, I can't bring myself to lie—not with Jase standing there. He has been so honest—more truthful than he ought to be—with me. I know it's stupid, but I don't want to deceive him.

"No one," I say, and though I will probably regret the words later, they feel right now.

Torvus grunts, then turns his back to us. The silence is torture. I stare at the back of his thick neck, at the thick arms attached to his thick body, and try not to think about how easily he could break my thinness.

Jase shifts. Just as I'm beginning to wonder whether that was it—whether Torvus has finished interrogating me—he turns and pierces me with a threatening glare.

"Jase will take you back to your mother's finca in the morning. Don't tell anyone what you've seen."

I take a moment to ponder his words—uncomfortably, beneath his stern gaze—determined to avoid offering him any more revealing information.

*Don't tell anyone what I've seen.* Sounds simple. The obvious, glaring hole in his strategy is that he can't stop me from telling, and I know that he knows it. So why wouldn't he keep me here? Why not just kill me? Now he knows I'm a Candidate, with ties to the Matriarch. He has seen my Alexia uniform—ties there, too. It doesn't make sense. . . .Why would he let me go? Is he so sure I will keep silent?

Jase purses his lips to one side, apologetically. He's fond of me. Truly, he has been as kind to me as . . . as *Treowe*, which is more than a compliment. Would Torvus spare me on account of Jase?

I glance again at the benevolent Brute. *Bats*, the two *have* to be related. The similarities are too striking not to be connected somehow. Can Brutes have sons? No, women have babies, not Brutes. That much, at least, Dom Bakshi taught me. Then . . . how did all these Brutes get here? When we were in the tree this morning, didn't Jase say the young ones "came"?

My thoughts multiply like mice and prove as hard to catch too. They skitter and scamper in circles, like rodents trapped in a barn with a prowling cat. I fight to chase them away, at least for now. I owe Torvus an answer.

"I won't."

The words are past my lips before I really, truly consider whether I can keep that promise. Will I tell? Will I have to? Will I want to? I don't know. But I do know this: I have to make Torvus believe his secrets are safe with me.

"Good," Torvus says. His eyes pass over my face slowly, studying it, the way Mother reads her book of scriptures. For a long moment he seems lost in his thoughts, and their weight drags the sternness from his face. He almost looks *sad*.

Then, as suddenly as if one of the mice in my mind scuttled into his, he looks away, grunting again.

"Continue to keep her out of sight until morning," he barks at Jase.

Jase shifts uncomfortably, his gaze sweeping the floor. I warrant "continue to" means I should have been out of sight to this point, which implies our little jaunt from Callisto to the kitchen and on to the chute *probably* defied a previous directive.

"A couple of the boys . . . may have seen her this afternoon," Jase says, deepening his voice, trying to sound more authoritative. I fight amusement, intrigued both by his show of toughness and the courage it took to disobey his leader's orders to show me a good time.

"'*May* have?'" Torvus rumbles.

"*Did*. Did see her. Fin . . . and his hunting party." Though clearly caught, I admire that Jase meets Torvus's boiling gaze.

Torvus's voice ignites with fresh anger. "When are you going to learn to follow orders?"

"I'm sorry. I . . . "

Torvus takes one long stride toward Jase, and I wonder for a terrifying moment if he will strike him. "Sorry is going to get you killed, boy."

Though they are nearly equal in height, Torvus's bulk, and temper, dwarf Jase. I want to help him somehow, to aid this Brute who has shown me kindness.

"It was my fault," I blurt out.

Both sets of eyes turn to me, but I don't back down. "I . . . snuck out . . . I was scared and . . . tried to get to my horse. Jase didn't—and Rohan, they didn't do anything wrong." I raise myself up to my full height, trying to speak with the confidence a lie can never produce, and I think it works . . . until Torvus begins to chuckle—not maliciously, but it's not comforting either.

"And you what—disarmed Rohan on your way through the door? Lies don't become you, girl."

He mumbles something angrily as he turns his back on me again; I can't quite catch his words. If it weren't preposterous, I could almost imagine he said, "*Not you, and not your mother.*"

In the ensuing silence, those bothersome, skittering rodents return. Torvus mentioned "your mother's finca" earlier. Now I question how he knows that my mother has a finca. Jase knows where I live; how he got that information I couldn't guess, but maybe he told Torvus. But what if that's backwards? If I heard what I think I did, Torvus has some familiarity with Mother. And my association with her doesn't sound positive.

I turn to Jase, hoping for reassurance, or at least a clue as to what I should do next, but he stares blankly at a dusty tabletop. His defeat unnerves me more than Torvus's hefty presence. I want the ever-smiling Jase back. And I want to shout at Torvus that I'm not a liar, but the defense rings thin—a vain plea, hurled from one just caught in a lie. In fact, anything I imagine saying now—"I didn't see anything," or "I'm not a threat to you"—could be taken for another falsehood. So I stay silent.

When Torvus speaks again, I can't miss his words this time: "You've been a fool, Jase."

I can almost feel a puff of breath rush past my skin: Jase's very spirit, sucked out of his body by his leader's scathing words. His shoulders slump, his gaze glued to the tabletop.

"*Never* let them blind you." Torvus's livid words fill the small house in one last gush of frustration, pressing against me and the walls and the sparse furnishings. He overturns a small table with a flick of his hand. The action seems to deflate his gust of anger, and with a heavy sigh he says, "What's done is done. Better to inform the others than let Fin spread rumors. Announce a fire meeting. Keep her secluded until then. Can you handle that?"

Jase lifts his eyes to meet Torvus's. "Yes." Though he answers evenly, without flinching, I'm struck by the realization that even these formidable Brutes experience emotions familiar to me: inadequacy, courage, joviality, care, and most astounding of all, *fear*.

Jase takes hold of my good arm too tightly as he leads me toward the door, for Torvus's benefit I assume, because as soon as we return to the speckled light and thrumming green outside, he lets go completely. I inhale an exhilaratingly fresh breath of air, like one returning to the surface of the sea after a deep swim.

Rohan stands from the crate. "Sounds like that went well." His cheeky comment coaxes Jase's familiar grin from hiding. The warmth of it brings mine along.

---

Day is already losing ground to evening as Rohan heaves the rope pulley, lifting us back into the mahogany canopy. Jase is off telling the others about the "fire meeting"—whatever that is—and gave Rohan strict orders to keep me hidden until then. After Jase disseminated this information, Rohan reminded him that he had, in fact, heard the whole conversation.

With a day of experiences to color my understanding, I'm free to enjoy the slow journey through giant branches and emerald leaves as long as my arm. I don't need Rohan to steady me this time. I take a wide stance and ride the slightly swaying platform, drawing on my experience as a rider to stay balanced. Although the other huts we pass still appear empty, we have company. A flock of scarlet macaws startle at our approach; they burst from the tree in a flutter of blue-tipped wings, their long, red tail feathers trailing behind. The birds' throaty, gargled squawks disrupt a band of spider monkeys, who in turn scramble up and away, swinging on vines with able-bodied limbs. The monkeys' squeals interrupt a sloth's sleep next, but his moss-streaked, furry body barely moves. He only turns his head toward the commotion, then nods off again.

Just before the platform reaches his hut, the sun dips below the mountaintops. The resulting light waves illuminate the sky above and around us with a vibrant, blush-colored sheen. We come to a stop, but Rohan doesn't move toward the door. He rests his forearms on the edge of the railing instead, staring out toward Nedé.

We watch the sunset from within it, above the whole world. Like our current view, everything has carried an air of the supernatural today, in this parallel universe where the wild Jungle holds delicate secrets, water flows through caves, and I am nearly touching a Brute who seems to prove everything I know about them wrong.

Trying not to be obvious, I watch him take it all in. It seems to move him—all the nature and light and lofty perspective. The glowing embers of evening play on his face as well as on the heavens, and I'm struck by . . . by the allure of *him*. His jaw, his breadth, an unruly strand of hair that brushes his cheekbone—he simultaneously sparks and soothes a piece of me I didn't know existed before today.

His eyes flicker in my direction, and I quickly dart mine elsewhere, pretending fascination with some glorious sight just past him and to the left.

*Don't be stupid, Reina Pierce. Evening and morning light—you can't trust them, remember? He's a Brute.*

To the east, beyond the Jungle, stepped foothills melt into a green puddle of flat farmland, interrupted only by an occasional snake-like ridge, dark thread of river, or shining lake. Beyond still, the Halcyon Sea's great expanse diminishes to a hazy line of horizon.

That's where I belong. I belong in Nedé. But the Arena, Finca del Mar, even Bella Terra, feel as distant as they appear. They are part of that *other* world—a world to which I will return tomorrow. Will all that feels so immediate, so magical now, seem as foreign to me then as home does at this moment?

"Have you ever been there? To Nedé?" My voice breaks something of the magic, the way the birds began a chain reaction of disruption, and I'm suddenly sorry for speaking at all.

Rohan shakes his head.

"Then how do you know about the Gentles?"

He takes long enough to respond for me to wonder if I should have asked. His answer confirms my suspicion.

"I know Jase is real free in what he tells you because he's . . . 'cause he's Jase, and he . . . " His voice trails off, thinking better of whatever he was going to say. "I can't answer all the questions you have. Not about camp, not about Torvus, not about us."

I plan to nod, but the prospect of not getting a single answer overpowers my assent. "One—can you answer just *one* question?"

Rohan doesn't reply. Learning from Jase, I take that as an opportunity to try.

"Why do some of you . . . " How can I consolidate twenty questions into one? "Why do some of you seem *good*, when others, like Dáin, hurt people?"

Rohan straightens, making the platform sway.

"We're *men*, that's why." The matched intensity of his words and gaze startle me, the return of electricity when he steps closer more so. "We can't be forced to be any certain way. We are what we are. We can be violent, or we can be . . . *gentle*, but that choice is ours. No one has taken it from us."

I try to process his answer, but rational thought becomes increasingly difficult with those dark eyes boring into mine. Why do I feel all melty inside? I turn away to sort through his words in peace—to break whatever spell he has cast on me—but he doesn't let me.

"I answered your question," he says. "Now you have to answer one of mine."

"That's fair."

He stares out into the quickly fading light, as if bashful to ask. "Now that you've been here, with us, which do you think is better?"

"What do you mean? Between good and dangerous?"

"No. Between us and the Gentles—which is *better*?"

The weight of his question defies gravity, hanging in the air like a swirl of smoke or a flash of light. I consider the only Brutes I have for reference: Jase, with his affable, endearing smile; Torvus's rock-splitting voice; the implausible quality in Rohan that draws me to him, even now. But then I remember the helpless panic produced by Dáin's body pinning mine down, his hand around my throat, and the fear—even the memory of that fear—could make me want to wish away every Brute in existence. Their danger— their possibility of evil—overshadows all else. Not Treowe, not any Gentle in Nedé, has ever incited terror. Annoyance, ambivalence, maybe even superiority, but never fear.

Rohan takes my shoulders gently and turns me to face him.

"Which is better?" he asks again.

The echoes of panic and half my resolve melt instantly in his surprisingly warm urgency. Rohan makes me feel something that defies logic. But still . . .

"I don't know," I whisper.

And it's the most honest answer I can give.

———

Jase appears in the tree hut doorway, a sooty smudge striping his cheek, like a wild thing fresh from the Jungle.

"It's time," he announces.

I'm relieved for the distraction. Whatever the "fire meeting" entails must be more entertaining than watching Rohan whittle the end of a stick. He hasn't so much as looked at me since we came inside half an hour ago. Still, Jase must sense my unease, because he says, "Don't worry. It's going to be fun."

*Fun?* I raise an eyebrow. Something tells me Jase interprets just about everything as "fun," diminishing my confidence in the night's activity. But I meet his smile with a half-hearted grin of my own, for his sake.

―――――――

The ring of stones we passed earlier today seems to have grown exponentially, expanded by the raging duel between fire and night within it. Red and yellow flames spread wide and low, reaching nearly every crevice of the pit. The battle of light and dark twists violently, casting eerie shadows on the dozens of faces encircling it. The place is packed with Brutes of all ages. Some crouch in the dirt; others perch on low tree branches. A few of the eldest balance precariously on the rocky perimeter, thrusting long poles laden with meat chunks into the fire. The resulting savory smoke would make my mouth water if it weren't suffocating me.

The din of their voices overtakes even the loud buzz of nighttime insects and animals. Laughter and shouts cut through the Brutes' collective jawing.

"Give me some of that meat!"

"Who's got the chicha?"

"Get off me, you big tapir!"

"Grab Pip before he gets burned!"

As we approach the mayhem, I slide behind Rohan, using his body as a screen. We skirt the crowd that way—Jase to my right and Rohan in front, so close my nose occasionally brushes his thin shirt. They lead me to a small dais adjacent to, and slightly higher than, the pit. There Torvus presides over the chaos in a large wooden chair at the center of the platform, gulping from a coconut shell. As we approach, the leader throws the shell aside, stands, and motions to the assembly. Immediately they fall silent.

Rohan steps aside, once again deferring to Jase the task of leading me to Torvus, exposing me to curious stares. Now I am the seagull among frigate birds—the only part of this wild scene that doesn't belong. The spectacle. The anomaly.

Though the firelight limits my vision, the whites of a hundred wide eyes shine eerily back at me.

On the platform, I stand sandwiched between Torvus on my right, Jase on my left. As the others wait expectantly for their leader to speak, the chorus of nocturnal creatures and crackle of the enormous fire are magnified tenfold.

"We have a visitor," Torvus thunders. "A woman of Nedé."

A quiet murmur ripples through the half-light. A cub boldly chirps, "Is she the Rescuer?"

Torvus grunts. "Silence!" Yet a moment later he answers the little Brute's question without malice. "No. She was a victim of . . . "

"She was no victim," a voice yells from the darkness. "She chased *me*."

A shadowy form ambles into the firelight, which illuminates a mop of thick, red hair. Not even the orange warmth of the blaze can hide his skin's paleness or mask the hate in Dáin's eyes. And he's pointing his harpy-beaked club at me.

My hand instinctively flies to my belt, and I curse to find it empty. If I had my bow, a blade—anything—I'd draw it and put an end to this evil thing. But defenseless as I am, I take a step backward instead. Jase grabs my arm.

"It's okay. Trust me. You're safe with us," he tries to reason. And though everything in me wants to snatch one of his many weapons and fight, or run, I force my feet to stay on the platform.

"You are not welcome here," Torvus booms. "You're no longer one of us."

"Not welcome?" Dáin sneers, sarcasm dripping from his words. "Isn't that a little extreme?"

"Not for a traitor! The rest of you, let this be a warning: anyone who defies my orders leaves this camp, left to eat hog plum and sleep with the cats."

"Yes, yes. I know. I'm only here for one small matter, and then I'll be on my way."

Torvus scowls but allows Dáin to continue.

"I thought I would pay you one last visit to ensure you do what you know you must, Torvus." He thrusts the club toward me. "I'm here to make sure she dies."

Rohan draws a blade from his back and steps slowly, deliberately toward the platform. He watches Torvus, though, not me. He eyes his leader closely, waiting for a command. I don't doubt he'd relish the opportunity to clock Dáin again. Jase tightens his grip on my bicep, for comfort or direction, I'm not sure.

Dáin takes another step forward. "You know what's at stake, Torvus. If you let her live—to go warn that snake—you'll give me no choice but to expedite my plans." He canvasses the ring of Brutes, all listening in stunned silence. "And I believe there are others here who would rather join me than die at the hands of the Alexia."

"Hot-headed fool!" Torvus's hands ball into fists. "You have no idea who this girl is. Do you think you can eradicate a termite mound by batting at it? You don't think about the consequences!"

Dáin flushes as he marches toward us. Now Jase whips me behind him and Torvus closes the gap, creating a two-Brute shield. Still, my heart thuds against my rib cage.

"At least I'm doing *something*," Dáin jeers, "instead of hiding out in the Wilds like . . . like a spineless Gentle!"

A few snicker—probably Fin and his friends. I expect Torvus to lose it, to go after Dáin and break him the way I know he could, but the massive Brute doesn't move.

"Muscle is pointless without a purpose," he growls, his age, anger, and strength colliding in a low, raspy urgency. Then, loud enough for everyone to hear clearly, he offers: "Who wants to go? Choose now who you stand with. The clan, or this traitor."

I can't imagine why anyone would follow Dáin over Torvus. What merit does this vengeful Brute hold over his leader? Who could follow someone who kills innocent people, who burns and destroys without cause? And yet . . . Fin is the first to walk through the veil of inferno toward my attacker, followed by at least ten others. The remaining majority shift uncomfortably.

"Thanks for the new recruits, Torvus. That worked out even better than I hoped," Dáin says, running his fingertips along the sharp teeth lining his club. "We'll be on our way then." He twirls the weapon once as he walks away. "Take good care of the enemy."

Silence stretches uncomfortably, until the defectors can no longer be heard traipsing through the brush.

I let out the breath I didn't realize I was holding.

"Real *fun*," I whisper to Jase, still hiding behind him.

He kicks my foot playfully, breaking some of the tension for us both. As he guides me forward to the platform's edge, Torvus addresses the remaining "clan."

"I make no apologies for my decision to let this woman live. To take life out of fear would make us no different than them. She will be returned to her home tomorrow. She has given her word to keep silent about what she has seen." He turns to me. "And only a coward goes back on one's word."

Torvus thrusts his right hand toward me, a Nedéan sign of

camaraderie. The gesture surprises me. How would a Brute know of such conventions? I'm also fully aware of the weight his action holds. If I respond in kind, I pledge my friendship with this leader. In effect, I vow to keep my word. *Can I?*

I don't have time to deliberate—no other choice. I extend my own arm, fingers barely able to grasp the bulk of his forearm pressed against mine, and seal my silence.

If you study a thick, rainy-season cloud long enough, you can watch it expand with multiplying moisture and electricity. Water vapor, high in the air, gathers steadily until the fledgling cloud cannot bear its own restless weight anymore and pours its guts onto the earth below.

A kind of rainstorm comes now—the uneasy tension of the previous minutes releasing in a gale of riotous energy.

A cheer swells from the gathering as Torvus nods solemnly, and someone hits a drum. Another joins the rhythm, deeper in pitch, and then a third and a fourth of a higher timbre. As Torvus retakes his seat, Jase plops down on the wood slats of the platform, letting his feet dangle over the edge. I join him, not sure what else to do.

Youthful Brutes pass meat and chicha around the renewed hubbub. A medium-sized Brute with a snakeskin fastened around his waist hands me and Jase skewers bulging with chunks of blackened meat. I nod my thanks, genuinely grateful for something edible. But how *does* one eat it? I glance at Jase for clues. He takes each end of the stick in his hands and bites right into the middle. I raise an eyebrow at him.

"Really? You eat it like *that*?"

"Oh, I'm sorry, should we eat it like *this*?" he teases, nibbling at the tip of charred flesh.

"Alright," I say, taking the challenge with exaggerated eagerness. I rip through the middle of my meat, filling my cheeks and letting the grease drip down my chin. Rich smokiness, with a hint of foreign spices, careens into my taste buds. It certainly tastes better than it looks.

"That's more like it," Jase says, beaming.

Still the drums pound, joined now by other instruments. They aren't much to look at, but serve their purpose: the clearing mushrooms with lively grating, whistling, thudding, scraping, and trilling. The music coaxes a handful of Brutes, finished with their meals, to dance around the edge of the fire ring. Their legs swing and stomp, crouch and spring, their hands spinning sticks and slapping each other in time to the music. The air pulses with the sound of their song; my heart beats in rhythm to the bass.

Someone lights the end of a torch and begins to spin it, faster and faster, until the fire blazes in a ring. He twirls the burning circle over his head, between his legs, and back up again. Two others join this new fire dance, at once dangerous and mesmerizing.

I'm suddenly struck by a memory of the Exhibition at Finca del Mar, how the dancers' delicate movements and bold leaps forced my heart to do the same. Their art was beautiful, smooth, sacred. This dance moves me too, though it is wild, playful, loud, and largely improvisational. Another contrast strikes me: how vastly different these Brutes are than those portrayed in the play—those enormous cloaked figures who snatched dancers without remorse.

*What if we have them all wrong?*

No—not all. We haven't completely misrepresented them. Dáin's reappearance underscores that. He doesn't even care about his own people, let alone women, or Nedé, or anything but himself. He'll hurt whoever gets in his way in order to destroy us. I can't be blinded to their true nature, even if their kind does include a bit of . . . this.

When the dancers collapse, exhausted, into their seats, another group takes their place, mimicking much of the same movement, but adding jumps and flips. In time, still others try their hand at the complicated movements.

I wonder where they learned all of this. Did Torvus teach them? I glance behind me, hoping to catch something in his expression, but the large wood chair sits empty now, a soft spotted pelt lining the place where he had been presiding.

"Will Torvus come back?" I ask Jase.

"Naw, probably not. He gets tired of our antics after a while. Besides, I think you remind him too much of—" he catches himself, and uncharacteristically chooses different wording— "of someone."

It's difficult to hear him over the drums, so I don't try further conversation.

A few minutes later, a cub approaches me with a shy smile, then boldly grabs my arm. He tugs at me, trying to pull me to my feet. I think I know where this is going. I plead silently with Jase, but he just laughs out loud, nodding to the little one.

"Fine," I yell at Jase, grabbing his arm in turn. "If I'm going, you are too!"

I've never been one for dancing. I mean, all women in Nedé have *opportunity* to dance, through classes, at celebrations and such, but I have much better agility on a horse than on my own two feet. Still, something breaks my inhibition—maybe the dark, maybe the drums, maybe the drink—and I let them lead me to the edge of the ring. I try to mimic their movements, letting my uninjured arm swing in wide circles, stomping my feet and bouncing in time to the drums in rigid form, but eventually what comes more naturally seeps out of my pores, and I just let my body do what it wants to do.

The Brutes don't seem embarrassed by my lack of skill. In fact, they laugh and cheer, urging me on until I'm too tired to dance another step. I half tumble back to the platform, laughing and teasing Jase, "Now *that* was 'fun.'"

He grabs a green coconut from a pile as we return, and when we sit, he hacks the top of it open with a machete before offering it to me.

"Here."

I gulp the bittersweet liquid as if I've never tasted it before, washing down the smoke and dryness, letting my heartbeat slow. My smile must match Jase's. In fact, I can't remember a time I felt happier, more free.

I take in all the strange and wonderful faces—dirty, angular, wide, narrow, young, large—and notice one staring back at me.

The dark brown of Rohan's eyes dances with the reflection of the flames. Only the faintest smile plays on his lips, but he seems pleased. At least, I don't think he's *unhappy*. He watches me watch him, and for some reason, I can't look away, even though my heart does cartwheels and my stomach flutters.

*I should look away.*

But I can't seem to. The sight of him intrigues me—all angles and bulk, courage and deep complexity. I want to know what thoughts run through his mind. And as the seconds pass, that feeling of wanting him close—that ridiculous draw I experienced in the cave, within the sunset—returns and multiplies. He's so . . .

Jase clears his throat, and I flush with embarrassment. My cheeks burn as if I just got caught doing something wrong, and I don't even know what it was. Embarrassment douses the prickles of electricity until I'm left with a puddle of soggy embers.

"Come on," he says. "You should get some rest. We'll have to start out early tomorrow."

———

Just when I believe I've caught it, sleep bounds away again, though I've forced myself to lie motionless on this stiff cot for hours. I blame my insomnia on the intrusive volume of nocturnal Jungle choruses and the shoulder that throbs from my reckless dancing. But sleeplessness is just as likely the result of the rhythmic breathing of two Brutes who sleep mere feet from me. Bright moonlight shifts through clouds and leaves, settling on their bodies in patchy luminosity. They sleep soundly—a happy, enviable state of being.

I was given Dáin's cot, which unnerves me more than I let on. Knowing his body lay on the same woven surface now cradling my skin makes it crawl. But with the bulk of Rohan and the kindness of Jase here with me, I let my mind wander to less disturbing thoughts. That's the idea, anyway, though it seems my mind has nowhere else to wander than troubling or inconclusive paths.

Knowledge is a funny thing: sometimes you learn information, only to realize you have more questions than answers to show for your trouble. The past thirty-or-so hours fall into that category. When I chased Dáin's mob toward the Wilds, I learned two things: that against all probability Brutes presently exist, and not only that, they were indeed responsible for the attack on Jonalyn's finca. What I have unlearned, though, outstrips that new information like a mudslide.

I am no longer certain whether Brutes are categorically self-serving, evil beasts. I don't know where these particular Brutes—some as small as my saddlebag—come from. Or, if Rohan is right to believe Gentles aren't born Gentle, how *they've* come to exist. I can't imagine what the cub meant by asking if I was the "Rescuer," or why Jase is more familiar with me than I with him. I can't reconcile Dáin's intent to kill me with Torvus's honorable refusal to do so, even though, tactically speaking, it would have been wise. And I don't know what I will do when I reach Bella Terra and then Finca del Mar. Will I keep this a secret—all of this wonderful, terrifying information? Will I keep my word to Torvus?

These questions feel important, I suspect with good reason. They demand answers, which will likely have enormous implications. But there's one more question—seemingly simple compared with the others—that knots my insides more than the rest.

Rohan stirs, flipping deftly on his narrow bed. I wonder for a moment if his eyes will open—hope they'll open—but within seconds his chest resumes rising and falling in deep, slumbering breaths. With him safely asleep, I study the curve of his lips, the thick line of eyelashes below his closed lids, the texture of his deep bronze skin. I wonder how it would feel if the hand under his cheek were replaced by my own. And that most difficult question of all gnaws at me afresh:

*Which is better?*

Brute? Or Gentle?

Though the comparison is too simplistic, I imagine Treowe reclining in the room with us anyway, and in my mind's eye I abandon Rohan's rugged bulk to consider Tre's round face, his weathered hands and slight frame. Even in my imagination he offers me a one-dimpled smile and a red hibiscus flower, echoing how I perceive his nature, I suppose. Tre is always looking for ways to make me feel special. He has never once yelled at or threatened me. He tempers my spirit, and my crabbiness, with his consistent calm. Perhaps that's why we enjoy each other so.

Tre embodies *safety*, and if I forget the Jungle and what I've discovered here, when I become Matriarch—yes, *when*—then I can help Tre. I could convince the Council to change our laws, and then he and I could always be friends. Now that I've been to the Brutes' camp, surely I could lead the Alexia here to contain them. Not kill them, of course—except Dáin—but hide them, let them live out their lives in peace. No one else would have to know of their existence. Women would be safe from Dáin and any Brute who could become like him.

And yet . . . Some invisible hand turns my chin from my imaginary Treowe back to Rohan's irresistible, slumbering form. A strange ache claws at my resolve.

This one—he can't have my allegiance. *I can't let him have it.* I don't trust what he would do with it.

Then what of this urge to slip my hand under his cheek, to cradle his face in my palm? And when I think of Jase's grin and the wildness of Tree Camp, why am I nearly sorry morning must come?

# CHAPTER SEVENTEEN

Camp was noticeably silent as the three of us descended the tree shortly after dawn. The Jungle may be the only place where morning is quieter than night, both animals and Brutes sleeping off the evening's diversions.

We dismount the platform, wind through the main camp, pass the abandoned fire ring, gray with ash and strewn with bones, and finally reach a grassy clearing. Callisto's nickers break the comparative quiet, like the voice of an old friend come to visit. Caked dirt patches add new patterns to the white sections of her hair, and her mane is so matted with barbs it could catch a fish, but, by Siyah, she's never looked so fine to me. I let her nuzzle me with her wet nose, though it smears my once-black vest with horse slobber and half-chewed leaves.

I reach out to rub her neck, but a crusty patch of blood stops me.

"What's this?" I mumble.

I don't remember her being injured there before. No, this is new. A bead of glistening red drips from the small wound. I stretch my fingers toward it to investigate.

"No!" Rohan yells, grabbing my hand, too hard.

"Ow!" I yell back.

"Don't touch it."

I yank my hand from his grip and snap, "What—you going to tell me Brutes are afraid of a little blood?"

Jase steps between us, trying to diffuse our tempers. "Bats," he says, soberly. He peers closely at Callisto's neck without touching the wound. "Vampire. She'll probably be fine, but just in case, you shouldn't touch her blood. And if she shows signs of any . . . " His voice trails off.

"Any *what*?" I press, failing to keep alarm from my voice.

"If she . . . starts acting strange, then you'll have to . . . " Jase seems reluctant to continue, and I stare at him, dumbfounded.

"*What?* What will I have to do?"

"You'll have to kill her," Rohan finishes. His matter-of-factness makes me madder.

"*Kill* her?"

"She'll probably be fine," Jase reassures, not very convincingly. "The odds are small that she'll get sick."

They don't know me—don't know the depth of my love for this horse. Her death would undo me. A Brute couldn't possibly understand that. Could they?

Rohan pours water from a smooth leather flask, washing the wound. Callisto doesn't seem bothered by the attention. Is that a good sign?

"How will I know? If she's sick, will she show it?"

"Likely," Jase answers. "We've never had horses, so I can't say for sure. But other animals, they get twitchy, or act strange, or freeze up. We call it 'the crazies.' Each animal shows it differently. But you'll at least get home. At *least.*"

I rub a hand down my horse's nose. Clumps of dried mud scratch my skin.

"I'm sure she'll be fine," Jase reiterates, placing a hand on my shoulder. "Here, I'll help you put the seat on it," he says, reaching for the saddle.

I almost correct his vocabulary but, not wanting him to feel silly, thank him instead.

Jase lifts the leather Alexia saddle onto Callisto's back, and I slip my arm out of its sling to buckle the cinch and breast straps, followed by the headpiece.

Despite the soreness last night, my shoulder moves better today, and I leave the sling behind. That slimy paste of Rohan's works wonders.

With Callisto properly saddled, I hand Jase the reins. He has already explained that he'll lead me, blindfolded, out of the Jungle. The prospect of being steered chafes my independence, but if it means avoiding another tranquilizer dart, he can lead me like a lamb all the way to the Sea. Besides, I'm past worrying that Jase will do me wrong.

Rohan places a bundle of dried meat and three mangoes in my saddlebag, then steps toward me, a length of cloth tucked into his waistband. My blindfold, I gather.

"Be careful out there," he says.

The implication takes a moment to register, but as his words sink in, my frustration with him a moment ago melts like butter in a pan. "You're not coming?"

He shakes his head. "Torvus's orders."

"Ah."

Why does that disappoint me? And for the love of Siyah, why won't my eyes meet his? I took the liberty of staring at this Brute long into the night; now, in daylight, I can barely bring myself to look at him.

"I want you to take this," he says, drawing a white bone dagger from a leather sheath on his leg.

The sturdy handle is carved with astonishing precision, intricately etched in a basket weave design. Above the guard, the two-sided blade—as long as his forearm—curves slightly at the tip. It's the work of a skilled artist, if *artist* can describe a weapon-maker.

"It's . . . impressive." I fumble for words, amazed that he made this himself and that, though it probably took weeks or months to finish, he offers it to me.

"Don't use it on Jase," he quips.

I'm thankful he doesn't seem to expect a grand show of gratitude, because I don't know what else to say. In fact, Rohan doesn't wait for further response at all. He's already behind me, preparing my blindfold.

I slide the dagger into a sheath on my otherwise-empty belt, and Rohan seals out the sun with a dense, scratchy fabric. The last thing I see is the massive mahogany tree, dotted with huts, stretching its sturdy limbs proudly over Tree Camp.

"*Please* be careful," Rohan's deep voice whispers, his hair brushing my ear, sending a shiver of prickles down my neck. His hands, rough and strong, slide from my shoulders to my biceps, which he squeezes lightly before releasing me. His touch shouldn't make me feel this way.

*He can't have it. He can't have your allegiance, Rei.*

———

It's easy to lose track of time when one is blindfolded on the back of a horse. The curious Jungle sounds—jabbering, tweeting, knocking, clucking, warbling—eventually become monotonous without eyes to find their sources, and I grow weary of trying to get my bearings. And so it feels like days, not hours, have passed by the time Callisto stops under me and Jase says, "You can take the blindfold off."

Hours of sightless travel have made me a little punchy, and I bemoan, "Really? Oh, can't I leave it on? I'm growing rather fond of it."

He smacks my leg, and Callisto shifts sideways at his unintentional directive. I laugh as he scrambles over a log to keep the reins.

Moments pass before my eyes adjust fully to the light, though the surrounding trees and brush shield us from the midday sun. Through a gap in the branches ahead, lowlands roll through Nedé, the wide swath cut by Highway Volcán blazing a trail toward its center. A dark smudge next to the road must be all that's left of the finca Dáin attacked two days ago. At least I have my bearings, even if they do bring a rush of unwelcome reality.

"Torvus told me to take you to your finca, but if I go with you, we'd have to take a much longer route so I could stay out of sight. Even that would be tricky, though, with your horse."

I hadn't considered any of this. "Of course," I say, as if I had. "I can find my way from here."

"I figured you could," he says, handing me my bow, quiver, and short sword. I hand the sword back, its place on my belt already occupied.

"Keep it. You can add it to your collection," I tease.

As I arrange my bow and quiver, something he said dogs me. "Jase?"

He looks up expectantly, his hazel eyes shining like glossy stones.

I want answers.

"You've been there before—to Bella Terra. That's why you know the way. You were hiding in the teak trees while I rode."

His smile fades. "You knew?"

"I may not have been quite as unconscious as I looked," I confess, cheeks heating with embarrassment. "I recognized Rohan the night of the attack—right before he drugged me. And your voice was familiar too. But why were you at Bella?"

He sighs, his eyebrows drawing in on themselves like the plant we toyed with yesterday. There it is again, his desire to tell me everything, to spell it out, plain as day. Why would he feel the need to keep secrets from me? It's like he's trying to protect me.

*Trying to protect me.* Just like—

"*Mother*," I whisper aloud, the answer I've been seeking since the night of the attack falling into my lap like a ripe custard apple. His eyes hold the shape and color of Mother's. Of mine. No wonder they seem so familiar. *He* seems so familiar.

Jase's bronze cheeks flush the tiniest pink. He turns abruptly, clearly uncomfortable. I dismount Callisto so I can make him look at me. So I can study him and see that I'm not going crazy.

"Jase, *why* were you at Bella Terra?"

He meets my gaze, and I will him to hold it. We stare at each other for a long moment, every second of which solidifies my suspicions. I could be looking into Mother's eyes from my four-poster bed, her form bent over a smaller version of me, her songs soothing me into sleep.

"Is she your—? How? How can you be—?"

"I told you, Reina," he says softly, "it's not for me to tell."

Bewilderment and anger heat my blood, which was already near boiling from hours of cooking in the Jungle. He has to be connected to Mother somehow, though I don't know how that's possible. *Why won't he just answer my questions?* Why is everyone always keeping things from me, like I'm a child?

256

"Fine," I snap, turning back to Callisto.

"Reina," he pleads, circling around me and blocking me from my horse. "I'm sorry. I really am. Don't be mad."

"Mad? Why would I be *mad*? You've only told me to trust you a hundred times since I met you, but you won't extend the same courtesy to me. You're right—there's nothing to be upset about."

He weighs my words, considering their validity. He knows I'm right. Well, he sees that I believe I'm right, which is almost the same thing.

"Okay," he relents, but he clearly remains conflicted, and that hurts me more than waiting for answers. I want him to explain, but deep down I know that telling everything isn't always right, or even kindest. I'm forcing his hand. I'm pitting him against his conscience, which contradicts mine.

"I only went there that one time," he begins, "after Torvus told me the Rescuer was—"

Guilt forces me to cut in.

"No—don't. Don't tell me. I'm sorry." As the rush of anger drains, my mind clears. "I . . . I do trust you. At least, I'll try to."

*And I'll go to the source for the answers I need,* I resolve silently. *I'll ask Mother.*

After a long second, Jase wraps his arms around me. The gesture's unexpectedness, and firm tightness, take me off guard, but I welcome it and return it. The sensation reminds me a bit of Treowe's hug in the Finca del Mar garden, yet carries an added assurance Tre couldn't offer. My best friend gave me solidarity. He knew me and sensed I needed comfort. Jase's strong embrace conveys confidence along with care, and that makes me braver.

I glance at his eyes one more time before mounting Callisto, just to make sure I'm not crazy. There it is, clear as sea water. Now that I recognize the similarity, I'm baffled I didn't catch it sooner.

"Will I see you again?" I ask, taking up the reins.

He shrugs his shoulders. "Don't know. I hope so. But if not, I'm glad I met you, Reina Pierce." Then he adds, hastily, as if embarrassed by his insensitivity, "Though I'm sorry about the circumstances."

I only look back once as I make my way down to the valley, toward Highway Volcán and everything I've ever known. But he has already disappeared into the green veil of the Jungle—vanished, as if the past three days never happened.

Part Four

# CHAPTER EIGHTEEN

WHEN WE WERE CHILDREN, Marsa claimed that when the moon was fat, "She'd finally had enough to eat." Of course, after circling around the world a dozen or so times, she'd lose all that beautiful excess and need some more of Marsa's fine cooking. I'm glad to have caught the bright moon stuffed nearly full tonight. The extra light proves useful, illuminating the road in the final hours of my journey and minimizing, albeit slightly, my fear that Dáin will jump out at me from the bushy growth flanking both sides of Highway Volcán.

When I trekked to the western edge of Nedé last week with Trinidad's patrol, the journey from Bella Terra to the border took scarcely half a day. Today, weighed down with worry that pushing Callisto too hard might cause her to fall prey to "the crazies," the reverse trip takes considerably longer.

We've travelled under the moon's gluttony for hours by the time the shadowed outlines of the twin rain trees appear, marking the lane home. I've passed under these leafy guards hundreds of times, and under normal circumstances, I'd notice their presence little more than the familiar bend up ahead. But recent events, and the enormous secret I've vowed to bear, have destroyed my happy oblivion, and tonight the rain trees' branches appear ghostly, dripping with vines and spiky bromeliads, backlit as they are by moonlight.

Callisto knows her way home, and once I've turned her toward it, there'd be no point in holding her back if I wanted to. Which I don't. I'm as anxious for my simple bed—and answers from Mother, if she'll give them—as Callisto is for her grassy pasture.

My eagerness to return practically defines irony. Less than two months ago, I couldn't wait to leave.

Do all women feel similarly when they set off to make lives of their own for the first time? Is it only once they've selected a destiny and begun a lifetime of work for Nedé's prosperity that they appreciate everything that came before?

A slight breeze stirs up the familiar scents of orange blossom, earthy animal musk, and watery Jabiru. I breathe it in like I've never smelled it before. Even the aroma of home has become strangely sacred in my absence. I suppose it helps to know this stop will be brief. I have to soak in all the beauty of home I can before returning to whatever waits for me in Phoenix City.

I deposit Callisto's tack and my weapons in the barn, then turn her out to sleep in the field before picking my way carefully through the paddocks toward the warm glow of a villa window. I enter through the kitchen door, the least creaky entrance in the house, hoping not to disturb anyone. To my surprise, Marsa occupies the kitchen table, husking roasted cacao beans by lamplight. The rich smell sparks an instant craving for a hot cup of creamy chokola, despite the dry season heat. The broad woman hums a tune, like a true Nedéan, her melody trailing away when she sees me.

"Merci Seigneur!" she murmurs, gathering herself up and charging across the kitchen. "Where have you been, petit?"

I had assumed I would see Mother first, and so during the long hours on Highway Volcán, I rehearsed what I would say to her, how the story would go, and what carefully-phrased questions I'd ask so as not to break my promise to Torvus unless absolutely necessary. Marsa's presence, and her knowledge of my disappearance, has thrown a monkey in the tree, and I'm dumbfounded for a moment, trying to decide what details—if any—I should explain.

"*Well?*" she prods, pressing her hands into her wide hips.

"I . . . got separated from my group . . . and I got hurt. But I'm alright now."

She takes me by the shoulders to look me up and down and, satisfied that I have all my limbs, attends to what is, in Marsa's opinion, the second highest priority.

"You need to eat something, manje."

"Yes please," I say, now keenly aware of my hunger and grateful for her eternal attentiveness to my stomach.

Marsa plates two savory pastries, bitter greens, and a slab of mango, and pours a glass of creamy goat's milk. I eat it greedily, and Marsa resumes hulling seeds and humming. Only once I've finished—barely refraining from licking the plate—does she speak again.

"Leda needs to know you've returned."

"I'll go tell her on my way to bed."

"She's not here, petit."

"Where is she?"

"Don't know. An Alexia came yesterday morning, said you were missing. Dom Leda got up quickly to go searching for you. Said she'd be back in a few days' time."

A few days? What did she expect to do, canvass the whole border herself? Her connections as head Materno and Center coleader might provide her with lodging, but where did she plan to search? What help would she be?

Still, that Mother went looking for me—alone, no less—doesn't make me resent her protection as I expected it would. Doesn't even make me grumpy toward her. In fact, her absence simply comes as a blow. I have questions I need her to answer. And, more than that, I think . . . I was looking *forward* to seeing her . . . was wanting to kiss her soft cheek—*imagine*—and hear her voice. She would probably say something pedantic, or quote something from her scripture-book, but in my present rosy-colored state of nostalgia, I might have tolerated even that. I miss Mother. *My* mother.

"But Jonalyn's here yet, in her room," Marsa continues, and at the sound of my sister's name, hope returns. Of course—Jo's here. I can finally, *finally* see her.

"Thank you, Marsa," I say, pushing myself from the table, almost tripping over my own feet in haste. Three steps down the hall, I toss over my shoulder, "It's good to see you."

———

The last room on the left side in the daughters' wing has housed only memories for so long that it feels odd to open the door and find Jonalyn sleeping there. My eldest sister left Bella to become a Materno nearly five years ago, young and lovely, determined to make Mother proud, promising to visit as often as she could. I tried not to resent that her duties managing the finca and having babies often kept her from making good on her promise to come see us, but my noble efforts proved futile. At least she succeeded at her first goal: Mother is more than proud of her. She beams whenever anyone mentions her eldest daughter.

Now Jonalyn has been forced home, her petite body tucked under a light blanket, and I want it to hold her there always. The large, whitewashed room smells like her again, tinged with orange blossom and plumeria, reminding me of years gone by when she would let me brush her hair while we sat crisscross on the narrow bed that cradles her now. Low lamplight settles on her features like dusk, and a long braid of dark hair hangs loosely over one shoulder. If it weren't for the faded pink blotches and crescent-shaped wound cupping her face, forehead to cheek, there'd be no sign of an attack.

In the corner, nestled atop a makeshift bed of thin cushions, her two-year-old daughter, Cassia, sleeps soundly. Soft brown curls stick to her kissable cheeks, and her fist clutches a cloth doll.

My sister's hand rests instinctively on an abnormally rounded abdomen as she sleeps. By Siyah! I had no idea she was carrying another child. Surviving an attack had to be traumatic enough. But to do so pregnant? No wonder her recovery has been slow.

I lower myself onto the edge of Jo's bed, and she stirs, then starts, pulling herself upright in a panic.

"Shhh," I comfort. "It's just me." I'm afraid I didn't consider how waking to a black-clad Alexia might give a sleeping somebody a fright.

Recognition softens her look of terror. "Oh, Rei!"

She tries to throw her arms around me, but her belly proves difficult to maneuver, and we settle for a side hug. I know little of Materno matters, but her stomach is huge; she must be getting close.

"I'm so glad you're okay," she breathes.

"So am I," I tease quietly, so as not to wake Cassia. "Sorry I scared you. I saw light through the door and thought you might be awake."

She glances sheepishly toward the small oil lamp. "I know it's wasteful, but I can't seem to sleep without it these days."

Her twenty-three years seem doubled tonight. Whatever happened the night of the attack must have been awful for weariness to settle so deeply into dark rings under her eyes.

"I'm so sorry—about what happened to you. And to the others."

Her eyes glisten, but she doesn't cry. She has Mother's softness in many ways, but my sister's fiery sense of justice burns through whatever tears might otherwise have come now.

"They were monsters, Rei," she says, her voice even lower. "*Monsters.*"

"What did they do?" I ask, wanting and not wanting to know.

"They were rifling through everything, taking whatever they wanted, attacking anyone who tried to stop them. One lit the villa on fire. Another had Serena pinned to the ground. I hit him in the face with a rake, but that didn't stop him; it just made him mad. He hit me over and over with a club."

My blood chills until bumps cover my skin, making every hair stand on end.

"What did he look like?" I hear myself ask, but I already know the answer. He had red hair and a freckled face, and his club had the hooked beak of a harpy eagle.

Her answer confirms my guess.

Violent anger bubbles and churns in my chest like a volcano preparing to blow. *How could he?* That monster. If I ever see him again, I'll . . . I'll run him through myself!

I swallow my rage, force it down, for Jo's sake.

"I almost lost the baby. Mother brought one of the Center nurses here. She saved my life, and my child's. Now she insists I stay in bed until my time to deliver."

Crickets thrum outside her open window, and I wonder what question I could ask that wouldn't make her relive any more horrific memories. After a moment, she breaks the silence for me.

"Reina . . . they were *Brutes*. And when you didn't come back,
I feared they got to you too."

She grips my hand so tightly her knuckles blanch. I hope my
face isn't equally drained of color as I consider how to answer.
I finally understand Jase's tortured hesitancy. I ache to tell her
everything, to confess I know who hurt her and what he tried
to do to me, to share the wonders I witnessed in the Jungle, that
some of the Brutes showed me kindness, and that one of them has
our mother's eyes. But then I remember my vow to Torvus, and
though I question whether I was wise to give it, I'd be disregarding
the Virtues if I broke my word, at least before I'm sure I need to.
So I feign ignorance in an act worthy of Ad Artium.

"How do you know they were Brutes?"

Now Jonalyn seems unsure, and I wonder if her disclosure was
a test. Was she fishing to see what I knew before deciding how
much to share?

"Can you keep a secret, Rei?"

"Of course."

"Mother told me. After the attack, she said it wasn't right to
keep the truth from me anymore. And now that you've been out
there—have seen what they can do, I think you should know too."

Panic fills me. *Now that you've been out there—have seen what
they can do* . . . Does she know where I've been? She would have
heard there was an attack near our patrol. She couldn't possibly
know the rest. I play off my unease as she continues.

"Mother already knew about the Brutes' existence; in fact, she
said there are more of them. She told me it was better if she didn't
share everything, but she insists they're not all as evil as the monsters that attacked us. And Rei—" she squeezes my hand tighter
still as she whispers— "she's connected to them somehow."

*Mother—connected to the Brutes.* I wish this piece of information shocked me more than it does. My surprise at Jonalyn's

revelation would have been exponentially greater before my world went all cockeyed a few days ago.

"How?" I ask, hopeful that I might not have to wait till Mother returns to get answers after all.

"I don't know." She shakes her head. "But she said that once I deliver the baby she'll explain more. She's probably worried any more stress will do me in." She smiles weakly.

"She's right," I say. "You should rest. I'm sure Mother will explain when she can."

I smooth a stray piece of her hair, and I feel like the older sister, comforting Jo the way she always did me. She seems amused by this role reversal too.

"I've never heard you defend Mother before," she says.

"Yeah, well, I guess Candidacy does that to a girl. All that diplomacy and dagger-throwing—and dodging Grandmother's icy glares—gives some perspective, you know?"

To hear her laugh again brings me great joy, but her smile quickly turns thoughtful.

"Do you want it, Reina? Can you really see yourself as Grandmother's successor? As the Mother of Nedé?"

"Two months ago, absolutely not. But things have . . . changed since then." It feels so strange to say it, to voice my growing desire to succeed the Matriarch, especially to someone who has only ever known me as a child, as a little sister. "I know I have much to learn, but I believe I could help Nedé."

She reads my face and nods. "Then I hope you win," she says. Her sincerity moves me. "Just don't kill Diablo as your first executive execution, or Ciela will incite a coup."

Laughter seems a fitting way to end the conversation; we could almost forget everything that went before and go on like we both belong here again. I tuck the blanket snugly around her and kiss her forehead goodnight.

My teak forest course seems to have shrunk in my absence, though my nostalgia for it has grown. So has my embarrassment, now that I've run the real thing, but I won't dwell on that. This morning is meant to be fun.

The obstacles all stand where I left them, though eager vines have already wound around a few of the supports, and one shoddy crossbeam has toppled.

Callisto shifts eagerly under me. I can't express my relief when I found her happily chewing grass in the field this morning. I think if she were sick, I'd see signs by now. So I decided to run her through our old training grounds to celebrate.

I don't need to retrieve my make-do weapons from the shed. I have plenty of the real thing now: my Alexia bow and quiver, plus the bone dagger from Rohan, which will serve well as a short sword. I'm conscious too of my uniform, though dirty and in need of mending. It symbolizes an accomplishment: taking hold of the dream that propelled me through a thousand laps on this course. And now, I am practically an Alexia.

"Chya!" I squeeze Callisto, and she leaps at the chance to showcase her improvement too.

The change in both of us is obvious. My horse flies through the course with practiced ease, nimbly trotting through the lattice of logs, running through a curtain of dried vines, sailing over the gap that used to present a challenge. My hand moves swiftly from quiver to bow string and back again, sending a steady stream of arrows toward every tree trunk target lining the perimeter. Arrow after arrow meets its mark. I have Trinidad's meticulous instruction to thank, though I'm sure it didn't hurt that I visualized Dáin's twisted face on every target.

Thinking of Trin reminds me that she still doesn't know where

I am. I should head back to the Arena as soon as possible this morning, even though that means I won't be here when Mother returns. I owe it to Trin. But first, there's one more person I need to see.

---

On the bank of the Jabiru, I watch the murky green water rush and swirl by. A tall piece of grass tickles the back of my arm. I yank it from the ground and wrap it around my finger, then let it spring off, over and over as I wait. I'm thinking about Little Boo and how I want to see him before I go when I hear . . .

"Hello, Rei." Treowe's voice is more welcome than any "home" sound I've heard yet. I grin at him as he slides down the trunk next to me.

"You got my message."

"Old Solomon looked like he might keel over, right there in the horse muck," he chuckles.

I had figured Tre would see Callisto in the barn when he went in to clean stalls this morning. But I wasn't sure how to tell him to meet me now, in the morning, a time we've never dared meet before. I never would have dreamed of being so bold a season ago. But I'm past all that now. I've seen too much—*un*learned too much—to care about convention. So this morning I simply walked up to Old Solomon and told him to have Treowe meet me "as soon as possible." Solomon was understandably shocked, but my next sentence puckered his face like he'd bitten into a green banana: "He'll know where."

I smile and hand Tre a mango, pretending as best I can that no time at all has passed since our last picnic—that the forces of the Matriarchy and the Jungle have not torn us from each other, haven't unsettled deep places in my soul. He takes the fruit with a one-dimpled smile, and we sit with our thoughts for a while.

I think back to a hundred other breaks we've shared here on the grassy hill overlooking the river, under our favorite fig tree. The shade has always offered respite from the humid heat of Nedé afternoons, as we talk about all the things best friends do, stuffing our faces with mangoes and dried fish, or bread and hard cheese. Our picnics, and his friendship, are the only things I've ever really loved about my life at Bella Terra. At least, until I left and learned the truth. Now I'm finding more to appreciate.

But, despite the nostalgia of being here with him, I can't long pretend that nothing has changed.

There's something about a good friend that compels you to bare your soul. And since I can't, my uncertainty and angst trickle out as a tentative question. "Would you ever hurt me, Tre?"

I can't look at his face when I ask him this. I don't need to see it anyway. I can already picture his eyes narrowed in confusion. Hurt me? Of course he would never hurt me. Why would someone who lives to serve the women of Nedé hurt any of us? Let alone my best friend. But I have to ask. What I have heard and seen has been fermenting in my mind like a vintage chicha, swelling and pressing, searching for a way out—maybe impairing my judgment like chicha too.

Out of the corner of my eye I catch his head whip around, an unruly clump of hair landing over his face. He pushes it back with a calloused hand.

"Hurt you?" The defensiveness in his voice makes the timbre even higher than normal. "Rei, what are you talking about?"

"I don't know. I . . . was just wondering if you think you would—if you ever *could*—hurt me."

Once out, the words sound ridiculous, and I wish I would have put more thought into how this conversation might go before opening my big mouth. But it doesn't matter now—the words are alive, giving voice to the fear and confusion that has gnawed at me since the Jungle. I trace my neckline with absentminded fingertips, remembering the pain Dáin inflicted, the suffocating panic, my helplessness.

Tre tips my chin up gently, forcing me to meet his gaze—a surprisingly bold gesture. "I would never do anything to hurt you. Not *anything*. You know that."

I can't blame the hurt evident in his tone, or even the mist glazing his eyes. Why did I even ask? I knew the answer. It's just . . . Rohan's question—I can't get it out of my mind.

"I'm sorry, Tre," I say quickly, hoping to keep him from the precipice of typical Gentle emotion. "I know you wouldn't. I'm just paranoid, with the raids and everything. But of course that isn't any of the Gentles. It couldn't be."

Tre seems appeased by my backpedaling, and I sigh inside with relief. He's literally the last person I would ever want to hurt. Besides, I know he doesn't have the answers I'm looking for and never will. Maybe I never will either. So it's best to just forget about all that for now, and instead breathe in the simple beauty of our few stolen moments before I must return to the chess game being played by the Candidates in Phoenix City.

"It's okay," he says, taking my hand and rubbing the top gently with his thumb. The sensation grounds me, and I'm shamed by his undeserved kindness. "I wish I knew who was doing it too. But you never need to question my care for you."

I smile appreciatively, and we settle back against the tree.

After a long moment, Tre turns to face me again. It seems to take him some courage, but he manages to say, "I was hoping you'd bring it up, but . . . and it's okay if you don't want to . . . "

"Out with it."

He sighs. "I know you were missing. I overheard Dom Pierce telling Old Solomon when she left. What happened, Rei?"

*What happened?* Such a simple question. One I should have seen coming.

But I have no simple answer to offer in return. Though I could dismiss his question with denial, that doesn't seem fair. He's my truest friend. But I've also made a promise, and what would it benefit Tre to possess the truth anyway? It would only put him in harm's way.

"It's better you don't know."

"Okay," he says, meeting my eyes with such trust that I have to fight not to blurt out the whole of it. "You're safe. That's the important thing."

I nod, trying to express reassurance. Tre doesn't know that those very words, rearranged, are testing my entire worldview: *Is my safety*, I wonder, *the safety of all of Nedé's women, truly most important?* If so, my promise to Torvus is less so, and I should tell the Matriarch everything. The Alexia should then dismember Dáin piece by piece with his own razor-backed club for what he's done, and annihilate the rest of the Brutes so that none of them can ever choose to harm us again.

Relief accompanies the prospect of the world returning to the way I've always known it to be. But the fantasy is short lived, replaced by the memory of Rohan's dark eyes, the strange and compelling angles of his face, illuminated by firelight. Jase's wholehearted acceptance and easy laughter. The small, stick-swinging, lizard-chasing cubs. Do *they* deserve to die?

What did Rohan say? Brutes can be violent or they can be gentle—they choose. *No one has taken it from us*, he said. If that's true—if hurting women isn't compulsory—then just because some of their kind *have* doesn't mean they all *would*. Besides, when Grandmother shot that Gentle, didn't it reveal wickedness in her heart too? Maybe we all have evil somewhere inside, at least a little. In light of all my resentment and shortness with Mother—angel though she be—plus my inability to keep the Virtues—that would make sense.

Minutes drift downstream with the river's current, and still Tre rubs the back of my hand. I stare at the gesture with new eyes. He has always been even-tempered, kind, helpful, *gentle*. But if Rohan is right, my friend wasn't born as such. Was Rohan suggesting that without some kind of interference, my mild-mannered companion would be a Brute too?

A sudden ache stabs at my insides. What would that imply about our friendship? Has Tre had any choice? Or is our relationship merely a by-product of some kind of alteration? The possibility shatters my heart more than any other. Forced devotion is not devotion at all. That I know for certain.

I need answers. Though part of me wishes we could just stay here in this moment forever—avoid whatever change, whatever heartbreak, might come—I need to go.

"You'd better get back," I say reluctantly. "Old Solomon's going to keel right over if you're gone too long."

He shrugs as he gets up. "That'd be better than a phase-out."

He says it with a twinkle, but his joke pricks my conscience, reminding me of the Center and the terrible choice every Gentle must make: stinger or phase-out, if they even live long enough to decide. My stomach churns from all of it—sadness over Tre's fate, worry that our friendship has been an obligatory sham, guilt for keeping the Jungle secret, and worst of all, realizing that no matter how much I want to erase what I now know, I can't. And because of that, nothing will ever be the same. Not between me and Tre. I suspect all my relationships will be altered in some way.

I stand with him, and he gives me a soft hug. I kiss his cheek, intentionally this time, not like in the Finca garden, when it just happened.

"You're a good friend, Treowe," I say. I know the words aren't new, but they carry new meaning. Then I turn to walk away.

"Can I always be your friend, Rei?" His urgent plea stops me as surely and abruptly as if he had grabbed my arm.

I want it to be true, but I know there's only one way to make it so.

"If I win," I say.

"Then win, Rei of Sunshine. Whatever it takes, please win."

---

Back on Highway Volcán, a toucan's distinct call distracts me, mercifully, from my tangled thoughts. I scan a nearby tree for her, easily spotting the lime green and red of her horn-like beak. Such a strange appendage. I never tire of the birds, despite their intrusive chatter. Her black back humbly defers all the attention to the party colors of her chest and beak. Those brighter hues—vivid yellow, red, orange, blue, and green—bring to mind the Matriarch's brilliant, airy robe. The bird calmly plucks a palm fruit with the tip of her stately beak, pauses, then tosses it up to herself and swallows it whole, doing it again and again, until the branch is stripped bare. The bird's eating habits only underscore the comparison, and I am suddenly not very fond of toucans.

Why am I so nervous to see Grandmother? I have no reason to suspect she would know more than I tell her, and yet a hollow, jittery sensation dogs me when I imagine encountering her upon my return. Maybe I won't need to. Surely the Mother of Nedé has enough matters of state to attend to without also taking too much of an interest in her granddaughter getting "lost" on border patrol. One can hope.

A storm builds in the heat of midafternoon. By the time I've reached the outskirts of Phoenix City, the clouds melt to the earth, pattering the cobbled stones. The smell of brick and sky collide. They dance to the serenade of ten thousand drops hitting one hundred surfaces in tandem: leaves, brick, grass, leather, horse.

The rain intensifies when I turn off Calle del Sol and onto another wide road toward the Arena. I'm hoping to find Trin, to let her know I'm okay.

When I hitch Callisto and pass through the high, stone archway, I'm not surprised to see her training a contingent of Alexia in the center of the Arena, ambivalent to the downpour. What I didn't expect was the relief, the fierce affinity, that warms me at the sight of her. Trin's strong voice carries authority across the expanse of the Arena, challenging her charges to run faster, throw harder, and shoot straighter, but her tone isn't cruel. Not like Adoni's can be. Speaking of, I don't see the Alexia leader anywhere.

I make my way across the waterlogged sand, but Trin sees me before I reach her. She doesn't make a big show of it—that's not the Alexia way—but I can tell she's glad to see me. Maybe as much as I am her. Water drips from the ends of soggy, gold-tipped braids, but her face is as bronze and striking as ever.

"I'm back," I say, lamely.

"Where the bats have you been?" she barks, like Marsa sometimes does when she's piping mad and relieved at once.

"Missed you too."

Her anger diffused by my sarcasm, she slaps my back.

"It's good to see you, Candidate."

"Same."

"But really—where have you been? What happened?"

Here we go. Time to tell my carefully curated tale. A true story—just not the *whole* true story.

"Callisto was having trouble keeping up, and I saw a suspicious group running toward the Jungle. I figured they had something to do with the attack, so I chased them. But I got knocked off Callisto and hurt my shoulder."

"Knocked off? How?"

"A trap."

"What kind of trap? Any detail might help."

Why didn't I anticipate a more curious interrogator? I try to think quickly, evaluate the necessity of—and potential danger in—the added details without delaying a response. "Some kind of rope, thrown at her legs. I didn't get a good look before they drugged me."

Trin's eyes widen. "They *drugged* you?"

Hmmm . . . maybe that last part should have been omitted? I force myself to stay calm, act like I meant to provide that information.

"Poison-tipped dart."

I'm completely off script now. I avoided lying to my sister, and Treowe too, but they didn't press for details I haven't properly sifted through.

"When I woke up, they were gone. It took me a while to find my way out of the Wilds, and then I came here. Well, I stopped home first, and then came here."

I've crossed a threshold—abandoned the world of truth and stepped into a false reality, one where I must keep track of my lies so as not to contradict myself. What's worse, I don't even know if I'm doing the right thing in keeping the truth from Trin. But it's too late now.

She looks me over, assessing my physical condition. Her eyes linger near my hip, then narrow.

"Where'd you get that?" she asks.

Well, isn't that helpful? I left Rohan's dagger hanging from my belt. Of course Trinidad wouldn't overlook the white handle protruding from the leather casing.

*Think, Reina. Leave no chink in your story.*

"I found it . . . while I made my way out of the Jungle."

She seizes the handle and unsheathes it in one fluid motion. She turns the blade in front of her, testing its sharpness with her thumb.

"We found a similar weapon at an attacked finca some time ago, but nothing like this. It's impressive."

I didn't have anything to do with its creation, and yet I feel validated somehow. Why should it make me proud to be associated with him?

Trin looks me square in the eye. "What else can you tell me? They were close enough to drug you. Did you see anything that could help us find them?"

No clever turn of phrase can sidestep this question, because the only answer is yes. I *have to* give her something. *Think, Reina!*

"I . . . uh . . . " My eyebrows scrunch with concentrated effort. "Yes—it was dark, but I think one—the leader—had red hair."

"Anything else?"

"No," I lie, pretending to be upset that I can't offer more. "That's all I saw."

She holds my gaze, completely hiding her thoughts. Does she believe me? She sucks her teeth, and I wonder if our rapport is the only thing keeping her from pressing further. When she hands me the dagger instead of keeping it for Adoni, I am sure of it.

"Adoni took a patrol to the border to search for you. I'll ride out and tell her you've returned. Go back to Finca del Mar. The other Candidates are already there."

I nod, the motion sending trickles of rain into my eye sockets.

"Reina," she says. Hearing my name in her voice rings odd. "I'm sorry I didn't find you. I looked everywhere. I only came back to get reinforcements. Adoni insisted she return to the border herself. I had to stay. I want you to know . . . it didn't feel right leaving you behind."

I've never seen Trin so . . . tender. I hadn't once considered she might feel guilty for losing a Candidate and, maybe it's selfish, but her remorse relieves me. I feel *less* bad knowing I'm not the only one squeezed by the constricting force of regret. My relief, however slight, makes room for a little sass.

"Don't go all Materno on me now," I jest. "It's alright. Everything turned out okay in the end."

"Yes, I suppose it did." Trin straightens up, resuming her usual toughness. "One more thing," she says, lowering her voice, though I doubt anyone can hear us in this rain. "Be careful." She leans in, until the water from her hair drips onto my shoulder. "I don't have any specific information, but I suspect Matriarch Teera has set some of the Candidates against each other, testing their allegiance."

"I guessed as much," I say.

"You may be safer because you're related, but I wouldn't count on it."

Neither would I, but I don't say so. "Thanks, Trin."

"I don't know what you'll be walking into when you arrive. Stay alert and watch your back. Especially where Jamara's concerned. You've seen the price she's willing to pay to win."

"But she already had her test—Bri has the scars to prove it."

Trin arches an eyebrow. "Who says there's only one?"

# CHAPTER NINETEEN

THE CLOUDS FINALLY RUN OUT OF RAIN and race across the horizon to collect more. In their wake, Finca del Mar's massive, white plaster walls and ornate hardwood trim shimmer with millions of water droplets in the golden evening light. Compared to Bella Terra, the Matriarch's home has always seemed luxurious—perhaps even excessive. But now, comparing the finca to Tree Camp, the words "grotesquely indulgent" come to mind. Who could ever need all this?

The Finca's ambivalence to the Virtues aside, it curiously reminds me of that other, wild place. The smallest similarities spark memories of the Jungle, like the abundant palm fronds shaking off their bath in the sea breeze. Or the cluster of bird-of-paradise flowers with their pokey, feathery heads. Every emerald green hedge. Even the rain tree plays games with my mind, standing like a toy version of the giant mahogany towering over the Brutes. Why does the entire Finca seem a manicured, sanitized version of the Wilds?

As Callisto carries me down the long driveway, I force my mind to focus. If Trinidad is right, I have to concentrate—I have to forget the Jungle. Eyes open. Mind sharp.

As I approach the sprawling villa, I notice again the plaque above the threshold, the aged patina of its bronze, Latin words lending extra solemnity: *Protect the weak. Safety for all. Power without virtue is tyranny.* They are Tristan Pierce's words, standing guard over every Matriarch, every woman who has ever walked through Finca del Mar's doors. If I succeed, I will pass under Nedé's maxim for the rest of my days. I straighten under the weight of the words. I still believe in them. But do they yet ring true in Nedé?

Does Nedé still protect the weak? The weakest among us are Gentles, and we treat them ill. Are all safe in Nedé? I doubt the Jungle Brutes would be safe here. Is our power grounded in virtue? Only if the women who hold the power are. Matriarch Teera will do *anything* "for the good of Nedé," or so she reminds us. Perhaps that's virtuous, I don't know.

Domus emerges from nowhere, meeting me at the oversized pond at the base of the villa steps. He claps his hands together.

"Dom Pierce," he says, rather enthusiastically for a Gentle. "It is *good* to see you. Come, come, off your horse."

I oblige. "Thank you, Domus," I say warmly, and when I remember that I'm not supposed to thank him, I don't care. Then I do care, remembering that I have to act the part if I'm to have any chance at Apprentice. I hand him the reins matter-of-factly.

"Take her to Neechi. He'll know what to do for her."

"Of course," he says, unsuccessfully hiding some personal amusement.

Right—I shouldn't be on first-name terms with the stablehand either. You'd think that after nearly two months of this I'd be able to bridle my backward ways. But I can't seem to treat the Gentles with indifference—let alone contempt—no matter how vital it is that I do so.

"The Matriarch will want to see you. I'll have the kitchen set another place at dinner. It is *good* to see you, Dom Pierce," he says again. He bows, then leads my mare toward the stables.

*If only Grandmother will feel the same.*

---

I knock three times on the oversized door of the Matriarch's office, the echo reverberating in my hollow chest. *Fear is irrational, Reina. You haven't done anything wrong.*

"Come in." As usual, her terse voice implies the opposite.

I've never actually entered Grandmother's office, not on any of my visits to Finca del Mar. The room is bigger than I imagined, maybe ten meters long and almost as wide. Plaster textures the walls with smooth, fan-like strokes, and everywhere there is gleam and parchment. Mounds of parchment. Grandmother presides at the largest desk I've ever seen. She also hangs on the wall behind herself, in an enormous portrait depicting her as a much younger woman. The painting draws me in. She looks . . . lovely. Strong, but somehow less fearsome. Perhaps her long, cinnamon-colored hair softens her. Or her rounder curves. Or perhaps the expression on her youthful face. I've never seen Grandmother with a smile so genuine. So when I look down again at the silver-haired, wiry woman below, with the high-arched eyebrows and pinched lips, I decide to pretend I'm talking to the *other* Matriarch. The inanimate one suspended on the wall.

"Rein—Dom Pierce." Her surprise is quickly replaced by a cool transcendence. "You look awful."

"Matriarch Teera," I reply, dipping my head in feigned deference. "I feel worse."

She stands, her desk remaining between us. "Explain what transpired to separate you from the Alexia patrol."

I'm glad I wasn't expecting her to waste time on a happy reunion, or I might be hurt by her all-business demeanor.

"We encountered an attack. I pursued several figures into the Jungle, but they threw me from my horse with a trap."

Grandmother looks angry and irritated—her version of thoughtful. She's concentrating very hard on my words, perhaps sifting through unseen matters. After a moment she asks, "How far into the Jungle did you go?"

My chest pounds. I hate not knowing how much she knows. What if there's more to the question—something that could trap me later?

"I don't know exactly." That's mostly true anyway. I was unconscious on the way in, blindfolded on the way out.

"You don't *know?*" Sarcasm drips from her voice like water from a soggy cloud.

*C'mon, Reina, act like a Matriarch! You can't let her see you sweat.* I force resolve into my voice, match her sarcasm with condescension of my own.

"Being knocked out has a way of hindering clear thinking, if you know what I mean. I was drugged—with a dart."

As my words sink in, even the wrinkles in Grandmother's face freeze, one eyebrow levitating above the other.

"Indeed," she says.

Her evenness unsettles me, and I wonder what she's more upset by: the fact that I was drugged, or that I dared raise my voice at her. I can only hope she'll assume my Alexia training has simply toughened me up, taught me not to mince words.

I prepare to parry another question, but none comes. Instead she skirts her desk and, as if intentionally trying a different angle, moves to stand uncomfortably close to me.

"Unthinkable," she says. "That must have been very difficult for you."

"It was."

"And if any information that would help the good of Nedé *does* come to mind, of course you will notify me immediately." She tilts her head to one side and taps a finger under my chin.

"Yes, of course."

"Well, now that you've returned, you will join the other Candidates in your daily routine until Nedé's two hundredth anniversary celebration Saturday next."

"Where you will choose your Apprentice," I finish for her, trying to look more confident than I feel.

"Yes." The weight of her hand on my shoulder startles me. "Though I doubt my selection will surprise anyone." She gives me a curt little smile.

My face flushes, but I hold her eyes. Maybe I didn't muddle this after all. Maybe I somehow convinced her I do have what it takes. A new emotion emerges from the aftermath of worry: hope. And hope is a powerful ally.

---

As I climb the marble staircase to the second floor, en route to the Senator's Suite, a thought that nagged me on my ride from Bella Terra this afternoon resurfaces. I was remembering the bizarre sensitive plant I discovered with Jase, which made me wonder whether there'd be an entry about it in the field guide I stumbled upon that day I perused the third floor. And *that* made me curious whether some of those other books might have answers I don't know to look for. At least, they might be interesting.

If I hurry, I might have just enough time to revisit them and still wash my dirt-caked skin before dinner. I take the second flight of stairs two-by-two, reach the third-floor landing, and half sprint down the hallway of paintings. Around the corner, I find the red velvet sofas of the sitting room looking as clean and lonely as the day I happened upon them, weeks ago now.

Dust-free books line the far shelf, seemingly undisturbed as well. I read over their titles again, grabbing the field guide and one about horses. Near the end of the shelf, a mid-sized book with no title strikes me as odd. I don't remember seeing it there before, but then, I didn't spend much time studying the shelf before Domus startled me out of my wits.

I pinch the worn, brittle leather spine, and pull it down gently, worried the whole thing might fall apart in my hands. I carefully split it down the middle. Surprisingly, ill-formed handwriting fills the lines with fading ink. This isn't a book; it's a log of some sort. And it smells like age. I read:

*February 27, 2070*

*This month marks three years in Nedé. The haven continues to flourish without any sign of danger. It's better than I imagined, really. In fact, there's so much peace it may finally be breaking through the decades of terror I endured before the Coalition. I'm beginning to notice an unfamiliar feeling: hope. It pops up in unexpected places, at unexpected times. I only wish Sasha were alive to see this place. She would have loved the gecko that lives in my cabana, though she'd never agree to calling me "Matriarch."*

*The rain's starting again, so we'll have to pause construction of the first Hive. Progress has been slow, but eventually it will house several hundred Gentles . . . .*

The entry continues, with more preceding and following—pages and pages of what I can only assume are Tristan Pierce's own musings.

Tristan was our first Matriarch. She knew better than anyone what it took to rule Nedé. I'd be crazy not to glean her knowledge, learn from her secrets. I'm greedy now to devour it, as if the leather-bound words hold the key to following in her footsteps toward the Matriarch's seat—never mind answering my questions.

I can't help myself. I return the other books and tuck the log under my arm instead. A shot of adrenaline makes me jittery. Though not necessarily forbidden, the priceless treasure isn't mine, so—should anyone find me with it and ask questions—I rehearse my excuses for having it all the way down the wide, smooth steps back to the second floor. I'm almost too nervous to look behind me when I enter my room and quietly close the door. I carefully place the log in a dresser drawer under a scarf, and quickly shut it in, as if the act signifies my getting away with it.

*Rei, you'd make a terrible thief,* I chide myself. But something tells me this deviance will be worth my shot nerves.

---

I arrive at dinner clean, but late. I don't care if Dom Russo fusses about it, though. Having a maniacal Brute threaten me with a tooth-backed club minimizes the terror of a woman wearing a pelt-print dress.

The Candidates have already begun eating their delicately garnished seafood ceviche by the time I enter the botanical dining room. Nari starts as I pull a chair next to her.

"Reina? You're back!" She leaps up and hugs me eagerly. I wasn't expecting *that*, but welcome the gesture nonetheless.

"Yes—just," I explain.

Bri doesn't stand, but she looks as pleased as I've ever seen her. "I'm glad you made it," she says. "Otherwise *that* witch," she flips her head toward Jamara, "would've had an open road to ruining the Matriarchy." She frowns at Jamara, who doesn't even look up from her plate.

"I see nothing changed while I was gone," I direct at Bri, but my sarcasm carries no bite. In fact, I feel a sudden, strange affinity for the fiery girl from Amal.

Glancing around the table, I notice one Candidate is missing. "Where's Yasmine?"

Nari's face falls. "She withdrew from the Candidacy a few days ago. She . . . took a 'fall,'" her eyes flicker discreetly toward Jamara, "while we were on border patrol."

"*Fall?*" Bri gapes, chased by a string of curses. Discreet is not in her constitution. "You know," she says, piercing Jamara with a scathing look, "it takes a real *brute* to hurt someone like Yasmine."

I wince at the insult—it carries a different connotation to me now.

Jamara severs a shrimp from its tail with her teeth. She doesn't respond to Bri. Doesn't even acknowledge her.

Bri's right. What kind of threat would Yasmine have been to any of us? She had a knack for history and Politikós—her mind held worlds of information—but we all knew the Matriarch would never accept her fragile disposition. She wasn't going to win. And yet, instead of protecting the weak, Jamara pushed her out by force?

That means Trinidad had it right: Jamara will keep fighting to win. And none of us is safe from her.

Bri finishes her tirade with a long gulp of chicha. Turning to me, she asks, "So what happened to you, anyway?"

I give the three Candidates a simple form of my story, with

few details and a good measure of ambivalence. Thankfully they don't pry for more. Bri just quips, "Lucky you made it back *just* in time . . . to sit on your butt all week while the Matriarch figures out who she'll choose at Nedé's little party."

"You don't think she has chosen yet?" Nari asks.

Bri shrugs, then looks at me. "Depends whether she has all the information she needs to decide."

Nari looks thoughtful, but I get Bri's meaning exactly: Have we all been tested? And as far as I know, I'm the only one whose loyalty might still be in question.

---

I exhale as my body slides between the cool, silken sheets. I won't deny that I've missed the plushness of this bed, and the salty, fresh breeze that blows through the seaward windows each night.

By warm lamplight, I remove Tristan Pierce's logbook from the dresser drawer and open the brittle leather cover, ravenous to know everything about our revered first Matriarch—any tidbit that could give me an edge . . . or answer my questions. The first entry reads,

*April 11, 2050*

*Doc Ferrelli said I should try writing my thoughts because it will help put the past to rest. Sounds like bull to me, but I'm not as screwed up as I was before I started seeing her, so I guess I should try whatever she asks. Doc also says I should turn my "negative energy" into a "constructive outlet." "Be the master of your emotions, and you will find solutions," she says. I told her I find voodoo dolls constructive. She didn't look amused.*

*April 18, 2050*

*Another nightmare. This time they all held me down in a pit of mud—every man who's ever hurt me. How can I be the "master of my emotions" when I'm being raped in my sleep? And the only "solution" I can think of is to hunt them down and kill them slowly.*

I suppose this is more of a personal diary than a log. I skim through the next few pages, which mostly detail Tristan's horrific dreams. With each page turned, my confusion grows. *This is our first Matriarch?* She sounds nothing like the noble, driven, selfless founder I've heard about, sung about, practically idolized since childhood. This Tristan seems unstable at best, vengeful more likely.

From what I can gather, she must have been hurt terribly by Brutes. Especially one she called a "father."

*December 9, 2052*

*With Dr. Ferrelli's help, I feel more like the old Tristan. I guess the shrink has some sense. Having a "solution" to focus on has helped me master my emotions. Or at least channel them. Though maybe that's the same thing? Seven months ago I formed a Safety Coalition, in honor of Sasha, for women who have been hurt by men. So far we have about twenty women who meet at Doc's office when she's not using it. It feels good to help others.*

*October 30, 2054*

*Those slimy narcissists on Capitol Hill actually passed it. Of course they're spinning it like this law is liberating women's choice, but all the Sexual Liberation Act does is legalize their sick lusts. Now men can pimp girls no matter their age—film it, make VR*

*of them—whatever they want. And we're powerless to stop them.*
*They're not men. They're brutes. I'm afraid this is the beginning of*
*the end for women. But what can we do?*

I have no idea what most of this means, but I've heard the word
"men" before. Rohan had said *they* were men—the Brutes in the
Jungle. The potential implications produce a headache, but I force
myself to keep reading and try not to jump to conclusions. Yet.

Tristan catalogs more dreams, and a fight she had with her best
friend, Melisenda, because she won't leave someone who has hurt
her. Several pages later I read,

*November 6, 2055*

*As I suspected, crimes against women have escalated since the bill*
*was passed. Europe, Asia, Africa—they're all following suit. It's like*
*the psycho sickos opened Pandora's box and all the perverted evil*
*in the world has been unleashed. All over the world women are*
*being trafficked, filmed, pimped, raped. Not that the media reports*
*it much anymore. It's old news. I only know how bad it is because*
*the Safety Coalition is exploding with new members. So when the*
*occasional headline does show up, I pin it up at my new office, so*
*I don't forget what they're capable of.*

The stress of the day and the coolness of night cause my eyelids
to droop. Every other page I have to pinch my arm to stay awake,
but I won't stop. Years pass under my tracking, sleepy eyes.

*January 31, 2063*

*The Coalition continues to spread like wildfire. New chapters*
*spring up daily around the world. We have millions of members,*

and the executive leadership team is up to 247 women, representing every country in the world, and all fifty states. At our secret meeting last month, they vowed with me to stand up for women everywhere against men's appetites. We must do something, for all those who are powerless to protect themselves.

February 3, 2063

Doc Ferrelli has advised me to "find solutions" so many times in the hundreds of hours I've spent on her couch that the inane phrase is drilled into my psyche. But what solutions? So many women have been devastated and abused at the hands of men. But we control nothing. Not the money, not the power, not the justice system. Probably the only thing men don't have a hand in is pushing babies out.

February 24, 2063

I've been thinking: women do control the birthing process. Except for doctors, I've never heard of a man who wasn't squeamish about a baby coming out of his playground. What if we could use that to our advantage?

March 1, 2063

Mel thinks I'm crazy (nothing new), but she says it's possible, at least theoretically, to create a vaccine that would block testosterone in infant boys. Apparently other applications of testosterone-blocking injections already exist, in cancer treatment and gender therapy. She was hesitant, of course—doesn't want to set me back in my "mental progress," wonders about the ethics, yada yada—but she

*agreed to do some research and run the theory past a few other
female lab technicians.*

*July 24, 2064*

*Mel did it. She figured it out: a vaccine for infants that prevents
testosterone from reaching viable levels, AND another "vaccine"
for existing testosterone-carrying men that obliterates their
sperm. I have a meeting today with my contact at Xavier
Pharmaceuticals to see what it would take to mass produce, and
my media maven assures me that with the right positioning,
fake reports of the "Scrotia Virus"–more contagious than
coronaviruses and AIDS combined!–will easily go viral. Pun
intended. Mel and I had a good laugh brainstorming slogans
that would convince male government officials to mandate
the vaccine. I guarantee a threat of impotence will have men
lining up around the block for their shots. Side note: it's a
little disconcerting how easily our vaccine "additives" and
"preservatives" have passed through federal testing. Either Mel
is really good at what she does, or there are more holes in these
regulations than Swiss cheese.*

I don't know what "testosterone" is, but I suspect I've just found
my first answer: the vaccine *is* what makes Gentles different from
Brutes. I rub my temples to stay awake. To find out more. Another
entry, sandwiched between a string of nightmares, reads,

*November 7, 2064*

*I introduced the framework for "The Liberation" at the Safety
Coalition's leadership council last month. The response was
overwhelmingly positive. Some have reservations, but after*

*meeting with each leader individually the past few weeks, they
have accepted the truth: for the safety and survival of women,
we must do something. Men are broken. Maybe they weren't a
hundred years ago, I don't know. But something has changed in
the twenty-first century. Maybe they've corrupted their own DNA
with their unchecked addiction to the "new drug," as a movement
from my mother's era put it. Sometimes I wonder how the world
would be different if they'd stopped the flood before it started—
maybe put an end to online pornography before it warped into an
addiction of pandemic proportions.*

Still the entries come, some filled with names, others detailing
the merits of what I assume are locations. Most have pencil marks
through them. A dozen pages later, the name Siyah catches my
attention. It's tucked within an entry dated August 1, 2065:

*I knew that Iranian coalition member was fierce, but Siyah
Assad has stopped at nothing to enact the Liberation in one of
the most difficult regions to coerce. She and most of her 5,000
ninja rangers disguised themselves, wearing facial hair and
dressing as men to slip in and out of military sites, banks, and
hospitals throughout the Middle East. I hear they can shoot
bows like blasted Robin Hood—never mind slit a man's throat
without a sound. She approached me at our last meeting,
strongly suggesting we form a military detail wherever we
create the safe haven. I told her I knew just the black boots
for the job.*

Siyah must have been as brave as we are taught, though I might
prefer Dom Bakshi's legend to imagining our first Alexia leader
soundlessly *slitting a man's throat*. Still, I can see why she has a
constellation named after her.

The very next entry reads,

*August 4, 2065*

*I can't share details even here, but the SC representative of a certain country has approached me with a solution to our greatest problem: where to go once the Liberation has been executed. Because of her position, she can grant us land that will be touted as a top-secret military base dealing with toxic biochemicals. It will give us everything we need: land, resources, privacy, a lab, and a place to store the Bank. There's even a horse breeding facility on site, though I don't know what we'll do with that. Preparations will begin immediately. Mel secured a list of fertility centers by country, and we have tasked the respective national leaders with discreetly destroying each one. Our own bank will be the only one in existence, and all that we need to begin anew. Seventy-four SC members have already committed to join me. The sisterhood is rising.*

The next entry is the one I first chanced upon—marking Tristan's third year in Nedé. This time I keep reading.

*... The rain's starting again, so we'll have to pause construction of the first Hive. Progress has been slow, but eventually it will house several hundred Gentles.*

*In keeping with our stellar luck, our last working military truck gave up the ghost. Without access to parts, dwindling gas stores, and, honestly, no one who knows how to fix it anyway, we had no choice but to scrap the last of the four vehicles for metal. With the commitment to simplicity "we" agreed on, I knew the luxury would be short-lived. At least Nedé is less than 125 miles north to south, 45 Jungle to sea—whatever that is in kilometers (another compromise Mel convinced me of in the name of "solidarity").*

*On the upside, it looks like that horse breeding stable has
come in handy after all. Lex Sterling, the Coalition member from
Kentucky, has been experimenting with those thoroughbreds she
squeezed onto our boat and the local breed we inherited with the
land. Cree-lo? Cree-oy? With any luck, she thinks we'll have a
good-sized herd in a few years. Siyah has requested some of the
mixed horses for her Alexia as soon as they're old enough to ride.*

*The gentled boys show signs of thriving, after the initial
problems with the inoculations were resolved. But Mel's
predictions—that they'd be weak from lack of muscle mass,
generally unmotivated, brittle-boned, and eternally baby-faced—
were correct. She is working to remedy these unfortunate side
effects of removing their testosterone, but that's proving difficult
with our limited resources. She warns me that their longevity is
unlikely—heart disease will be prevalent as they age, and they won't
likely live past forty. But I'll take a Gentle for forty years over a
Brute for eighty every time.*

My head spins faster than a dog chasing its tail. I read the entry
again. And then a third time. I picture Old Solomon, wrinkled and
limping. I see the Gentles in the Center waiting room, sick, weak,
and broken. *We did this to them? She* knew *they would become this
way?* I read on . . .

*Unlike the setbacks with the Gentles, the "life serum," as Mel
termed it, has worked perfectly. The Bank is safely stored and the
lab up and running in our new Center for Health Services. As per
the Coalition's request, Mel was careful to procure enough sperm
to produce billions of offspring, in a variety of nationalities, and
the resulting babies have been beautifully diverse, though with
similarities (obviously) to the mothers. In half-a-dozen generations,
she thinks racial lines such as "black" and "white" will be a thing*

*of the past, replaced by a beautiful, equalizing "Nedéan Brown"—
women truly united. Twenty-three founding members agreed to
be our first Maternos. In the future, we should only need thirty
percent or so of the population to take on the role—averaging ten
live births, roughly half Gentles—but even I realize the necessity
of having more babies in these early years to get this society off
the ground, and I've consented to do my part. Mel relayed to me
that my announcement of my intention to birth a child—me, have
a kid!—convinced sixteen more to do likewise. The increase in
recruitment was so effective she thinks I should make it a law that
all Matriarchs should have at least one or two children to model
proper sacrifice. To give Materno a good name. I hate to say it, but
she's probably right.*

If our beautiful Nedéan brown skin is a result of the life serum,
does that mean the Gentles aren't the only ones who've been altered?
Has everything we experience in Nedé been tampered with? And I
had no idea our first Matriarch was as hesitant to fulfill her duties
of birthing a child as our eighth. I wonder whether Tristan resented
her duties to her child, Acacia Pierce, the way Teera squirmed
under the expectation to raise my own mother and aunt.

A strange vacancy yawns open where my Nedéan pride once
stood firm. I've come to accept that Teera isn't the hallowed keeper
of the Articles and Virtues I once thought she was. But Tristan
Pierce? *Bats*—is nothing sacred?

The next few pages dabble in matters of state: annual rains, a
terrible fever, a military threat, the formation of the Alexia. Despite
the possibility that any entry could offer another mind-bending
revelation, eventually my lids blink closed and refuse to reopen. As
sleep overtakes me, I dream I'm running, running, running from a
red-haired Brute with a syringe the size of a mahogany tree.

# CHAPTER TWENTY

WHEN THE SUN NUDGES ME with her gentle alarm, I jolt awake. She's much too bright for dawn. In fact, it appears I slept through breakfast. Second morning in a row. I read long into the night again, poring over Tristan's book, finally reaching its anticlimactic conclusion. The final entries grew increasingly dull. Still, I couldn't stop reading. What if I missed something important between the mundane lines of Nedé's early history? Something that would help me understand how Brutes got here . . . or that would explain why I get jittery when I recall the feel of Rohan's body pressed against me on the raft.

My feet hit the cool tile floor, and I'm pulling a breezy shirt over my head in five seconds. I'm in no mood to play Candidate today, my mind equally hazy from tiredness and dates, names, and logistics, but I have to make an appearance. And I'm off to a poor start. I'm keenly aware how every move could help, every misstep could hinder, my standing in Grandmother's eyes.

Yesterday Dom Russo begrudgingly gave me the day off when I claimed I was exhausted from the whole "going missing" ordeal. Truthfully, my mind was too full of questions to put up with socializing. I convinced myself I needed to find peace on the back of my pinto mare. The cadence of Callisto's gait always opens my mind to breathe. It sounded good in theory, anyway. The actual result of our hours-long ride was too much time to think. Too many moments to wonder what Tristan's words meant—what horrors did women live through to feel their only option was to create Nedé? Too many opportunities to replay every conversation I've had in the past week.

Craziest of all, the further I rode, the more fiercely I had to fight a ridiculous urge to turn my horse toward Highway Volcán and ride all the way to the Jungle Wilds. I kept telling myself, *They're Brutes, Reina. They're the reason Tristan was half out of her mind. They're threats to our safety.* And yet I could barely restrain my stupid self from the detour. Am I going mad?

I don't understand the illogical part of me that wishes to be back, that actually *wants* to return to the danger. I fear them, but I'm drawn to them.

My cheeks go hot every time I recall one particular Brute and the way he looked at me in the sunset glow high in the mahogany tree. It's not just Rohan I want to see, though. It's Jase, too. And the muddy-faced small Brutes, all monkey-play and mischief, and even Torvus, with his strength like a mountain. They possess some . . . *quality* that makes me wonder whether—even as I've discovered so much of who I am these past two months—I've been missing a larger piece of me my whole life.

When we were kids, my sisters and I liked to play on a rocky island that would appear near the edge of the Jabiru when the river was low. Sometimes we would try to dam up the smaller section of water that ran between the shore and the island. Ciela was always most determined. She'd bark orders at Jo and me: "Get that rock over there!" "We need more sand and leaves!" "Quick—the water's coming through!" Sometimes we'd succeed at holding the current back just long enough to wade in our newly created pool of shallow, green water. But eventually the river always won out. No matter how strong our defense, the water would push and wiggle a stone loose, and that would trigger a chain reaction of dismemberment. A dam is only as strong as its weakest point.

Tristan's journals may have dislodged a rock in the strong dam of my belief in Nedé—of everything it is and was—but I suspect the weakening began in the deluge of events triggered by my arrival here all those weeks ago. The visit to Hive I, where Grandmother shot a Gentle without cause. The Center, where I saw what becomes of the sick and dying sons of Nedé. Or maybe it was even before that. Maybe Mother prevented my ability to blindly believe in our system by her quiet refusal to treat Gentles with cruelty or disregard. Whatever the cause, the weakest part of my dam has been compromised, and it crumbles around me—the water pushing and rushing and drowning me.

If the Matriarchy hid the truth about the Gentles from us— that *they're* the ones altered, not the Brutes—what else might it be hiding? What role did the foremothers really play? Was there ever even a Great Sickness? I shove the questions down as I pull up a pair of linen pants, return the diary to my dresser drawer, twist my hair into a scarf, and jog toward the door. I won't get answers unless I'm chosen. If I become Matriarch, then surely I'll have access to everything Grandmother knows.

Speaking of Grandmother, I hear her muffled voice as I take the last flight of stairs two-by-two into the great room, past her office, and start down the hall toward the classroom.

"What did you find?" she asks crisply.

Curiosity gets the better of me, and I backtrack to Winifred's cage, deciding the pet macaw looks famished and needs a snack immediately. Luckily she snaps a seed from my outstretched fingertips without squawking a greeting.

Adoni's now-familiar voice replies, "I took a patrol to the border as soon as Trinidad reported her missing. We were short on evidence, but then I got lucky. In their lust for blood the Brutes were careless; they raided another finca not far from where Dom Pierce got separated from her group. I followed the smoke and caught up with the culprits just before they found cover in the Jungle."

Adoni pauses, and I hold my breath. I know I should pull myself away before someone sees me eavesdropping, but her next words freeze me solid.

"I apprehended one of them. He's the Brute we've been looking for—the leader. He matches the description given by witnesses at other raid sites . . . and according to my second-in-command, the description your granddaughter gave."

*Adoni caught a Brute.*

Maddening curiosity draws me from my rainbow-feathered alibi toward the closed door, one tiny step at a time.

"Where is he?" Grandmother asks.

"The underground Arena cells."

"Who else knows?"

"Only my second and I know of his capture or his location." Her voice changes slightly, and she sounds a little less like the mighty Alexia leader, and more like a curious woman. "I wouldn't have believed it if I hadn't caught one, Teera. He's nothing like I imagined." And then, in her usual, hardened tone, "You will want to see the thing, I assume. There will be decisions to make, and quickly."

"The only matter of business is how to wipe them off the earth as quickly as possible." I imagine the Matriarch's terseness matches an extra pucker to her lips. But she adds, more thoughtfully, "And to ensure no one else has made contact with them."

Silence stretches uncomfortably. Are they finished then? I take a step back, unnerved by the prospect of Adoni walking out the door to find me behind it, but then Grandmother speaks again.

"Tell me about the commander in charge of Reina's patrol. Could there have been any negligence on her part? Anything she might be keeping from you?"

In the space of time it takes Adoni to answer, Trinidad's golden eyes flash before mine, stern and brave. She's the closest ally I have at the Arena—no, more than that: a friend—and if she gets in trouble for what I did, or for what I didn't tell her, I'll never forgive myself. For a terrifying second I consider barging into Grandmother's office to demand she leave Trinidad out of this— if I were a braver woman I would—but cowardice extinguishes the impulse.

"I . . . " Adoni begins, audibly taken aback. "I have no reason to suspect Trinidad handled the situation ill. She's a fine Alexia and the best of commanders. However, if you have reason to believe she is keeping something from me, I will have no problem *interrogating* her further."

"No," the Matriarch says slowly. "Not yet."

I dry my slick palms on my linen pants and force myself to breathe quietly.

"Adoni, you know how I feel about my granddaughter. However, something in her demeanor upon her return makes me wonder if she's keeping something from me."

"Keeping something?"

"It could be nothing—you know how young women are, flighty and dramatic. But I refuse to be played for a fool."

"Of course, Matriarch."

"Yes . . . I believe it's time to test how loyal Reina is to the ideals of Nedé . . . and to *me*."

---

I managed to sneak to the classroom without being caught, though I can't imagine my color returned to normal before I arrived. Thankfully, nothing out of the ordinary happened during the brief lesson with Dom Russo, where she trained the four remaining Candidates on proper protocol for the two hundredth anniversary celebration next weekend. Nothing unusual happened this afternoon either, while Dom Tourmaline fitted me for what she attests is the "crowning glory of her career," to wear at said celebration. And nothing happened during dinner, as I pushed Cajun stir-fry in circles around my plate, forcing myself to take a few bites.

In fact now, during my customary evening ride on Callisto, I almost wonder whether I imagined the whole conversation. Did I *really* hear Grandmother say it was time to test my loyalty?

The sunset in the west washes the ocean in the east with an understated, muted-mango sheen as I ride. Stunning. Refreshing. I almost feel like myself again as we sprint the last hundred meters across the sand, buzzed by the salt wind rushing past us, then make our way back to the stables in the fading light.

I'm not surprised to find Neechi organizing tack when I approach, balancing on a ladder to hang a bridle on a high hook. He's here nearly every time I return from my rides, and we've developed a quiet familiarity.

After making sure we're alone, I ask, "Did you see the sunset?"

Neechi doesn't respond as he climbs down the ladder, and even though he knows I can put Callisto away on my own, he comes to take her anyway.

"I can—" I start, but Neechi silences me with a finger to his lips.

"Dom Reina," he whispers, his usually smooth, lilting voice pulled tight, "walk with me to her stall."

This is so unlike Neechi that I agree without a fuss. He walks slowly, biding his time and fidgeting with Callisto's neck rope.

"You will be tested soon," he says, barely loud enough to be heard.

"How do you know that?"

He brushes the question out of the air dismissively. Such details aren't the concern, so I squeeze my lips together. All the same, I bet Domus had a hand in relaying the information, through the Gentles' secret communication lines.

"Listen to me, Dom Reina," Neechi says, and the intensity of his voice arrests me.

I squeeze a handful of Callisto's mane, grounding myself for whatever might come next. I've never heard him speak like this, his voice quivering with emotion.

"You must do *whatever* she asks of you. You must! Do you understand? You will do good as Matriarch, enough good to make up for anything she requires."

We reach Callisto's stall, but I am frozen in place, trying to process his words. Neechi places a hand over mine, still tangled in horse hair.

"Please, Dom Reina," he pleads. "If you care about us at all, you must do as she says. He—we, we will all understand. It must be done. You are our best hope."

Goose bumps prickle across my bare arms, but I somehow manage a dazed nod. Neechi pulls Callisto forward, and I release her to his care. The way he goes about his business, a chance observer would have no idea we had been talking at all. I can tell he's nervous, that he'd rather I leave, so I do, though now that the initial shock has subsided some, I'm burning to make him explain whatever he's not telling me.

As I follow the path toward the sprawling villa, day's last light vanishes under heavy night. A nocturnal chorus—timid compared with the Jungle, but familiar—begins its slow build. A breeze rustles rows of hibiscus bushes as I pass. I pick a flower, the petals tightly curled together for the night, and I spin the thin stem between my fingers.

Grandmother *will* test me. And even though I'm not surprised by the Gentles' ability to secure classified information—they've certainly done it before—I still find it puzzling they would know of what nature the test will be. Neechi's uncustomary urgency worries me too. But the most pressing matter as I enter the villa is this: When will it happen?

I don't have to wonder long. When I reach the Senator's Suite, Domus waits outside the door.

"Dom Pierce," he says, with a stiff little bow. Apology seems to accompany what comes next: "The Matriarch requests your presence at the Arena tomorrow morning. Nine o'clock sharp."

---

Passing under the stone archway of the Arena, I imagine crossing the threshold with a younger version of myself beside me, little Reina, anxious to see one of the Alexia demonstrations she loves. As we step into the enormous stone vault of bravado and bravery—full of shouts and song, the smell of horses and perfume, women of all shapes and varying manners—she suddenly notices the Alexia uniform and bow I wear—chosen deliberately today to show Teera the strength I've found. I don't miss the awe in her innocent, curious eyes. She slowly tucks a strand of unruly hair behind her ear—the one that always falls over her face—and gingerly fingers my leather belt. Her bright eyes are round as full moons, in awe of the intricate bone dagger hanging from the loop. I wore that deliberately too, though I may later regret my impulsiveness. I smile at her gaping mouth, her delight over my weapons.

The scene melts around me, leaving only the empty, hard silence of the morning. But the essence of the emotion remains: I'm not who I once was. And, Alexia or not, whatever Grandmother requires, I will rise to the challenge.

I step over the last stone tile and onto the sandy, bright Arena floor. I'm not surprised to see the toucan's party colors billowing in the center, flowing on the silken robe of Nedé's eighth Matriarch. Swirls of yellow, green, blue, red—a silver, nine-pointed star—they pierce the monotony of brown earth and grey stone, demanding attention. Grandmother faces away from me, bending over something obscured from my view. Four Alexia stand by. I recognize all of them. Adoni, Fallon, Merced, Trinidad. *Trinidad!* I want to yell to her now—to apologize for lying, for possibly putting her in danger. To tell her what a fool I've been. But this isn't the time or place.

At Adoni's prompting, the Matriarch turns toward me, arms outstretched in a strangely warm greeting.

One's grandmother shouldn't fill a person with apprehension, but mine does. At least I'm not as nervous as I was last night. Light has the power to chase away nighttime monsters. So I hold my chin high and take wide strides toward my Matriarch until I can see the silver lines of her high, angled eyebrows and the translucent brown, wrinkled skin, thin as a bat's wings, that holds her all together.

"Reina," she croons. She wraps her arms around my shoulders, pulling me against her chest in an embrace. My body stiffens. She called me *Reina.* And a hug? Something isn't right. What is she trying to do—be a grandmother for once? I don't trust it. I strain to get a look at whatever's behind her, but only glimpse a corner of rough fabric before she steps back, her robe screening the object once again.

"My dear," she begins, "you are my granddaughter, and I have the highest trust in you."

Her words sound like a cup of palm nectar—too sweet to drink. This has to be an act. She has *never* been this nice to me.

"I'd be negligent not to allow every Candidate the opportunity to prove her utmost devotion to the ideals of Nedé," she continues. "You must understand that by giving you this opportunity, I confer on you a great honor. You will demonstrate what I already believe is inside you: a heart that beats for Nedé."

She steps aside, finally revealing what has been hidden behind her gauzy, flitting robe: A strangely lumpy sack, tall as a torso, covering all but two knees pressed into the dirt.

My jaw tightens instinctively, but once I recognize the likely visible tension in my face, I force myself to relax. She mustn't see anything in me but strength. Neechi's words tumble forward and back in my mind, like seaweed caught in the tide: *Whatever it takes. Whatever it takes. Whatever it takes.* I have to prove to her an allegiance I do not possess in order to act on the loyalty I have for *all* of Nedé—for Mother and Marsa, my sisters and Trinidad, the Brutes in the Jungle and the Gentles. *Especially* the Gentles.

"During your time as a Candidate, you have been educated in the history of Nedé."

I nod. Inside I squirm—does she know just *how much* I've been educated? No, she couldn't.

"You and I—every woman in Nedé—live in safety because our foremothers purchased that freedom for us. They were forced to make very difficult decisions. Decisions that involved life and death. Our society flourishes today because they did not shrink away from either, and in so doing, they righted the wrongs of their world."

Grandmother walks a slow circle around her prisoner as she continues, "While on patrol you became aware that a new threat has come against Nedé. The particulars of this threat are not important at this time. All you need know is that this danger must be eradicated immediately. And *I* need to know you'll stand with me against it, regardless of your personal affections."

She says the last words slowly, in all the coolness I know to be her true self. I should be afraid, but a growing relief slows my racing heart. I'm putting the pieces together . . .

I know more than she suspects about this "new threat": the Brutes in the Jungle. And Adoni said the one she captured—the Brute she believes to be the leader—was being kept in an underground cell here. And I know who that is. So I know who cowers under that sack. And I would be more than happy to kill him. Slowly, quickly—in any way she wants me to. I will rid Nedé of Dáin's evil, avenge the attack on my sister, and prove my "allegiance," all at the same time. I've never killed anyone, but I have to pass the test if I'm going to help them. For Treowe's sake. And Mother's small ones. For Neechi and all the Gentles. And if I must kill, then what a stroke of luck that it won't cost me my soul.

When I speak, the strength of my voice reflects my reemerging rage toward Dáin.

"Of course. Any threat to the safety of Nedé must be disposed of immediately."

I don't wait to see if Grandmother will produce a gun, as she did at the Hive courtyard the day of Nari's test. To show just how ready I am to do the Matriarch's bidding, I slide the bow from my back and put adequate distance between me and the target. My will is set, my face hard. I nock an arrow smoothly, sliding it into place with deft, practiced fingers. I widen my stance and lift the bow, ready to see Dáin's freckled, snarling face. Ready to inflict the same terror in him that he inflicted on me the night he held me down and choked me and glared at me with hungry, wicked eyes. I'm ready to stop his cold heart from ever beating again.

Grandmother wasn't expecting me to acquiesce so eagerly. I see it on her face. But satisfaction quickly replaces surprise.

"I knew you wouldn't embarrass me," she says. She nods at Adoni, who grabs the top of the sack with two hands and tugs. The cloth slides up his sides, arms, neck, and over his head.

But it's not Dáin's eyes that meet mine. These eyes are soft, familiar, steady. And it's not Dáin's harsh, scarred face that glistens with sweat. This face is round and kind, chapped from working in the sun. And it's not Dáin's wild red hair that hangs damp in the muggy air. This hair is golden as dried straw, and a clump of it hangs helplessly over one eye. My body threatens to collapse under me.

"*Treowe*," I whisper.

His face drips with perspiration, but his eyes hold the strength of . . . of a Brute. Without a sound those eyes shout at me, *Do it, Reina. You have to do this*. But he only nods, knowingly, assuring me that he knows I must.

*Remember who you are, Reina.* My mother's voice comes softly in recollection, like a whisper that stirs you from sleep.

*I don't know who I am!* I want to scream back. But maybe now I do . . .

I've always suspected I had more of my grandmother in me than my mother would like. Now I realize I also have more of Mother in me than suits my grandmother. I am no tyrant. I cannot kill an innocent person, not for something as small as my own safety.

But what about the safety of many? Doesn't it make sense to sacrifice one soul for the chance to liberate thousands? Especially when this brave martyr begs me to do it? Neechi believes it is worth it. *For the love of Siyah!* He knew this was coming. He knew it! Why didn't he tell me it would be Tre?

Of course I know the answer. Neechi thinks my becoming Matriarch is their only chance at a different life. But he's a Gentle. Of course he would think so.

Yet . . . Tristan Pierce thought so too. Two hundred years ago she faced the same difficult decision—a decision between life and death. *And now I must make it for myself.* She believed it was worth sacrificing some for the safety of the weak and vulnerable. But she only had to sacrifice evil Brutes—twisted men like Dáin— didn't she? *I'd have to execute an innocent Gentle. No, more than a Gentle—a faithful friend. One who has only ever shown me kindness, served my family, overlooked my stupid pride. A Gentle who . . . who would die for me.*

I stare into his eyes—furious at what he's asking of me. I recognize a power there that Teera never will, but only because Tre taught me to see beyond a Gentle's roles and weaknesses to appreciate his surprising, overlooked strengths.

For a split second I consider the four Alexia around Grandmother, toy with the urge to beg them for some kind of assistance. Each stands at attention, eyes forward, back straight. Not even Trinidad looks at me. But I know that expression— steely, irked, resigned. She wore it when Jamara was beating the life out of Bri and Adoni wouldn't stop it—right before she intervened. *I wish she would do something now.* But what? This is *my* moment of testing. *My* opportunity to prove my loyalty to the good of Nedé. And the good of Nedé—all of Nedé—is for me to take Grandmother's place as Matriarch.

Grandmother raises an eyebrow. "Not what you were expecting?" Her left nostril flares slightly.

I've delayed too long. Even if I shoot now, Grandmother will know I hesitated. *Will it be too little too late?*

I squeeze the bow grip until my fingernails dig into my palms. My vision blurs with hot tears. *Stupid Treowe! Why did you have to be so good to me?* A tremor shakes my arm as I lift the bow. He is unfathomably calm, and as silent as the first time I met him, when he knelt in the dirt beside me to bury the kid goat. His sun-spot freckles washed out in the bright light, he looks scarcely older now, but clearly, his mild strength has grown. *Faithful Treowe.* I curse silently. He lifts his chin toward the sun and closes his eyes, readying himself for the blow.

For a brief moment I think of the sun and Siyah and wonder if I could shoot out that enormous ball of light. If I were immortal, I could save my friend. But I can't, I'm not, I can't. I can't save him. In the end, my hesitations buckle under reality: if I don't shoot him, Grandmother will. Or worse. I'd be a fool to think otherwise.

I pull the bowstring back centimeter by centimeter until my pointer and middle fingers tremble against the corner of my mouth. Then I set my jaw, close my eyes, and let the arrow fly.

Part Five

# CHAPTER TWENTY-ONE

HE'S DEAD. *He's dead. He's dead.*

The words pulsate through my mind—my entire body—as rhythmic and deep and thick as my blood. The verdict feels red like my blood too. Red, like the spreading circle over Treowe's chest where my own arrow pierced his heart.

I lie prone atop my bed in the Senator's Suite as night falls, the silk coverlet stuck to my clammy, dusty skin, my forehead pressed against the back of my hands. Perhaps this kind of grief would be better sorted atop Callisto, but I can't go to the stables. I'm not ready to see Neechi, and there's nowhere else that affords any privacy. Who cares where I grieve anyway? No matter where I go, my eyes will sting from crying out every tear they can produce, my throat will still burn from the violent rejection of everything in my gut. Down to my core, every centimeter of me not numb with grief would still ache with the recollection of what I've done.

*She would have killed him, Reina,* I tell myself again. *Probably tortured him and then killed him.* And I believe that's true. But the knowledge does little to assuage my conscience as I lie here, hour after hour, replaying what transpired on the Arena floor.

The particulars of the test unfolded so suddenly, I scarcely had time to think. If I had stalled longer, could I have found a crack in the Matriarch's test big enough to slip through? If I had been smarter, quicker, surely I could have found a way to outwit Grandmother at her own game, the way Nari quoted the constitution instead of killing the Gentle in the Hive courtyard.

There must have been another way. For the hundredth time I scan the scene in my memory, hoping to find—dreading I'll find—some contingency I missed. I turn a complete circle in my reconstructed scene, considering every possibility—running, refusing, even shooting my blasted Grandmother instead—but each scenario ends in Tre's death and the certain loss of the Apprenticeship.

Reason clamors to be heard: the only way to help the Gentles is to become the next Matriarch. And the only chance I had—I *have*—of being chosen is to prove my loyalty to the current one.

Still, my internal critic screams back, *Even if there was no other way to stop her, what kind of monster kills her best friend?*

I squeeze my eyes tighter, head pounding in a fresh wave of pain. No more tears exist, or I'd shed them all over again.

I remember Neechi's hushed voice in the stable—was that just last night?—begging me to do whatever Teera required. Assuring me "it" must be done. If I had known then what he meant—what he was asking of me—I would have refused him right then and there. Without the disadvantage of panic, I would have made a more virtuous decision.

He must have known as much, or he would have told me what was coming.

If I weren't so numb, I'd be furious with Neechi for keeping the truth from me—for letting me walk into the test blind, completely unaware of what Grandmother would demand of me. I'd be angry with Treowe, too, for his . . . his . . . for his stupid selflessness. I'd be mad that he didn't fight. That he *wanted* me to go through with his execution, knowing it would wreck me to pieces. But grief leaves me limp with exhaustion and regret, sapping the strength required for anger.

A soft knock wakes me from the fitful sleep that came on the heels of a restless night. I ignore it, too groggy to care who is at my door. The taps come again, and a third time, but apart from opening my eyes enough to note the bright light of late morning, I don't stir. Moving sounds hard. Hours of sleeping facedown have stiffened every limb and joint.

The doorknob turns slowly, and a Gentle in a powder blue linen suit steps in, hair trimmed short, his skin wrinkled with premature age. Domus closes the door quietly behind him. He balances a small, silver tray, which he places on the dresser before moving to the foot of my bed.

"Forgive my impertinence, Dom Reina," he says softly, "but I took the liberty of bringing you breakfast."

Impertinence indeed. He could be whipped or put in the stocks for entering without permission. But his gesture—risking trouble to help me—doesn't anger me. And from what I've learned of Domus, I'm barely surprised that he knows I'm in my room with no intention of coming to breakfast.

"Thank you," I manage, the dry rasp of my voice strangely foreign. Without so much as a glance in his direction I close my eyes again, waiting for him to vacate the room now that he has completed his good deed. I *want* him to leave me alone.

"Reina," he begins again, his risky omission of my proper title genuinely vulnerable. "I suspect this won't mean much to you now, but . . . " His voice cracks midsentence, and when he continues, his words are wet with grief. "He chose this. He knew it was coming, and he didn't run. I provided him a stinger, but he refused. Treowe went willingly, believing—*knowing*—you are our best hope." He comes closer, touches my shoulder lightly. "Don't waste his sacrifice."

His talk of Tre jars me fully awake, but I still can't bring myself to move or say a word. A moment later, he leaves my bedside and opens the door.

"You'll be expected at the morning lesson," he says quietly. "Please consider making an appearance."

The door clicks shut, and silence envelops me once again.

With considerable effort I roll to my side, facing the wall of windows that look out over the Halcyon Sea, shimmering like turquoise-tinted glass in the morning light.

As much as I long to lie in bed all day, let loose all the tears replenished while I slept, drown my guilt in grief, Domus has forced me to face a grounding question: *What am I going to do with Tre's sacrifice?*

Yes, I killed him, and I regret it with every fiber of my being. But I am still a part of this Succession. Three other Candidates hope their names will be announced as Matriarch Teera's Apprentice tomorrow. But if they succeed, I don't. And if I don't, his death will be for nothing. What *I did* will be for nothing.

*I can't let it be for nothing.*

I push myself up from the bed and drag my legs over the edge and, once a wave of dizziness subsides, shuffle to the windows. Through dry, swollen eyes I see Grandmother in the garden below my second-story suite, posing among the foliage for a painting. Winnifred perches on her bent forearm like a feathered accessory.

The scarlet macaw's bright red, blue, and yellow plumage comple-
ment the equally bold colors of the matriarchal robe. I consider
Teera's straight back, the slight lift of her chin, the high arc of her
thin eyebrows. If it weren't for the silver gray hue of her ear-length
hair, or the thinness of her sagging skin, she could be decades
younger than her seventy-six years.

I recognize the artist, a slight woman with hair dyed almost
bone white, as a soloist from the Exhibition of the Arts we attended
during training. A paint-smeared smock covers her simple shift
dress, and her long hair twists up into a topknot. She dabs and
brushes a canvas nearly as tall as her subject with practiced strokes,
transforming the bright hues mottling her palette into colorful
details.

I wonder if this commission will be the last portrait of Nedé's
eighth Matriarch. This must be how Teera wants to be remembered: strong, yet so welcoming, so nurturing, even a flight animal
deigns to rest on her arm. Someday, perhaps a hundred years from
now, those who view this relic will assume as much. They will marvel at this Matriarch who built the Alexia to unmatched strength,
who constructed the Arena and instituted the demonstrations, yet
who embodied safety and care for her people.

But I know the truth. I know how this Matriarch put a bullet
in a Gentle's head when Nari refused to execute his "punishment."
I know this woman who talks secretively with Adoni. This leader
who surrounds herself with those she can control. This monster
who asked her own granddaughter to murder an innocent friend.

I wish I could spit in her face.

Winifred stretches one blue-tipped wing, then the other, lazily
spreading her elegant plumage and revealing a short row of clipped
flight feathers. Grandmother only brings her outside, poses with
her, because she knows she can't fly away. Even her pet must be
controllable.

As much as I have come to despise her, I need Matriarch Teera to believe she has my loyalty. She must be certain she can control me before she'll choose me.

Before I left on patrol last week, I doubted she'd feel the need to assess my loyalties at all, at least not the way she had tested the other Candidates she was seriously considering, Nari and Jamara. But when I returned from the Jungle, my alibi, or my demeanor, must not have convinced her completely, because she did test me. And I'd be a fool to think I can hide away and mourn without further alerting her suspicions.

But if I can resume my part in this game, pretending I haven't been shattered like a felled tree, then how could she doubt my allegiance? I gave up my conscience to prove it to her. From her perspective, she has what she wants: a devoted trainee who will perch on her arm like a pet.

I breathe deeply next to the open window, inhaling jasmine and salt air, forcing life back into my lungs. I have to go on living . . . proving . . . winning. I have to believe that Tre wanted it this way. If he sacrificed himself so I could help the Gentles, at least I can follow his example.

I punch the wall, hard. Kick it for good measure. Then I open the armoire and choose a pale yellow sundress—the least mournful item of clothing I can find—and slip it over my head. I soak my face in a basin of cold water to relieve the red puffiness and braid my hair over one shoulder. Anyone who knows me would suspect I had been crying, but luckily for me, no one here fits in that category. Anyway, it's the best I can do.

I practice smiling in the mirror, forcing my face to hide my real feelings, just to make sure I can actually do it before seeing anyone. When my lip starts to quiver, I slap my cheek in protest. I can't think of what I'm about to do as betraying Tre's memory. If Domus is right, only resilience will honor it.

# CHAPTER TWENTY-TWO

I'M THE LAST TO SLIP INTO MY SEAT around the table when I enter the lecture room downstairs. Dom Russo stops speaking when I enter, shooting me a particularly sour glare.

"As I was saying," she resumes, "the surrey will take you from the Finca to the Arena directly after lunch tomorrow. Meet by the pond with . . . "

I try to listen, but my mind quickly drifts to the first day of the Succession, where we gathered in this very room. That first day I was tempted to like Jamara because she reminded me a little of Marsa, but I have no such illusions now. The tall, thick Candidate from Kekuatan will stop at nothing to win this Succession, even if it means beating my face to a pulp. I know she knows I'm watching her, but she doesn't move a muscle, just keeps staring straight ahead. If she were to win the Apprenticeship, Nedé would be subject to an even more ruthless, vengeful Matriarch than the one we have now.

Next to Jamara, Nari runs a finger along her feather pen, a scrap of parchment proof that she's taking this Succession seriously to the very end. Unlike Jamara, I've warmed to Nari over the past seven weeks. She's kinder than Jamara, bolder than Yasmine, and not completely annoying like Bri.

The latter picks at her fingernails, not bothering to appear interested as Dom Russo drones on about proper ceremony etiquette. Her blond bangs curve over her forehead, framing her eyes and slight nose, and I suddenly realize she's quite lovely. I haven't noticed, I guess, because I've been too busy either gawking at her nerve or trying to refrain from punching that pretty face.

"After the Alexia demonstration, Matriarch Teera will rise and address . . . " Dom Russo's voice floats into and back out of my attention.

How strange that after tomorrow, I may never see these women again. If I—*when* I win, Bri, Jamara, and Nari will return home to their respective Provinces and carry on the same destinies they left. Nari will keep repurposing materials into new innovations. Bri will continue her Politikós aspirations in Amal—maybe even try for Senator someday. And Jamara will go back to ensuring Nedé's tens of thousands of Gentles serve the rest of us with meek obedience.

Given what Jamara's capable of, the thought of her serving in Gentles Regimen unsettles me. Now that I know Gentles aren't born Gentles, I'm doubly torn by the way they are treated at the Hive, how they languish at the Center. I can only imagine the conditions of the phase-out facilities.

The Gentles' plight reminds me of Treowe, of course, and grief begins bleeding over my soul like spilled ink. I bite the tip of my thumb hard to keep it at bay.

"Dom Pierce?" The Jaguar presses, mercifully chasing the shadow back into the recesses of thought.

"Hmm?"

"I asked whether you can tell me what the Apprentice's robe signifies."

I search my mental catalog of lectures amassed from dozens of hours sitting in this room, with files covering everything from interprovince relations to sanitation systems, but come up short, and the silence lengthens into awkwardness. Thankfully, Nari comes through with a timely save.

"If I may, the robe represents the Matriarch's hope of conferring her full title to her Apprentice in a year's time. The pattern of the Apprentice's robe matches the Matriarch's to signify that she will follow in her mentor's footsteps, while it is shorter and sleeveless to recognize that power has not yet been transferred."

I blink at Nari in silent gratitude; she offers a slight, knowing smile in return.

*I have got to get it together.* I pinch my thigh to snap out of my head. I have to at least look like I know what I'm doing, even if I'm running at quarter speed today.

"Correct, Dom Kwan. And once the robe is conferred on the new Apprentice, the rest of you will graciously applaud Matriarch Teera's choice. We will have no poor losers, understood?" She pinches her lips even tighter than normal, fixing Bri with an irritated stare. Bri blinks back innocently. "At the end of the ceremony, surreys will be waiting behind the Arena to escort you back to Finca del Mar. To preserve decorum, and to respect the new alliance between Matriarch and Apprentice, the Candidates not chosen will pack their belongings immediately and prepare to vacate the premises directly after the Matriarch's private celebration in the great room. Please remember to inform your relatives that, while they are invited to attend the party with you, lodging is reserved for the Apprentice's family and the Matriarch's distinguished guests."

Bri snorts. "No room for us, eh? Don't want any 'poor losers' having access to the chicha?"

But having been assaulted by two of the Candidates in this room, I'm not opposed to the idea of clearing the villa after the big announcement. I don't know who I can trust.

Visibly flustered, Dom Russo ignores Bri's comment. "Are there any questions about the order of events tomorrow, or what is required of you?" When none of us respond, she concludes with uncharacteristic softness, "Best of luck to the four of you. It has been an honor to instruct you the past month and a half. Nedé will be in good hands, whichever of you Teera chooses."

But I notice her gaze skips over Bri.

I can't say I agree. I'm terrified of what Nedé could become if certain Candidates were chosen. Neechi is right, isn't he? I *am* the Gentles' only hope of turning the tide. And it's probably time to tell him I understand.

———

I head down the hall and into the great room, then slip out a glass door that leads into the backyard garden.

At first I don't notice Grandmother, peering over the artist's shoulder, admiring her finished portrait. Domus stands by in his blue suit, holding a silky shade umbrella over the pair.

"Reina," she calls, without taking her eyes from the painting, "tell me what you think."

Startled, and wary of speaking to the woman I presently hate more than anyone in the world, I'm forced to join her vantage point. The large canvas teems with vivid colors, brushed smooth as silk threads. In the artist's depiction, Grandmother's mouth curves up into what could almost be called a smile, though I doubt it did any such thing during the entire session. Winifred's white-ringed black eyes seem to look on her Domina with admiration, another artistic leap, and her long tail feathers drip from Teera's arm like graceful red jewels. Green elephant ears, yellow cassia, and violet orchids encircle the pair, echoing the bright colors of Teera's robe. The picture unfolds just as I imagined it would, portraying our eighth Matriarch as equal parts beauty, strength, and approachability, even with the true-to-life, sharply peaked eyebrows. Nedé's motto scrolls across the top of the portrait in gold lettering: *Protect the weak. Safety for all. Power without virtue is tyranny.* And at the bottom, *Teera Pierce, 8th Matriarch of Nedé, 2221–2267.*

I swallow my dissent, playing the part of enamored Candidate rather than betray my bitterness. "It's a work of art," I say, because that's true.

"Yes," Teera says thoughtfully. After a moment, she addresses the artist. "Have it hung in the south entrance of the Arena tomorrow morning so we can show off your craftsmanship, Freja." She hands Winifred to Domus, then turns down the path toward the sea, rather than back to the villa. I'm about to make a quick exit toward the stables when she addresses me again.

"Come, Reina. I wish to speak with you."

Stuffing down reluctance, I obediently follow. It's the first time I've been this near her since the Arena, and my stomach coils with loathing. We travel the geometric mosaic path to a more secluded section of the garden before she speaks again.

"I am a woman of firm conviction, Reina, but I'm not above reflection. The Gentle was a traitor, and justice begged to be done. Still, I have considered what I asked of you yesterday and wonder if it wasn't unfair of me to require you to punish someone you . . . *knew.*"

Anger explodes in my chest like boulders falling in the Jabiru. How could she say Treowe—faithful Treowe—was a traitor? Guilty of what? Being my friend? He was more innocent than she'll ever be. It takes every ounce of my resolve not to do something I'll regret. But I force my mind away from the cliff and try to keep my wits about me. She's apologizing, which means she either means it, or I need to figure out what card she's trying to play.

She continues, "I believe your mother's abominable neglect of the Articles created an unhealthy environment for you and your sisters that warped your perceptions of duty. I blame myself, really. If I had stifled Leda's rebellion when I first suspected her weakness . . ." She pauses, likely mentally recounting the ways she could have "stifled" her daughter, then snaps, "Regardless, because of your poor upbringing, perhaps it was unfair to ask you to carry out that sentence in particular, without knowing the details of what has been happening in Nedé."

First she discredits Treowe, now Mother? Does she despise everyone who embodies goodness? I muster all my nerve so I can stop and face her when I speak.

"You needed to know you could trust me when it counted. I hope you know now that you can." I hold her gaze with more boldness than I've ever had with her before. "I won't let you down, *Matriarch*."

She studies my face a moment, and though she's notoriously hard to read, I think I might have done it. I think I've convinced her I mean it.

"Good," she says quietly, almost too pensively, and I'm reminded of that evening we shared dinner in this garden. The evening she announced she had selected me as a Candidate. *She chose me for a reason*, I remind myself now. She wants me to succeed. As long as it serves her purposes, anyway.

"I do want to count on you, Reina, which is why there mustn't be any secrets between us." Then, as if suddenly struck by some trifling matter, she adds, "Adoni mentioned you found a weapon during the incident on patrol. Do you still have it?"

Rohan's bone dagger. I kick myself again for forgetting it on my weapons belt when I stopped to see Trin at the Arena. Of course she would tell Adoni. And why wouldn't Adoni tell Teera?

"Yes, I . . . I meant to give it to Adoni," I lie, "but she wasn't at the Arena when I passed through. It's in my room now, but I can take it to her tomorrow, at the ceremony, if you wish."

Grandmother drums her fingers against her elbow, considering. "Reina, I believe it will take time for you to trust me completely, but perhaps it will help if I trust *you* with some information first." She lowers her voice, for effect I gather, as no one is within earshot. "We've captured the one responsible for the attacks on Nedé soil, including, we suspect, the unspeakable raid on Jonalyn's finca. I am interested in the weapon because it likely belongs to one of . . . them."

I know this already, but I put on my best make-believe surprised face. I feign ignorance with my next question too: "*Them*? Who are they? Gentles?"

She seems about to answer but thinks better of sharing more than she needs to. "I will tell you . . . after *tomorrow*. Once the two hundredth anniversary celebration is out of the way, we'll devote every resource to restoring complete peace in Nedé. The asset we've acquired will be of particular use in leading the way."

She said "we'll." Surely that's a good sign.

"Of course," I say. "And . . . this 'asset' will cooperate?"

"My dear, anyone can be persuaded if the right tactics are employed."

Perhaps the words aren't directed at me, but they knock the wind from my lungs regardless. Yes, anyone can be persuaded to do anything. Anything at all. I hate her and her manipulative tactics.

I would pity her next target if it wasn't Dáin, the only being who could possibly tie with her for most loathsome human under the stars.

She tips her head and tries at a thin smile. "We will have much to discuss, but for now, you need to trust that what I asked of you was for the good of Nedé."

It takes all the restraint I have to nod obediently, but I manage, garnering an awkward pat on my shoulder from Grandmother. When she turns back toward the villa, I resume step beside her, brooding in silence, unable to think of anything to say that won't land me in a cell. So I mentally count the tiles underfoot until we reach the villa, where Grandmother excuses herself to her office.

As soon as she's out of sight, I practically run toward the stables. This charade had better be worth it.

———————

"How *could* you?"

I let the words hang, fierce and low, in the earthy air of the open-beam stable. A mottled gray horse stands crosstied in the breezeway, tail twitching, as a short Gentle in dirty linen trousers brushes her down. I know he's heard me, but he doesn't pause a stroke or offer so much as a grunt.

Taking long steps over the smooth-raked dirt, I come nearer and repeat my question. "How *could* you, Neechi? You knew it was Tre, you knew we were friends, and you let me walk into her trap completely blind!" Now I fight to keep my voice low, a flood of tears held barely at bay, knowing we're not truly safe to talk openly anywhere at Finca del Mar. This is Grandmother's turf.

"Not completely," he finally says, with his soft voice, which usually soothes but now infuriates me. "I told you what we felt you needed to know."

"And why did you get to decide what I needed to know? Huh? You're a Gentle!"

I wish the words back as soon as they pass my lips. Insulting him is low, even for a girl awash in grief. If I was less prideful, or less hurt, I'd apologize.

His eyes trace the dirt for a moment before speaking, and I feel as small as an ant.

"What *he* wanted you to know," he says finally, then returns to brushing loose hairs from the mare. "He made us promise not to tell you."

How can I argue with the dead? Tre knew I would have refused if I'd had more time to think it through. Right or wrong, it's not Neechi's fault.

"Domus said he offered him a stinger. Why didn't he take it and . . . die in peace?"

"Because he believed you'd be the best Matriarch Nedé's ever seen. A Matriarch who cares about Gentles, that would change everything for us. Would that chance ever come again? He refused the stinger because he knew he'd die either way, so he figured it best to let you prove yourself to Matriarch Teera." He stops brushing to meet my eyes. "I would have done the same."

I see the tear tracks now, glistening down his round, caramel cheeks. How many tears has he cried over this?

Maybe I can't judge what these Gentles did. I wasn't taken from my mother to live in a Hive. I've never been forced to clean sewage, wait on fussy elites, or sleep in subpar housing. I'll probably live to old age in perfect health and strength, never experiencing brittle bones or mystery ailments that kill me after three or four decades of life. I've not been *altered*, without my consent or even knowledge. Can I resent them for wanting hope?

I soften my voice with effort. "I don't understand how the Matriarch . . . Why Treowe, Neechi? How did she know?"

"I can't say what she knows, Dom Reina, but the Alexia can question us for any reason, and we usually have no reason to lie. She could know anything that has been seen by one of us."

A memory flashes—the day Tre brought my leather bag to the finca from home. Behind a hedge, he told me about Jonalyn, thanked me for being his friend. If one of those gardeners had actually seen . . .

My eyes clench, recalling the shy smile my small kiss coaxed. My lack of restraint—is that how she knew? Of all the stupid, impulsive . . . and if Tre had known then what my gift would cost, would he have been so pleased?

I shake my head, trying to dislodge the memory. But the thought of other Gentles watching my every move is disconcerting, especially since my talking with Neechi is also a violation of Article II.

"And how did you know?" I ask.

Neechi lowers his voice to a hushed whisper so I have to lean in to hear him. "The Alexia's farrier comes once a week from the Arena to tend to the Matriarch's horses. He tells me things of interest—a Gentle who's been hurt, a Senator caught with another woman, someone put in the cells—and I share with Domus what I think needs sharing. That's how Domus knew the Matriarch had Treowe."

Gentles permeate Nedé like silent fixtures, moving like gears and wires and knobs to make Nedé run. They're passive people, which, according to Tristan's journal, is also due to the vaccine. I'm ashamed to admit I'm surprised they have enough shrewdness to listen, or enough curiosity to gossip amongst themselves.

Neechi looks bashful. "Some of us wish things could be different for us, but what can we do? We don't have much, but our mouths still work. We talk, and we hope that someday the information will prove useful. And we pray that someday, somebody will do something for us. We're not fighters, Dom Reina. We don't have it in us. And until Matriarch Teera, we were mostly content to live our short lives serving Nedé. We don't want trouble. But for all the good she's done in Nedé, our lives have gotten worse. She doesn't treat us like past Matriarchs. At least, that's what I've heard."

"And that's why you need me? Because I'll *do* something?"

He nods. "Do you see now?"

"Sure, I see. I see that I had to kill my best friend because I'm the only one crazy enough to care about him." I bite my lip and stare at the wall studded with tack. "I'm sorry . . . I just need a ride, okay?" Neechi offers a conceding nod, and steps aside to let me pass. I make a break for Callisto's stall before the tears come again.

My pinto mare's head hangs over the wide-beam gate, eager at the sound of my voice. I run a hand down her neck and kiss her velvety nose.

"There's my girl," I whisper. "I haven't forgotten about you."

Callisto seems as alert as always—eyes clear, one ear twitching. No sign of anything abnormal, five days since I found the wound crusted with blood. I just wish I knew how long I have to wait before I can stop worrying about her getting "the crazies," as Jase called it.

I slip a neck rope over her head and lead her out the gate. Since Neechi has a horse in the breezeway, and because I think we've said everything that needs to be said for now, I exit to the right, then circle back to catch the trail that leads to the shore.

In five minutes Callisto's hooves are pressing into rough sand, and I can finally breathe. The Halcyon Sea laps the shoreline with small, gentle waves, its enormous liquid body stretching away from us clear to the horizon. There's something freeing in feeling the weight of smallness, and nothing makes me feel small like the ocean.

I gulp down the salt air as Callisto breaks into a run. She loves this as much as I do. I curl my fingers into her windblown mane and close my eyes, letting the rhythm of her hoofbeats keep pace for my heart.

It's not fair of them to expect me to save them. Who am I? What can I actually do?

Regardless of what I'm able to accomplish, of course I *want* to help them. "Protect the weak" took on new meaning after the Hive visit, where I saw how young Gentles live, and the Center, where I learned how they die: sick, too young, neglected, alone.

The wind whips the heat of regret from my skin, at least momentarily, uncovering a fresh resolve. *Tre is dead, but I will honor him. I will, I will, I will.*

# CHAPTER TWENTY-THREE

A STRANGELY COMFORTING, FAMILIAR BLEND OF SPICES draws me into the dining room for the Candidates' last meal together. Preoccupied with choosing a seat, it takes me a moment to recognize why the aroma doesn't fit this space. But once I've settled next to Nari and spread the crisp cloth napkin across my lap, I realize the scents of allspice, oregano, and chicken don't pair with the capiz chandelier of Finca del Mar's dining room. They're more likely to belong in my mother's rustic kitchen. Yet here we are, offered plates of savory chicken and rice among the meticulously pruned dwarf orange trees, giant orchids, and gleaming silverware of the indoor arboretum. I'm tempted to think the chefs called it quits a night prematurely and left us comfort food for our loss, until a Gentle slides a cobalt glass plate in front of me. Even the rice looks more polished somehow. Marsa is the best of the best, but this meal marries the simplicity of *arroz con pollo* with elegance in a way she has no reason to recreate.

The familiar smells hint at Bella Terra and widen the gaping hole of loss inside. Bella and Tre are intertwined in my memory, and the thought of the former permanently lacking the latter about breaks me. I'll see Mother tomorrow, though, after the celebration. That's something. My sisters, too. Well, Ciela at least. I'm sure Jonalyn is still on bed rest.

The soothing indoor waterfall, trickling down the wall opposite me, holds my attention until Jamara and Bri take their seats, blocking my view. Then the food on my plate becomes strangely mesmerizing.

As usual, Nari attempts small talk as we begin our meal, trying to break the awkward silence between us. "I heard you weren't well last night, Reina. Feeling better today?"

"Yes, thank you." I even smile a little, hoping to convince her.

Bri stares at me from across the table, chewing slowly. "I didn't think you had it in you," she blurts in her casually sharp way. Leave it to Bri to bring up the one subject I was intent on avoiding.

"What do you mean?" I ask innocently, fixing her with my best "shut up or I'll kill you" glare.

"Oh, nothing. I mean, I just thought you were a little soft toward Gentles. Owing to your *mother's* influence. But I guess it was just part of your do-gooder routine after all."

Nari turns to me, her brow knit in confusion. "Did something happen?"

If it were just Bri and me, my throat wouldn't feel as tight as a twisting vanilla tendril. Bri knows Grandmother has systematically tested us, and our shared knowledge feels safer because she has as little regard for the Matriarch as I do. But I'm reluctant to talk about my test in front of Nari, the one remaining Candidate who refused to do what Grandmother asked of her. Though her refusal didn't save that Gentle's life in the end, it showed her mettle. She proved she'd stand for what she believed was right. I thought I would too. But now . . . I'm ashamed of myself, I guess. I can't explain my underlying reasons, and without them I really am a monster. And Jamara—I don't want her to know anything about me, period. It would be better if I despised her; worse, I fear her.

But now that Bri has bared the subject like a skinned fish, I have to answer Nari. I sit on my hands to steady them.

"I was asked to . . . execute justice on a threat to Nedé," I say, forcing steadiness into my voice.

Nari covers her mouth, the corners of her eyes creased with concern. "And . . . *did you?*"

I can tell by the flatness of her tone she's already guessed the truth. I let myself nod. Stoic Jamara shifts in her seat, and her brow creases in . . . surprise? Worry? Confusion? Hard to tell, but I mark her betrayal of *any* emotion as noteworthy.

Nari leans back and stares at the ceiling. Candlelight bounces off the capiz shells of the chandelier, giving her face a soft, mottled glow. The aura suits her.

With no one else brave, or stupid, enough to initiate conversation, I finally scoop a forkful of garnished chicken and rice into my mouth. I'm instantly back in my mother's kitchen, gathered round her rough-hewn table, the rice, beans, plantains, and pastries passed family-style to women and Gentles alike. Was it nearly two months or an eternity ago that I said goodbye to the place I never thought I'd miss? Now I'd trade waking up to infernal Diablo over the silk sheets and fine clothes of my tenure here any day. But time only moves forward, not back, and that life ran its course. Just like my innocence.

I shove in another bite to keep my mouth from telling Nari everything. I don't know why I care so much what she thinks of me. That's not true. I do know. I care because I wish I were more like her. And I crave her admiration because it would compliment my character.

When she turns her attention back to me, none of us misses her troubled expression, but she drops the subject anyway. "Well, one more day," she concludes blandly, raising a thin-stemmed glass of bubbly chicha. "To the Succession."

We raise our glasses, reluctantly clinking each against the others. I toast Nari, then Bri, who downs her glass in two gulps. But when I stretch my glass across the table to Jamara, her wordless glare sends a chill through my body, despite the warmth of the arboretum. Her eyes hold mine in a death grip of pure, cold hate.

"May the best Candidate win," she whispers.

———

The next morning I'm once again at the mercy of Dom Tourmaline, subjected to her bizarre and painful "beautifying" treatments in preparation for the celebration. The Dom is certainly an expert—anyone who could make this Amal girl look the part of distinguished Candidate must be cousins with magic. I just wish it weren't such a hassle to look pretty.

I'm not intimidated by her eccentric vibe or expressionless face like the first time we met. Now I recognize her image as an artist embodying her craft: a moving, breathing statue. Despite the overapplied makeup and obtrusive orange hair, her intelligence still shines through her eyes.

I'm back in the torture chair, trying to stifle yelps while she strips hair from my forearms, when a knock interrupts us. Domus enters with an apology, crossing the dressing room in shuffled steps.

"Dom Reina," he says with a little bow of his wrinkled head. "This came for you."

I take a small envelope from his hand but don't thank him—not in front of Dom Tourmaline. If my coolness makes him worry I hate him for his part in hiding the truth from me, so be it. He can see that I'm here, making a go at this thing instead of guzzling grief in my room. I heeded his reprimand. That must be gratitude enough.

Inside the unsealed envelope, a short note on plain parchment bears my mother's handwriting.

*Dearest Reina,*

*How sorry I am to miss the festivities today. Jonalyn has begun labor and, given her condition, I cannot leave her side. I trust you'll understand, but please know how I wish to be there with you. I pray the outcome is what's best for you and all Nedé. If you stay on at Finca del Mar, I will visit soon.*

*Love you, Rei of Sunshine,*
*Mother*

Embarrassment and anger rise in my chest—not due to Mother's words, but because my stupid eyes sting with salt, threatening to let loose tears. It was easier not caring. I didn't miss her when I couldn't stand her. I shove the letter into a pocket and breathe deeply, trying to stave off emotion.

"Not bad news, I hope," Dom Tourmaline probes.

"Oh, no. It's . . . my mother won't be coming to the celebration. It's fine. Really. My sister is having a baby—early, I think— and she has to be with her."

"Are you close with your mother, then?"

"No, not really. But I . . . I think we will be closer now that I'm not living at home. I'm sorry she won't be here, anyway."

The truth is, I do miss her, but I also need to know what Jonalyn meant by Mother being "connected" with the Brutes. And why Jase has her eyes. And why Torvus knows of her. And I was hoping to get that chance today.

"I understand," the Dom muses. "We all have to make our way in this world. Sometimes letting go proves more difficult than we anticipated."

"Exactly."

She finishes smoothing a blessedly cool oil over my de-haired limbs, then directs me to another chair surrounded by an assortment of makeup cases and hair accessories.

The soft brushes and jewel-toned cakes of powder call to mind the last time I served as Dom Tourmaline's canvas. The Exhibition of the Arts flew in the face of one of Nedé's core Virtues; simplicity was replaced by Grandmother's affinity for finery and abundant chicha. But today's celebration is more ceremony than party, and I doubt the Senators would be as forgiving if the Candidates arrived too fancied up.

"Why bother with all of this?" I wave a hand up and down my body. "It's not like it will help my chances."

She sucks in a sharp breath, as if I've punched her in the gut. "Why bother? *Why . . . ?*" She sweeps a strand of hair up to the crown of my head, clipping it a little too roughly with a metal band, and mutters, "Some women have no vision."

"I didn't mean . . . I just figure Grandmother's decision is probably made, so . . . ?" I let my voice trail away, certain my apology isn't working.

She braids, twists, and clips several more sections of hair in silence, moving around my head until she's right in front of me. When she secures the last lock, she suddenly crouches down, meeting my eyes with her own.

"You're a smart woman, Dom Pierce, not unlike your mother. Certainly you can guess why this matters. What was my commission, *hmmm?*"

"Um . . ." Put on the spot, and completely taken off guard by her sudden switch of demeanor, I search the annals of our first conversations for an answer. "To make me look better than the goats I lived with?"

"That was necessary, yes. But what else?"

"So I wouldn't embarrass Grandmother."

She tips her head and raises an eyebrow. While she waits for me to figure out what I've missed, she fingers the cobalt feathers of her hairpiece, smoothing nonexistent ruffles. Of course. It's always about—

"Control," I say. "She wants to know I'd do anything—change anything—be just what she wants."

Dom Tourmaline straightens, selects a small gold band from among her accessories, and clamps it somewhere in the maze of braids.

As if the past minute didn't happen, she says in her more familiar, ethereal tone, "I may not be able to dress you in a gown fit for the occasion, but I assure you, Dom Pierce, I have spared no attention to detail."

She removes a silk sheath from the outfit hanging on the armoire, revealing the most beautiful "plain clothes" I've ever seen.

"Dom Tourmaline . . . "

At first glance, the dress appears basic enough. The ivory silk, sleeveless bodice with a high neckline falls into sheer, asymmetrical silk panels from waist to midcalf. But muted turquoise, green, yellow, and crimson splashes hint just softly enough at the Matriarch's own robe without insinuating privilege. Seamless black riding pants peek out below the hem, paired with my favorite feature of the entire ensemble: a pair of black leather riding boots, ornate with custom tooling.

"It's customary for each Candidate to wear something representative of her destiny, but as you hadn't chosen one before you were selected, I took the liberty of fashioning something after what yours could be."

What mine *could be*. Apprentice. Alexia. Hero. Matriarch.

A new look for a new destiny.

As I slip into her masterpiece, I consider the countless hours she must have spent designing and dying the fabric, stitching the pants, commissioning the boots—all for me. All to convince Matriarch Teera that I am what she wants me to be. *Why?*

Dom Tourmaline guides me to a mirror so we can observe the result. I still don't care for all the fussing, pulling, buffing, smoothing, and painting, but Dom Tourmaline has accomplished every task Grandmother gave her. Once again, the girl in the mirror holds my attention. A strange muse steals my concentration: her beauty holds my attention the way Rohan's form held it. My gaze traces every angle and curve, admiring the art of me, the way I admired the strength of him.

Heat creeps into my cheeks, and I will myself to banish the memory of watching him sleep. *Not here, not now, Reina.* I have to keep my mind focused on today. This could be the biggest day of my existence—the day I am chosen as Apprentice to the Matriarch—the day I begin the journey of becoming Nedé's ninth ruler—the first day of the rest of my life. Besides, *he can't have your heart, Reina Pierce. He's not safe.*

I find Dom Tourmaline's face in the mirror's reflection. One corner of her lips turns up ever so slightly. She's pleased. Rightly so.

"It's perfect," we say in unison.

# CHAPTER TWENTY-FOUR

*Long live Nedé, the Brutes are no more,*
*And peace shall ever rule;*
*Bring virtue and sacrifice,*
*All women now rejoice,*
*Tyranny is dead, we'll forge fast ahead . . .*

A MATCHLESS CHORUS OF VOICES carries the tune, reverberating around the Arena as thousands of women from across Nedé celebrate our unity, diversity, victory, and all-around grit. Nedéans love to sing, but the abundant chicha at the celebration raises their voices louder and prouder, even without instrumental accompaniment.

The four arched entrances, along with every railing and baluster, drip with garlands and swags of palm, monstera, bougainvillea, bird-of-paradise, and laceleaf. Orange and red flags unfurl from posts around the Arena, dancing and snapping in the breeze like birds in flight. With blue sky above, and obstacles for the Alexia demonstration waiting below, the whole scene fills my heart with such euphoria I'm tempted to sing as loud as the rest.

From a circular stage positioned in the center of the obstacles, ten feet high and triple that across, Freja leads us in the final lines of the Nedéan anthem as eloquently as at the Exhibition. Her voice paints the words as smoothly as her brushes stroked the canvas in the garden.

*Living as one, with our Gentle sons,*
*Nothing more can they take,*
*The future's now ours to make.*

I want to give myself fully to the moment. But even as I sing the lines, I can't help but fixate on the words. Once simply an anthem of our collective pride in Nedé—my love included—now I squirm at the suggestion that "Brutes are no more," "Tyranny is dead," and we are living "as one, with our Gentle sons." And if those are lies, what other false ideals have I believed without question?

The Candidates, attended by Dom Russo, sit on our own private balcony, directly across from the Matriarch's box, where we can watch the determiner of our fate from afar. As the song ends, Teera stands, stretching her arms wide toward the crowd like an enormous embrace.

"Women of Nedé, it is my great honor to congratulate you on two hundred years of peace, prosperity, and productivity. The foremothers sacrificed much to escape the tyranny of the ancient world, facing their fears to usher in a new age of reason and virtue. They built Nedé with their own hands: a land in which all may live peacefully, all may reach their full potential—women and Gentles alike. We have proven our superiority to the Brutes of old, who used lies to entice and violence to enslave. But the Brutes are no more, and what we have created, on the shoulders of our predecessors, outshines anything that came before!"

A cheer erupts from the crowd, and I'm forced to clap along. A chant begins on one end of the Arena, quickly engulfing the crowd like a rolling wave: "Nedé stands for peace! Nedé stands for virtue!"

Matriarch Teera smiles, but knowing Grandmother, she's enduring the interruption rather than appreciating it.

"Nedé stands for peace! Nedé stands for virtue!"

Eventually the Mother of Nedé raises her hands to hush her unruly children.

"Indeed, Nedé stands for peace and for virtue, and during my tenure as Matriarch I have worked to ensure those ideals remain safe from any threat. Many others who share that passion have committed their lives, their destinies, to maintaining order in Nedé: the Alexia, Nedé's crowning jewel!"

A series of loud *pops* coincide with her final words, and billows of flower petals burst from unseen canisters, showering cantering Lexanders with a rainbow of petals as they burst through each of the four archways. The four groups stream around the perimeter, then weave in and out of each other in a practiced dance. The complicated choreography continues: the horses gallop and turn, weave and jump with skill matched only by their riders. Adoni sits tall on her pure black mare, Nyx, whose bridle and saddle shine with beads the same bright colors as the petals stuck in her mane and tail. Adoni readies her bow, and the other Alexia follow suit. Soon the Arena floor is crisscrossed with flying arrows, zinging past riders and piercing painted targets.

For a moment the scent of leather and horse, the mixture of adrenaline and wonder, combine, and I'm eight years old again, sitting next to Grandmother in silent awe of the sleek horses and daring riders. But now, after three weeks of Candidate training with the Alexia, I no longer doubt I could do it—I could be one of them. I owe my newfound confidence to one unique woman. I scan the Arena and spot gold-tinged Midas rounding the near corner. Trinidad's tight, gold-tipped curls bounce in time to her horse's beat. She somehow keeps her bow perfectly steady as she rides, easily striking another target. To cheers from the crowd, she swings her right leg over Midas's back, balancing on her left foot in a single stirrup, to hit a moving target directly behind them.

I've never watched my unlikely mentor show off—not since knowing who she was, anyway. Watching her nail trick after trick proves how lucky I am to have been trained by her, *and* how far I have yet to go.

Still, the show of skill and my affinity for the riders almost makes me hope the pending announcement doesn't pan out in my favor. For a few short seconds I fantasize about taking Adoni up on her offer to return to the Arena as a recruit. I curl and stretch my toes in the custom-made riding boots. If not for my duty to Tre and the other Gentles, I'd jump off this platform right now and go swear allegiance to Adoni. In another life—in a world before the Succession—I was born to be Alexia. I was made to wear leather and carry a bow and sword. And though Adoni would never give Callisto the chance, she was born to run with these horses, decorated in beads and embossed leather and running her heart out.

The thought of Callisto reminds me of the danger of sickness, which transports me to the morning I found blood on her neck, which, in turn, reminds me of Jase and Rohan. And why does everything seem to go back to Rohan?

*He's not safe.*

Even though Matriarch Teera's opening speech was laced with

troubling hypocrisy, the foremothers did away with Brutes for a reason. Dáin is all the example I need of their terrorizing potential.

Dáin. I squeeze fistfuls of my gauzy skirt, immediately feeling naked without a weapon. But there's no need. He's likely chained in a cell under this very Arena floor. I only know the hidden cells exist because of my mother. As the Matriarch's daughter, she knows things—most of which I gather she'd rather forget, but still, the cells under the Arena came up once, somehow, and I've always wondered why they exist. There's already a jail and stocks in Phoenix City, in plain sight. Why would Grandmother have *secret* cells? Could they have been made for the Brutes? And if so, how long has she known they exist?

Questions about the Brutes, how the vaccine affects Gentles, and what must be done churn my mind like a spoon stirring a water glass into a swirling whirlpool. The next spare hour I find I'll read Tristan Pierce's journal again, try to steady the spinning inside, make sure I didn't miss any other clues our first Matriarch might have left behind.

When every obstacle has been conquered and every target resembles a pincushion, Matriarch Teera rises again, booming, "Your Alexia!" The black-clad peacekeepers circle and bow to deafening cheers.

Dom Russo pokes my back with a bony finger, hissing, "Hurry up, Dom Pierce." It's time to take the stage. As I step double time to catch up with the other Candidates, the Matriarch begins the speech that will seal our fates.

"Forty-six years ago," she begins, "I was chosen to represent the people of Nedé."

Her voice dims as I duck into the passageway, taking the stairs two by two and bumping into Bri at the bottom.

She jabs, "Professional to the end, *Reina*."

"Annoying to the end, Brishalynn."

She half-smirks, half-smiles, holding my gaze a moment as we line up across the eastern archway, awaiting our cue. I really don't get that girl.

I have nothing to say to Jamara, but if this is to be my last interaction with the Candidates before becoming Apprentice, I want to say something to Bri and Nari. But what? That I know I'm probably going to win, and I hope we can still be friends? That if somehow I don't win, I hope Nari does? That I'm sorry for not being a better friend? What sort of farewell does one give women you hope to beat and will likely never see again?

"I've been glad to know you all," I say, immediately embarrassed by my lame attempt.

Bri rolls her eyes, Jamara ignores me, but Nari squeezes my arm. "You too," she says, before facing the Arena floor.

Matriarch Teera's concluding remarks reach the alcove, and Dom Russo sweeps a hand at us, signaling the time has come. The four remaining Candidates march side by side toward the stage to a chorus of musical instruments and thousands of cheering, slightly inebriated women. We climb eight stairs to the stage, then stand in a circle, backs to each other, staring out at our potential future subjects. I face the northern section of the Arena, where the Alexia and their horses stand at attention against the far wall. I catch Trin's eye and try not to smile. She nods slightly, mouthing the words, "You've got this, Candidate." I silently take up the refrain, *You've got this, Reina. You've got this.*

"The four Candidates before you," Teera resumes, "have undergone rigorous training in each of our most vital destinies to ensure Nedé's legacy of wise, courageous leadership continues for years to come. After careful evaluation and consideration, per Article I of the Constitution of Nedé, I hereby choose as my Apprentice . . . "

Only the whip-snap of colorful flags interrupts the silent hush over the Arena. Sweat beads on my shoulders, dripping carelessly down my back. "Please," I beg my mother's God, *"please let me help them."*

" . . . Jamara Makeda of Kekuatan Province."

The crowd erupts in another chorus of cheers, whistles, and whoops, and musicians take up the Nedéan anthem again.

My knees threaten to buckle under me, and a wave of dizziness nearly takes me down.

*Jamara?*

Of course they would cheer—they don't know her. They have no idea what she's done, what she's capable of. I'm supposed to congratulate her—we all are. As I wait my turn, I can't resist turning toward Grandmother. I don't cry, don't plead. I don't even glare. All the confusion inside me manifests in a stupid, blank stare. I know she notices me, but ever the stately one, she doesn't so much as grace me with a glance.

Nari goes first, gripping Jamara's forearm in the traditional Nedéan way. "Congratulations, Dom Makeda. May you represent us well."

Jamara smiles, the closest thing to a genuine smile I've ever seen on her wide, dark face, even showing her teeth.

"Well, well," Bri says when it's her turn, "if you didn't pull it out of your backbiting—" She finishes the uncouth slam by whistling through her teeth, and I wonder if she's contemplating punching Jamara's out. It would serve her right, after what she did to Bri. She would have killed her if I hadn't let my monkey-butt self get knocked out in her stead.

Bri steps aside, and it's my turn. Jamara's tunic is stiff and pale green—both the texture and color recalling the uniform of Gentles Regimen, her former destiny. I reluctantly grip her forearm, searching for the words I never thought I'd say. *Be mature. She won. Don't be a sore loser,* I coach myself. But if it weren't blistering hot outside, ice might form in the space between our eyes.

"Congratulations, Dom Makeda," I force out. "May you serve Nedé well." I space the words without really meaning to; it's just that each one requires monumental effort.

Instead of releasing her grip, Jamara squeezes my arm more tightly. "The best Candidate won after all, Dom Pierce," she hisses through a stately smile, "and you had better stay out of her way."

# CHAPTER TWENTY-FIVE

THE SURREY RIDE BACK TO FINCA DEL MAR passes in a jostling blur. At least Dom Russo had the good sense to arrange private transportation after the announcement. The wheels rattle down the stone driveway, between rows of stick-straight palms, toward the sprawling villa. I detest the perfection of it more than ever. Anger burns in my veins like the rising, heavy heat of midafternoon.

Before the driver has time to stop the horses, I jump from the surrey and storm past the pond-like fountain, splashing a handful of water on my way to the front door. Nedé's motto, hung above the threshold, goads me.

*Protect the weak. Justice for all.*
*Power without virtue is tyranny.*

What hope do we have now? Grandmother's disdain for Gentles is evident. But the Candidate—no, the *Apprentice*—from

Kekuatan is no better. Jamara proved that she will do anything for power. I can't think of a single virtue I admire about her.

Inside the villa, I blaze straight for the marble staircase to the second floor, taking the stairs in leaps, storm across the breeze-way to the north wing, and pound three times on the enormous mahogany door of the Matriarch's suite. It's risky—I've never dared come to her private quarters before—but I know she'll be here, getting ready for the after-party that begins in an hour, and I need to speak with her. I need to know. If I wasn't sure the door would be locked, I'd barge right through it.

After a long pause, she inquires, "Who is it?"

"It's Reina."

The silence drags on three seconds past hopeless, but then, wonder of wonders, she opens the door.

Grandmother has changed into a peach silk robe, though her celebration hair and makeup remain intact. One thin eyebrow raises, as if in warning. "Yes?"

"May I come in?"

She spins away, leaving me to close the door behind us. "What do you want?"

I glance around the room to get my bearings. Like the Senator's Suite, the eastern wall comprises floor-to-ceiling windows, boasting shimmering sea views and ample sunlight. Velvet furniture creates a seating area in front of the windows, and there's a small kitchen, and a large library, and an enormous bed piled high with both pillows and a pinch-faced woman wearing a jaguar-print robe.

*Dom Russo?*

The implications take a moment to settle, and when they do, my stomach lurches. I tighten my jaw so it won't hang open. Every new facet of Grandmother I discover further undermines my respect for her. The Mother of Nedé, disregarding yet another core virtue—self-restraint—the very virtue she has punished others severely for defying? It's sickening.

Grandmother grows impatient. "Did you come in here to stare, or have you something intelligent to say?"

"I'd like to speak to you—alone."

She considers for a moment, then nods toward her advisor, who excuses herself to another room, closing the door behind her.

"I suppose you want to know why I didn't choose you," Grandmother says coolly.

"I know Candidates aren't entitled to an explanation, but as your granddaughter, after you brought me here, after all you said, I think I deserve to know why."

"Very well."

*Very well?* It worked? She's actually going to tell me? I play off my shock like I knew my boldness and sound logic would convince her.

She crosses the room to the kitchen, opens a cabinet, and pours two glasses of chicha. I decline the one she offers me, garnering a knowing smirk from the old woman.

"I was going to choose you, you know." She sips the bubbly, amber liquid, letting it settle on her tongue before continuing. "Despite Leda's pathetic influence, you showed promise. Adoni said you handled yourself well in the Arena, and even Russo conceded you had the potential to be a competent understudy. After you executed the Gentle, I was properly convinced you'd make me proud after all."

My mouth feels suddenly dry and I swallow with difficulty. "So what changed?"

She turns again to the glass like we have all the time in the world. I wonder how much she's already consumed today.

"Trust changed, Reina. I needed to know I could rely on you to tell me everything, that you could be counted on to respect the bounds of my authority." She moves toward a stack of books on a desk near the window.

"But you *can* trust me. I've given you everything and taken nothing in return."

"Taken *nothing*?" Her hand rises along with her voice, and I fear a blow is coming. Instead she thrusts a book in my face. "Is this nothing?"

I recognize the faded leather binding: Tristan's journal.

"How dare you enter my private office and take anything of mine?"

"I didn't . . . " I stammer. "I'd never go into your office . . . I promise, I . . . I did read it, but I didn't steal it. I found it upstairs."

Her eyes narrow to slits and her nostrils flare, just enough for me to notice.

"Found it?" she quietly seethes. I liked the yelling better.

"In the little library on the third floor."

She seems to be putting pieces together silently, then, in a fit of fury, she throws her crystal glass against the wall. It explodes in a shower of iridescent shards.

I might not have stolen it, but the fact that I didn't let on how much I knew when she questioned me after the Jungle has already condemned me. There's no use trying to convince her of my innocence. She might not realize just how much I know, but she knows I kept something from her, and there's no reversing that. So I air my own useless suspicions before she can accuse me of anything else.

"Why were you in my room?"

I immediately recognize how silly this question is. She's the Matriarch—she can go wherever the bats she pleases. But perhaps all the chicha works in my favor, because she says, "I was collecting this." She retrieves Rohan's dagger from a drawer in the desk, then turns it this way and that in the light, contemplating the craftsmanship. I want to rip it from her hands.

"You don't know what they're like," she says, returning to the cool, composed cadence I'm used to. "I'm assuming you read it—" she flits a hand at the tattered leather book— "but you don't know the half of it, Reina. There are other records you'll never be privy to, not now." She sets down the weapon, and I'm relieved she doesn't throw that against the wall too.

"You probably think I'm too hard on the Gentles, but if you understood the alternative, you wouldn't blame me. You're full of ideals and mercy, just like your mother, but you have no idea the horrors they're capable of. If the *Gentles* themselves knew the vile creatures they were saved from becoming, they'd beg for the vaccines. But we can't give them that choice. No, they must never have that choice. We who are wise and full of self-control must make the decision for them, to protect them from themselves, and us from them."

I take a risk to feel out the scope of her awareness. "How many are there? Out there, now?"

"Does it matter? It only takes one Brute to bring evil back into the world, Reina. *Just one.* And I will double the force of the Alexia if I must to stomp every ember of their threat into the ground."

Seconds pass between us, eyes locked, tension as taut as a bow-string. This game she plays—the coolness and twisting, telling but not divulging—in the course of Candidacy I've picked up a nuance or two myself. I could hold my ground, could fire back some insult, but I need her to yet doubt what I know. The wisest move would be none at all. So I hold her gaze with measured calm.

"Of course, Matriarch."

The dagger glows white against the oiled mahogany desk. No matter how stupid the impulse, it takes tremendous self-control not to swipe it before turning on my heel and marching out the door.

---

I keep my composure across the breezeway and down a long, narrow hall, straight to the Senator's Suite. Once inside the relative security of my room—my *former* room—I barely hold it together. The mountain of pillows and silk bedding beckons me, but instead I throw open drawers and rummage through the armoire until I find the leather rucksack I brought from Bella Terra nearly eight weeks ago.

I stuff it with a couple of new shirts, my old riding pants, and a backless jumpsuit à la Dom Tourmaline which I tolerated slightly more than the other impractical clothes she curated for me. In the remaining space, I shove in one hairbrush, two scarves, and a carved wooden monkey with a crooked smile, then button the flap. That's it—all I take with me from nearly two months of training: a stuffed bag and an empty heart.

A knock startles me, until I recognize the three evenly spaced raps as Domus's.

"Come in."

He closes the door silently behind him before giving a tight little bow. "Dom Reina, I . . . am very sorry about this turn of events."

And then I lose it—I really lose it. All the implications I've been avoiding since the announcement crash through my chest, leaving an aching hole in their wake.

"He died for nothing, Domus, *nothing!*" Tears quickly spill over and down my cheeks, making a mess of Dom Tourmaline's carefully applied powders and creams. "He sacrificed himself so I could win, so I could help you, and I failed. I killed him, and I still failed."

Domus edges closer, like a timid old dog, squeezing his hands together and crying too, but without the fuel of anger his tears come softly, almost apologetically. Sometimes the placidity of Gentles infuriates me, but for once I am grateful he expresses his grief gently, or I might completely lose it.

After a minute filled with only the sounds of regret and sorrow, Domus says, "The important thing now . . . Dom Reina, I overheard your conversation with the Matriarch."

"How—?"

Like Neechi, he brushes my question aside with a wave of his hand. "I put the journal in the library. Many years ago your mother, kind Dom Leda, showed me the book." He says Mother's name with the tenderest of affection. "I can't read, of course, but she told me it contained important information—very important information—and that someday, if another woman came to Finca del Mar who showed us kindness, I should . . . *help* that person find it too."

"My mother?" Shock seals up my tear ducts fast.

Domus nods. "I knew you should have it. You're very much like her, you see. I thought you should know where it came from. And I wanted to say my goodbyes."

It takes me a moment to realize he's not referring to my leaving the Finca tonight. "What do you mean, Domus?"

He sighs, his gaze dropping to his polished leather shoes. "It's my time, Dom Reina." When I still don't catch on, he continues, "She knows one of us moved it. No matter who she suspects, she won't take any chances."

"Domus," I whisper, but any following words drown before they reach my throat. He's right. Grandmother would easily dispose of ten Gentles to root out one traitor. And she only knows about it because I denied I took it.

"All this blood on my hands."

"No," he says firmly. "Not on your hands. On hers. Don't you take it as your own. I'd do it again. You might not be Apprentice, but I know you'll do something good with what I showed you. It won't be for nothing. You'll see."

Whether he's trying to convince me or himself, I'm not sure either of us is persuaded.

"What if we got you out of here? I could take you to my mother's place."

"No. Running would make it worse for the others. If she believes she caught the traitor, her anger will die down faster. Besides," he smiles wistfully, "I'm an old Gentle. Lived longer than most, with more comforts than any. It's time, and I'll meet my end with the courage Treowe showed when he met his."

It's so painfully unfair. I take his dark, wrinkled hands in mine. They feel like leather, etched as bark. "Then thank you, Domus, for everything."

He nods, pats my hand with his, then turns toward the door.

A sudden thought arrests me. "Domus, what about Neechi?"

His wiry eyebrows bunch with weary concern. "I don't know. His chance is better than ours in the villa. Better not to tell him so he has nothing to hide."

The door clicks closed, and the tears start again. I have to do something, but what?

Outside my windows, guests have begun milling in the garden, Senators and friends of the Matriarch, families of the Candidates, and whoever else Grandmother invited to continue the celebration.

I slip out of the colorful, symbolic dress Dom Tourmaline made for the ceremony, replacing it with something similar from the armoire, but in a more appropriate color for my mood: pitch black. I retain the custom pants and boots she designed, so that I could almost pass for an Alexia, if not for the sheer skirt trailing from the tight, sleeveless bodice, speckled with constellation-like silver specks.

I leave my hair as it is too, full of twists and braids, and secured with shiny, metal bands, thankful that Dom Tourmaline's artistry was clearly Alexia-inspired today. Rummaging around a drawer, I find a few cakes of powder and attempt to remedy the worst of the tear damage.

I turn in a complete circle, taking one last look at the opulence I nearly called home. Then I swing the rucksack over my shoulder, and head to the one place I know I shouldn't go.

———————

I'll have only a few minutes before I'm expected in the great hall, so I practically run over the tile path that winds through the sprawling seaside garden to the open-air stable.

I've never been so relieved to see that Gentle brushing down a mare in the breezeway.

When Neechi sees me, a smile stretches across his wide face. "Good news?"

I duck into a stall next to him so we can talk quietly. It's still risky, but I have no choice.

"No, not good news." His face falls like a sudden downpour, but I don't have time to explain. "Listen, Neechi, I don't have much time. I need you to do something for me. I need you to have Callisto ready for me tonight." I hand over my sack of belongings. "I don't know when I'll be back, but make sure she's fed and brushed down, okay?"

"Of course, Dom Reina," he says, but there's a question in his tone I can't blame. I could have come and got my horse with or without Neechi's "preparations." All I need for my horse is a neck rope, for crying out loud. I'm just hedging, trying to decide whether to tell him.

I consider Neechi, with his short frame, kind eyes, and worn hands. And I consider losing his friendship—the way I've lost Tre, the way she'll kill Domus. I can't let this Gentle's death be my fault too.

"I need you to do something else," I whisper. "You know Old Solomon, and how he works at my mother's place? You must have some way of finding out how to get there, right? You need to get there, Neechi. I want you to leave Finca del Mar, tonight if you can, and find your way to Bella Terra. Tell Dom Leda I sent you—you'd be a great help to Old Solomon—and tell her I'll explain soon. Could you make it there, without being caught?"

Neechi rubs the back of his neck with one hand, and returns to brushing with the other. "It's a risk."

"It's worth a shot," I try again. "You're not safe here."

He chuckles, but without humor. "I've never been safe here, Dom Reina." He looks up from the horse. "But I appreciate you looking out for me."

I want to press him further, make him promise, but I'm out of time.

"I have to go. Please try, Neechi. For me?" Yet as I step through the bulletwood gate, I doubt I'll ever see that soft-spoken stable-hand again.

# CHAPTER TWENTY-SIX

THE GREAT HALL IS ALREADY HALF FULL of guests when I try to slip in unnoticed. The party doesn't match the opulence and grandeur of the Exhibition during training, but no Finca del Mar party would be complete without talented musicians, vibrant bouquets, decadent foods, and an ample supply of chicha.

I don't recognize many of the guests, so I scan the clusters of women dotting the room, looking for an easy entry point. Nari seems deep in conversation with someone who could be a relative. I need someone to converse with, primarily to avoid having to talk with those I'd rather evade. Top on my list of dodge-at-all-costs: Grandmother, who stands shoulder to shoulder with Jamara, introducing her protégé to a group of influentials, including my Aunt Julissa. I'm so intent to skip the potential of encountering them that Bri—who sips a glass of chicha with several Senators at the opposite end of the hall—becomes a viable option. I load a plate with fruit tartlets and chèvre and try my luck.

Shockingly, as I approach the group Bri breaks away and takes my arm, all familiar-like, so that anyone watching would think we were the best of friends reunited after months apart. But this is Bri, and as she guides me casually across the room, I know she's up to something even before she leads us into the unoccupied dressing room where Dom Tourmaline styled me just this morning.

With the door closed behind us, she drops the facade like a hot rock. "What the bats happened?"

"What?"

"*What*? What could you possibly have done to screw it up? You had it. We all knew you were her choice."

"I thought you didn't want me to win."

Ignoring my deflection, she continues a puzzled tirade. "You were the only one who completed your test. Nari couldn't do it, Jamara got stopped short, but you . . . I thought you . . . didn't you . . . ?"

"Yes, I did it," I snap miserably, throat tightening with anger. "I shot him."

Genuine confusion softens Bri's hard expression. "Then what happened?" she asks again, barely above a whisper.

I stall a moment, weighing how much to tell her, if anything. But what does it matter now? Apart from my promise to Torvus not to tell anyone about *them*, I'm under no obligation to hide the truth. Besides, Bri already knows about the raids—she was on the same patrol that chased the column of smoke to the burning finca.

"I read Tristan Pierce's journal, Bri. I found it, and I read it, and I discovered there's a lot of things we haven't been told. She caught me with it."

A subtle shift occurs between me and my fellow Candidate from Amal. Perhaps now that I'm no longer a threat to her, she can stomach me easier. Or maybe we've been through too much together for her to keep up the act any longer. Whatever her reasons, she drops the bravado, the obnoxious needling. At least for now.

"What did it say?" she asks.

I take a deep breath and hope to Siyah I'm not making a mistake.

"A lot of things. Mostly that Gentles aren't born dull-headed and lazy—they're made that way by a vaccine. I think it's that shot they give the babies at the Center."

She tugs at a strand of hair as she considers this information. Her mind must be spinning. Why wouldn't it be? I've had weeks to put the pieces together—and a whole unconventional childhood to prepare me to see the Gentles as human. But strangely, she doesn't seem very broken up over the revelation.

"So what?" she finally counters. "They have to keep them from becoming Brutes somehow, right? Whether it was all at once ages ago, or whether we have to keep doing it over and over, either way, we're keeping Gentles from becoming Brutes. Why would knowing that keep Teera from choosing you?"

I consider her question. I turn it over and over, then back to front again. I realize I'm afraid of the answer, terrified by the implications of my doubt.

"I guess because she's not sure which I think is better."

Bri slaps her forehead and lets her fingers drag down her face, finally resting over a gaping mouth.

"Not sure which is better? Monsters who hurt women or Gentles who serve them? Yeah, tough choice."

"It's not that simple."

She shakes her head in disbelief. "Maybe your mother did turn you soft." But there's no sarcasm in her voice. Pity instead, which is always worse.

The only way to convince Bri I'm not crazy would be to tell her about the Brutes I met, which I can't, not without breaking my word. If she could hear Jase's easy laughter, or watch the way Rohan tended to my shoulder, if she had witnessed the cubs tromping innocently through the Jungle, or listened to the drums and cheers around the fire, then maybe she'd be as conflicted as I am.

"What if they weren't all monsters?" I send the probe out gently, pretending I just thought to ask myself this very question.

"Then the foremothers wouldn't have had to do what they did," she says with confident finality. "But if you're asking those kinds of questions—geez, Reina—it's no wonder you scared off Teera."

"I didn't say . . . "

"Shut up," she cuts in with a hint of the old Bri. "Whatever you said or didn't say, you'd better get out of here. Soon. If she chose Dom Evil because she can't trust you, you think she's going to let you just walk away, knowing whatever you know that she doesn't want you to know? Hmmm?"

"She's my grandmother," I start to defend, but I don't need Bri's epic eye roll to tell me what a stupid argument that is.

"And even if she doesn't invent some reason to dispose of you," she continues, "*Jamara* will have no problem finishing what Adoni interrupted. Once that witch is Matriarch, none of us are safe. I bet she'll even finish off Yasmine, just to be cruel."

I cringe at the thought of Jamara's probable rampage of revenge. "Where are *you* going to go?"

Bri shrugs. "Doesn't matter. Figure I've got a year at least until she takes over Nedé. Teera doesn't give five rats about me. She didn't even test me, remember? I'm no threat to her. But she might change her mind if she catches me talking to your traitorous butt. We'd better get out there." She pauses as she reaches for the door handle. "Don't get yourself killed, okay?"

"Yeah," I say. "You too."

A few steps outside the dressing room we part, taking opposite, nonchalant paths through the crowd to minimize any association.

I wander aimlessly at first, pretending to be absorbed with my hors d'oeuvres and the nearby musicians. A flavor, or scent, or chord—something triggers a memory, and I'm transported to the dance-drama at the Exhibition in this very room—the tale of one woman whose bravery changed everything. They made Tristan seem so perfect. A brave hero, liberating women everywhere from the Brutes' evil.

I wanted to be like her then. I wanted my bravery to change the course of history too. That was before I found her journal—filled with nightmares and self-doubt—and discovered the price she was willing to pay for safety. It was before I danced around a fire ring with Brutes. That was before "bravery" ended in murdering my best friend. Before I failed.

The room grows hot, and I amble closer to the double doors that exit into the garden. Surely I've endured enough polite nods and awkward wandering to get credit for not being a sore loser. I'm ready to get out of here. But I don't reach fresh air before catching Jamara's watchful eye. Victoriously attached to the Matriarch, she appraises me coolly, her back straight as a teak tree, her thick arms protruding like branches from the green tunic falling to her ankles. She purses her full lips, and her nostrils flare slightly. Teera's quintessential understudy. I don't know whether to laugh at the blatant plagiarism of intimidation techniques or to be afraid. No, I won't give her the satisfaction of fear tonight, but I'm not stupid either—I'll stay as far away from Jamara Makeda as I can manage. Starting now.

I slip outdoors into the fading light of evening and inhale sharply the heavy, plumeria-tinged air. It fills my lungs like freedom. Strings of lights make up for the fading sun, reflecting off waxy leaves and illuminating the mosaic tiles underfoot. My feet follow the familiar path while my mind wonders about another familiarity: my sister Jonalyn. I wish I could ride all the way to Bella Terra tonight—to see her and Mother, Cassia and the new baby, too, to sleep in my old bed and wake to Ciela's stupid rooster. But home is the first place Grandmother would expect me to go, and while I have no reason to think she'd come after me, Bri's words have me nervous. Besides, the time has come to choose my destiny. The Succession proved a timely delay of the inevitable, but I can't avoid the decision any longer. And after today, I don't want to.

The stables are quiet and empty, dark too, with only traces of the last ambient light of day. No stablehand oils saddles in the breezeway, or rakes stalls, or brushes horses, and hope flutters in my chest. It's late enough that Neechi could have simply gone to his quarters for the night, but still, there's a chance he listened. And I'll take what hope I can get.

Callisto nickers, and I head straight to her stall, letting her nuzzle my cheek and giving her velvety nose a kiss. No surprise, she's smooth and clean, and a circle of rope hangs on a peg outside her gate next to my rucksack. She stamps a hoof restlessly.

"What's wrong, girl? You anxious to go too? I don't know why. Neechi spoiled you rotten."

She stomps again, then shakes her head. I reach a hand out to calm her, but her agitation makes me nervous. Does she sense something?

Not wasting any time, I lead her out of the stall, slip on the neck rope, shoulder the leather sack, and make a straight shot for the Arena.

———

Darkness settles over the barracks by the time I knock on the rust-red door marked with a faded yellow 2. A slight lapse in planning—I hadn't accounted for the fact that the Arena would be deserted for the night by the time I arrived, or the unfortunate fact that I didn't actually know where Trin lived. Lucky for me, I chanced upon three Alexia strolling past the paddock where I took the liberty of turning out Callisto for the night, and they pointed me in the right direction. This plan is really going to stink if she's not home.

I'm about to knock a second time when the lock clicks and the door swings inward. An unfamiliar Trinidad appears behind it, dressed in a silk camisole and simple linen shorts, arms bare of metal bands, her copper-tipped curls stretched straight in a miniature ponytail perched atop her head. Only her peculiar gold eyes hint at the fierce Alexia we witnessed today in the Arena.

"Reina?"

"Hey," I begin awkwardly. I'm aware of the chance I'm taking, and it makes me self-conscious. It's not like Trin and I are *friends*. She did take me under her wing during training, and she seemed genuinely glad I didn't die in the Jungle, but showing up at her private quarters is territory we've never covered. I clearly don't have many options at this point.

"Can I come in?"

She shrugs, then steps back from the door to let me pass. I exhale in relief. This is a start.

The apartment might fit inside my room at Bella Terra, with only a bed and dresser in one corner, a compact table and two chairs under a window, and a small sofa, all made from matching hardwood.

Once Trin closes the door behind us, she relaxes some. "I can't believe she didn't choose you." Just like Trin to get right to the point. "I thought for *sure* she'd choose you, Candidate."

I chuckle, precisely because it's not funny. "That makes two of us."

I invite myself to take a seat on the sofa, and Trin pulls out a chair.

"So what does Adoni think of her new boss?"

It's her turn to smirk. "She's not happy about it. Apprentice Makeda seems just the sort of woman who would order you to turn around so she can stab you in the back. But Adoni has . . . bigger problems at the moment."

I nod impartially, knowing better than to ask, wishing she'd explain more. But I have a pretty good guess what shape those "bigger problems" take, and where one of them is now.

She glances at my bag. "So, what brings you here?"

A flush of unexpected nerves betrays me, and I have to squeeze my hands together to keep them from shaking. I take a steadying breath. Might as well be out with it. "I want to join the Alexia."

She leans over her knees, resting her chin on splayed fingers as she considers me.

"Why?"

*Why?* Such a simple question, and once I had a simple answer. When I used to press Dom Bakshi for help deciding on a destiny—exasperating her with my indecision—I wanted to join the Alexia because they were bold. Daring. The antithesis, I thought, of Materno—of my mother and what I assumed she wanted for me. Then, during Candidate training, I discovered the Alexia were even more than I thought—that they, perhaps more than any other destiny, strive for the Virtues I myself want to embody.

But now? Now that I've seen Teera's tight grip on the defenders of Nedé—know of her plans to use the Alexia to annihilate the Brutes—why *would* I willingly align myself with the sword in her hand?

I close my eyes, remembering how easily she coerced me into doing her bidding, scared she could do it again. No—I didn't shoot Tre for Teera's sake—I did it for him, for a greater good. I did it because I still care about the Virtues. And as long as most of the Alexia do too, maybe Nedé has a chance to right its wrongs. It's worth the risk.

I sigh, slowly, trying to tease out an explanation that will make sense to Trin.

"Because," I say, "as long as women like you wear the bow, I believe the Alexia can still be the destiny it was when your nana carried her dagger." And that's true—as much truth as I can give her tonight.

Trin nods slowly, deep thought and casual clothes giving her a strangely ordinary appearance. Yet even now, stripped of costume and bravado, my unlikely mentor commands respect.

"You can talk with Adoni in the morning," she says, standing. "You have somewhere to sleep tonight?"

"No."

"It's too late to get you into the barracks. You can have the couch."

She doesn't wait for an answer before pulling a thin blanket from a tiny closet and throwing it at my face. "You better not snore."

––––––––––

The next morning Trin finds me a proper Alexia vest to complete the pants and boots from Dom Tourmaline I'm still wearing, then sends me to get my horse while she fillets two avocados in her miniature kitchen. The creamy green flesh replaces a proper breakfast during the short walk to the Arena. By the time we cross under the now-familiar stone archway, the air already lies hotter and heavier than a pregnant sow.

The expanse of gravel and training apparatuses already bustle with a growing crowd of Alexia, more than I expected.

Trin inclines her head, sweat already giving her mocha skin a dewy sheen. "We get the week's patrol orders today. You should talk with Adoni before she thinks you're crashing the party."

The Alexia leader isn't difficult to find. Counting the thick, black braid looping from the top of her head down one shoulder, she stands almost a full head above the others. I lead a slightly antsy Callisto across the Arena floor toward her. I muster confidence as I approach, which I find less difficult than on the first day of Candidate training. Adoni's still slightly terrifying, but I believe I've earned some measure of her respect. At least, I hope I have.

When she sees me coming, she doesn't stop sharpening her short sword until I'm close enough to see the individual black and green scales on her dragon tattoo. The beast curls around her bicep and over her broad shoulder, reminding me why she's in charge around here.

There was a time when I wondered whether my indecision meant I was made for something outside the confines of a single destiny. But standing here among these strong, capable, virtuous women, I suspect I could spend my whole life just trying to do this one justice.

I clear my throat, then swallow the last of my pride. "You told me once that if things didn't work out with the Succession, I'd have a place with you. Does the offer stand?"

She slides the blade into a sheath dangling from her belt as she straightens, expressionless. Then, with the slightest twist of her mouth she asks, "Did you forget that offer didn't extend to your mutt?"

"Don't tell me you're afraid she's going to show up Nyx."

I smile, but regret the quip as soon as it leaves my mouth. Adoni isn't exactly the kind to appreciate a good joke. And the truth is, I know I'm going to have to let Callisto go. I've known for a long time, however stubbornly I've resisted. My fingers instinctively curl around the strands of her two-tone mane. It's time to choose my destiny, even if that means parting with the best horse in the course of human history.

"I do remember," I admit. "And if she can't stay, I'll take her to my mother's finca as soon as I get the chance."

Adoni nods, then looks me up and down, appraising my build. "You need more training," she sniffs. Then, to someone behind me, asks, "You want her?"

Trinidad stands watch behind me, suited up with bow and quiver. The Alexia second-in-command scrunches her nose in false reluctance, rubbing a hand over a gold armband. "I guess I could, if no one else will take her." She winks at me.

Adoni doesn't react to the familiarity between Trin and me. "Once she's ready, assign her a detail." Then, to me, "Avoid notice if you can. Get that horse out of here, and whatever you do, don't show your face at the Finca." She thrusts her forearm toward me. I take my time reaching out, allow myself to feel the press of each finger into her sinewy muscle, and savor this moment I've dreamed of for far too many years. "Welcome to the Alexia, Reina Pierce."

And with that, I'm in.

I don't know what I'm going to do tomorrow—how I'll move forward under the crushing weight of what I've done, tormented by the realizations plaguing me. But today I'll honor Tre's memory.

*Protect the weak.*

I'll trade the wooden sword he crafted for me years ago for one of steel, exchange my ipê-string bow for the precision weapons of the Alexia.

*Safety for all.*

I'm one of them now. I'm finally one of them.

*Because power without virtue is tyranny.*

# Glossary

**Acacia** *(uh KAY shuh)* **Pierce**—daughter of Tristan Pierce; second Matriarch of Nedé

**Ad Artium** *(ad AHRT tee uhm)*—destiny of Nedé specializing in the arts

**Adoni** *(uh DO nee)*—leader of the Alexia

**Agricolátio** *(A gri ko LAH tee o)*—destiny of Nedé specializing in horticulture

**Alexia** *(uh LEX ee uh)*—destiny of Nedé specializing in peacekeeping

**Amal** *(uh MAHL)*—southwestern Province of Nedé, meaning "hope"

**Angelica**—Alexia

**Apprentice**—the Matriarch's choice of successor, selected from among four Candidates; trains under the Matriarch for one year, after which time she assumes the Matriarchal role and title

**Arena**–Alexia training facilities

**Bella Terra** *(BAY yuh TER uh)*–Materno finca managed by Leda Pierce; Reina's home

**Bolas** *(BO luhs)*–a hunting weapon made by attaching each end of a medium-length rope to a sphere made of a heavy material; used to capture animals by entangling their legs

**Brishalynn** *(BREE shuh lin)* **"Bri" Pierce**–Succession Candidate representing Amal

**Brute**–an ungentled male, thought to be extinct

**Callisto** *(kuh LI sto)*–Reina's pinto horse, a Paint and Lexander mix

**Calle del Oeste** *(KAI yay del o ES tay)*–Nedéan thoroughfare running north to south along the western border

**Candidate**–one of four women chosen to compete in the Succession, in which the Matriarch chooses a successor

**Cassia** *(CA see uh)*–Reina's niece; daughter of Jonalyn Pierce

**Center for Health Services**–aka the Center; facility in Phoenix City responsible for medical and Materno services

**Chicha** *(CHEE chuh)*–an alcoholic beverage made from fermenting fruit and/or grains

**Ciela** *(see AY luh)* **Pierce**–Reina's older sister; lab technician at the Center for Health Services

**Dáin** *(DAY in)*–Brute

**Divisadero** *(di vi suh DE ro)* **Mountains**–mountain range marking Nedé's western border

**Dr. Karina Novak** *(kuh REE nuh NO vak)*–doctor; coleader of the Center for Health Services with Leda Pierce

**Dr. Ferrelli** *(fer EL ee)*—Tristan Pierce's psychiatrist

**Dom** *(DAHM)*—shortened form of *Domina*, a title of respect given to women of distinction (adult women who have chosen a destiny) in Nedé

**Dom Bakshi** *(buhk SHEE)*—Reina's tutor; educator of Bella Terra's Gentles

**Dom Russo** *(roo SO)*—advisor to Matriarch Teera

**Dom Tourmaline** *(TUR muh leen)*—personal stylist to Matriarch Teera, assigned to Reina during the Succession

**Domus** *(DAHM uhs)*—Gentle 37628; major domus (finca manager) of Finca del Mar

**Estrella** *(uh STRAY yuh)*—Leda's horse

**Fabricatio** *(fa bri CAH tee o)*—destiny of Nedé dealing with manufacturing

**Fallon** *(FA luhn)*—Alexia

**Fik'iri** *(fik EE ree)*—northeastern Province of Nedé, meaning "love"

**Finca del Mar** *(FEEN kuh del MAHR)*—the Matriarch's estate

**Finglas** *(FIN glahs)*—aka Fin; Brute

**Gentles Regimen**—destiny of Nedé specializing in Hive oversight and Gentles' vocational training

**Halcyon** *(HAL see ahn)* **Sea**—body of water marking Nedé's eastern border

**Highway Volcán** *(vol CAHN)*—main Nedéan thoroughfare running east from Phoenix City to Nedé's western border

**Hive**—live-in training facility for Gentles ages seven to fourteen

**Initus** *(IN i toos)* **Ceremony**—Nedé-wide celebration at the Arena to commemorate the fourteen-year-old Gentles' departure from their respective Hives to begin vocations

**Innovatus** *(in o VAH toos)*—destiny of Nedé dealing with innovation, particularly repurposing materials and maintaining technologies necessary "to increase convenience without compromising our core virtue of simplicity," as per Article V of the constitution

**Jabiru** *(JAH buh roo)* **River**—river running from the Divisadero Mountains to the Halcyon Sea, dividing Amal and Lapé provinces from Kekuatan and Fik'iri

**Jamara Makeda** *(juh MAHR uh muh KEE duh)*—Succession Candidate representing Kekuatan

**Jase** *(JAYS)*—Brute

**Jonalyn** *(JON uh lin)* **Pierce**—aka Jo; Reina's eldest sister; Materno; finca manager in Kekuatan

**Julissa** *(jyoo LI suh)* **Pierce**—Matriarch Teera's younger daughter; Reina's aunt

**Jungle**—the land outside Nedé's borders, characterized by unexplored, dense vegetation

**Kekuatan** *(kuh KOO uh tahn)*—northwestern Province of Nedé, meaning "strength"

**La Fortuna** *(lah for TYOO nah)*—Materno finca belonging to Jonalyn Pierce

**Lapé** *(lah PAY)*—southeastern Province of Nedé containing Phoenix City, meaning "peace"

**Leda** *(LEE duh)* **Pierce**—Reina's mother; daughter of Matriarch Teera; codirector of the Center for Health Services

**Lexander** *(LEX an dur)*—breed of horse developed by Lex Sterling; a Criollo-Thoroughbred mix prized by the Alexia

**Little Boo**—Gentle 85272; nurtured by Leda Pierce at Bella Terra

**Marsa Museau** *(MAHR suh myoo ZO)*—aka Dom Marsa, or just Marsa; chef at Bella Terra; second mother to Reina and her sisters

**Materno** *(muh TER no)*—destiny of Nedé specializing in the birth and care of children

**Melisenda "Mel" Juárez** *(me li SEN duh HWAH rez)*—best friend of Tristan Pierce; lab technician

**Merced** *(mer SED)*—Alexia

**Midas**—Trinidad's horse

**Nari Kwan** *(nahr EE KWAHN)*—Succession Candidate representing Lapé

**Nedé** *(ne DAY)*—the haven formed by the Safety Coalition in 2067 for the preservation and protection of women

**Neechi** *(NEE chee)*—Gentle 54901; stablehand at Finca del Mar

**Nyx** *(NIX)*—Adoni's horse

**Phase-out facility**—a place for Gentles who are no longer useful to live out their remaining days

**Pippin**—aka Pip; Brute

**Politikós** *(po LI ti kos)*—destiny of Nedé specializing in politics

**Reina** *(RAY nuh)* **Pierce**—daughter of Leda Pierce; granddaughter of Matriarch Teera; Succession Candidate

**Rio del Sur** *(REE o del SUR)*—river running from the Divisadero Mountains to the Halcyon Sea, marking Nedé's southern border

**Rohan** *(RO hahn)*—Brute

**Safety Coalition**—organization which fought for the safety and survival of women, founded in 2052 by Tristan Pierce

**Scientia and Medicinae** *(see EN tee uh and med uh KEE nee)*—destiny of Nedé specializing in science and medicine

**Siyah Assad** *(see YAH uh SAHD)*—former operative for the Safety Coalition; first Alexia leader

**Solomon**—aka Old Solomon; Gentle 29811; major domus (i.e., lead Gentle) at Bella Terra; former preeminent horse trainer for the Alexia

**Stinger**—slang for a quietus injection, which ends a Gentle's life. An option for Gentles who are no longer useful and/or who suffer from debilitating pain

**Succession**—the competition by which the Matriarch chooses a successor from among four Candidates, one from each Province

**Teera** *(TEE ruh)* **Pierce**—Eighth Matriarch of Nedé

**Torvus** *(TOR vuhs)*—Brute leader

**Treowe** *(TREE o)*—aka Tre *(TRAY)*; Gentle 61749; finca worker at Bella Terra

**Trinidad** *(TRIN uh dad)*—Alexia second-in-command

**Tristan Pierce**—founder of the Safety Coalition; first Matriarch of Nedé

**Valya** *(VA lyuh)*—Alexia

**Yasmine Torres** *(yaz MEEN TOR rez)*—Succession Candidate representing Fik'iri

# Acknowledgments

I<small>F GRATITUDE WERE A TREE</small>, mine would resemble a giant mahogany, its branches representing the countless people who believed in and supported the creation of this series. A few deserve special recognition, no doubt more than I can do justice to here.

Paul Daniel, for being my number-one fan, most helpful critic, and for having superior plot ideas ninety percent of the time.

My beautiful girls, Ryan and Logan, for taking an interest in this project from the beginning, helping draw maps and costumes and showing your support, even when my passion for this book took from our time together.

Andrew Wolgemuth, for being willing to take yet another leap with me. Here's to hoping for fireworks.

Don Pape, for believing, pushing, reading, and celebrating.

Nicci Jordan Hubert, your insights astound me, and your belief in this book inspired me to push up that last mountain to take this story from passable to great.

Ashley Paulus, for immersing yourself in the world of Nedé and being as excited to talk about the characters as I am. Emily Smith, for using your literary superpowers to provide such helpful critique.

April Carey, for giving me a push at the right time. Tammy Tilley and Jen Schuler, for your early feedback that kept me writing. And Alicia Coogan, Amy Geer, Betsey Ekdahl, Claire Zasso, Elizabeth Hooper, Emily Marschner, Emily Weimer, Genevieve Nelson, Jen Johnson, Jenny Brannan, Jocey Pearsey, Linn VanEusen, Noël Brower, Ryan Minassian, and Sarah Bosman, for having keen eyes and incredibly helpful feedback. This book is better because of your contributions, and I am indebted!

A special thank-you to Daniel Frost, for bringing Nedé to life in one of the most beautiful book maps ever.

Wander publishing team, I'm beyond grateful for your partnership. A special thank-you to Linda Howard, for believing in this project from the beginning, and Sarah Rubio, for caring about every single detail of Nedé as much as I do. Eva Winters, for spinning your talents into this award-worthy cover. And every talented teammate who has had a hand in the creation and marketing of this book, your passion and talents inspire me.

Alycia Burton, for awakening me to the beauty of free riding, and your horse Goldrush, the inspiration for Callisto. Monty Roberts, whose inspiring story taught me the benefits of horse gentling. John Carr, for sharing your remarkable knowledge of horses and the Belizean jungle (and for lending Gold Coin, so I could ride right into it). Kassai Lajos, who blew my mind with the human capabilities of horse archery and taught me that the best horse archers are not the best riders nor the best archers; they are the people who can treat them as one. And Dr. Grant Horner: *Tu es optimus.*

And my deepest, most heartfelt gratitude to the One for whom this was written. Here's my "small lunch." Multiply it or eat it—it's all the same to me.

# A Note from the Author

I CARE DEEPLY ABOUT WOMEN. Of course I'm biased. Not only am I female, I gave birth to two more. I care for my daughters' safety, honor, and futures even more than my own. But I also care equally for men, and believe that selfless masculinity, unleashed, has the power to change the world. My heart aches over the great divide between us—the blaming, shaming, and fear. I believe there's a better way—a partnership that brings out the best in us all, a world in which we choose the good of others above our own desires.

Most authors dream that their words will somehow make a difference in this world, and I'm no different. But words sail further when tethered to action. That's why I'm donating half of all my earnings from this book to the Corban Fund, which supports organizations seeking to end violence against women and promote change, like the A21 Campaign, the National Center on Sexual Exploitation, and Fight the New Drug.

Men aren't better than women; women aren't better than men. We both have the capacity to choose good, so let's do more of that.

*Safety for all,*
*Jess*

# About the Author

JESS CORBAN graduated from college with a degree in communications and, perhaps more instructive, thirteen stamps in her passport. After college, a chance interview at a small publisher for an even smaller position sparked a love for writing that turned into twelve nonfiction books (under various pseudonyms). Now Jess lives with her husband and two daughters in the Sierra Nevada Mountains of California, where she finds inspiration in a sky full of stars and hiking the Canyon of the Kings. *A Gentle Tyranny* is her debut novel. Connect with Jess at JessCorban.com.

# POWER WITHOUT VIRTUE IS TYRANNY.

THE EXCITING CONCLUSION TO
THE NEDÉ RISING SERIES

AVAILABLE WHEREVER BOOKS ARE SOLD

# The Quotable Feynman

# The
# Quotable
# Feynman

*edited by*
## MICHELLE FEYNMAN

PRINCETON UNIVERSITY PRESS
PRINCETON AND OXFORD

Requests for permission to reproduce material from this work should be sent to Permissions, Princeton University Press

Published by Princeton University Press, 41 William Street, Princeton, New Jersey 08540

In the United Kingdom: Princeton University Press, 6 Oxford Street, Woodstock, Oxfordshire OX20 1TW

press.princeton.edu

Cover image of Richard P. Feynman photographed by and © 1984 Faustin Bray, faustin@sound.photosynthesis.com.

Library of Congress Cataloging-in-Publication Data

Feynman, Richard P. (Richard Phillips), 1918-1988, author.
[Quotations. Selections]
The quotable Feynman / edited by Michelle Feynman.
pages     cm
Includes index.
ISBN 978-0-691-15303-2 (hardcover : alk. paper)   1.  Feynman, Richard P. (Richard Phillips), 1918-1988—Quotations.
I.   Feynman, Michelle, editor.    II.  Title.
QC16.F49A25 2015
081—dc23          2015022699

British Library Cataloging-in-Publication Data is available

This book has been composed in BodoniStd-Book

Printed on acid-free paper. ∞

Printed in the United States of America

1  3  5  7  9  10  8  6  4  2

*To Ava and Marco*

# Contents

*A Brief Note on Sources*                                      *ix*
*Foreword, by Brian Cox*                                        *xi*
*Reflections on Richard Feynman, by Yo-Yo Ma*                  *xv*
*Preface: My Quotable Father, by Michelle Feynman*           *xvii*
*Chronology*                                                *xxiii*

Youth                                                           3
Family                                                         15
Autobiographical                                               23
Art, Music, and Poetry                                         51
Nature                                                         57
Imagination                                                    83
Humor                                                          89
Love                                                          103
Philosophy and Religion                                       109
Nature of Science                                             123
Curiosity and Discovery                                       165
How Physicists Think                                          185
The Quantum World                                             197
Science and Society                                           213
Mathematics                                                   223
Technology                                                    241
War                                                           249
*Challenger*                                                  261
Politics                                                      271

Doubt and Uncertainty                      281
Education and Teaching                     293
Advice and Inspiration                     317
Intelligence                               327
The Nobel Prize                            333
Worldview                                  345
The Future                                 355
Honoring Richard Feynman                   363

*Acknowledgments*                          *383*
*Photo Credits*                            *387*
*Sources*                                  *389*
*Index*                                    *397*

# A Brief Note on Sources

Richard Feynman has been called the great explainer. This book of quotes characterizes my father's approach to scientific problem solving, his philosophy, and his communication style. Taken by topic, these quotes provide a richer, deeper understanding of how he thought, emphasize what he thought was important, and give shining examples of how he expressed himself.

Sources were his many published works, his personal papers that occupy 14 file drawers, and dozens of hours of recorded lectures. A number of important quotes also came from interviews that he did with Charles Weiner for an oral history project for the American Institute of Physics from 1966–1973. I, along with research assistants Anisha Cook and Janna Wennberg, who were instrumental in the book's shape over the final summer, gathered thousands of quotes and then sorted them into the 26 topics that make up this book.

While no collection of quotations drawn from written works, notes, correspondence, and lectures can fully capture my father's wide-ranging thoughts on various topics, it is my hope this compilation will provide the reader with a sense of his clarity, his humor, his unique way of looking at the world.

Michelle Feynman

# Foreword

If you go into any physics department at any university in the world and ask the undergraduates which scientist they most aspire to be like, I think a majority would say "Richard Feynman." Einstein might come a close second. I would say Feynman.

Richard Feynman was one of the greatest physicists of the 20th century. His 1965 Nobel Prize, shared with Julian Schwinger and Sin-Itiro Tomonaga, was awarded for their work in developing the theory of quantum electrodynamics, which to this day stands as our most precise description of the interaction between light and matter. We wouldn't understand atoms without it. Feynman's name is most closely associated with the theory because of his introduction of Feynman diagrams. Every physicist working at CERN, or any modern particle physics laboratory, has been taught how to use Feynman diagrams. They are the foundation of our understanding of the subatomic world, allowing us to calculate what will happen when particles collide and even to predict the existence of new ones, like the Higgs Boson. I cannot imagine particle physics without them, and they probably wouldn't exist today without Feynman; I don't think anyone else would have come up with them. They are intuitively obvious after they have been explained to you, and yet you get the feeling that you'd never have invented them yourself. This was Richard Feynman's particular genius; exploring nature using a sort of internalized intuitive magic. His approach was summarized famously by his friend and colleague Hans Bethe: "There are two types of genius.

Ordinary geniuses do great things, but they leave you room to believe that you could do the same if only you worked hard enough. Then there are magicians, and you can have no idea how they do it. Feynman was a magician."

Quantum electrodynamics alone is enough to place Feynman firmly among the greats, but there are plenty of Nobel Prize–winning physicists whose names few undergraduates would even recall, let alone hero worship. The reason for the unique esteem in which Richard Feynman is held, I think, can be found in this book. It is his incisive, humble logic; razor-sharp precision deployed with humanity; wonder catalyzing discovery; a deep love of nature and a powerful desire to understand how it works. When I read his words, which should be read in a New York workingman's accent, I hear the reassuring clarity of an old engineer who's popped 'round to fix your plumbing. There is no artifice, no obfuscation, no attempt to bamboozle or self-aggrandize; just a feeling that this person will get the job done with a minimum of fuss. Richard Feynman thought about physics like that. I often quote him in my own books because I can never put my feelings about physics quite as clearly as he could. There is a beautiful interview broadcast by the BBC in 1981 called "The Pleasure of Finding Things Out," in which Feynman is asked about the possibility of discovering a "Theory of Everything" — a complete mathematical framework which describes all of Nature at the most fundamental level.

"People say to me, 'Are you looking for the ultimate laws of physics?' No, I'm not. I'm just looking to find out more about the world, and if it turns out there is a simple ultimate law which explains everything, so be it; that would be very nice to discover. If it turns out it's like an onion with millions of layers and we're just sick and tired of looking at the layers, then that's the way it is! And therefore when we go to investigate we shouldn't pre-decide what it is we are trying to do except to find out more about it. . . . My interest in science is to simply find out more about the world."

That is, for me, a perfect description of science. Take delight in the small, rather than adopting futile intellectual postures in the face of the intricate infinite delicacy of nature and you might make a little progress. Reading his words, you will hear that message over and over again. I am a simple man, and I like to think carefully about simple things. That's a real physicist talking.

This direct simplicity certainly didn't preclude lyricism when it came to describing the process of doing science. Some of my favorite quotes are those that reveal Feynman's inner picture of the scientific endeavor: "We live in a heroic, a unique and wonderful age of excitement. It's going to be looked at with great jealousy in the ages to come. How would it have been to live in the time when they were discovering the fundamental laws?" This is suffused with, to use a cliché often hurled at scientists, child-like wonder, and Feynman was absolutely comfortable with such a double-edged compliment. "I hate adults."

Feynman was also a polemicist, deploying his deliberate linguistic clarity to powerful effect whenever he got the chance. I can think of few physicists who would write, in an introductory lecture on electromagnetism: "From a long view of the history of mankind, seen from, say, ten thousand years from now, there can be little doubt that the most significant event of the 19th century will be judged as Maxwell's discovery of the laws of electrodynamics. The American Civil War will pale into provincial insignificance in comparison with this important scientific event of the same decade." I love this. I read it as an entirely appropriate swipe at the futility of provincial wars, prefiguring Carl Sagan's *Pale Blue Dot*, the great lament for parochial human stupidity written three decades later: "The Earth is a very small stage in a vast cosmic arena. Think of the rivers of blood spilled by all those generals and emperors so that in glory and triumph they could become the momentary masters of a fraction of a dot."

   In these pages, then, you will catch a glimpse of genius, read the thoughts of one of history's great polymaths and one of the greatest scientists who ever lived. I hope you will learn a lot, as I have, and perhaps emerge with a little additional curiosity, wonder, humility, and respect for the natural world. Having said that, "I don't wanna take this stuff seriously. I think we should just have fun imagining it and not worry about it."

Brian Cox
Professor of Particle Physics
The University of Manchester

# Reflections on Richard Feynman

There seems to be an insatiable public appetite to feel a closeness with the giant mind and personality of Richard Feynman. This curiosity transcends generations, crosses disciplines and cultures. Over a quarter of a century after his passing, he remains alive in the public consciousness, his books are still in print, his legendary lectures are online, scientists are continuing to grapple and tangle with many of the theories he put forth decades ago.

So where does the longevity of his aura come from? I can only offer a sliver of a snapshot.

Over three decades ago, I used to see Richard backstage at concerts. He came not because he liked cello playing particularly, but because his beloved young daughter, Michelle, played, and of course, what doting father wouldn't want to please his daughter? Sometimes we would pass time bantering about what truth is in science and art, and he would always say, "In science you have to prove it." And then he would regale us with stories of his adventures playing the bongo drums. Once we went to the house and he showed us his beautiful drawings of the human figure. He talked about how his desire to go to Tuva came about from playing a geography game. He was always energetic, attentive, and present.

One of my heroes, as I was growing up, was the great cellist Pablo Casals. I was particularly impressed when he remarked that he was a human being first, a musician second, and a cellist third. I was similarly taken when I read one of Richard's quotes: "You cannot develop a personality with physics alone; the rest of your life must be worked in."

Therein lies a clue to the longevity of Richard Feynman. Yes, he was one of the all-time great physicists, but he also paid attention to life and love, to his children, to his family, to the sensuality of the human figure, to the primal complexities of drumming, to his entire environment. While he paid close attention to problems we face and generate, he also knew that humans are a subset of nature, and nature held for him the greatest fascination — for the imagination of nature is far, far greater than the imagination of man, and nature guards her secrets jealously.

Thus, for him, it was worth the years of work to extract some of those secrets in order to pass them on in the most direct and understandable form to the rest of us. Because he worked his whole life into his personality, we could identify with his humanness and therefore stay with him as he took us on the most spectacular journey of all, the never-ending quest to understand everything.

Surely you must still be joking, Mr. Feynman!

Yo-Yo Ma
Cellist

# Preface

# My Quotable Father

I recently came across a few of my notebooks from high school and college and found scribbles from my time in the classroom. By turns funny, uplifting, heartbreaking, and occasionally annoying, those excerpts from my life of years ago remind me of a particular moment or a class much more quickly than do my actual class notes — there is something very powerful about a concise statement. And so I have always loved quotes.

One of my favorite quotes from my father came in a birthday card he gave me when I turned 18: "Go forth!" he wrote. When I read those words, I remember my reaction — pride and excitement, mixed with some apprehension. I also recall that he usually didn't bother himself with the trivialities of birthday cards; he left that to my mother, which made this particular quote that much more poignant.

My father left me his words. From them I remember both his outlook on life and his voice, positive and clear. He was someone who didn't worry about small problems. His advice here — leave it; let it go — is inspiring:

> And we all do stupid things, and we know some people do more than others, but there is no use in trying to check who does the most.

I'm often asked what kind of father he was, and although I occasionally teased him for not remembering what I thought were pertinent details of my life (age, school, etc.), he was always happy and ready to spend time with me. He might have had a reputation for not suffering fools gladly, but I remember him as a funny, energetic, kind, playful, patient man. I recall his wise advice about finding a career, very similar to a letter he wrote to a high school student in 1984:

> It is wonderful if you can find something you love to do in your youth which is big enough to sustain your interest through all your adult life. Because, whatever it is, if you do it well enough (and you will, if you truly love it), people will pay you to do what you want to do anyway.

Whenever I read his words, I hear his voice. It still makes me laugh to think that he used the phrase "cooked up" in his Nobel Prize lecture:

> I never used all that machinery which I had cooked up to solve a single relativistic problem.

I am charmed by my father's use of expressions that are no longer in rotation, and I am mesmerized by his distinct rhythm of speaking. I remember a few archaic expressions from when I was growing up — the refrigerator was the "icebox," for goodness' sake! Or "They go all around Robin Hood's barn to come around here" to describe a round-about path.

I know he was fascinated by Las Vegas. He incorporated stories from visits there in his lectures. I really love the following excerpt because he was such an expert at breaking grammatical rules. The rhythm really sets the scene:

Example. I'm in Las Vegas, suppose. And I meet a mindreader, or, let's say, a man who claims not to be a mindreader, but more technically speaking to have the ability of telekinesis, which means that he can influence the way things behave by pure thought. This fellow comes to me, and he says, "I will demonstrate this to you. We will stand at the roulette wheel and I will tell you ahead of time whether it is going to be black or red on every shot."

I believe, say, before I begin, it doesn't make any difference what number you choose for this. I happen to be prejudiced against mindreaders from experience in nature, in physics. I don't see, if I believe that man is made out of atoms and if I know all of the — most of the — ways atoms interact with each other, any direct way in which the machinations in the mind can affect the ball. So from other experience and general knowledge, I have a strong prejudice against mind readers. Million to one.

Now we begin. The mind reader says it's going to be black. It's black. The mind reader says it's going to be red. It's red. Do I believe in mindreaders? No. It could happen. The mindreader says it's going to be red. It's red. Sweat. I'm about to learn something . . .

It was also revealing to see how he spent his leisure time. Was I surprised to see quotes that revealed his penchant for always working on physics? Not really. It was a switch he couldn't turn off. I remember he always seemed to be thinking about physics. When he didn't have a pad of paper, it was common to find equations on scraps of paper — even margins of the newspaper. Even when he was very young, he recalled, he was annoyed at being pulled away from working.

I didn't get to do as much as I wanted to, because my mother kept putting me out all the time, to play.

That one really made me laugh. These next two exemplify his open, honest attitude and how he loved nothing better than thinking about physics:

> It is a nice problem, however, and I often spend time on airplanes trying to figure it out. I haven't cracked it yet.
>
> It must have been a day or so later when I was lying in bed thinking about these things that I imagined what would happen if I wanted to calculate the wave function at a finite interval later.

I've always been impressed by his humility:

> I suffer from the disease that all professors suffer from — that is, there never seems to be enough time, and I invented more problems than undoubtedly we'll be able to do, and therefore I've tried to speed things up by writing some things on the board beforehand, with the illusion that every professor has: that if he talks about more things, he'll teach more things. Of course, there's only a finite rate at which material can be absorbed by the human mind, yet we disregard that phenomenon, and in spite of it we go too fast.

I remember so much advice from my father: Think about a math problem to see whether your answer makes sense. Work to be direct and honest in communication. Aim to be friendly and kind. Realize that life is an exciting adventure. Find something to do that you love. Work hard. And always, *always* remember your sense of humor! I have not always been able to laugh at myself, but it was something at which my father excelled. I remember his once trudging through an airport, luggage in tow, laboring to make a connecting flight home. He muttered to himself, "Flying is for the birds!" — and, realizing just how true that was, laughed and regained his equanimity. Of all the advice he dispensed, perhaps his exhortation to remember one's sense of humor is the most crucial. Doing so has helped me cope with difficult moments in my own life.

Strangely enough, I came across one of my father's quotations about *his* father that sums up how I feel about *my* father:

> Not having experience with many fathers, I didn't realize how remarkable he was.

I will be forever grateful to my father for sharing his life with me — from the charming, silly, playful moments to the serious.

Michelle Feynman, 2014

# Chronology

1918        Born in New York on May 11

1939        Graduates from MIT, begins graduate studies
            at Princeton

1940–41     Research assistant, Princeton University

1942        Receives PhD from Princeton

1942        Marries Arline Greenbaum

1943–45     Works on Manhattan Project, Los Alamos,
            New Mexico

1945        Arline dies

1945–50     Professor of theoretical physics, Cornell University

1950        Visiting professor at Caltech; takes a year teaching
            in Brazil

1950–59     Professor of theoretical physics at Caltech

1952        Marries Mary Louise Bell

1954        Wins Albert Einstein Award

1956        Divorces Mary Louise

1959        Gives lecture "There's Plenty of Room at the
            Bottom"; offers two nanotechnology challenges

1959        Becomes the Richard Chase Tolman Professor of
            Theoretical Physics at Caltech

1960        Marries Gweneth Howarth

1961–63     Delivers freshman lectures on physics at Caltech
            that become The Feynman Lectures on Physics

1962        Wins the E. O. Lawrence Award

1962        Son, Carl Richard Feynman, born

| 1963 | Delivers John Danz Lectures leading to *The Meaning of It All* |
| 1964 | Delivers Messenger Lectures at Cornell University, which become the text for *The Character of Physical Law* |
| 1965 | Elected foreign member of the Royal Society |
| 1965 | Wins Nobel Prize |
| 1968 | Daughter, Michelle Catherine Feynman, born |
| 1972 | Wins Oersted Medal for teaching |
| 1973 | Wins Niels Bohr International Gold Medal |
| 1979 | Delivers Sir Douglas Robb lectures on Quantum Electrodynamics at Auckland University, New Zealand, which become *QED: The Strange Theory of Light and Matter* |
| 1985 | Serves as a member of the Presidential Commission investigating the *Challenger* space shuttle accident |
| 1985 | Publishes *Surely You're Joking, Mr. Feynman!* and spends fourteen weeks on the *New York Times* best-seller list |
| 1988 | Dies in California on February 15 |

# The
# Quotable
# Feynman

# Youth

I didn't get to do as much as I wanted to, because my mother kept putting me out all the time, to play.

*– Surely You're Joking, Mr. Feynman!*, p. 17

When I was a kid, I had this notion that you could take the importance of the problem and multiply it by your chance of solving it. You know how a technically minded kid is, he likes the idea of optimizing everything anyway, if you can get the right combination of those factors, you don't spend your life getting nowhere with a profound problem, or solving lots of small problems that others could do just as well.

– *Omni* interview, February 1979

Don't despair of standard dull textbooks. Just close the book once in a while and think what they just said in your own terms as a revelation of the spirit and wonder of nature. The books give you facts but your imagination can supply life. My father taught me how to do that when I was a little boy on his knee, and he read the *Encyclopaedia Britannica* to me!

– Letter to Rodney C. Lewis, August 1981 (*Perfectly Reasonable Deviations from the Beaten Track*, pp. 332–333)

I went to take the calculus book out, and the teacher — sorry, the librarian — said, "Child, you can't take this book out. Why are you taking this book out?" I said, "It's for my father." And so I took it home, and I tried to learn a little bit. My father looked at the first few paragraphs and couldn't understand it, and this was rather a shock to me — a little bit of a shock, I remember. It was the first time I realized that I could understand what he couldn't understand.

– Interview with Charles Weiner, March 4, 1966 (Niels Bohr Library and Archives with the Center for the History of Physics)

I learned very early the difference between knowing the name of something and knowing something.

— *What Do You Care What Other People Think?*, p. 14

When I was a child and found out Santa Claus wasn't real, I wasn't upset. Rather, I was relieved that there was a much simpler phenomenon to explain how so many children all over the world got presents on the same night.

— *Los Angeles Times*, November 27, 1994

When I was young, what I call the laboratory was just a place to fiddle around, make radios and gadgets and photocells and whatnot. I was very shocked when I discovered what they call a laboratory in a university. That's a place where you are supposed to measure something very seriously. I never measured a damn thing in my laboratory.

— Future for Science interview

[On his first talk:] I remember getting up to talk, and there were these great men in the audience and it was frightening. And I can still see my own hands as I pulled out the papers from the envelope that I had them in. They were shaking. As soon as I got the paper out and started to talk, something happened to me which has always happened since and which is a wonderful thing. If I'm talking physics, I love the thing. I think only about physics, I don't worry where I am; I don't worry about anything, and everything went very easily.

— Future for Science interview

The moment I realized that I was now working on something new was when I read something about quantum electrodynamics at the time, and I read a book, and I learned about it. For example, I read Dirac's book, and they had these problems that nobody knew how to solve. I couldn't understand the book very well because I wasn't up to it, but at the last paragraph at the very end of the book, it said, "Some new ideas are here needed!" And so there I was! Some new ideas were there needed, so I started to think of new ideas.

– Interview with Yorkshire Television program, "Take the World from Another Point of View," 1972

[To one of his former high school teachers:] Another thing that I remember as being very important to me was the time when you called me down after class and said, "You make too much noise in class." Then you went on to say that you understood the reason, that it was that the class was entirely too boring. Then you pulled out a book from behind you and said, "Here, you read this, take it up to the back of the room, sit all along, and study this; when you know everything that is in it, you can talk again." And so, in my physics class I paid no attention to what was going on but only studied Woods' *Advanced Calculus* up in the back of the room. It was there that I learned about gamma functions, elliptic functions, and differentiating under an integral sign. A trick at which I became an expert.

– Letter to Abram Bader, November 1965 (*Perfectly Reasonable Deviations from the Beaten Track*, pp. 176–177)

[CBS] asked me what I thought of the New York School System, and I said that I am only good in physics and I do not know the

New York School System except for the particular school that I went to thirty years ago. I thought that my high school was very good. There was a great variety of science courses offered for those times — advanced math, physics, chemistry, and biology. Several teachers gave me direct encouragement, good advice, and taught me special things outside the regular courses. I had a good time in high school.

  – Letter to Miriam Cohen, November 1965

[To his aunt:] It is good to hear from someone who has known me for so long. You have gone through all the stages with mother, from ruined linen towels to mom's worrying about whether I would blow up the house with my laboratory.

  – Letter to Jesse M. Davidson, December 1965 (*Perfectly Reasonable Deviations from the Beaten Track*, p. 181)

[On his father:] He was rational; he liked the rational mind and things that could be understood by thinking.

  – Interview with Charles Weiner, March 4, 1966 (Niels Bohr Library and Archives with the Center for the History of Physics)

When I got to kindergarten, which was much later — I was six years old — they had a thing in those days which was "weaving." They had a kind of colored paper — square paper with quarter-inch slots made parallel. And you have quarter-inch strips of paper. One was the weft and the other was the warp. You're supposed to weave it and make designs that were regular and interesting. And apparently that's extremely difficult for a child. I was especially commented on; the teacher was very excited and surprised. I made elaborate patterns — correctly, without any difficulty, whereas it was so difficult for most of the children that they don't do that in kindergarten anymore.

— Interview with Charles Weiner, March 4, 1966 (Niels Bohr Library and Archives with the Center for the History of Physics)

My father would often take me to the Museum of Natural History — that was a great place. We would look at the dinosaur bones and stuff like that — it was great!

— Interview with Charles Weiner, March 4, 1966 (Niels Bohr Library and Archives with the Center for the History of Physics)

[On his father describing glaciers:] He understood! The thing that was very important about my father is not the facts but the process — the meaning of everything. How we find out; what is the consequence of finding such a rock? With a vivid description of the ice, which is probably not exactly right! Perhaps the speed was not ten inches a year but ten feet a year — I never knew; he never knew. But he would describe anyway, in a vivid way, and always with some kind of lesson about it. Like, "How do you think we find these things out?"

— Interview with Charles Weiner, March 4, 1966 (Niels Bohr Library and Archives with the Center for the History of Physics)

[On his sister, also a physicist:] She would hear us talking, and she would ask me, and I would explain it to her. It wasn't so direct in her case.

> – Interview with Charles Weiner, March 4, 1966 (Niels Bohr Library and Archives with the Center for the History of Physics)

I was always very upset if something went bad or if I was bad — I always tried to be a good boy.

> – Interview with Charles Weiner, March 4, 1966 (Niels Bohr Library and Archives with the Center for the History of Physics)

Arithmetic was very easy; it was too easy. For instance, when I was ten or eleven, one day I was called from a class to a previous class that I had been in by a previous teacher to explain to the class how to do subtraction. I had "invented," (they claim) a better way of doing subtraction than they were using that she liked. She had forgotten it, in the meantime, so I was called from class to explain it to her.

> – Interview with Charles Weiner, March 4, 1966 (Niels Bohr Library and Archives with the Center for the History of Physics)

[On his friend Bernard Walker:] I had a friend who was as interested in science as I was, so we did much together — I was about twelve. We studied together, we'd argue together, we did chemistry experiments.

> – Interview with Charles Weiner, March 4, 1966 (Niels Bohr Library and Archives with the Center for the History of Physics)

I was not good at athletics. This always bothered me — I felt like a sissy because I couldn't play baseball. It was to me, at a childish age, a very serious business. I had trouble learning how to ride a bicycle . . . . Every once in awhile, I would get kicked out of the group. We had a hut, and each time I was kicked out of the group, I would invent something, like a periscope for the hut or a design for a second story or something.

– Interview with Charles Weiner, March 4, 1966 (Niels Bohr Library and Archives with the Center for the History of Physics)

We put sodium ferrocyanide — sodium ferrocyanide? — or something, in the towels, and another substance, an iron salt, probably alum, in the soap. When they come together, they make blue ink. So we were supposed to fool my mother, you see. She would wash her hands, and then when she dried them, her hands would turn blue. But we didn't think the towel would turn blue. This was all in the Cedarhurst era. Anyway, she was horrified. The screams of "My good linen towels!" But she was always cooperative. She never was afraid of those experiments.

– Interview with Charles Weiner, March 4, 1966 (Niels Bohr Library and Archives with the Center for the History of Physics)

[On boiling water:] I remember using the developing trays, which were waxed, so that they were insulated, putting water in them, and boiling it — and watching the most beautiful phenomenon at the end, when all the water boils away, and the last bit of water, it's dry, is making sparks, because it's breaking the circuit. And the sparks move around, because it breaks here, but the water flows, you see, and it flows here and connects, and then it makes another spark here, and finally, these lines of salt, and beautiful yellow and blue sparks! It's a very beautiful thing. In fact, now that you remind me, I think I'll have to set one up and see what it looks like, after all these years. I used to boil water all the time with this thing.

— Interview with Charles Weiner, March 4, 1966 (Niels Bohr
   Library and Archives with the Center for the History of Physics)

I had lots of trouble, because I remember, my friend and I — the man drew on the blackboard (I still remember, you know, he's going to explain how a projection system works, you know, the projector that makes pictures on the wall) — so he drew a light bulb, and he draws a lens and so on to explain. Then he draws lines coming out of the light bulb parallel, the rays of light going parallel to each other. So, I don't remember whether it was I or my friend, but one of us said, "But that can't be right. The rays come out from the filament radially, in all directions." I don't know if I used the word "radially," but anyway, we explained. He turned around and said, "I say they go parallel, so they go parallel!" Well, this didn't sit well with us, because I knew, certainly, that no matter what he said, the rays didn't go parallel.

— Interview with Charles Weiner, March 4, 1966 (Niels Bohr
   Library and Archives with the Center for the History of Physics)

[On the Great Depression:] There was also the attitude that you should do something, work — you know, the idea that to hang around and do nothing was somehow . . . . There was a feeling of some sort of responsibility to earn money. I can't explain it.

– Interview with Charles Weiner, March 4, 1966 (Niels Bohr
  Library and Archives with the Center for the History of Physics)

I always kept up this ability to work very quickly with the mathematics, so as to get rid of the homework.

· – Interview with Charles Weiner, March 5, 1966 (Niels Bohr
  Library and Archives with the Center for the History of Physics)

I don't know much about the "general theory of intelligence," but I do remember when I was young I was very one-sided. It was science and math and no humanities (except for falling in love with a wonderful intelligent lover of piano, poetry writing, etc.).

– Letter to Dr. William L. McConnell, March 1975 (*Perfectly
  Reasonable Deviations from the Beaten Track*, p. 281)

I was inspired by the remarks in these books [Heitler and Dirac]; not by the parts in which everything was proved and demonstrated carefully and calculated, because I couldn't understand those very well. At the young age what I could understand were the remarks about the fact that this doesn't make any sense, and the last sentence of the book of Dirac I can still remember, "It seems that some essentially new physical ideas are here needed." So, I had this as a challenge and an inspiration. I also had a personal feeling, that since they didn't get a satisfactory answer to the problem I wanted to solve, I don't have to pay a lot of attention to what they did do.

– From *Nobel Lectures, Physics 1963–1970*, Elsevier Publishing Company, Amsterdam, 1972

At the age of thirteen I was converted to non-Jewish religious views.

– Letter to Tina Levitan, January 1967 (*Perfectly Reasonable Deviations from the Beaten Track*, p. 234)

You see, what happened to me, what happened to the rest of us is we started for a good reason, but then we're working very hard to do something, and to accomplish it, it's a pleasure, it's excitement.

– UCSB talk, "Los Alamos from Below," February 1975

# Family

I have a nice cozy house with a good family in it.

– Letter to professors Gilberto Bernadini and Luigi A. Radicati
(*Perfectly Reasonable Deviations from the Beaten Track*,
p. 209)

I was happily surprised by your present of the beautiful photograph, which is now in my office. Thank you very much. When I came home with it and showed it to my son (who is twelve years old) he was delighted with it. I asked him what it was — after a few moments he said, "probably a diffraction pattern from a laser from a regular pattern of square holes." I could have killed him! I was afraid to ask him for the focal length of the lens used!

– Letter to Sheila Sorensen, October 1974

Another thing my father told me — and I can't quite explain it, because it was more an emotion than a telling — was that the ratio of the circumference to the diameter of all the circles was always the same, no matter what the size. That didn't seem too unobvious, but the ratio had some marvelous property. There was a mystery about this number that I didn't quite understand as a youth, but this was a great thing, and the result was that I looked for pi everywhere.

– National Science Teachers Association Fourteenth Convention lecture, "What Is Science?" April 1966

[On his son:] He's a lot like me, so at least I've passed on this idea that everything is interesting to at least one other person. Of course, I don't know if that's a good thing or not, you see?

– *Omni* interview, February 1979

[Advice to a father about a son:] The two of you — father and son — should take walks in the evening and talk (without purpose or routes) about this and that. Because his father is a wise man, and the son I think is wise too for they have the same opinions I had when I was a father and when I was a son too. These don't exactly agree, of course, but the deeper wisdom of the older man will grow out of the concentrated energetic attention of the younger. Patience.

   – Letter to Mr. V. A. Van Der Hyde, July 1986 (*Perfectly Reasonable Deviations from the Beaten Track*, p. 415)

[On his son:] He talks a blue streak. He could win a Nobel Prize for talking.

   – *South Shore Record*, October 28, 1965

I was surprised to read your comment about my meeting the press that you did not mention how cute and wonderful my little boy looks. Could that be modesty?

   – Letter to Dr. Richard Pettit, MD, the doctor who delivered son Carl, November 1965 (*Perfectly Reasonable Deviations from the Beaten Track*, p. 186)

[Advice to a father:] Do not be too mad at Mike for his C in physics. I got a C in English Literature. Maybe I never would have received a prize in physics if I had been better in English.

   – Letter to Arnold Phillips, November 1965 (*Perfectly Reasonable Deviations from the Beaten Track*, p. 185)

[Advice to a father about a son:] Let him go, let him get all distorted studying what interests him the most as much as he wants. True, our school system will grade him poorly — but he will make out. Far better than knowing only a little about a lot of things.

- Letter to Mr. V. A. Van Der Hyde, July 1986 (*Perfectly Reasonable Deviations from the Beaten Track*, p. 415)

I have worked on innumerable problems that you would call humble but which I enjoyed and felt very good about because I sometimes could partially succeed.

- Letter to Koichi Mano, February 1966 (*Perfectly Reasonable Deviations from the Beaten Track*, p. 201)

We bought a new camping van that we drive around. We like to camp out in the desert and so on and it's decorated all around with these diagrams.

- BBC interview, "Scientifically Speaking," April 1976

[On his father:] When I got older, he'd take me for walks in the woods and show me the animals and birds and so on. He'd tell me about the stars and the atoms and everything else. He'd tell me what it was about them that was so interesting. He had an attitude about the world and the way to look at it which I found was deeply scientific for a man who had no direct scientific training.

- Future for Science interview

My father had taught me to worship pi; to be awe-inspired by pi. He loved pi because there was such a strange ratio and it was such a simple thing with a circle.

– Future for Science interview

[On his father:] He had ways of looking at things. He used to say that suppose we were Martians and we came down to earth and then we would see these strange creatures doing things, what would we think? For instance, he would say, to take an example, suppose that we never went to sleep. We're Martians, but we have a consciousness that works all the time and finds these creatures who for eight hours a day stop and close their eyes and become more or less inert. We'd have an interesting question to ask them. We'd say "How does it feel to do that all the time? What happens to your ideas? You're running along very well, you're thinking clearly — and what happens? Do they suddenly stop? Or do they go more and more slowly and stop or exactly how do you turn off thoughts? Then later I thought about that a lot, and I did experiments in college to try and find out the answer to that — what happened to your thoughts when you went to sleep.

– Future for Science interview

Not having experience with many fathers, I didn't realize how remarkable he was. How did he learn the deep principles of science and the love of it, what's behind it, and why it's worth doing?

– *What Do You Care What Other People Think?*, p. 14

[On his father:] Before I was born, he said to my mother that this boy is going to be a scientist. You can't say things like that in front of women's lib these days, but that is what they said in those days. But he never told me to be a scientist. The way he did it when I was very small, he'd tell me things.

    – Future for Science interview

# Autobiographical

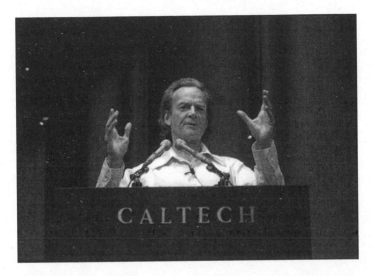

Some people say, "How can you live without knowing?" I do not
know what they mean. I always live without knowing. That is easy.
How you get to know is what I want to know.

– "The Uncertainty of Science," John Danz Lecture Series, 1963

I remember the work I did to get a real degree at Princeton and the guys on the same platform receiving honorary degrees without work — and felt an "honorary degree" was a debasement of the idea of a "degree which confirms certain work has been accomplished." It is like giving an "honorary electricians license." I swore then that if by chance I was ever offered one I would not accept it.

> — Letter to Dr. George W. Beadle (*Perfectly Reasonable Deviations from the Beaten Track*, p. 233)

The work that I do, none of it is secret. It is internationally known; it's transmitted by letter, back and forth, and by magazines all over the world.

> — Interview for Viewpoint

Please appreciate that it is not a matter of deep principle to me, so that if my resignation causes you any major difficulties, feel free to disregard my preferences. But your flock will contain one very peculiar, sad and reluctant bird.

> — Letter to Dr. Detlev W. Bronk and the National Academy of Sciences, August 1961 (*Perfectly Reasonable Deviations from the Beaten Track*, p. 109)

It is most interesting and revealing to pick up the morning newspaper and read about oneself, especially when it is so well written and complimentary.

> — Letter to Dr. Irving S. Bengelsdorf (*Los Angeles Times*), April 1967

I'd average about 20 minutes of doing nothing, and then I'd open it, you see; well, I opened it right away to see that everything was all right and then I'd sit there for 20 minutes to give myself a good reputation that it wasn't too easy, there was no trick to it, no trick to it. And then I'd come out, you know, sweating a bit, and say "It's open. There you are." And so forth.

> – UCSB talk, "Los Alamos from Below," February 1975, regarding his hobby of safecracking

In order to work hard on something, you have to get yourself believing that the answer's over there, so you'll dig hard there, right? So you temporarily prejudice or predispose yourself, but all the time, in the back of your mind, you're laughing. Forget what you hear about science without prejudice. Here, in an interview, talking about the Big Bang, I have no prejudice, but when I'm working, I have a lot of them.

> – *Omni* interview, February 1979

[After discussing calculating the position of Venus:] I don't know about the philosophy of Mayans — we have very little information due to the efficiency of the Spanish conquistadores and, well, mostly their priests, who burned all the books. They had hundreds of thousands of books and there's three left. And one of them has this Venus calculation, and that's how we know about that. Just imagine our civilization reduced to three books — the particular ones left by accident, which ones?

> – "QED: Photons — Corpuscles of Light," Sir Douglas Robb Lectures, University of Auckland, 1979

I am a stick-in-the-pleasant-mud type of guy.

> – Letter to professors Gilberto Bernardini and Luigi A. Radicati, February 1966 (*Perfectly Reasonable Deviations from the Beaten Track*, p. 209)

Old friends should tell each other what they are doing.

> – Letter to Morrie Jacobs, November 1965 (*Perfectly Reasonable Deviations from the Beaten Track*, p. 179)

But whatever way I did it, I wouldn't give a damn. I know I didn't care to find out what way you had to do it, because it seemed to me, if I did it, I did it.

> – Interview with Charles Weiner, March 4, 1966 (Niels Bohr Library and Archives with the Center for the History of Physics)

It is interesting that human relationships, if there is an independent way of judging truth, can become unargumentative.

> – "The Uncertainty of Science," John Danz Lecture Series, 1963

But I never thought of theoretical physics as being a field that's split-able, in those days — just anything in theory. Because, you see, my mathematical talents had finally overcome my experimental talents. I used to play around, but I played around less and less and did more and more analysis, mathematical, like these theorems and these papers, so I was becoming theoretical instead of experimental.

> – Interview with Charles Weiner, March 5, 1966 (Niels Bohr Library and Archives with the Center for the History of Physics)

I think it is very important to resist accepting too much of unimportant details and inanities. Some wisdom and skill is required to avoid throwing the baby with the bath. But, otherwise, we have too much to think about and cannot concentrate our small minds on the problems.

  – Letter to Mr. Jim Barclay, January 1967

It's hard to work in secrecy; there's a kind of schizophrenia involved in the sense that you have to remember what it is that you know that you're not allowed to say. And what happens is that you lean over backwards to avoid saying things until you become inarticulate on certain subjects, because if you start to talk about a subject which you heard something secret, you're afraid to say anything about it for fear that maybe that was one of the things that was secret. So I don't like secrets.

  – Interview for Viewpoint

[On philosophers:] It isn't the philosophy that gets me, it's the pomposity. If they'd just laugh at themselves!

  – *Omni* interview, February 1979 (*The Pleasure of Finding Things Out*, p. 195)

I find it psychologically very distasteful to judge people's "merit."

  – Letter to Dr. Detlev W. Bronk and the National Academy of Sciences, August 1961 (*Perfectly Reasonable Deviations from the Beaten Track*, p. 108)

My lament was that a kind of intense beauty that I see given to me by science, is seen by so few others.

> – Letter to Mrs. Robert Weiner, October 1967 (*Perfectly Reasonable Deviations from the Beaten Track*, p. 248)

I suspect that there are plenty of ingenious people able to deal, as well as I, with the problems that you mention, who are at present employed as anything from manager to criminal.

> – Letter to Jarrold R. Zacharias, Laboratory for Nuclear Science and Engineering (*Perfectly Reasonable Deviations from the Beaten Track*, p. 82)

It was such a shock to me to see that a committee of men could present a whole lot of ideas, each one thinking of a new facet, while remembering what the other fellow said, so that, at the end, the decision is made as to which idea was the best — summing it all up — without having to say it three times. So that was a shock. These were very great men indeed.

> – On his experience with the Manhattan Project, "Los Alamos from Below," 1976

I enjoyed leafing through your magazine *Science and Children*, but find I must decline your invitation to write an article for it. I find that my talents are much better in the line of dancing and being an escort than in writing articles for a magazine of that type.

> – Letter to Diane Ruth (*Science and Children*), June 1966

So I made my decision, not to be a member of an honorary society, if it's an honorary society only. If this damned thing did anything, it would be all right.

– Interview with Charles Weiner, June 28, 1966 (Niels Bohr Library and Archives with the Center for the History of Physics)

[On *Surely You're Joking, Mr. Feynman!*:] I was telling all these stories to a friend. There was no idea that I was telling them to anybody else, so there was no correcting or worrying about how stupid it looked or how clever or whether I was egotistical or an idiot in the story. It didn't make any difference. I'd tell it the way it happened to me. Then Ralph got the idea to write them down, so he arranged them a little bit and kept them sounding like me.

– "The Remarkable Dr. Feynman," *Los Angeles Times Magazine*, April 20, 1986

Now that I am burned out and I'll never accomplish anything, I've got this nice position at the university teaching classes which I rather enjoy, and just like I like reading *Arabian Nights* for pleasure, I'm going to play with physics, whenever I want to, without worrying about any importance whatsoever.

– *Surely You're Joking, Mr. Feynman!*, p. 173

I'm not much good at this show business, but we'll see what happens.

– Audio recording of Feynman Lectures on Physics, Lecture 12, November 7, 1961

I knew I'd be a scientist somehow.

> – Interview with Charles Weiner, March 4, 1966 (Niels Bohr Library and Archives with the Center for the History of Physics)

Things aren't really so tough; it is just fun having crazy adventures. I get a kick out of life and so sometimes odd things befall me.

> – Letter to Mary Bowers, November 1960

Mulaika would rejoice in knowing that I am sitting here with one of the most beautiful "shiners," I, at least have ever seen. Apparently the bars in Buffalo are tougher than even the chili and sailors near the Brooklyn Navy Yard.

> – Letter to Bert and Mulaika Corben, 1948

Probably, it was just the kind of time everyone has in California, but it seemed to me to be especially good.

> – Letter to Professor E. O. Lawrence, July 1947 (*Perfectly Reasonable Deviations from the Beaten Track*, p. 76)

The Brazilians were impressed with my Portuguese, in fact the lectures were given in the language which they referred to as Feynman's Portuguese.

> – Letter to Professor Joe Keller, September 1949

[Regarding a request to do a talk:] Oh heck, we know each other well enough, what I mean is I don't feel like doing it.

– Letter to Dr. Victor F. Weisskopf, April 1962

The first morning I drove in was tremendously impressive; the beauty of the scenery, for a person from the east who didn't travel much, was sensational. There are the great cliffs; you've probably seen the pictures, I won't go into much detail. These things were high on the mesa and you'd come up from below and see these great cliffs and we were very surprised. The most impressive thing to me was that as I was going up, I said that maybe there were Indians even living here, and the guy who was driving the car just stopped; he stopped the car and walked around the corner and there were Indian caves that you could inspect.

– UCSB talk, "Los Alamos from Below," February 1975

I go down to the dormitory place to get rooms assigned, and they say you can pick your room now. I tried to pick one; you know what I did? I looked to see where the girl's dormitory was and I picked one that you could look out across. Later I discovered a big tree was growing right in front of it.

– UCSB talk, "Los Alamos from Below," February 1975

Well, the bachelors, and the bachelor girls, the people who lived in the dormitory, felt they had to have a faction because a new rule had been promulgated — no women in the men's dorm, for instance. Well, this is absolutely ridiculous. All grown people of course. What kind of nonsense? So we had to have political action.

   – UCSB talk, "Los Alamos from Below," February 1975

The trouble with playing a trick on a highly intelligent man like Mr. Teller is the time it takes him to figure out from the moment that he sees there is something wrong to till he understands exactly what happened is too damn small to give you any pleasure!

   – UCSB talk, "Los Alamos from Below," February 1975

I can't forget Hawaii. I look at my old face mask and gloves and long to be with the fish of Hanauma Bay again.

   – Letter to Dr. San Fu Tuan (University of Hawaii), September 1973

I met some very great men beside the men on the evaluation committee, the men I met in Los Alamos. And there are so many of them that it's one of my great experiences in life to have met all these wonderful physicists.

   – UCSB talk, "Los Alamos from Below," February 1975

I don't know anything, but I do know that everything is interesting if you go into it deeply enough.

   – *Omni* interview, February 1979

There is a difference between the name of the thing and what goes on.

  – National Science Teachers Association Fourteenth Convention
    lecture, "What Is Science?" April 1966

Perhaps it is just that I enjoy being peculiar.

  – Letter to Dr. Detlev W. Bronk and the National Academy of
    Sciences, August 1961 (*Perfectly Reasonable Deviations from
    the Beaten Track*, p. 108)

It is my policy to keep up the standard of my own published work.

  – Letter to Alladi Ramakrishnan, January 1962 (*Perfectly Rea-
    sonable Deviations from the Beaten Track*, p. 130)

Please be assured that I am not interested in propaganda or persuading people. We agree that we should be interested only in what is right in science.

  – Letter to F. Harrison Stamper, February 1962

Words can be meaningless. If they are used in such a way that no sharp conclusions can be drawn, as in my example of "oomph," then the proposition they state is almost meaningless.

  – "The Uncertainty of Science," John Danz Lecture Series, 1963

One might say that, in case you are beginning to believe that some of the things I said before are true because I am a scientist and according to the brochure that you get I won some awards and so forth, instead of looking at the ideas themselves and judging them directly. In other words, you see, you have some feeling toward authority. I will get rid of that tonight. I dedicate this lecture to showing what ridiculous conclusions and rare statements such a man as myself can make. I wish, therefore, to destroy and image of authority that has previously been generated.

– "The Unscientific Age," John Danz Lecture Series, 1963

Among the many things I know very little about, one is what one should do to prepare oneself to be a theoretical physicist.

– Letter to Eric W. Leuliette, September 1984 (*Perfectly Reasonable Deviations from the Beaten Track*, p. 369)

There must always be a parallel between a general theorem and a special example of a kind. In fact, I personally find — people are different; some people think abstractly very well — I don't. I always have to have examples to understand something the first time I hear it, and then I generalize from the examples. Other people like the general thing and then use it on the thing.

– Esalen lecture, "Quantum Mechanical View of Reality (Part 1)," October 1984

I didn't do experiments, I never did, I just fiddled around. I made radios and gadgets. I fiddled around. Gradually, through books and manuals, I began to discover there were formulas applicable to, say, electricity in relating the current and resistance.

– National Science Teachers Association Fourteenth Convention lecture, "What Is Science?" April 1966

The result of this is that I cannot remember anybody's name, and when people discuss physics with me, they often are exasperated when they say, "The Fitz-Gronin effect" and I ask, "what is the effect?" I can't remember the name.

– National Science Teachers Association Fourteenth Convention lecture, "What Is Science?" April 1966

I love the subject of physics and it has been my desire to try to share the delights of understanding it with any minds that were able to, male or female, and I don't believe that there's any reason, I never have believed that there's any reason that we know of, that there's a difference in the ability of one or another person to understand the physics.

– Oersted Medal acceptance speech, 1972

I'm sorry that I am unable to give you a recommendation for a nomination for the Niels Bohr Medal, but I have always made it a principle of never recommending or criticizing a colleague.

– Letter to Mr. Bjorn Andersen, February 1976

One day I'll be convinced there's a certain type of symmetry that everybody believes in, the next day I'll try to figure out the consequences if it's not, and everybody's crazy but me.

– *Omni* interview, February 1979

I don't know the effect I'm having. Maybe it's just my character; I don't know. I'm not a psychologist or sociologist, I don't know how to understand people, including myself.

– *Omni* interview, February 1979

On the program it says this is a keynote speech. I telephoned when I heard that I was going to give a keynote speech to ask, "What does that mean?" and they said that would be the after-dinner speech, and I said "No." So they moved to now, but they didn't change the title, and I don't know what a keynote speech is. I do not intend in any way to suggest what should be in this meeting as a keynote of the subjects or anything like that. I have my own things to say and to talk about, and there's no implication that anybody needs to talk about the same thing or anything like that.

– MIT conference, May 1981

All these things I don't understand — deep questions, profound questions; however, physicists have kind of a dopey way of avoiding all of these things.

– MIT conference, May 1981

Some new kind of thinking is necessary, but physicists, being kind of dull-minded, only look at nature and don't know how to think these new ways.

– MIT conference, May 1981

I never think, "This is what I like, and this is what I don't like," I think "This is what it is, and this is what it isn't," and whether or not I like it is really irrelevant, and I have extracted it out of my mind.

> – "QED: Photons — Corpuscles of Light," Sir Douglas Robb Lectures, University of Auckland, June 1979

I will not be able to speak the way I usually speak because I speak too fast, so I will have to speak slowly and have not got time to say a great deal.

> – "The Computing Machines in the Future," Nishina Memorial Lecture, August 1985

You tell them about how some people used to believe in witches, and of course nobody believes in witches now, and you say, "How could people believe in witches?" and then you turn around and you say, "Oh, what witches do we believe in now? What ceremonies do we do? Every morning we brush our teeth! What is the evidence that brushing teeth does us any good with cavities? As the Earth turns in orbit, there's an edge between light and dark, and on that edge, all the people — they're on that edge doing the same ritual for no good reason. Just like in the Middle Ages they had other rituals, and you're trying to picture this perpetual line of tooth brushers going around the Earth!

> – Interview with Yorkshire Television program, "Take the World from Another Point of View," 1972

The pleasure in physics, for me, is that it's revealed that the truth is so remarkable and amazing. I have this disease, and many other people who have studied far enough to begin to understand a little about how things work are fascinated by it, and this fascination guides them on to such an extent that they've been able to convince governments to keep supporting them in this investigation that the race is making!

> – Interview with Yorkshire Television program, "Take the World from Another Point of View," 1972

I have tried many different ways of understanding the physical universe.

> – Letter to Richard D. Farley, August 1975

[Response to a colleague's suggestion for an autobiography:] Actually your suggestion has put a bee in my bonnet which I hope dies before it puts me to work.

> – Letter to Dr. Erik M. Pell, March 1976

It is my greatest pleasure to think anew about things, and I am delighted to discover that I have infected you with the same pleasure.

> – Letter to Dr. Frank Potter, November 1984 (*Perfectly Reasonable Deviations from the Beaten Track*, p. 371)

You ask me on what I think about life, etc., as if I had some wisdom. Maybe, by accident, I do — of course I don't know — all I know is I have opinions.

> – Letter to Mr. V. A. Van Der Hyde, July 1986 (*Perfectly Reasonable Deviations from the Beaten Track*, p. 413)

Thank you for your letter about my KNXT interview. You are quite right that I am very ignorant about smog and many other things, including the use of the finest English.

– Letter to Raymond Rogers, January 1966 (*Perfectly Reasonable Deviations from the Beaten Track*, p. 209)

There's a great deal of intimidation by intellectuals in a country of less intellectual people. It comes in the form of pompous studies and pompous words to describe ideas that are fairly simple or have very little content. If someone says they do not understand one of these ideas, they're often put down, which must be hard for those who don't have too much confidence in their own intelligence.

– *U.S. News and World Report* interview, February 1985

I can write under pressure. It's the only way I really can write.

– "Joy of the Chase," *The Daily Telegraph*, July 5, 1988

What about me? I had to come right back here to teach classes after being waited on hand and foot by two beautiful nymphs and their assistant commandos. It was tough.

– Letter to Mariela Johansen, January 1975

My wife and I think I am crazy.

– Letter to Mariela Johansen, January 1975

If you go in the same direction as everybody else, you have a whole host of people that you gotta get ahead of.

– CERN talk, December 1965

Those people who have for years been insisting in the face of all obvious evidence to the contrary that the male and female are equally capable of rational thought may have something.

> – National Science Teachers Association Fourteenth Convention lecture, "What Is Science?" April 1966

I decided to stay at Caltech forever. I couldn't bear missing guys running around all excited with discoveries.

> – *The Daily Times*, October 5, 1966

I know that that fraternity was a very important thing in my life. I know it — I mean, as far as social things — because, although it was hard to do, it forced me to do it. It's easy to not do it, it's scary, and it's easy to not to do it, but they made sure I did it. They taught me to dance. And so the confidence came relatively rapidly after a while.

> – Interview with Charles Weiner, March 5, 1966 (Niels Bohr Library and Archives with the Center for the History of Physics)

[On English classes:] Yes. I didn't see why I had to worry about that now. After all, how do you spell something? Suppose I make a mistake? (This was my attitude — it was the attitude at the time.) You make a mistake in spelling. What does it mean? It means that the damn language is irrational. It's just a stupid method of spelling. Some guy ought to make some progress. If those English professors would sit around and figure out how to straighten out the spelling, instead of teaching this idiocy all the time — they had no feeling of progress, no feeling of development, like the sciences or anything.

> – Interview with Charles Weiner, March 5, 1966 (Niels Bohr Library and Archives with the Center for the History of Physics)

[On college courses:] I'm trying to emphasize that my humanities effort was always somehow to figure out how I could, by using science, escape the humanities. I fought it to the bitter end.

> – Interview with Charles Weiner, March 5, 1966 (Niels Bohr Library and Archives with the Center for the History of Physics)

I cannot conceive that antagonism could result from the way I expressed myself, but only perhaps from the fact that I did express myself.

> – Letter to Bill Whitley (KNXT), May 1959 (*Perfectly Reasonable Deviations from the Beaten Track*, p. 101)

The physical world was real, and the mathematics, I had become enthralled with, but not for itself, really — you know what I mean? It was fascinating, but my real heart was somewhere else. So I decided, I have to get my hands dirty, I can't stand these abstract things. So I changed to electrical engineering, because there was something that was real. But then some few months later, I realized I'd gone too far, and that somewhere in between — that physics was the right place. So I moved around a little bit at the beginning, and ended up with the physics course.

> – Interview with Charles Weiner, March 4, 1966 (Niels Bohr Library and Archives with the Center for the History of Physics)

I went to a scientific school, MIT. And the fraternity, when you first join, they try to, if you think you're smart, keep you from feeling that you're too smart by giving you what looked like simple questions, to try to figure out what actually happens. It's like training for imagination. It's kind of fun.

– BBC, "Fun to Imagine" television series, 1983

I always tried to do it myself, because I'd learn something, maybe get a different idea. I never looked it up.

– Interview with Charles Weiner, March 5, 1966 (Niels Bohr Library and Archives with the Center for the History of Physics)

It turned out that the notes I took at conferences were never very useful for anything, and I don't take much notes at conferences any more.

– Interview with Charles Weiner, February 4, 1966 (Niels Bohr Library and Archives with the Center for the History of Physics)

You've got plenty of room and not too many people, and it looks like it ought to be good! Anyway, you do, and don't forget you have Rutherford, so it's okay!

– On life in New Zealand, "QED: Photons — Corpuscles of Light," Sir Douglas Robb Lectures, University of Auckland, June 1979

Yes, I shall write an article on "Energy" for you. However, instead of the proposed compensation of $225 plus 25 copies of my contribution, I should instead like to receive one set of the complete new encyclopaedia when it comes out.

– Letter to Warren E. Preece (*Encyclopaedia Britannica*), January 1970

People often think I'm a faker, but I'm usually honest, in a certain way — in such a way that often nobody believes me!

– *Surely You're Joking, Mr. Feynman!*, p. 41

My talents do not include competence for advising in International Relations.

– Letter to Clarence Streit, January 1966

Any vague theory that is not completely absurd can be patched up by more vague talk at every point that brings up inconsistencies — and if we begin to believe in the talk rather than in the evidence we will be in a sorry state.

– *Feynman Lectures on Gravitation*, p. 22

So I graduated. And I had to wear an academic outfit in order to graduate. And also I remember that they teased me, that Princeton didn't know what they were going to get — that Princeton was an elegant place, and I was just, you know, a rough guy, and so on. Not really worry about it, but I did take it seriously, that there was a matter of — you know, Princeton has a certain elegance. And I was not an elegant person.

– Interview with Charles Weiner, March 5, 1966 (Niels Bohr Library and Archives with the Center for the History of Physics)

I was OK, but I was kind of a rough, kind of a simple character, as far as society goes. But I wasn't worried about it. I was just sort of half-proud of it.

– Interview with Charles Weiner, March 5, 1966 (Niels Bohr Library and Archives with the Center for the History of Physics)

It used to worry me — how do I look, what am I like? So I got out of that when I was at MIT. Probably the usual growing up, although I have reasons, I claim to understand it a little bit in terms of this fight and so on. But anyway I did change at MIT, my personality, my fear of girls; my young and timid frightened and somewhat insecure character disappeared.

> – Interview with Charles Weiner, March 5, 1966 (Niels Bohr Library and Archives with the Center for the History of Physics)

I believe, although I can't guarantee it, that most of my education as a graduate student was through my own studying, through worrying about problems, through talking to friends, and very little courses. And that's the way it was in those days.

> – Interview with Charles Weiner, March 5, 1966 (Niels Bohr Library and Archives with the Center for the History of Physics)

When I was at MIT, I had read a lot. I didn't explain that. I forgot to. I was in the library a lot. I read advanced books. That's the way I taught myself, I read lots of stuff — I was very avid for reading and studying and learning. I read about general relativity, I learned it from a book, and I read a lot of quantum mechanics along with Welpin, and all this stuff, by reading.

> – Interview with Charles Weiner, March 5, 1966 (Niels Bohr Library and Archives with the Center for the History of Physics)

I had a great faith in that way of looking at the world — scientific — make sure what the reality is, don't get mixed up.

> – Interview with Charles Weiner, March 5, 1966 (Niels Bohr Library and Archives with the Center for the History of Physics)

I can tell an amusing story — you can always later throw it away, you know? I finally arrived in Ithaca at 2 a.m. or 12 something, in the night. I got off the train, and I slung my suitcase onto my shoulder as I always used to. Then I said: "Wait a minute now. You're a professor, and you have to try and behave like one." A porter asked me: "Can I carry your suitcase?" "No, I carry my own." Then I realized: I've got to start living in a dignified way. So I let him carry it to a taxi, and I sat rather elegantly in the back of the taxi, and the guy says, "Where to?" I say, "Biggest hotel in town, please."

> – Interview with Charles Weiner, June 27, 1966 (Niels Bohr
>   Library and Archives with the Center for the History of Physics)

You see, I'm a one-sided fellow. I understand and love the sciences. But there are many fields of intellectual things that I don't really go for, like literature, psychology, philosophy, and so on, unless it's done in a very sort of scientific way. I'm very one-sided. I'm not a wide guy, only very wide in the sciences, but very much in the sciences and limited.

> – Interview with Charles Weiner, June 27, 1966 (Niels Bohr
>   Library and Archives with the Center for the History of Physics)

I don't like the non-technical problems. They're not to my liking. I just don't feel good about them. So I don't have much to do with it and have never, therefore, done much consulting.

> – Interview with Charles Weiner, June 28, 1966 (Niels Bohr
>   Library and Archives with the Center for the History of
>   Physics)

I don't mean I don't believe in thinking about what I'm doing. Talking about it is another matter. I don't like to talk about it anymore.

> – Interview with Charles Weiner, June 28, 1966 (Niels Bohr Library and Archives with the Center for the History of Physics)

I was consulted on a problem of safety for nuclear energy peacetime plants. I was thinking of designing one at the General Electric Co. The reason that I was involved, of course, was because I was involved in the safety at Los Alamos. And so I felt, you ought to help out if you know about these things for peacetime use in business.

> – Interview with Charles Weiner, June 28, 1966 (Niels Bohr Library and Archives with the Center for the History of Physics)

I'm a very complicated man. I mean, I've got all kinds of side things, infinite amounts of them.

> – Interview with Charles Weiner, June 27, 1966 (Niels Bohr Library and Archives with the Center for the History of Physics)

Bob Wilson came in and said that he had been funded to do a job that was a secret and he wasn't supposed to tell anybody, but he was going to tell me because he knew that as soon as I knew what he was going to do, I'd see that I had to go along with it.

> – "The Remarkable Dr. Feynman," *Los Angeles Times Magazine*, April 20, 1986

But what I did immorally, I would say, was not to remember the reason that I said I was doing it, so when the reason changed — Germany was defeated — not the singlest thought came to my mind about that that now I have to reconsider why I am continuing to do this. I simply didn't think, okay?

– BBC, "The Pleasure of Finding Things Out," 1981

Theoretical physics is a human endeavor, one of the higher developments of human beings — and this perpetual desire to prove that people who do it are human by showing that they do other things that a few other humans do (like playing bongo drums) is insulting to me.

– Letter to Tord Pramberg, January 1967, regarding photos in a physics book of Feynman drumming (*Perfectly Reasonable Deviations from the Beaten Track*, p. 230)

You know, the real problem — you have to appreciate, really, all my time in these schools and around there — was the lack of supplies. Perhaps it was good, so that I had plenty of time to worry about elementary things before I was swamped by advanced things. I couldn't get books. The library had no calculus book. When they got it, it was within a week or two, I'm sure, that I took it out — the first guy to take it out. The first calculus book that was in town.

– Interview with Charles Weiner, March 4, 1966 (Niels Bohr Library and Archives with the Center for the History of Physics)

That was also what you worried about — that girls would think you were a sissy. Dumb, but that's life.

– Interview with Charles Weiner, March 5, 1966 (Niels Bohr Library and Archives with the Center for the History of Physics)

I am not happy as a member of a self-perpetuating honorary society.

> – Letter to Dr. Detlev W. Bronk and the National Academy of Sciences, August 1961 (*Perfectly Reasonable Deviations from the Beaten Track*, p. 108)

At the very beginning, we had terribly important secrets. We'd worked out lots of stuff about uranium, how it worked, and all this stuff was in documents that were in filing cabinets that were made out of wood that had on them little ordinary, common padlocks.

> – UCSB talk, "Los Alamos from Below," February 1975

I do remember one moment. I was in my pajamas, working on the floor with papers all around me, these funny-looking diagrams of blobs with lines sticking out. I said to myself, wouldn't it be funny if these diagrams really are useful, and other people start using them, and *Physical Review* has to print these silly pictures?

> – *Omni* interview, February 1979, regarding the Feynman Diagrams

It was radioactive; it was plutonium. And we stood at the door of this room talking about it. There was a new element that was made by man that had never existed on the earth before, except for a very short period possibly, at the very beginning.

> – UCSB talk, "Los Alamos from Below," February 1975

I must explain that because I am a scientist does not mean that I have not had contact with human beings. Ordinary human beings. I know what they are like. I like to go to Las Vegas and talk to the showgirls and the gamblers and so on. I have banged around a lot in my life, so I know about ordinary people.

– "The Unscientific Age," John Danz Lecture Series, 1963


[When asked if he would like to read his prepared obituary:] I have decided it is not a very good idea for a man to read it ahead of time; it takes the element of surprise out of it.

– "The Cult of Richard Feynman," *Los Angeles Times Magazine*, December 2, 2001, p. 16

# Art, Music, and Poetry

For far more marvelous is the truth than any artist of the past imagined it. Why do the poets of the present not speak of it? What men are poets who can speak of Jupiter if he were a man, but if he is an immense spinning sphere of methane and ammonia must be silent?

– *Feynman Lectures on Physics*, vol. 1, pp. 3–6

I understood at last what art is really for, at least in certain respects. It gives somebody, individually, pleasure. You can make something that someone likes so much that they're depressed, or they're happy, on account of that damn thing you made! In science, it's sort of general and large: You don't know the individuals who have appreciated it directly.

– *Surely You're Joking, Mr. Feynman!*, p. 267

If you mean that this is an age of science in the sense that in art, in literature, and in people's attitudes and understandings and so forth that science plays a large part, I don't think it is a scientific age at all.

– "The Unscientific Age," John Danz Lecture Series, 1963

I think most kids in high school are very mature. Because I know my friends who were in literature — you know, who wrote — and my friends who wrote plays, and they would read the great plays. They wouldn't read the children's plays, you know. It's the same thing. Anybody that's any good in high school already knows that they have to look at the real stuff.

– Interview with Charles Weiner, March 4, 1966 (Niels Bohr Library and Archives with the Center for the History of Physics)

I have a friend who's an artist and he's sometimes taken a view which I don't agree with very well. He'll hold up a flower and say, "Look how beautiful it is," and I'll agree. But then he'll say, "I as an artist can see how beautiful a flower is. But you, as a scientist take it all apart, and it becomes dull." I think he's kind of nutty. First of all, the beauty that he sees is available to other people — and to me too, I believe. Although I may not be quite as refined aesthetically as he is, I can appreciate the beauty of a flower. But at the same time, I see much more in the flower than he sees. I can imagine the cells inside, which also have a beauty. There's beauty not just at the dimension of one centimeter; there's also beauty at a smaller dimension. There are the complicated actions of the cells, and other processes. The fact that the colors in the flower have evolved in order to attract insects to pollinate is interesting; that means insects can see the colors. That adds a question: Does this aesthetic sense we have also exist in lower forms of life? There are all kinds of interesting questions that come from a knowledge of science, which only adds to the excitement and mystery and awe of the flower. It only adds. I don't understand how it subtracts.

– *What Do You Care What Other People Think?*, p. 11

I wanted very much to learn to draw, for a reason that I kept to myself: I wanted to convey an emotion I have about the beauty of the world.

– *Surely You're Joking, Mr. Feynman!*, p. 261

The artists of the Renaissance said that man's main concern should be for man, and yet there are other things of interest in the world. Even the artists appreciate sunsets, and the ocean waves, and the march of the stars across the heavens. There is then some reason to talk of other things sometimes.

– *The Character of Physical Law*, p. 13

Bongo playing has never been "music" to me — I don't read notes or know anything about conventional music — it has just been fun making noise to rhythm — not much "intelligence" in the intellectual sense is involved.

– Letter to Dr. William L. McConnell, March 1975 (*Perfectly Reasonable Deviations from the Beaten Track*, p. 281)

I am sorry not to want to send you a drawing, because it has been my policy not to sell them to people who want them because it is a physicist who made them.

– Letter to Dr. William L. McConnell, March 1975 (*Perfectly Reasonable Deviations from the Beaten Track*, p. 282)

Mr. Auden's poem only confirms his lack of response to Nature's wonders for he himself says that he would like to know more clearly what we "want the knowledge for." We want it so we can love nature more.

– Letter to Mrs. Robert Weiner, October 1967 (*Perfectly Reasonable Deviations from the Beaten Track*, p. 248)

And the crassness of our time, so much lamented, is a crassness that can be alleviated only by art, and surely not by science without art. Art and poetry can remind the mind of beauty and gradually make life more beautiful.

– Letter to Mrs. Robert Weiner, October 1967 (*Perfectly Reasonable Deviations from the Beaten Track*, p. 248)

I had never thought of that idea that many possible viewpoints not obviously equivalent is a sign also of greatness in art.

– Letter to Jay A. Young, August 1966

The value of science remains unsung by singers, so you are reduced to hearing — not a song or poem, but an evening lecture about it. This is not yet a scientific age.

– "The Value of Science," December 1955

The fact that I beat a drum has nothing to do with the fact that I do theoretical physics.

– Letter to Tord Pramberg, January 1967, regarding photos in a physics book of Feynman drumming (*Perfectly Reasonable Deviations from the Beaten Track*, p. 230)

[On Nobel Prize work:] It is true that most of the work was done in the quiet and peaceful atmosphere at Telluride — a quiet and peace which I was perpetually trying to dispel by jungle rhythms.

– Letter to Erik M. Pell, November 1965

The human mind as it evolved, it evolved from an animal, and it evolves in a certain way that it is like any new tool in that it has its diseases and difficulties. It has its troubles, and one of the troubles is that it gets polluted by its own superstitions that it confuses itself, and that the discovery was finally made of a way to keep it sort of in line so that they can make a little progress in some direction rather than to go around in a circle and to force itself into a hole.

– Galileo Symposium, "What Is and What Should Be the Role of Scientific Culture in Modern Society," September 1964

# Nature

Poets say science takes away from the beauty of the stars — mere globs of gas atoms. I too can see the stars on a desert night, and feel them. But do I see less or more? The vastness of the heavens stretches my imagination — stuck on this carousel my little eye can catch one-million-year-old light. A vast pattern — of which I am a part . . . . What is the pattern, or the meaning, or the why? It does not do harm to the mystery to know a little about it.

– *Feynman Lectures on Physics*, vol. 1, pp. 3–10

The point of my remarks about poets was not meant to be a complaint that modern poets show no interest in modern physics — but that they show no emotional appreciation for those aspects of Nature that have been revealed in the last four hundred years.

– Letter to Mrs. Robert Weiner, October 1967 (*Perfectly Reasonable Deviations from the Beaten Track*, p. 248)

Physicists are trying to find out how nature behaves.

– *Omni* interview, February 1979

If we look out from physics, which of course is the center of the universe, and see what surrounds us . . .

– Audio recording of Feynman Lectures on Physics, Lecture 3, October 3, 1961

If you want to burn a diamond in air, you can — but you're kind of dopey.

– Audio recording of Feynman Lectures on Physics, Lecture 1, September 26, 1961

But it illustrates that, if we screw up the geometry sufficiently, it is possible that all of gravitation is related in a way to pseudo forces.

– Audio recording of Feynman Lectures on Physics, Lecture 12, November 7, 1961

Things on a small scale behave nothing like a large scale at all. That's what makes physics hard, and very interesting.

– Audio recording of Feynman Lectures on Physics, Lecture 2, September 29, 1961

Nature, as a matter of fact, seems to be so designed that the most important things in the real world appear to be a kind of complicated accidental result of a lot of laws.

– *The Character of Physical Law*, p. 122

There is the value of the worldview created by science. There is the beauty and the wonder of the world that is discovered through the results of these new experiences.

– National Science Teachers Association Fourteenth Convention lecture, "What Is Science?" April 1966

The nucleus is very small. The atom in its diameter is $10^{-8}$ cm, and the nucleus in its diameter is in the order of magnitude is 10 to the $^{-13}$ cm. What does that mean? If you had an atom, and you wanted to see the nucleus, you'd have to expand it, magnify it, so the whole atom is the size of this room and then the nucleus is a bare speck that you can just about make out with the eye — 1/100th of an inch across.

– Audio recording of Feynman Lectures on Physics, Lecture 2, September 29, 1961

So close is life to life. The universality of the deep chemistry of living things is indeed a fantastic and beautiful thing. And all the time we human beings have been too proud to recognize our kinship with the animals.

– "The Uncertainty of Science," John Danz Lecture Series, 1963

It is easy to demonstrate that if Nature was nonrelativistic, then if things started out that way then it would be that way for all time, and so the problem would be pushed back to Creation itself, and God only knows how that was done.

– Dirac Memorial Lectures, "The Reason for Antiparticles," 1986

For a successful technology, reality must take precedence over public relations, for nature cannot be fooled.

– Report of the Presidential Commission on the Space Shuttle *Challenger* Accident, Volume 2: Appendix F, June 1986

There's a very large number of stars in the galaxy. If you tried to name them, one a second, naming all the stars in our galaxy — and I don't mean all the stars in the universe, just this galaxy here — it takes three thousand years. And yet, that's not a very big number. Because if those stars were to drop one dollar bill on the earth during a year, each star dropping one dollar bill, they might take care of the deficit which is suggested for the budget of the United States.

– BBC, "Fun to Imagine" television series, 1983

[In response to a child's question, "What happens when an irresistible force meets an immovable object?":] They shake hands.

   — From notes for "About Time" program, 1957

All things that we make are Nature. We arrange it in a way to suit our purpose.

   — "The Computing Machines in the Future," Nishina Memorial
     Lecture, August 1985

We drop an egg on the sidewalk: it splatters in all directions. On the other hand if we had a smear of egg on the sidewalk, we would not expect it to come together to form a complete egg and ride back into our hand. So it would be obvious that the laws of nature appear different if we were to reverse the direction of time.

   — From notes for "About Time" program, 1957

The biological example of writing information on a small scale has inspired me to think of something that should be possible. Biology is not simply writing information; it is doing something about it. A biological system can be exceedingly small. Many of the cells are very tiny, but they are very active; they manufacture various substances; they walk around; they wiggle; and they do all kinds of marvelous things — all on a very small scale.

   — "There's Plenty of Room at the Bottom," December 1959

The origin of the force of gravitation is a problem which puzzles me too, and I do not think that we thoroughly understand it at all.

– Correspondence with R. I. Elliott on gravitation, January 1949

Trying to understand the way nature works involves a most terrible test of human reasoning ability. It involves subtle trickery, beautiful tightropes of logic on which one has to walk in order not to make a mistake in predicting what will happen.

– "The Uncertainty of Science," John Danz Lecture Series, 1963

Imagination reaches out repeatedly trying to achieve some higher level of understanding, until suddenly I find myself momentarily alone before one new corner of nature's pattern of beauty and true majesty revealed. That was my reward.

– From Les Prix Nobel en 1965 [Nobel Foundation], Stockholm, 1966

For instance, I stand at the seashore, alone, and start to think.
There are the rushing waves
mountains of molecules
each stupidly minding its own business
trillions apart
yet forming white surf in unison.
Ages on ages

before any eyes could see
year after year
thunderously pounding on the shore as now.
For whom, for what?
On a dead planet, with no life to entertain.
Never at rest
tortured by energy
wasted prodigiously by the sun
poured into space.
A mite makes the sea roar.
Deep in the sea
all molecules repeat
the patterns of one another
till complex new ones are formed.
They make others like themselves
and a new dance starts.
Growing in size and complexity
living things
masses of atoms
DNA, protein
dancing a pattern ever more intricate.
Out of the cradle
onto the dry land
here it is
standing:
atoms with consciousness;
matter with curiosity.
Stands at the sea
wonders at wondering: I

a universe of atoms
an atom in the universe.

— "The Value of Science," December 1955

While we're admiring the human mind, which is something we enjoy doing — it's always someone else's human mind that we enjoy admiring — we should take some time off to stand in awe of nature, of a nature which can follow with such completeness and generality such an elegantly simple principle as the law of gravitation.

— Audio recording of Feynman Lectures on Physics, Lecture 7, October 17, 1961

It is characteristic of the physical laws that that have this abstract character. Just like the conservation of energy is a theorem about quantities which you have to add together without a machinery, so the great laws of mechanics are quantitative mathematical laws for which no machinery is available.

— Audio recording of Feynman Lectures on Physics, Lecture 7, October 17, 1961

[On his father:] He went on to say that in the world whenever there is any source of something that could be eaten to make life go, some form of life finds a way to make use of that source; and that each little bit of left over stuff is eaten by something.

— National Science Teachers Association Fourteenth Convention lecture, "What Is Science?" April 1966

We have learned from much experience that all philosophical intuitions about what nature is going to do fail.

— *The Character of Physical Law*, p. 53

We used to laugh at the Greeks who claimed that the planets had to go in circles because it was a perfect figure. If they were talking in the modern times they would use group theoretic arguments and would imply that from a point of view of the planet the sun looks always the same, or that we have invariance under a combined time displacement and rotation. But the planets do not go in circles! Nature is not "symmetrical" and the question is why not?

— Programme of American Physical Society Annual Meeting, 1950

Nature uses only the longest threads to weave her patterns, so each small piece of her fabric reveals the organization of the entire tapestry.

— *The Character of Physical Law*, p. 34

The apparent enormous complexities of nature, with all its funny laws and rules, each of which has been carefully explained to you, are really very closely interwoven. However, if you do not appreciate the mathematics, you cannot see, among the great variety of facts, that logic permits you to go from one to the other.

— *The Character of Physical Law*, p. 41

We look at the stars: all the light that we see, that little tiny and influent spreads from the star over this enormous distance of three light years, for the nearest star. On, on, on, this light from the star is spreading, the wave-fronts are getting wider and wider, weaker and weaker, weaker and weaker, out into all of space, and finally, the tiny fraction of it comes in one square eighth of an inch, a tiny little black hole, and does something to me so I know it's there.

– BBC, "Fun to Imagine" television series, 1983

All the intellectual arguments that you can make will not communicate to deaf ears what the experience of music really is.

– *The Character of Physical Law*, p. 58

What is it about nature that lets this happen, that it is possible to guess from one part what the rest is going to do? That is an unscientific question: I do not know how to answer it, and therefore I am going to give an unscientific answer. I think it is because nature has a simplicity and therefore a great beauty.

– *The Character of Physical Law*, p. 173

There is always another way to say the same thing that doesn't look at all like the way you said it before. I don't know what the reason for this is. I think it is somehow a representation of the simplicity of nature.

– From *Nobel Lectures, Physics 1963–1970*, Elsevier Publishing Company, Amsterdam, 1972

Perhaps a thing is simple if you can describe it fully in several different ways without immediately knowing that you are describing the same thing.

– From *Nobel Lectures, Physics 1963–1970*, Elsevier Publishing Company, Amsterdam, 1972

Nature has always looked like a horrible mess, but as we go along we see patterns and put theories together; a certain clarity comes and things get simpler.

– *QED: The Strange Theory of Light and Matter*, p. 149

You can know the name of a bird in all the languages of the world, but when you're finished, you'll know absolutely nothing whatever about the bird. You'll only know about humans in different places, and what they call the bird. So lets look at the bird and see what it's doing — that's what counts.

– *What Do You Care What Other People Think?*, p. 14

If you take an apple and magnify it to the size of the earth, then the atoms in the apple are approximately the size of the original apple.

– *Feynman Lectures on Physics*, Vol. 1, pp. 1–3

Nature doesn't care what we call it, she just keeps on doing it whatever way she wants.

– Audio recording of Feynman Lectures on Physics, Lecture 1, September 26, 1961

The fact that there's no perpetual motion at all is a general statement of the conservation of energy law.

– Audio recording of Feynman Lectures on Physics, Lecture 4, October 6, 1961

If you want to talk about Nature, you're going to talk about something complicated and dirty, and therefore at first approximations, ever increasing in accuracy.

– Audio recording of Feynman Lectures on Physics, Lecture 12, November 7, 1961

Nature is, no doubt, simpler than all our thoughts about it.

– Yorkshire Television interview, "Take the World from Another Point of View," 1972

I'm trying to find out, not how nature could be, but how it is. See what's right.

– Yorkshire Television interview, "Take the World from Another Point of View," 1972

And so it can be that distances and times all seem to change, and things will be frightening and disturbing and disguise a sense of time as different from your sense of time, but its only because there is something left. There's another view in which the time is added together with the space, which makes this a new sense but requires an enormous amount of imagination, because we haven't any analogous experience of this kind.

– Audio recording of lecture on relativity, Douglas Advanced Research Laboratory, 1967

If it were a common experience for biological systems to move that fast, then no doubt inside the brain there would be evolved a special wiring that would not, in fact, require us to learn the theory of relativity; it would be an innate feeling that this is right.

– Audio recording of lecture on relativity, Douglas Advanced Research Laboratory, 1967

This rather trivial understanding of relativity could have easily been understood the moment perspective was understood, and the famous old kingdom legends about the guys who feel the elephants, you know, as a rope, because he's holding on to the tail, or as a leaf because he's holding on to the ear, and so on, is just simply the same idea that things depend upon your point of view.

– Audio recording of lecture on relativity, Douglas Advanced Research Laboratory, 1967

Energy is a very subtle concept. It is very, very difficult to get right.

– National Science Teachers Association Fourteenth Convention lecture, "What Is Science?" April 1966

Is it unbelievable that a part of the brain can make do much "thinking" and interpreting and we would be unaware of it and not be able to control it? Maybe. But maybe not. The simplest animal must be able to think at this kind of level if he sees at all.

– On human and animal eyesight, in a letter to Edwin H. Land (Polaroid Corporation), May 1966 (*Perfectly Reasonable Deviations from the Beaten Track*, p. 224)

Relativity is not simply that things depend upon your point of view; it is.

– Audio recording of lecture on relativity, Douglas Advanced Research Laboratory, 1967

Light has weight, a finite weight proportional to its finite mass — neither zero nor infinity. Any object as it speeds up gets heavier until at light speed it is infinitely heavier than it would be at rest. But light never is at rest so the argument doesn't apply to light. In gravitational fields light falls, very slightly, and the images of stars seen very near the sun (during an eclipse) are slightly out of place because the light doesn't go in straight lines, but curves slightly down toward the sun as it goes by, because it falls.

– From notes for "About Time" program, 1957

The world is a spinning ball, and people are held on it on all sides, some of them upside down. And we turn like a spit in front of a great fire. We whirl around the sun. That is more romantic, more exciting. And what holds us? The force of gravitation, which is not only a thing of the earth, but is the thing that makes the earth round in the first place, holds the sun together, and keeps us running around the sun in our perpetual attempt to stay away. This gravity holds its sway not only on the stars, but between the stars; it holds them in the great galaxies for miles and miles in all directions.

– "The Uncertainty of Science," John Danz Lecture Series, 1963

The principle of relativity can be stated this way: that the motion of bodies among themselves in an enclosed space is the same whether the enclosed space is standing still or is moving uniformly at a constant speed in a straight line.

> – Audio recording of lecture on relativity, Douglas Advanced Research Laboratory, 1967

The internal machinery of life, the chemistry of the parts, is something beautiful.

> – "The Uncertainty of Science," John Danz Lecture Series, 1963

What looks still to our crude eyes is a wild and dynamic dance.

> – "The Uncertainty of Science," John Danz Lecture Series, 1963

All other aspects and characteristics of science can be understood directly when we understand that observation of science is the ultimate and final judge of the truth of an idea.

> – "The Uncertainty of Science," John Danz Lecture Series, 1963

If you have any appreciation for the complexities of nature and for the evolution of life on earth, you can understand the tremendous variety of possible forms that life would have.

> – "The Unscientific Age," John Danz Lecture Series, 1963

Our psychological feeling of the flow of time then has been converted to a definite physical idea of a quantity which we can measure accurately and can speak of equal intervals of time.

– From notes for "About Time" program, 1957

So now when we ask how old is the universe we had better ask where.

– From notes for "About Time" program, 1957

The question is whether two events which appear to occur simultaneously to me, appear also simultaneously to anyone else. This question is the question as to whether there is an absolute meaning to "the present" because the present is all those events which are occurring at the same time as "now." If a different set of events occur "now" from your point of view then we will have to say that the present for me and you is not the same and has no absolute significance.

– From notes for "About Time" program, 1957

You are lucky you have such a deep interest in nature, and even if you find it is much more complicated and difficult to understand than you thought, when you learn more about it, it is also in certain ways more simple and beautiful than what you can imagine.

– Letter to student Charles E. Tucker, April 1967

You all know something about the wonders of science — it isn't a popular audience I'm talking to — so I won't try to make you enthusiastic once again with the facts about the world; the fact that we are all made of atoms, the enormous ranges of time and space that there are, the position of ourselves historically is a result of a remarkable series of evolution, the position of ourselves in the evolutionary sequence, and further the most remarkable aspect of our scientific world view is its universality in this sense, although we talk about our being specialists that we are really not.

– Galileo Symposium, "What Is and What Should Be the Role of Scientific Culture in Modern Society," September 1964

That the fact that our knowledge is in fact universal is something that is not completely appreciated, that the position of the theories are so complete that we hunt for exceptions and we find them very hard to find — in the physics at least — and the great expense of all these machines and so on is to find some exception to what is already known.

– Galileo Symposium, "What Is and What Should Be the Role of Scientific Culture in Modern Society," September 1964

Do you have any ideas about the mesons and fundamental particles? The meson theory ideas I have are either just phenomenological observations or childish modifications of electrodynamics. Surely Nature has a better imagination than to use the pseudoscalar field theory!

– Letter to Professor L. Landau, November 1954

There was another thing someone could measure in classical physics, which was something like the speed — actually it's called the momentum: it's the speed times the mass, which tells you how well something coasts!

– Esalen lecture, "Quantum Mechanical View of Reality (Part 1)," October 1984

So there came a time, perhaps, when for some species the rate at which learning was increased reached such a pitch that suddenly a completely new thing happened; things could be learned by one animal, passed on to another and another fast enough that it was not lost to the race. Thus became possible an accumulation of knowledge of the race. This has sometimes been called time-binding.

– National Science Teachers Association Fourteenth Convention lecture, "What Is Science?" April 1966

This phenomenon of having a memory for the race, of having an accumulated knowledge passable from one generation to another, was new in the world. But it had a disease in it. It was possible to pass on mistaken ideas. It was possible to pass on ideas which were not possible to the human race.

– National Science Teachers Association Fourteenth Convention lecture, "What Is Science?" April 1966

Then a way of avoiding the disease was discovered. This is to doubt that what is being passed from the past is in fact true, and to try to find out *ab initio*, again from experience, what the situation is, rather than trusting the experience of the past in the form in which it was passed down.

– National Science Teachers Association Fourteenth Convention lecture, "What Is Science?" April 1966

The trees are made of air, primarily. When they are burned, they go back to air, and in the flaming heat is released the flaming heat of the sun that was bound in to convert the air into tree, and in the ash is the small remnant of the part which did not come from air, that came from the solid earth.

– National Science Teachers Association Fourteenth Convention lecture, "What Is Science?" April 1966

And I'm not happy with all the analyses that go with just the classical theory because nature isn't classical, dammit, and if you want to make a simulation of nature, you'd better make it quantum mechanics, and by golly it's a wonderful problem because it doesn't look so easy.

– MIT conference, May 1981; "Simulating Physics with Computers"

There's an enormous range of this one property — the wavelength — a range of phenomena that's this complete, enormous spectrum. The eye sees a very narrow range of this spectrum, and it's all put together with this one theory of electromagnetic waves. I'm going to talk about that part of it, and I'm going to call it "light" instead of saying "electromagnetic radiation." Light, what we see, is only one little part, but the physicist's point of view is the accident that the human eye happens to be sensitive to waves from here to here is not essential. The phenomena are the same — it's a whole range!

– "QED: Photons — Corpuscles of Light," Sir Douglas Robb Lectures, University of Auckland, June 1979

If you want to know the way nature works, we looked at it happily, and that's the way it looks! You don't like it? Go somewhere else — to another universe where the rules are simpler!

– "QED: Photons — Corpuscles of Light," Sir Douglas Robb Lectures, University of Auckland, June 1979

It's always possible that tomorrow somebody's going to figure it out, but it's going to be very difficult and very strange.

– "QED: Photons — Corpuscles of Light," Sir Douglas Robb Lectures, University of Auckland, June 1979

As much as we admire the human mind, we must also stand in awe of Nature which follows with such completeness and generality such an elegantly simple principle as this law of gravitation. And what is this law? That every object in the universe attracts every other with a force that is proportional to the mass of each and varies inversely as the square of the distance between them.

– In personal notes

Things that are very common and observed all the time and which appear perfectly obvious are quite different in this world. It turns out that what we thought was obvious is wrong, and it's much more complicated — or not more complicated but just different! In fact, sometimes it's simpler and more beautiful.

– "QED: Electrons and Their Interactions," Sir Douglas Robb Lectures, University of Auckland, June 1979

Most elastic things, like steel springs and so on, is nothing but this electrical thing pulling back: You pull the atoms a little bit apart when you bend something, and then they try to come back together again. But rubber bands work on a different principle. There are some long molecules, like chains, and other little ones that are shaking all the time, that are bombarding them. And the chains are all kind of kinky. When you pull open the rubber band, the strings get straighter. But these strings are being bombarded on the side by other atoms that are trying to shorten them by kinking them. So it pulls back, it's trying to pull back. It pulls back only because of the heat!

　– BBC, "Fun to Imagine" television series, 1983

I've always found rubber bands fascinating. To think, when they've been sitting on an old package of papers for a long time, holding those papers together, its done by a perpetual pounding-pounding-pounding of the atoms against these chains, trying to kink them and trying to kink them, year after year.

　– BBC, "Fun to Imagine" television series, 1983

The world is a dynamic mess of jiggling things.

　– BBC, "Fun to Imagine" television series, 1983

We're so used to circumstances in which these electrical phenomena are all canceled out, everything is sort of neutral, where pushing and pulling is sort of dull, but nature has these wonderful things: magnetic forces and electrical forces.

　– BBC, "Fun to Imagine" television series, 1983

You must compare your ideas with Nature; she tells you yes or no. She produces phenomena that require explanation. You cannot make your own assumptions and analyze the consequences.

– Letter to Mr. Robert Bonic, January 1974

[On the laws of gravitation:] The only applications of the knowledge of the law that I can think of are in geophysical prospecting, in predicting the tides, and nowadays, more modernly, in working out the motions of the satellites and planet probes that we send up, and so on; and finally, also modernly, to calculate the predictions of the planets' positions, which have great utility for astrologers who publish their predictions in horoscopes in the magazines. It is a strange world we live in — that all the new advances in understanding are used only to continue the nonsense which has existed for 2,000 years.

– *The Character of Physical Law*, p. 27

Astronomy is older than physics. In fact, it got physics started by showing the beautiful simplicity of the motion of the stars and planets, the understanding of which was the beginning of physics.

– *Feynman Lectures on Physics*, vol. 1, p. 59

I think Nature's imagination is so much greater than man's, she's never gonna let us relax!

– BBC, "Fun to Imagine" television series, 1983

The most remarkable discovery in all of astronomy is that the stars are made of atoms of the same kind as those on Earth.

– *Feynman Lectures on Physics*, vol. 1, p. 3

Of course, men want knowledge for many other purposes also, to make war, to make a commercial success, to help the sick or the poor, etc., motives of various values. These obvious motives and their consequences the poets do understand and do write about. But emotions of awe, wonder, delight and love which are evoked upon learning Nature's ways in the animate and inanimate word, together (for they are one) is rarely expressed in modern poetry where the aspect of Nature being appreciate is one which could have been known to men in the Renaissance.

– Letter to Mrs. Robert Weiner, October 1967 (*Perfectly Reasonable Deviations from the Beaten Track*, p. 248)

How is it possible, by looking at a piece of nature, to guess how another part must look, where you've never been before? It's only in modern times that man has really been able to guess what nature is going to do in situations that he's never looked at before.

– BBC, "Strangeness Minus Three," 1964

This universe has been described by many, but it just goes on, with its edge as unknown as the bottom of the bottomless sea of the ancients' idea — just as mysterious, just as awe-inspiring, and just as incomplete as the poetic pictures that came before.

– "The Uncertainty of Science," John Danz Lecture Series, 1963

I like science because when you think of something you can check it by experiment: "Yes" or "No," nature says, and you go on from there progressively. Other wisdom has no equally certain way of separating truth from falsehood.

– Letter to Beata Kamp, February 1983 (*Perfectly Reasonable Deviations from the Beaten Track*, p. 356)

We are so used to looking at the world from the point of view of living things that we cannot understand what it means not to be alive, and yet most of the time the world had nothing alive on it. And in most places in the universe today there probably is nothing alive.

– "The Uncertainty of Science," John Danz Lecture Series, 1963

What makes you so sure that the new discovery of the interrelationship between nuclear forces is going to be so wonderful? How do we know it isn't going to be some complicated, dirty, or simple thing? We don't know. We keep on trying anyway. We're not sure. It's worth the risk. Because it very likely will be peculiar and if it is, it'll be very interesting.

– BBC, "Strangeness Minus Three," 1964

# Imagination

I don't know why it is that some people find science dull and difficult, and other people find it fun and easy, but there's one characteristic that I get a big kick from, and that is that it takes so much imagination to try to figure out what the world is really like.

– BBC, "Fun to Imagine" television series, 1983

I would like not to underestimate the value of the world-view which is the result of scientific effort. We have been led to imagine all sorts of things infinitely more marvelous than the imaginings of poets and dreamers of the past. It shows that the imagination of nature is far, far greater than the imagination of man.

– "The Value of Science," December 1955

It was thought in the Middle Ages that people simply make many observations, and the observations themselves suggest the laws. But it does not work that way. It takes much more imagination than that. So the next thing we have to talk about is where the new ideas come from. Actually, it does not make any difference, as long as they come.

– "The Uncertainty of Science," John Danz Lecture Series, 1963

It is surprising that people do not believe that there is imagination in science. It is a very interesting kind of imagination, unlike that of the artist. The great difficulty is in trying to imagine something that you have never seen, that is consistent in every detail with what has already been seen, and that is different from what has been thought of; furthermore, it must be definite and not a vague proposition. That is indeed difficult.

– "The Uncertainty of Science," John Danz Lecture Series, 1963

The game I play is a very interesting one. It's imagination, in a tight straightjacket, which is this: that is has to agree with the known laws of physics.

– "Tiny Machines," Esalen Institute

I find myself trying to imagine all kinds of things all the time, and I get a kick out of it, just like a runner gets a kick out of sweating. I get a kick out of thinking about these things. I can't stop!

– BBC, "Fun to Imagine" television series, 1983

I think with science, one of the things that makes it very difficult is that it takes a lot of imagination.

– BBC, "Fun to Imagine" television series, 1983

The great part of astronomy is the imagination that's been necessary to guess what kind of structures, what kinds of things, could be happening to produce the light and the effects of the light, and so on, of the stars we do see.

– BBC, "Fun to Imagine" television series, 1983

Many times in science, by using imagination, you've imagined something which could be, according to all the known knowledge of the law, and you don't know whether it is yet or not.

– BBC, "Fun to Imagine" television series, 1983

We have to imagine how things might look from another point of view. A point of view that perhaps we have never been able to take.

– Audio recording of lecture on relativity, Douglas Advanced Research Laboratory, 1967

It requires careful study of the detailed experiments, and lots of thought, to lift our imagination to the point to see this. Otherwise, we would be fine. If we were able to move, say, very rapidly, then we would be able to see all these things quite directly.

– Audio recording of lecture on relativity, Douglas Advanced Research Laboratory, 1967

It's much more interesting for me (unless I'm working on it) to leave a mystery a mystery, rather than to make believe I know an answer to it.

– BBC, "The Pleasure of Finding Things Out," 1981

Knowledge is of no real value if all you can tell me is what happened yesterday. It is necessary to tell what will happen tomorrow if you do something not only necessary, but fun. Only you must be willing to stick your neck out.

– "The Uncertainty of Science," John Danz Lecture Series, 1963

Our imagination is stretched to the utmost, not as in fiction, to imagine things which are not really there, but just to comprehend those things which are there.

– *The Character of Physical Law*, pp. 127–128

The stuff of fantasizing in looking at the world, imagining things, which really isn't fantasizing because you just try to imagine the way it really is, comes in handy sometimes.

– BBC, "Fun to Imagine" television series, 1983

I gotta stop somewhere, to leave you something to imagine!

– BBC, "Fun to Imagine" television series, 1983

# Humor

I am Professor Feynman, in spite of this suit-coat.

– Galileo Symposium, "What Is and What Should Be the Role of
Scientific Culture in Modern Society," September 1964

A poet, I think it is, once said,
The whole universe is in a glass of wine
I don't think we'll ever know in what sense he meant that —
for the poets don't write to be understood —
but it is true that if you look at a glass of wine closely enough
you will see the entire universe.
There are the things of physics:
the twisting liquid, the reflections in the glass,
and our imagination adds the atoms.
It evaporates, depending on the wind and weather.
The glass is a distillation of the earth's rocks,
and in its composition, as we've seen,
the secret of the universe's age,
and the evolution of the stars.
What strange array of chemicals are in the wine?
How did they come to be?
There are the ferments, the enzymes,
the substrates, and the products.
And there, in wine, was found the great generalization:
All life is fermentation.
Nor can you discover the chemistry of wine
without discovering, as did Pasteur,
the cause of much disease.
How vivid is the claret, pressing its existence
into the consciousness that watches it.
And if our small minds, for some convenience,
divides this glass of wine, this universe, into parts —
the physics, biology, geology, astronomy, psychology, and all —
remember that Nature doesn't know it.
So we should put it all back together,

and not forget, at last, what it's for.
Let it give us one final pleasure more:
drink it up and forget about it all!

> – *Feynman Lectures on Physics*, pp. 3–10

Although my mother didn't know anything about science, she had a great influence on me as well. In particular, she had a wonderful sense of humor, and I learned from her that the highest forms of understanding we can achieve are laughter and human compassion.

> – *What Do You Care What Other People Think?*, p. 19

My wife couldn't believe I'd actually accept an invitation to give a speech where I'd have to wear a tuxedo. I did change my mind a couple of times.

> – *Omni* interview, February 1979

I am glad to hear you think the show is O.K., but very surprised to learn that I have a "professional approach." What profession? T.V. personality? Well, all I know I learned from my director. Maybe you mean by "professional approach" that I act like a steel wastecan can!

> – Correspondence with Philip Daly (BBC), August 1964

Thank you for the invitation to attend the "Conference on Color, Flavor, and Unification" to be held on November 30. Since you give the year 1975 and offer to pay airfare, may I assume we are taking a trip back in time via the *Enterprise*? I am happy to accept in any case.

– Letter to Dr. Gordon Shaw, May 1979

[While drawing arrows:] The arrows are called amplitudes, so I may say amplitude rather than arrow. It's just a word, and we can have any word we want, like it says in Lewis Carroll!

– Esalen lecture, "Quantum Mechanical View of Reality (Part 2)," October 1984

There are $10^{11}$ stars in the galaxy. That used to be a huge number. But it's only a hundred billion. It's less than the national deficit! We used to call them astronomical numbers. Now we should call them economical numbers.

– *Feynman Lectures on Physics*

I think that it is much more likely that the reports of flying saucers are the results of the known irrational characteristics of terrestrial intelligence rather than of the unknown efforts of extra-terrestrial intelligence.

– *The Character of Physical Law*, pp. 165–166

But you can appreciate the difficulties that the chemists have and also appreciate why the names are so long. It's not because they want to be obstinate, it's because they have an extremely difficult problem, to describe this thing in words. Why they don't just draw the pictures all the time, I don't know.

– Audio recording of Feynman Lectures on Physics, Lecture 1, September 26, 1961

What's wrong with that? That's an excellent way to do things: to take a good flying guess at it first and then check it.

> – Audio recording of Feynman Lectures on Physics, Lecture 8, October 20, 1961

Everybody who comes to a scientific lecture knows they are not going to understand it, but maybe the lecturer has a nice, colored tie to look at. Not in this case!

> – *QED: The Strange Theory of Light and Matter*, p. 9

Never say you'll give a talk unless you know clearly what will you will talk about and roughly what you will say.

> – Notes

For those who want some proof that physicists are human, the proof is in the idiocy of all the different units which they use for measuring energy.

> – *The Character of Physical Law*, p. 75

If we look up at the sky: to many ancient people, it appeared like the surface of a dome in which there are points of light. And this idea that it could be a shell with points of light on it is not self-evidently crazy. It's only the result of a great deal of astronomical observation that permits the idea that that's not what we're looking at.

> – Audio recording of lecture on relativity, Douglas Advanced Research Laboratory, 1967

One of the biggest and most important tools of theoretical physics is the wastebasket.

– Future for Science interview

It was a complete surprise to me when he said, "I wanted to tell you that you won the prize." "Won?" I said, "hot dog!" You see? So he says, "It's interesting to hear a serious scientist saying something like, hot dog." I said, "Listen, you call up any serious scientist and tell him he won $15,000, he'll say hot dog."

– Interview with Charles Weiner, June 28, 1966 (Niels Bohr Library and Archives with the Center for the History of Physics)

Hence, blow on soup if you want to cool it off.

– Audio recording of Feynman Lectures on Physics, Lecture 1, September 26, 1961

You're on the air, they say. Of course, it's got nothing to do with the air. You can have radio broadcasts without any air.

– Audio recording of Feynman Lectures on Physics, Lecture 2, September 29, 1961

All these particles are really chicken tracks in a cloud chamber.

– Audio recording of Feynman Lectures on Physics, Lecture 2, September 29, 1961, Q&A

If you can't see gravitation acting here, you have no soul!

– Audio recording of Feynman Lectures on Physics, Lecture 7, October 17, 1961

The Greeks got somewhat confused — they were helped by, of course, some very confusing Greeks.

> – Audio recording of Feynman Lectures on Physics, Lecture 8,
>   October 20, 1961

The question is, how would you answer her if you were the cop? Well, if you're really the cop, then no subtleties are involved; it's very simple. You say, "tell that to the judge."

> – Audio recording of Feynman Lectures on Physics, Lecture 8,
>   October 20, 1961

I am human enough to tell you to go to hell.

> – Letter to Tord Pramberg, January 1967, regarding photos in
>   a physics book of Feynman drumming (*Perfectly Reasonable
>   Deviations from the Beaten Track*, p. 230)

I have been thinking about educating the people who do cosmology and 1) can write Chapter 25 with a manuscript to you April 1, 1969, 2) can talk into a tape recorder and you can make what you can out of the mess, 3) hope you quit bothering me, you bastard. In case of the first two, all best regards.

> – Letter to Allan Sandage, February 1969

I always get the impression when I come east that the east is backward. If we had a room this hot in the west, we would air-condition it.

> – "Current Algebras and Strong Interactions," 1967

[After a microphone malfunction:] Now I predict that the probability that I'll have a microphone of that kind next time is very low!

– "QED: Fits of Reflection and Transmission," Sir Douglas Robb Lectures, University of Auckland, 1979

It is always possible to follow the right lines after the events.

– Programme of American Physical Society Annual Meeting, 1950, regarding priests' reading sheeps' liver lines to predict the future

When you work hard, there are moments when you think, "At last, I've discovered that mathematics is inconsistent!" But pretty soon you discover the error, as I finally did.

– *Feynman's Tips on Physics*, p. 63

[Standing in front of three press microphones:] Why three microphones? It is ridiculous. Why not tap three lines off one microphone, if you need three.

– Press conference, April 23, 1963

I get the compliments, and all you get is some remark like "and there was no buffoon commentator asking you dumb questions," or the like. Little did most people (even some in the business) realize how it was actually done. They all believed the illusion that all I had to do was open my mouth and talk for an hour.

Like all true art, the artist disappears, and it looks natural and wonderful.

– Letter to Christopher Sykes (BBC), March 1983

My schedule is such lately that I must refuse to get bogged down reading someone else's theory; it may turn out to be wonderful and there I'd be with something else to think about.

– Letter to Francis Crick, March 1978 (*Perfectly Reasonable Deviations from the Beaten Track*, pp. 317–318)

Something I think theoretical physicists should be ashamed of: when you think of how much money is being put into these experiments and the big apparatus and so forth, and here we just sit around with a beautiful theory and mumble about it and can't calculate any numbers! We shouldn't get our salaries, I think. Or maybe they should be raised — we'd work faster!

– "QED: New Queries," Sir Douglas Robb Lectures, University of Auckland, 1979

There are certain kinds of men in every field that I can talk to as well as I can talk to a good scientist.

– Interview with Yorkshire Television program, "Take the World from Another Point of View," 1972

If you give more money to theoretical physics, it doesn't do any good if it just increases the number of guys following the comet head.

– CERN talk, December 1965

So while I was a professor, I could act very much like a student, even a freshman. I could be mistaken for a freshman in a perfectly legitimate way.

– Interview with Charles Weiner, June 27, 1966 (Niels Bohr Library and Archives with the Center for the History of Physics)

If the doctor says, "This guy's got bumps sticking out," you do something. But he says, "He's a little bit nuts," you're afraid to ask questions. Very amusing.

– Interview with Charles Weiner, June 28, 1966 (Niels Bohr Library and Archives with the Center for the History of Physics)

Well, unfortunately, you see I have always been unfashionable. How this parton* thing has been so successful that I have become fashionable. I have to find an unfashionable thing to do.

– Interview with Charles Weiner, February 4, 1973 (Niels Bohr Library and Archives with the Center for the History of Physics)

---

*The parton model was proposed by Feynman and James Bjorken in the 1960s to address new discoveries on hadron collision.

This conference was worse than a Rorschach test: There's a meaningless inkblot, and the others ask you what you think you see, but when you tell them, they start arguing with you!

> – *Surely You're Joking, Mr. Feynman!*

[In response to a fan letter:] I am now unique — a physicist with a fan who has fallen in love with him from seeing him on TV. Thank you, oh fan! Now I have everything anyone could desire. I need no longer be jealous of movie stars. [Letter signed: Your fan-ee (or whatever you call it — the whole business is new to me), Richard P. Feynman]

> – Letter to Ilene Ungerleider, August 1975 (*Perfectly Reasonable Deviations from the Beaten Track*, p. 286)

I just love the smell of rats because it's the spoor of exciting adventure.

> – Letter to Gweneth and Michelle Feynman, February 1986 (*Perfectly Reasonable Deviations from the Beaten Track*, p. 402)

So I have invented another myth for myself: that I'm irresponsible. I'm actively irresponsible. I tell everybody I don't do anything. If anybody asks me to be on a committee to take care of admissions, "No, I'm irresponsible. I don't give a damn about the students." Of course I give a damn about the students, but I know that somebody else will do it.

> – Interview with Yorkshire Television program, "Take the World from Another Point of View," 1972

It is gratifying to be honored by one's friends and neighbors. I have found, however, that winning awards always brings about some pitfalls and obstacles. I had to go to Sweden to accept one award and had to get up at 7 a.m. to accept another.

– Chamber of Commerce Outstanding Citizen Award acceptance speech

This is a tremendous idea — that you should do some careful experiments instead of deep philosophical arguments and find something out.

– Audio recording of Feynman Lectures on Physics, Lecture 7, October 17, 1961

I therefore don't have much to say. But I will talk a long time anyway.

– Programme of American Physical Society Annual Meeting, 1950

There are also of course in the world a number of phenomena that you cannot beat that are just the result of a general stupidity. And we all do stupid things, and we know some people do more than others, but there is no use in trying to check who does the most.

– "The Unscientific Age," John Danz Lecture Series, 1963

[In response to a fan letter:] One gets a nice feeling when reading letters from people who enjoyed something you did, and the glow doesn't usually wear off by lunchtime.

– Letter to J. S. Paxton, January 1982

For example, there is the absurdity of the young these days chanting things about purple people eaters and hound dogs, something that we cannot criticize at all if we belong to the old flat foot floogie and a floy floy or the music goes down and around. Sons of mothers who sang about "come Josephine, in my flying machine," which sounds just about as modern as "I'd like to get you on a slow boat to China." So in life, in gaiety, in emotion, in human pleasures and pursuits, and in literature and so on, there is no need to be scientific, there is no reason to be scientific. One must relax and enjoy life.

– "The Unscientific Age," John Danz Lecture Series, 1963

It is odd, but on the infrequent occasions when I have been called upon in a formal place to play the bongo drums, the introducer never seems to find it necessary to mention that I also do theoretical physics.

– *The Character of Physical Law*, p. 13

# Love

It's necessary to fall in love with a theory, and like falling in love with a woman, it's only possible if one does not completely understand her.

– CERN talk, December 1965

Beautiful blonde or no beautiful blonde, I am still not married so I can still work at physics.

– Letter to Dr. Ted A. Welton, October 1948

If I'm sitting next to a swimming pool and somebody dives in and she's not too pretty, so I can think of something else, I think of the waves and things that have formed in the water.

– BBC, "Fun to Imagine" television series, 1983

There are other things in which scientific methods would be of some value; they are perfectly obvious but they get more and more difficult to discuss — such things as making decisions. I do not mean that it should be done scientifically, such as in the United States the Rand Company sits down and makes arithmetical calculations. That reminds me merely of my sophomore days at college in which in discussing women we discovered that by using electrical terminology — impedance, reluctance, resistance — that we had a deeper understanding of the situation.

– Galileo Symposium, "What Is and What Should Be the Role of Scientific Culture in Modern Society," September 1964

[On what he was most proud of:] I was able to love my first wife with as deep a love as I was able to.

– The *Los Angeles Times*, February 16, 1988

My mother taught me, said I must step out of the bus first and help her out, and all this stuff, and I worried about: what am I going to talk about? I still remember what we talked about. It's so silly, because, you know this first experience. She asked me if I played the piano, and I told her I had tried to learn, and I used to take lessons, for a little while. After I was older — after many long months of this I could only play something called "Dance of the Daisies," or fairies or something, and this didn't seem to me a very good thing, and so I didn't do piano. This and that, we talked about. Later, as we were saying good-bye, she said, "Thank you for a lovely evening." I was so impressed. I was so happy. Then I found out, on my second date, that the girl said, "Thank you for a lovely evening." On my third date, when we were saying good-night, just at the door, I said to her, "Thank you for a lovely evening," and she got paralyzed, unable to say anything, because that was what she was just about to say. So I quickly learned the formal from the truth, you see.

– Interview with Charles Weiner, March 4, 1966 (Niels Bohr Library and Archives with the Center for the History of Physics)

I was frightened of girls when I went there. I remember when I had to deliver the mail. I'm just trying to tell you the differences. It's interesting, how social attitudes develop. When I had to deliver the mail; to take the mail out from upstairs. It happened to be a time when some of the juniors had a few girlfriends, two girlfriends. There were just sitting on the steps talking, and I just didn't know how the heck I was going to be able to carry those letters past them. Girls scared me. This whole business scared me.

– Interview with Charles Weiner, March 5, 1966 (Niels Bohr Library and Archives with the Center for the History of Physics)

[On his first wife:] This probably happens to everybody, but anyway to me it seemed like independent and personal, that her feminine softness and different view of the world — and she was an artist, too — of what was valuable, what was beautiful, and so on, were things that I didn't ordinarily have direct interest in — like the lack of interest in humanities, in a way. But because of her interest in these things and the love that was developing between us, I paid a lot of attention to these matters, and softened up. I became a better guy as a result of the relationship and of listening to her ideas.

– Interview with Charles Weiner, March 5, 1966 (Niels Bohr Library and Archives with the Center for the History of Physics)

# Philosophy and Religion

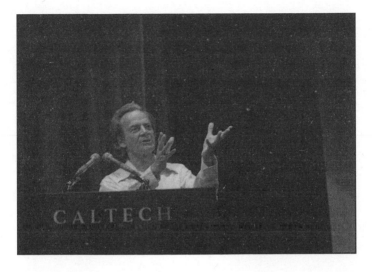

Philosophers say a great deal about what is absolutely necessary for science, and it is always, so far as one can see, rather naive, and probably wrong.

– *Feynman Lectures on Physics*, pp. 2–7

The science creates a power through its knowledge, a power to do things: You are able to do things after you know something scientifically. But the science does not give instructions with this power as to how to do some good as against how to do evil.

> – Galileo Symposium, "What Is and What Should Be the Role of Scientific Culture in Modern Society," September 1964

The question enters many people's minds as to whether they will ever understand something which they like to call subjective consciousness or a personal conscience.

> – UC Berkeley Lectures, "Time and Physics in Evolutionary History," spring 1968

How can we maintain that inspiration without a metaphysical theory, without necessarily believing certain ideas, such as that Christ rose from the dead, or something like that. Is that necessary in order to believe that the idea that you should help your neighbor, or that you should do unto your neighbor as he does to you; is it necessary to believe that Christ rose from the dead, in order to live like a Christian?

> – Interview for Viewpoint

Nevertheless, a very great deal more truth can become known than can be proven.

> – From *Nobel Lectures, Physics 1963–1970*, Elsevier Publishing Company, Amsterdam, 1972

I, a universe of atoms, an atom in the universe.

– "The Value of Science," December 1955

It doesn't seem to me that this fantastically marvelous universe, this tremendous range of time and space and different kinds of animals, and all the different planets, and all these atoms with all their motions and so on, all this complicated thing can merely be a stage so that God can watch human beings struggle for good and evil — which is the view that religion has. The stage is too big for the drama.

– Interview for Viewpoint

I would say the world-view of the physicists is not encroaching on any of the assumptions of biology or religion or whatever.

– UC Berkeley Lectures, "Time and Physics in Evolutionary History," spring 1968

You cannot define *anything* precisely. If we attempt to, we get into that paralysis of thought that comes to philosophers who sit opposite each other, one saying to the other, "you don't know what you are talking about!" The second one says, "What do you mean by *know*? What do you mean by *talking*? What do you mean by *you*?" and so on.

– *Feynman Lectures on Physics*, Lecture 8, October 20, 1961

I really didn't intend to insist that ethics and science are separate, but rather that the fundamental basis of ethics must be chosen in some non-scientific way. Then, when this is chosen, of course, science can help to decide whether we should or should not do certain things. Science can help us see what might happen if we do them, but the question as to whether we want something to happen depends on a choice of the ultimate ethical good.

– Letter to Professor Lawrence Cranberg, March 1965

But it turns out that falsehood and evil can be taught as easily as good.

– "The Uncertainty of Values," John Danz Lecture Series, 1963

Peace is a great force for good or for evil. How it will be for evil, I do not know. We will see, if we ever get to peace.

"The Uncertainty of Values," John Danz Lecture Series, 1963

Scientists are explorers, philosophers are tourists.

– *No Ordinary Genius*, p. 260

The proponents of one idea have looked with horror at the actions of the believers of another. Horror because from a disagreeing point of view all the great potentialities of the race were being channeled into a false and confining alley. In fact, it is from the history of the enormous monstrosities that have been created by the false belief that philosophers have come to realize the fantastic potentialities and wondrous capacities of human beings.

– "The Uncertainty of Values," John Danz Lecture Series, 1963

Looking back at the worst times, it always seems that they were times in which there were people who believed with absolute faith and absolute dogmatism in something. And they were so serious in this matter that they insisted that the rest of the world agree with them.

– "The Uncertainty of Values," John Danz Lecture Series, 1963

I say that we do not know what is the meaning of life and what are the right moral values, that we have no way to choose them.

– "The Uncertainty of Values," John Danz Lecture Series, 1963

All I am trying to do is cast some doubt of confusion into the principle that survival permits ethics without question and that all people will agree that survival is the real determinate of good. If you can see that there may be some doubt about that, who would resolve the doubt for science?

– Letter to Professor Lawrence Cranberg, March 1965 (*Perfectly Reasonable Deviations from the Beaten Track*, p. 150)

Well, then how about the vocabulary. Have we got too many words? No, no. We need it to express ideas. Have we got too few words? No. By some accident, of course, through the history of time, we happened to have developed by accident the perfect combination of words.

– "The Unscientific Age," John Danz Lecture Series, 1963

This problem of moral values and ethical judgments is one into which science cannot enter.

– "The Unscientific Age," John Danz Lecture Series, 1963

To see generosity you must be generous enough not to see the meanness, and to see just meanness in a man you must be mean enough not to see the generosity.

– Letter to Reverend John Alex and Mrs. Marjorie Howard, December 1965 (*Perfectly Reasonable Deviations from the Beaten Track*, p. 184)

If you thought you were trying to find out more about it because you're going to get an answer to some deep philosophical question, you may be wrong. It may be that you can't get an answer to that particular question by finding out more about the character of nature. My interest in science is simply to find out about the world.

– BBC, "The Pleasure of Finding Things Out," 1981

I do not wish to accept membership in the American Philosophical Society. My reasons are entirely personal and reflect in no way on my opinion of the society. On the contrary, I feel it is a fine organization.

– Letter to George W. Corner and the American Philosophical
   Society, July 1968

What, then, is the meaning of it all? What can we say today to dispel the mystery of existence?

– "The Uncertainty of Values," John Danz Lecture Series, 1963

I agree that science cannot disprove God. I absolutely agree. I also agree that a belief in science and religion is consistent. I know many scientists who believe in God. It is not my purpose to disprove anything.

– "The Uncertainty of Values," John Danz Lecture Series, 1963

It seems to me that there is a kind of independence between the ethical and moral views and the theory of the machinery of the universe.

– "The Uncertainty of Values," John Danz Lecture Series, 1963

Because a little knowledge is dangerous, that the young man just learning a little science thinks he knows it all.

– "The Uncertainty of Values," John Danz Lecture Series, 1963

It seems that the metaphysical aspects of religion have nothing to do with the ethical values, that the moral values seem somehow to be outside of the scientific realm.

   – "The Uncertainty of Values," John Danz Lecture Series, 1963

Men, philosophers of all ages, have tried to find the secret of existence, the meaning of it all. Because if they could find the real meaning of life, then all this human effort, all this wonderful potentiality of human beings, could then be moved in the correct direction and we would march forward with great success. So therefore we tried these different ideas. But the question of the meaning of the whole world, of life, and human beings, and so on, has been answered very many times by very many people. Unfortunately all the answers are different, and the people with one answer look with horror at the actions and behavior of the people with another answer.

   – Galileo Symposium, "What Is and What Should Be the Role of Scientific Culture in Modern Society," September 1964

We do not know what the meaning of existence is. When we say at the result of studying all of the views that we have had before we find that we do not know the meaning of existence; but in saying that we do not know the meaning of existence, we have probably found the open channel.

   – Galileo Symposium, "What Is and What Should Be the Role of Scientific Culture in Modern Society," September 1964

What science is, is not what the philosophers have said it is.

> – National Science Teachers Association Fourteenth Convention
>   lecture, "What Is Science?" April 1966

In religion, the moral lessons are taught, but they are not just taught once — you are inspired again and again, and I think it is necessary to inspire again and again, to remember the value of science for children, for grownups, and everybody else, in several ways.

> – National Science Teachers Association Fourteenth Convention
>   lecture, "What Is Science?" April 1966

A man cannot live beyond the grave.

> – National Science Teachers Association Fourteenth Convention
>   lecture, "What Is Science?" April 1966

Now, we know that, even with moral values granted, human beings are very weak; they must be reminded of the moral values in order that they may be able to follow their consciences. It is not simply a matter of having a right conscience; it is also a question of maintaining strength to do what you know is right. And it is necessary that religion give strength and comfort and the inspiration to follow these moral views. This is the inspirational aspect of religion. It gives inspiration not only for moral conduct — it gives inspiration for the arts and for all kinds of great thoughts and actions as well.

> – "The Relation of Science and Religion," May 1956

It is a great adventure to contemplate the universe beyond man, to think of what it means without man — as it was for the great part of its long history, and as it is in the great majority of places. When this objective view is finally attained, and the mystery and majesty of matter are appreciated, to then turn the objective eye back on man viewed as matter, to see life as part of the universal mystery of greatest depth, is to sense an experience which is rarely described. It usually ends in laughter, delight in the futility of trying to understand. These scientific views end in awe and mystery, lost at the edge in uncertainty, but they appear to be so deep and so impressive that the theory that it is all arranged simply as a stage for God to watch man's struggle for good and evil seems to be inadequate.

– "The Relation of Science and Religion," May 1956

Although I believe that from time to time scientific evidence is found which may be partially interpreted as giving some evidence of some particular aspect of the life of Christ, for example, or of other religious metaphysical ideas, it seems to me that there is no scientific evidence bearing on the golden rule. It seems to me that that is somehow different.

– "The Relation of Science and Religion," May 1956

Western civilization, it seems to me, stands by two great heritages. One is the scientific spirit of adventure — the adventure into the unknown, an unknown which must be recognized as being unknown in order to be explored; the demand that the unanswerable mysteries of the universe remain unanswered; the attitude that all is uncertain; to summarize it — the humility of the intellect. The other great heritage is Christian ethics the basis of action on love, the brotherhood of all men, the value of the individual — the humility of the spirit. These two heritages are logically, thoroughly consistent. But logic is not all; one needs one's heart to follow an idea.

– "The Relation of Science and Religion," May 1956

One thing that Von Neumann gave me was an idea that he had which was interesting. That you don't have to be responsible for the world that you're in, and so I have developed a very powerful sense of social irresponsibility as a result of Von Neumann's advice. It's made me a very happy man since.

– UCSB talk, "Los Alamos from Below," February 1975

The uncertainty that is necessary in order to appreciate nature is not easily correlated with the feeling of certainty of faith which is usually associated with deep religious belief.

– "The Uncertainty of Values," John Danz Lecture Series, 1963

Most people are bad, you know, in one way or another — but they are not always bad, and they have other good points to compensate.

– Correspondence with Mimi Phillips, published in the *Wheeling News Register*, October 5, 1958

At thirteen I was not only converted to other religious views but I also stopped believing that the Jewish people are "the chosen people."

– Letter to Tina Levitan, February 1967 (*Perfectly Reasonable Deviations from the Beaten Track*, p. 236)

We have everybody here who's coming, I guess, but I see somebody that isn't here — how do you like that? Now that's an old philosophical question, isn't it, whether you can see someone that isn't here? I remember arguing at Princeton with the graduate students for hours and hours — the philosophy students as to what you were talking about when you said there was no chicken in the icebox. That's why I have nothing to do with philosophers.

– Esalen lecture, "Quantum Mechanical View of Reality (Part 1)," October 1984

In my opinion, it is not possible for religion to find a set of metaphysical ideas which will be guaranteed not to get into conflicts with an ever advancing and always changing science which is going into an unknown. We don't know how to answer the questions; it is impossible to find an answer which someday will not be found to be wrong. The difficulty arises because science and religion are both trying to answer questions in the same realm here.

– "The Relation of Science and Religion," May 1956

So I often wonder: What is the relation of integrity to working in the government?

– *What Do You Care What Other People Think?*, p. 218

One thing is that I have no more stomach for philosophical questions and political questions. One of the reasons is I got — I shy away from them much more positively than I ever did before. I won't even discuss them. I don't know why.

– Interview with Charles Weiner, June 28, 1966 (Niels Bohr Library and Archives with the Center for the History of Physics)

Why make yourself miserable saying things like, "Why do we have such bad luck? What has God done to us? What have we done to deserve this?" all of which, if you understand reality and take it into your heart, are irrelevant and unsolvable. They are just things that nobody can know. Your situation is just an accident of life.

    – *What Do You Care What Other People Think?*, p. 51

In this age of specialization, men who thoroughly know one field are often incompetent to discuss another. The great problems of the relations between one and another aspect of human activity have for this reason been discussed less and less in public. When we look at the past great debates on these subjects, we feel jealous of those times, for we should have liked the excitement of such argument. The old problems, such as the relation of science and religion, are still with us, and I believe present as difficult dilemmas as ever, but they are not often publicly discussed because of the limitations of specialization.

    – "The Relation of Science and Religion," *Engineering and Science*, May 1956

# Nature of Science

You ask, are we getting anywhere? I'm reminded of a situation when I was asked the same thing. I was trying to pick a safe. Somebody asked me, "How are you doing? Are you getting anywhere? You can't tell until you open it. But you have tried a lot of numbers that you know don't work.

– Panel discussion, particle physics conference, Irvine, California, 1971

[On the relation of physics to other sciences:] Anyway, you see it's all so interconnected it's not worth calling them different names except for convenience.

> – Audio recording of Feynman Lectures on Physics, Lecture 3,
>    October 3, 1961, Q&A

For today all physicists know, from studying Einstein and Bohr, that sometimes an idea which looks completely paradoxical at first, if analyzed to completion in all detail and in experimental situations, may, in fact, not be paradoxical.

> – From *Nobel Lectures, Physics 1963–1970*, Elsevier Publishing
>    Company, Amsterdam, 1972

I am familiar with a number of experimental physicists and they are sort of men of the earth. Therefore, I have always suspected that, one day, working far away from theorists, close to their big machines, they will get the idea of a new experiment: an experiment which will test the oracle. They would like to see what would happen, just for the fun of it, if they falsely report that there exists a certain bump, or an oscillation in a certain curve, and see how the theorists predict it. I know these men so well that the moment I thought of that possibility I have honestly always been concerned that some day they will do just that. That you can imagine how absurd the theoretical physicists would sound, making all these complicated calculations to demonstrate the existence of such a bump, while these fellows are laughing up their sleeves. For these reasons, I have found myself almost incapable of making calculations of the type that most other people make. I am afraid they will catch me out!

> – Programme of American Physical Society Annual Meeting, 1950

There's so much distance between the fundamental rules and the final phenomena that it's unbelievable that the final variety of phenomena can come from such a steady operation of simple rules.

  – Interview with Yorkshire Television program, "Take the World from Another Point of View," 1972

Scientific knowledge enables us to do all kinds of things and to make all kinds of things. Or course if we make good things, it is not only to the credit of science; it is also to the credit of the moral choice which led us to good work. Scientific knowledge is an enabling power to do either good or bad — but it does not carry instructions on how to use it.

  – "The Value of Science," December 1955

We like to say that the world outside is real or what we can measure is real and if you look at it a bit longer you realize that the only thing that is real is what you felt you measured and how you feel that that the outside world could have easily been an illusion of the brain.

  – UC Berkeley Lectures, "Time and Physics in Evolutionary History," spring 1968

A scientific argument is likely to involve a great deal of laughter and uncertainty on both sides, with both sides thinking up experiments and offering to bet on the outcome.

  – "The Uncertainty of Science," John Danz Lecture Series, 1963

It's one of the advantages of modern society: that we don't have to cope with these difficult technical problems.

– Audio recording of lecture on relativity, Douglas Advanced Research Laboratory, 1967

But there is nothing in biology yet found that indicates the inevitability of death.

– Galileo Symposium, "What Is and What Should Be the Role of Scientific Culture in Modern Society," September 1964

Now you can see why it is I feel a bit uncomfortable when someone asks to give a talk: "Please tell us the latest things," because then, of course, I'm talking about the problems we have in understanding the insides of a proton! So, that gives us some idea as to why it is I feel so uncomfortable talking all the time about things we don't know much about, and nobody asks me about the stuff we do know everything about!

– "QED: Photons — Corpuscles of Light," Sir Douglas Robb Lectures, University of Auckland, June 1979

The only way to have real success in science, the field I'm familiar with, is to describe the evidence very carefully without regard to the way you feel it should be. If you have a theory, you must try to explain what's good and what's bad about it equally. In science, you learn a kind of standard integrity and honesty.

– *What Do You Care What Other People Think?*, pp. 117–118

You say, the trouble with the teachers of physics is that they don't explain quantum mechanics like this, that the particles behave like waves, or they behave like billiard balls, or they behave like — I don't know what. They don't behave like anything that you know of, you see. So it's impossible to describe the things except in analytic ways.

– Audio recording of Feynman Lectures on Physics, Lecture 2, September 29, 1961

As usual, nature's imagination far surpasses our own, as we have seen from the other theories which are subtle and deep. To get such a subtle and deep guess is not so easy. One must be really clever to guess, and it is not possible to do it blindly by machine.

– *The Character of Physical Law*, p. 162

Yeah, well, you shine a light in the corner and that's exciting when you run in there but if you get stuck to a wall then there's no use — you have to find another way out, right?

– Interview with Charles Weiner, February 4, 1966 (Niels Bohr Library and Archives with the Center for the History of Physics)

Physics is not mathematics, and mathematics is not physics. One helps the other. But in physics you have to have an understanding of the connection of words with the real world. It is necessary at the end to translate what you have figured out into English, into the world, into the blocks of copper and glass that you are going to do the experiments with. Only in that way can you find out whether the consequences are true.

    — *The Character of Physical Law*, p. 55

Now this power to do things carries with it no instructions on how to use it, whether to use it for good or for evil. The product of this power is either good or evil, depending on how it is used.

    — "The Uncertainty of Science," John Danz Lecture Series, 1963

In general, we look for a new law by the following process. First we guess it. Then we compute the consequences of the guess to see what would be implied if this law that we guessed is right. Then we compare the result of the computation to nature, with experiment or experience, compare it directly with observation, to see if it works. If it disagrees with experiment it is wrong. In that simple statement is the key to science. It doesn't make any difference how beautiful your guess is. It does not make any difference how smart you are, who made the guess, or what his name is — if it disagrees with experiment it is wrong.

    — *The Character of Physical Law*, p. 156

The mathematicians are exploring in all directions, and it's quicker for a physicist to catch up on what he needs than to try to keep up with everything that might conceivably be useful.

    — *Omni* interview, February 1979

We are trying to prove ourselves as wrong as quickly possible, because only in that way can we find progress.

— *The Character of Physical Law*, p. 158

Discovering the laws of physics is like trying to put together the pieces of a jigsaw puzzle. We have all these different pieces, and today they are proliferating rapidly. Many of them are lying about and cannot be fitted with other ones. How do we know that they belong together? How do we know that they are really all part of one picture? We are not sure, and it worries us to some extent, but we get encouragement from the common characteristics of several pieces. They all show blue sky, or they are all made out of the same kind of wood.

— *The Character of Physical Law*, p. 83

What is necessary "for the very existence of science," and what the characteristics of nature are, are not to be determined by pompous preconditions, they are determined by the material with which we work, by nature herself. We look, and we see what we find, and we cannot say ahead of time successfully what it is going to look like.

— *The Character of Physical Law*, p. 147

If science is to progress, what we need is the ability to experiment, honesty in reporting results — the results must be reported without somebody saying what they would like the results to have been — and finally — an important thing — the intelligence to interpret the results.

— *The Character of Physical Law*, p. 148

So my antagonist said, "Is it impossible that there are flying saucers? Can you prove that it's impossible?" "No," I said. "I can't prove that it's impossible. It's just very unlikely." At that he said, "You are very unscientific. If you can't prove it impossible then how can you say that it's unlikely?" But that is the way that is scientific. It is scientific only to say what is more likely and what is less likely, and not to be proving all the time the possible and impossible.

– *The Character of Physical Law*, pp. 165–166

When you're putting ideas together which are vague and hard to remember, it's like — I get this feeling very much — it's like building those houses of cards, and each of the cards is shaky, and if you forget one of them, the whole thing collapses and you don't know how you got there. You have to build them up again. If you are interrupted, and you forget how the cards go together (the cards being different parts of the idea, or different kinds of idea that have to go together to build up the main idea), it's quite a tower, and it's easy to slip. It needs a lot of concentration — solid time to think.

– BBC, "The Pleasure of Finding Things Out," 1981

It's a much deeper and warmer understanding, and it means you can be digging somewhere where you're temporarily convinced you'll find the answer, and somebody comes up and says, "Have you seen what they're coming up with over there?", and you look up and say, "Jeez! I'm in the wrong place!" It happens all the time.

– *Omni* interview, February 1979

The idea is to try to give all the information to help others to judge the value of your contribution: not just the information that leads to judgment in one particular direction or another.

– "Cargo Cult Science," Caltech commencement address, 1974

Scientific integrity. A principle of scientific thought that is utter honesty.

– Notes

The principle of science, the definition almost, is the following: the test of all knowledge is experiment. Experiment is the sole judge of "proof."

– Audio recording of Feynman Lectures on Physics, Lecture 1,
    September 26, 1961

In this complicated array of moving things, you can imagine it's something like trying to watching a great chess game being played by the gods. And you don't know what the rules of the game are, but all you're allowed to do is watch the playing. Now of course if you watch long enough, you may eventually catch on to a few of the rules. The rules of the game is what I mean by fundamental physics.

– Audio recording of Feynman Lectures on Physics, Lecture 2,
    September 29, 1961

If they tell us that a certain situation must always produce the same result, that's all very well. But if when we try it and it doesn't occur, then it doesn't occur. We just have to take what we see.

– Audio recording of Feynman Lectures on Physics, Lecture 2,
    September 29, 1961

Because science is good, let's say, it doesn't mean that which is not science is not good.

  – Audio recording of Feynman Lectures on Physics, Lecture 3, October 3, 1961

Incidentally, psychoanalysis is not a science: it's a medical business, it's like witch doctory. It has a theory as to what causes disease — lots of different spirits, and this and that. Let's say the witch doctor has a theory that the disease is caused by a spirit which comes through the air; it's true, something does come in through the air — but it's not the same kind of spirit, and it is not gotten rid of say, by shaking a snake over it, but quinine does help malaria. So, if you're sick, I would advise that you go to the witch doctor because he is the man in the tribe who knows the most about the disease; on the other hand, it is not a science.

  – Audio recording of Feynman Lectures on Physics, Lecture 3, October 3, 1961

It's easy enough to make up a theory by talking.

  – Audio recording of Feynman Lectures on Physics, Lecture 7, October 17, 1961, Q&A

It wasn't that I knew that I was smart. It was just that — you see, scientific things are rationally right.

  – Interview with Charles Weiner, 1966, March 4, 1966 (Niels Bohr Library and Archives with the Center for the History of Physics)

Yeah, I'm always interested in the relationship, the practical business — that the thing does not mean anything really unless there's some way to make something go.

- Interview with Charles Weiner, March 4, 1966 (Niels Bohr Library and Archives with the Center for the History of Physics)

You must know, if you know how to play chess, that it's easy to learn all the rules, and yet it's very hard to select the best move, or to understand why Alekhine did that. And so, in the same manner, only much worse is it in nature, that we may be able to find all the rules — actually, we do not have all the rules, we know that we don't have all the rules — every once something like "castling" or something is going on, that we still don't understand.

- Audio recording of Feynman Lectures on Physics, Lecture 2, September 29, 1961

Because there are many people who feel that the way to do it is to find out what problem the big guys are working on, and work right there. It isn't such a good scheme. You can be chasing the wrong thing, if you haven't thought about it yourself.

- Interview with Charles Weiner, March 5, 1966 (Niels Bohr Library and Archives with the Center for the History of Physics)

If it's physics, it's interesting. See, everything fits together.

- Interview with Charles Weiner, March 5, 1966 (Niels Bohr Library and Archives with the Center for the History of Physics)

But the beautiful experiment, which I still remember, in the lab, was this. There was a ring. You know, other experiments — dropping with the apparatus, with spark caps, with wheels, with all kinds of things. There was a hook on the wall; I mean a nail driven into the wall, and a ring of metal, a metallic ring, an amelus, whatever you call it, like a big washer, a big thing. It said: "Hang on the wall, measure the period, calculate the period from the shape, and see if they agree." I loved that. I thought that was the best doggoned thing. I didn't care as much — I'm just trying to remember now — I liked the other experiments, but they involved the sparks and all the other hocus pocus, which was too easy. With all that equipment, you could measure the acceleration of gravity. But to think that physics is so good, not that you can figure out something carefully prepared, but something as natural as a lousy old ring hanging off a hook — it impressed me, that I had now the power to tell what something as dumb as that was going to do.

   – Interview with Charles Weiner, March 5, 1966 (Niels Bohr Library and Archives with the Center for the History of Physics)

The situation is, as it always is when we're near the answer, it looks much simpler than it has any right to be. And we have to understand that simplicity. And why we think it must be more complicated. Our minds are too complicated, somehow.

   – Yorkshire Television interview, "Take the World from Another Point of View," 1972

I have a principle in strong interaction theories; if the theory is complicated, it's wrong.

— Panel discussion, particle physics conference, Irvine, California, 1971

I'm not at all pessimistic that the answer will ultimately fall out. You can't fail. Nature cannot resist the perpetual penetration by experiment, and those apes which sit crudely and clumsily watching what's happening, sooner or later are going to see, after their noses are rubbed in the answer, what it is.

— Panel discussion, particle physics conference, Irvine, California, 1971

You can recognize truth by its beauty and simplicity.

— *The Character of Physical Law*, p. 171

Some theorists do not understand the relation of theory and experiment — and where lies the true source and test of all their knowledge?

— Letter to Dr. Blas Cabrera, September 1982 (*Perfectly Reasonable Deviations from the Beaten Track*, p. 349)

In science (unlike business or any other pursuits) we are all working together cooperating to try to understand Nature and we have learned to be very careful to recognize and commend anybody who gets a really useful new idea.

— Letter to Dr. Rafael Dy-Liacco, June 1978 (*Perfectly Reasonable Deviations from the Beaten Track*, p. 321)

New ideas are always fascinating, because physicists wish to find out how Nature works. Any experiment which deviates from expectations according to known law commands immediate attention, because we may find something new.

– Letter to Mr. L. Dembart (*Los Angeles Times*), January 1986 (*Perfectly Reasonable Deviations from the Beaten Track*, p. 397)

Most of our problems are man-made, of this type.

– Audio recording of lecture on relativity, Douglas Advanced Research Laboratory, 1967

In fact, an engineer is probably best defined as a man who knows how to convert energy from one unit to another.

– Audio recording of lecture on relativity, Douglas Advanced Research Laboratory, 1967

The complications of relativistic arguments is that you have two points of view. The common thing that a novice does is shift back and forth between the two during a calculation.

– Audio recording of lecture on relativity, Douglas Advanced Research Laboratory, 1967

It is amazing how little predictive ability theoretical physics has, even when it relies solely upon well-established fundamental principles.

– Letter to Dr. Hans Bethe, June 1951

There is today, in my opinion, no science capable of adequately selecting or judging people. So I doubt that any intelligent method is known.

> – Letter to Mr. Douglas M. Fowle, September 1962 (*Perfectly Reasonable Deviations from the Beaten Track*, p. 135)

Physicists looking at psychology, through force of habit, try to suggest some simple element be found to study, rather than the whole human brain at once.

> – On human and animal eyesight, in a letter to Edwin H. Land (Polaroid Corporation), May 1966 (*Perfectly Reasonable Deviations from the Beaten Track*, p. 223)

More and more people find fundamental physics a relatively uninteresting subject. So it is left in an incomplete state, with a few working very slowly at the edge on the question of what is the third order tensor field that has a coupling constant $10^{30}$ times smaller than gravity?

> – MIT centennial, "Talk of Our Times," December 1961

The purpose of scientific thought is to predict what will happen in given experimental circumstances.

> – Letter to F. Harrison Stamper, April 1962

It is not always a good idea to be too precise.

> – "The Uncertainty of Science," John Danz Lecture Series, 1963

The most obvious characteristic of science is its application, the fact that as a consequence of science one has a power to do things.

– "The Uncertainty of Science," John Danz Lecture Series, 1963

But if a thing is not scientific, if it cannot be subjected to the test of observation, this does not mean that it is dead, or wrong, or stupid. We are not trying to argue that science is somehow good and other things are somehow not good.

– "The Uncertainty of Science," John Danz Lecture Series, 1963

Incidentally, the fact that there are rules at all to be checked is a kind of miracle; that it is possible to find a rule, like the inverse square law of gravitation, is some sort of miracle.

– "The Uncertainty of Science," John Danz Lecture Series, 1963

Science is not a specialist business; it is completely universal.

– "The Uncertainty of Science," John Danz Lecture Series, 1963

The speed at which science has been developing for the last 200 years has been ever increasing, and we reach a culmination of speed now.

– "The Unscientific Age," John Danz Lecture Series, 1963

That something is unscientific is not bad, that is nothing the matter with it.

– "The Unscientific Age," John Danz Lecture Series, 1963

Unlike other scientific subjects, there has not been a general detailed development of our ideas of time. We do not know a great deal more than is known from common sense. Everyone knows how it flows inexorably onward and the scientist in all his studies has found relatively little to add to our knowledge of that mystery.

– From notes for "About Time" program, 1957

Scientific problems like to separate into two kinds. One, to understand the origin of the arrangement of things as we find them, and two, to understand how they will behave if started in a given circumstance.

– From notes for "About Time" program, 1957

It is interesting that this thoroughness, which is a virtue, is often misunderstood. When someone says a thing has been done scientifically, often all he means is that it has been done thoroughly.

– "The Uncertainty of Science," John Danz Lecture Series, 1963

Suppose Galileo were here and we were to show him the world today and try to make him happy, or see what he finds out. And we would tell him about the questions of evidence, those methods of judging things which he developed. And we would point out that we are still in exactly the same tradition, we follow it exactly — even to detail of making numerical measurements and using those as one of the better tools, in the physics at least. And that the sciences have developed in a very good way directly and continuously from his original, in the same spirit as he developed. And as a result there are no more witches and ghosts.

– Galileo Symposium, "What Is and What Should Be the Role of Scientific Culture in Modern Society," September 1964

Now, it might be true that astrology is right. It might be true that if you go to the dentist on the day that marks as at right angles to Venus, that it is better than if you go on a different day. It might be true that you can be cured by the miracle of Lourdes. But if it is true it ought to be investigated. Why? To improve it. If it is true then maybe we can find out if the stars do influence life; that we could make the system more powerful by investigating statistically, scientifically judging the evidence and objectively more carefully.

– Galileo Symposium, "What Is and What Should Be the Role of Scientific Culture in Modern Society," September 1964

Science is a long history of learning how not to fool ourselves.

– Quoted in K. C. Cole, *The Universe and the Teacup: The Mathematics of Truth and Beauty*, 1998

I believe that we must attack these things in which we do not believe. Not attack by the method of cutting off the heads of the people but attack in the sense of discuss.

– Galileo Symposium, "What Is and What Should Be the Role of Scientific Culture in Modern Society," September 1964

I am thoroughly convinced that the world-view of physics is adequate to describe the phenomena of experiences of other sciences.

– UC Berkeley Lectures, "Time and Physics in Evolutionary History," spring 1968

In physics we believe very nicely that we have a theory by which if you tell us the initial conditions, we will predict what will happen in the future.

– UC Berkeley Lectures, "Time and Physics in Evolutionary History," spring 1968

Other theories, subjects, have a thing called the past as a fundamental part of that theoretical structure. But physics does not usually require a study of the past in order to analyze what is going to happen next.

– UC Berkeley Lectures, "Time and Physics in Evolutionary History," spring 1968

There is a way of thinking about the past that makes it the present, which makes a theory of the past really a predictive theory as to what will happen in the future.

– UC Berkeley Lectures, "Time and Physics in Evolutionary History," spring 1968

There is this relation of physics and biology in which we all talk so much and we try to describe the biological world always describing things outside. We always try to describe you, never me.

– UC Berkeley Lectures, "Time and Physics in Evolutionary History," spring 1968

If there is such a consciousness, then we have a large number of questions about how did it evolve, how extensive is it, how spread is it throughout the natural world among other animals or even the natural world and so on. It produces more questions than answers. Nevertheless there are many of you I suspect who have some kind of a feeling that everything is real from the inside as it is in a light.

– UC Berkeley Lectures, "Time and Physics in Evolutionary History," spring 1968

We're not trying to find out for certainty what the world looks like but just what we've seen so far.

– Esalen lecture, "Quantum Mechanical View of Reality (Part 1)," October 1984

We suspend an assumption that we are able to say that "this is an either this or that condition" when you haven't made any observation yet. And then we can continue to think straightforwardly, and that's the most efficient way we know.

– Esalen lecture, "Quantum Mechanical View of Reality (Part 1)," October 1984

That is what science is; the result of the discovery that is worthwhile rechecking by new direct experience, and not necessarily trusting the race experience from the past.

– National Science Teachers Association Fourteenth Convention lecture, "What Is Science?" April 1966

There is also a value of science in the value which it teaches the value of rational thought, as well as the importance of freedom of thought; the positive results that come from doubting that the lessons are true.

– National Science Teachers Association Fourteenth Convention lecture, "What Is Science?" April 1966

Usually when we publish things, things that we publish in the technical journals are very carefully polished and all of the routes and side alleys and back thoughts and so on that you had are taken out. You do not describe your personal adventure and succession of ideas. Any references that are given are given to the first man who thought of the thing, not the guy who told you about it, and so on.

– CERN talk, December 1965

I think that maybe that's why young people make success. They don't know enough. Because when you know enough it's obvious that every idea that you have is no good.

– CERN talk, December 1965

All they're doing is they're taking the physical world and they're slicing it up to analyze it. And this one you slice a different way, and no matter which way you slice it, it's the same bologna, so you should look at the bologna, not the slice process.

– CERN talk, December 1965

Say, look, what a wild and wonderful tour I took to come back to nothing. I did not ever solve the problem of infinite self-energy; it's still just as infinite as it was before I began.

– CERN talk, December 1965

Each of the theories we have in the world seem to be possible to write in many different ways and to look at from very many different physical views.

– CERN talk, December 1965

It seems to me quite marvelous that the laws of physics are of such a kind that they can be written in another way that isn't obviously the same and yet is the same. I will, just for the fun of it, will propose — although I have to think about it more to see whether it's sensible — that that's because it's simple, and that a simple thing is something that an be described in two different ways and you don't know that you're describing the same thing. Whereas if you take a complicated thing, in order to fully describe it, you've said so much about it, that there's no other way that you could see that it looks different.

– CERN talk, December 1965

When you look at things from different physical points of view, if you'll not sell your soul to one of them, which is what I was doing, but take them all, then you're that much greater.

– CERN talk, December 1965

The odds that your theory will be in fact right and that the general thing that everybody's working on will be right, is low. But the odds that you, Little Boy Schmidt, will be the guy who figures a thing out, is not smaller.

– CERN talk, December 1965

It's very important that we do not all follow the same fashion. Because although it's ninety percent sure that the answer lies over there, where [Murray] Gell-Mann is working, what happens if it doesn't, and if everybody's doing this?

– CERN talk, December 1965

If you've made up your mind to test a theory, or you want to explain some idea, you should always decide to publish it whichever way it comes out. If we only publish results of a certain kind, we can make the argument look good. We must publish BOTH kinds of results.

– "Cargo Cult Science," Caltech commencement address, 1974

In spite of the fact that science could produce enormous horror in the world, it is of value because it can produce something.

– "The Value of Science," December 1955

Science is a way to teach how something gets to be known, what is not known, to what extent things are known (for nothing is known absolutely), how to handle doubt and uncertainty, what the rules of evidence are, how to think about things so that judgments can be made, how to distinguish truth from fraud, and from show.

These are certainly important secondary yields of teaching science, and physics in particular.

– "The Problem of Teaching Physics in Latin America," 1963

It might not be that way, in which case you're looking for whatever the hell it is that you find!

– *Omni* interview, February 1979

The whole idea you started with is gone! That's the kind of exciting thing that happens from time to time.

– *Omni* interview, February 1979

So far, physics has tried to find laws and constants without asking where they came from, but we may be approaching the point where we'll be forced to consider history.

– *Omni* interview, February 1979

The lesson you learn, as you grow older in physics is that what we can do is a very small fraction of what there is.

– *Omni* interview, February 1979

We have an illusion we can do any experiment we want. We all, however, come from the same universe evolving, and we don't really have any "real" freedom. For we obey certain laws and have come from a certain past.

– MIT conference, May 1981

There's also the possibility that you don't understand because you get a bit confused. You're sure that you must have misinterpreted what I said or something like that, and you get turned off. Let me assure you that most of the time you did interpret correctly what I said because it's going to be so shocking the way Nature actually works that you're not going to believe that either.

– "QED: Photons — Corpuscles of Light," Sir Douglas Robb Lectures, University of Auckland, June 1979

Science — pure science, that is — cannot flourish, or at best can only flourish by accident.

– Notes for talk on "Science in America"

It is natural to explain new ideas in terms of what is already in your own head, but all these concepts are piled on top of each other: this idea is taught in terms of that idea, and that idea is taught in terms of another idea, which comes from counting, which can be different for different people!

– *What Do You Care What Other People Think?*, p. 59

When the argument for the existence of a term is solely to explain a single experiment, it is a question of physical taste.

– Programme of American Physical Society Annual Meeting, 1950

At each meeting it always seems to me that very little progress is made. Nevertheless, if you look over any reasonable length of time, a few years say, you find a fantastic progress and it is hard to understand how that can happen at the same time that nothing is happening in any one moment. I think that it is something like the way clouds change in the sky — they gradually fade out here and build up there and if you look later it is different.

– Programme of American Physical Society Annual Meeting, 1950

It is clear to everyone today that physics is almost entirely in the hands of the experimenters. I think, nevertheless, that we should appreciate that theory is supposed to have a predictive value.

– Programme of American Physical Society Annual Meeting, 1950

If you try to test modern theory on its predictive value, you find that it is very weak.

– Programme of American Physical Society Annual Meeting, 1950

When a new particle or a new fact is discovered, notice that all the theorists do one of two things: they either form a group, or disperse.

– Programme of American Physical Society Annual Meeting, 1950

One should look very hard for an "expected" failure. I have probably been converted from my prejudice that it must fail, just in time to be caught off base by an experiment next month showing that it indeed does.

– "The Present Situation in Quantum Electrodynamics," Solvay conference, 1961

In the South Seas there is a cargo cult of people. During World War II, they saw airplanes land with lots of good material, and they want the same thing to happen now. So they've arranged to make things that look like runways, put fires along the sides, made a wooden hut for a man to sit in, with two wooden pieces on his head like headphones and bars of bamboo sticking out like antennas — he's the controller. They wait for the airplanes to land. They're doing everything right. The form is perfect. But it doesn't work. So I call these things "cargo cult science" because they follow all the apparent precepts and forms of scientific investigation, but they're missing something essential.

– *U.S. News and World Report* interview, February 1985

Scientific progress to discovering new things often results by noticing small deviations from the predictions of old theories, and this cannot be done unless the predictions are very precise and detailed.

– "The Qualitative Behavior of Yang–Mills Theory in 2+1 Dimensions," January 1981

If you've heard about the atom being a little solar system, the nucleus at the center like the Sun and the planets going around like electrons, then you're back in nineteen hundred and something.

– "QED: Electrons and Their Interactions," Sir Douglas Robb Lectures, University of Auckland, June 1979

It's interesting how some people find science so interesting, and other people find it kind of dull and difficult. Especially kids, some just eat it up.

– BBC, "Fun to Imagine" television series, 1983

In the case of science, I think that one of the things that make it difficult is that it takes a lot of imagination. It's very hard to imagine all the crazy things that things really are like.

– BBC, "Fun to Imagine" television series, 1983

These are kind of disciplines in the field of science where you have to learn to know when you know and when you don't know and what it is you know and what it is you don't know. You gotta be careful not to confuse yourself!

– Yorkshire Television program, "Take the World from Another Point of View," 1972

The world is strange; the whole universe is very strange, but when you look at the details, you find out that the rules are very simple.

– Yorkshire Television program, "Take the World from Another Point of View," 1972

I think that that the numbers are a problem in astronomy — the sizes and numbers.

– BBC, "Fun to Imagine" television series, 1983

Newton, I would say, is a genius about something — a teacher about something. He's the guy who taught us how to think about science in a modern way so that we could make some progress. He's the one who distinguished very carefully between the facts that he would develop and experimentally determine, "This really happened!"

– "QED: Fits of Reflection and Transmission," Sir Douglas Robb Lectures, University of Auckland, 1979

You first have to tell me why a gram is as big as it is. And it's because somebody chose a gram during the French Revolution or something. They decided that such-and-such is a gram, and then the electron is so many grams!

– "QED: New Queries," Sir Douglas Robb Lectures, University of Auckland, 1979

That is one advantage we physicists have; we know what we found out a century ago.

– Letter to Dr. Robert S. Alexander, November 1965

I wanted to give you some appreciation of the wonderful world and the physicist's way of looking at it, which, I believe, is a major part of the true culture of modern times. (There are probably professors of other subjects who would object, but I believe they are completely wrong.) Perhaps you will not only have some appreciation of this culture; it is even possible that you may want to join in the greatest adventure that the human mind has ever begun.

– *Feynman Lectures on Physics*, Appendix

The present concentration of research facilities and scientific universities has obvious dangers.

– Letter to Professor M. L. Oliphant, regarding expanding research overseas (*Perfectly Reasonable Deviations from the Beaten Track*, p. 82)

Many physicists are working very hard trying to put together a grand picture that unifies everything into one super-duper model. It's a delightful game, but at the present time none of the speculators agree with any of the other speculators as to what the grand picture is.

– *QED: The Strange Theory of Light and Matter*, p. 150

If I am gambling in Las Vegas, and am about to put some money into number twenty-two at roulette, and the girl next to me spills her drink because she sees someone she knows, so that I stop before betting, and twenty-two comes up, I can see that the whole course of the universe for me has hung on the fact that some little photon hit the nerve ends of her retina.

– *Feynman Lectures on Gravitation*

[On what would mark the end of physics:] Looking for trouble — and you don't find any.

– MIT panel

[On his father:] He did teach himself a great deal: He read a lot and studied a lot because, as I know now, he understood a great deal about science.

– Interview with Charles Weiner, March 4, 1966 (Niels Bohr Library and Archives with the Center for the History of Physics)

Science not purposeful — research in engineering is. Our greatest advances come from researchers not aimed at use but just for fun, curiosity, and desire for understanding.

– Notes from Los Alamos

No need to stop atomic research to control bomb. Only real requirement is to control use to which research is put.

– Notes from Los Alamos

Problems of chemistry and biology are greatly helped if our ability to see what we are doing and do things on an atomic level is ultimately developed — a development which I think cannot be avoided.

– Notes

Not one exact statement in science about anything.

– Notes

What happens when physical ideas get into the outside world, and are applied to society and psychology and so on, is that they become distorted to such a point that they become trivial, obvious, dull, things of no precision or accuracy.

– Audio recording of lecture on relativity, Douglas Advanced Research Laboratory, 1967

You gotta stop and think about it, to really get the pleasure about the complexity — the inconceivable nature of nature.

– BBC, "Fun to Imagine" television series, 1983

I think that the discovery of electricity and magnetism and the electromagnetic effects which are finally worked out are probably the most fundamental transformation of the most remarkable thing in history, the biggest change in history.

– BBC, "Fun to Imagine" television series, 1983

In order to talk about the impact of ideas in one field on ideas in another field one is always apt to be an idiot of one kind or another. In these days of specialization, there are few people who have such a deep knowledge of two departments of our understanding that they don't make fools of themselves in one or the other.

  – "The Uncertainty of Science," John Danz Lecture Series, 1963

How can we say that only the best must be allowed in to join those who are already in, without loudly proclaiming to our inner selves that we who are in must be very good indeed. Of course I believe that I am very good indeed, but that is a private matter and I cannot publicly admit I do so, to such an extent that I have the nerve to decide that this man, or that, is not worthy of joining my elite club.

  – Letter to Dr. Detlev W. Bronk and the National Academy of Sciences, August 1961 (*Perfectly Reasonable Deviations from the Beaten Track*, p. 108)

I introduced you to the gauge theories, if you recall. But I must confess I'm not at all happy about them. They're like maps showing the different particles. An ordinary map that shows the mountain peaks doesn't tell you why the mountains are there. You still have to find out how the Earth works.

  – BBC interview, "Beyond Present Theories"

Science means, sometimes, a special method of finding things out. Sometimes it means the body of knowledge arising from the things found out. It may also mean the new things that you can do when you have found something out, or the actual doing of new things.

– "The Uncertainty of Science," John Danz Lecture Series, 1963

In learning science you learn to handle trial and error, to develop a spirit of invention and of free inquiry, which is of tremendous value far beyond science. One learns to ask oneself: "Is there a better way to do it?" (And the answer to this is not the conditioned reflex: "Let's see how they do it in the United States," because there must certainly be a better way than that!)

– "The Problem of Teaching Physics in Latin America," 1963

[On revelation:] Afterwards, you think "Why the devil was I so stupid and didn't see this?" Not only true of you but true of the history of science. You can always look at human history and wonder why they hadn't thought of it twenty years earlier or ten years earlier, depending on the pace.

– Yorkshire Television program, "Take the World from Another Point of View," 1972

I imagine experimental physicists must often look with envy at men like Kamerlingh Onnes, who discovered a field like low temperature, which seems to be bottomless and in which one can go down and down. Such a man is then a leader and has some temporary monopoly in a scientific adventure.

– "There's Plenty of Room at the Bottom," December 1959

Understanding space really means understanding how things might look from another point of view.

> – Audio recording of lecture on relativity, Douglas Advanced Research Laboratory, 1967

In no field is all the research done. Research leads to new discoveries and new questions to answer by more research.

> – Letter to student Mark Minguillon, August 1976 (*Perfectly Reasonable Deviations from the Beaten Track*, p. 306)

I believe most assuredly that the next science to find itself in moral difficulties with its applications is biology, and if the problems of physics relative to science seem difficult, the problems of the development of biological knowledge will be fantastic.

> – Galileo Symposium, "What Is and What Should Be the Role of Scientific Culture in Modern Society," September 1964

The world goes around because of differences of opinion and interests resulting in a division of labor — even volunteer labor. I hope everyone does not think as I do — if I found out they did, I would change my view. For from this variety of approaches real progress must come. We must try everything.

> – Letter to John M. Fowler, March 1966

I wouldn't say that my physics wasn't up to the prize, but I'm not up to it on a human side, being a Prize Winner and an Important Scientist. I'm not, that's all. I was a kid fooling around. I was in my pajamas working on the floor with paper and pencil and I cooked something up, OK?

– "The Remarkable Dr. Feynman," *Los Angeles Times Magazine*, April 20, 1986

So it's kind of fun to imagine that this intimate mixture of highly attractive opposites which are so strong that they cancel out the effects and it's only sometimes, when you have an excess of one kind or another that you get this mysterious electrical force. And how can I explain these electrical forces in any other way? Why should I try to explain it in terms something like jelly or other things which are made?

– BBC, "Fun to Imagine" television series, 1983

But we have to keep going, we find out more if we just keep going, so we keep going.

– Audio recording of Feynman Lectures on Physics, Lecture 7, October 17, 1961

Incidentally, may I say from the beginning that if a thing is not a science, it is not necessarily bad. For example, love is not a science. So, if something is said not to be a science, it does not mean that there is something wrong with it; it just means that it is not a science.

– Audio recording of Feynman Lectures on Physics, Lecture 3, October 3, 1961

I went down to the town to buy supplies and I was carrying a wastepaper basket and some other things, and [Leonard]

Eisenbud, who was a theoretical physicist — we met — he passed me on the street. "Ah," he said, "you look like you're going to be a good theoretical physicist. You've brought the right tools — there's an eraser and a wastebasket."

> – Interview with Charles Weiner, March 5, 1966 (Niels Bohr Library and Archives with the Center for the History of Physics)

[On Einstein:] He wore this sweater, without a shirt under it, no socks — just like everybody says — and was such a soft, nice man in the discussions, at all points. He was such an interesting man to talk to.

> – Interview with Charles Weiner, March 5, 1966 (Niels Bohr Library and Archives with the Center for the History of Physics)

You know that nature can look very, very strange, in the fundamentals, and yet produce in the end the natural phenomena in a way, very different looking than you would think at first. It's all right. You've got to think it out, you can't just jump to the conclusion that it's wrong.

> – Interview with Charles Weiner, March 5, 1966 (Niels Bohr Library and Archives with the Center for the History of Physics)

[On the first nuclear test:] I've always been impressed by acoustics. Acoustics have meaning for me. Not so much as the visual. When I heard the solidity of that crack, at 20 miles away, then I knew that that thing was something, and I got excited.

> – Interview with Charles Weiner, March 5, 1966 (Niels Bohr Library and Archives with the Center for the History of Physics)

I've found that my trouble is, I haven't been writing things up. I discover things, and then other people discover them later, and then it's not worth writing them up. For instance, I worked out the quantum theory of gravitation to an order infinitely higher — I mean, to a degree, to a detail, infinitely higher — than anybody else that I know. But it isn't complete. There are some slight weaknesses. So I haven't written it up. But it's crazy — that's five years old now. It should be written up.

> – Interview with Charles Weiner, June 27, 1966 (Niels Bohr
>   Library and Archives with the Center for the History of Physics)

What happens to it — this is interesting, this is the way science works, I found out — what happens to a person, when they believe something, is that they see a few that look like it, which are due to something else. Then they believe in the existence of the thing. Then all the rest of the things which are not good become corroborative evidence, not one bit of which is very strong, but seems to be in large amount. But the moment that you propose that it isn't true, all the corroborative evidence just disappears. I mean, it's just a very small business — it's just selection of a special plate, that looks like it's in the right direction. It is not strong. And so one can build up an argument and believe something, and think it has a large amount of weight, when actually if you go and look carefully at it the weight is very weak, and each item is weak and it doesn't add up to much.

> – Interview with Charles Weiner, June 28, 1966 (Niels Bohr
>   Library and Archives with the Center for the History of Physics)

I've always taken an attitude that I have only to explain the regularities of nature — I don't have to explain the methods of my friends. I don't have to learn the systems and methods of my friends — only the regularities of nature — and that's a very economizing way of proceeding.

– Interview with Charles Weiner, June 28, 1966 (Niels Bohr Library and Archives with the Center for the History of Physics)

Science is only useful if it tells you about some experiment that has not been done; it is no good if it only tells you what just went on.

– *The Character of Physical Law*, p. 164

Therefore psychologically we must keep all the theories in our heads, and every theoretical physicist who is any good knows six or seven different theoretical representations for exactly the same physics.

– *The Character of Physical Law*, p. 168

We are trained by Einstein and Bohr and so on, to appreciate that an idea which is prima facie absurd, can after time aligns enough, agree with experience. That is, things that look absolutely nutty, like lack of simultaneous time or uncertainty and so on, is perfectly possible.

– CERN talk, December 1965

We have a habit in writing articles published in scientific journals to make the work as finished as possible, to cover all the tracks, to not worry about the blind alleys or to describe how you had the wrong idea first, and so on.

– From *Nobel Lectures, Physics 1963–1970*, Elsevier Publishing Company, Amsterdam, 1972

Research is a method of attaining information. You don't make a bomb by research — you find out how to do it by research.

– Notes from Los Alamos

If you expect science to give you all the answers to the wonderful questions about what we are, where we are going, and what the meaning of the universe is, then I think you could easily become disillusioned and look for a mystic answer to these problems. How a scientist can want a mystic answer, I don't know.

– BBC, "The Pleasure of Finding Things Out," 1981

And so it is with science. In a way it is a key to the gates of heaven, and the same key opens the gates of hell, and we do not have any instructions as to which is which gate. Shall we throw away the key and never have a way to enter the gates of heaven? Or shall we struggle with the problem of which is the best way to use the key?

– "The Uncertainty of Science," John Danz Lecture Series, 1963

Control of scientific innovations means end of science. Science is source of all our engineering development — care not to kill it by control.

– Notes from Los Alamos

Science alone of all subjects contains within itself the lesson of the danger of belief in the infallibility of the greatest teachers of the preceding generation.

– National Science Teachers Association Fourteenth Convention lecture, "What Is Science?" April 1966

Well, these scientific views end in awe and mystery, lost at the edge in uncertainty, but they appear to be so deep and so impressive that the theory that it is all arranged as a stage for God to watch man's struggle for good and evil seems inadequate.

– "The Uncertainty of Values," John Danz Lecture Series, 1963

# Curiosity and Discovery

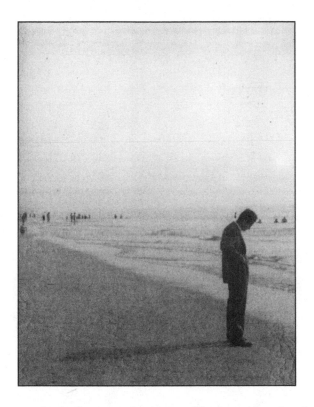

The more I ask why, it gets interesting. That's my idea, that the deeper a thing is the more interesting it gets.

– BBC, "Fun to Imagine" television series, 1983

I love challenges. I always have. In fact, later hobbies at the beginning were not scientific but were always challenges. Picking locks, cracking codes, analyzing hieroglyphics that nobody knows how to translate — you see, they're all the same now.

- Interview with Charles Weiner, March 4, 1966 (Niels Bohr Library and Archives with the Center for the History of Physics)

The other day, I was at the dentist, and he's getting ready with his electric drill to make holes, and I thought, I better think of something fast, or else it's gonna hurt! And then I thought about this little motor going around, and what was it that made it turn, and what was going on.

- BBC, "Fun to Imagine" television series, 1983

I think that to keep trying new solutions is the way to do everything.

- "The Uncertainty of Science," John Danz Lecture Series, 1963

I wonder why. I wonder why. I wonder why I wonder. I wonder *why* I wonder why I wonder why I wonder!

- *Surely You're Joking, Mr. Feynman!*, p. 48

The dream is to find the open channel.

- "The Uncertainty of Values," John Danz Lecture Series, 1963

What one fool can do, so can another, and the fact that some other fool beat you to it shouldn't disturb you: you should get a kick out of having discovered something.

— *Feynman Lectures on Computation*, pp. 15–16

Suppose people are exploring a new continent, OK? They see water coming along the ground, they've seen that before, and they call it "rivers." So they say they're exploring to find the headwaters, they go upriver, and sure enough, there they are, it's all going very well. But lo and behold, when they get up far enough they find the whole system's different: There's a great big lake, or springs, or the rivers run in a circle. You might say, "Aha! They've failed!" but not at all! The real reason they were doing it was to explore the land.

— *Omni* interview, February 1979

As long as I didn't know they discovered it, for that moment I knew something and I had found a law, and I could make predictions about nature, which is the aim that I had. And the fact that somebody else was already making the predictions, unbeknownst to me, in no way takes the pleasure away, in any way. So that was really a great moment. I would like more moments like that, but I don't have to ask the gods for everything.

— Interview with Charles Weiner, June 28, 1966 (Niels Bohr Library and Archives with the Center for the History of Physics)

Fiddling is the answer. Experimenting is fiddling around.

> – Interview with Charles Weiner, March 5, 1966 (Niels Bohr Library and Archives with the Center for the History of Physics)

This stuff of fantasizing and looking at the world, imagining things, which really isn't fantasizing because you're only trying to imagine things the way it really is, comes in handy sometimes.

> – BBC, "Fun to Imagine" television series, 1983

You come in to me now, in an interview, and you're asking me about the latest discoveries that are made. Nobody every asks about a simple, ordinary phenomenon in the street, you know, like, "What about those colors?" Or something like that. We could have a nice, interview, explain all about the colors. Butterfly wings and whole big deal. Don't care about that. You want the big, final result. Instead it's going to be complicated, because I am at the end of 400 years of very effective method of finding things out about the world.

> – Yorkshire Television interview, "Take the World from Another Point of View," 1972

The truth always is funny in the sense that it explains a lot more than you expected when you started to figure it out.

> – Audio recording of Feynman Lectures on Physics, Lecture 7, October 17, 1961, Q&A

I can't understand anything in general unless I'm carrying along in my mind a specific example and watching it go.

   – *Surely You're Joking, Mr. Feynman!*, p. 244

Man has been stopped before by stopping his ideas.

   – "The Uncertainty of Values," John Danz Lecture Series, 1963

Furthermore, in the search for new laws, you always have the psychological excitement of feeling that possibly nobody has yet thought of the crazy possibility you are looking at right now.

   – From *Nobel Lectures, Physics 1963–1970*, Elsevier Publishing Company, Amsterdam, 1972

The exceptions to any rule are most interesting in themselves, for they show us that the old rule is wrong. And it is most exciting then, to find out what the right rule is, if any, is.

   – "The Uncertainty of Values," John Danz Lecture Series, 1963

I have to understand the world, you see.

   – *Surely You're Joking, Mr. Feynman!*, p. 231

[On theoretical physics:] It's like exploring a new country and you cannot explore a country successfully if you care what you find because you might say to yourself "I don't think it's gonna come out the way I thought it was and so I'm gonna quit exploring." No, it's the fun of finding out what it's like rather than starting out with a pre-set idea and if you find that it isn't that way you get disappointed; that's a ridiculous thing, so I don't fill up my mind with ideas of which way it's going to go, I just try and find out as much as I can.

– BBC interview, "Scientifically Speaking," April 1976

We live in a heroic, a unique and wonderful age of excitement. It's going to be looked at with great jealousy in the ages to come. How would it have been to live in the time when they were discovering the fundamental laws? You can't discover America twice, and we can be jealous of Columbus. You say, yes, but if not America, then there are other planets to explore. That is true. And if not fundamental physics, then there are other questions to investigate.

– *Perfectly Reasonable Deviations from the Beaten Track*, p. 440

And it is a miracle that it's possible, by doing experiments over here, to predict what's going to happen over there. It is not as much a miracle to predict something if you know the laws about it. In other words, it's enough of a miracle that there are laws at all, but what's really a miracle is to be able to find the law. It's another kind of miracle. You see, knowing a law to figure out that such and such is going to do something, and then have nature do it — OK, that's pretty good. But to look at other aspects and to guess, and to know that there's a pattern under there, and to tell nature that in this experiment she's going to do that — not by deduction, strictly speaking, from what's known but by guessing from what's known — it seems a wonderful thing to me. And I always wanted to do that.

 – Interview with Charles Weiner, June 28, 1966 (Niels Bohr Library and Archives with the Center for the History of Physics)

It was because it was a challenge, for its own sake — completely, always, for its own sake. It was the excitement, the fun, of working this thing out.

 – Interview with Charles Weiner, March 4, 1966 (Niels Bohr Library and Archives with the Center for the History of Physics)

Even in my crazy book, I didn't emphasize — but it is true — that I worked as hard as I could at drawing, at deciphering Mayan, at drumming, at cracking safes, etc. The real fun of life is this perpetual testing to realize how far out you can go with any potentialities.

 – Letter to Mr. V. A. Van Der Hyde, July 1986 (*Perfectly Reasonable Deviations from the Beaten Track*, p. 414)

The way I think of what we're doing is, we're exploring — we're trying to find out as much as we can about the world. People say to me, "Are you looking for the ultimate laws of physics?" No, I'm not. I'm just looking to find out more about the world. If it turns out there is a simple ultimate law which explains everything, so be it; that would be very nice to discover. If it turns out it's like an onion, with millions of layers, and we're sick and tired of looking at the layers, then that's the way it is. But whatever it comes out, it's nature, and she's going to come out the way she is! Therefore when we go investigate it we shouldn't predecide what it is we're going to find, except to find out more.

– BBC, "The Pleasure of Finding Things Out," 1981

I often think about that, especially when I'm teaching some esoteric technique such as integrating Bessel functions. When I see equations, I see the letters in colors — I don't know why. As I'm talking, I see vague picture of Bessel functions from Jahnke and Emde's book, with light-tan js, slightly violet-bluish ns, and dark brown xs flying around. And I wonder what the hell it must look like to the students.

– *What Do You Care What Other People Think?*, p. 59

My interest in science is to simply find out more about the world, and the more I find out, the better it is. I like to find out.

– BBC, "The Pleasure of Finding Things Out," 1981

I'll never make that mistake again, reading the experts' opinions. Of course, you only live one life: You make all your mistakes, and learn what not to do — and that's the end of you.

– *Surely You're Joking, Mr. Feynman!*, p. 255

Since then I never pay any attention to anything by "experts." I calculate everything myself.

– *Surely You're Joking, Mr. Feynman!*, p. 255

It cannot interest you until you deeply understand the problem and its intricacies. Then every subject is interesting.

– Notes

The work is not done for the sake of an application. It is done for the excitement of what is found out.

– "The Uncertainty of Science," John Danz Lecture Series, 1963

Learn what the rest of the world is like. The variety is worthwhile.

– *Surely You're Joking, Mr. Feynman!*, p. 63

The next day at the meeting, I saw [Murray] Slotnick and said, "Slotnick, I worked it out last night, I wanted to see if I got the same answers you do. I got a different answer for each coupling — but, I would like to check in detail with you because I want to make sure of my methods." And, he said, "what do you mean you worked it out last night, it took me six months!" That was a thrilling moment for me, like receiving the Nobel Prize, because that convinced me, at last, I did have some kind of method and technique and understood how to do something that other people did not know how to do. That was my moment of triumph in which I realized I really had succeeded in working out something worthwhile.

– From *Nobel Lectures, Physics 1963–1970*, Elsevier Publishing Company, Amsterdam, 1972

It has to do with curiosity. It has to do with people wondering what makes something do something. And then to discover that if you try to get answers, that they're related to each other. The things that make the wind make the waves, and the motion of water is like the motion of air is like the motion of sand. The fact that things have common features, turns out more and more universal. What we're looking for is how everything works. What makes everything work.

 – Yorkshire Television interview, "Take the World from Another Point of View," 1972

It's curiosity, as to where we are, what we are. It's very much more exciting to discover that we're on a ball, half of us sticking upside down, it's spinning around in space, there's a mysterious force which holds us on, going around a great big glob of gas that's burning, fueled by a fire that's completely different from any fire we can make (well, now we can make that fire — nuclear fire), but that's a much more exciting story to many people than the tales which other people used to make up, who worried about the universe; that we were living on the back of a turtle, or something like that. They were wonderful stories, but the truth is so much more remarkable. The pleasure of physics to me, is that it's revealed that the truth is so remarkable, so amazing.

 – Yorkshire Television interview, "Take the World from Another Point of View," 1972

The same thrill, the same awe and mystery, come again and again when we look at any problem deeply enough. With more knowledge comes deeper, more wonderful mystery, luring one on to penetrate deeper still. Never concerned that the answer may prove disappointing, but with pleasure and confidence we turn over each new stone to find unimagined strangeness leading on to more wonderful questions and mysteries — certainly a grand adventure!

— "The Value of Science," December 1955

[On physics problems:] Most of the time I don't solve them. Once in a great while I do. And since the problems I've chosen to work on are rather big, hard problems that nobody else has solved, when you solve something nobody else has solved, you've got a little pride. You get a kick out of doing it.

— "The Remarkable Dr. Feynman," *Los Angeles Times Magazine*, April 20, 1986

I don't know anything, but I do know that everything is interesting if you go into it deeply enough.

— *Omni* interview, February 1979

The only thing in the world is not applications. It's interesting in understanding what the world is made of. It's the same interest, the curiosity of man that makes him build telescopes. What is the use of discovering the age of the universe? Or what are these quasars that are exploding at long distances? I mean what's the use of all that astronomy? There isn't any. Nonetheless, it's interesting.

— Future for Science interview

A guy came into my room and found me leaning out of a wide-open window in the dead of winter, holding a pot in one hand and stirring with the other. I was curious as to whether jello would coagulate if you kept it moving all the time.

　– *What Do You Care What Other People Think?*, p. 56

I'm not answering your question, but I'm telling you how difficult a "why" question is. You have to know what it is that you're permitted to understand and allow to be understood and know, and what it is you're not.

　– BBC, "Fun to Imagine" television series, 1983

If you heat a rubber band, it will pull more strongly. For instance, if you hang a weight with a rubber band, and put a match to it, it's kind of fun to watch it rise.

　– BBC, "Fun to Imagine" television series, 1983

I love puzzles: One guy tries to make something to keep another guy out; there must be a way to beat it.

　– *Surely You're Joking, Mr. Feynman!*, p. 139

You should never be afraid that something new will come out. It will come out in due time, and then you'll try to understand it. Of course, it'll be very exciting!

　– Audio recording of Feynman Lectures on Physics, Lecture 3, October 3, 1961, Q&A

It's the way I study — to understand something by trying to work it out or, in other words, to understand something by creating it. Not creating it one hundred percent, of course, but taking a hint as to which direction to go but not remembering the details. Those you work out for yourself.

– *Feynman Lectures on Computation*, p. 15

Isn't interesting to live in our time and have such wonderful puzzles to work on?

– Letter to Dr. Victor F. Weisskopf, January–February 1961

He often started to talk about things like this: "Suppose a man from Mars were to come down and look at the world." It's a very good way to look at the world.

– National Science Teachers Association Fourteenth Convention lecture, "What Is Science?" April 1966

I kind of try to imagine what would have happened to me if I'd lived in today's era. I'm rather horrified. I think there are too many books that the mind gets boggled. If I got interested, I would have so many things to look at, I would go crazy. It's too easy. Maybe. Maybe not. Maybe this is just an old fashioned point of view.

– Interview with Charles Weiner, March 4, 1966 (Niels Bohr Library and Archives with the Center for the History of Physics)

And sometimes people say, "How is it you're suddenly working on this?" It's just that I finally got some success. I work often on a large range of things that don't work out. Then there's silence.

And then people say, "Why are you suddenly doing this?" Well, yeah, I finally got somewhere on this. It's not that I suddenly did it.

– Interview with Charles Weiner, June 28, 1966 (Niels Bohr Library and Archives with the Center for the History of Physics)

What we're looking for is how everything works and what makes everything work. And what happens first in history is that we discover first the things that are on the face of it that are obvious, and gradually we ask more questions and dig in a little deeper to things we need to do a little more complicated experiment to find out.

– Interview with Yorkshire Television program, "Take the World from Another Point of View," 1972

Many of the other people who tell you about Los Alamos know somebody up in some higher echelon of governmental organization or something, worried about some big decision. I worried about no big decisions. I was always flittering about underneath somewhere.

– UCSB talk, "Los Alamos from Below," February 1975

Maybe the reason we make so much progress in physics is because it's so easy.

– *Great American Scientists*, p. 24

I studied metallography, for instance, because it was a field I didn't know anything about. I was always interested to learn something about which I didn't know anything — to see what would happen, you know, in metallurgy, and metallography. I remember that course in particular. That's when I discovered for the first time the very great use of your knowledge of physics, the universality.

– Interview with Charles Weiner, March 5, 1966 (Niels Bohr
   Library and Archives with the Center for the History of Physics)

I think the right way, of course, is to say that what we have to look at is the whole structural interconnection of the thing; and that all the sciences, and not just the sciences but all the efforts of intellectual kinds, are an endeavor to see the connections of the hierarchies, to connect beauty to history, to connect history to man's psychology, man's psychology to the working of the brain, the brain to the neural impulse, the neural impulse to the chemistry, and so forth, up and down, both ways.

– *The Character of Physical Law*, p. 125

I can't answer adult questions. They're bad questions. Usually they want to know the meaning of some new word they've seen and it's something they'll never understand. I hate adults. Younger people are curious about nature.

– *Columbia Dispatch*, October 22, 1966

I decided that, when I was a kid, I used to enjoy the subject for the fun of it. I used to like nature and do it for the fun of it. So what I ought to do is play games with it, just whatever was curious and interesting to me — I should just play. You see? Just like I was when I was a kid — try to find a relation between things, do this, do that, whatever I felt like. I don't have to do this problem because it's important or that problem because it's important, or everybody expects me to do something.

> – Interview with Charles Weiner, June 27, 1966 (Niels Bohr
> Library and Archives with the Center for the History of Physics)

I don't really read a lot of what the other guy does. I read what his assumptions are and if they seem reasonable then I work out the conclusions. I don't need to read how he works out the conclusions most of the time.

> – Interview with Charles Weiner, June 28, 1966 (Niels Bohr
> Library and Archives with the Center for the History of Physics)

I don't wanna take this stuff seriously. I think we should just have fun imagining it and not worry about it. There's no teacher going to ask you questions at the end. Otherwise, it's a horrible subject.

> – BBC, "Fun to Imagine" television series, 1983, regarding par-
> ticle physics

Sometimes the truth is discovered first, and the beauty or "necessity" of that truth seen only later.

> – "Structure of the Proton," Niels Bohr Medal lecture given in
> Copenhagen, Denmark, October 1973

But if you keep proving stuff that others have done, getting confidence, increasing the complexities of your solutions — for the fun of it — then one day you'll turn around and discover that nobody actually did that one!

– *Feynman Lectures on Computation*, p. 16

I want to do scientific research — that is, to find out more about how the world works. And that is not a secret; that work is not secret.

– Interview for Viewpoint

The hardest part of the helium problem was done by physical reasoning alone, without being able to write anything. By just standing — you know, I remember kind of leaning against the kitchen sink, you see, and looking at it, and just thinking. And it was very, very interesting to be able to push through that doggoned thing without having stuff to write.

– Interview with Charles Weiner, June 28, 1966 (Niels Bohr Library and Archives with the Center for the History of Physics)

When you explain a "why," you have to be in some framework in which you've allowed something to be true. Otherwise, you're perpetually asking why.

– BBC, "Fun to Imagine" television series, 1983

You begin to get a very interesting understanding of the world and all its complications. If you try to follow anything up, you go deeper and deeper in various directions.

– BBC, "Fun to Imagine" television series, 1983

All we know, is that as we go along we find we can amalgamate pieces, and then find pieces that don't fit, and keep trying to put the jigsaw puzzle together. But whether there's a finite number of pieces, and whether there's a border to this jigsaw puzzle or not, is of course, not known. And it will never be known until we — if we do — ever finish the picture.

  – Audio recording of Feynman Lectures on Physics, Lecture 2,
    September 29, 1961

That was the beginning, and the idea seemed so obvious to me and so elegant that I fell deeply in love with it. And, like falling in love with a woman, it is only possible if you do not know much about her, so you cannot see her faults. The faults will become apparent later, but after the love is strong enough to hold you to her. So, I was held to this theory, in spite of all difficulties, by my youthful enthusiasm.

  – From *Nobel Lectures, Physics 1963–1970*, Elsevier Publishing
    Company, Amsterdam, 1972

We live in a heroic age. We live in a moment that'll never come again. These discoveries cannot be made twice. One doesn't discover America two or three times in succession, really, and one doesn't discover the laws of nuclear forces or electricity more than once.

  – BBC, "Strangeness Minus Three," 1964

That's the way it always is in these pinnacle discoveries. The big pile-up of stuff, all the old things that you've thought of before you try again and again, but the great discovery always involves a great philosophical surprise.

– BBC, "Strangeness Minus Three," 1964

The chance is high that the truth lies in the fashionable direction. But, on the off-chance that it is in another direction — a direction obvious from an unfashionable view of field theory — who will find it? Only someone who has sacrificed himself by teaching himself quantum electrodynamics from a peculiar and unfashionable point of view; one that he may have to invent for himself.

– From *Nobel Lectures, Physics 1963–1970*, Elsevier Publishing
   Company, Amsterdam, 1972

# How Physicists Think

There is always the possibility of proving any definite theory wrong;
but notice that we can never prove it right. Suppose that you invent
a good guess, calculate the consequences, and discover every time
that the consequences you have calculated agree with experiment.
The theory is then right? No, it is simply not proved wrong.

– *The Character of Physical Law*, p. 157

People are still designing new gyros, new devices, new ways, and it may well be that one of them will solve the problems, for instance, this inanity of having to have the axle bearings so accurate. If you play with the gyro for a while you will see that the friction on its axle is not small. The reason is, if the bearings were made too frictionless, the axle would wobble, and you'd have to worry about that tenth of a millionth of an inch — which is ridiculous. There must be a better way.

– *Feynman's Tips on Physics*, p. 129

It is important to realize that in physics today, we do not have any knowledge of what energy is.

– Audio recording of Feynman Lectures on Physics, Lecture 4, October 6, 1961

Thinking is nothing but talking to yourself inside.

– *What Do You Care What Other People Think?*, p. 54

Physicists like to think that now all you have to do is say, "These are the conditions, now what happens next?"

– *The Character of Physical Law*, p. 114

Everything I would do like this, I would always have a practical problem to exemplify it. I have always thought the thing was no good unless you could use it somehow.

– Interview with Charles Weiner, March 4, 1966 (Niels Bohr Library and Archives with the Center for the History of Physics)

A great deal of formulation work is done in writing the paper, organizational work, organization. I think of a better way, a better way, a better way of getting there, of proving it. I never do much — I mean, it's just cleaner, cleaner and cleaner. It's like polishing a rough-cut vase. The shape, you know what you want and you know what it is. It's just polishing it. Get it shined, get it clean, and everything else.

– Interview with Charles Weiner, March 4, 1966 (Niels Bohr Library and Archives with the Center for the History of Physics)

When I think about something, I go along in a certain way, and then I get balled up, and then I go back, and I think — I get mixed up easily. I easily get into confusion, which is the horror of the whole business when you're thinking. It's like building a pile of cards and the whole thing collapses, and you keep going and it collapses.

– Interview with Charles Weiner, June 28, 1966 (Niels Bohr Library and Archives with the Center for the History of Physics)

I try always to work with the least knowledge possible, with a little knowledge of what other people are doing, because I feel more happy being more individual, if I am not following the line and getting confused by what they say.

– Interview with Charles Weiner, June 28, 1966 (Niels Bohr Library and Archives with the Center for the History of Physics)

I don't like to judge other people, or their work, at all. I don't. I don't want to judge somebody else's work.

– Interview with Charles Weiner, June 28, 1966 (Niels Bohr Library and Archives with the Center for the History of Physics)

I'd been traveling every summer somewhere, and I thought this time, where am I going to go? And I said, the hell with it, I don't feel like traveling. Instead of traveling, I'll do biology experiments. I'll go into a different field, instead of going into a different country.

– Interview with Charles Weiner, June 28, 1966 (Niels Bohr Library and Archives with the Center for the History of Physics)

I had a principle that everything that I wrote, I should understand inside out; that there was just a little bit less written than what I knew; and that whatever I wrote would be right. I didn't like the papers that somebody would write; suggesting an idea which in three months they find is cockeyed.

– Interview with Charles Weiner, June 28, 1966 (Niels Bohr Library and Archives with the Center for the History of Physics)

It was to me a rather annoying thing, because I realized what it would mean is all this noise and all this trouble and wild business, you know? There'd be newspapermen for whom I had no respect, publicity for which I had no respect. This world is so full of hot air, and just extra propaganda junk today, that it's not real. I just don't want to get involved with all that stuff, and I didn't know how I was going to escape it. I still imagined that I could by not answering the phone. So I took the telephone off the hook.

– Interview with Charles Weiner, June 28, 1966 (Niels Bohr Library and Archives with the Center for the History of Physics)

It has turned out that many things that bothered me that I thought that I didn't understand because I didn't know enough about the subject, turned out that I didn't understand them because they weren't logical, they weren't valid.

– Interview with Charles Weiner, February 4, 1966 (Niels Bohr Library and Archives with the Center for the History of Physics)

But I don't work in a straight line. So I leap ahead in one direction and I'm expecting to close up with the other and make a finished product, OK? But the leap that went in the forward direction works. I think that's not all there is to it. I think I'll be able to make a bigger do, and I work on it, but it doesn't get any bigger. I get confused or something. But the leap ahead was very important.

– Interview with Charles Weiner, February 4, 1966 (Niels Bohr Library and Archives with the Center for the History of Physics)

You know how scientists, they usually look at the rest of the world, think of how absurd everything is, how stupid everybody is, how dopey the Navy guys are that measured the distances different, so ha-ha, but you should be ashamed of yourself, we should be ashamed of ourselves, for there's no difference, for example, in the ways we measure anything.

– Audio recording of lecture on relativity, Douglas Advanced
  Research Laboratory, 1967

If you're ever running for an airplane in a taxi, and you suddenly discover that you're using Daylight Saving Time instead of Standard Time or something like that, and you don't know whether you're going to make the plane or not, and you try to figure out, which way? You know how complicated it is.

– Audio recording of lecture on relativity, Douglas Advanced
  Research Laboratory, 1967

I took this stuff that I got out of your seal and put it in ice water, and I discovered that when you put some pressure on it for a while and then undo it it doesn't stretch back. It stays the same dimension. In other words, for a few seconds at least and more seconds than that, there is no resilience in this particular material when it is at a temperature of 32 degrees.

– Transcript of the hearing of the Presidential Commission on
  the Space Shuttle Accident, February 11, 1986

The thing that doesn't fit is the thing that's the most interesting, the part that doesn't go according to what you expected.

– BBC, "The Pleasure of Finding Things Out," 1981

The physicists should be ashamed of themselves: Astronomers keep asking, "Why don't you figure out for us what will happen if you have a big mass of junk pulled together by gravity and spinning? Can you understand the shapes of these nebulae?" And nobody ever answers them.

– *Feynman's Tips on Physics*, p. 127

I believe that has some significance for our problem.

– Transcript of the hearing of the Presidential Commission on the Space Shuttle Accident, February 11, 1986

Once I got into physics I forgot who I was talking to.

– Interview with Charles Weiner, June 28, 1966 (Niels Bohr Library and Archives with the Center for the History of Physics)

You will have to brace yourselves for this — not because it is difficult to understand, but because it is absolutely ridiculous: All we do is draw little arrows on a piece of paper — that's all!

– *QED: The Strange Theory of Light and Matter*, p. 24

The paradox is only a conflict between reality and your feeling of what reality ought to be.

– *Feynman Lectures on Physics*, vol. 3, pp. 18–19

Do you think that it is not a paradox, but that it is still very peculiar? On that we can all agree. It is what makes physics fascinating.

– *Feynman Lectures on Physics*, vol. 3, pp. 18–19

The real problem in speech is not precise language. The problem is clear language. The desire is to have the idea clearly communicated to the other person. It is only necessary to be precise when there is some doubt as to the meaning of a phrase, and then the precision should be put in the place where the doubt exists. It is really quite impossible to say anything with absolute precision, unless that thing is so abstracted from the real world as to not represent any real thing.

– "New Textbooks for the 'New' Mathematics," *Engineering and Science* 28, no. 6 (March 1965)

And you can re-create the things that you've forgotten perpetually — if you don't forget too much, and if you know enough. In other words, there comes a time where you'll know so many things that as you forget them, you can reconstruct them from the pieces that you can still remember. It is therefore of first-rate importance that you know how to triangulate — that is, to know how to figure something out from what you already know. It is absolutely necessary.

– *Feynman's Tips on Physics*, p. 39

There's a unit of time I must use here if I use miles here. $c$ equals the speed of light. If you wish, that formula tells you what I just said. Which was you convert time into miles by asking, what's the unit of time? The time to go one mile. You want to measure this in kilometers? Okay, and the unit of time is the time to go one kilometer. And if you use this interval to measure time, instead of seconds, then the formula's right.

– Audio recording of lecture on relativity, Douglas Advanced Research Laboratory, 1967

Incidentally, from the point of view of basic physics, the most interesting phenomena are of course, the new places, the places that don't work, not the places that do work. Because there's where we'll discover new rules.

– Audio recording of Feynman Lectures on Physics, Lecture 2,
    September 29, 1961

It will not do to memorize the formulas, and to say to yourself, "I know all the formulas; all I gotta do is figure out how to put 'em in the problem!"

– *Feynman's Tips on Physics*, p. 38

First, I'm going to tell you what the theory is; I'll tell you what it looks like, what we do to make the calculations, just what the thing is because otherwise how are you going to understand what "world picture" this thing is? And it is a "world picture" because it describes all the phenomena (except radioactivity and gravity) in the world! That's a lot of phenomena! It should explain, if everything is thoroughly understood, the laughter of the audience when you make a dummy remark!

– "QED: Photons — Corpuscles of Light," Sir Douglas Robb
    Lectures, University of Auckland, June 1979

In fact, the total amount that a physicist knows is very little. He has only to remember the rules to get him from one place to another and he is all right.

– *The Character of Physical Law*, p. 45

I learned that really physics is a very useful background for what looks like different fields; that the world is the same, the physical laws are not so un-useful, you know what I mean? They work. Yeah, they work, and you can use the ideas in different fields, and you are ahead of the other guys, because there are a large number of things that are self-evident to you that they have to learn. But of course, you have to learn by experience too. I'm not trying to say just — both together are much better than anybody. But it is true that studying physics is good all over the place.

– Interview with Charles Weiner, March 5, 1966 (Niels Bohr Library and Archives with the Center for the History of Physics)

It's a very hard job. It's lots of work. So what do we do it for? Because of the excitement, because of the fact that each time we get one of these things, we have a terrific — El Dorado — we have a new view of nature. We see the ingenuity, if I may put it that way, of nature herself. The peculiarity of the way she works. It takes a terrible strain on the mind to understand these things. And the real value of the development of the science, in this connection, the thing that makes me go on, is this, the difficulty of understanding it. That these apes, stand around looking at nature and find that to really catch on, they have to polish their minds to the last.

– BBC, "Strangeness Minus Three," 1964

I happen to know this, and I happen to know that, and maybe I know that; and I work everything out from there. Tomorrow I may forget that this is true, but remember that something else is true, so I can reconstruct it all again. I am never quite sure of where I am supposed to begin or where I am supposed to end. I just remember enough all the time so that as the memory fades and some of the pieces fall out I can put the thing back together again every day.

– *The Character of Physical Law*, p. 47

# The Quantum World

We physicists are always checking to see if there is something the matter with the theory. That's the game, because if there is something the matter, it's interesting! But so far, we have found nothing wrong with the theory of quantum electrodynamics. It is therefore, I would say, the jewel of physics — our proudest possession.

– *QED: The Strange Theory of Light and Matter*, p. 8

What I am going to tell you about is what we teach our physics students in the third or fourth year of graduate school — and you think I'm going to explain it to you so you can understand it? No, you're not going to be able to understand it. Why, then, am I going to bother you with all this? Why are you going to sit here all this time, when you won't be able to understand what I am going to say? It is my task to convince you not to turn away because you don't understand it. You see, my physics students don't understand it. That is because I don't understand it. Nobody does.

– *QED: The Strange Theory of Light and Matter*, p. 9

The science fiction writers who have interpreted my view of the positron as an electron going backward in time have not realized that the theory is completely consistent with causality principles and in no way implies that we can travel backward in time.

– Correspondence with David Paterson (BBC), February 1976

All my mature life I have been trying to distill the strangeness of quantum mechanics into simpler and simpler circumstances. I have given many lectures of ever increasing simplicity and purity.

– Letter to Dr. N. David Mermin, March 1984 (*Perfectly Reasonable Deviations from the Beaten Track*, p. 368)

Maybe gravity is a way that quantum mechanics fails at large distances.

– Letter to Dr. Victor F. Weisskopf, January–February 1961

Before and after are not absolute ideas; they depend on the point of view. It is similar to the question of what is in front and what is in back. If I turn a little bit, I can change the arrangement. Two things may appear to be at the same distance from one man, but appear to be at different distances from another. Likewise, it is true that two events which may appear to be at the same from one point of view may not do so from another. This leads us to the idea of the representation of time as a fourth geometrical dimension.

– From notes for "About Time" program, 1957

I really do believe that quantum mechanics is fundamentally correct, and that all this is simply psychological trouble. It is extremely difficult to get used to it because it's so much common sense and common knowledge that gets this idea that when you're not looking at something, it's either this way or that way. And to be able to say, "By God, you can't even say it's either this way or that way when you don't look at it? But it must be either" No, you can't say that, or you're going to get in trouble! They say that can't be so bad. It must be that Nature isn't quite like that.

– Esalen lecture, "Quantum Mechanical View of Reality (Part 1)," October 1984

Now I come to the greatest shame of theoretical physics. For the last twenty-five years, well it's more than that, it's nearly forty years, field theories have been in existence, and still no one can compute most of their consequences exactly. Even the predictions of Yukawa's field theory, for example, can't be calculated exactly. We can calculate approximately in electrodynamics only because the coupling is small. We make a series expansion in the coupling constant. When we can't make the series expansion we're too stupid to figure out what the consequences are. That's a sin. It's one of the reasons we are not making much progress.

– Caltech lecture on particles, 1973

One is presumptuous if one says, "We're going to find the ultimate particle, or the unified field laws," or "the" anything. If it turns out surprising, the scientist is even more delighted. You think he's going to say, "Oh, it's not like I expected, there's no ultimate particle, I don't want to explore it?" No, he's going to say, "What the hell is it, then?"

– *Omni* interview, February 1979

The behavior of things on a small scale by quantum mechanics is weird and wonderful and theoretical physicists have always tried to delight the general public with the wonders of the small world.

– "Theory and Applications of Mercereau's Superconducting Circuits," October 1964

The most interesting problems today — and certainly the most practical problems — are obviously in solid-state physics. But someone said there is nothing so practical as a good theory, and the theory of quantum electrodynamics is definitely a good theory!

– *QED: The Strange Theory of Light and Matter*, p. 114

And the best thing to do is to relax and enjoy this: the tiny-ness of us, and the enormity of the rest of the universe. Of course, if you're feeling depressed by that, you can always look at it the other way and think of how big you are compared to the atoms and the parts of atoms, and then you're an enormous universe to those atoms, and then you can sort of stand in the middle and enjoy everything in both ways.

– BBC, "Fun to Imagine" television series, 1983

We may think of two quarks and antiquarks with a sausage around them — but to move the sausage involves field inertia or effective mass proportional to the length of the sausage.

– "Mass Varying with Position," *Physics* 230, 1987 (R. P. Feynman Papers, California Institute of Technology Archives)

The principles of physics, as far as I can see do not speak against the possibility of maneuvering things atom by atom. It is not an attempt to violate any law; it is something in principle that can be done; but in practice, it has not been done because we are too big.

"There's Plenty of Room at the Bottom," December 1959

It is very important to know that light behaves like particles, especially for those of you who have gone to school, where you were probably told something about light behaving like waves. I'm telling you the way it does behave — like particles.

– *QED: The Strange Theory of Light and Matter*, p. 15

There was a time when the newspapers said that only twelve men understood the theory of relativity. I do not believe there ever was such a time. There might have been a time when only one man did, because he was the only guy who caught on, before he wrote his paper. But after people read the paper a lot of people understood the theory of relativity in some way or other, certainly more than twelve. On the other hand, I think I can safely say that nobody understands quantum mechanics.

– *The Character of Physical Law*, p. 129

The theory of quantum electrodynamics describes nature as absurd from the point of view of common sense. And it agrees fully with experiment. So I hope you can accept nature as she is — absurd.

– *QED: The Strange Theory of Light and Matter*, p. 10

Our first experiment to try to understand the proton as a complicated object, like a watch, was to knock two of these watches together at high energy and to look at what kind of gear wheels and so forth came out at what angles. This is the typical hadron-hadron collision, and it involves two unknowns, both the target and the missile.

– Oersted Medal acceptance speech, 1972

We have often made great advances at physics by recognizing that the complexity of things at one level is the result of the fact that these things are composed of simpler elements at another level.

  – "Structure of the Proton," Niels Bohr Medal lecture given in
    Copenhagen, Denmark, October 1973

[On the existence of quarks:] There are, however, a number of theoretical arguments against this idea. So strong are these arguments that at first they seemed to lead to paradoxes. But one by one we were learning how it may be possible to get around these paradoxes. We are perhaps getting the first glimpses of a truly dynamical theory of the hadrons.

  – "Structure of the Proton," Niels Bohr Medal lecture given in
    Copenhagen, Denmark, October 1973

If the experiments continue to confirm the need for quarks in protons then this is the way the theory will apparently develop: Quarks of three colors, so nine in all. And eight kinds of gluons. This part sounds elaborate but is mathematically simple. And a long-range force — which sounds simple but appears mathematically a bit unnatural. Suggestions to explain this long-range force, such as Kauffmann's, all seem a little awkward and not to have an inner beauty we usually expect from truth. But sometimes the truth is discovered first and the beauty or "necessity" of that truth seen only later.

  – "Structure of the Proton," Niels Bohr Medal lecture given in
    Copenhagen, Denmark, October 1973

Beside our eight gluons and nine quarks there would still be the electron, muon, photon, graviton, and two neutrinos, so we would still leave a new proliferation of particles to be analyzed by the next generation. Will they find them all composed of yet simpler elements at yet another level?

– "Structure of the Proton," Niels Bohr Medal lecture given in Copenhagen, Denmark, October 1973

The proton and neutron are only two out of about four hundred known varieties of things. This is a terrible mess, worse than chemistry in Mendeleev's time by about a factor of four or five!

– Caltech lecture on particles, 1973

If the predictions keep on working, then you can keep saying, "Yes, things are not really made out of partons, but they act as if they are made out of partons in this respect, and in that respect, and in that respect." That's what reality is in physics, an idea which fits an even wider class of experiments. In the days when people said things are made out of atoms, there were objections that you could get the same results from thermodynamics. Only the thermodynamics properties were right. In that particular case, as experiments went on and on, the proposition that things were made of atoms turned out to be of a much greater generality and correctness than just thermodynamics.

– Caltech lecture on particles, 1973

There has never been a satisfactory model of reflection of light from thin surfaces or, after that, from any other phenomenon.

Satisfactory in their old fashioned, classical view: a logical hocus-pocus has to be done quantum mechanically in order to describe these things.

– Esalen lecture, "Quantum Mechanical View of Reality (Part 2)," October 1984

The behavior of sub-nuclear systems is so strange compared to the ones the brain evolved to deal with that the analysis has to be very abstract: to understand ice, you have to understand things that are themselves very unlike ice.

– *Omni* interview, February 1979

If they'd explain that this is their best guess but so few of them do; instead, they seize on the possibility that there may not be any ultimate fundamental particle, and say that you should stop work and ponder with great profundity. "You haven't thought deeply enough, first let me define the world for you." Well, I'm going to investigate it without defining it!

– *Omni* interview, February 1979

I've entertained myself always by squeezing the difficulty of quantum mechanics into a smaller and smaller place.

– MIT conference, May 1981

The incompleteness of our present view of quantum electrodynamics should not blind us to the enormous progress that has been made.

– "The Present Situation in Quantum Electrodynamics," Solvay conference, 1961

In turns out that on the microscopic scale, all the laws of physics are exactly reversible: forwards in time, backwards in time — looks the same. But all those phenomena (and there are many of course: life and frying eggs are two examples) that go in one direction only have to be interpreted by the complexity of circumstances, that there are so many particles getting mixed up.

– "QED: Electrons and Their Interactions," Sir Douglas Robb Lectures, University of Auckland, June 1979

So what I'm going to talk about in this lecture is all of physics, really — all of known physics at the moment, plus a lot that's guessed. So the lecture's going to be even more extensive than the ones before because there I was dealing with only two particles, and now I have to deal with two dozen particles!

– "QED: Electrons and Their Interactions," Sir Douglas Robb Lectures, University of Auckland, June 1979

It's lucky we have such a large-scale view of everything that we can see them as things without having to worry about all these little atoms all the time.

– BBC, "Fun to Imagine" television series, 1983

When we were talking about the atoms, one of the troubles that people had with the atoms was that they're so tiny, and it's so hard to imagine the scale. That the size of what the atoms are, compared to an apple, is the same scale as the size of the apple compared to the earth. And that's kind of a hard thing to take. You have to go through these things all the time, and people find these numbers inconceivable. And I do, too!

– BBC, "Fun to Imagine" television series, 1983

[On atoms:] Now, what you do is, you just change your scale. You're just thinking of small balls; you don't try to think of exactly how small they are too often, or you get kind of a bit nutty.

– BBC, "Fun to Imagine" television series, 1983

It was about the beginning of the 1900s that it was discovered that light, as a matter of fact, behaves like particles, which was a terrible shock after great success with the wave theory. And then the problem of trying to see the how particles could make these wave-like phenomena so easily explained by waves became known as the "wave–particle duality." Light behaves like particles on Thursdays and like waves on Tuesdays, and that, of course, is not a satisfactory theory.

– "QED: Fits of Reflection and Transmission," Sir Douglas Robb Lectures, University of Auckland, 1979

I remember being so distinctly impressed by the boldness and novelty of using quantum mechanics to describe such macroscopic things.

– Letter to Dr. Scully, February 1974

If we will only allow that, as we progress, we remain unsure, we will leave opportunities for alternatives. We will not become enthusiastic for the fact, the knowledge, the absolute truth of the day, but remain always uncertain. In order to make progress, one must leave the door to the unknown ajar.

– Galileo Symposium, "What Is and What Should Be the Role of Scientific Culture in Modern Society," September 1964

But the thing that's unusual about good scientists is that they're not so sure of themselves as others usually are. They can live with steady doubt, think "maybe it's so" and act on that, all the time knowing it's only "maybe."

— *Omni* interview, February 1979

Multiply the importance of a problem by your ability to do something about it.

— Notes

The behavior of things in the small scale is so fantastic! It is so wonderfully different! So marvelously different than anything that behaves on a large scale.

— BBC, "Fun to Imagine" television series, 1983

When these new ideas of relativity and quantum mechanics were developed early in this century they appeared so strange that many conservative people hoped they would ultimately be proven wrong, but the last half-century of experiment of ever greater energy, scope and accuracy, have only continued to confirm them.

— "Structure of the Proton," Niels Bohr Medal lecture given in Copenhagen, Denmark, October 1973

I have tried to explain that all the improvements of relativistic theory were at first more or less straightforward, semi-empirical shenanigans. Each time I would discover something, however, I would go back and I would check it so many ways, compare it to every problem that had been done previously in electrodynamics (and later, in weak coupling meson theory) to see if it would always agree, and so on, until I was absolutely convinced of the truth of the various rules and regulations which I concocted to simplify all the work.

– From *Nobel Lectures, Physics 1963–1970*, Elsevier Publishing Company, Amsterdam, 1972

What happens inside will be the same whether that thing is standing still or is coasting along at a uniform speed.

– Audio recording of lecture on relativity, Douglas Advanced Research Laboratory, 1967

I never objected to what other people would immediately have objected to, you know. All the books would say we can't use advanced waves because this would mean effects would precede causes. But things like that never bothered me. I don't give a darn. I never thought in terms of cause and effect necessarily, anything.

– Interview with Charles Weiner, March 5, 1966 (Niels Bohr Library and Archives with the Center for the History of Physics)

[On quantum mechanics:] We can't pretend to understand it since it affronts all our commonsense notions. The best we can do is to describe what happens in mathematics, in equations and that's very difficult. What is even harder is trying to decide what the equations mean. That's the hardest thing of all, but then that is what makes this business of the physics of the nucleus so exciting. That's why I do it. No one can honestly say this is going to lead to practical knowledge. We can't say we're going to get a new source of energy. We do it because it's what we're good at and because it is a great adventure in imagination.

– BBC, "Horizon: The Hunting of the Quark," May 1974

It used to be thought that atoms were small, and that was a limit of measurement, but at the present time, with the new instruments and design during all this time, we've been able to make instruments that can test this theory. Now the distances can be described this way: If the atom is made one hundred kilometers on a side, then we're measuring with one-centimeter accuracy.

– "QED: Photons — Corpuscles of Light," Sir Douglas Robb Lectures, University of Auckland, June 1979

Doing these particle experiments is easy — it's far more difficult to analyze the results what they mean. What could you make of a collision in which two mini cars crashed head on at high speed and produced a Rolls Royce — or two Rolls Royces crashing to make a motor cycle?

– BBC, "Horizon: The Hunting of the Quark," May 1974

# Science and Society

You cannot understand science and its relation to anything unless you understand and appreciate the great adventure of our time. You do not live in your time unless you understand that this is a tremendous adventure and a wild and exciting thing.

– "The Uncertainty of Science," John Danz Lecture Series, 1963

It is necessary to teach both to accept and to reject the past with a kind of balance that takes considerable skill.

    – National Science Teachers Association Fourteenth Convention lecture, "What Is Science?" April 1966

The conclusion from all the researchers is that all people in the world are as dopey as can be and the only way to tell them anything is to perpetually insult their intelligence.

    – "The Unscientific Age," John Danz Lecture Series, 1963

In any decision for action, when you have to make up your mind what to do, there is always a "should" involved, and this cannot be worked out from "If I do this, what will happen?" alone. You say, "Sure, you see what will happen, and then you decide whether you want it to happen or not." But that last stop, the decision whether you want it to happen or not, is the step the scientists cannot help you with.

    "The Uncertainty of Science," John Danz Lecture Series, 1963

I think that to say these are scientific problems is an exaggeration. They are far more humanitarian problems. The fact that how to work the power is clear, but how to control it is not, is something not so scientific and is not something that the scientist knows so much about.

    – "The Uncertainty of Science," John Danz Lecture Series, 1963

I have a large number of uncomfortable feelings about the world.

   – "The Unscientific Age," John Danz Lecture Series, 1963

The attitude of the populace is to try to find the answer instead of trying to find a man who has a way of getting at the answer.

   – "The Unscientific Age," John Danz Lecture Series, 1963

To be prejudiced against mind reading a million to one does not mean that you can never be convinced that a man is a mind reader.

   – "The Unscientific Age," John Danz Lecture Series, 1963

I would like to point out that people are not honest. Scientists are not honest at all, either. It's useless. Nobody's honest. Scientists are not honest. And people usually believe that they are. That makes it worse. By honest I don't mean that you will only tell what's true. But you make clear the entire situation. You make clear all the information that is required for somebody else who is intelligent to make up their mind.

   – "The Unscientific Age," John Danz Lecture Series, 1963

Who are the witch doctors? Psychoanalysts and psychiatrists, of course. If you look at all of the complicated ideas that they have developed in an infinitesimal amount of time, if you compare to any other of the sciences how long it takes to get one idea after the other.

If you consider all the structures and inventions and complicated things, the ids and the egos, the tensions and the forces, and the pushes and the pulls, I tell you they can't all be there. It's too much for one brain or a few brains to have cooked up in such a short time.

— "The Unscientific Age," John Danz Lecture Series, 1963

Newspaper articles and popularization books tend to try to "explain" the latest views in a way that is simplified to be easy to understand, but what is understood then is wrong; sometimes only a little bit wrong but enough to throw you off.

— Letter to student Charles E. Tucker, April 1967

To find the proper place of scientific culture in modern society is not to solve the problems of modern society. There are a large number of problems that have nothing much to do with the position of science in society, and it is a dream to think, if you do think that at all, that to simply decide that one aspect, as to how ideally science and society should be matched, is somehow or other to solve all the problems.

— Galileo Symposium, "What Is and What Should Be the Role of Scientific Culture in Modern Society," September 1964

This world view all of us try from time to time to communicate to our unscientific friends and we get into difficulty most often because we get confused in trying to explain to them the latest questions, such as the meaning of the conservation of CP, whereas they don't know anything about the most preliminary things. For four hundred years since Galileo we have been gathering information about the world which they don't know.

   – Galileo Symposium, "What Is and What Should Be the Role of
      Scientific Culture in Modern Society," September 1964

The great majority of people, the enormous majority of people, are woefully, pitifully, absolutely ignorant of the science of the world they live in, and they can stay that way, I don't mean that, I say to heck with them, what I mean is that they are able to stay that way without it worrying them at all — only mildly — so from time to time when they see CP* mentioned in the newspaper they ask what it is. An interesting question of the relation of science to modern society is just that — why is it possible for people to stay so woefully ignorant and yet reasonably happy in modern society when so much knowledge is missing to them?

   – Galileo Symposium, "What Is and What Should Be the Role of
      Scientific Culture in Modern Society," September 1964

As I'd like to show Galileo our world, I must show him something with a great deal of shame. If we look away from the science and look at the world around us we find out something rather pitiful.

---

*CP stands for charge parity. Physicists once believed that the laws of physics for a particle and an antiparticle are the same as long as you make the particles symmetrical with respect to position, but this belief was found to be incorrect by James Cronin and Val Fitch in 1964, leading to the pair's winning the 1980 Nobel Prize in Physics.

That the environment that we live in is so actively, intensely unscientific.

– Galileo Symposium, "What Is and What Should Be the Role of Scientific Culture in Modern Society," September 1964

I believe that the science has remained irrelevant because we wait until somebody asks us questions or until we are invited to give a speech on Einstein's theory to people who don't understand Newtonian mechanics, but we never are invited to give an attack on faith-healing or on astrology on what is the scientific view of astrology today.

– Galileo Symposium, "What Is and What Should Be the Role of Scientific Culture in Modern Society," September 1964

I believe that we should demand that people try in their own minds to obtain for themselves a more consistent picture of their own world, that they not permit themselves in the luxury of having their brain cut in four pieces or two pieces even, and on one side they believe this and on the other side they believe that, but never try to compare the two points of view. Because we have learned that, by trying to put the points of view that we have in our head together and comparing one to the other, we make some progress in understanding and in appreciating where we are and what we are.

– Galileo Symposium, "What Is and What Should Be the Role of Scientific Culture in Modern Society," September 1964

I think we live in an unscientific age in which almost all the buffeting of communications and television words, books, and so on are unscientific. That doesn't mean they are bad, but unscientific. As a result, there is a considerable amount of intellectual tyrant in the name of science.

  – National Science Teachers Association Fourteenth Convention
    lecture, "What Is Science?" April 1966

People think that experts know what they are doing. But most experts, whether in the stock market, education, sociology, or some parts of psychology, don't know more than the average person. They do studies, follow certain methods, and have results.

  – *U.S. News and World Report* interview, February 1985

Publicity is an evil thing — once it starts to work — its practitioners don't know when to stop and it gets bigger and bigger.

  – Letter to Jeanne Henry, July 1974

Although you say, "I'd love to get all the publicity we can stand," I personally cannot stand publicity and my wish would be the exact opposite. I'd love no publicity at all. We will both have to compromise a bit.

  – Letter to Jeanne Henry, July 1974

There seems to be some interest in the world about how it is, how it feels and so on to do physics and so on. And various psychologists are always breathing down our neck to discover the mode, how creativity works.

  – CERN talk, December 1965

I read your article very carefully, and I must say that the *Pakistan Observer* contained one of the best and clearest articles about what we did to win the Nobel Prize. All the big newspapers and news systems really do not carry anything like an attempt of the truth or explanation of the real situation. It takes a local paper and a man who really understands what things are about, to create a serious and sensible article that is not just full of pleasantries and trivia.

– Letter to Dr. A. M. Harun-ar Rashid, November 1965

It is unfair to use me to promote your own company.

– Letter to Jeanne Henry, July 1974

One of the ways of stopping science would be only to do experiments in the region where you know the law.

– *The Character of Physical Law*, p. 158

Right or wrong, I got the idea that the traditions of science are not — they're fragile. The traditions of scientific thought, I don't believe they're fragile. I think they're very fragile, and easily lost, and that science really has a value. The viewpoint that's involved, the objectivity, the way of doing things is valuable, see? So I thought it was of value, and that it might be destroyed. It could be destroyed because maybe people without this tradition would be the only ones left that would have any power.

– Interview with Charles Weiner, June 27, 1966 (Niels Bohr Library and Archives with the Center for the History of Physics)

People have this feeling that scientists know more about this than they do. It is not true. It's like the Wizard of Oz. You look behind and you see he's an ordinary fellow like you are.

> – Interview with Charles Weiner, June 28, 1966 (Niels Bohr Library and Archives with the Center for the History of Physics)

If success resulted from using such a scientific attitude, a country might be encouraged to go on and develop a re-interest in the problems of science itself.

> – MIT centennial, "Talk of Our Times," December 1961

I find that the lures that are put out in industry often exceed the reality.

> – Interview with Charles Weiner, March 5, 1966 (Niels Bohr Library and Archives with the Center for the History of Physics)

Is science of any value? I think a power to do something is of value. Whether the result is a good thing or a bad thing depends on how it is used, but the power is a value.

> – "The Uncertainty of Science," John Danz Lecture Series, 1963

# Mathematics

I wish you ladies and gentleman out there knew some of this mathematics. It's not just the logic and accuracy of it all you're missing — it's the poetry too.

– BBC interview, "A Novel Force in Nature"

Take this neat little equation here. It tells me all the ways an electron can make itself comfortable in or around an atom. That's the logic of it. The poetry of it is that the equation tells me how shiny gold is, how come rocks are hard, what makes grass green, and why you can't see the wind. And a million other things besides, about the way nature works.

 – BBC interview on the gauge theories, "A Novel Force in Nature"

It's not an accidental large number, like the large number which is the ratio of the volume of the earth to the volume of a flea.

 – Audio recording of Feynman Lectures on Physics, Lecture 7, October 17, 1961

A vector is like a push that has a certain direction, or a speed that has a certain direction, or a movement that has a certain direction — and it's represented on a piece of paper by an arrow in the direction of the thing.

 – *Feynman's Tips on Physics*, p. 23

You know, it's not true that what is called "abstruse" math is so difficult. Take something like computer programming, and the careful logic needed for that — the kind of thinking that mama and papa would have said was only for professors. Well, now it's part of a lot of daily activities, it's a way to make a living; their children get interested and get hold of a computer and they're doing the most crazy, wonderful things!

— *Omni* interview, February 1979

But you see, from the beginning I was disconnected. I was trying to find a formula for adding the integers together because I wanted the formula. I didn't care; it didn't mean anything to me, that this was worked out by the Greeks or even by the Babylonians in 2000 BC. This didn't interest me at all. It was my problem and I had fun out of it, you see. It was always that way. I was always playing my own independent game.

— Interview with Charles Weiner, March 4, 1966 (Niels Bohr Library and Archives with the Center for the History of Physics)

To those who do not know mathematics it is difficult to get across a real feeling as to the beauty, the deepest beauty, of nature. C. P. Snow talked about two cultures. I really think that those two cultures separate people who have and people who have not had this experience of understanding mathematics well enough to appreciate nature once.

— *The Character of Physical Law*, p. 58

Errors in algebra, differentiation, and integration are only nonsense; they're things that just annoy the physics, and annoy your mind while you're trying to analyze something. You should be able to do calculations as quickly as possible, and with a minimum of errors. That requires nothing but rote practice — that's the only way to do it.

– *Feynman's Tips on Physics*, p. 19

It is remarkable, but at this time it is possible to say that there is no experimental discrepancy at all between the physics theories anywhere and the results of the experiment. That doesn't mean we can compute everything. The rules of the game by which we make the computation are underneath everything. That's the way nature works. It's simple.

– "QED: Photons — Corpuscles of Light," Sir Douglas Robb Lectures, University of Auckland, June 1979

Now the idea is this: We want to see the momentum distribution of the partons inside. Imagine a swarm of bees coming toward you. Suppose you scatter radar from the swarm. The different bees would have different velocities, and when you scattered radar from them, you'd see a distribution of frequencies scattered from a monochromatic radio wave by a moving bunch of bees, you can get the distribution momentum of the bees inside the swarm.

– Caltech lecture on particles, 1973

Mathematics is a language plus reasoning; it is like a language plus logic. Mathematics is a tool for reasoning.

– *The Character of Physical Law*, p. 40

Euclid said, "There is no royal road to geometry." And there is no royal road. Physicists cannot make a conversation to any other language. If you want to learn about nature, to appreciate nature, it is necessary to understand the language that she speaks in. She offers her information in only one form; we are not so unhumble as to demand that she change before we pay attention.

  – *The Character of Physical Law*, p. 58

So I got more and more interested in the mathematical business associated with physics. In addition, mathematics itself had a great appeal for me. I loved it all my life.

  – Furture for Science interview

To use mathematics successfully one must have a certain attitude of mind — to know that there are many ways to look at any problem and at any subject.

  – "New Mathematics," written for the California State Department of Education, 1965

You need an answer for a certain problem: the question is how to get it. The successful user of mathematics is practically an inventor of new ways of obtaining answers in given situations.

  – "New Mathematics," written for the California State Department of Education, 1965

What is the best method to obtain the solution to a problem? The answer is, any way that works.

  – "New Mathematics," written for the California State Department of Education, 1965

Mathematics is not a science from my point of view, in the sense that it's not a natural science. It's an unnatural science, perhaps.

– Audio recording of Feynman Lectures on Physics, Lecture 3, October 3, 1961

The final result of taking the limits is written still another way, as $\frac{ds}{dt}$. Now, it gets even more abstract. These ds are again not to be divided out. And if I tell you to call them an eensy weensy bit of time and distance, the mathematicians will get very angry at me. But it works fine. You can use it. If you imagine that these two are smaller than anything at all, then you've got the right idea.

– Audio recording of Feynman Lectures on Physics, Lecture 8, October 20, 1961

Now you're doing calculus. That's high-class calculus. Differentiating things. Nothing to it.

– Audio recording of Feynman Lectures on Physics, Lecture 8, October 20, 1961

You can work out your own table of integrals by differentiating until you're green around the gills, and you'll find for every formula with a differential, you've got an integral formula if you turn it around.

– Audio recording of Feynman Lectures on Physics, Lecture 8, October 20, 1961

Unlike the case of mathematics in which everything can be defined and then you don't know what you're talking about — in fact, the glory of mathematics is that you don't know what you're talking about. The glory is that the laws, the arguments, and the logic are independent of what it is.

– Audio recording of Feynman Lectures on Physics, Lecture 12,
   November 7, 1961

I never get my signs right — you may not either, but at the end you can figure it out.

– Audio recording of Feynman Lectures on Physics, Lecture 13,
   November 10, 1961

I'm always checking things while I calculate because I make so many mistakes. One way to check it is to do the mathematics very carefully; the other way to check it is to keep seeing whether the numbers that come out are sensible, whether they describe what's really happening.

– *Feynman's Tips on Physics*, p. 63

The apparent ease with which I do this is false: I swear I did it more than once before I got it right!

– *Feynman's Tips on Physics*, p. 62

Remember, whenever you're stuck in a mathematical analysis, you can always do it by arithmetic!

– *Feynman's Tips on Physics*, p. 82

I knew that one of the great problems of geometry was trisecting an angle. So the heck with learning all these little bits and pieces, we would go ahead and do the big problem, you see! That's a way to learn, though — I'm telling you.

- Interview with Charles Weiner, March 4, 1966 (Niels Bohr Library and Archives with the Center for the History of Physics)

It wasn't anything brilliant, it's just that I was facile at mathematics, mathematical manipulating like a guy that's good at doing arithmetic fast in his head. That kind of stuff. It's very useful to be able to do.

- Interview with Charles Weiner, March 5, 1966 (Niels Bohr Library and Archives with the Center for the History of Physics)

The only thing I could think of was, this stuff was good to teach somebody else, but it wasn't good itself. I still have that feeling about mathematics.

- Interview with Charles Weiner, March 5, 1966 (Niels Bohr Library and Archives with the Center for the History of Physics)

I can't gamble. I understand the mathematics of the odds. I believe firmly that the games are presumably fair. They're honest. If they're honest, there's no game to it, because it's just a question of how the dice go, and it isn't interesting to me. It's just accident.

- Interview with Charles Weiner, June 27, 1966 (Niels Bohr Library and Archives with the Center for the History of Physics)

I don't know why number theory does not find application in physics. We seem to need instead the mathematics of functions of continuous variables, complex numbers, and abstract algebra.

- Letter to Mr. Robert Boeninger, May 1969

I cannot understand mathematics very well as I have told you, and must have physical examples, but that is just the way my mind works.

   – Letter to Bert and Mulaika Corben, 1948

Thinking I understand geometry and wanting to cut a piece of wood to fit the diagonal of a five-foot square, I try to figure out how long it must be. Not being very expert, I get infinity — useless nor does it help to say it may be zero because they are both circles. It is not philosophy we are after, but the behavior of real things. So in despair, I measure it directly — lo, it is near to seven feet — neither infinity nor zero. So, we have measured these things for which our theory gives us numbers close to what we measure. We are seeking the formula that gives the square root of fifty.

   – Letter to Barbara Kyle, October 1965 (*Perfectly Reasonable Deviations from the Beaten Track*, p. 152)

I am not interested in what today's mathematicians find interesting.

   – Letter to Dr. John A. Wheeler, May 1966

Set theory is used sometimes, but not very often, in practical matters. Its greatest uses and beauty appears in the study of the logical foundations of mathematics.

   – Letter to Alexander Calandra, September 1965

A pure mathematician is very impractical — he is not interested (in fact, he is purposely disinterested) in the meaning of the mathematical symbols and letters and ideas, but is only interested in logical interconnection of the axioms, while the user of mathematics has to understand the connection of mathematics to the real world.

– "New Mathematics," written for the California State Department
of Education, 1965

The successful user of mathematics is practically an inventor of new ways of obtaining answers in given situations.

– "New Mathematics," written for the California State Department
of Education, 1965

There are many ways of doing a problem but, unfortunately, there also are definite known fixed ways of doing the problems. What we have been doing in the past is teaching just one fixed way to do arithmetic problems instead of teaching the flexibility of mind; that is, the various possible ways of writing down a problem, the possible ways of thinking about it, and the possible ways of getting at the problem.

– "New Mathematics," written for the California State Department
of Education, 1965

In order to use mathematics one must have a deeper understanding of the relation of mathematical objects to real things and this deeper understanding is opposed to a tendency to try to make all of the different kinds of mathematical applications represent the same thing.

– "New Mathematics," written for the California State Department
of Education, 1965

Strictly and technically, if it be known, the theory of the fundaments of mathematics is not in a completely satisfactory state and involves some very great complications.

– "New Mathematics," written for the California State Department of Education, 1965

I might, perhaps, mention why some attention is paid to different base systems besides base 10. The point is only to increase again mathematical experience. To make clear to children that the base 10 is an accident of human history and that there is nothing special about the number 10.

– "New Mathematics," written for the California State Department of Education, 1965

If I were giving a talk on mathematics, I would have already answered you. Mathematics is looking for patterns.

– National Science Teachers Association Fourteenth Convention lecture, "What Is Science?" April 1966

So he knew all his arithmetic, and he was very good at it, and that was a challenge to me. I kept practicing. We used to have a little contest. Every time we'd have to calculate anything, we'd race to the answer, he and I, and I would lose. After several years I began to get in there once in a while, maybe one out of four. You have to notice the numbers, you see — and each of us would notice a different way. We had lots of fun.

– On his experience with the Manhattan Project, "Los Alamos from Below," 1976

Of course you'd notice something funny about a number like if you have to multiple 174 by 140, for example. You notice that 173 by 141 is like the square root of 3, times the square root of 2, which is the square root of 6, which is 245. But you have to notice the numbers, you see, and each guy would notice a different way — we had lots of fun.

– UCSB talk, "Los Alamos from Below," February 1975

There were these high priests that could predict Venus, and the normal men, who you will imagine said, said, "God, how do they do this? This is marvelous, it frightens me, I can't learn arithmetic, this is impossible," and so forth. Now if there had been in those days an attempt at pedagogy, in other words, the priests trying to explain to the laymen what they were doing, they could explain they were only counting or doing the equivalent of counting.

– Esalen lecture, "Quantum Mechanical View of Reality (Part 2)," October 1984

I will show you how to make these calculations as if you were taking beans out of pots!

– Esalen lecture, "Quantum Mechanical View of Reality (Part 2)," October 1984

I think we've understood all we can from that point of view; what we've found in this century is different enough, obscure enough, that further progress will require a lot of math.

– *Omni* interview, February 1979

I don't believe in the idea that there are a few peculiar people capable of understanding math, and the rest of the world is normal. Math is a human discovery, and it's no more complicated than humans can understand.

– *Omni* interview, February 1979

Math is just a language.

– In personal notes

Math may permit wildly different apparent starting points.

– In personal notes

The rules of algebra are things studied by mathematicians, and mathematicians have tried to find all the objects you could possibly find which obey those rules! The rules were originally made for counting apples; it was improved by using negative numbers; it was improved still further by inventing fractions.

– "QED: Fits of Reflection and Transmission," Sir Douglas Robb
   Lectures, University of Auckland, 1979

[On complex numbers:] It's interesting that mathematicians all this mathematics for these crazy numbers without having anything to directly apply it to in physics and that it should turn out to be so fundamental to the bottom laws of physics using such funny numbers.

– "QED: Fits of Reflection and Transmission," Sir Douglas Robb
   Lectures, University of Auckland, 1979

We have, today, become very sophisticated. In the early days, when mathematics was first developing and it was said that a number is something like when you count the number of apples or people or something like that, then the idea of half of a person was somewhat of a problem. But nowadays there's no difficulty at all, and nobody has any moral or discomforting, gory feelings when they hear there are 3.2 people per square mile in a certain region.

– "QED: Fits of Reflection and Transmission," Sir Douglas Robb Lectures, University of Auckland, 1979

You'd be surprised how many numbers you could make by playing with pi's and 2s and 5s and so on, and if you haven't got anything to guide you except the answer, you can make it come out to even several decimal places by suitable jiggling about. It's surprising how close you can make an arbitrary number by playing around with nice numbers like pi.

– "QED: New Queries," Sir Douglas Robb Lectures, University of Auckland, 1979

Now, you say, is that the correct way to do it? There is no such thing! There is no "correct" way to do anything. A particular way of doing it may be correct, but it is not the correct way.

– *Feynman's Tips on Physics*, p. 58

On looking back over the work, I can only feel a kind of regret for the enormous amount of physical reasoning and mathematically re-expression which ends by merely re-expressing what was previously known, although in a form which is much more efficient for the calculation of specific problems. Would it not have been much easier to simply work entirely in the mathematical framework to elaborate a more efficient expression? This would certainly seem to be the case, but it must be remarked that although the problem actually solved was only such a reformulation, the problem originally tackled was the (possibly still unsolved) problem of avoidance of the infinities of the usual theory. Therefore, a new theory was sought, not just a modification of the old. Although the quest was unsuccessful, we should look at the question of the value of physical ideas in developing a new theory.

   – From *Nobel Lectures, Physics 1963–1970*, Elsevier Publishing
     Company, Amsterdam, 1972


When I was in high school, we had an algebra team, and I was on the algebra team. It was a crazy thing, where we'd meet together with another school, and they'd open from an envelope problems that somebody invented somewhere, and they'd announce, "This problem is 45 seconds," or maybe "two and a half minutes," and they would write it on the board. You had 15 seconds to think and then you'd work like a demon, and you'd put a circle around your answer. It didn't make any difference how you got the answer. This is what I loved. I used to practice, to do this, and I would get very, very fast. The ability to do algebra fast, which later became the ability to do calculus fast, always stood me in good stead.

   – Interview with Charles Weiner, March 5, 1966 (Niels Bohr
     Library and Archives with the Center for the History of Physics)

It seems to me if you say $2x = 32$, I know what it means. $x$ always represents some number, so if the number happens to be up there as an exponent, does it make any difference? I mean, we knew about exponents. Does it make any difference the problem?

> – Interview with Charles Weiner, March 4, 1966 (Niels Bohr
> Library and Archives with the Center for the History of Physics)

When I was at MIT, I would read books on fields that I didn't know, like general relativity and so on — or even in the encyclopedia, when I'd pull stuff out of the article — I seemed to have a sense to pull, in electrostatics, a lot of stuff, but when it went to the calculation of the capacitance of an elliptical condenser, which was quite complicated, it didn't bother me that I didn't understand it. I knew that was not so interesting as the general theorems about the laws of the inverse square, and, you know, I had some way of knowing what was important and what was not.

> – Interview with Charles Weiner, March 4, 1966 (Niels Bohr
> Library and Archives with the Center for the History of Physics)

My father taught me about pi before I had learned in the school the decimals for fractions, and explained decimals. See, I was really ahead in arithmetic. I remember him telling me about pi as a great and marvelous mystery. Everything was always dramatic — that all circles have the same ratio of the distance around to the distance across, and that this number, this strange number, is of very great significance, and is a marvelous number. So pi was like in gold letters, you see.

> – Interview with Charles Weiner, March 4, 1966 (Niels Bohr
> Library and Archives with the Center for the History of Physics)

Pure mathematics is just such an abstraction from the real world, and pure mathematics does have a special precise language for dealing with its own special and technical subjects. But this precise language is not precise in any sense if you deal with real objects of the world, and it is only pedantic and quite confusing to use it unless there are some special subtleties which have to be carefully distinguished.

– "New Mathematics," written for the California State Department of Education

# Technology

There is a computer disease that anybody who works with computers knows about. It's a very serious disease and it interferes completely with the work. The trouble with computers is that you "play" with them!

— *Surely You're Joking, Mr. Feynman!*, p. 127

The right answer must be determined by experiment, and pure speculation has no place — but not being able to experiment I could not keep my mind from wandering on the plane. So I should like to report on my pure speculations just for fun, not in the sense that I think these things are necessarily so, but only for the fun of thinking how exciting it might be.

– Letter Edwin H. Land (Polaroid Corporation), May 1966
(*Perfectly Reasonable Deviations from the Beaten Track*, p. 221)

Computers, however, can't yet "catch on" to what is being said, the way a person does. They need to be told in excruciating detail exactly what to do. Perhaps one day we will have machines that can cope with approximate task descriptions, but in the meantime we have to be very prissy about how we tell computers to do things.

– *Feynman Lectures on Computation*, p. 3

[On quantum computers:] What we really need to worry about is not the absolute energy, but the energy that's lost — that is, the free energy that produces chaos or irregularities. This concern is just like what somebody said to me about my atomic computer. You've estimated the energy, he said, but you've forgotten how much energy it takes to manufacture the computer. Well fine. Let's say that's the $mc^2$ of all the atoms. But when I'm done computing after 100 years, I'm going to get that energy back again.

– "Tiny Computers Obeying Quantum Mechanical Laws," *New Directions in Physics: The Los Alamos 40th Anniversary Volume*, 1987

I want to talk about the possibility that there is to be an exact simulation, that the computer will do exactly the same as nature. If this is to be proved and the type of computer is already explained, then it's going to be necessary that everything that happens in a finite volume of space and time would have to be exactly analyzable with a finite number of logical operations.

– "Simulating Physics with Computers," *International Journal of Theoretical Physics*, May 1981

The discovery of computers and the thinking of computers have turned out to be extremely useful in many branches of human reasoning. For instance, we never really understood how lousy our understanding of language was, the theory of grammar, and all that stuff, until we tried to make a computer work which would be able to understand language.

– MIT conference, May 1981

[On the *Challenger* explosion:] The fact that this danger did not lead to catastrophe before is no guarantee it will not the next time, unless it is completely understood.

– "Feynman Takes NASA to Task," *Pasadena Star-News*, June 11, 1986

A computer is a high-class, super-speed, nice, streamlined filing clerk.

– Esalen lecture, "Computers from the Inside Out," October 1984

It is always better to make the machines smaller, and the question is how much smaller is it still possible to make machines according to the laws of Nature, in principle. I will not discuss which and what of these things will actually appear in the future. That depends on economic problems and social problems, and I am not going to try to guess at those.

– "The Computing Machines in the Future," Nishina Memorial
  Lecture, August 1985

The idea of the telescope is to focus the light from a bigger area into a smaller area, so we can see things that are weaker, less light.

– BBC, "Fun to Imagine" television series, 1983

Good machining is essential to building good apparatus for the precise and careful measurements required in physics to discover Nature's Laws.

– Letter to Raymond Rogers, January 1966 (*Perfectly Reasonable
  Deviations from the Beaten Track*, p. 208)

There is a great deal of work to try to develop smarter machines, machines which have a better relationship with the humans so that input and output can be made with less effort than the complex programming that's necessary today. This goes under the name of artificial intelligence, but I don't like that name.

Perhaps the unintelligent machines can do even better than the intelligent ones.

– "The Computing Machines in the Future," Nishina Memorial
  Lecture, August 1985

I mentioned something about the possibility of time — of things being affected not just by the past but also by the future, and therefore that our probabilities are in some sense "illusionary." We have only the information from the past, and we try to predict the next step, but in reality it depends on the near future, which we can't get at, or something like that.

– MIT conference, May 1981

For fun again and intellectual pleasure, we could imagine machines tiny like few microns across wheels and cables all interconnected by wires, silicon connections, so that the thing as a whole, a very large device, moves not like the awkward motions of our present stiff machines but in a smooth way of the neck of a swan, which after all is a lot of little machines, the cells all interconnected and all controlled in a smooth way. Why can't we do that ourselves?

– "The Computing Machines in the Future," Nishina Memorial
  Lecture, August 1985

[On investigating the *Challenger* explosion:] The main thing I learned at that meeting was how inefficient a public inquiry is: Most of the time, other people are asking questions you already know the answer to — or are not interested in — and you get so fogged out that you're hardly listening when important points are being passed over.

– "Feynman: Frustrated by the Slow Pace of Probe," *Pasadena Star-News*, January 29, 1989

It is not necessary to understand the way birds flap their wings and how the feathers are designed in order to make a flying machine. It is not necessary to understand the lever system in the legs of a cheetah, that is, an animal that runs fast, in order to make an automobile with wheels that go very fast. It is, therefore, not necessary to imitate the behavior of Nature in detail in order to engineer a device which can in many respects surpass Nature's abilities.

– "The Computing Machines in the Future," Nishina Memorial Lecture, August 1985

Have you ever asked yourself what you are made of? If you answer, flesh and bones, then I'll ask what they're made of — you'll say molecules, proteins, perhaps even DNA. What are those molecules made of — atoms: We are all a pile of atoms.

– BBC, "Horizon: The Hunting of the Quark," May 1974

# War

There is a responsibility for all of us for the way the world has come out, but we didn't have enough sense to think of a way of avoiding it.

– "900 at Caltech, JPL Declare Support for Nuclear Arms Freeze," *The Los Angeles Times*, October 16, 1982

People said, "Don't you feel guilty?" afterwards. No, because at that moment is when I did my thinking of the seriousness of the situation in the world, of the possibilities of making a bomb, of the dangers that would result if the other side were to have done it if we didn't, and it seemed to me absolutely clear that we must really make an effort to save the world from the other possibility. It's true, it turned out later that they weren't doing very well, but there was no way at the time to know, because it was possible. We showed it was possible. It was not impossible, therefore, that they would do it, and if they did, that would be terrible.

- Interview with Charles Weiner, March 5, 1966 (Niels Bohr Library and Archives with the Center for the History of Physics)

On the other hand, as a possibility of a large release of power, now it's often said that science makes the bomb. It isn't. It's engineering which makes the bomb. The reason to make the bomb was a military reason during the war. It's true that scientists worked on it, but they weren't working on science, they were being engineers during the war. They were taken away from the laboratories in order to do this.

- Interview for Viewpoint

A further result of the calamity of war might be a universal antagonism toward physics, as a result of the destruction which people might blame the scientists for having made possible.

– MIT centennial, "Talk of Our Times," December 1961

I would like an opportunity to describe, instead of the horror of the things I helped to make, rather some of the hopes and values also created which might arise if the war problem could be solved.

– Notes on the atom bomb

The practical attainment during the war of the transmutation of the elements and the release of subatomic energy has once again emphasized that the discoveries of science are never good or bad in themselves. It is a question of what use we make of the discoveries. Science gives us power. We can utilize it either to further good or to further evil. And the release of nuclear energy is the release of a most tremendous power. It is potentially of extreme value, or as we have seen, is capable of unprecedented destruction.

– Notes from Los Alamos

A discussion of the future of atomic energy is a discussion of the problems arising in making the choices.

– Notes from Los Alamos

Because knowledge can be applied to war and war is bad is no reason to seek to stop war by suppressing knowledge. Even if we kept science going here and not leaking out, we couldn't prevent its advance in other hands. We sit, others act.

– Notes from Los Alamos

Most bitter debate centers around control of information, development of military weapons and research into new knowledge.

– Notes from Los Alamos

Problem is science gives power for good or evil. We are concerned it may be used for evil. Monopolization by the military does not strike any sane man that the choice is to develop the good ends — but is forcing science to develop in just those directions in which it can be made most destructive.

– Notes from Los Alamos

Scientists discovered energy locked in atoms and dreamed of the age of its release. The great atomic age was ushered in in a mathematic and horrible fashion. The greatest problem by all odds is that of war and peace.

– Notes

I don't know myself whether I am for nuclear testing or against nuclear testing. There are reasons on both sides. It makes radioactivity, and it's dangerous, and it's also very bad to have a war. But whether it's going to be more likely to have a war because you test, I don't know. Whether preparation will stop the war, or lack of preparation, I don't know.

– "The Unscientific Age," John Danz Lecture Series, 1963

All the equipment from different research was being put together to make the new apparatus to do the experiment to try to separate the isotopes of uranium.

– UCSB talk, "Los Alamos from Below," February 1975

Bomb has great danger — war — any nation can and will develop atomic power.

– Notes from before Los Alamos

It is the lesson of the last war not to think of people as having special inherited attributes simply because they are born from particular parents, but to try to teach these "valuable" elements to all men because all men can learn, no matter what their race.

– Letter to Tina Levitan, February 1967 (*Perfectly Reasonable Deviations from the Beaten Track*, p. 235)

Although in my field at the present time I'm a slightly famous man, at the time I was not anybody famous at all. I did not even have a degree when I started to work on my stuff associated with the Manhattan Project.

– UCSB talk, "Los Alamos from Below," February 1975

All the science stopped during the war except the little bit that was done in Los Alamos.

– UCSB talk, "Los Alamos from Below," February 1975

All the things they'd thought of in Berkeley about the atomic bomb, and nuclear physics and all these things, and I didn't know very much about it. I had been doing other kinds of things. And so I had to do an awful lot of work.

– UCSB talk, "Los Alamos from Below," February 1975

I never traveled on an airplane before; I traveled on an airplane. They strapped the secrets, with a little thing with a belt on my back!

– UCSB talk, "Los Alamos from Below," February 1975

I have a great deal of respect for these military guys because I never can decide anything very important in any length of time at all.

– UCSB talk, "Los Alamos from Below," February 1975

We always were in a hurry. I have to explain that everything we did, we tried to do as quickly as possible.

– UCSB talk, "Los Alamos from Below," February 1975

I told them what we were doing, and they were all excited. We're fighting a war. We see what it is. They knew what the numbers meant. If the pressure came out higher that meant there was more energy released and so on and so on. They knew what they were doing.

– UCSB talk, "Los Alamos from Below," February 1975

I'd sit in a restaurant in New York, for example, and looked at the buildings and how far away, I would think, you know, how much the radius of the Hiroshima bomb damage was and so forth. How far down there was down to 34th Street. All those buildings, all smashed and so on. And I got a very strange feeling. I would go along and I would see people building a bridge. Or they'd be making a new road, and I thought, they're crazy, they just don't understand, they don't understand. Why are they making new things, it's so useless?

– UCSB talk, "Los Alamos from Below," February 1975

The attitude is that this business about how you open safes is not something that everybody should know because it makes everything very unsafe, it's very dangerous to have everybody know how to do this.

– UCSB talk, "Los Alamos from Below," February 1975

I worked on the Los Alamos project during World War II. After the first successful test there was tremendous excitement. Everyone had parties; we all ran around. I sat on the end of a jeep and beat drums. One man, Bob Wilson, was just sitting there and moping. When I asked him why, he said, "It's a terrible thing that we made."

– *U.S. News and World Report* interview, February 1985

[On the atomic bomb:] Maybe, by some miracle, those who have the responsibility to control this thing will begin to realize — or maybe already realize — its uselessness. In that case, the bomb may turn out to have been useful in stopping us from the age-old historical exercise of destroying each other.

  – *U.S. News and World Report* interview, February 1985

[On the Los Alamos project:] Suppose scientists hadn't gone ahead and, instead, had said, "It will be such a serious problem for humankind later that we don't think that we should do it." What a scream there would have been if Hitler and his crew had managed to make the bomb and used it to dominate the world.

  – *U.S. News and World Report* interview, February 1985

It's very annoying to have everybody ask you for an opinion, and you're supposed to be wise all of a sudden, and I know I'm not wise all of a sudden.

  – "The Remarkable Dr. Feynman," *Los Angeles Times Magazine*,
    April 20, 1986, p. 37

I made the decision to work on the Manhattan Project at the beginning of the war because I thought the Germans would do it. I don't know whether that was the right decision.

  – "The Remarkable Dr. Feynman," *Los Angeles Times Magazine*,
    April 20, 1986

From a scientific point of view, the Manhattan Project was not what I would have ordinarily wanted to do; it was engineering more than science. It was very exciting to meet all the great men and smart characters that you read about. It's a similar response I have to the commission. I wouldn't have wanted to do the commission aside from the feeling of duty, but once I decide that I'm stuck and I've got to do it, then I've got to work hard. But if you gave me half a chance, I'd quit. It's exciting, once you're stuck in it. It's like asking somebody who is almost having an automobile accident whether it's exciting. You're damn tootin' it's fun trying to steer between the cars, isn't it? Only he'd rather not have to do that.

  – "The Remarkable Dr. Feynman," *Los Angeles Times Magazine*,
     April 20, 1986, p. 37

[Opposing bilateral nuclear arms freeze:] [Reagan is one of the] experts, especially in government, who don't know what they're doing.

  – Quoted in *Star-News*, October 16, 1982

The terror and danger of the atomic bomb has been told over many times.

  – Notes

The atomic bomb is essentially just a very big bomb 1000 times more energetic than the biggest block buster.

  – Notes

A nation will very soon be able to declare the death sentence to half the population of any other nation and within the day carry out the execution.

– Notes

Slight hope that it might be blessing in horrible disguise by bringing the lukewarm idealism toward cooperation between people into the reality born of necessity

– Notes

It has always been clear that cooperation was very desirable.

– Notes

The slight hope that the horror of the atomic bomb could possibly finally convince mankind the folly of division.

– Notes

[On the Los Alamos project:] What happened to me — what happened to the rest of us — is we started for a good reason, then you're working very hard to accomplish something, and it's pleasure, it's excitement. And you stop thinking, you know; you just stop.

– "The Feynman Legend," *The Los Angeles Times*, February 17, 1988

This same business with the bomb and this pessimism kept with me for several years and, by 1950, I still was pessimistic about the world and was pretty sure that I had it right, that nobody was getting anywhere and we were all going around in circles and that we were going to have trouble. Then when we'd have trouble with Russia and so on, we'd bomb each other out, and the Northern Hemisphere would be in a bad way.

– Interview with Charles Weiner, June 27, 1966 (Niels Bohr Library and Archives with the Center for the History of Physics)

[On the nuclear bomb:] As far as I know — maybe other people don't agree — there was in my experience no serious difficulty produced because information was maintained as secret that was essential to a more or less fundamental understanding, or was kept secret too long. There were important things which were released gradually — but in time, so to speak.

– Interview with Charles Weiner, June 27, 1966 (Niels Bohr Library and Archives with the Center for the History of Physics)

We scientists are clever — too clever — are you not satisfied? Is four square miles in one bomb not enough? Men are still thinking. Just tell us how big you want it!

– Notes

And that's one thing I did learn, that if you have some reason for doing something that's very strong and you start working on it, you must look around every once in a while and find out if the original motives are still right.

– Future for Science interview

# *Challenger*

RICHARD FEYNMAN

Nothing short of a subpoena from Congress will get me to Washington again.

– Letter to David Acheson, 1986 (*Perfectly Reasonable Deviations from the Beaten Track*, p. 405)

When using a mathematical model, careful attention must be given to uncertainties in the model.

- *Star-News*, Opinion, June 18, 1986

[On the Rogers Commission:] I feel like a bull in a china shop. The best thing is to put the bull out to work the plow. A better metaphor will be an ox in a china shop, because the china is the bull, of course.

- Letter to Gweneth and Michelle Feynman, February 12, 1986 (*Perfectly Reasonable Deviations from the Beaten Track*, p. 402)

If in this way the government would not support them, then so be it.

- Report of the Presidential Commission on the Space Shuttle *Challenger* Accident, Volume 2: Appendix F, June 1986

NASA owes it to the citizens from whom it asks support to be frank, honest, and informative, so that these citizens can make the wisest decisions for the use of their limited resources.

- Report of the Presidential Commission on the Space Shuttle *Challenger* Accident, Volume 2: Appendix F, June 1986

[On the Rogers Commission:] I'm a little disturbed that I felt a sense of duty.

   – "The Remarkable Dr. Feynman," *Los Angeles Times Magazine*,
      April 20, 1986


[On the Rogers Commission:] During the discussion earlier there are various pious remarks about how we as individuals, or better, small groups (called subcommittees), can go anywhere we want to get info. I try to propose I do that (and several physicists tell me they would like to go with me) and I have set my affairs so I can work intensively full time for a while. I can't seem to get an assignment, and the meeting breaks up practically while I am talking, with the Vice Chairman (Armstrong) remark about our not doing detailed work.

   – Letter to Gweneth and Michelle Feynman, February 12, 1986
      (*Perfectly Reasonable Deviations from the Beaten Track*, p. 399)


Sunday, I go with Graham and his family to see the Air and Space museum which Carl liked so much — we are in an hour before the official opening and there are no crowds — influence; after all, the acting head of NASA.

   – Letter to Gweneth and Michelle Feynman, February 12, 1986
      (*Perfectly Reasonable Deviations from the Beaten Track*, p. 401)


[On Rogers's leniency with fraternizing with the press:] I was pleased by his reaction, but now as I write this, I have second thoughts. It was too easy after he explicitly talked about the importance of no leaks, etc. at earlier meetings. Am I being set up? (See, darling, Washington Paranoia is setting in.) If, when he wants to stop or discredit me, he could charge me with leaking something important. I think it possible that there are things in this that somebody might be trying to keep me from finding out and might try to discredit me if I get too close.

– Letter to Gweneth and Michelle Feynman, February 12, 1986
 (*Perfectly Reasonable Deviations from the Beaten Track*, p. 401)

[On Rogers:] I am probably a thorn in his side.

– Letter to Gweneth and Michelle Feynman, February 12, 1986
 (*Perfectly Reasonable Deviations from the Beaten Track*, p. 401)

[On the Rogers Commission:] At this rate we will never get down close enough to business to find out what happened.

– Letter to Gweneth and Michelle Feynman, February 12, 1986
 (*Perfectly Reasonable Deviations from the Beaten Track*, p. 401)

[On the Rogers Commission:] I am determined to do the job of finding out what happened — let the chips fall.

– Letter to Gweneth and Michelle Feynman, February 12, 1986
 (*Perfectly Reasonable Deviations from the Beaten Track*, p. 401)

[On the Rogers Commission:] My guess is that I will be allowed to do this, overwhelmed with data and details, with the hope that so buried with all attention on technical details I can be occupied, so they have time to soften especially dangerous witnesses, etc. But it won't work because (1) I do technical information exchange and understanding much faster than they imagine, and (2) I already smell certain rats that I will not forget because I just love the smell of rats.

– Letter to Gweneth and Michelle Feynman, February 12, 1986
*(Perfectly Reasonable Deviations from the Beaten Track*, p. 402)

Official management, on the other hand, claims to believe the probability of failure is a thousand times less. One reason for this may be an attempt to assure the government of NASA perfection and success in order to ensure the supply of funds. The other may be that they sincerely believed it to be true, demonstrating an almost incredible lack of communication between themselves and their working engineers.

– Report of the Presidential Commission on the Space Shuttle
*Challenger* Accident, Volume 2: Appendix F, June 1986

It appears that there are enormous differences of opinion as to the probability of a failure with loss of vehicle and of human life. The estimates range from roughly 1 in 100 to 1 in 100,000. The higher figures come from the working engineers, and the very low figures from management. What are the causes and consequences of this lack of agreement? Since 1 part in 100,000 would imply that one could put a Sshuttle up each day for 300 years expecting to lose only one, we could properly ask "What is the cause of management's fantastic faith in the machinery?"

– Report of the Presidential Commission on the Space Shuttle
*Challenger* Accident, Volume 2: Appendix F, June 1986

The argument that the same risk was flown before without failure is often accepted as an argument for the safety of accepting it again. Because of this, obvious weaknesses are accepted again and again, sometimes without a sufficiently serious attempt to remedy them, or to delay a flight because of their continued presence.

– Report of the Presidential Commission on the Space Shuttle *Challenger* Accident, Volume 2: Appendix F, June 1986

It would appear that, for whatever purpose, be it for internal or external consumption, the management of NASA exaggerates the reliability of its product, to the point of fantasy.

– Report of the Presidential Commission on the Space Shuttle *Challenger* Accident, Volume 2: Appendix F, June 1986

The O-rings of the Solid Rocket Boosters were not designed to erode. Erosion was a clue that something was wrong. Erosion was not something from which safety can be inferred.

– Report of the Presidential Commission on the Space Shuttle *Challenger* Accident, Volume 2: Appendix F, June 1986

An entirely automatic landing is probably not as safe as a pilot-controlled landing.

– Report of the Presidential Commission on the Space Shuttle *Challenger* Accident, Volume 2: Appendix F, June 1986

We find that the attitude to system failure and reliability is not nearly as good as for the computer system. For example, a difficulty was found with certain temperature sensors sometimes failing. Yet 18 months later, the same sensors were still being used, still sometimes failing, until a launch had to be scrubbed because two of them failed at the same time.

– Report of the Presidential Commission on the Space Shuttle *Challenger* Accident, Volume 2: Appendix F, June 1986

The action of the jets is checked by sensors, and, if they fail to fire the computers choose another jet to fire. But they are not designed to fail, and the problem should be solved.

– Report of the Presidential Commission on the Space Shuttle *Challenger* Accident, Volume 2: Appendix F, June 1986

If a reasonable launch schedule is to be maintained, engineering often cannot be done fast enough to keep up with the expectations of originally conservative certification criteria designed to guarantee a very safe vehicle. In these situations, subtly, and often with apparently logical arguments, the criteria are altered so that flights may still be certified in time. They therefore fly in a relatively unsafe condition, with a chance of failure of the order of a percent.

– Report of the Presidential Commission on the Space Shuttle *Challenger* Accident, Volume 2: Appendix F, June 1986

Let us make recommendations to ensure that NASA officials deal in a world of reality in understanding technological weaknesses and imperfections well enough to be actively trying to eliminate them.

– Report of the Presidential Commission on the Space Shuttle *Challenger* Accident, Volume 2: Appendix F, June 1986

We have also found that certification criteria used in Flight Readiness Reviews often develop a gradually decreasing strictness. The argument that the same risk was flown before without failure is often accepted as an argument for the safety of accepting it again. Because of this, obvious weaknesses are accepted again and again, sometimes without a sufficiently serious attempt to remedy them, or to delay a flight because of their continued presence.

– *Pasadena Star-News*, Opinion, June 18, 1986

Out of a total of nearly 2,900 flights, 121 failed (1 in 25). This includes, however, what may be called early errors, rockets flown for the first few times in which design errors are discovered and fixed. A more reasonable figure for the mature rockets might be 1 in 50. With special care in the selection of the parts and in inspection, a figure of below 1 in 100 might be achieved but 1 in 1,000 is probably not attainable with today's technology. NASA officials argue the figure is much lower.

– *Pasadena Star-News*, Opinion, June 18, 1986

In fact, previous NASA experiments had shown, on occasion, just such difficulties, near accidents and accidents, all giving warning that the probability of flight failure was not so very small.

– *Pasadena Star-News*, Opinion, June 18, 1986

Why do we find such an enormous disparity between the management estimate and the judgment of the engineers? It would appear that, for whatever purpose, be it for internal or external consumption, the management of NASA exaggerates the reliability of its product, to the point of fantasy.

– *Pasadena Star-News*, Opinion, June 18, 1986

The fact that this danger did not lead to a catastrophe before is no guarantee that it will not the next time, unless it is completely understood. When playing Russian roulette, the fact that the first shot went off safely is little comfort for the next.

– *Pasadena Star-News*, Opinion, June 18, 1986

I report to Rogers that I have these close relatives with press connections and is it OK to visit with them? He is very nice and says, "Of course."

– Letter to Gweneth and Michelle Feynman, February 12, 1986
  (*Perfectly Reasonable Deviations from the Beaten Track*, p. 401)

I am not interested in my personal comfort; rather the well being of the country.

– Correspondence with Rogers ("Mr. Feynman Goes to Washington," 1986)

# Politics

We all know that they don't know what they're doing in Washington. It's not that they're fools; it's just that nobody knows how to handle many of the problems. A lot of experts have studied these subjects. But they know much less than they will admit. If somebody ran for office saying that they didn't have answers, nobody would pay any attention to him. Everybody wants an answer. But someday, maybe, everybody will slowly come around to the realization that the experts don't know almost everything.

– *U.S. News and World Report* interview, February 1985

If it can be controlled in thermonuclear reactions, then it turns out that the energy that can be obtained from a quart of water a second is equal to the all the electrical power generated in the United States. With a faucet running at 15 gallons of water a minute, you have the fuel to supply all the energy in the United States that's used today. Therefore, it's up to the physicist to figure out how to liberate us from the need for having energy. And in can be done, in practice.

– Audio recording of Feynman Lectures on Physics, Lecture 4, October 6, 1961

[On the electron's negativity:] It's the scale I want to measure, and I use the "minus" because of Benjamin Franklin, who chose to call the electron "minus." Okay? So we're stuck with that since 1776. And lots of other things we're stuck with since 1776. And some of them they're not so concerned as I am.

– "QED: New Queries," Sir Douglas Robb Lectures, University of Auckland, 1979

Science is an international human effort, and there would be no "American science" were it not for scientific development in the rest of the world.

– Letter to Mr. Stuart Zimmer, February 1982 (*Perfectly Reasonable Deviations from the Beaten Track*, p. 344)

This is in the attitude of the mind of the populace, that they have to have an answer and that a man who gives an answer is better than a man who gives no answer, when the real fact of the matter is, in most cases it is the other way around. And the result of this is that the politician must give an answer. And the result of this is that political promises can never be kept. It is a mechanical fact, it is impossible. The result of that is that nobody believes campaign promises. And the result of that is a general disparaging of politics, a general lack of respect for the people who are trying to solve problems.

– "The Unscientific Age," John Danz Lecture Series, 1963

They decided to do something utterly illegal, which was to censor mail of people inside the United States, in the Continental United States, which they have no right to do. So it had to be set up very delicately, as a voluntary thing. We would all volunteer, not to seal our envelopes that we would send our letters out with. We would accept, it would be all right, that they would open letters coming in to us; that was voluntarily accepted by us.

– UCSB talk, "Los Alamos from Below," February 1975

For a very quick summary, I see nothing wrong with nuclear power except questions of the possibility of explosions, sabotage, stealing fuel to make bombs, leaking stored radioactive spent rods, etc. But all these are technical or engineering questions, about which we can do a great deal.

– Letter to student Mark Minguillon, April 1976 (*Perfectly Reasonable Deviations from the Beaten Track*, pp. 304–305)

The television industry can be proud to be a part of the tradition of freedom of expression of this country.

– Letter to Bill Whitley (KNXT), May 1959 (*Perfectly Reasonable Deviations from the Beaten Track*, p. 101)

The government of the United States is not very good, but it, with the possible exception of the government of England, is the greatest government on the earth today, is the most satisfactory, the most modern, but not very good.

– "The Uncertainty of Values," John Danz Lecture Series, 1963

I don't think of the problem as between socialism and capitalism but rather between suppression of ideas and free ideas. If it is free ideas and socialism is better than communism, it will work its way through. And it will be better for everybody. And if capitalism is better than socialism, it will work its way through.

– "The Uncertainty of Values," John Danz Lecture Series, 1963

According to the Constitution there are supposed to be votes. It isn't supposed to be automatically determinable ahead of time on each of the items what's right and what's wrong. Otherwise there wouldn't be the bother to invent the Senate to have the votes. As long as you have the votes at all, then the purpose of the votes is to try to make up your mind which is the way to go.

– "The Unscientific Age," John Danz Lecture Series, 1963

There is a system of laws and juries and judges. And although there are of course many faults and flaws, and we must continue to work on them, I have great admiration for that.

– "The Unscientific Age," John Danz Lecture Series, 1963

Universal education is probably a good thing, but you could teach good as well as bad — you can teach falsehood as well as truth. The communication between nations as it develops through a technical development of science should certainly improve the relations between nations. Well, it depends what you communicate. You can communicate truth and you can communicate lies. You can communicate threats or kindness.

– Galileo Symposium, "What Is and What Should Be the Role of Scientific Culture in Modern Society," September 1964

My theory is that loss of common interest — between the engineers and scientists on the one hand and management on the other — is the cause of the deterioration in cooperation.

– "Mr. Feynman Goes to Washington," 1987

I expect to stay away from the President's Board of Master Plumbers as much as possible, and I hope you do not draft me.

– Letter to Congressman Barber B. Conable Jr., November 1965

You write that true Americans have a big generous heart, which shows only what a big and generous heart you have. For you must know that a great nation, at least one where the British ideas of freedom flourish, is very complex, and side by side lie the great and the mean, the generous and the selfish, just as they lie side by side in each man.

- Letter to Reverend John Alex and Mrs. Marjorie Howard, December 1965 (*Perfectly Reasonable Deviations from the Beaten Track*, p. 184)

No government has the right to decide on the truth of scientific principles, nor to prescribe in any way the character of the questions investigated. Neither may a government determine the aesthetic value of artistic creations, nor limit the forms of literary or artistic expression. Nor should it pronounce on the validity of economic, historic, religious, or philosophical doctrines. Instead it has a duty to its citizens to maintain the freedom, to let those citizens contribute to further adventure and the development of the human race.

- "The Uncertainty of Values," John Danz Lecture Series, 1963

I decided at the time, I believe, that the morally right thing to do was to protect ourselves; I felt there was a great evil around, and that this evil would only grow if it had more technical power. The only way that I knew how to prevent that was to get there earlier so that we could prevent them from doing it, or defeat them.

- BBC, "The Pleasure of Finding Things Out," 1981

Mr. Hollingsworth shows nerve in calling me an AEC specialist. Is every scientist in the country working for the Atomic Energy Commission?

– Letter to Lewis L. Strauss, July 6, 1956

[On the Rogers Commission:] I have a unique qualification — I am completely free and there are no levers that can be used to influence me and I am reasonably straightforward and honest. There are exceedingly powerful political forces and consequences involved here. But although people have explained that to me from different points of view I disregarded them all, and proceed with apparently naive and single-minded purpose to the one end: first, why, physically, the shuttle failed, leaving later the question of why humans made, apparently, bad decisions when they did.

– Letter to Gweneth and Michelle Feynman, February 12, 1986
(*Perfectly Reasonable Deviations from the Beaten Track*, p. 398)

[After a UN meeting on atomic energy:] Ever since then, I've had a much better idea how government works, and what the hell's the matter with it. I mean, that those things that are vital to be decided are decided too easily. I mean, it's great that a man can decide so quickly. So can a die decide quickly? It's just — it's bad. It was a very serious thing.

– Interview with Charles Weiner, June 27, 1966 (Niels Bohr Library and Archives with the Center for the History of Physics)

There are an awful lot of light decisions of historical importance.

– Interview with Charles Weiner, June 27, 1966 (Niels Bohr Library and Archives with the Center for the History of Physics)

[On company workers:] They have a conflict, and tensions, and usually they either give up completely, or there's another tension that happens. If they get 100 percent involved in the company work, then another trouble happens. There's always some guy on top of them, the boss, who is dumber technically than they are, and who makes the decision as to what they ought to do, and whether what they do is worthwhile.

– Interview with Charles Weiner, June 28, 1966 (Niels Bohr Library and Archives with the Center for the History of Physics)

The real question of government versus private enterprise is argued on too philosophical and abstract a basis. Theoretically, planning may be good. But nobody has ever figured out the cause of government stupidity — and until they do (and find the cure), all ideal plans will fall into quicksand.

– *What Do You Care What Other People Think?*, pp. 90–91

So, very delicately, amongst all these liberal-minded scientific guys agreeing to such a proposition, we finally got the censorship set up.

– UCSB talk, "Los Alamos from Below," February 1975

The other thing that gives a scientific man the creeps in the world today are the methods of choosing leaders — in every nation. Today, for example, in the United States, the two political parties have decided to employ public relations men, that is, advertising men, who are trained in the necessary methods of telling the truth and lying in order to develop a product. This wasn't the original idea. They are supposed to discuss situations and not just make up slogans. It's true, if you look in history, however, that choosing political leaders in the United States has been on many different occasions based on slogans.

– Galileo Symposium, "What Is and What Should Be the Role of Scientific Culture in Modern Society," September 1964

# Doubt and Uncertainty

But I don't have to know an answer. I don't feel frightened by not knowing things, by being lost in a mysterious universe within any purpose, which is the way it really is, so far as I can tell. It doesn't frighten me.

– BBC, "The Pleasure of Finding Things Out," 1981

[Doubt] is not a new idea; this is the idea of the age of reason. This is the philosophy that guided the men who made the democracy that we live under. The idea that no one really knew how to run a government led to the idea that we should arrange a system by which new ideas could be developed, tried out, tossed out, more new ideas brought in; a trial and error system. This method was a result of the fact that science was already showing itself to be a successful venture at the end of the 18th century. Even then it was clear to socially minded people that the openness of the possibilities was an opportunity, and that doubt and discussion were essential to progress into the unknown.

– "The Value of Science," December 1955

I can live with doubt, and uncertainty, and not knowing. I think it's much more interesting to live not knowing anything than to have answers which might be wrong. I have approximate answers, and possible beliefs, and different degrees of certainty about different things, but I'm not absolutely sure of anything.

– BBC, "The Pleasure of Finding Things Out," 1981

American ideals of freedom are the same as the ideals of scientific development. The ultimate development of the potentials of mankind requires an allowance for error.

– Notes for talk on "Science in America"

Now, we scientists are used to this, and we take it for granted that it is perfectly consistent to be unsure, that it is possible to live and *not* know. But I don't know whether everyone realizes this is true. Our freedom to doubt was born out of a struggle against authority in the early days of science. It was a very deep and strong struggle: permit us to question — to doubt — to not be sure. I think that it is important that we do not forget this struggle and thus perhaps lose what we have gained.

– "The Value of Science," December 1955

This business about not understanding is a very serious one that we have between scientists and an audience. And I want to work with you because I want to tell you something: Students do not understand it either, and that's because the professor doesn't understand it, which not a joke but very interesting.

– "QED: Photons — Corpuscles of Light," Sir Douglas Robb Lectures, University of Auckland, June 1979

People who hear that all I'm going to do is make a couple of arrows on a board to calculate the chance that something happens — say that this guy doesn't know physics. But this is the guy that knows that that's what you have to do and admits, therefore, that he doesn't know why he's doing what he does. And you can have the confidence that when I say I don't know what I'm doing, probably no one else does either.

– "QED: Fits of Reflection and Transmission," Sir Douglas Robb Lectures, University of Auckland, 1979

Everything has to be checked out very carefully. Otherwise you become one of those people who believe all kinds of crazy stuff and doesn't understand the world they're in. Nobody understands the world they're in, but some people are better off at it than others.

– "This Unscientific Age," John Danz Lecture Series, 1963

It is in the admission of ignorance and the admission of uncertainty that there is a hope for the continuous motion of human beings in some direction that doesn't get confined, permanently blocked, as it has so many times before in various periods in the history of man.

– "The Uncertainty of Values," John Danz Lecture Series, 1963

It would have been unscientific not to guess.

– "The Uncertainty of Science," John Danz Lecture Series, 1963

Does this mean that physics, a science of great exactitude, has been reduced to calculating only the probability of an event, and not predicting exactly what will happen? Yes.

– *QED: The Strange Theory of Light and Matter*, p. 19

I think it's much more interesting to live not knowing than to have answers which might be wrong. I have approximate answers and possible beliefs and different degrees of uncertainty about different things, but I am not absolutely sure of anything and there are many things I don't know anything about, such as whether it means anything to ask why we're here. I don't have to know an answer. I don't feel frightened not knowing things, but being lost in a mysterious universe without any purpose, which is the way it really is, as far as I can tell.

   – BBC, "The Pleasure of Finding Things Out," 1981

I think that when we know that we actually do live in uncertainty, then we ought to admit it; it is of great value to realize that we do not know the answers to different questions. This attitude of mind — this attitude of uncertainty — is vital to the scientist, and it is this attitude of mind which the student must first acquire. It becomes a habit of thought. Once acquired, one cannot retreat from it anymore.

   – Galileo Symposium, "What Is and What Should Be the Role of
     Scientific Culture in Modern Society," September 1964

I've learned how to live without knowing. I don't have to be sure I'm succeeding, as I said before about science, I think my life is fuller because I realize that I don't know what I'm doing. I'm delighted with the width of the world!

   – *Omni* interview, February 1979

[On "typewriter science":] Some intellectual sits at the typewriter and writes it all out as if the information were really known. The intellectual never says, "I don't know this," or "I'm not really sure." If he were to do so, he couldn't sell his articles because somebody else would come along and say that they have all the answers.

   – *U.S. News and World Report* interview, February 1985

All scientific knowledge is uncertain. This experience with doubt and uncertainty is important. I believe that it is of very great value, and one that extends beyond the sciences. I believe that to solve any problem that has never been solved before, you have to leave the door to the unknown ajar. You have to permit the possibility that you do not have it exactly right. Otherwise, if you have made up your mind already, you might not solve it.

– "The Uncertainty of Science," John Danz Lecture Series, 1963

So what we call scientific knowledge today is a body of statements of varying degrees of certainty. Some of them are most unsure; some of them are nearly sure; but none is absolutely certain.

– "The Uncertainty of Science," John Danz Lecture Series, 1963

It is not possible to predict exactly what'll happen in any circumstance.

– Audio recording of Feynman Lectures on Physics, Lecture 2, September 29, 1961

The thing you can't face is not knowing what somebody's cooking up. That's hard, not knowing. But any real thing, you just sit there, take it for reality, and see what you do under the circumstances.

– Interview with Charles Weiner, March 5, 1966 (Niels Bohr Library and Archives with the Center for the History of Physics)

There is no harm in being uncertain. It is better to say something and not be sure than to not say anything at all.

– "The Uncertainty of Science," John Danz Lecture Series, 1963

It is of paramount importance, in order to make progress, that we recognize this ignorance and this doubt. Because we have the doubt, then we propose looking in new directions for new ideas.

– "The Uncertainty of Science," John Danz Lecture Series, 1963

If we were not able or did not desire to look in any new direction, if we did not have a doubt or recognize ignorance, we would not get any new ideas.

– "The Uncertainty of Science," John Danz Lecture Series, 1963

What we call scientific knowledge today is a body of statements of varying degrees of certainty.

– "The Uncertainty of Science," John Danz Lecture Series, 1963

I feel a responsibility as a scientist who knows the great value of a satisfactory philosophy of ignorance, and the progress made possible by such a philosophy, progress which is the fruit of freedom of thought. I feel a responsibility to proclaim the value of this freedom and to teach that doubt is not to be feared, but that it is to be welcomed as the possibility of a new potential for human beings.

– "The Uncertainty of Science," John Danz Lecture Series, 1963

I want to maintain here that in the admission of ignorance and the admission of uncertainty that there is a hope for the continuous motion of human beings in some direction that doesn't get confined, permanently blocked as it has so many times before in various periods in the history of man.

– "The Uncertainty of Values," John Danz Lecture Series, 1963

The only way that we will make a mistake is that in the impetuous youth of humanity we will decide we know the answer.

– "The Uncertainty of Values," John Danz Lecture Series, 1963

All my life I have been inspired by Galileo and his struggle with the Church, his struggle for a freedom to doubt, and the struggle that went along with other people connected with Galileo.

– Galileo Symposium, "What Is and What Should Be the Role of Scientific Culture in Modern Society," September 1964

One way of looking at the uncertainty in the world is supposing that these things are there but that we only see them crudely. This idea we have to get rid of it doesn't work!

– Esalen lecture, "Quantum Mechanical View of Reality (Part 1)," October 1984

The thing that's unusual about scientists is that while they're doing whatever they're doing, they're not so sure of themselves as others usually are. They can live with steady doubt, think "maybe it's so" and act on that, all the time knowing it's only "maybe."

– *Omni* interview, February 1979

I believe that a scientist looking at nonscientific problems is just as dumb as the next guy and when he talks about a non-scientific matter, he will sound as naive as anyone untrained in the matter.

– "The Value of Science," December 1955

When we are talking to each other at these high and complicated levels, and we think we are speaking very well, that we are communicating, but what we are really doing is having a some kind of big translation scheme going on, translating what this fellow says into our images, which are very different.

– BBC, "Fun to Imagine" television series, 1983

There is no harm in doubt and skepticism, for it is through these that new discoveries are made.

– Letter to Armando Garcia, December 1985 (*Perfectly Reasonable Deviations from the Beaten Track*, p. 396)

In physics the truth is rarely perfectly clear, and that is certainly universally the case in human affairs. Hence, what is not surrounded by uncertainty cannot be the truth.

– Letter to the editor of the California Tech, February 1976

You may think that it might be possible to invent a metaphysical system for religion which will state things in such a way that science will never find itself in disagreement. But I do not think that it is possible to take an adventurous and ever-expanding science that is going into an unknown, and to tell the answer to questions ahead of time and not expect that sooner or later, no matter what you do, you will find that some answers of this kind are wrong.

– "The Uncertainty of Values," John Danz Lecture Series, 1963
  (*The Meaning of It All*, pp. 46–47)

Science is the belief in the ignorance of experts.

– National Science Teachers Association Fourteenth Convention
  lecture, "What Is Science?" April 1966

When you're thinking about something you don't understand, you have a terrible, uncomfortable feeling called confusion. It's a very difficult and unhappy business. And so most of the time you're rather unhappy, actually, with this confusion. You can't penetrate this thing. Now, is the confusion because we're all some kind of apes that are kind of stupid, trying to figure out how to put the sticks together to reach the banana and we can't quite make it, the idea. And I get that feeling all the time, that I'm an ape trying to put the two sticks together. So I always feel stupid. Once in a while, though, the sticks go together on me and I reach the banana.

– Swedish television interview on Nobel Prize winners, 1965

To make progress in understanding, we must remain modest and allow that we do not know. Nothing is certain or proved beyond all doubt. You investigate for curiosity, because it is unknown, not because you know the answer. And as you develop more information in the sciences, it is not that you are finding out the truth, but that you are finding out that this or that is more or less likely.

– "The Relation of Science and Religion," May 1956

The fact that you are not sure means that it is possible that there is another way someday.

– "The Uncertainty of Values," John Danz Lecture Series, 1963

We absolutely must leave room for doubt or there is not progress and there is no learning. There is no learning without having to pose a question. And a question requires doubt. People search for certainty. But there is no certainty. People are terrified — how can you live and not know? It is not odd at all. You only think you know, as a matter of fact. And most of your actions are based on incomplete knowledge and you really don't know what it is all about, or what the purpose of the world is, or know a great deal or other things. It is possible to live and not know.

– "The Role of Scientific Culture in Modern Society"

# Education and Teaching

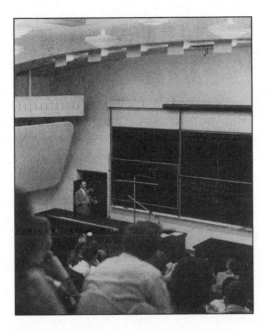

I don't believe I can really do without teaching. The reason is, I have to have something so that when I don't have any ideas and I'm not getting anywhere I can say to myself, "At least I'm living; at least I'm doing something; I'm making some contribution" — it's just psychological.

– *Surely You're Joking, Mr. Feynman!*, p. 165

You'll learn infinitely better and easier and more completely by picking a problem for yourself that you find interesting to fiddle around with some kind of thing that you heard that you don't understand, or you want to analyze further, or want to do some kind of a trick with — that's the best way to learn something.

– *Feynman's Tips on Physics*, p. 15

In teaching science you are telling new minds about the most wondrous world they live in, you are passing on the greatest ideas man has ever contemplated: the fathomless space, the infinite gyrations of the atoms, the web of interaction of all life, and of life with the inanimate. And this vast sea of knowledge is surrounded on all sides by much vaster areas of ignorance, which are not things to fear but challenges to learn about.

– Notes for talk on "Science in America"

In fact, it's impossible in the long run to do everything by memory. That doesn't mean to do nothing by memory — the more you remember, in a certain sense, the better it is — but you should be able to recreate anything that you forgot.

– *Feynman's Tips on Physics*, p. 41

This is, as a matter of fact, the way you start on any complicated or unfamiliar problem: You first get a rough idea; then you go back when you understand it better and do it more carefully.

— *Feynman's Tips on Physics*, p. 77

When it came time for me to give my talk on the subject, I started off by drawing an outline of the cat and began to name the various muscles. The other students in the class interrupt me. "We know all that!" "Oh," I say, "you do? Then no wonder I can catch up with you so fast after you've had four years of biology." They had wasted all their time memorizing stuff like that, when it could be looked up in fifteen minutes.

— *Surely You're Joking, Mr. Feynman!*, p. 72

I often remember vividly my most enjoyable trip. Many things bring it to mind — like the dark blue T-shirt in my drawer at home — or the interference picture in my office — or just now when my secretary asked me if I wanted to talk to students at a nearby university (USC 20 miles) or high school. My answer was that I will talk to students anytime they are near enough to home, or are at Vancouver, B.C.

— Letter to Mariela Johansen, April 1975

The students may not be able to see the thing I want to answer, or the subtleties I want to think about, but they remind me of a problem by asking questions in the neighborhood of that problem. It's not so easy to remind yourself of these things.

— *Surely You're Joking, Mr. Feynman!*, p. 166

Don't look up the answer; just figure it out. After all, it's only nature; she can't beat you. If you think hard enough, you'll figure it out.

– Audio recording of Feynman Lectures on Physics, Lecture 30, February 20, 1962

Learn by trying to understand simple things in terms of other ideas — always honestly and directly. What keeps the clouds up, why can't I see stars in the daytime, why do colors appear on oily water, what makes the lines on the surface of water being poured from a pitcher, why does a hanging lamp swing back and forth — and all the innumerable little things you see all around you. Then when you have learned to explain simpler things, so you have learned what an explanation really is, you can then go on to more subtle questions.

– Letter to Master Ashok Arora, January 1967 (*Perfectly Reasonable Deviations from the Beaten Track*, p. 230)

It has nothing to do with what you're supposed to learn. All it is is that you can learn something, and it's just useful to learn as much as possible. However, it's imperative to learn a certain minimum amount in order to go on and learn something else.

– Audio recording of Feynman Lectures on Physics, Lecture 17, November 28, 1961

I am going to try and tell what the world of light and electrons looks like from the point of view of modern physics. This is quite an order, and I may fail badly — but let us try.

– On his lecture topic for the Sir Douglas Robb Lectures, June 1979

Those are just names, and people use them, so we'll use them.

– Audio recording of Feynman Lectures on Physics, Lecture 30, February 20, 1962

Foreign languages have been taught all over for so long! Are there not studies of methods and results — inconclusive studies at least that show that any method is worse than any other that can be used to prove or disprove anything? That is just what you need to generate doubt and humbleness and an atmosphere more conducive to uncertainty.

– Letter to Dr. Amos J. Lessard, February 1983

If you understand something, you can remember it, when you work it out yourself.

– Interview with Charles Weiner, March 5, 1966 (Niels Bohr Library and Archives with the Center for the History of Physics)

As I get more experience I realize that I know nothing whatsoever as to how to teach children arithmetic. I did some write some things before I reached my present state of wisdom.

– Letter to Beryl S. Cochran, April 1967 (*Perfectly Reasonable Deviations from the Beaten Track*, p. 241)

I don't know anything about small children. I have one, so I know that I don't know.

– National Science Teachers Association Fourteenth Convention lecture, "What Is Science?" April 1966

You'll see I'll never get anywhere with the physics if I keep talking about all this stuff. But it's interesting. So what? So it doesn't make any difference. So you learn something else.

– Audio recording of Feynman Lectures on Physics, Lecture 14, November 14, 1961

It is necessary to learn words. It is not a science. That doesn't mean just because it is not a science that we don't have to teach the words. We are not talking about what to teach; we are talking about what science is. It is not science to know how to change centigrade to Fahrenheit. It's necessary, but it is not exactly science. In the same sense, if you were discussing what art is, you wouldn't say art is the knowledge of the fact that a 3-B pencil is softer than a 2-H pencil. It's a distinct difference. That doesn't mean an art teacher shouldn't teach that, or that an artist gets along very well if he doesn't know that.

– National Science Teachers Association Fourteenth Convention lecture, "What Is Science?" April 1966

It's natural to explain an idea in terms of what you already have in your head. Concepts are piled on top of each other: This idea is taught in terms of that idea, and that idea is taught in terms of another idea, which comes from counting, which can be so different for different people!

– *What Do You Care What Other People Think?*, p. 59

Interest is an emotion — like love. It is not a property of a subject.

– Notes

In any thinking process there are moments when everything is going good and you've got wonderful ideas. Teaching is an interruption, and so it's the greatest pain in the neck in the world.

  – *Surely You're Joking, Mr. Feynman!*, p. 165

In psychology there is a profound question of what type of facility is it that permits a child to learn a language from simply hearing it spoken and seeing it used. We are far from knowing how it is done. It is even very hard to see how it can be done. But it is done by every child. We cannot expect to solve such problems by studying machines. Nevertheless, it is an intriguing academic investigation to see, at least in principle, some way that it might be done by a machine.

  – Letter to R. B. Leighton, April 1974

You ask, how can this guy teach, how can he be motivated if he doesn't know what he's doing. As a matter of fact, I love to teach. I like to think of new ways of looking at things as I explain them, to make them clearer — but maybe I'm not making them clearer. Probably what I'm doing is entertaining myself.

  – *Omni* interview, February 1979

One does not learn a subject by using the words that people who know the subject use in discussing it. One must learn how to handle the ideas and then, when the subtleties arise which require special language, that special language can be used and developed easily. In the meantime, clarity is the desire.

  – "New Mathematics," written for the California State Department of Education

They treated me so nicely in Vancouver that now I now the secret of how to really be entertained and give talks: Wait for the students to ask you.

   – *Surely You're Joking, Mr. Feynman!*, p. 303

I don't know what's the matter with people: they don't learn by understanding; they learn by some other way — by rote or something. Their knowledge is so fragile.

   – *Surely You're Joking, Mr. Feynman!*, pp. 36–37

I am a successful lecturer in physics for popular audiences. The real entertainment gimmick is the excitement, drama and mystery of the subject matter. People love to learn something, they are "entertained" enormously by being allowed to understand a little bit of something they never understood before. One must have faith in the subject and in people's interest in it.

   – Letter to Ralph Bown, March 1958, *Perfectly Reasonable Deviations from the Beaten Track*, p. 98

I believe that all of the exercises in all of the books, from the first to the eighth year, ought to be understandable to any ordinary adult — that is, the question that one is trying to find out should be clear to every person.

   – "New Mathematics," written for the California State Department of Education

Physics has a profound effect on all the other sciences. So that students from many other sciences find themselves studying it.

> – Audio recording of Feynman Lectures on Physics, Lecture 3, October 3, 1961

See, with all these things the big trouble is the words. They sound like something terrible, but the idea isn't really so bad.

> – Audio recording of Feynman Lectures on Physics, Lecture 8, October 20, 1961

That's just symbols — you have to know the idea.

> – Audio recording of Feynman Lectures on Physics, Lecture 8, October 20, 1961

Don't copy it down; just listen to what it says. Otherwise you don't understand anything when it's finished.

> – Audio recording of Feynman Lectures on Physics, Lecture 15, November 17, 1961

Nobody knows how to teach physics, or to educate people — that's a fact, and if you don't like the way it's being done, that's perfectly natural. It's impossible to teach satisfactorily: For hundreds of years, even more, people have been trying to figure out how to teach, and nobody has ever figured it out.

> – *Feynman's Tips on Physics*, p. 15

I suffer from the disease that all professors suffer from — that is, there never seems to be enough time, and I invented more problems than undoubtedly we'll be able to do, and therefore I've tried to speed things up by writing some things on the board beforehand, with the illusion that every professor has: that if he talks about more things, he'll teach more things. Of course, there's only a finite rate at which material can be absorbed by the human mind, yet we disregard that phenomenon, and in spite of it we go too fast.

– *Feynman's Tips on Physics*, p. 71

One of the things one learns in school which is incorrect is that problems are relatively easy, if they're formed, you can set 'em up, you can solve them — which isn't at all true.

– Interview with Charles Weiner, March 5, 1966 (Niels Bohr Library and Archives with the Center for the History of Physics)

I thought that one of the troubles with all the courses in physics was that they just said: You learn all this, you learn all that, and when you come out the other end you'll understand the connections. But there's no map, "guide to the perplexes," you see. So I want to make a map. But it turns out it's not a feasible design. I mean, I just never made such a map.

– Interview with Charles Weiner, June 28, 1966 (Niels Bohr Library and Archives with the Center for the History of Physics)

But there must be people living who aren't listening to the lectures of some professor, who are sitting just reading the book and thinking for themselves. They must get something out of it. So if I keep some hope that that's worth something to them, maybe I can feel better about the whole thing.

– Interview with Charles Weiner, June 28, 1966 (Niels Bohr Library and Archives with the Center for the History of Physics)

What I really was doing was teaching myself. I wasn't interested in publishing at all. But I did discover a lot of things. You see, I thought everybody else knew all these things. In the meantime I was trying to teach myself. So I learned a lot of things that weren't known, or a few things that weren't well known. And I checked — things that people have noticed later as being simple, sometimes I noticed a little ahead. But the main thing I was doing was teaching myself.

> – Interview with Charles Weiner, February 4, 1966 (Niels Bohr Library and Archives with the Center for the History of Physics)

I finally figured out a way to test whether you have taught an idea or you have only taught a definition. Test it this way: You say, "Without using the new word which you have just learned, try to rephrase what you have just learned in your own language."

> – National Science Teachers Association Fourteenth Convention lecture, "What Is Science?" April 1966

To learn a mystic formula for answering questions is very bad.

> – National Science Teachers Association Fourteenth Convention lecture, "What Is Science?" April 1966

A child should be given a child's answer. "Open it up; let's look at it."

> – National Science Teachers Association Fourteenth Convention lecture, "What Is Science?" April 1966

I have your letter of February 6, requesting my views on teaching science to youngsters. I have just one suggestion — never mind all the big talk about materials — get a good teacher and back her up. There's no other way!

> – Letter to Douglas O'Brien (Sunset Hill Elementary School), March 1967

I don't wish to spare the time on the non-science students. Anything I say would be either easily available by reading or talking to the science students, or else it would be over their heads.

> – Letter to Franklin W. Stahl (University of Oregon), April 1961

(In response to a child's question, "Does time exist?") Suppose it didn't. Then what?

> – From notes for "About Time" program, 1957

When we come to consider the words and definitions which children ought to learn, we should be careful not to teach "just" words. It is possible to give an illusion of knowledge by teaching the technical words which someone uses in a field which sound unusual to ordinary ears, without at the same time teaching some ideas or some facts using these words which require the special words in the special way and with the special care that they have been defined.

> – "New Mathematics," written for the California State Department of Education, 1965

This ends the main points that I wanted to make — the first that there must be a freedom of thought; second, that we do not want to teach just words, and third, that subjects should not be introduced without explaining the purpose or reason or without producing any yield as the subject is studied during the first eight years of school.

> – Unpublished extended version of "New Mathematics," written for the California State Department of Education, 1965

Students have a resilience and a skill at recognizing "all that jazz" as just "jazz." It was a child who understood the emperor's clothes!

> – Letter to Richard Godshall, March 1966 (*Perfectly Reasonable Deviations from the Beaten Track*, p. 218)

I believe that a book should be only an assistance to a good teacher and not a dictator.

> – Letter to Richard Godshall, March 1966 (*Perfectly Reasonable Deviations from the Beaten Track*, p. 218)

Stay human and on your pupil's side.

> – Letter to Richard Godshall, March 1966 (*Perfectly Reasonable Deviations from the Beaten Track*, p. 218)

It would be very good for the students to learn that science is an ongoing subject with new research always modifying old ideas, and I myself would be happy to see the careful criticism of my ideas that your physicists have made.

> – Letter to Sandor Solt, April 1969 (*Perfectly Reasonable Deviations from the Beaten Track*, p. 251)

Simple questions with complicated answers are always asked by dull students. Only intelligent students have been trained to ask complicated questions with simple answers — as any teacher knows (and only teachers think there are any simple questions with simple answers).

> – Letter to Professor Michael H. Hart, December 1980 (*Perfectly Reasonable Deviations from the Beaten Track*, p. 330)

I have much experience only in teaching graduate students in physics, and as a result of that, I know that I don't know how to teach.

> – National Science Teachers Association Fourteenth Convention lecture, "What Is Science?" April 1966

We decided that we don't have to teach a course in elementary quantum mechanics in the graduate school any more. When I was a student, they didn't even have a course in quantum mechanics in the graduate school, it was considered too difficult a subject. When I first started to teach, we had one. Now we teach it to undergraduates. We discover now that we don't have to have elementary quantum mechanics for graduates from other schools. Why is it getting pushed down? Because we are able to teach better in the university, and that is because the students coming up are better trained.

> – National Science Teachers Association Fourteenth Convention lecture, "What Is Science?" April 1966

I think it is very important — at least it was to me — that if you are going to teach people to make observations, you should show that something wonderful can come from them.

> – National Science Teachers Association Fourteenth Convention lecture, "What Is Science?" April 1966

I now know that it's possible for a night's work of a graduate student to be done in ten seconds by a professor.

– CERN talk, December 1965

There are many new plans in many countries for trying to teach physics, which shows that nobody is satisfied with any method. It is likely that many of the new plans look good, for nobody has tried them long enough to find out what is the matter with them; whereas all the old methods have been with us long enough to show their faults clearly.

– "The Problem of Teaching Physics in Latin America," 1963

The fact is that nobody knows very well how to tell anybody else how to teach. So when we try to figure out how to teach physics we must be somewhat modest, because nobody really knows how. It is at the same time a serious problem and an opportunity for new discoveries.

– "The Problem of Teaching Physics in Latin America," 1963

Science is an activity of men; to many men, it is a great pleasure and it should not be denied to the people of a large part of the world simply because of a fault or lack in the educational system.

– "The Problem of Teaching Physics in Latin America," 1963

From memorizing, knowledge is not understood, and the beauty of nature is not appreciated. It does not tell how things were found out, or reveal the value of an inventive free mind.

– "The Problem of Teaching Physics in Latin America," 1963

I understand I am supposed to make some response and so I planned a talk on my philosophy of teaching. After pondering it at great length, I discovered I had nothing but clichés and unimportant things, to say, and so I called up to ask if I could talk on something else, and so I would like to talk on something in physics itself rather than to talk about teaching because I don't know anything about teaching.

– Oersted Medal acceptance speech, 1972

Say you've got a disease, Wener's granulomatosis or whatever, and you look it up in a medical reference book. You may well find that you then know more about it than your doctor does, although he spent all that time in medical school, you see? It's much easier to learn about some special, restricted topic than a whole field.

– *Omni* interview, February 1979

I'm disappointed with my students all the time. I'm not a teacher who knows what he's doing.

– *Omni* interview, February 1979

My task is to explain all this and convince you not to turn away because it appears incomprehensible. That's what it takes four years for us to do to a student: to get him so he doesn't run away because it looks crazy. The thing that's exciting about this is that Nature is strange as it can be in this sense!

– "QED: Photons — Corpuscles of Light," Sir Douglas Robb Lectures, University of Auckland, June 1979

I sometimes feel that it would be much better not to educate our children in such subjects as mathematics and science. If we left youngsters alone, there would be a better chance that, by accident, the kids would find a good book or an old textbook or a television program that would excite them. But when youngsters go to school, they learn that these subjects are dull, horrible, and impossible to understand.

– *U.S. News and World Report* interview, February 1985

[On school textbooks:] They don't try to make subjects easier to understand. They try to make it easier to know what to do to pass the test and please the teacher.

– *U.S. News and World Report* interview, February 1985

One has the advantage of using questions to finish the lecture.

– "QED: Fits of Reflection and Transmission," Sir Douglas Robb Lectures, University of Auckland, 1979

My theory is that an excited and enthusiastic teacher teaching in a new and experimental situation — trying new things out — exudes so much in personality and energy that the students (or some students, at least) cannot help but respond. They respond magnificently.

– Letter to Mr. Robert Bonic, January 1974

General education is required for such a large number of students that a very large number of teachers are needed. Because there are so many teachers and because only a few people are really outstanding in anything, we must realize that most teachers must be either mediocre or dull. This is not a criticism of the profession — it is merely a matter of arithmetic.

– Letter to Mr. Robert Bonic, January 1974

It is too easy to memorize a lot or read a lot and not really understand anything.

– Letter to Apostolos Tournas, February 1985

About your attempts at teaching: It is so difficult isn't it — you can lead the horses to water but you can't make the damn fools drink!

– Letter to Malcolm Joseph, January 1982

One of my little pleasures in life is to go to the Van Nuys High School once or twice a year to answer questions for the science students of Mr. Coutts' classes. This activity was initiated many years ago by Mr. Coutts, and I look forward to doing it every year. The questions are on anything: relativity, black holes, clouds, spinning tops, magnetic force, you name it. The class is alive and very interested and seems to enjoy it as much as I.

– Letter to Ms. Melinda Jan, April 1985 (*Perfectly Reasonable Deviations from the Beaten Track*, p. 380)

[Advice to a student:] If your professors and fellow students seem to know some things but seem to be oblivious to other things, that does not exclude you from learning what they know whilst remaining deeply aware of what they are blind to.

– Letter to Mr. Alan Woodward, March 1982 (*Perfectly Reasonable Deviations from the Beaten Track*, p. 345)

Most theorists don't know that wire space is a problem. For them a wire is an idealized thin string that doesn't take up any space, but real computer designers soon discover that they can't get enough wires in.

– "The Remarkable Dr. Feynman," *Los Angeles Times Magazine*, April 20, 1986

When the student doesn't understand the professor, usually the student thinks it's because he's dopey and didn't catch on. This time it was because the professor wasn't saying anything that was sensible.

– "Tiny Computers Obeying Quantum Mechanical Laws," *New Directions in Physics: The Los Alamos 40th Anniversary Volume*, 1987

Easy to teach that any subject is dull — very rare but not impossible to teach a subject is interesting.

– Notes

Biology is not simply writing information; it is doing something about it.

– "There's Plenty of Room at the Bottom," December 1959

If you look closely enough at anything, you will see that there is nothing more exciting than the truth, the pay dirt of the scientist.

– "The Uncertainty of Science," John Danz Lecture Series, 1963

You teach the value of a free, inquiring, and discovering mind — the kind of mind that built America and that America was built for.

– Notes for talk on "Science in America"

There may be some idea that's difficult to understand the first time you study it. For example, Einstein's theory or something like this. And a man trying to learn it can't understand it. Later he finally understands it — say, when he goes to teach it, he finally understands it. He thinks that his particular way of understanding it is a very much clearer than the way it was presented to him before. Therefore, big deal, he puts out a paper — new way of looking at it! Actually, it's not a new way. I mean, maybe it is a little bit new, but it's very personal, and it's not sufficiently different.

> – Interview with Charles Weiner, March 5, 1966 (Niels Bohr Library and Archives with the Center for the History of Physics)

I worked hard at teaching in the beginning, and they were OK. I think the students were satisfied. Later, you give the same course over again, and you don't work so hard if you don't reorganize it. I got more and more careless about teaching. And if I teach something I've taught before, it's not any longer a good course, because I borrow so much stuff from before; and I'm so lazy about correcting papers and preparing the courses, I don't think they're any good any more. I think I'm getting less and less careful as a teacher, relatively. I mean, I'm still useful, but I think I used to be good, really good, relatively. And now I'm lazy.

> – Interview with Charles Weiner, June 27, 1966 (Niels Bohr Library and Archives with the Center for the History of Physics)

There's an awful lot of rote learning, and a lot of mistaking knowledge for the right technical words and so on, you know. A guy who says the right words is thought to know something. I didn't bother but I could have taught my child, after he learned to talk, to say — and I thought I would, just for the fun of it, to demonstrate this, but I didn't bother the poor boy — but it's not at all impossible to teach a child to say that pi is the ratio of the circumference to the diameter of a circle. It's just as easy to teach him that as to teach him a nursery rhyme. And then to say that pi is numerically equal to 3.14159. That way you can get fooled. You haven't the slightest idea what you're talking about, and you sound just fine.

— Interview with Charles Weiner, June 28, 1966 (Niels Bohr Library and Archives with the Center for the History of Physics)

I never know when I'm lecturing or teaching what the response is.

— Interview with Charles Weiner, June 28, 1966 (Niels Bohr Library and Archives with the Center for the History of Physics)

Teach them the culture of our government and our times, and prepare the better of them to be able to watch and appreciate or perhaps to take part in the greatest adventure that the human mind has ever embarked on.

— Notes for talk on "Science in America"

Today we do not have the power of expression to tell a student how to understand physics physically. We can write the laws, but we still can't say how to understand them physically. The only way you can understand physics physically, because of our lack of machinery for expressing this, is to follow the dull, Babylonian way of doing a whole lot of problems until you get the idea. That's all I can do for you. And the students who didn't get the idea in Babylonia flunked, and the guys who did get the idea died, so it's all the same!

  – *Feynman's Tips on Physics*, p. 50

If we're going to explain this theory, the first question is will you understand it? Will you understand the theory? When I tell you first that the first time we really fully explain it to our physics students, they're in the third year graduate physics, then you think the answer's going to be no. And that's correct: You will not understand it.

  – "QED: Photons — Corpuscles of Light," Sir Douglas Robb
    Lectures, University of Auckland, June 1979

I think we should teach them that the purpose of knowledge is to appreciate wonders even more. And that the knowledge is just to put into correct framework the wonder that nature is.

  – On teaching science to the public, Galileo Symposium, "What
    Is and What Should Be the Role of Scientific Culture in
    Modern Society," September 1964

If the professors of English will complain to me that the students who come to the universities, after all those years of study, still cannot spell "friend," I say to them that something's the matter with the way you spell friend.

  – "This Unscientific Age," John Danz Lecture Series, 1963

# Advice and Inspiration

If you have any talent, or any occupation that delights you, do it, and do it to the hilt. Don't ask why or what difficulties you may get into.

> — Letter to student Frederich Hipp, April 1961 (*Perfectly Reasonable Deviations from the Beaten Track*, p. 120)

You have no responsibility to live up to what other people think you ought to accomplish. I have no responsibility to be like they expect me to be. It's their mistake, not my failing.

– *Surely You're Joking, Mr. Feynman!*, p. 172

You ask me if an ordinary person could ever get to be able to imagine these things like I imagine them. Of course! I was an ordinary person who studied hard. There are no miracle people. It just happens they get interested in this thing and learn all this stuff, but they're just people.

– BBC, "Fun to Imagine" television series, 1983

[On revelation:] The hope of that gold — that can keep you going.

– Yorkshire Television program, "Take the World from Another Point of View," 1972

Know how to solve every problem that has been solved.

– Written on blackboard when he died

Just because Feynman says he is pro-nuclear power, isn't any argument at all worth paying attention to because I can tell you (for I know) that Feynman really doesn't know what he is talking about when he speaks of such things. He knows about other things (maybe). Don't pay attention to "authorities," think for yourself.

> – Letter to student Mark Minguillon, August 1976 (*Perfectly Reasonable Deviations from the Beaten Track*, p. 305)

Any real knowledge has to have been found out somehow. If an expert tells you that "a great man invented it" and the ideas cannot be explained, then be suspicious.

> – *U.S. News and World Report* interview, February 1985

All you have to do is, from time to time — in spite of everything, just try to examine a problem in a novel way. You won't "stifle the creative process" if you remember to think from time to time. Don't you have time to think?

> – Letter to Michael E. Stanley, March 1975 (*Perfectly Reasonable Deviations from the Beaten Track*, p. 283)

Find and pursue something interesting that delights you especially, so you become a kind of temporary expert in some phenomenon that you heard about. It's the way to save your soul — then you can always say, "Well, at least the other guys don't know anything about this!"

> – *Feynman's Tips on Physics*, p. 41

To know when you know, and when you don't know, and what it is you know and what it is you don't know, you gotta be very careful not to confuse yourself.

> – Yorkshire Television interview, "Take the World from Another Point of View," 1972

You should, in science, believe logic and arguments carefully drawn and not authorities.

– Letter to Beulah E. Cox, September 1975 (*Perfectly Reasonable Deviations from the Beaten Track*, p. 290)

Study hard what interests you the most in the most undisciplined, irreverent and original manner possible.

– Letter to J. M. Szabados, November 1965 (*Perfectly Reasonable Deviations from the Beaten Track*, p. 206)

Work as hard and as much as you want on the things you like to do the best. Try to keep the other grades from going to zero if you can.

– Letter to V. A. Van Der Hyde, July 1986 (*Perfectly Reasonable Deviations from the Beaten Track*, p. 415)

It is wonderful if you can find something you love to do in your youth which is big enough to sustain your interest through all your adult life. Because, whatever it is, if you do it well enough (and you will, if you truly love it), people will pay you to do what you want to do anyway.

– Letter to Eric W. Leuliette, September 1984 (*Perfectly Reasonable Deviations from the Beaten Track*, p. 369)

For some people when you are young you only want to go as fast, as far, and as deep as you can in one subject — all the others are neglected as being relatively uninteresting. But later on when you get older you find nearly everything is really interesting if you go into it deeply enough. Because what you learned as a youth is that one thing is even more interesting as you go deeper.

> – Letter to Mr. V. A. Van Der Hyde, July 1986 (*Perfectly Reasonable Deviations from the Beaten Track*, p. 283)

Work hard to find something that fascinates you. When you find it, you will know your lifework.

> – Letter to student Mike Flasar, November 1966 (*Perfectly Reasonable Deviations from the Beaten Track*, p. 229)

Don't think of what "you want to be," but what you "want to do."

> – Letter to V. A. Van Der Hyde, July 1986 (*Perfectly Reasonable Deviations from the Beaten Track*, p. 415)

I have just one wish for you: the good luck to be somewhere where you are free to maintain the kind of integrity I have described, and where you do not feel forced by a need to maintain your position in the organization, or financial support, or so on, to lose your integrity. May you have that freedom.

> – "Cargo Cult Science," Caltech commencement address, 1974

[On social elegance of people:] It isn't true that it's very fancy and everybody believes in it, and that you're some kind of a funny guy because you don't quite get in the swing. There are a lot of people in it that are smiling, or that even are elegant and superior, that understand what it is — that it's a show. But you don't know that at first.

> – Interview with Charles Weiner, March 5, 1966 (Niels Bohr Library and Archives with the Center for the History of Physics)

Do not read so much, look about you and think of what you see there.

> – Letter to Master Ashok Arora, January 1967 (*Perfectly Reasonable Deviations from the Beaten Track*, p. 230)

You cannot develop a personality with physics alone; the rest of life must be worked in.

> – Letter to Mr. Alan Woodward, March 1982 (*Perfectly Reasonable Deviations from the Beaten Track*, p. 345)

A man may be digging a ditch for someone else, or because he is forced to, or is stupid such a man is "toolish" but another working even harder may not be recognized as different by the bystanders but he may be digging for treasure. So dig for treasure, and when you find it you will know what to do.

> – Letter to student Mike Flasar, November 1966 (*Perfectly Reasonable Deviations from the Beaten Track*, p. 229)

Remain a thoughtful person and you will remain free. For freedom is a consistency of thought and action.

> – Notes for a commencement speech

Do not remain nameless to yourself — it is too sad a way to be. Know your place in the world and evaluate yourself fairly, not in terms of the naive ideals of your own youth, nor in terms of what you erroneously imagine your teacher's ideals are.

– Letter to Koichi Mano, February 1966 (*Perfectly Reasonable Deviations from the Beaten Track*, p. 201)

I can't believe I ever said I like to hear from old friends — or maybe I did — but I hate to answer letters!

– Letter to Dr. N. H. Spector, September 1985

No problem is too small or too trivial if we can really do something about it.

– Letter to Koichi Mano, February 1966 (*Perfectly Reasonable Deviations from the Beaten Track*, p. 201)

I entered MIT in mathematics, changed to electrical engineering for a while and then settled in physics. What field of physics? Aside from deciding I liked theoretical work best, I have wandered around from stresses in molecules to quantum theory electrodynamics, theory of liquid helium, nuclear physics, turbulence in the flow of water (I didn't succeed in the last two problems so nothing is published), and recently particle physics. You do any problem that you can, regardless of field.

– Letter to student Mark Minguillon, August 1976 (*Perfectly Reasonable Deviations from the Beaten Track*, pp. 306, 309)

What do I advise? Forget it all. Don't be afraid. Do what you get the greatest pleasure from. Is to build a cloud chamber? Then go on doing things like that. Develop your talents wherever they may lead. Damn the torpedoes full speed ahead!

– Letter to student Frederich Hipp, April 1961 (*Perfectly Reasonable Deviations from the Beaten Track*, p. 120)

Tell your son to stop trying to fill your head with science — for to fill your heart with love is enough.

– *No Ordinary Genius*, p. 161

We've learned from experience that the truth will come out. Other experimenters will repeat your experiment and find out whether you were wrong or right. Nature's phenomena will agree or they'll disagree with your theory. And, although you may gain some temporary fame and excitement, you will not gain a good reputation as a scientist if you haven't tried to be very careful in this kind of work. And it's this type of integrity, this kind of care not to fool yourself, that is missing to a large extent in much of the research in cargo cult science.

– "Cargo Cult Science," Caltech commencement address, 1974

It is therefore of first-rate importance that you know how to "triangulate" — that is, to know how to figure something out from what you already know. It is absolutely necessary.

– *Feynman's Tips on Physics*, p. 39

The best thing to do is what seems best to you, not me, so that you will motivate your students by your own confidence, interest, and personality. It is not good to seek criticism from other personalities.

– Letter to Professor P. Mitra, December 1973

If you feel that you or your friends know enough to give advice, suggest curricula, etc., that is your business. If not, then mind your own business, and go home and give your own physics students the best damn course you can.

– Letter to John M. Fowler, March 1966


We are going to suppose something: that all the energies are positive. If the energies were negative we know that we could solve all our energy problems by dumping particles into this pit of negative energy and running the world with the extra energy.

– Dirac Memorial Lectures, "The Reason for Antiparticles," 1986

# Intelligence

After all, I was born not knowing and have only had a little time to change that here and there.

– Letter to Armando Garcia, December 1965 (*Perfectly Reasonable Deviations from the Beaten Track*, p. 396)

Ordinary fools are all right, you can talk to them, and try to help them out. But pompous fools — guys who are fools and are covering it all over and impressing people as to how wonderful they are with all this hocus-pocus, THAT, I CANNOT STAND!

– *Surely You're Joking, Mr. Feynman!*, p. 284

There's no talent, no special ability to understand quantum mechanics, or to imagine electromagnetic fields, that comes without practice and reading and learning and study. I was born not understanding quantum mechanics — I still don't understand quantum mechanics!

– BBC, "Fun to Imagine" television series, 1983

The whole idea that the average person is unintelligent is a very dangerous idea. Even if it's true, it shouldn't be dealt with they way it's dealt with

– "The Unscientific Age," John Danz Lecture Series, 1963

I don't know what it is exactly, but it's interesting how when you do something foolish, you protect yourself from knowing of your own foolishness.

– "The Remarkable Dr. Feynman," *Los Angeles Times Magazine*, April 20, 1986

I'm a very curious man, and I watch phenomena that happen all the time. You often wonder what it would be like to be going a little crazy. And I had this experience of going crazy, or of something wrong with my mind, and I didn't notice it. The same mind that is weakening has lost its analytical ability to watch itself. So I was simply rationalizing every failure. I didn't have the sense to realize what was perfectly obvious: A person doesn't get old in a week!

– UCSB talk, "Los Alamos from Below," February 1975

Even if you're one of the last couple of guys in the class, it doesn't mean you're not any good. You just have to compare yourself to a reasonable group, instead of to this insane collection that we've got here at Caltech.

– *Feynman's Tips on Physics*, p. 18

The first one has to do with whether a man knows what he is talking about, whether what he says has some basis or not. And my trick that I use is very easy. If you ask him intelligent questions — that is, penetrating, interested, honest, frank, direct questions on the subject, and no trick questions — then he quickly gets stuck. It is like a child asking naive questions. If you ask naive but relevant questions, then almost immediately the person doesn't know the answer, if he is an honest man.

– "This Unscientific Age" John Danz Lecture Series, 1963

We are not that much smarter than each other.

– Quoted in the *New York Times Magazine*, James Gleick, September 26, 1992

I'm an explorer, okay? I get curious about everything, and I want to investigate all kinds of stuff.

– BBC, "No Ordinary Genius," 1993

What I cannot create, I do not understand.

– Written on blackboard when he died

I've learned to draw and I read a little bit, but I'm really still a very one-sided person and I don't know a great deal. I have a limited intelligence and I use it in a particular direction.

– *What Do You Care What Other People Think?*, p. 11

No matter how carefully we select the men [only men were admitted to Caltech in 1961], no matter how patiently we make the analysis, when they get here something happens: It always turns out that approximately half of them are below average! Of course you laugh at this because it's self-evident to the rational mind, but not to the emotional mind — the emotional mind can't laugh at this. When you've lived all the time as number one or number two (or even possibly number three) in high school science, and when you know that everybody who's below average in the science courses where you came from is a complete idiot, and now you suddenly discover that you are below average — and half of you guys are — it's a terrible blow, because you imagine that it means you're as dumb as those guys used to be in high school, relatively. That's the great disadvantage of Caltech: that this psychological blow is so difficult to take.

– *Feynman's Tips on Physics*, p. 17

# The Nobel Prize

I don't like honors. I appreciate it for the work that I did, and I know that there's a lot of physicists who use my work. I don't need anything else. I don't think there's any sense to anything else. I don't see that it makes any point that someone in the Swedish Academy decides that this work is "noble enough" to receive a prize. I've already got the prize: The prize is the pleasure of finding the thing out, the kick in the discovery, the observation that other people use it. Those are the real things.

– BBC, "The Pleasure of Finding Things Out," 1981

You know, I did this work in 1949. I guess they just ran out of winners and looked back over the old stuff.

> – *South Shore Record*, October 28, 1965

And so, you Swedish people, with your honors, and your trumpets, and your king — forgive me. For I understand at last — such things provide entrance to the heart. Used by a wise and peaceful people, they can generate good feeling, even love, among men, even in lands far beyond your own. For that lesson, I thank you. *Tack!*

> – From Les Prix Nobel en 1965 [Nobel Foundation], Stockholm, 1966

So what happened to the old theory that I fell in love with as a youth? Well, I would say it's become an old lady, that has very little attractive left in her and the young today will not have their hearts pound anymore when they look at her. But, we can say the best we can for any old woman, that she has been a very good mother and she has given birth to some very good children. And, I thank the Swedish Academy of Sciences for complimenting one of them. Thank you.

> – From *Nobel Lectures, Physics 1963–1970*, Elsevier Publishing Company, Amsterdam, 1972

One of the pleasant things about winning the prize is to hear from former students.

> – Letter to Loren A. Page, November 1965

I was delighted too when I heard about the Nobel Prize, thinking as you did that my bongo playing was at last recognized.

> – Letter to Sandra Chester (*Perfectly Reasonable Deviations from the Beaten Track*, pp. 163–164)

There were all kinds of things, serious and humorous, telegrams and letters. And in each of them I saw happiness on the part of the people who were sending it and some real feeling of affection, which kind of overwhelmed me and made me feel real love for all these people, because they all seemed to be so good-hearted and so happy about the congratulations. I didn't realize that to have everything come at once like that, it really makes you feel good. So that was the good part of the whole thing, the letters. That was the good part.

> – Interview with Charles Weiner, June 28, 1966 (Niels Bohr Library and Archives with the Center for the History of Physics)

We have not quantitatively checked this theory with the gluons — it might be wrong. We have only got a few experiments to check the W-Boson — that might be wrong. On the other hand, why does it look like it could be the same thing repeated? One: the limit of the imagination of man. When he sees a new theory and a new phenomenon, he tries to fit it with that theory, and until he's done enough experiments, he doesn't know that it doesn't work. So when he gives a lecture in 1979 in New Zealand, he thinks it works!

> – "QED: New Queries," Sir Douglas Robb Lectures, University of Auckland, 1979

Some guy who made a lot of money on dynamite wants to make himself a big thing and put his name on the big prize so everybody will remember the name "Nobel," and for that I got to be annoyed. The hell with it.

– "Nobel Prize: Another Side of the Medal," *The Los Angeles Times*, October 7, 1983

Appearances, dinner with the King, meet the King, get the Prize, tatata, all this stuff, see. And the worst of it was that I ridicule kings and things like that. I ridicule ceremony. I used to. I still do. I laugh at it. And here I have to be a party to it. It's not very consistent to laugh at it when somebody else is doing it, but when you're in it, because you're receiving a prize and so on, you're going to go right along without some kind of — You know, you used to laugh, and here you are, the Big Boy, right in the middle of it, not laughing anymore, ha ha ha!

– Interview with Charles Weiner, June 28, 1966 (Niels Bohr Library and Archives with the Center for the History of Physics)

The real mistake that one makes when one wins the prize is to take it all too seriously for example, this speech. I worried very hard — is it appropriate to give such a speech? It don't make a goddamn bit of difference. It isn't really very serious. It doesn't make any difference what you say. After all, may I remind you that I have never in my life read the Nobel lecture of anybody? They're published, but who reads them?

– Interview with Charles Weiner, June 28, 1966 (Niels Bohr Library and Archives with the Center for the History of Physics)

If somebody says, "We need a Nobel Prize winner to sign a letter to Russia on the Jews," I say, "I'm willing to sign a letter to Russia on the Jews but I'm not willing to be a Nobel Prize winner signing a letter to Russia on the Jews."

> – Interview with Charles Weiner, February 4, 1966 (Niels Bohr Library and Archives with the Center for the History of Physics)

Now it turns out that after you win the prize, you're supposed to give a talk on what you did to win the prize. I should think that they knew the reason when they gave you the prize, but apparently they're a bit uncertain or something.

> – CERN talk, December 1965

[On learning of the Nobel Prize:] The telephone rang, the guy said I'm from some broadcasting company. I was very annoyed to be awakened. That was my natural reaction. You know, you're half awake, and you're annoyed. So the guy says, "We'd like to inform you that you've won the Nobel Prize." And I'm thinking to myself — I'm still annoyed; see — it didn't register. So I said, "You could have told me that in the morning." So he says, "I thought you'd like to know." Well, I said I was asleep and put the telephone back.

> – "Nobel Prize: Another Side of the Medal," *The Los Angeles Times*, October 7, 1983

I picture myself as an ordinary guy, and I hate to be discovered. I hate to find that the way I picture myself isn't the way they're picturing me. They have me as some kind of Nobel Prize winner, but I still really haven't caught on that I'm any different than I was before.

– Future for Science interview

It bothers me that everyone always chooses "Nobel prize winners" as important examples of scientists. Why do we pay such attention to the choice of the members of the Swedish Academy? That may be OK for the unknowing public, but surely a science teacher can make his own independent choices of which scientists excite his imagination and which men he would like to call to the attention of his students.

– Letter to Mr. Stuart Zimmer, February 1982 (*Perfectly Reasonable Deviations from the Beaten Track*, p. 340)

I just get tired of being a "Nobel Prize Winner" from time to time.

– Letter to Mr. Stuart Zimmer, February 1982 (*Perfectly Reasonable Deviations from the Beaten Track*, p. 340)

It is very hard to be pushed out of the ivory tower; the light is so strong that it hurts. What hurts worse is to think of myself in tails receiving something from the King of Sweden, while the television cameras are watching.

– Letter to Betsy Holland Gehman, November 1965 (*Perfectly Reasonable Deviations from the Beaten Track*, p. 187)

Well isn't it exciting to hear from old school mates; that is one of the best parts of winning the Nobel Prize. All kinds of people that

I used to know and like, that I haven't heard from in a long time, come out of the woodwork.

 – Letter to Wanna M. Hecker, November 1965

I used to be able to go to any old high school and answer questions at the physics clubs. But now, they don't even ask me. They're afraid. They wouldn't ask a Nobel Prize winner to talk to a physics club. And if some student finally gets up the nerve to do it, what happens is, I say OK. And when I go there, it's not just the physics club but the whole damn school is there. The principal finds out or the physics teacher finds out what the kid in the physics club has done, and they say, "Oh, he's such an important man, everybody should be interested in this guy." It's kind of out of proportion. I'm not up to it.

 – "The Remarkable Dr. Feynman," *Los Angeles Times Magazine*,
  April 20, 1986

[On winning the Nobel Prize:] You can't escape it. A guy calls you up in the middle of the night, and my first reaction was, I won't accept. But then I realized that if I said that I'd make a bigger stink than if I took it. You're stuck. It's not fair to be stuck like that. There's no reason why your privacy and everything has to be interfered with.

 – "Nobel Prize: Another Side of the Medal," *The Los Angeles
  Times*, October 7, 1983

[After Nobel Prize:] We had hundreds of letters, from friends all over the world, and relatives — like a relative of mine happened to be on a ship, you know, going from Spain to somewhere and, oh gee, he practically busted a gasket, and sent a big telegram. I got telephone calls from Mexico City that I can't hear because the telephone system was no good. I still tried to get back and tell that person I really liked it, and thank them for the call, but I don't know the address so I'm stuck. It was hard to hear but I finally understood who it was. All kinds of crazy stuff. Very nice letters. They were all full of — kind of happy. Everybody was excited. Each letter indicated some excitement in the house, whoever it was.

> – Interview with Charles Weiner, June 28, 1966 (Niels Bohr
> Library and Archives with the Center for the History of Physics)

At the dancing afterwards — you see, I had to get some release from the formalities — I overdid it then. When I got informal, I just went wild, you see. So when the dancing began, we started, I danced with my wife; then I danced with somebody else, a sister of a Nobel Prize winner. I didn't get to dancing with the Princess, because I had a — you know, I wouldn't even try.

> – Interview with Charles Weiner, June 28, 1966 (Niels Bohr
> Library and Archives with the Center for the History of Physics)

When I danced with my wife, when I danced with the daughter of a Nobel Prize winner, they were taking pictures, all the time — click, flash, flash. When I danced with this girl, which I did twice as many dances as I did with anybody else altogether — no pictures. Nothing. Not in the paper. Not a picture. Nothing. Apparently there's something wrong with this, you see, and they protect the Nobel Prize winners from their dumb idiosyncrasies. But this was my idea of relaxing, of informality. I had to do something because I had to get out from under, you know what I mean? It was fun. It was funny.

– Interview with Charles Weiner, June 28, 1966 (Niels Bohr Library and Archives with the Center for the History of Physics)

The prize was a signal to permit them to express, and me to learn about, their feelings. Each joy, though transient thrill, repeated in so many places, amounts to a considerable sum of human happiness. And, each note of affection released thus one upon another has permitted me to realize a depth of love for my friends and acquaintances, which I had never felt so poignantly before.

– From Les Prix Nobel en 1965 [Nobel Foundation], Stockholm, 1966

Hell, if I could explain it to the average person, it wouldn't have been worth the Nobel prize.

– *People*, July 22, 1985

[To a reporter after being woken up to be told about his winning the Nobel Prize:] This is a heck of an hour. I could have found out later this morning.

– *California Tech*, Caltech student newspaper, October 1965

Yeah, "give us a quote" is really what they're trying to say. And I couldn't figure a way of saying it. I gradually developed a way, but it was rather too late — saying I'd worked on the interaction of radiation and matter. That sounds good and doesn't say anything.

– Interview with Charles Weiner, June 28, 1966 (Niels Bohr Library and Archives with the Center for the History of Physics)

# Worldview

The first principle is that you must not fool yourself — and you are the easiest person to fool.

– "Cargo Cult Science," Caltech commencement address, 1974

Cleverness, however, is relative.

> – Audio recording of Feynman Lectures on Physics, Lecture 4, October 6, 1961

All the time you're saying to yourself, "I could do that, but I won't" which is just another way of saying that you can't.

> – *Surely You're Joking, Mr. Feynman!*, p. 68

I learned very early the difference between knowing the name of something and knowing something.

> – *What Do You Care What Other People Think?*, p. 14

It is necessary, I believe, to accept this idea, not only for science but also for other things; it is of great value to acknowledge ignorance. It is a fact that when we make decisions in our life, we don't necessarily know that we are making them correctly; we only think that we are doing the best we can — and that is what we should do.

> – "The Relation of Science and Religion," May 1956

There is no authority who decides what is a good idea.

> – "The Uncertainty of Science," John Danz Lecture Series, 1963

What Do You Care What Other People Think?

– *What Do You Care What Other People Think?*

It's good to know I have such loyal, permanent rooters no matter what I do, good or bad.

– Letter to Evie Frank, December 1965

In order to talk to each other, we have to have words, and that's all right.

– National Science Teachers Association Fourteenth Convention lecture, "What Is Science?" April 1966

Every morning at six I have this silly habit of going out and jogging slowly (6 mph) around for 5 or 6 miles. I haven't figured out why — I don't know whether it makes me feel good or what. I always feel good, but I did before I started jogging too.

– Letter to Mariela Johansen, January 1975

There has been much talk about the way scientists look at love and so on, and I think it isn't really quite right, that science is not a dull, hard, cold business, but as a matter of fact I believed then, and I still believe, that if used right it gives you a way of looking at the world and at the meaning of things that are happening to you that gives you some control and calmness in otherwise difficult situations, and so on.

– Interview with Charles Weiner, March 5, 1966 (Niels Bohr Library and Archives with the Center for the History of Physics)

I have a philosophy that it doesn't do any good to go and make regrets about what you did before but to try and remember how you made the decision at the time.

   – Interview for Viewpoint

[On Hans Bethe:] Like most Europeans he was a very serious man. And that means that he thinks better, it's legitimate to talk about intellectual subjects at a beer party. That's all it means.

   – CERN talk, December 1965

We are lucky to live in an age in which we are still making discoveries.

   – *The Character of Physical Law*, p. 127

If you thought that science was certain — well, that is just an error on your part.

   – *The Character of Physical Law*, p. 77

It does not do harm to a mystery to know a little about it.

   – *Feynman Lectures on Physics*, vol. 1, p. 3

The brotherhood we are attempting this week is not a viewpoint to have for seven days. Nor is it simply a concept to be kept in mind for all time. Brotherhood must be a program of action, a program of real and active cooperation between the peoples of the world. And this cooperation is not simply a desirable thing.

Cooperation is a necessity for the survival of a just fraction of the vast population of the earth — you, and I, included.

– Notes from before Los Alamos

I am curious on how reliable old memories are and wonder how much we make up in our own mind when we review events. Maybe we remember saying what we would have liked to say.

– Letter to Dr. Judah Cahn, March 1983 (*Perfectly Reasonable Deviations from the Beaten Track*, p. 362)

And there's something that struck me, it's very curious: I suspect that what goes on in every man's head might be very, very different.

– BBC, "Fun to Imagine" television series, 1983

I share sorrow in the loss of a man's life, which added significance and interest to all human life.

– In a telegram to Dr. Aage Bohr, regarding the death of Dr. Neils Bohr

If in some cataclysm, all of the scientific knowledge is to be destroyed and only one sentence is to be passed on to the next generations of creatures, what would be the best thing, the thing that contains the most information in the least number of words? I believe it is the atomic hypothesis, or the atomic fact, or whatever you want to call it, that all things are made out of atoms, little particles that move around, are in perpetual motion, attract each other when they are some distance apart, but repel being squeezed into one another. In that one sentence, you'll see that there is an enormous amount of information about the world if just a little imagination and thinking is applied.

> – Audio recording of Feynman Lectures on Physics, Lecture 1,
> September 26, 1961

The worthwhile problems are the ones you can really solve or help solve, the ones you can really contribute something to. A problem is grand in science if it lies before us unsolved and we see some way for us to make a little headway into it. I would advise you to take even simpler, or as you say, humbler, problems until you find some you can really solve easily, no matter how trivial. You will get the pleasure of success, and of helping your fellow man, even if it is only to answer a question in the mind of a colleague less able than you.

> – Letter to Koichi Mano, February 1966 (*Perfectly Reasonable
> Deviations from the Beaten Track*, p. 198)

The world is a dynamic mess of jiggling things if you look at it right.

> – BBC, "Fun to Imagine!" television series, 1983

What I am trying to do is bring birth to clarity, which is really a half-assedly thought-out pictorial semi vision thing.

> – Quoted in James Gleick, *Genius: The Life and Science of
> Richard Feynman*, 1992, p. 244

The grand ages of different civilizations are characterized by people's enormous confidence in success, their belief that they have some new thing that is different, and their certainty that they are developing it by themselves.

– MIT centennial, "Talk of Our Times," December 1961

It is quite certain that many things are inherited but it is evil and dangerous to maintain, in these days of little knowledge of these matters, that there is a true Jewish race or specific Jewish hereditary character.

– Letter to Tina Levitan, February 1967 (*Perfectly Reasonable Deviations from the Beaten Track*, p. 235)

To select, for approbation, the peculiar elements that come from some supposedly Jewish heredity is to open the door to all kinds of nonsense on racial theory. Such theoretical views were used by Hitler. Surely you cannot maintain on the one hand that certain valuable elements can be inherited from the "Jewish people," and deny that other elements which other people may find annoying or worse are not inherited by these same "people."

– Letter to Tina Levitan, February 1967 (*Perfectly Reasonable Deviations from the Beaten Track*, p. 235)

The error of anti-Semitism is not that the Jews are not really bad after all, but that evil, stupidity and grossness is not a monopoly of the Jewish people but a universal characteristic of mankind in general.

– Letter to Tina Levitan, February 1967 (*Perfectly Reasonable Deviations from the Beaten Track*, p. 235)

[On his mental health after the bomb:] I would see people building a bridge and I would say, "They don't understand." I really believed that it was senseless to make anything because it would all be destroyed very soon anyway, but they didn't understand that. And I had this very strange view of any construction that I would see. I always thought how foolish they are to try to make something. So I was really in a kind of depressive condition.

– BBC, "The Pleasure of Finding Things Out," 1981

The error of pro-Semitism is not that the Jewish people or the Jewish heritage is not really good, but rather the error is that intelligence, good will, and kindness is not, thank God, a monopoly of the Jewish people but a universal characteristic of mankind in general.

– Letter to Tina Levitan, February 1967 (*Perfectly Reasonable Deviations from the Beaten Track*, p. 235)

The way my two children responded to my stories was very different, but I don't know that it was because one was a boy and the other a girl. I think people are very different and that if I had two sons they would respond differently too — maybe.

– Letter to Dorothy Weeks, February 1983 (*Perfectly Reasonable Deviations from the Beaten Track*, p. 358)

# The Future

Why repeat all this? Because there are new generations born every day. Because there are very great ideas developed in the history of man, and these ideas do not last unless they are passed purposely and clearly from generation to generation.

– "The Uncertainty of Science," John Danz Lecture Series, 1963

When we get stuck in a certain place, it's a place where History will not repeat herself. And that makes it even more exciting, because whatever we're going to look at — the method and the trick and the way it's going to look — is going to be very different than anything we've seen before, because we've used all the methods from before.

– Yorkshire Television interview, "Take the World from Another Point of View," 1972

If we thought the past was a long time, the future seems incomprehensibly longer.

– From notes for "About Time" program, 1957

We can always say to other people: "That was very clever of you to have explained why the world just has to be the way we have found it to be so far. But what is it going to look like tomorrow?" Our philosophy's vigor comes from the fact that we are still struggling.

– MIT centennial, "Talk of Our Times," December 1961

Fundamental physics has a finite lifetime. It has a while to go. At the present moment, it is going with terrific excitement, and I do not want to retire. But I'm taking advantage of the fact that I live in the right age.

– MIT centennial, "Talk of Our Times," December 1961

We like improved production, but we have problems with automation. We are happy with the development of medicine, and then we worry about the number of births and the fact that no one dies from the diseases we have eliminated. Or else, with the same knowledge of bacteria, we have hidden laboratories in which men are working as hard as they can to develop diseases for which no one else will be able to find a cure. We are happy with the development of air transportation and are impressed by the great airplanes, but we are aware also of the severe horrors of air war. We are pleased with the ability to communicate between nations, and then we worry about the fact that we can be snooped upon so easily. We are excited by the fact that space can now be entered; well, we'll undoubtedly have difficulty there too. The most famous of all of these is of course the development of nuclear energy and its obvious problems.

– "The Uncertainty of Science," John Danz Lecture Series, 1963

We are here only at the very beginning of time for the human race. There are thousands of years in the past, and there is an unknown amount of time in the future. There are all kinds of opportunities, and there are all kinds of dangers.

– "The Uncertainty of Values," John Danz Lecture Series, 1963

From a long view of the history of mankind, seen from, say, ten thousand years from now, there can be little doubt that the most significant event of the 19th century will be judged as Maxwell's discovery of the laws of electrodynamics. The American Civil War will pale into provincial insignificance in comparison with this important scientific event of the same decade.

– *Feynman Lectures on Physics*, pp. 1–11

I am sorry to have to answer your question (as to whether I consider nuclear energy a curse or a salvation of mankind) that I don't really know. I look to the future neither with hope nor fear but with uncertainty as to what will be.

– Letter to Dr. David A. Marcus, February 1975 (*Perfectly Reasonable Deviations from the Beaten Track*, p. 279)

I hope for freedom for future generations, freedom to doubt, to develop, to continue the adventure of finding out new ways of doing things, of solving problems.

– "The Uncertainty of Values," John Danz Lecture Series, 1963

We are only at the beginning of the development of the human race; of the development of the human mind, of intelligent life, we have years and years in the future. It is our responsibility not to give the answer today as to what it is all about, to drive everybody down in that direction and to say, "This is a solution to it all." Because we will be chained then to the limits of our present imagination.

– Galileo Symposium, "What Is and What Should Be the Role of Scientific Culture in Modern Society," September 1964

We are at the very beginning of time for the human race. It is not unreasonable that we grapple with problems. But there are tens of thousands of years in the future. Our responsibility is to do what we can, learn what we can, improve the solutions, and pass them on.

– "The Value of Science," December 1955

I have often made the hypothesis that ultimately physics will not require a mathematical statement, that in the end the machinery will be revealed, and the laws will turn out to be simple, like the checker board with all its apparent complexities.

— *The Character of Physical Law*, pp. 57–58

People in the past, in the nightmare of their times, had dreams for the future. And now that the future has materialized, we see that in many ways the dreams have been surpassed, but in still more ways there are many of our dreams of today which are very much the dreams of people of the past.

— Galileo Symposium, "What Is and What Should Be the Role of Scientific Culture in Modern Society," September 1964

So there's a great deal that goes over from the one science to the other, and the most important thing that goes over is the character of the science, the critical character. It's very, very much the same. The sources of dirt and the sources of error are physically different. But you can still get an idea: does it make sense or doesn't it make sense?

— Interview with Charles Weiner, June 28, 1966 (Niels Bohr Library and Archives with the Center for the History of Physics)

Future always uncertain. Is there one?

— Notes

There are a few young men hoping to be theoretical physicists who will be inspired to take the attitude: "Those guys don't know what the hell they've been talking about all these years, they couldn't even solve the most simple problem. I'll show 'em how to do it." That's good, that might happen.

– Caltech lecture on particles, 1973

I had a calculus book once that said, "What one fool can do, another can." What we've been able to work out about nature may look abstract and threatening to someone who hasn't studied it, but it was fools who did it, and in the next generation, all the fools will understand it.

– *Omni* interview, February 1979

Each generation that discovers something from its experience must pass that on, but it must pass that on with a delicate balance of respect and disrespect, so that the race that is now aware of the disease to which it is liable does not inflict its errors too rigidly on its youth, but it does pass on the accumulated wisdom, plus the wisdom that it may not be wisdom.

– National Science Teachers Association Fourteenth Convention lecture, "What Is Science?" April 1966

If one were walking through a building to get from one side to the other and had not yet reached the door, one might argue, "Look, we have been walking through this building, we have not reached the door; therefore, there is no door at the other end." It seems to me that we are walking through a building, but we do not know whether it is an infinite building or a finite building, so there is still a possibility of a final solution. One thing that would happen, I think, if a final solution were found would be deterioration in the philosophy of science.

– MIT centennial, "Talk of Our Times," December 1961

My son is like that, too, although he's much wider in his interests than I was at his age. He's interested in magic, in computer programming, in the history of the early church, in topology — oh, he's going to have a terrible time, there are so many interesting things.

– *Omni* interview, February 1979

# Honoring Richard Feynman

He was the most original mind of his generation.

– Freeman Dyson of the Institute for Advanced Study in Princeton,
*New York Times*, February 17, 1988

He's the most creative theoretical physicist of his time and a true genius. He has touched with his unique creativity just about every field of physics.

– Sidney D. Drell, former president of the American Physical Society, *New York Times*, February 17, 1988

In science, as well as in other fields of human endeavor there are two kinds of geniuses: the "ordinary" and the "magicians." An ordinary genius is a fellow that you and I would be just as good as, if we were only many times better. There is no mystery as to how his mind works. Once we understand what he has done, we feel certain that we, too, could have done it. It is different with the magicians . . . . Even after we understand what they have done it is completely dark . . . . Richard Feynman is a magician of the highest caliber.

– Marc Kac, *Enigmas of Chance*, p. xxv

C.P. Snow described Feynman "as though Groucho Marx was suddenly standing in for a great scientist."

– "The Cult of Richard Feynman," *Los Angeles Times Magazine*, December 2, 2001

I would drop everything to hear him lecture on the municipal drainage system.

– David Mermin of Cornell, cited in *Lectures on Computation*, ed. Tony Hey

Dick made a conscious effort to look at problems from a different vantage point. It was deliberate.

– Thomas A. Tombrello, Caltech Oral History Archives, interview by Heidi Aspaturian, December 2010

I'm thinking how to measure how smart Feynman was, because it wasn't any standard sort of smart. It was this way of viewing the world obliquely, and he tried to get there deliberately. I think he worked really hard at that and succeeded in marvelous ways.

– Thomas A. Tombrello, Caltech Oral History Archives, interview by Heidi Aspaturian, December 2010

Well, Dick Feynman reinvented the wheel, but it turned out to be a much better wheel.

– Valentine L. Telegdi, Caltech Oral History Archives, interview by Sara Lippincott, March 2002

Feynman was not a theorist's theorist, but a physicist's physicist and a teacher's teacher.

– Valentine L. Telegdi, *Physics Today*, February 1989

He is a second Dirac, only this time human.

– Eugene Wigner, quoted by Robert Oppenheimer in a letter to Professor Raymond Birge, University of California, Berkeley, 1943

An honest man, the outstanding intuitionist of our age, and a prime example of what may lie in store for anyone who dares to follow the beat of a different drum.

    – Julian Schwinger, *Physics Today*, February 1989

I knew Feynman a bit, and I will say that Feynman could do in a day what 100 John Rigdens could never do. Never do.

    – John Rigden, interview with Dr. Dudley Herschbach, American
      Institute of Physics, 2003

He had a great reputation. He was already heralded as this very clever fellow from Princeton who knew everything. And he did know everything, you know. He did solve some problems for us, just like that.

    – Philip Morrison, interview with Charles Weiner, American
      Institute of Physics, 1967

You can talk to Feynman and his answers are precise and of the type that an experimental physicist can understand, or at least thinks he understands.

    – Carl Anderson, Caltech Oral History Archives, interview by
      Harriett Lyle, 1979

When Dick was faced with a problem in mathematics, he was tremendously intuitive. He would find ways to solve the problem, or to prove something that he'd conjectured was true. These ways would be quite original and would usually be considered completely unorthodox by the mathematical fraternity. But they worked. He understood mathematics well enough to invent new mathematics that was intrinsically correct. He didn't make mistakes at it; it's just that he developed novel ways to do things that fitted in with his experience, and achieved results that sometimes took other people quite a while to understand how he'd achieved them.

  – Charles A. Barnes, interview with Heidi Aspaturian, Caltech
     Oral History Archives, July–August 1987

Before he went off to Sweden to receive the Nobel Prize, he gave an absolutely wonderful lecture on the campus to the local people in the little theatre — Culbertson — that used to exist here on campus. It was a beautiful little building, and it held two or three hundred people, I guess. We were just fascinated while Dick made a very clear and extremely modest, typical Dick Feynman exposition of how he had got to the position that finally ended up with him being invited to Sweden to get the Nobel Prize. He explained that the way he got to the point of being able to formulate his rules for quantum electrodynamics was by doing every difficult quantum electrodynamics problem that people would bring to him.

  – Charles A. Barnes, interview with Heidi Aspaturian, Caltech
     Oral History Archives, July–August 1987

But whenever Dick went somewhere for discussions of difficulties with then standard theory, he would invite people to dig out problems that they couldn't solve or could only solve with incredible difficulty. The ones that were particularly useful to him were those that other people had solved, but only with enormous difficulty. By looking at these problems and learning how to solve them by his own methods, Dick evolved his own set of rules.

– Charles A. Barnes, interview with Heidi Aspaturian, Caltech Oral History Archives, July–August 1987

I remember Richard Feynman saying, "I could never figure out what all these other guys were doing, therefore I did it my own way." And, you know — to paraphrase Frost — that made all the difference with Dick.

– Thomas A. Tombrello, interview with Heidi Aspaturian, Caltech Oral History Archives, December 2010

Truly one of the most original people at Caltech.

– Thomas A. Tombrello, interview with Heidi Aspaturian, Caltech Oral History Archives, December 2010

With Dick, there was the Feynman effect. It's like the Chinese restaurant effect — ten minutes after dinner you're hungry again. With Dick, the lecture was so clear that you quit taking notes. And then five minutes after the lecture, you couldn't reproduce the lecture! I remember when Matt Sands and Leighton, people like that, were taking notes for the Feynman lectures in freshman physics. They often realized at the end of a talk that they couldn't reproduce it. They had photographs of the board. They had recorded what Feynman said. Still, there was something elusive about it. I'm not saying it was wrong or incomplete. It was subtle.

And you didn't realize the subtlety, because it was so smooth, it was so beautifully done. It was a piece of artwork. But you had to constantly be aware of the fact that because Dick made it seem so simple, you were missing key things. The Feynman effect. It was very interesting.

– Thomas A. Tombrello, interview with Heidi Aspaturian, Caltech Oral History Archives, December 2010

I had a very strange interaction with Feynman. We were discussing something, and he said to me, "If I don't absolutely know something about it, I don't say I know something about it." And this was meant in a very friendly way. You don't get offended by that.

– Samuel Epstein, interview with Carol Bugé, Caltech Oral History Archives, December 1985–January 1986

He made the person he was talking to feel charming and witty and suddenly feel that you could do high-level physics. And he was a wonderful listener.

– Jenijoy La Belle, interview with Heidi Aspaturian, Caltech History Archives, February–May 2008, April 2009

The students regarded him as their patron saint at Caltech, [and the reputation] is quite deserved.

– Steven C. Frautschi, interview with Shirley K. Cohen, Caltech History Archives, June 2003

I remember Feynman's story. They called him up and said, "You won the Einstein Prize." He said, "Well, what's that?" And they

said, "Well, you get $15,000. Don't you have anything to say?"
He said, "Hot dog!"

– Seymour Benzer, interview with Heidi Aspaturian, Caltech
Oral History Archives, September 1990–February 1991

I didn't know Dick well at all. I knew him well enough to call him
Dick, but that was about all; we hadn't had a lot of interaction. I
said, "Dick, what's special about the center of the galaxy? Why
should we see something like this? Is there something special
about that?" He was standing there and looking down at this
[chart on the floor]. He said, "That's where God lives."

– James A. Westphal, interview with Shirley K. Cohen, Caltech
Oral History Archives, July 1998

He had an enormous impact on me, not just intellectually but in kind
of seeking the truth. All these things underneath that drove him —
not just how smart he was — had a really big influence on me.

– Barry C. Barish, interview with Shirley K. Cohen, Caltech Oral
History Archives, July 1998

Feynman is a much more exuberant person and much more of an
extrovert, really. Life is just happiness for him, even if he's had all
these medical troubles. He just is a fundamentally happy person.

– Hans A. Bethe, interview with Judith R. Goodstein, Caltech
Oral History Archives, February 1982

The thing that always impressed me about Dick was that you
could ask him a question, and if it wasn't a very good question,

he would take it and turn it around and answer maybe another question that was a good question. You'd just learn an enormous amount from him.

— Alvin V. Tollenstrup, interview with David A. Valone, Caltech Oral History Archives, December 1994

And these new areas; when I was an undergraduate, nobody did quantum mechanics, except super-advanced PhD students. First they had to learn all sorts of fancy Hamiltonian mechanics and all sorts of stuff, it was thought then. You had to go through all that monkey business before you could hope to even begin quantum mechanics . . . . Richard Feynman, among other people, showed that you don't have to go through that other stuff. You just start talking about quantum mechanics and the kids lap it up.

— David S. Wood, interview with Shirley K. Cohen, Caltech Oral History Archives, May 1994

The faculty and the students are in many ways very much alike here. This I gradually began to learn in those postwar days, when everybody was new here or was restarting again after the war. The students of course, in a sense, copy the faculty, because the faculty are role models for them. Dick Feynman is the great example. They all love him, and rightly so.

— Rodman W. Paul, interview with Carol Bugé, Caltech Oral History Archives, February 1982

A lecture by Dr. Feynman is a rare treat indeed. For humor and drama, suspense and interest it often rivals Broadway stage plays. And above all, it crackles with clarity. If physics is the underlying "melody" of science, then Dr. Feynman is its most lucid troubadour.

– Irving Bengelsdorf, *Los Angeles Times* science editor, 1967

When people get Nobel Prizes, that's probably one of the chief problems that the division chairman has, trying to hold onto the best people on the staff, and trying to handle these offers that they are continually getting. And if they get a Nobel Prize, that doesn't help solve that problem. Except, I do want to say that in Feynman's case, he said he had made up his mind; he likes Caltech and he wants to stay here, no matter what offers he gets — and you can be sure he's gotten them from about every place in the world.

I heard that when he answered the phone, he said, "Are you going to give me an offer?" If the person said, "No, I'm not at all interested in that," then he'd go ahead and talk to him; otherwise he would say, "The answer's no," and hang up. Maybe that's a joke, but I heard that about Dick Feynman. He's a very loyal Caltech professor.

– Carl Anderson, interview with Harriett Lyle, Caltech Oral History Archives, January 1979

Everything in retrospect, all the physics that I use today, and it seems like 90% of it I must have learned from Feynman and I had never seen anyone work so quickly and so I had never come across a physicist like that. Certainly nobody at Princeton or at Oxford was like this. And he was pretty fast and terrible when he was young. He is not much less fast or terrible now. And, you know when an idea popped into his head it would take literally no more than 5 or 10 minutes to work this kind of thing out.

– Robert Hellwarth, interview with Joan Bromberg, May 1985,
   American Institute of Physics

One of the great things about Feynman was the fun it was in taking up a problem and discussing it, kicking things around, laughing. I can recall his delight in one of the tricks played when he was a student at MIT, students getting together and hoisting a car and leaving it up on the roof of one of the buildings for the administration to deal with. [laughs] And the same delight he got in opening safes. I think I've told the story about the two safes at General Electric in Schenectady that Feynman opened while the security man was looking on . . . . I think that sense of fun that Feynman had — he explained afterward about how so many people use numbers like e and pi and their license number and the telephone number. Those were the numbers that he first tried to use with the greatest chance of solving the safe opening problem.

– John Wheeler, interview with Kenneth W. Ford, American
   Institute of Physics, March 1994

The people I know admired his breadth of interest, his curiosity and his love of life. Most of us tend to have much narrower lives than he, and many of us regret at times that we don't have the breadth of experience and relationships he did.

– Kip Thorne, "The Cult of Richard Feynman," *Los Angeles
   Times Magazine* December 2, 2001, p. 16

It was going along in an orderly way, but it was clear that the outspoken people were against it. Then Feynman got up, finally, and said, "I've been thinking about this and I think it's a terrible mistake. It's not Caltech. We would be giving the wrong message. And I think we should immediately squash it. It doesn't matter whether we've made mistaken commitments. We should just not do it." And that was the vote, essentially — that was the resolution. What Feynman said carried the day. It was pretty persuasively said.

– Fred Anson, reminiscing on the vote about whether to establish an army research center at Caltech, interview with Shirley K. Cohen, Caltech Oral History Archives, February 1997

He was quite a character with a sense of humor that just wouldn't quit.

– Childhood friend Joseph Heller, interview with Shelley Erwin, Caltech Oral History Archives, May 2010

I recall that Dick used to ask his class a question. He'd say, "OK. You have a lawn sprinkler, and you turn on the water, and the sprinkler rotates while shooting out oblique jets of water. Now, suppose you put this same sprinkler in a swimming pool and start to suck the water out through it. Would the sprinkler still be rotating?" It would make a great difference — like day and night. Things like that made the category of separated flows very interesting . . . I think it was a graduate course, but I cannot remember exactly which class. I was there when he asked us this question, and I thought, "Ah, that's a great teacher." A lawn sprinkler — everybody sees those, daily. But he just changed the direction of the water flow in the hose and we had to say what would happen.

- Theodore Y. Wu, interview with Shirley K. Cohen, Caltech Oral History Archives, February–March 2002

But the one person here who had a tremendous influence on me and whom I considered unique was Feynman. He had an enormous impact on me, not just intellectually but in kind of seeking the truth. All these things underneath that drove him — not just how smart he was — had a really big influence on me.

- Barry C. Barish, interview with Shirley K. Cohen, Caltech Oral History Archives, May/July 1998

I had Dick Feynman for mathematical physics. I used to go around to all his seminars when I was an undergrad, even. I couldn't understand any of the mathematics at all, but every once in a while he'd stop and he'd say, "What this really means is . . .," and I could understand that.

- Carver Mead, interview with Shirley K. Cohen, Caltech Oral History Archives, July 1996

He liked teaching, but he didn't like to supervise. The way he told it to me once was, that if he could formulate a problem sufficiently straightforwardly for a graduate student to do for a thesis, he could do it himself in one evening. If he could get a problem that clearly set, he couldn't refrain from doing it.

– Robert F. Christy, interview with Sara Lippincott, Caltech Oral
  History Archives, June 1994

I think during my time on the faculty at Caltech, the interesting thing to me there was the great movement forward in the pedagogy. In teaching those core courses, so-called. In terms of physics, I think it was largely due to Feynman. It used to be thought that a student, before he could have a hope of even starting to learn anything about quantum mechanics, had to go all through a great long rigmarole of classical mechanics at very sophisticated levels and so on. And Feynman showed that that's not true. You don't have to do that. . . . The material they're given and what they learn here now is far, far advanced, compared to when I was an undergraduate. You know, it's like the difference between the Model T Ford and the latest car, or the Wright brothers' airplane and a 747.

– David S. Wood, interview with Shirley K. Cohen, Caltech Oral
  History Archives, June 1994

Feynman invented a whole new way of doing quantum mechanics, and his diagrams didn't spring from any contact with the mathematicians; in fact, Dick has generated things. And he sometimes made remarks that mathematicians don't really help very much. He got very angry about the way mathematics was taught in the California schools. He was on a committee or something, for the governor or somebody. So you see, the whole thing turned around.

– William A. Fowler, John Greenberg, and Carol Bugé, Caltech
  Oral History Archives, May 1983–May 1984

You can talk to Feynman and his answers are precise and of the type that an experimental physicist can understand, or at least thinks he understands.

– Carl Anderson, interview with Harriett Lyle, Caltech Oral History Archives, January 1979

I discussed this matter with Feynman once, who is perhaps that physicist in the United States who most understands this side of physics. He has this kind of attitude to see whether the thing is right. But we discussed this and he said, "Well, among the younger generation nowadays there are very few people who would dare to publish a thing which contained contradictions." Practically nobody would, because he would say, "Then I will very soon be criticized by the other fellows who would say, 'There is your contradiction, you must be wrong.'" But then to say, "Well, I know that I must be wrong; certainly there is a contradiction, but damn it, I can see that it's right." Now, of course, you can again say that that is a very funny attitude. How can you know it? You cannot prove it; it contains contradictions.

– Werner Heisenberg, interview with Thomas S. Kuhn, American Institute of Physics, February 1963

[On Feynman humor:] I have no quarrel with this aspect of Dick Feynman's personality; like most other people, I found it delightful. But it leaves out so much: not only his scientific genius, but his deep love of nature, his passion for teaching, and above all his extraordinary standards of personal integrity, not *always* present at the highest levels of creativity. . . . Whatever else Dick Feynman may have joked about, his love for physics approached reverence.

— Laurie M. Brown, *Physics Today*, February 1989

[On his personality:] I had a glimpse of it on British television years before when I had no idea who Feynman was other than an American professor who might have been invented by Arthur Miller to do monologues on such matter — and, come to that, anti-matter — in which I had no special interest, no background, and no insight, but which was made mysteriously captivating. Later on, that personality came through intoxicatingly in his taped reminiscences published as *Surely You're Joking, Mr. Feynman!*; the physicist not of the faculty club but of the saloon.

— Tom Stoppard, "Stage View," *New York Times*, November 27, 1994

I recall the time I first saw Richard, for only a few hours just forty-five years ago. He was on his way to New Mexico, I expect, passing through the Chicago Laboratory of the Manhattan district. A half-dozen theorists gathered to meet him; his reputation had preceded him from Princeton. One or two people showed him difficult integrals they hoped he could solve, a little like asking the visiting strong man to loosen some rusted gate. He performed as hoped, but it was not the kind of light in which his wonderful zest for the rhythms and the puzzles of the world could be made out. But I saw that clearly later, at Los Alamos and around our shared old office in Cornell, and I came to love and admire his amazingly original, generous, honest, and playful mind, and a spirit that seemed like his gestures to dance through life.

— Philip Morrison, personal letter of condolence, February 1988

Dick Feynman's contributions to physics have made an extraordinary impact on our work: his development of quantum electrodynamics, his invention of the path-integral formulation of quantum field theory, his essential contributions to the theory of the weak interactions, his invention of the parton model for deep inelastic electron-proton scattering, and his extraordinary insights into the nature of high energy collisions which led to the unraveling of the quark and gluon structure of matter. His work touched virtually every area of physics.

Through his teaching and remarkable personality, Feynman taught us that physics is not only profound but also intuitive and comprehensible. We are also proud of his service to his country and the courage he showed on the *Challenger* investigation. Few scientists have made more impact on science and society. We treasure his memory.

– The SLAC (Stanford Linear Accelerator Center) Theoretical Physics Group, personal letter of condolence, February 1988

In the score of years that I knew him, as weekly lecturer at the Labs every Wednesday, as critic, consultant, and very human being, he was a great inspiration, a great mind, and a great spirit. Often he would show the greatest patience and kindness in transforming an innocent but ill-informed or stupid question into a rich and brilliant one, saving the questioner from embarrassment. His great humor matched his great intellect. He will live forever in the minds of this and all future generations of physicists and of all educated people.

– Bernard Soffer, Hughes Aircraft Company Research Laboratories, personal letter of condolence, February 1988

Dick had such a dynamic and colorful personality. He had great enthusiasm for learning. He was known as one of the world's most brilliant physicists and original thinkers, yet he was concerned to make science understandable and fascinating to others, thereby making him one of Caltech's most outstanding and favorite teachers. He was very creative in explaining the most esoteric concepts so that ordinary people could understand. Feynman stories are legend here, always told with affection and admiration.

– Sunney I. Chan, Chairman of the Faculty, California Institute of Technology, personal letter of condolence, February 1988

Dick was the best and favorite of several "uncles" who enriched my childhood. During his time at Cornell, he was a frequent and always welcome visitor at our house, one who could be counted on to take time out from conversations with my parents and other adults to lavish attention on the children. He was at once a great player of games with us and a teacher even then who opened our eyes to the world around us.

– Henry Bethe, personal letter of condolence February 1988

# Acknowledgments

There are many people to thank for their assistance.

First, my two researchers were incredible — Anisha Cook and Janna Wennberg. I was so very lucky to have your help on this project. I find it impossible to imagine I could have done this without the two of you and your hours of hard work. Thank you for your efforts.

I can always count on an honest assessment of my work from my friend Gregory Feldmeth, assistant head and long-time history teacher at Polytechnic School. I really appreciate his tireless efforts helping me with this project. He was instrumental in critically reviewing the sorting of quotes into categories, assisting with the painstaking task of removing duplicate quotes, and helping me create a timeline of my father's life. I was grateful to have his counsel and company. Polytechnic Upper School English teacher Grace Hamilton was incredibly generous with her time and expertise while assisting with the preface. Another friend, Richard White, Polytechnic School physics and computer science teacher extraordinaire, recommended the unstoppable team of Janna and Anisha, and was giving with his advice and technical ingenuity. I can understand why these three teachers are beloved by students.

Leslie Carmell, director of communications at Polytechnic School, is a dream to work with. She has been enormously supportive to me, and I am so grateful for her eagle eye and always-insightful suggestions. My colleagues are exceptional — Jennifer

Godwin Minto, Barbara Bohr, John Yen, as well as the host of talented teachers and staff at Polytechnic School. I am fortunate to work there.

Melanie Jackson, I am glad I have a wonderfully intelligent and kind literary agent such as you to advocate for me.

Thank you to my brother, Carl Feynman, for his confidence in me to complete this project.

Ralph Leighton was very accommodating and emailed audio files of *The Feynman Lectures on Physics* as he digitized them and was very, very helpful with his suggestions and advice. Christopher Sykes was impressive with his ideas and knowledge about sources of various quotes. Adam Cochran from Caltech was instrumental with communication with Caltech — everything from getting permissions to connecting me with people who were helpful, thorough, and efficient. Shelley Erwin and Loma Karklins from the Caltech archives were exactly that. Thank you for your knowledge and assistance. Tony Hey was kind enough to dig through his personal archives and scan a transcript from a panel discussion that was difficult to find. Ann Rho, senior director of development at Caltech, was eager to help, and was a good person with whom to brainstorm ideas. Alan Alda, thank you for your friendship and support. I am grateful to Kip Thorne for his guidance, not the least of which was putting me in touch with Brian Cox!

Brian Cox has a communication style reminiscent of my father's, and I am delighted he agreed to write a foreword for this book.

Yo-Yo Ma is a long-time family friend whom I'll describe as kindness personified. My father and I spent many hilarious evenings backstage and at dinner after attending Yo-Yo's concerts (the tradition continues — I now go with my children), and Yo-Yo dedicated a series of concerts to my father shortly after my father died. I'm not sure why I thought it was a good idea to burden my friend who is a professional cellist to write something for this book, but I'm impressed that he didn't back down from the challenge.

The last few years have not been easy, and I have become increasingly grateful for — and at times, dependent on — my fantastic friends. It seems like a long list, and I'm only sad that I can't thank *all* the people who have meant so much to me over the last few years. I am blessed to be part of a wonderful community. I want to thank Megan Foker — I don't know where I would be without her. She helped me through a challenging period in my life and did it with such humor, grace, and equanimity that it was easier to remain balanced. Everyone needs a friend like Megan. I appreciate Rick Foker's help with their family so Megan could spend time with me. I'm proud that my community includes: Heather and Tom Unterseher, Cheryl Wold and Paul Wennberg, Electra and Peter Lang, Jane Kaczmarek, Stacy and Michael Berger, Dyanne di Rosario-Halsted and Chris Halsted, Tim Hartley and Jason Lyon, Tiffany and Marc Harris, Mario Miralles and Brenda Bork, Ralph Leighton and Phoebe Kwan, Kevin and Kristen Tyson, Scott Lee and Karen Wong, Francisco Miralles, Susan Blaisdell, Dorothy Shubin, Carl and Paula Feynman, Charles Hirshberg and Alison Adler, and Joan Feynman. You are my support team. Your friendship, love, and support have buoyed my spirits over the years. John Murlowski, you came along at exactly the right moment and knew just how to help and support me.

Finally, I'd like to thank my children, Ava and Marco Miralles, for their fantastic ideas, burgeoning independence, and general helpful attitudes about the project. I love you.

# Photo Credits

Page xxi: Photo by Ursula deSwart, courtesy Michelle Feynman and Carl Feynman

Page 3: Courtesy Michelle Feynman and Carl Feynman

Page 15: Courtesy Michelle Feynman and Carl Feynman

Page 23: Lecturing at Caltech Seminar Day, May 1978
Courtesy California Institute of Technology

Page 51: Courtesy Michelle Feynman and Carl Feynman

Page 57: Courtesy Michelle Feynman and Carl Feynman

Page 83: Photographer Richard Hartt, Courtesy California Institute of Technology

Page 89: Formal Nobel portrait, 1965, Clemens of Copenhagen
Courtesy California Institute of Technology

Page 103: Courtesy Michelle Feynman and Carl Feynman

Page 109: Lecturing at Caltech Seminar Day, May 1978
Courtesy California Institute of Technology

Page 123: Courtesy Michelle Feynman and Carl Feynman

Page 165: Courtesy Michelle Feynman and Carl Feynman

Page 185: With Paul Dirac at Relativity Conference in Warsaw, July 1962
Courtesy California Institute of Technology

Page 197: Photographer Clemens of Copenhagen
Courtesy Michelle Feynman and Carl Feynman

Page 213: Courtesy Michelle Feynman and Carl Feynman

Page 223: Photographer Richard Hartt.
Courtesy California Institute of Technology

Page 241:  Courtesy Michelle Feynman and Carl Feynman
Page 249:  Courtesy Michelle Feynman and Carl Feynman
Page 261:  Courtesy California Institute of Technology
Page 271:  Courtesy California Institute of Technology
Page 281:  Courtesy Michelle Feynman and Carl Feynman
Page 293:  Courtesy California Institute of Technology
Page 317:  Courtesy California Institute of Technology
Page 327:  Courtesy Michelle Feynman
Page 333:  Hughes Aircraft Company
Page 345:  Courtesy Michelle Feynman and Carl Feynman
Page 355:  Courtesy Michelle Feynman and Carl Feynman
Page 363:  Courtesy Michelle Feynman and Carl Feynman

# Sources

American Physical Society Annual Meeting, 1950

Audio recording of lecture on relativity, Douglas Advanced Research Laboratory, 1967

BBC, "Fun to Imagine" television series, 1983

BBC, "Horizon: The Hunting of the Quark," May 1974

BBC, "The Pleasure of Finding Things Out," 1981

BBC, "Strangeness Minus Three," 1964

BBC interview, "A Novel Force in Nature"

BBC interview, "Scientifically Speaking," April 1976

*California Tech*, Caltech student newspaper, October 1965

Caltech lecture on particles, 1973

"Cargo Cult Science," Caltech commencement address, 1974

CERN talk, December 1965

*The Character of Physical Law*, MIT Press, Richard P. Feynman, 1965

"The Computing Machines in the Future," Nishina Memorial Lecture, August 1985

"The Cult of Richard Feynman," *Los Angeles Times Magazine*, December 2, 2001

Dirac Memorial Lectures, "The Reason for Antiparticles," 1986

Esalen lecture, "Computers from the Inside Out," Esalen Institute, produced by Faustin Bray/ Sound Photosynthesis Mind@Large Catalog

Esalen lecture, "Quantum Mechanical View of Reality (Part 1)," Esalen Institute, produced by Faustin Bray/ Sound Photosynthesis Mind@Large Catalog, Z440-07, 1984

Esalen lecture, "Quantum Mechanical View of Reality (Part 2)," Esalen Institute, produced by Faustin Bray/ Sound Photosynthesis Mind@Large Catalog, Z440-07, 1984

Esalen workshop, "Tiny Machines," Esalen Institute, produced by Faustin Bray/ Sound Photosynthesis Mind@Large Catalog

Eugene Wigner, quoted by Robert Oppenheimer in a letter to Professor Raymond Birge on November 4, 1943, University of California, Berkeley

"Feynman: Frustrated by the Slow Pace of Probe," *Pasadena Star-News*, January 29, 1989

*Feynman Lectures on Computation*, Perseus Publishing, Richard P. Feynman, edited by Tony Hey and Robin W. Allen, 1996

*Feynman Lectures on Gravitation*, Addison-Wesley Publishing, Richard P. Feynman, edited by Fernando B. Morinigo and William G. Wagner, 1995

*Feynman Lectures on Physics*, Addison Wesley, Richard P. Feynman, edited by Robert B. Leighton and Matthew Sands, 1963

"The Feynman Legend," *The Los Angeles Times*, February 17, 1988

"Feynman Takes NASA to Task," *Pasadena Star-News*, June 11, 1986

*Feynman's Tips on Physics*, Basic Books, Richard P. Feynman, edited by Michael A. Gottlieb and Ralph Leighton, 2013

Future for Science interview, R. P. Feynman Papers, California Institute of Technology Archives

Galileo Symposium, "What Is and What Should Be the Role of Scientific Culture in Modern Society," September 1964

*Great American Scientists*, Prentice Hall, Editors of Fortune, 1960

Interview of Alvin V. Tollestrup by David A. Valone on December 23, 1994, Caltech Oral History Archives

Interview of Barry C. Barish by Shirley K. Cohen on July 21, 1998, Caltech Oral History Archives

Interview of Barry C. Barish by Shirley K. Cohen, May–July 1998, Caltech Oral History Archives

Interview of Carl Anderson by Harriett Lyle, January 9–February 8, 1979, California Institute of Technology Archives

Interview of Carl Anderson by Harriett Lyle on January 30, 1979, Caltech Oral History Archives

Interview of Carver Mead by Shirley K. Cohen on July 17, 1996, Caltech Oral History Archives

Interview of Charles A. Barnes by Heidi Aspaturian, July–August 1987, Caltech Oral History Archives

Interview with Charles Weiner, March 4, 5 and June 27, 28, 1966; February 4, 1973, Niels Bohr Library and Archives with the Center for the History of Physics

Interview of David S. Wood by Shirley K. Cohen on May 25, 1994, Caltech Oral History Archives

Interview of David S. Wood by Shirley K. Cohen, June 1994, Caltech Oral History Archives

Interview of Fred Anson by Shirley K. Cohen on February 26, 1997, Caltech Oral History Archives

Interview of Hans A. Bethe by Judith R. Goodstein on February 17, 1982, Caltech Oral History Archives

Interview of James A. Westphal by Shirley K. Cohen, July 8–29, 1998, Caltech Oral History Archives

Interview of Jenijoy La Belle by Heidi Aspaturian, February–May 2008, and April 2009, Caltech History Archives

Interview of John Rigden by Dr. Dudley Herschbach on May 21, 2003, American Institute of Physics, College Park, MD, www.aip.org/history/ohist

Interview of John Wheeler by Kenneth W. Ford on March 15, 1994, American Institute of Physics, College Park, MD, www.aip.org/history/ohist

Interview of Joseph Heller by Shelley Erwin on May 5, 2010, Caltech Oral History Archives

Interview of Philip Morrison by Charles Weiner on February 7, 1967, American Institute of Physics, College Park, MD, www.aip.org/history/ohist

Interview of Robert F. Christy by Sara Lippincott, June 1994, Caltech Oral History Archives

Interview of Robert Hellwarth by Joan Bromberg on May 28, 1985, American Institute of Physics, College Park, MD, www.aip.org/history/ohist

Interview of Rodman W. Paul by Carol Bugé on February 17, 1982, Caltech Oral History Archives

Interview of Samuel Epstein by Carol Bugé on December 19 and 26, 1985, and January 10, 1986, Caltech Oral History Archives

Interview of Seymour Benzer by Heidi Aspaturian, September 11, 1990–February 1991, Caltech Oral History Archives

Interview of Steven C. Frautschi by Shirley K. Cohen on June 17, 2003, Caltech History Archives

Interview of Theodore Y. Wu by Shirley K. Cohen, February–March 2002, Caltech Oral History Archives

Interview of Thomas A. Tombrello by Heidi Aspaturian on December 26–31, 2010, Caltech Oral History Archives

Interview of Valentine L. Telegdi by Sara Lippincott on March 4, 9, 2002, Caltech Oral History Archives

Interview for Viewpoint by Bill Stout for KNX Television, ca. 1959

Interview of Werner Heisenberg by Thomas S. Kuhn on February 13, 1963, American Institute of Physics, College Park, MD, www.aip.org/history/ohist

Interview of William A. Fowler by John Greenberg and Carol Bugé, May 1983–May 1984, Caltech Oral History Archives

Julian Schwinger, in his obituary of Feynman in February 1989, *Physics Today*

Les Prix Nobel en 1965 [Nobel Foundation], Stockholm, 1966

"Mass Varying with Position," *Physics* 230, 1987 (R. P. Feynman Papers, California Institute of Technology Archives)

MIT centennial, "Talk of Our Times," December 1961

MIT conference, May 1981; "Simulating Physics with Computers," *International Journal of Theoretical Physics* 21

National Science Teachers Association Fourteenth Convention lecture, "What Is Science?" April 1966

"New Textbooks for the 'New' Mathematics," *Engineering and Science* 28, no. 6, March 1965

*New York Times* obituary, February 17, 1988

"900 at Caltech, JPL Declare Support for Nuclear Arms Freeze," *The Los Angeles Times*, October 16, 1982

*No Ordinary Genius, The Illustrated Richard Feynman*, W. W. Norton, edited by Christopher Sykes, 1994

*Nobel Lectures, Physics 1963–1970*, Elsevier Publishing Company, Amsterdam, 1972

Oersted Medal acceptance speech, 1972

*Omni* interview, February 1979

Panel discussion, particle physics conference, Irvine, California, 1971

*Pasadena Star-News*, Opinion, June 18, 1986

*People*, July 22, 1985

*Perfectly Reasonable Deviations from the Beaten Track*. Basic Books, Richard P. Feynman, edited by Michelle Feynman, 2005

"The Present Situation in Quantum Electrodynamics," Solvay conference, 1961

"The Problem of Teaching Physics in Latin America," 1963

"The Qualitative Behavior of Yang–Mills Theory in 2+1 Dimensions," January 1981

"QED: Fits of Reflection and Transmission," Sir Douglas Robb Lectures, University of Auckland, 1979

"QED: New Queries," Sir Douglas Robb Lectures, University of Auckland, 1979

"QED: Photons—Corpuscles of Light," Sir Douglas Robb Lectures, University of Auckland, 1979

*QED: The Strange Theory of Light and Matter*, Princeton University Press, Richard P. Feynman, 1985

"The Relation of Science and Religion," May 1956

"The Remarkable Dr. Feynman," *Los Angeles Times Magazine*, April 20, 1986

Report of the Presidential Commission on the Space Shuttle *Challenger* Accident, Volume 2: Appendix F, June 1986

*South Shore Record*, October 28, 1965

"Structure of the Proton," Niels Bohr Medal lecture given in Copenhagen, Denmark, October 1973

*Surely You're Joking, Mr. Feynman!* W. W. Norton, Richard P. Feynman and Ralph Leighton, edited by Edward Hutchings. 1985

Swedish television interview on Nobel Prize winners, 1965

"Theory and Applications of Mercereau's Superconducting Circuits," October 1964

"There's Plenty of Room at the Bottom," December 1959

"Tiny Computers Obeying Quantum Mechanical Laws," *New Directions in Physics: The Los Alamos 40th Anniversary Volume*, 1987

Tom Stoppard, "Stage View," *New York Times*, November 27, 1994

UC Berkeley Lectures, "Time and Physics in Evolutionary History," spring 1968

UCSB talk, "Los Alamos from Below," February 1975

"The Uncertainty of Science," John Danz Lecture Series, 1963

"The Uncertainty of Values," John Danz Lecture Series, 1963

Unpublished personal correspondence and notes

"The Unscientific Age," John Danz Lecture Series, 1963

*U.S. News and World Report* interview, February 1985

"The Value of Science," December 1955

*What Do You Care What Other People Think?*, W. W. Norton, Richard P. Feynman and Ralph Leighton, 1988

Yorkshire Television program "Take the World from Another Point of View," 1972

# Index

Page numbers in italics refer to images.

abstruse math, 225–226
academic advising, 326
academic path, 42, 324
admission committee duties, 100
*Advanced Calculus* (Woods), 7
aesthetic sense, 54
Albert Einstein Award, 370–371
algebra rules, 236
American Philosophical Society
    membership, 115–116
amplitudes, 93
Andersen, Bjorn, 36
Anderson, Carl, 367, 373, 378
Anson, Fred, 375
antiquarks, 202
anti-Semitism, 352. *See also* Jewish
    people
arithmetic, 10, 234–235, 298
art, 53
artificial intelligence, 245–246
assumptions, 144, 181
astrology, 141, 219
astronomy, 79, 80, 86, 94, 151,
    191–192. *See also* stars
athletic ability, 11
atom, 60, 149, 202, 205, 207, 211,
    247, 350–351
atom bomb. *See* Los Alamos;
    Manhattan Project

atomic energy, UN meeting, 278
Atomic Energy Commission, 278
atomic research, 154. *See also* Los
    Alamos; Manhattan Project
authority, 32–33, 319–320
awards: Albert Einstein Award, xxiii,
    370–371. *See also* Nobel Prize

Barish, Barry C., 371, 376
Barnes, Charles A., 367–369
base systems, 234
Bengelsdorf, Irving, 372–373
Bonner, Seymour, 370–371
Bessel functions, 173
Bethe, Hans, 349, 371
Bethe, Henry, 381
Big Bang, 26
bilateral nuclear arms freeze, 258
biology, 62, 127, 143, 154, 157,
    312
Bjorken, James, 99
Bohr, Niels, 125, 161
bomb-making. *See* Los Alamos;
    Manhattan Project
bongo playing, 54–55, 96, 102,
    *197*, 336
brain, 70
Brazil lecture, 31
Brown, Laurie M., 378–379

Buffalo, New York, 31
burn-out, 30

calculus, 7, 48–49, 229, 361
California Institute of Technology
    (Caltech), 41, *85*, 331; loyalty,
    373
camping van, 19
capacitance, of elliptical condenser,
    239
capitalism, 275
cargo cult science, 149–150, 325
Casals, Pablo, xv–xvi
*Challenger* explosion: probability of
    failure, 244, 266–267; on Rogers
    Commission activity, 246–247,
    263–266, 278, 380; technical
    failures, 267–269
Chan, Sunney I., 381
charge parity, 218
chemistry: childhood experiments,
    11–12; explanatory challenges
    of, 93, 154
Christian ethics, 119. *See also*
    religion
Christy, Robert F., 376–377
civilizations, 351–352
Civil War, 358
Columbus, 171
communism, 275
company workers, 279
complex numbers, 236
computer programming,
    225–226
computers: communicating ability,
    243–244; miniaturization,
    245, 246; quantum computers,
    243
conference attendance, 43

Conference on Color, Flavor, and
    Unification, 92–93
confusion, 291
conservation of energy law, 65, 69
consulting, 47
cooperation, 349–350
Corben, Mulaika, 31
Cornell University, arrival, 46
cosmology, 96
Cox, Brian, xi–xiv
creativity, 220
Cronin, James, 218
curiosity, 174–177, 180, 329–330

Daylight Saving Time, 191
death, 127
definition, 112
differentiation (calculus), 229
discovery, 168, 183–184
division of labor, 157
dogmatism, 114
dormitory living, 32–33
doubt, 283–284, 292
Drell, Sidney D., 365
Dyson, Freeman, 363

Earth, 68, 125
education, universal, 276
Einstein, Albert, 125, 159,
    161
Eisenbud, 158–159
elasticity, 78, 177
electrical forces, 78, 158
electricity, 155
electron charge, 273
*Encyclopaedia Britannica*,
    43–44
engineer, 137
engineering technology, 247

English classes: literature, 18; spelling, 41, 315

enjoyment of life, 102

Epstein, Samuel, 370

equation, 225

ethics: and science, 113; and survival, 114

evolution of life, 72

existence, 117

experimental physicists, 126. *See also* physicists

experimentation: idea generation, 137; paradoxical ideas, 125; purpose, 139; scientific truth, 81, 132

exploration, 168, 171

exponents, 239

extra-terrestrial intelligence, 93

faith-healing, 219

fan-base, 100, 101

Feynman, Carl (son), *xxi*, 17, 18, 353, 362

Feynman, Michelle (daughter), ix, xvii–xxi, *xxi*

Feynman, Richard: air travel, 255; American Institute of Physics oral history project, ix; athletic ability, 11; aunt, 8; autobiographies, 39 (see also *Surely You're Joking, Mr. Feynman!*); childhood, *3, 15*, 180–181; Cornell University arrival, 46; dating, 106; daughter (Michelle Feynman), xvii–xxi, *xxi*, 353; father, 5, 8–9, 17, 19–21, 65, 153, 239; fatherhood, xviii, xxi, 18, 19; fraternity life, 41, 42–43;

graduate education, 44, 45, 307; high school algebra team, 239; honesty, 370; humor, 378–379, 380; intellectual interests, 46–47; intelligence, 366, 367; intuitiveness, 367–368; jogging habit, 348; kindergarten learning, 8–9; Las Vegas experiences, xviii–xix; life chronology, xxiii–xxiv; memory of names, 36; mental health, 353; mistaken identity, 99; mother, 11, 92, 106; musical interest, xv–xvi (*see also* music); National Academy of Sciences resignation, 25; Nobel Prize (*see* Nobel Prize); personality, 27, 34, 44–45, 371, 379, 381; photographs, *89, 109, 123, 165, 185, 197, 213, 225, 241, 249, 261, 271, 281, 327, 333, 345, 355, 363;* playfulness, 374, 379; as polemicist, xiii–xiv; Portuguese skills, 31; post–World War II pessimism, 259; professional approach, 92; religious views, 14, 120, 371; reputation, 367; research philosophy, xi–xiii, 188–190; role model, 372; self-perception, 37, 37–38, 40, 44–45, 178, 331; self-teaching, 304; sister, 10; son (Carl Feynman), *xxi*, 17, 18, 353, 362; speech patterns, 38; teacher role, 293, 295, 300–302, 307, 369–370, 372–373, 375–377; undergraduate education, 42, 44, 324; university position, 30,

Feynman, Richard (*Continued*)
40, 41, *83, 173, 293, 317;* wives,
40, 92, 105, 107, 341–342;
work ethic, xix–xx, 177–179;
worldview, 345, 347–353;
writing style, 40, 188, 189
Feynman diagrams, xi, 49
Fitch, Val, 218
Fitz-Gronin effect, 36
flying saucers, 93, 131
fools, 329
foreign languages, 298
Fowler, William A., 377
Franklin, Benjamin, 273
fraternity life, 41
Frautschi, Steven C., 370
fundamental physics, 132, 357

galaxy, 61, 93
Galileo, 141, 289
gambling odds, 231
gauge theories, 156
gender differences, 41, 106
generalization, 35
general theory of intelligence, 13
generosity, 115
genius, xi–xii, 365
geometry, 230–231, 232
gluons, 204–205, 336
God, 61, 112, 116, 119
government: versus private
enterprise, 279; role, 277
gram (measure), 152
gravitation: applications, 79;
elegance, 65, 77; experiment,
135; inverse square law, 139;
light in, 71; origin of
force, 63

gravitons, 205
Great Depression, 12–13
Greeks, 96
Greenbaum, Arline (first wife), 105,
107
gyros, 187

Hadron collision, 99, 203
Hawaii, 33
Heisenberg, Werner, 378
helium, 182
Heller, Joseph, 375
Hellwarth, Robert, 373–374
Higgs Boson, xi
high school algebra team, 239
Hiroshima bomb damage, 256
Hitler, 352
honesty, 216
honorary degrees, 25
honorary society membership, 30
Howarth, Gweneth (third wife), 40,
92, 341–342
human beings: and animals, 60–61;
future time span, 358–360
humanitarian problems, 215
human mind, 56
human relationships, 27
humor, xx–xxi, 378–379

ignorance: admission of, 284, 285;
growth potential, 288–289
imagination, 63, 83, 85–87, 151
Indian caves, 32
industry attraction, 222
information sharing, 132
inspiration, and religion, 111
intellectual tyranny, 40, 219–220, 329
interest, 299

interviews, 98, 169
inverse square law of gravitation, 139
irresistible force, 62

Jewish people, 120, 338, 352
judicial system, 276

Kac, Marc, 365
Kauffmann's long-range force, 204
keynote speeches, 37
knowledge: accumulation, 75, 361;
      of experts, 220, 222; power, 87,
      126; purposes, 80; universality,
      74
KNXT interview, 40

La Belle, Jenijoy, 370
laboratory, 6
language: clarity of, 192–193,
      300; learning process, 300; of
      science, 299, 305
large numbers, 225
Las Vegas visits, xviii–xix, 50
laws of electrodynamics, 359
laws of mechanics, 65
learning: difficult ideas, 313; of
      interest, 320, 321–322; process,
      297; rote learning, 313–314; of
      special topics, 309; styles, 304
leisure activities, 19, 55, 56, 96, 102,
      *197*, 336
life, 39
light: in gravitational fields, 71;
      reflection, 205–206; wavelength,
      76
limits (calculus), 229
Los Alamos: dormitory living, 32–33;
      mail censure, 274; physicists,
33; safety, 47; security, 49;
      wartime research, 254; work
      attitude, 177–179. *See also*
      Manhattan Project
love, 105–107, 158

Ma, Yo-Yo, xv–xvi
magnetic forces, 78
magnetism, 155
Manhattan Project: academic training
      at entry, 254; arithmetic use,
      234–235; committee, 29;
      destructive capacity, 256,
      258–259; moral stand, 48, 251,
      257–258, 259; plutonium, 50;
      secrecy, 260; work patterns,
      255, 256
Massachusetts Institute of
      Technology: fraternity life, 41,
      42–43; keynote speech, 37;
      personal development, 45
mathematical model accuracy, 263
mathematics: abstractness,
      42; appreciation of, 226;
      calculation errors, 226–227,
      230; characteristics, 227, 236;
      consistency, 97; and physics,
      129, 130, 227–228; poetry in,
      223; as problem solver, 66, 228,
      233; teaching approaches, 233;
      young students, 310. *See also*
      *individual concepts*
Mead, Carver, 376
meanness, 115
memorization, inefficiency of,
      296, 308
memory: doing by, 295; of names, 36
Mermin, David, 365–366

Meson theory, 74
metallography, 180
microphone usage, 97
modern society, problems of, 217
momentum, 74
moral values, 115, 117, 118
Morrison, Philip, 367, 379
muons, 205
music: bongo playing, 54–55, 56, 96, 102, *197,* 336; experience of, 67; piano-playing, 106

NASA resource allocation, 263. See also *Challenger* explosion
National Academy of Sciences, 25
nature: as accidental result, 60; complexities, 66, 69, 72, 73, 128; nebulae shapes, 191–192; nonrelativistic nature, 61; quantum mechanics simulation, 76; rules, 134; simplicity, 67–68, 69; understanding of, 63
neutrinos, 205
Newton, Isaac, 152
New York School System, 8
New Zealand, 43
Niels Bohr Medal recommendations, 36
Nobel Prize: felicitations, 336, 337, 339–341; Feynman reaction, 95, 101, 333, 335–336, 339–340, 342–343; lecture, xviii, 13–14, 67–68, 111–112, 125, 162, 170, 174–175, 183, 184, 209–210, 238, 337; newspaper reports, 221; research work, xi, 336, 368; source, 337; work environment, 56

nuclear arms freeze, 258
nuclear energy: future expectations, 359; interrelationships, 81; peacetime plants, 47; wartime development, 252
nuclear testing, 160, 253
nucleus, 60
number theory, 231

obituary, 50
Onnes, Kamerlingh, 157
ordinary people, 50

*Pakistan Observer,* 221
*Pale Blue Dot* (Sagan), xiv
paradoxical ideas, 125, 192
particles. *See individual particles*
Parton model, 99, 227, 380
Paul, Rodman W., 372
peace, 113
personality, 27
philosophers: critique of, 28, 109, 121; versus scientists, 113
physicists: experimental physicists, 126; goals, 59; humanity of, 94; knowledge of, 195; world-view, 37, 112
physics: ability to understand, 36; versus astronomy, 79; fascination in, 38–39; fundamental physics, 133, 138; future expectations, 360; graduate education, 199; limitations, 147–148; and mathematics, 129, 130, 227–228; versus other sciences, 125, 302; predictive ability, 142–143, 285; problem-solving, 175–176; reversibility of laws, 207; solid-state physics,

201–202; teaching of, 301, 302, 308, 314–315. *See also* theoretical physics

pi, 17, 20, 237, 239, 313–314

planetary movement, 66

plutonium, 50. *See also* Los Alamos; Manhattan Project

poetry: of Auden, 55; by Feynman, 63–64, 91–92; nature in, 80; and science, 57

political party structure, 279–280

political questions, 121–122

politicians, expectations of, 274

Portuguese language skills, 31

positron, 199

precise language, 192–193

prejudice, 26

President's Board of Master Plumbers, 276

Princeton University, 44

private enterprise, versus government, 279

problem-solving for learning, 296, 315

projection system, 12

proton, 203–205

psychiatrists, 219

psychoanalysis, 133

psychoanalysts, 216–217

publicity, 190–191, 220

public-speaking, 6, *23*, *109*

publishing, 144, 146, 160, 162

pure mathematicians, 232–235

pure mathematics, 240

puzzles, 177

quantum computers, 243

quantum electrodynamics theory: Dirac's book, 7, 13–14;

Feynman contributions, xi, xii; incompleteness of, 206–207; nature in, 203; strength of, 202

quantum mechanics: fundamental accuracy, 200; macroscopic descriptions, 208; teaching of, 128, 199, 372; undergraduate courses, 307, understanding of, 203, 210–211, 329

quantum theory of gravitation, 160

quarks, 202, 204

question types, 307, 330

radio broadcasts, 95

Reagan, Ronald, 258

relativity, 70, 71, 138, 209–210

religion: certainty of faith, 120; Christian ethics, 119; conflict with science, 117, 118–119, 121, 290–291; moral lessons, 118; role in life, 111

renaissance artists, 54

research, 162

research facilities, 153

resilience of material, 191

Rigden, John, 367

rituals, 38

Rogers Commission. See *Challenger* explosion

Rorschach test, 100

rote learning, 313–314. *See also* learning

rubber bands, 78, 177

rules, exception to, 170

Sagan, Carl, xiv

Santa Claus, 6

school systems, 8

Schwinger, Julian, xi, 367

science: in decision-making, 105; definition, 132, 156; and ethics, 113, 116–117; and God, 116, 163; ignorance of, 217–218; imagination and, 83, 151; interest in, 115, 151; as international effort, 273; irrelevance, 219; language of, 299, 305; logic in, 321; non-science, 139, 158; power of, 111, 144, 222, 253; religious conflict, 117, 118, 119, 121, 290–291; structural interconnection, 180; success in, 128, 150, 162–163; teaching of, 147, 163, 295; traditions, 221; uncertainty of, 213; universality, 140; young students, 310

*Science and Children*, 29

science fiction writers, 199

scientific discovery, 35

scientific innovations, 163

scientific integrity, 132

scientific lectures, 94, 127–128

scientific method, 127, 131, 140

secrecy in work, lack of, 28, 182

self-positionality, 324

set theory, 232

Snow, C. P., 226, 365

social elegance, 322–323

socialism, 275

Soffer, Bernard, 380

solid-state physics, 201–202

South Seas, 149–150

space, and time, 69

specialization, 122, 155

Standard Time, 191

Stanford Linear Accelerator Center, 380

stars: beauty of, 57; galactic expanse, 61, 93; light from, 67. *See also* astronomy

Stoppard, Tom, 379

stupidity, 101

sub-nuclear systems, 206

success, in science, 128

summer travel, 189

*Surely You're Joking, Mr. Feynman!*, xxiv, 5, 30

survival, 114

table of integrals, 229

teaching: desire for, 293, 300; entertainer role, 301; high school, 7; as interruption, 300; philosophy of, 309, 311; time effect, 313; time management, 302–303

Telegdi, Valentine L., 366

television industry, 275

textbooks, 5, 310

theoretical physicists, 98, 99, 158–159, 161, 360–361

theoretical physics: as higher human development, 48; limitations, 200–201; perception of, 27, 35; predictive ability, 138, 149, 171–172; research approach, 170–171

theory, development of, 44, 129, 134, 136, 146, 185, 239–240

Theory of Everything, xii

theory of relativity, 70, 72, 203

thermonuclear reactions, 273
Thorne, Kip, 374
time: absolute meaning, 73; direction
    of, 62; as fourth geometrical
    dimension, 200; limited
    knowledge, 140; measurement,
    193; and space, 69
Tollenstrup, Alvin V., 372
Tombrello, Thomas A., 366, 369–370
Tomonaga, Sin-Itiro, xi
trees, 75–76
triangulation, 325
truth, 72, 81, 136, 169, 181, 184, 290
typewriter science, 286

ultimate particle, 201
uncertainty, 283, 286–288
United Nations atomic energy
    meeting, 278
United States of America: Civil
    War, 358; government, 275;
    ideals of freedom, 283; national
    complexity, 276–277; political
    party structure, 279–280
universal education, 276
universe: age, 73; beyond man,
    119; expanse, 80; poetry on,
    91–92
universities: concentration of, 153;
    general education requirement,
    310–311

uranium: information security, 49;
    isotope separation, 254

vector, 225
Venus, 26
vocabulary, 114–115
Von Neumann, 120
voting, 275

Walker, Bernard, 10
wavelength, 76
wave–particle duality, 202–203, 208
W-Boson, 336
weaving, 9
Western civilization, heritages,
    119–120
Westphal, James A., 371
Wheeler, John, 374
Wigner, Eugene, 366
Wilson, Bob, 47–48, 256
wire space, 312
witch doctors, 216–217
witches, 38
Wood, David S., 372, 377
words, value of, 34
World War II. *See* Manhattan Project
writing habit, 40
Wu, Theodore Y., 375–376

younger people, 180
Yukawa's field theory, 200–201